Apocalypse USA:
Civil War 2: The Death Walker War

"A Dickensian-style adventure satire with millions of
flesh-chomping zombies."

—Wei Lin on Books, Singapore

"The high-stakes suspense of a Jack Ryan novel combined with the
pulse-pounding horror of The Walking Dead."

—ARC reader, Liverpool

2033: the year America's traitorous Deep State teams up with anarchist Antifa to strike a death blow to the wounded and tottering Republic.

Witness deadly factional fighting, mass assassinations, federal, state, and local governments violently divided and ready to do battle. All the while, a stealthy bioweapons attack worms its way through the guts of the Heartland.

In the miiddle of this growing insanity arrives intrepid London Juggernaut reporter Ellie Sato on her first trip to the USA. Will she be able to survive and rescue her friends while the continent crumbles around her?

Reader Suitability:
Scenes of violence, moderate profanity, and torture.
Recommended for 18+

APOCALYPSE: USA

THE DEATH WALKER WAR

RK SYRUS

"You Deep State scum, one day you swampy cocksuckers will unleash a chaos you can't control! What will you do then? You cocksucking motherf—" *[US Federal Prisoner 89945#005 was re-gagged.]*

—Document leaked from the Congressional Committee for True Facts investigating the seditious myth of the so-called "Deep State," circa 2031

"They keep telling us it weren't no war... but it was."

—A survivor, Kansas City, Missouri, 2033

Map of lower 48 states showing approximate

Red (Republican)

vs

Blue (Democrat)

political divisions.

1

Abdelkader heard sounds coming down from the dark roof of the artificial cave, the chafing of leathery wings, the rasp of small talons on custom-made metal perches, and sharp screeches.

Bats, he thought. "Disgusting creatures."

"But so useful, General," said Dr. Baldur.

Abdelkader realized he must have spoken out loud. He hadn't meant to. He made sure the silicone gel attaching his prosthetic mask around his lips was firmly pressed down; he did not want to lisp like a homosexual.

"I am no general. The Pangean war for Europe is over. We lost," he said flatly, his words returning no echo through the din coming from the stone walls above. *But*, he thought, *an even greater prize is at hand.* It *had* to be...

"They're resting now, full." The awkward scientist's sycophantic chattering interrupted Abdelkader's thoughts. The younger, round-faced man craned his neck back to study the colony through a night-vision device. "They're easy to feed." He chuckled. "Thank you for letting me use this species," Dr. Baldur said. "I'd hate to have to take care of a colony of insectivore bats. Way out here, I mean."

The younger, vain, and skinny virologist was an Uyghur, one of the unfortunate millions of ethnic Muslims trapped in mainland China. As a boy, he had escaped from a PRC concentration camp with all his vital organs unharvested and still inside his body cavities. He ended up working in India's pharmaceutical industry.

Abdelkader was suspicious of the depth of Dr. Baldur's genetic manipulation skills and more importantly, his commitment. *We'll see about you, you pretty young man. Soon we'll see.*

An indistinct moan came from the next chamber. Abdelkader already sensed what was around the corner. A CIA drone strike had melted off half his face, his exposed olfactory nerves now extra sensitive. He was able to make out distinct smells: blood, urine, sweat, and fear.

"Do you need more? Bats, I mean."

"Not yet, sir. They're not fussy eaters and do not mass that much, though it is a fact, an interesting trait, that they can consume more than half their body weight in blood during a twenty-minute lunch."

Abdelkader had not known this, and it was indeed an interesting fact. "Afterward, can they still fly?"

"As soon as they suck a host's blood, their digestive system begins excreting excess water."

Bat piss. That must be the particularly sour smell coming from the food chamber. Abdelkader peeked in to see the shaved head of a child, a ball gag filling its toothless mouth. The rubber ball was transected by a feeding tube. Despite the nutrients being force-fed to him or her, the child did not look well; its eyes were swollen shut and looked ridiculously puffy set in the emaciated face. The naked creature's slim shoulders were caked with dried vampire bat excrement and unhealed sores.

"I'll get you some fresh food. Even bats deserve better than this. Unwholesome as they are, they are part of our army now."

What army is that? Abdelkader mused. The attack on Europe had failed because French President Rapace put his own desire for revenge above the plan to wipe the continent clean of its infestation of nationalists, Christians, Jews, and traitor Muslims.

But there were other ways to force a just utopia on unwilling and subhuman oppressors. His small rogue Pangean force would soon teach that to the most sinful, narcissistic, and greedy nation in all history. A four-hundred-year-old poisonous strangle vine planted in 1619, whose roots fed on the bodies of tens of millions of black slaves, lapped up the blood of uncountable victims of Indigenous genocide, and continued to gorge insatiably on the misery of the world's poorest. America was rotting from the inside; toppling it required only a push.

Dr. Baldur shut the outermost door gently so as not to disturb the members of the colony clinging to the ceiling.

"Gen— I mean, sir, you may dislike bats, but we both know who will come to hate them more… Americans!"

Abdelkader stared. Baldur spoke with a zest for terror he was only mimicking and a desire for vengeance he had not earned. The man had not even gotten a proper haircut—he kept his woolly locks fastened in a ridiculous man bun.

Abdelkader continued to stare. Silence dragged.

Finally, the scientist gave another tittering laugh and said, "Of course t-they hate them already. Americans… ever since the 2020, uh, pandemic. And bats, especially the bloodsucking species, they've never had a good rep—"

"I have to go to the other side." Abdelkader was referring to the north end of the island, where Baldur was not permitted. "What have you to show me?"

"Right this way. I think you'll be pleased. We've made progress."

They walked down a winding corridor. The facility lay under the salt pans covering the island's surface. The first shallow excavations had been made by pirates to hide treasure, and these were then made larger by slaves escaping from the mainland. Finally, a Venezuelan anarchist group had built a sophisticated bioweapons laboratory deep inside metamorphic rock and sediment. They walked past plastic sheeting that covered bare rock walls.

"Is it finished?"

"Almost certainly…"

Then Dr. Baldur glanced back at the door they had just come out of. A fixed smile lay frozen on his face, and a little sweat trickled down from the edge of his man bun. The food sources for the vampire bats had their heads shaved so that their hair would not entangle with the delicate wings of the flying parasites. Perhaps Dr. Baldur was afraid his usefulness to the project would soon end, and he was imagining himself shaved bald, beaten to a pulp, his teeth extracted, chained to a wall, waiting to be fed on.

"But you will need me every step of the way," Dr. Baldur said. "Every step, yes, toward victory, sir."

"Don't let me doubt that."

They passed through a final pressurized door. The air here was much cooler than in the passage leading away from the bat colony. Everywhere Abdelkader looked, temperature, humidity, and radiation monitors hung from walls and sat on lab tables.

No sooner had the door hissed closed behind them than a small Indonesian woman in a mask and gown spun around. She was so shocked at their sudden appearance that she dropped a handful of red-capped test tubes. One after another, they hit the concrete floor and shattered.

Abdelkader swore in Algerian Arabic. Suppressing his rage, he held his breath as he looked left and right for a respirator. There were none. His next impulse was to shoot the stupid girl, who stood staring at him from behind her face shield with her dark, dull eyes. He put his hand on the grip of his pistol, then noticed what the scientist was doing.

Dr. Baldur glanced at the shards on the floor and the glistening blue liquid spreading across the floor, and he laughed. Abdelkader had his other hand clamped over his mouth and fake nose. His face got hotter as raw exposed blood vessels pushed up against the silicone of his synthetic face.

"What?" Abdelkader said, dropping his hand. He felt foolish and that only fanned his rage. "That's not the virus?"

"Oh, it is," Dr. Baldur said in a whiny keening voice. "It certainly is." He chuckled again. "This is from the most potent batch of A/P-32 we've ever cultured." The scientist patted the lab assistant out of the way and handed her a dustpan and broom. "That's what I meant to tell you. It does everything you wanted: It can penetrate any respirator and filtration system, it spreads undetectably by asymptomatic transmission. No antigen test now available will be able to identify it."

"How do you know? Westerners, especially the Americans, have become more vigilant against invading viruses than hijacked planes. Homeland

Security claims their health-check vigilance at ports, airfields, and land crossings has made the USA an 'antiviral Fort Knox.'"

"I, er, sent some volunteers in. They infected themselves and passed screening centers in Miami, Honolulu, and Los Angeles."

"Why wasn't I told?" If anyone came to suspect what they were doing… Without proper precautions, all Abdelkader's work, all the Pangeans' remaining resources could be vaporized by an airstrike that would sink this flat little pancake of an island under the Caribbean Sea. His voice rose to a higher pitch as his fire-damaged lungs gasped, "Why did you do that?"

"It was a double-blind operation. The subjects did not even know what they were doing. I assure you."

Quickly, as though trying to create a distraction before he said something else to displease Abdelkader, Dr. Baldur picked up another red-capped tube from the big table in the center of the lab where the strangest creature sat peering at them with mismatched, beady eyes.

"I haven't seen that before," Abdelkader said crossly. As the mutant rodent's eyes—one blue, one green—met his own he felt his anger melt away into revulsion. The creature had tufts of orange-reddish hair and in place of paws it stood unsteadily on four tiny human hands.

"That?" Baldur cackled nervously. "That's Avi, a giant Luzon rat we've 'humanized' for… for certain avenues of scientific inquiry."

The little hands even had human-looking fingernail beds and revealed, as the hybrid pawed at the glass of its cage, whorls of fingerprints.

Abdelkader had a strong urge to shoot the hybrid; instead he asked, "It came out like that? From gene splicing?"

"Oh nonono, we don't have the equipment, or the time. I only modified parts of his immune system. The scalp and forearms came from aborted fetuses and while surgery is not my specialty I, *zip*, just spliced them on."

Baldur must have noticed Abdelkader's persistent look of disgust, he hastily added, "But of course we used only tissue from aborted infidels, the spawn of Caracas whores."

"And playing with this abomination hasn't distracted you from your main task," Abdelkader said menacingly.

"The pathogen AC-32. It's marvelous. Made to order. After a period of gestation in a human, it deploys an adeno-associated virus, which crosses the brain–blood barrier and delivers… You haven't told me what you intend as the final viral package." Perhaps to take attention away from the big rat who was pawing at his cage with both tiny human hands, Dr. Baldur looked at the wall to the north end of the island. "But whatever is the final viral payload, it will be more certain of getting to its destination than a FedEx package." He breathed in deeply, as though the musty air that hung in the subterranean room were as fresh and healthy as the sea air blowing across the island above them.

Dr. Baldur sounded like Abdelkader's seven-year-old son reading out of the encyclopedia, before the American bomb incinerated those books along with the rest of his home and family. Avoiding the glances of the clumsy lab assistant, Abdelkader looked around. There was a thick book on the table with dozens of Post-it notes attached, open to pages filled with biochemical formulas and diagrams. No author was listed, it was entitled: *Biological and Chemical Weapons: Their Joys and Pitfalls.*

"Is this your creation, Doctor?" He prodded the leather-bound text. "Or are you copying from the work of better minds?"

Dr. Baldur made some face-saving reply, which Abdelkader did not hear. He was making a mental note to bring in a new lab technician from the Venezuelan mainland. The sloppy Indonesian woman would be feeding the vampire bats before sundown. He turned and walked back to the pressure door.

"T-this is what you asked for. It meets, exceeds even, all the specifications for the non-lethal pathogen you so wisely tasked me to create." The scientist kept jabbering. "This version of Pegivirus C is as likely to spread death as pure water."

"Dr. Baldur, that is exactly what I want. I do not intend to spread death," Abdelkader said with cold vehemence. "That's too merciful for America. I intend to spread madness and utter damnation."

He left the virus lab and headed straight for the north end of Isla La Tortuga.

2

SIX MONTHS LATER, JANUARY 17, 2033
CITIZEN-JUGGERNAUT NEWSROOM
CHURCH OF THE IMMACULATE CONCEPTION,
MAYFAIR, LONDON

ELLIE SATO

Ellie!" Smitty, the paper's managing editor, yelled up at the ceiling from a reclining position atop his unreasonably complicated-looking back-pain-therapy chair. "You're late for assignments. Again."

Ellie Sato struggled down the last wobbly steps of the spiral staircase to the basement of the former Catholic church.

"Sorry. Ah!" Her heel became wedged in a loose floorboard, and in the process of unwedging it, she nearly toppled over. "Is it any excuse that I own the *Juggernaut*?"

"Not in the least," John Favre said. His rotund body was topped off by a tangle of graying ringlets that made the staff reporter look like an unkempt sheepdog. He was sitting behind a formerly grand old desk that must have belonged to a bishop. It had been carved in the shape of Notre Dame Cathedral and was still recognizable despite many parts having been chopped off for firewood by homeless drug addicts.

"We're determined to treat you more shabbily than ever in our ongoing protest against Tory elitism," added the only other full-time newsroom employee they could afford, Ed Flappe. His equally rotund and bald figure spoke from a beanbag chair that was nearly squashed flat due to multiple leaks of dried beans which might have been inside since the 1970s.

"Sorry, Smitty," Ellie said. "But they had a brand-new set of guard friars upstairs. They wouldn't let me in at first, said I looked like a tart."

Smitty lifted his head from his headrest. "Enough dither dather. Gather round the story assignment slug board," he said, nearly tipping over. "Gah! When in heaven's name will you get the flooring fixed, Ellie?"

"If you hadn't gotten into an argument with our former investor, Mr. Oliphant, we might have been able to afford to get back into the Gherkin Tower offices."

Ranulph Oliphant, the wealthiest man in Scotland, had invested in the *Juggernaut* after Ellie had helped him save Europe from obliteration by the mad fiend President Rapace and his evil Pangean allies. The partnership fell apart when Smitty took his mandate to copy the *Daily Mail*'s sensationalism too far.

"How was I to know he'd take offense at being prodded out of the closet?"

"Ran wasn't in any closet," Ellie said. "He's a widower, and you hit on a very sensitive nerve with the article that alleged his country estate Oliphant Green 'boasted a bevy of lady-boys and sex workers that made the aristocratic depravities of Longleat look like Easter at a nunnery.'"

"It was our best-selling issue," John said.

"The pornographic pictures you dimwits published were taken in a Bangkok brothel during the 1970s, before Ran Oliphant was born," Ellie protested.

"They expressed the substance of the piece better than any facts would have," Ed said. John nodded agreement.

Ellie stalked over the warped floorboards to a chewed-up couch sitting in front of a large flat-screen display, which took up nearly an entire wall.

"You're just lucky I had enough money to pay him back or else he'd have repossessed that back-support chair and everything else we have. He was really cheesed off."

"Remind me to thank you for your financial faith in old-school journalism," Smitty said, guiding the mechanized casters of his chair over to where she was standing. The device, which had cost thousands, was the best thing he'd ever found to keep his spine discs in place and saved him boatloads of agony. "On a day when you arrive to work on time."

After she had paid Ran back out of her advance royalties on her best-selling book *The Pangean Protocol*, which threw light on the insane French president and a perverted Pope, there was just enough left over for a down payment on this church building. The property had fallen into receivership when the English Catholic Church was bankrupted by sex-abuse lawsuits.

In order to qualify for the mortgage on the former church building, Ellie had to lease the upstairs to the Bodmin Greyfriars, a revived order of friars from Bristol. They ran a soup kitchen and provided security for the whole block. These charitable services were particularly needful since the formerly very posh Mayfair area had fallen on hard times and was besieged by rape gangs and drug dealers.

As Ellie watched from the couch, one of the news story assignment slugs crawled off the edge of the whiteboard, fell to the floor, righted itself, and started slowly oozing its way toward Smitty. It left a silvery trail of goo behind it.

"Oh!" Smitty exclaimed, leaning over far enough to make Ellie worry that he might throw his back out. "Who filled the robot slugs with slime?"

Ellie picked up the long wriggling mechanoid by its squishy rubber outer shell. LED lights on the backs of the toys were pulsating with names of story ideas. This one said: *LIBERTY MELTDOWN*

About a foot in length, the sophisticated robot slugs were a legacy of their ill-advised spending spree. As to the prankster using them to mess up the interior of the newsroom, there was a distinct scarcity of suspects. Predictably, both Ed Flappe and John Favre tried to blame their unpaid intern.

"I would take a hard look at Esmunda," Ed said.

"She's dodgy, that one," John agreed. "Check her desk for bottles of fake slime."

"Some Inspector Morse and Sergeant Lewis you two are," Ellie said. "Esmunda put in her notice last night. Seeing the friars in their cassocks and listening to their Gregorian chanting every day was giving her bad dreams."

That left them severely understaffed. Until she herself had become a flinty-eyed capitalist media owner, Ellie had had little idea how important unpaid labor was to a business. She picked up the robotic slug, turned off its movement function, and stuck it back on the whiteboard.

"Look at the mess," Smitty kept on. "I'm going to trash those things."

"Y'can't," Ed and John said nearly in unison.

"They're part of our sacred newspaper heritage," Ed said. "The term 'slug' refers to short captions denoting news assignments and comes from the days when they used lead bars in the Linotype machine to print newspapers."

Ellie's Louboutin stuck to the filthy floor; her foot nearly popped out again. "Gah! Out they go," she exclaimed and then noticed what was written on the story assignment board. "And what's all this? You've conflicted me out of everything."

The board, with mechanical slugs for headlines, read:

MANIACS LOOSE IN LONDON: Will the Tories' closure of most UK care facilities for the mentally infirm soon mean a looney living in your skip bin? [E. Sato barred – medical conflict]

LIBERTY MELTDOWN: The climate crisis caused the melting of NY's Statue of Liberty last summer and the disintegration of Sydney's Opera House last week (good riddance). Why are Big Ben and Nelson's Column not affected? Is global warming leaving the underachieving UK behind? Will America or China win the Space Mirror Race to cool planet Earth before it's too late? [E. Sato barred – financial conflict]

THERE CAN BE ONLY 1 (USA): After the (most recent) unprecedented cockup of the US Presidential election, no less than 3 candidates have a possible chance of being sworn in to office. UK bookies are giving nearly equal odds to all in the days leading up to the crucial US Supreme Court ruling, which shall decide the matter. [E. Sato barred – travel restriction]

TAX GRIFTER (UK-NATIONAL): Millionairess author cheats HMR out of taxes with spurious donation scheme. [E. Sato – upper class privilege conflict]

CROYDON CAT MANGLER (UK-LOCAL): The cruelly mutilated corpses of innocent felines have been piling up for nearly two decades. Will Scotland Yard ever stop this perennial pet persecutor?

"Not everything, Ellie," Smitty said placatingly.

"I'm not doing the Cat Mangler," she said. "That story's as old as the hills. All you do is sit and have tea with seniors who talk about little Bink-Bink who disappeared years ago." Ellie looked down the list. "Why am I barred from the maniacs story?"

"Um… because you are one of the mentally damaged, you live in a care home, dear," Smitty said soothingly.

"I'm living in an emergency psychiatric care home in order to keep it open while my very good friend is, er, away."

"You couldn't be there because the mansion's worth a hundred million pounds and comes with its own staff," John said.

"There's only one butler, and I've never seen him," Ellie shot back, determined to prove her egalitarian status. "The rest are robots."

"Well, Ellie, even though it's a voluntary outpatient situation, you're still technically mental," Smitty said. "The National Union of Journalists code also prohibits you from reporting on climate change because your financial disclosure form shows you own shares in an oil company."

"I thought the company made palm oil moisturizer."

"And, of course, I'm not letting you go overseas to that train wreck America's become lately," Smitty said protectively. "Not after you were nearly killed in the Middle East and then again barely survived your misadventures on the continent. No more!"

Ellie looked at the penultimate story idea.

"Tax grifter?" she said with rising alarm and indignation. "Is that supposed to be me?"

"Well, you did get a phony British Museum tax credit didn'tcha?" Ed said, fiddling with a spare slug robot and a bottle of glue under his desk.

"That was the idea of Ran's accountants. I donated my Namiki collector's fountain pen to the museum, and they're going to loan it to the Tokyo National Museum."

A Turkish oligarch had once offered her nearly £2 million for it just before she'd nearly let it get destroyed during the 96-Hour War. Ever since then, she had been afraid to take it out of the vault at London's Appelboom pen store.

"All the money I saved I put right back into the *Juggernaut,* after you scunned off our only investor, Mr. Oliphant. I'm up to my eyeballs in debt."

"Neither a borrower nor a lender be," John said with the mock wisdom of a newsroom sage.

"Easy for you to say. You lot are only drawing pay because I took over as the newspaper's publisher."

"Spoken like a selfish toff. As though it's the working man's fault when your nefarious financial schemes are exposed." Ed put a slug on the banister and sent it crawling up to the friary.

Ellie spent the next hour looking at evidence photographs depicting mangled cat corpses and taking calls from the head friar, who threatened to stop paying rent unless she hired a better cleaning service. Smitty wheeled over to her, then flicked a switch which made the chair give him a full-body rubdown, which he seemed to be enjoying to the point of public indecency.

"Don't look so glum, Ellie," Smitty said, the vibrating chair making his voice quaver. "I've promised your parents I will, henceforth, keep you far away from any more of these self-harming far-flung adventures."

3

TAVISTOCK MANOR AND MENTAL SANITORIUM
MAYFAIR, LONDON

Ellie left the offices of her newspaper late in the evening and had a few minutes to reflect on the wisdom of becoming a business owner, landlord, and celebrity author all in the space of a few months. She looked at the deconsecrated former Catholic Church. After expensive renovations, it looked much better than it had during her first visit, when she and her then-housemate had broken in in pursuit of a story on local drug gangs.

Initially, she had thought that working in the same basement where she'd seen a man shot and had been attacked by a grooming-gang child rapist brandishing a sword would compound her nightmares. However, her psychiatrist, whose sister happened to be an estate agent who was representing the vacant property, convinced her it would be empowering to defy her demons. Her doctor was also adamant, after learning exactly how much of an advance her publisher had offered her for *The Pangea Protocol*, that Ellie borrow to purchase the property instead of merely leasing it.

"The only way to truly defeat your PTSD and banish your inchoate fears is to take a serious financial risk. That is my professional opinion," Dr. Katz, BM BCh (Oxon), MBiomed, FRCPsych, had told her as he texted his sister about Ellie's keen interest in closing the acquisition as soon as was practical.

It was nine p.m. by the time Ellie finally dragged herself up the stairs of Tavistock Manor on Grosvenor Square. The only lights glimmering in the park came from a few robot dog walkers. She wondered if Chestnut, her adopted Labradoodle, was among them. She was too tired to go searching. She was working so much she felt her dog had become more attached to the manor's butler, Mr. Surghit.

As she reached the top of the ornate granite stairs, she fumbled for her handset in case the bags under her eyes were so bad the security system's facial-recognition program would once again refuse to recognize her. The double mahogany doors swung silently open.

She looked left and right, hoping to get a glimpse of the heretofore invisible Mr. Surghit. There was no one on the polished marble of the grand foyer. Ellie worked longer hours than anyone, and since the *Juggernaut's* volunteer intern had quit, she also got paid the least. Exploiting the working class was becoming a drag.

Suddenly, a shaggy form bounded down the marble staircase. Chestnut leapt up at her, his top half soaking wet. He must have escaped a shampoo session. His rear half was caked with mud and some gunky brown residue Ellie hoped was just moldering leaf residue.

"Not now, Chestnut. Go! Go finish your bath. I don't want the robots chasing you all night."

It was only then that she noticed a pair of steely bureaucratic eyes watching her from a wing-backed chair at the end of the entrance hall. He was sitting as motionless as the portrait of the Earl of Scarborough, on the wall behind him, and if Ellie hadn't looked right at him, she might have walked right past.

"Oh, Mr. Delingpole, what a pleasant, er, surprise."

What the devil could the NHS fellow want at this hour?

"Hello, Ms. Sato," he said without moving his lips. He uncrossed his very long, thin legs, which made even his slim trousers look baggy as he cautiously approached her. True, in the recent past she had locked him in an office while helping a serial poisoner escape, but since then, they'd been polite if not cordial.

"I guess you're here to have a look about," Ellie said as brightly as she could manage. A threatening growl came from her pet. "Don't be like that,

Chestnut. You like Mr. Delingpole. It's his aftershave that made you want to attack him, and he's not wearing any tonight."

She prodded the wary Labradoodle back toward the service lift inside of which a dog-grooming robot was waiting.

"I don't see why you bothered popping by," Ellie went on. "As of January 31st, Tavistock's going back to whatever it was before the previous government forced it to become an outpatient hospital for the mentally infirm."

The building's owner, a fellow from India, had taken full advantage of the Labour-Marxist's convoluted property tax regime. Now that the Tories were back in, there was no financial advantage to housing mad people. The only other patient, Ms. Annunciata China, had been locked away in solitary confinement until they sorted out that mass-murder nonsense. Luckily Dr. Katz had diagnosed Ellie as suffering from PTSD and registered her as a halfway-house patient that allowed them to keep Tavistock open, and most importantly, rent free.

"Yes, yes," Delingpole said. "We'll need you to take an inventory of any NHS equipment on the premises and ensure its safe return to the relevant departments. If anything is missing or damaged, I'm afraid we'll have to bill you."

"Me? I'm the patient here."

"You did sign the surety form."

Oh, brilliant, now she had another job.

"That's not fair."

Delingpole approached her while fiddling with a clipboard full of forms with microscopic writing on them; he was clearly intent on getting her to sign some more sureties.

"In my experience, neither life nor insanity are fair," he said slowly, with the sort of fainthearted menace all government people eventually acquire. "Can you please sign these in triplicate?"

Ellie took the clipboard and looked around for a decent pen. There was no chance she was going to sign her name with the ballpoint Delingpole had handed her; it was so manky it might well have been used as a dipstick to check a car's oil levels. How did one get oneself snapped into a comfy straitjacket and put in a relaxing-sounding padded cell? She could use a—

What now?

A crash sounded from three or four flights up.

"Well, thanks for popping in." Ellie handed the ministry man his bowler hat, his clipboard, and umbrella. "Seems I'm needed upstairs. Just mail me those forms."

"One last thing," he said as she prodded him toward the doors. "You haven't heard from *her*, have you?"

"Why, you haven't lost her again, have you?"

"Oh, no. We've taken steps." Delingpole reached into his mac overcoat and took out an overlarge handset. On its screen were feeds from surveillance cameras labeled:

St. Bartholomew's remote cam-link

NHS Client Annunciata Romanov China (she/her) # 485 777 3456

There were four different angles, including an infrared night-vision camera—all were trained at the exterior of Ms. China's asylum cell.

"She won't cause any more mayhem."

More crashing sounded from the central staircase, followed by a rain of what looked like caramelized popcorn. Chestnut dashed away from the lift and began snapping it up.

"Hope not, ha. We've got mayhem a-plenty without good ol' Annunciata about. Good night—"

"We know you've been in to see her at the Old Bailey. If she should contact you again…"

"I'll ring you straight away. Mind the steps down to the street." Ellie finally shut the door and glanced upstairs with growing trepidation.

Once she had both Chestnut's forelegs and hindquarters back in the Jacuzzi soaker tub, she ventured onto the fourth floor, which had recently been remodeled into a place where mad people could snack and do relaxing arts and crafts.

"Esmunda!" Ellie shouted over the music. The *Juggernaut*'s former intern was over by the antique French sofa, doing what looked like a twerking lap dance in front of a scruffy-looking boy in ripped jeans who was holding a beer bottle.

"Oh, hi," Esmunda said, blowing a strand of pink-dyed hair out of her beady little eyes.

"We agreed, uh, didn't we? No guests after six, right?"

"These aren't guests, they're me mates! Whooo!" Esmunda grabbed her mate's beer and drained it.

Despite misgivings, Ellie had let Esmunda stay here because she had seemed so eager to work in journalism and complained her crushing student debt and the awful London housing market had forced her to live at the seafood market under a crab fridge. She had promised to help around the house and asserted that Ellie would barely notice she was there among the bajillion rooms of the mansion. Tonight, Ellie certainly noticed Esmunda as well as the unmistakable smell of a very unwholesome synthetic cannabis called Spice.

"When you're through giving lap dances, could you help me inventory some of the NHS stuff?"

At the mention of work, Esmunda was instantly shocked into nasty rebelliousness. "I quit the *Juggernaut*. You're not the boss of me anymore." Then she looked as though she were holding in a belch for a moment, crossed her eyes, and burst out laughing.

"Where are the nice kids like Attie Jr.?" Ellie fumed as she retreated back through her own bedroom door, which she had to keep locked since the night she had come home to find a pair of tattooed nonbinary people doing nonbinary things to each other in her bathroom.

After checking under the bed for passed-out partygoers, and texting Mr. Surghit to triple the house's antiviral protocols, Ellie sank into the plush folds of the four-poster bed, which probably cost more than her parents' residence in Northumberland. She had snaked a long silk-covered pillow around both sides of her head, which nearly blocked out the drill rap music coming from down the hallway, and had just sunk into a long dark meditation on where exactly she would be living in a few weeks when she had to vacate Tavistock, when a demanding tapping came from the window.

Outside, hanging in the dark, was the bulbous shape of a small dirigible. Her back let her know it resented having to, once again, stand upright as Ellie stepped slowly over and cranked open the mullioned glass panes. The night air wafting in was chilly and carried a scent from the flower beds below. A plastic, birdlike beak jabbed forward once again to knock on the glass and pecked her in the forehead.

"Ouch."

As soon as she detached the square envelope from its plastic undercarriage, the delivery balloon sped off into the night sky.

The envelope was made of heavy cardstock and featured bright colors suitable for a surprise birthday greeting. Ellie debated opening it right away. The way her day was going, she doubted the contents would be festive. Then from between the folded creases of the envelope, she noticed a muted flickering light. It was a video card.

There's no chance of getting any rest until I've opened it, she thought, ripping the cover asunder. It was probably from a bill collector who had decided to get creative with their demand letters.

She opened the package and found herself face-to-face with the lantern-jawed, tiny-eyed, large-eared close-shaven head of the Chippenham Cannibal. Though it had been several years since his infamous crime spree, which had begun with him butchering and eating his aged and abusive father and then playing marbles with local kids using the victim's eyeballs, his meek and simple gap-toothed grin was unmistakable. He stared politely out from the surface of the animated greeting card, which could play brief snippets of video captured by a handset.

"Oy, hi. Ah… y'needs come ter see yer friend," the Cannibal said without preamble. "Here's what ter bring…"

4

TAVISTOCK MANOR
MAYFAIR, LONDON

Ellie awoke the next morning to the sounds of a poorly tuned lawnmower sputtering away in the park. She was pleasantly surprised to see her blister packs of Benzodiazepine and Selective Serotonin something or other untouched on her bedside table.

Ever since her long journey through the bone-strewn catacombs under Paris, she'd felt off her head. Not all the time, but mostly in the evening. It had been more difficult without the odd comfort of her now-incarcerated roommate Anna.

When Ms. Annunciata China lost her final appeal and was sent back to a high-security asylum, Ellie had to insist on being declared insane or Tavistock Manor would have lost its charitable status, and they'd have had to move to somewhere without an eight-car garage and an army of mechanical servants.

Pretending to have a disturbed personality turned out not to be so hard. She told the NHS psychiatrist a tame version of some of the things she'd actually witnessed during the past few years, and the sympathetic lady had immediately whipped out her prescription pad and referred her to the top London specialist, Dr. Katz.

The drugs helped—at first. Then Ellie noticed she was feeling like a light bulb that needed sixty watts but was only getting twenty. It was also quiet. Chestnut rarely caused any doggie fuss, and she never saw the only full-time human on the Tavistock staff. This was about when Esmunda showed up carrying two suitcases with the long talons of an aggressive old macaw named Magellan clamped on her shoulder.

The *Juggernaut* intern had followed her home from the cathedral; she looked too pitiful to just turn away, and Ellie ended up letting her in as though she'd been expected. Her medication had dulled her faculties to the point she was no longer wary of wayward youths who smoked synthetic weed first thing in the morning.

What should have been another warning sign came when Ellie had dropped a vintage Montblanc 146 onto the Venetian marble floor. It fell point first, as all fountain pens do, and was damaged so badly the factory in Hamburg sent her a stern email saying they were doubtful that they could save it, suggesting that in the future, she limit herself to Bic ballpoint pens. This brazen snub did not affect her at all.

Then, the very same day, she had gone to Appelboom Pens, where the proprietor Luc told her Diamine Ink Company was discontinuing their Orange Ogre color—which she had never really cared for—and she went into a crying fit that lasted the whole of the afternoon.

She decided to get a second opinion on her course of treatments. Through a double layer of electrified wire mesh of the Old Bailey's holding cell, Ellie discussed her medicinal misgivings with Ms. China who, despite her own mental condition, knew more about pharmaceuticals and chemistry than anyone else in Europe. Ms. China ridiculed her for not being able to handle "kiddie-portion psychotropics."

Ellie decided that her fuzzy-headedness would not do for someone who had employees who depended on her and a commercial mortgage with very severe penalties for default. For a week, she had tried to wean herself off the meds but kept reaching for them at night, until one evening she found Mr. Surghit had installed a holographic system that projected the starry night sky onto her bedroom ceiling.

Of course! Most of her issues stemmed from the twenty-four hours she'd spent in the Paris Catacombs, alternately being shot at, nearly raped, drowned, and buried alive under the remains of six million dead French people. Her repressed pernicious claustrophobia subsided, as did her reliance on psychotropics. She penned a hearty thank-you note to Mr. Surghit in a shade of Oxford-blue ink, which she felt conveyed her sincerity.

The next morning, the note was gone from the hall table, replaced by a combination walking handweight/throwing toy, which Chestnut enjoyed immensely.

As her head cleared, she realized she should ask her personal banker why her net balances always seemed to remain negative. That was still a pending item on her list the evening she received the polite request from the Chippenham Cannibal.

The morning light streamed in through the partly curtained windows as Ellie lay in bed considering her best course of action. Suddenly an astounding racket coming from the hallway made her want to crawl back under the covers. It sounded as though the animals were overthrowing the keepers at a zoo. She got her robe on and poked her head out.

"Chestnut! Don't let that mean old Magellan tease you."

Esmunda's monstrously sized macaw had taken to mercilessly pestering the normally serene and somewhat naïve Labradoodle. The unnaturally cruel winged beast would send its droppings flying into his food and water bowls and also onto Chestnut's curly golden-brown fur from all angles without warning.

"Magellan, you old scoundrel, stop that or I'll..." Ellie stopped herself. She didn't want to have video posted online of her threatening to have a bird's wings clipped, especially an elderly creature who was reportedly older than she was. "Or I'll ask Esmunda to be very strict with you."

"Lick me! Right there!" the bird said in a horrible screeching voice, the words echoing through the marble stairwell.

Magellan was standing atop a suit of armor on the landing above, scanning her with one coal-black eye while bobbing his head up and down in a lascivious manner. The atrocious avian seemed to revel in the helpless rage of humans and dogs alike.

"Lick me! Right there!"

"Ezzie!" she called out generally. Her houseguest could pop up anywhere, having claimed every room as her own—except, for now, Ellie's bedroom. "I'm going out now."

Only the chortling of the beastly bird answered her, echoing up and down the central stairwell. Ellie checked she had the items the Chippenham Cannibal had asked her to bring to the asylum: her passport for identification, a large Hermes scarf, and a pair of rubber-soled deck shoes.

The surprisingly polite fellow, whose pre-cannibalism name was Harry Goodrum, had explained there had been some changes to security procedures at the asylum, and she would need these items when she arrived during visiting hours. The need for better identification, she could understand. As for the footwear, perhaps they were asking people to remove their shoes as they did in the airport in order to check them for explosives and germs.

Though she didn't recall mentioning her planned visit to anyone, Mr. Surghit had a cab waiting.

"'Lo, ma'rm," said the friendly puce-faced driver from the front compartment. "'Fraid it's a Persimmon viral alert t'day. M'conveyance has to complete the full cycle while you watch according to Public Carriage Office regulations."

"I'm familiar with the drill," Ellie said, looking at her watch. St. Bartholomew's was not far, and whatever it was Ms. China had to discuss wouldn't take more than fifteen or twenty minutes. She'd just tell Smitty she'd been interviewing Cat Mangler victims' owners and was certain she could make it to the cathedral by ten.

After six months of Taupe Alert, the "Daily Viral Load Caution" for central London had notched up to Persimmon. As a result, the rear of the cab had to cycle through an extra ultraviolet-light self-cleaning routine before the door would unlock.

The driver, who like many cabbies had become a talented amateur virologist, regaled her with interesting species captured in his car's antiviral filters.

"A week ago, in the back, right where you're sittin', they found a Tasmanian whooping cough bug," he said through the speaker from inside his sealed-off driver's compartment. "Blasted thing was enormous, some seven hundred nanometers, nearly had to get me flyswatter out."

They sped off.

Just in case someone at St. Bartholomew's would be handling her shoes, Ellie had invested in a new pair of Fendi half boots and a pair of Gucci slip-ons from Harrods via their online shopping portal the previous evening. They had been delivered by drone before she got up.

Inside the ozone-smelling cab, she looked at her newest wardrobe acquisitions. These boots said "best-selling author who happens to own London's oldest newspaper and is in no way stuck up about it" while the slippers said "I'm not a madhouse inmate, just visiting." At only £390 and £299 respectively, with some kind of discount or points credit on her Harrods card, not to mention free delivery, they were really solid wardrobe investments. Additionally, with no payments due for sixty days, she could take advantage of Viral High Alert sales day and pay it all off when the *Juggernaut* spun out a profit, which everyone assured her it soon would.

Fleet Street Books rolled by, but she was unable to politely gloat at the display stack of *The Pangea Protocol* in the window. Some lunatics dressed in flowing red cloth with their faces painted like harlequins and carrying Extinction Climate Rebellion signs were dumping clods of grass and dirt onto the steps of the Barclay's Bank next to the bookshop.

"If the environment were a bank, it would have been saved already!" yelled one enormous woman with blue hair through a loudspeaker. Two (probably) men wearing red tights were performing a very odd ballet dance, which carried over onto the road. Their cab was delayed until the police could nonviolently coax them back onto the sidewalk.

One of the probably-men was not happy. He shouted at the officer, "Viruses are the CURE, humans are the DISEASE!"

The cab driver turned back to her, speaking through the partition, "Barmy lot, huh? Diggin' up perfectly good grass and dumpin' it in the middle o' town. Who's gonna clean that mess? Not them university do-nothings."

As they drove away, a piercing shriek chased them along. From the glimpse Ellie got out the back window, she saw one of the protestors had epoxied himself to the Barclay's front door. He had been so filled with zeal to save the planet he'd applied adhesive to his cheek and ear as well as his clothing. The authorities were wondering what to do with him when some people tried to leave the bank via the door the protestor was attached to. This resulted in considerable pain.

They pulled up at the Giltspur Street entrance to the medical complex a few minutes later.

"'Ere y'go. Saint Bartholomew's. This was the fictional meeting place of one Sherlock Holmes and one Dr. Watson in *A Study in Scarlet*."

Did she look like a tourist? Maybe the poor man was angling for a larger gratuity. Because of the additional sanitizing cycles, the day would undoubtedly yield him fewer fares.

"Oh, not here, please," Ellie said. "By the pharmacy entrance, please."

"Are y'sure? That's where they keep the dangerous lunatics."

"Yes," Ellie said, taking a deep breath as she gathered her things and added thirty percent to the fare, which her business card was able to pay, somewhat to her surprise.

Unlike the main entrance, which served the teaching hospital and two medical museums, the pharmacy area had no robotic golf cart conveyances to whiz people about. Instead, the back alley featured armed guards on patrol and barbed wire along the rooftops.

At the entrance kiosk, a squat-looking female guard sat behind the tempered glass. She did not seem interested in the passport Ellie politely held up.

"Okay, Sato, E. You're on the list. Legal stenographer for a patient's solicitor. You're early."

"Am I? Yes, I am." Ellie considered correcting the mix-up, but the fat metal doorway popped open. A bit disappointed not to be recognized as a famous author and media mogul, she pushed through the vertical turnstile bars and entered the visitor's scrutiny area, ready to be scrutinized.

They did not ask her to remove her half boots, but they did put her bag through a few complex-looking scanning machines.

"No gifts for inmates," the man at the console said, tapping the outline of her slip-ons.

"I have, er, bunions. Terrible little things," Ellie said. "Sometimes they take my mind off my legal stenography scribbling, so I put those on."

Ellie just went with the mistake they'd made about her job. If she tried to correct them, they'd keep her there an hour sorting things out. The security examiner shrugged his beefy shoulders as she collected her things on the other side of the full-body scanner.

"Stall number eighteen, way in the back," he called after her. "The convic— I mean, patient will be let in by a different entrance."

This place had tighter security than where they'd held former French President Rapace, and he'd tried to kill five hundred million people. The lady guard from the front desk, who looked much slimmer than she had through the Plexiglas, came to escort her.

"Don't mind him," she said in a soothing chirpy voice. "He's an employee transfer from Belmarsh Prison. We're really just a hospital with a little added protection for the patients."

Ellie wondered whether there was a news story here. Nearly half of young British women aged seventeen to nineteen reported having some form of mental illness, and the *Juggernaut* needed to reel in that demographic to capture more advertising spend.

"I'm early, you said. Can you show me around?" Ellie asked. "If it's allowed, of course."

The guard's name was Juanita. She was from the Philippines and seemed heartened by Ellie's interest in the facility.

"This is the quiet room," Juanita said. "If anyone feels as though their senses are overloading and they need to harm themselves or others, they can pop in here."

Through mirrored one-way glass, Ellie saw a figure squatting in the middle of a padded room, rocking gently back and forth. Details were hard to make out in the dim light, but it seemed the deranged man was squatting on a floor mat and chewing something that looked like cardboard and then spitting the resulting soggy bits into a lumpy pile. She could only see the back of his head, but something about his bald spot seemed familiar...

"Oh my. Has that patient been here long?" Ellie was suddenly worried about Ms. China. At the Old Bailey, she had seemed much like her old self, but that was weeks ago. Would Ellie find her in as poor shape as this drooling wretch?

"Him?" Juanita said, indicating the man swaying on the padded floor.

"Oh, no, that's our attending psychiatrist, Dr. Katz. I guess he had a stressful night shift again."

"You don't say," Ellie said vaguely. She was thinking it would probably not be a good idea to mention that Dr. Katz was her very own psychiatrist.

They moved on to the second floor.

"Before the renovation, acute adult mental health clients went to Gordon Hospital," Juanita said proudly. "But demand outstripped supply, and Gordon had to convert all their activity rooms into wards. Here, we still have space for fun."

A large rectangular head leered at Ellie from the window into the next room on their tour.

"Hi, sir," Ellie said as she waved politely. The hulking and very alert-looking Chippenham Cannibal was a mite more intimidating in person than he had been in the animated greeting card message.

"This is our showpiece, the most advanced occupational therapy facility in Europe," Juanita said proudly. "It features finger painting, sing-along karaoke, and a wide variety of crafts facilitated by a cutting-edge molecular 3D printer, which St. Bartholomew's received by anonymous donation."

From inside the arts and crafts area, the Cannibal waved back and then raised overly large hands to rearrange the cap he was wearing. It looked quite ornate, with bells and crescent-shaped moons hanging from peaked ends.

"Why is he wearing a fool's cap?"

"Your client, Ms. China, is putting on *Macbeth* for the annual winter play. She's quite an overachiever. Keeps us all on our toes."

Ellie suddenly thought of something drilled into her head by that dusty old spinster, Ms. Welk, who taught drama at her middle school.

"Wait a moment, there's no fool in Shakespeare's *Macbeth*."

"We know," Juanita said sympathetically, smiling as she laid her hand on the thick glass in front of the large, merry-looking man. "But who's going to tell him?"

The Cannibal giggled, and mirroring her gesture, he also put his hand on the glass, then shook his head, which sent his cap ornaments dancing silently around his head.

"You have male and female patients together?"

Juanita nodded. "Everyone has their own private room and a cubicle bath. The ministry decided to house everyone together because so many biological males were demanding to be put in women's facilities, and everyone was at a loss as to what to do with the ungendered. Besides, we really feel it helps them adjust to going back out in the real world, eventually."

In the case of the jolly cannibal, Ellie hoped that eventuality was many decades distant.

Juanita escorted Ellie through a maze of brightly lit, white-tiled corridors until they got to a door stenciled with a big black *18*.

"Solicitor's privacy extends to you, so there'll be no camera inside, but there are several in the hallway, so in the unlikely event you, er, feel yourself under threat, just stick your hand out the little window and signal. Someone will be along as soon as they can."

The room was narrow and L shaped. Two chairs were bolted to either side of a pedestal desk similarly affixed to the bare floor. Ms. China must hate this place after having lived at luxurious Tavistock.

The lock clicked, and the other door opened. A hairy, liver-spotted hand jangled some keys. It took Ellie a moment to realize the guard was not being playfully menacing with his jangling—he was so old, and possibly suffering from a bout of Parkinson's, that he could not keep his hands still. Ms. China breezed past him and sat down.

"Ellie!" Ms. China said, a pensive but determined expression on her face. "You came. Thank you very much."

It was often hard to judge the other woman's mood, mostly due to the whorls of gold and silver tattoos over every inch of her body and face, and the four extra pupils tattooed on her eyes, two on each eyeball. When speaking with her, Ellie mostly looked at her dimpled chin. She spared a glance at her hands, which were normally tipped with long, sharp, and envenomed false nails. These had, thankfully, been removed prior to her incarceration. There was nothing to worry about, Ellie told herself.

"Of course I came, you're my most, uh, unique friend." Ellie was feeling a bit guilty for having convinced Ms. China to turn herself in after they defeated the Pangeans. Then she was struck by a distinct change in Ms.

China's appearance. "Oh, you've let your hair grow… and you've colored it. It looks like mine… Oh, Annunciata… What are you—"

There were two small plastic tubes in Ms. China's nostrils. The moment Ellie spotted them, the other woman broke open a glass ampule of something that filled the air with lavender scent. Ellie managed to get halfway to her feet and had inhaled half a breath before remembering that inhaling was the last thing she should do. She felt her body go numb all over and slumped back down on the cheap plastic chair bolted to the concrete floor of the asylum.

5

ST. BARTHOLOMEW'S HIGH-SECURITY PSYCHIATRIC HOSPITAL
LONDON

Ellie sat immobilized, staring straight ahead, unable to even glance in a different direction. Ms. China, her ex-roommate and now definitely ex-friend, rummaged around inside the baggy seafoam-green-colored hospital jumpsuit. As she did so, a silver zombie Hello Kitty locket dangled out, hanging from her long neck on the end of a length of hospital-issued non-strangling tissue twine.

After a moment, Ms. China brought out a flat oval. It was rubbery looking and had eyeholes on either side. The talented poisoner and former MI6 operator Ms. China began to peel apart the two layers.

"Here we have me for you, and you for... me," she said, poking her flattened nose into shape.

Whatever Ms. China had sprayed into the air left Ellie conscious but unable to will herself to take any voluntary action. She was, however, able to feel upset, and hoped her silent gaze expressed her disappointment in the woman's evident relapse to antisocial behavior.

"I'm really sorry about this," Ms. China said, as she affixed very familiar-looking Eurasian features over her own tattooed ones. "But I just have to. Maybe one day you'll understand."

Ellie was certain she would not. Yet when Ms. China spoke, she had the odd compulsion to do something besides sit flaccidly in her stupid seat. Her shoulder jerked spasmodically, and her right hand flopped off her lap to hang limply down.

"Oops," the other woman whispered as she patted down the silicone version of Ellie's forehead over her own. "I have to be careful what I say, my own version of scopolamine, which I call Obediens serum, makes people highly suggestible. Eleanor: lean your head back."

Ellie tilted her head back and felt an odd rush of accomplishment, as though she had for the first time been able to tie her shoelaces by herself. The feeling did not last, rather it made her eager for another similar sensation.

Ms. China gently affixed the rubbery version of her face over Ellie's, smoothing the adhesive silicone right up to her hairline.

"You were the only person I could think of," her captor said as she found a mirrored surface in one of the brackets holding down the interview desk. "I have to book it before they discover the 3D printer I had an associate of mine donate is capable of making chemical compounds and masks as well as plastic tubby toys."

Then Ms. China made Ellie undress.

"You can keep your underwear."

Ellie was thankful to be stopped before she was completely naked. Next, she put on the St. Bartholomew's jumpsuit, which was made of horrible fabric and not one of her best colors. Ms. China checked Ellie's watch, which was now on her wrist.

"It's show time," the madwoman mused, and Ellie felt a sharp jab on her wrist.

"I'm sorry for that too. Now listen closely: you are to count slowly to three hundred, no cheating, and then you are to tap on the door to the prisoner wing and go inside. Keep your head down. The screw on duty is an old geezer who only ever looks at my ass, which is comparable to your ass."

Ms. China now looked like a highly botoxed version of Ellie. She checked herself over one last time and tied the large tastefully patterned Hermes scarf around her head.

The serum made Ellie eager to hear more instruction.

"Once you are in my cell, number 609, you will lie down on the bunk facing the wall and not move until the serum wears off."

She looked into each of Ellie's glazed but hopefully wrath-filled eyes and then tapped on the visitor's door to be let out. As the lock clicked, Ms. China looked back. She was about to say something more, then changed her mind, put on sunglasses and a surgical mask, and was let out by a St. Bartholomew's attendant who was not Juanita.

Ellie sat in her chair, counting, and quietly fuming, and counting, half expecting several polite and beefy guards to burst in any moment with Ms. China in handcuffs and a straitjacket, her stupid ruse having unraveled before she had gotten outside.

265... 266...

How could anyone be fooled by Ms. China's disguise? Her hair was completely off, and she walked like a creepy pickpocket not with the smooth gait of someone who had runway model training. Of course... with those sunglasses and that dumb mask even Ellie might have mistaken her for herself.

295... 296...

The fake Ms. China face stuck on top of Ellie's own was becoming maddeningly itchy. Despite this, and the seething resentment at having been, once again, drugged and fooled by her former housemate, she had to admire the madwoman's nerve and inventiveness. Ellie also wondered why she would risk escaping. From what she'd heard, Ms. China's lawyers were upbeat about obtaining a court order to have her released back into the outpatient program.

300.

Like a puppet with invisible strings, she got up off the plastic chair, walked to the door, and rapped on it with a hand that couldn't quite make a fist.

She heard the old screw shuffling up to the door. The duffer, as predicted, only looked at her rear, though what pervy stimulus it could provide, cloaked as it was in the baggy prisoner's outfit, she couldn't imagine.

Can't you tell the difference, you sad wanker? Ellie thought furiously.

You're ogling a Eurasian woman with two good legs, not a Scottish one with one biomechanical false leg.

At cell 609, she turned smartly left, and before the door clanked shut, was obediently lying down on the thin mattress atop the poured-concrete bunk and facing a cinderblock wall.

What if I have to pee?

Without further instructions, her somnambulated body merely lay sideways on the cot. Her mind, on the other hand, was seething. How could she do this? Other than Annunciata's son, Attie Jr., who was living with his grandparents in North Carolina, Ellie was probably her only friend.

And what was with this elaborate escape ruse? Judging by the lengths she had gone to 3D print a serviceable replica of both their faces, and to brew this Obediens serum—which probably wasn't something you could nick from the dispensary—there had to be a larger game afoot.

Ellie stared at concrete blocks inches from her face, which concentrated her mind wonderfully. The only possible motive Ellie could impute to Ms. China had to do with Attie Jr. That was not much to go on. Then she recalled the Cannibal's instruction to bring her passport, which hadn't been asked for at the St. Bartholomew's security desk. Ms. China wasn't just escaping the hospital, she was planning to escape to America!

The realization burned inside her until she heard the old screw shuffling along outside. He did not come in, but he did mumble, "Gotta get me pack of fags... can' 'member where I left..."

Ellie repeated this fragment silently, over and over until she convinced her lazy somnambulistic self she needed to get some cigarettes straightaway. As soon as this thought penetrated, it was as though someone had twitched on a marionette string. Her left leg slipped off the bunk and onto the floor.

6

ST. BARTHOLOMEW'S HIGH-SECURITY PSYCHIATRIC HOSPITAL
LONDON

Oh, I'm going mental for a fag... I want one.

Her small inner voice repeated what she had heard the asylum guard say, twisting it into a command. Would she actually be able to trick the part of her brain that was being made ultra-suggestible by the Obediens serum?

Moving in a dreamlike state, Ellie observed herself getting up off her bunk bed and walking the few steps to the door. Remarkably, it was unlocked.

Right... madhouse activity hours.

She thought briefly about imagining an itch on her nose so that her somnambulist self would have the urge to scratch it and hopefully remove the silicone mask of Ms. China plastered over her own. It did not work—she was only intent on getting a smoke. Thereafter, she decided against trying to change direction, afraid she might end up just standing there knocking her head against a door jamb, which was unlikely to garner much attention in this place.

The corridor was empty. Just as she felt her feet slowing down and her enthusiasm for a smoke fading, she heard muted chuckles of polite laughter coming from a door. A sign hung on it, lettered in soothing pastel colors.

Occupational Therapy
Help US help YOU
to develop Purposeful, Effective, and Nourishing
Routines, Patterns, and Roles.

Go… in. There are bound to be smokes there, go! Ellie urged her numb body.

It was the same area she had passed earlier on the other side of the security glass, the one with activity tables and the shiny new 3D printer. She only recognized one person, and despite her misgivings she imagined he had scads of cigarettes to lend. She shuffled over to him. In a moment, she was staring at the broad T-shirt-clad chest of the Chippenham Cannibal. Her mouth felt as though it had been shot through with dentist's anesthetic. Even if she had been able to speak, she wasn't exactly sure what she would say.

She got the Cannibal's attention. He looked down, the bells on his cap tinkled. She continued staring at a spot above the neckline of his T-shirt. If she couldn't speak, perhaps she could mime her desire.

Her hand raised itself to her lips and made a theatrical puffing motion. The Cannibal bent down. His deep-set coal-black eyes looked like twin navels, his puffy face so full of engorged spider veins he would not need any rouge makeup before going on stage. He examined her.

Despite having been on heavy medication for more than a decade, and having an unquenchable taste for the flesh of his first-order relatives, the Cannibal was no numpty. He scanned her, hairline to neckline. Drawing himself up, he thought a moment, then grabbed her hand and pulled her toward the toilet stall.

Oh, Mr. Cannibal!

A number of terrible perverted urges which the poor deluded fellow might want to satisfy on her very pliable body flashed through Ellie's mind. Fear and terror, however, did not dispel the Obediens serum.

Behind them, the door to the stall slid closed quietly, and Ellie had some very unfavorable thoughts about the wisdom of making these institutions coed. The space was very confined. The Cannibal slithered his hand down, brushing the pants of her jumpsuit, and then, having found what he was after, he brought up a bottle of ammonia.

"You're not her," he said quietly.

He uncapped the bottle and gave her a whiff, then another, then another. Ellie coughed. It was a brilliant, miraculous feeling. A minute later, she was able to raise her hands to the rubbery replica of Ms. China's face. She still felt sluggish.

"Oh, thank you, Mr. Cann— I mean, sir," she said, trying to keep herself from hyperventilating as her companion looked at her, hard.

"You're not her," he said in a growling whisper.

"Maybe we should, uh, alert someone," Ellie said, edging toward the door.

A fat hairy arm stopped her.

"She got out?"

"Anna? I do believe she did, yes, so I have to go and get her back in."

The Cannibal looked at the fluorescent lighting, his black eyes glittering. "No."

"No?" Ellie felt she should have remained in her nice, safe solitary cell.

"No," the Cannibal repeated, more thoughtfully this time. "If she… Ms. Anna China… she was nice to me. Helped me make this hat, taught me Shakespeare. No one ever dunnat before."

"She does have her good moments, but I don't see how—"

"If they find out she's escaped, she'll be for it. Get in loads of trouble. We gots to do somethin'."

"We will, we will," Ellie assured him as she started to peel off her silicone mask from the bottom. "First let me—"

"No." The Cannibal pushed her hands down again. "I got a way, but you just keep her face on fer now."

"Wh-why?"

To this point, and Ellie's eternal gratitude, the fellow had not done anything untoward. In fact, quite the opposite, as he had known how to counteract psychotropic drugs with simple cleaning supplies. However, she was just hoping, more like imploring, that the Cannibal did not want to play out some weird fantasy that involved Ms. China.

"We're going to save our friend," he said.

"From who?"

"From herself," the Cannibal whispered as he opened the door a crack to check if anyone was lurking outside. "C'mon."

They managed to walk right past Juanita. It was rather easy for Ellie to remain inconspicuous on the other side of a three-hundred-pound fellow wearing a cap that jingled merrily with every step.

They went past the quiet room, where Ellie's psychiatrist was still squatting on the floor. He now had a much larger mound of chewed-up, saliva-lubricated cardboard bits in front of him, and his fingers were mushing them into small circles.

Oh, poor Dr. Katz, she thought. When he was giving her medical and financial advice, he had always seemed so sure of himself.

Dr. Katz's suit jacket and pants were hanging outside the isolation room. The Cannibal expertly brushed up against them as he passed, and a moment later Ellie felt a keycard pressed into her hand. As they passed two orderlies, he smiled and pretended to play an invisible flute while jingling his cap.

The keycard opened a door at the end of a corridor.

"In here, please, Miss."

She was greeted by the strong scent of food rotting in compost bins. Ellie cringed, her nose and mouth feeling odd contracting under the surprisingly adhesive and pliable mask.

"Been thinin' about gettin' out and about, m'self," the Cannibal said, gesturing to a mechanism near the ceiling. "Camera's broken. No one ever watched along here anyhoo. Staff cuts."

The brawny man heaved a grate up from the floor. Ellie was distinctly reminded of her catacomb-induced claustrophobia psychosis.

"Is this really, uh…?"

"Bes' way. Only way ter help our friend." The way he said that might have indicated a romantic attraction for Britain's most talented poisoner and bioweapons expert. On the other hand, it might merely have been professional admiration. Ellie hadn't been there long enough to figure out the nuances of the dating scene inside St. Bartholomew's.

"Did you do all this by yourself?"

Without much forethought, Ellie climbed down through the open drain grating. Drawing upon her recent knowledge of underground excavations, she could tell this area had been excavated professionally without the alterations being detectible from within the garbage room.

"Nope," the Cannibal said, lowering himself down and prodding her on without bothering to reseal the grate above them. "This was the work o' the Fiddler."

She gathered this person did not play violin for the London Philharmonic.

"Is he about somewhere about, this Fiddler?"

"Nope. I mean, yes. Well, y'see, he was gonna get out, and he 'fessed ter me he was gonna keep fiddlin'. Old people, pigs, babies, didn't care what he fiddled."

"Uh, where is he now?" Ellie did not want any more surprises while she struggled to figure out what she was doing and whether it was at all a good thing.

"He's ri' there. Holdin' the door fer us, y'might say." The gloomy light coming through apertures in the manhole cover above revealed a professionally satisfied smirk on her companion's face. It was the first time Ellie had seen a hint of the marauder Mr. Goodrum must have been at one time. It soon vanished, replaced by his customary ruddy-cheeked, chummy grin. He indicated a space up ahead.

The metal grating leading out from the widened shaft was jammed open by what looked like a crumpled cardboard box. However, upon closer inspection, Ellie noticed the "box" was wearing a moldering jumpsuit. A good portion of the reek down there must have been coming from the decomposing body of the former inmate, the Fiddler. It was likely the two of them had planned an escape, then had a falling out just before executing the final phase.

The remains of the Fiddler were sitting, nearly folded in half. His desiccated, completely bald head was squashed between his legs, his face touching his groin. His skinny arms were clasped over his head as though frozen in the act of warding off a blow. One of his legs was sticking out toward Ellie. As she approached, she noticed the cloth of that pants leg was cut off at the hip.

"He ain't gonna fiddle no more. Ho-ho," the Cannibal said, prodding the corpse's foot out of Ellie's way. He jingled his cap and declared, "'An thou hadst been set i' th' stocks for that question, thou'dst well deserv'd it'."

After quoting from *King Lear*, the Cannibal levered the portcullis-style hatchway all the way open. As she passed the Fiddler's remains, she averted her eyes from the extended leg, which had been shoved into a narrow beam of light coming from above. The exposed leg was missing a large chunk of flesh that had been removed from the bare thigh in a professionally carved-out strip the size of a generous sirloin steak.

Feeling the clammy, humid chill of the gloomy improvised tunnel more than ever, Ellie squeezed into a gap full of thick dusty cables and bare concrete. This had to be the space between the foundations of two buildings. She was somewhat hopeful that the space was too small for her companion and yet was at the same time fearful it might not be.

When they had been sneaking out from the asylum, long before the last chance for her to raise the alarm had come and gone, Ellie had determined that she was responsible for Ms. China being in the dreadful place.

In Paris, after stealing a vital vial of blood from the former French president, she had convinced Ms. China to give herself up rather than remain a fugitive. Something urgent had driven her friend to take such extreme measures to escape. Ellie had to find out what it was and bring her back.

With a few contortions of his barrel-chested frame and a grunt, her break-out partner squashed himself through after her. Worming their way along the next dirty, narrow, and damp space, they approached a small metal square set in the concrete wall: an access hatch. To where?

A foot-long crowbar had been positioned there, probably by the Fiddler. The Cannibal took it up and levered the hatch's rusty hinges off their mounts. Mold and grime fell, but there was little noise as it gave way. He ushered Ellie forward into a much larger room. This one was bathed in a greenish glow. She found herself among rows and rows of shelves. The stale air was tinged with an antiseptic-type smell.

"Gah," Ellie gasped as her eyes adjusted to the light.

In front of her was a large jar filled to the top with viscous liquid, and floating inside were two skulls fused together just behind the jawline. The two human foreheads were grossly bulbous and misshapen, the teeth and jaws tiny and underdeveloped: tiny conjoined twins whose skeletons had been preserved in formaldehyde.

"We're in the Pathology Museum," the Cannibal said from behind her as he squeezed through. "Mind you don't break anythin."

7

BARTS PATHOLOGY MUSEUM
LONDON

Edging past the specimen jar holding the horribly deformed skulls of the conjoined twins, Ellie had a moment to think about her plan from here on out. She realized she didn't have one.

In her defense, she had been turned into a highly suggestible sleepwalker and been cajoled into breaking out of a facility for the criminally insane by a fellow who had snacked on a filet steak carved from the leg of his previous break-out partner. Her brain was a bit addled.

From behind her, the Cannibal whispered, "Give us a hand."

Ellie put her shoulder to the large specimen jar and slid it out of the way, the greenish preservative fluid sloshing back and forth. The partial remains of the former Siamese twins slowly twirled around to look the other way, farther into the gloom of the large exhibition storage room.

"Dunna whut kind 'o security systems they got ineer," her companion said as he crept forward on his hands and knees. "I never got this far a'fore."

"I'll be quiet as a mouse," Ellie said. "Uh, perhaps you should leave your cap."

"Yer righ," the Cannibal said, his long white teeth flashing dully in the greenish light. "I keep forgettin' it's on. Soft and comfortable. You made it...

I mean Anna made it for me with that mervelous machine we got in the activity area."

Suddenly seized by guilt that she had somehow contributed to the Terror of Chippenham having escaped custody, Ellie felt compelled to say, "It was, ah… a really nice place, from what I saw. St. Bartholomew's Hospital, I mean. Juanita the attendant seemed first rate. You don't think you'd be more comfortable back there? I won't tell anyone about the Fiddler."

The man's smile vanished. He pushed her through into the aisle between seemingly endless specimen jars which stretched up to the high ceiling and went on for row after row.

"Go back? Now? Are ye off yer nut?"

Ellie bit the inside of her cheek to stop herself from replying. As she did so, the Ms. China mask came away from her face, and when she pressed it back, it seemed to be losing adhesion. She wouldn't be able to wear it much longer.

"I just meant—"

"Oh, I know. Like everyone else, except Anna, you're judgin' me." He took a moment to look around. "Bin that way all me life. I got big bones, canna help it. Da, he put me on one diet after another, put a padlock on the fridge, yelled at me, made me sleep in the yard, in th' dog's house, roof leaks, I got cold, and wet, and hungry. I got so hungry…"

"Just please promise me you won't harm anyone, anyone else, while you're out and about. Do it for Anna," Ellie said in a last-ditch attempt to ease her conscience.

"Harm? Me?" he said, sounding slightly offended but at least no longer dwelling on his rather harsh upbringing.

Without further conversation, he stalked around the shelves to a less cluttered area of the warehouse. This looked like a workshop suited to maintaining exhibits and preparing them for display in the public areas of the Pathology Museum.

In the middle, sitting atop a side table, was a plastic model of a female. It was posed as a dead body in a mock-up of a countryside crime scene complete with fake grass and leaves. The Cannibal's deep-set beady eyes measured the room, studied the doors on their level and the landing above. Without warning, he stripped the rubber corpse naked. The Cannibal took the dress and rolled it into a tight ball. He studied Ellie.

"Of course, I'm doin' this for Anna. You make sure you do righ'. Bring her back safe 'n' sound. Whatever comes, righ'?"

"I will, sir. Whatever comes."

"Good. Now scream as loud as y'can."

The Cannibal's face lit up with an enthused grin as he seized both her arms with his beefy hands and picked her up off the floor. She didn't need much encouragement to wig out, and she screamed.

"Tha's good. I hear 'em coming," her captor said, dragging her along the shelves toward a dimly lit fire exit. The building was ancient, and there was a wrought-iron gantry walkway all around the second level of the storage room. Lights came on above, and then a door burst open.

Flashlight beams lanced down at them.

"Oy! What are you muckin' about?" came a shout from above.

"Get back!" bellowed the Cannibal. "Get back or I'll kill me hostage!"

Ellie felt herself spun around, ostensibly being used as a human shield; but it seemed that the Cannibal was making sure the security guards and their body cameras got a good look at the scene and the silicone face she was wearing.

"Let her go! There's nowhere to run."

"How about I run you to Hell!" The Cannibal cackled, and with his free hand, he jammed the flower dress from the fake corpse into Ellie's hands. He leaned over her and whispered, "Now bite me."

What now?

"Bite me, and hard," he whispered. "They need to see blood."

Ellie sure as heck did not need to see, feel, or taste blood. His arm closed over her nose and mouth. She had no choice, closing her eyes and biting down on the big man's hairy forearm.

After uttering a soft chuckle and forcing his flesh harder against her bared teeth, he cried out theatrically: "You bitch, you bit me! I will fix you!"

With ferocious velocity, he flung her at the fire escape door. Her midsection hit the crossbar handle, and the air whooshed out of her lungs as the door swung open. Cold evening air spackled with rain hit the back of her neck.

Skidding to her knees on the wet cobblestones of the alley, she looked back and saw the Cannibal had grabbed a specimen jar containing what looked like a spindly spiderlike arm terminating in a large hand with ten or twelve fingers. He threw it at the guards rushing down the circular stairs. In doing so, he managed to knock over a rack of shelving. It fell against the next one and the next like dominoes, effectively blocking the fire exit. He was sealed in.

As Ellie got to her feet, the Cannibal took a light fixture from the exhibit table and smashed it onto the flammable preservative solution sloshing all over the floor. Ellie's last sight of Chippenham's most famous son was him heaving himself up on a teetering shelf, fool's cap back on his head, bellowing with glee as he threw one specimen jar after another at his pursuers.

The heavy fire exit door was on a spring-loaded mechanism. It swung shut, locking her out. Ellie looked at the bundle in her hand. Then she remembered to remove her face. Ms. China's prosthetic had lost most of its stickiness, and it peeled off easily. She threw the balled-up mess down a sewer grate, briefly noting that the lipstick on the now grossly distended lips didn't look too bad and had certainly resisted smudging. She'd have to ask after the brand, if she was ever reunited with her irascible friend.

The upper windows of the museum began belching smoke. Ellie looked left and right—the alley remained deserted. The Cannibal had done his part, it was now all up to her. Having discarded any ideas of modesty, Ellie doffed her seafoam-green St. Bartholomew's jumpsuit and put on the purloined flower dress. It fit like a pup tent, but at least it hid her ridiculous-looking hospital slippers.

A police car sped past the mouth of the alley, which was the only way out. As she tried to avoid members of the Met, she ran straight into a fireman. He looked at her with suspicion.

"Are you, uh, injured, madam?"

"Me?" Ellie remembered she had her Asian face back on. The crappy flower dress was perfect. "Me no injury, no. I cleaning crew, in museum working. Awful man come, try burn place. You go! Go fire put out."

Fooled by her haphazard accent, the man let her pass and waved to a fire truck approaching down the narrow street.

Multiple sirens howled, coming closer with every undulating whine. Rain poured down, soaking her borrowed polyester dress with every wind-blown watery gust. Ellie leaned against the side of a building on the other side of the avenue and considered her predicament. Her shivers of cold and fading adrenaline rush were threatening to send her into hypothermic shock. Ellie decided she had found herself in an extremely tight situation—she had a plethora of pressing problems, ones only very rich people could help her solve.

8

POSTMAN'S PARK
LONDON

The cold, rain-spattered bench Ellie sat on faced a wall covered with ceramic tiles commemorating "Deeds of Heroic Self-Sacrifice committed by Ordinary Britons." The two tiles she could see read:

Alice Ayres
daughter of a bricklayer's labourer
who by intrepid conduct
saved 3 children
from a burning house
in Union Street Borough
at the cost of her own young life.
April 24, 1885

John Cranmer, Cambridge
aged 23 a clerk in
the London County council
who was drowned near Ostend
whilst saving the life of
a stranger and a foreigner.
August 8, 1901

Ellie doubted the deeds of the Chippenham Cannibal would ever be commemorated on this wall, though he had almost certainly been recaptured or killed while helping her escape so that Ellie might find their mutual friend before it was too late.

A few hundred meters away, the last dregs of the smoke from the fire Mr. Goodrum had started in the museum's storage room rose into the drizzling ashtray-gray sky. For the fiftieth time, Ellie rearranged her legs on the hard surface of a bench near the small roof guarding the historic plaques from the elements. Her teeth chattered more uncontrollably as the drenched coldness of her borrowed flower dress and undergarments smushed against her goose-pimpled skin.

She looked left and right. There were only passing cabs and an inventive bicyclist who had rain wipers attached to his face visor.

The Cannibal's improvisations and quite believable acting had likely succeeded in covering for Ms. China. Any video of the incident would clearly show that Ellie, wearing Ms. China's face, was the man's hostage in an escape gone awry.

Ran Oliphant was taking his time getting here. After she dashed away from Barts Pathology Museum and the fire brigades, she had tried to borrow someone's handset. This was made much more difficult by the fact she looked like an evictee from a homeless camp. Her hair was a soaking mess, she smelled of formaldehyde, and she had bits of sticky silicone on her face. Even her eco-friendly asylum-issued slippers were biodegrading in the wet.

When she had gotten a few blocks away from the fire, having received a few nasty stares through the windows of cabs and sending a couple running into a shop to avoid the crazy homeless Eurasian lady, she'd come upon a courier's scooter. There was no phone on it, but strapped to the handlebars was a weatherproof texting device.

It flashed: *"URGENT get u ass back to the Aroma/India u forgot the vindaloo takeaway dumbass."*

Fortunately there was a general texting function, and she had time to dash off her own urgent message to Mr. Oliphant's YouChatter identity, which was the only one she could remember. Then she erased the text before the delivery fellow came back and, holding her single piece of clothing close to her body, made her way to the nearby Postman's Park rendezvous.

What was keeping them? Wealthy people were supposed to be idle.

She couldn't go back to Tavistock. Ellie, wearing her own face, was the last person known to have seen Ms. China before the shambolic escape. The authorities would definitely want to speak to her last visitor. Explaining what really happened was certain to set Ellie up for an involuntary committal. She already had an NHS mental health minder. At worst, she'd be held complicit in Ms. China's escape and any crimes the talented chemist and prolific prisoner was at the moment doubtlessly committing.

She huddled miserably in Postman's Park until… until…

"You all right, then, miss?"

Someone in an N-100 mask was nudging her foot with his own. She must have dozed a bit, after the unavoidable rush of adrenaline stemming from watching innumerable jars holding human specimens explode in formaldehyde fireballs, not to mention the residual effects of the Obediens serum she'd been dosed with. She had felt unutterably sleepy.

The man's virus mask looked like an elephant's trunk drawn by a six-year-old. Of course. London's viral count alert had been elevated to Persimmon. Germaphobes would be masking up.

"I'm, ah—"

"Stop prodding that poor Japanese girl!" a woman's shrill voice yelled from the entrance to the park.

Her would-be rescuer muttered a muffled apology, and he slunk off in the opposite direction from an oncoming figure who was definitely weirder looking than him. Mr. Oliphant's chief scientist and personal shopper, Dr. Melanie François, came ambling past the park's central fountain toward her. Her hair was as massive as ever and held tightly coiled within a dozen tubes of aluminum foil. Her left arm was covered by a shoulder-length opera glove, while her right arm was bare except for a paper stencil pattern which was stuck to it and flapping around as she moved.

"Look at you, Ellie Sato! You're a sight!"

Ellie would have responded with a cutting retort had her teeth not been chattering so much. Melanie took off her own pink brocaded vest, which was hardly warmer than the flower dress, and put it around her.

"Ran's in the van a block away. He hates getting wet," she said, leading her toward Little Britain Street. "When you texted, you warned us to be extra discreet."

"I-I-I'm sure no one's p-p-paying any mind," Ellie chattered as they moved toward a large, thankfully warm-looking, Mercedes Sprinter executive van.

Once inside, she fell under the hawklike gaze of Mr. Oliphant, the telecom oligarch. Despite being very fit, the middle-aged sandy-haired Scotsman looked a bit more care-worn than when she had seen him last during their settlement negotiations over the fate of his investment in the *Juggernaut*.

Between sips of hot Earl Grey tea—not her favorite—Ellie managed to relate the considerably astonishing events which had just befallen her. When she was done, Ran Oliphant and Melanie looked at one another.

Finally, he said, "If that doesn't just take the biscuit. Ms. Sato, you never seem to become tangled up in anything commonplace, do you?"

Now Melanie and Ran had a story for her. Two days earlier, Ran had received a secret urgent message sent to the same YouChatter username Ellie had just messaged. It had obviously been Ms. China posing as Ellie.

"And…" Ellie said, bracing herself for the reply. "What did she ask for?"

Hopefully it wasn't anything too expensive. Though, given her present financial burdens, if Ellie felt morally obliged to pay back whatever had been stolen, Ran would have to accept installments.

"Nothing much. Only a quick flight to Washington DC." Ran scrolled through the items on his digital day planner. "You arrived safely… twelve minutes ago."

As the driver of the Mercedes van circled Trafalgar Square, Melanie gave her a quick health checkup, and Ellie prodded her own sluggishly moving mind to come up with an action plan that would not muck things up further.

"Right, right," Ran Oliphant said into a handset and then ended the call. "My publicity guy has contacts at the Met, and they have contacts with the city police." The oftentimes dour-looking businessman gave her a reproachful look. "Mr. Harry Goodrum escaped the fire."

He started to poke at his handset screen again.

"That's, er, good, I guess?" Ellie said as Melanie prepared to stick a medical swab deep into her sinuses.

"I'm calling Scotland Yard directly so you can help put the Chippenham Cannibal back where he belongs before he harms anyone."

Ellie nearly gagged on the long swab as she exclaimed, "Oh, no, no, you mustn't."

Melanie, the former medical student, finally withdrew the swab and put it inside a testing device.

"I mustn't help catch a mad killer?" Ran said rather testily.

"Don't you see? There's something about… Ms. China's not dumb. I mean, she wrote the world's most definitive textbook on biological and chemical warfare."

"That's not helping," Melanie whispered.

"I mean…" Ellie said after swallowing back cold saliva dislodged by the cotton-tipped probe. "First of all, the Cannibal, Harry, promised me he would not harm anyone. And I believe he has reformed his ways, to a large degree." Ellie decided not to mention her accomplice seemed satisfied with limiting himself to dining on bad people like the Fiddler who probably deserved it.

"We owe it to Ms. China," she added hastily before Ran connected with 999. "Without Anna's help, we never would have stopped the schemes of those terrible Pangeans in Europe. Millions would have died."

Ran paused, thinking. "I suppose… and it was sort of satisfying watching her torture my old business enemy Dr. Licht. What's your idea?"

"Uh—"

Thankfully, at that moment, the mobile viral analyzer gave a poignant *ping*. Getting the results of various tests Melanie had performed gave Ellie time to silently brainstorm.

Melanie watched chemical formulas flickering across her mobile screen. "Your viral scans are negative. There's very little left in your system of whatever Ms. China gave to you that put you in a catatonic state. If we ever find her, I wouldn't mind getting the recipe for that."

"Melanie," Ran growled.

"For completely ethical purposes, of course."

Ellie pushed Ran's phone away before he was able to massively complicate the pickle she was in.

"The only thing that would motivate Anna to go to such lengths would be her son, Attie Jr." Ellie shook her head and looked at the streetlamps flickering past the van's windows. "But he's in one of the Carolinas over there, with his grandparents. Why would she go to Washington?"

"Dunna about that," Ran said, picking up a different handset. "But I do know who else is in that city at the moment—Army Sergeant Bryan. You remember him?"

Ellie vividly recalled the moment the large African albino had burst in to the PKK terrorist stronghold in Turkey after the Kurdish resistance had kidnapped her in Ankara. At first sight of him, she'd thought he was an alien. She'd met albino fashion models before, but the soldier's glowing blue cybernetic eyes really left a memorable first impression. She nodded.

"He's there escorting his goddaughter, Sienna, and a group of students on some sort of civics field trip."

Ellie caught on. "And they live near Attie Reidt's family. Do you think the boy is with them, and that's why...?"

Ran's large thumbs slowly typed a text message. "It's five in the afternoon there..."

Sarge Bryan responded right away.

"Yes, Ms. China's son is with them," Ran said, summarizing the texted reply. "No, they haven't seen her, or, for that matter, you, Ellie."

Melanie rolled her eyes as her tin-foil-covered hair snakes quivered. "By now Ms. China's silicone Ellie mask is probably really degraded and wrinkled. Tell Sarge Bryan to be on the lookout for a very old Eurasian woman."

Ran ignored his assistant.

"He says they'll move to a more secure hotel room but doesn't expect any problems. He's a guest of a business associate of mine, Mr. Barracude. They're under very high security given the tense political situation in America right now. Mr. Barracude's wife, Janice Jones, is the current administration's chief of staff and might be the next vice president depending on how their Supreme Court rules in the next day or so."

Ellie thought she recalled Ms. Jones from some fashion magazine covers.

"Doesn't her husband own makeup companies?"

"And half the eastern US seaboard," Ran added. "I'll tell Sarge to expect the real you in about... ten hours."

They drove to Mayfair and dropped Melanie off a discreet distance away from Tavistock Manor. Ellie had to get hold of a few items of clothing that didn't smell of cinders and formaldehyde. She watched through the windscreen as Mr. Surghit let Melanie in straightaway, as though he'd been expecting her. She couldn't see any secret police agents lurking, but that didn't mean there weren't any.

"I just thought of something," Ellie said, thinking that the spasms her back was going through might be alleviated by lying on the nice four-poster bed inside the mansion. "I'm already in America. They have computers tracking people's passports, don't they? I'd rather not be put back in a detention cell."

"Well," Ran said, picking up his normal phone, "we can always call the authorities, but without Ms. China in hand, not to mention Mr. Goodrum, you may find yourself in a heap of legal trouble. We know where Ms. China is headed. You've got to get to her first and convince her to give herself up to the British embassy, then everything can get sorted."

They circled Grosvenor Square a few times, then met Melanie at the back of the manor. She was pulling two large suitcases that came up nearly to her shoulders.

"I didn't know what you'd need or how long you were going for, so I grabbed a bit of everything essential. Your nice butler left these cases out in the hall before I even asked for them."

In the meantime, Ran had been in contact with Tennyson Sewart of the Foreign Office, whom Ellie had met briefly in Turkey before the 96-Hour War in the Middle East. Sewart was a school friend of Ran's, and he agreed to reactivate Ellie's diplomatic travel credentials as long as his department incurred no costs, got credit for any fugitives captured, and Ellie agree to take full blame if anything went wrong.

Ran helped the chauffeur heave the two enormous trunks inside the van. "In the States, you'll be the guest of Mr. Barracude."

"Thanks," Ellie said. "What's he like?"

"You recall Dr. Licht?"

"The fellow who at the last minute sold us out to the evil Pangeans and nearly got us and Europe vaporized last year?"

"Barracude's a lot like him, but less..." Ran crinkled his nose, searching for the right word. "Less polished, more American."

"You'll like him," Melanie gushed. "He probably hasn't personally killed anyone since he emigrated from Brazil."

Ellie and Ran looked at her.

A few blocks later, they pulled up to a crusty old building on St. James's Street.

"The driver will take you to the airport," Ran said, sliding the van door open. "I'm spending the rest of the night here at White's Gentlemen's Club, where thankfully no girls are allowed."

"And..." Melanie said suggestively. The pair had been working together so long that Ran knew instantly what she was getting at. His lips compressed.

"And, Ms. Sato, if you need anything or become further entangled by any more of these astonishing problems that seem to follow after you... I'd take it as a personal favor if you'd call someone else. Ladies, good night."

The van's door closed automatically, and Melanie grabbed Ellie's hand.

"He doesn't mean that. He's just being a grumpy widower." She nodded to the driver, the motion sending her hair wobbling. The raindrops had caused the long foil snakes in it to sag down and now made her head look like a silvery willow tree. "America! Oh, I wish I were going with you. I just can't leave Ranny alone when he's in one of his moods. He might do something dreadful... like marry an actress."

"Without your help, I'd be down at Scotland Yard answering questions forever," Ellie said, wondering whether she should risk sneaking back to Tavistock to get some more essential clothing and fashion items. "When he's in a better mood, please thank him."

"You can do that yourself. You should be back in a jiff."

9

ZULIA STATE, VENEZUELA

ABDELKADER

The one thing Abdelkader knew about Americans was that their love of guns and fighting amongst themselves was exceeded only by their insatiable lust for drugs. Opioids, meth, and cocaine were the lifeblood of that failing white supremacist republic. The enemy population's demand to constantly be high gave him and the weapons of his personal intifada a route into "Fortress America."

"Is smaller load, this, than we normally take," said Munoz, their Venezuelan pilot, as they heaved a three-foot-square box out of the darkness and on board the smuggler's small plane.

"It's heavy enough," Abdelkader said. He and his Pangean associates were wearing their Middle Eastern faces to blend in with the swarthy South Americans. Dr. Baldur was not part of their inner circle, so he had only his own pudgy, sweating face to wear. Abdelkader had him put on a respirator and not speak.

"We could still fit some... oh." The Venezuelan smuggler noticed the weight readout in the small cockpit jump as the box was rolled into place and strapped down.

"As you can see, there is no weight to spare," Abdelkader said, strapping himself into the seat that had the best view of the cockpit and the cargo.

This was the riskiest part of their journey. Had there been any alternative, he would have left Dr. Baldur back at Isla La Tortuga feeding the colony of vampire bats, but he needed him to confirm how effective the six-month-long initial phase of their operation had been before unleashing the second and final wave.

The scientist, who had grown soft around the middle during his time working night and day in the underground lab, could not keep himself from chattering.

"This is a very interesting aircraft design," Dr. Baldur said, his voice muffled by his filtration mask. "It is an Indian design, yes?"

Munoz looked back. He probably had a few hundred kilos of coke or the newly popular synthetic opioid Red Mist secreted in the jungle close to the makeshift airstrip. Despite knowing about Abdelkader's connections to the powerful and dangerous ruling junta in Caracas, perhaps Munoz also had ideas about hijacking their mysterious cargo. All thoughts of a double-cross had likely vanished when the greedy smuggler got a look at Abdelkader's heavily armed men.

"You like *Evita*, huh?" Munoz said, stroking the plane's carbon-fiber console. "She is a hybrid Chinese-Indian design with a coating of my own special anti-radar paint. No one ever challenge us on any flight, ever."

The flying wing design was capable of defeating the weaker parts of the Honduran air surveillance system. Abdelkader had spent the day confirming Munoz was paid up with his bribes to the cartels that were in control of the more sophisticated radar-tracking stations. Getting into the United States would be another matter. But that was where he had to take Dr. Baldur—to make a house call on a terminal patient called America.

10

ISLA LA TORTUGA, VENEZUELA

KOMANDIR ZVENA

Rodya! Look where you're stepping," Zvena yelled at his partner, who was hauling their landing craft up on the pure white sandy beach. "Your big feet are crushing turtle nests."

"Oh, sorry, Komandir." Rodion's mechanically assisted legs shifted his two-hundred-kilo weight as delicately as they could, avoiding further crushing of leatherback sea turtle burrows.

"And we only have ranks when we are in Moscow. In the field, we are *zelyonye chelovechki*, little green men, reporting directly to President Putin."

"Yes, sir, I mean Yari."

"Get up here." Zvena kneeled down among driftwood and lengths of dry, flaky seaweed. Satellite and drone imagery revealed the flat little island's subterranean facilities had recently been abandoned, but he was not going to walk into a trap, especially not one in a suspected bioweapons facility.

"Where do we start?" Rodion asked, trotting over and lying down heavily on his tactical vest, which was festooned with grenades and ammo pouches. "I'm surprised this island is still here. It's quite low but has not been swamped by rising water levels."

"Look closely," Zvena said as the orange early morning sun illuminated the slim gash of land floating improbably in the blue-green Caribbean Sea. "Someone has gouged out the middle part to build up the edges. It's the same geography as the hundreds of man-made islands in the South China Sea. Someone has taken the trouble to protect their investment here, and President Putin is curious to find out what that might be."

As a high-ranking officer in the all-cyborg Human+ division of Spetsnaz, Zvena had spent the last few years developing his own intelligence contacts separate and apart from the GRU's Directorate. Then, late in 2031, filthy Turks had launched a sinister and cowardly attack on Moscow hoping to cripple the Russian Federation. At the same time, the Pangeans attacked the European Union with a dark-matter doomsday weapon. In the process of defeating the threats, Zvena and his immediate subordinates, Rodion and Tata, were given the honor of being little green men, granted licenses to suppress threats to the Federation by any means necessary.

"Signal the *Suvorov*, we are going to the north end."

A stealth frigate, whose sloped superstructure barely protruded above the waves, had launched their landing craft half an hour ago. Since the collapse of the Venezuelan socialist dictatorship into a pliable but unstable narco-junta, Russia had taken over operations at most of the petroleum facilities in the country. With a view to protecting their investment from any planned counterrevolution or foreign coup, Russian agencies were constantly monitoring the region. Certain sources had revealed tantalizing information about mysterious activities on Isla La Tortuga, ones which seemed to be a significant departure from the normal turtle poaching and decadent beach orgies.

"Remote sensing says there are larger structures to the south," Rodion said.

"It would take days to make a search of them. North is the place the people who were here went just before they left the island. Time-lapse surveillance shows this area was kept almost completely isolated until then."

"They kept something here that only certain people were allowed to see?"

Seagulls hovered in place over them, gliding in the steady breeze, sending territorial squeals down at them.

"It's our best chance to quickly find any clues of what they were up to."

Their examination of the site would have to be complete before it was invaded by scientific personnel from regular Russian military intelligence; they would never share their information with cyborg units, even ones reporting to the president.

As they approached the hidden bunker, they stayed clear of the winding path leading from the southern facility. Along with their enhanced vision, caution was the best way to avoid booby traps. Zvena's boots kept sinking into the loose sand, and the two-hundred-meter walk became like a trudge through snow back home, except with a constant fishy-smelling wind pushing back at him.

"There's nothing," Rodion said after twenty minutes of searching in a grid pattern. "The sand has blown all over. The surveillance pictures were substandard resolution. How are we supposed to find anything?"

Zvena's shoulder joints creaked in the increased humidity as he shrugged. "It was the best intelligence we could steal from the Americans. All our satellites are busy watching our other enemies. Keep looking."

The third time they trudged through the twisted, wind-tortured scrub brush, Zvena's foot hit something. It was a hatch.

"We will need equipment. Call the OCEL."

Rodion tapped a panel on his forearm, and a minute later a six-legged mechanical mule came bounding across the sand dunes. The programmers had used behavior algorithms from dogs and other animals to control its movements. It loped up to Zvena and then crouched down on its forelegs at its heels, looking up at him through a dome from which sixteen sensors protruded like the eyes of a spider.

"He looks like he wants to play fetch," Rodion said, picking up a piece of driftwood.

O.C.E.L. meant "mule" in anglicized Russian and was an acronym given to this model by the Russian Foundation for Advanced Research Projects.

"Be serious, Rodya, stop playing," Zvena said shortly. They were on ground that had only hours ago been in the hands of an unknown, undoubtedly hostile, force. He had waited on calling in the equipment-bearing robot until he was sure there were no surface booby traps. "Get digging."

The OCEL was able to carry three times its own weight and had small rocket modules. The robot could also pick up objects on command. Back in Moscow, Zvena had it retrieve a tennis ball a few times, but only after he made sure no one else was watching.

With shovels and a compact jackhammer, they prised away the quick-dry cement that had been poured into the hatch opening.

"They've cut off the ladder," Rodion said, using his built-in cyborg night vision to peer into a ragged hole that went deep into the underbelly of the island.

Zvena confirmed there were stubs of melted metal.

"We do it the hard way, then," he said. "Tell the mule to dig in and attach descent lines."

With the robot assistant's legs deeply embedded in the sand, they attached steel cables to their webbing bets and ordered the OCEL to lower them down. Ten meters down Zvena was still dangling like bait on a fishing line and spitting out the sand which rained down incessantly.

"There is a landing." Rodion grabbed a railing and pulled Zvena after him onto a six-by-three scaffolding, which led to an arched hole in the wall of the silo-like structure.

Zvena was annoyed. "It's a long way down. Why stop he—"

A creature leaped out of the doorway and seized Rodion. Its head was shaved, and ragged clothes and gray flesh sagged from its arms and legs. With hydraulic-assisted reflexes, Zvena's friend slammed his fist down on the creature's shoulder and collarbone. They snapped, making dull cracks that echoed in the quiet space.

"*Idi na khuy!*" Rodion swore. *Go to the dick!*

After the initial surprise, it was clear the attacker was no threat. He was not armed, and his emaciated form was one fifth of Rodion's weight. Yet despite the crushing blow, was still alive.

"Wait, let's ask—"

Rodion preempted any questioning of the prisoner by grabbing the creature's rotting shirt and tossing him down into the shaft. The falling form bounced along the wall a few times before they heard him hit the bottom.

"Sorry, but that was really disgusting."

What puzzled Zvena was why his auditory and heat sensors had not picked up the presence of a hostile in such close quarters. He checked over the area again, prodding around corners with the titanium spear point of his Spetsnaz pike. There was nothing else in the hollow spaces next to the gantry platform.

"Keep descending. And Rodya, ask me before you do anything."

"Yes, Komandir."

The poor wretch had probably been a Venezuelan worker who helped construct this facility and then was sealed in when his bosses had abandoned Isla La Tortuga. Even if they had been able to interrogate the man, Zvena's ocular snapshots of the encounter revealed a crazy-looking figure who was nearly starved to death and whose brain was likely mush. They would not have gotten any reliable intelligence from him. The truth lay deeper.

As they approached the bottom, about fifty meters down, Zvena smelled something. Nothing registered on his digital olfactory sensors. He shook his head and spat. Sometimes the metal sensor strips in his sinuses got clogged with snot. Still nothing. But there was definitely a strange smell... he couldn't quite put his finger on it.

Suddenly a tentacle came up from the ground and encircled his leg. He pulled it away and leveled his pistol at... nothing.

"Enjoy your year without winter, Russian."

"Huh?"

The voice spoke English with a Turkish accent. But that man, that mutant, was dead.

"Rodya..."

Rodion was hanging from his harness, staring at a fungus that was growing out from the concrete. He was leaning forward, as if he was about to eat it.

More tentacles came from the wall and encircled Zvena's legs. This time he must have fired at them. The next time he could think, he looked down to find his gun was warm and out of ammunition. His sensors had registered no toxic gas, no radiation, yet somehow they were in a pit of madness. These were the same symptoms as reported by victims who survived the dark-matter energy weapon that had wiped out the city of Bordeaux in France.

Another tentacle leaped out and covered his mouth and nose. With lightning reflexes, he aimed his pistol at his head and pulled the trigger.

Click!

If his gun hadn't been empty, he would have shot his own jaw off trying to free himself from something that wasn't there. Periods of clarity were coming in ever shorter bursts. He looked over to Rodya; his partner was hanging by his tether, munching on a filthy mushroom like it was the sweetest candy.

The distant round blue hole of the sky shone many meters above. The tentacle had his arm, he pulled on it. He knew it wasn't there, but he couldn't get it out of his mind. With his free hand, he punched every button on his forearm command panel.

"*Robot vnimaniya. Raketa… pobeg pryamo seychas!*"

The tentacle slithered around his back and started strangling him. In front of Zvena, the Turkish mutant's huge round gray dead-fish eye loomed larger and larger until it was all he could see.

A tremendous crack to the back of his helmet was the next thing he felt. Zvena found himself flying through blue sky, not knowing if he was still hallucinating. He dangled like a four-hundred-pound fish on a line and bounced against something.

"Oh, Rodya, it's you," he mumbled.

Vaguely aware of rocket boosters roaring above him, he and his friend clashed together again like bolo balls on strings, and sank gently down to the sandy beach. The digital clock in the corner of his eye had skipped forward three minutes. Zvena spat out more sand.

Harsh fumes of burned rocket fuel mixed with sea air. He looked around. A few meters away, nearer the lapping ocean waves, was the mechanical mule. It was inert, having spent all of its fuel lifting them up out from the chasm of the silo and then lowering them down to the beach exfiltration point, per its emergency protocol. A seagull was trying to land on it to see if it was something edible. One of its six legs kicked out, scaring the bird away, then the robot lay still.

"Good… boy," Zvena managed to say. Then he looked around for Rodion.

The larger cyborg was slumped in a disheveled heap behind a fat dry log.

"Rodya. Wake up, stand up. The *Suvorov* will send a landing party. You are still Human+ division. Act respectable in front of the Navy people."

"Ahhh, Yari, my mouth tastes like shit!" Rodion dribbled bits of chewed toadstool down his chin.

Zvena's eyes were still not focusing properly. He blinked away sand as his ocular implants phased through heat vision and infrared mode. Something was strange about Rodya. He had either broken his arm or become a hunchback.

"Hey! Do a system check and run a toxin analysis. Who knows what kind of mushroom you were…"

The thing on Rodion's back came into clearer focus. At first Zvena thought it was a leatherback turtle having revenge on his partner for despoiling the nest of eggs. Then he noticed his comrade's eyes start to follow invisible patterns in the sky—he was zoning out again. Zvena extended his Spetsnaz pike and speared the strange scrabbling creature.

The object was the head, one shoulder, and right arm of the sole inhabitant of La Tortuga. The body parts were moving, and its mouth had clamped down on Rodion's body armor harness, cracking its long yellow rotting teeth on the ceramic back plates as it compulsively bit and bit and bit.

He levered the animated remains away from Rodion's back and then threw his pike like a javelin. It landed one hundred meters down on the beach, sticking upright in the wet sand with its little passenger still clawing, scrabbling, and biting at the shaft.

11

LONDON LUTON AIRPORT

Soooo," Melanie said, hugging Ellie at the steps up to the private jet, "if you do have any serious problems, you have my YouChatter handle, it will ring my lobes directly."

Eurolincx's scientist at large tugged on her big hoop earrings.

"You mean," Ellie said, "if I have any difficulty finding the criminally insane woman who just drugged me, stole my passport, and escaped a maximum-security mental hospital. And after I find her, convince her to quietly return with me before anyone realizes she's not wandering the streets of London in a daze?"

Ran Oliphant's contacts at the Met police said the authorities were under the impression that Ms. China had escaped the blaze at Barts Museum and was presumed to be hiding somewhere in a state of amnesiac shock.

"I meant more like if your host in America, Mr. Barracude, makes a pass at you," Melanie said. "He was pretty grabby the last time I met him, though that was before he was married to Janice. You'll like her. She had lots of clothes."

Thankfully, the stairs up to the private jet were an automated escalator. Ellie had far too many pains all over to even contemplate climbing up unassisted.

"I'm a veteran of the fashion scene," she called back. "I think I can handle one dirty old rich guy."

A pair of little red dolly bots came whizzing up to the Sprinter van. The chauffeur heaved Ellie's steamer trunks onto them, and they attached themselves to the aircraft stairs, then were pulled up to the cargo doors.

Once inside, Ellie concluded the plane's interior must have been designed to appeal to the Middle Eastern market. There was enough platinum and gold plating over every fixture that, had it been solid instead of decorative leaf, the plane would have been too heavy to ever get off the ground.

"*Bienvenue,* Ms. Sato," said a male steward who, despite wearing PPE covering and a face shield, looked as though he could be a magazine model. "Yours was a last-minute booking, therefore we were uncertain if you would require our full hygiene-pod service."

Private flight services had years ago adapted to catering to the most paranoid of wealthy hypochondriacs. As Ellie slumped into the nearest plush leather seat, she noticed the collapsed polyurethane bubble that would be inflated to form a hermetically sealed barrier suitable for the most germaphobic traveler.

"Oh, no, just whatever's easiest." Ellie could have mentioned that earlier in the day she had splashed through a drainage tunnel that contained at least one decomposing human body. Microbes were the least of her problems. "I will, however, be needing a shower if you have one."

"Of course," the steward said, looking relieved that he would not have to attend to a bubble-girl passenger. "I shall make certain everything is prepared for just after takeoff."

After a brief sprint down the runway and a moment of weightlessness that made her feel queasy and euphoric at the same time, Ellie thought to check her steamer trunks. She found them fastened to the side of the hallway between the sitting room and the bedroom.

"Oh, Melanie," she uttered under her breath as a half dozen mismatched high-heeled shoes came tumbling out of the first trunk. "That's the last time you're packing anything."

The contents of the second trunk were no better. Instead of being full of formal business wear, it was full of lingerie with a few bathrobes and fuzzy slippers thrown in. "Half this stuff isn't even mine." Ellie poked through crushed mounds of what had to be the contents of Esmunda's laundry hamper mixed in with leather and latex dominatrix outfits Ms. China had left in storage at Tavistock.

She used her lasts bits of energy to cobble together a jacket dress into a somewhat smart deplaning outfit and set it aside for their landing in about seven hours. Ellie walked past the oval windows, which were filled with a pitch-black night sky and a half moon which blazed stark bone white.

She'd never been in an airborne bathroom quite like the one clearly preferred by traveling sheiks. The central shower dais was surrounded by four kneeling pads, possibly for concubines or sex slaves. There were dozens of water jets with settings reading: Steam, Color, Aroma, Music, and Sensual Massage.

"What setting gets the muck off you fastest?" Ellie muttered.

"Sorry, could you repeat that, please?"

"Ah!"

The shower mechBrain's unexpected utterance caused her to bump her ribs against a nozzle, right where the fire door had hit her after the Cannibal had thrown her out of the museum.

Making some adjustments, she managed to use the enormous rainforest ceiling nozzle and the dozen side jets to clean off her grime-covered skin without scalding or drowning herself as loud techno music blasted from all around in sync with flashing neon lights.

She pulled on a Cinderella night dress and lay down on the king-sized bed set upon a dais shaped like the open mouth of a huge golden lion's head.

Chimes began softly and politely in the world of her dreams, then became more and more insistent.

"Already? No. Once more around the planet, please."

Unfortunately her medically trained flight attendants would not be put off.

"Sorry, ma'am," the steward said over the intercom. "Due to the Persimmon alert in the UK, America has raised their viral threat to 'Orange

Beta.' Therefore, I'm afraid to say we are obliged to run a PCR Ebola test and transmit certifications before landing, and the machine takes an hour to process."

There was a click, but the mic did not shut off. The steward's voice lost his fake perky charming tone, and he said, "I really think the Yanks like to jerk our chain with these alerts. And who is this woman? She's dressed like a supermarket skip-diver. If she hadn't voluntarily taken a shower I'd have filed a complaint with management... Is that thing still on?"

Click.

The Khóshekh virus scare during the Middle East's last war had spurred public health authorities to new heights of vigilance. She could either get this over with now or sit on the runway for an hour. She let the steward into the bedchamber. He was once again dressed in green scrubs, and in his hands he held an instrument resembling a long fondue fork.

"It's best to do this after you've just gotten up," he said apologetically. "Now, please tilt your head way back and say 'ah.' You may feel a pinch during the retrieval of the wee little biopsy sample we need. Try not to gag."

After the biopsy and blood sample, a robot barista brought Ellie a mocha, the top frothy surface of which had a picture of the Burj Khalifa drawn in white foam. Her fingers rubbed gently over the other, half-day older jab on her other arm. Ms. China must have taken a blood sample along with the rest of her identity.

With her scientific knowledge and extremely persuasive abilities, it would have been easy for Ms. China to swap out the sample her own air crew had ended up testing. They would compare that DNA with the data registered with her passport identity when confirming new arrivals in America did not have any horrible foreign diseases.

It was getting on two a.m. local DC time. Ellie's internal clock was so mixed up after her forced nap at St. Bartholomew's that she would welcome some normal jet lag. Despite the bruises on her ribs, which were blooming every shade of purple she could name, and the swelling of an ankle she hadn't noticed she twisted until she got up from the lion's maw bed, Ellie was encouraged. Perhaps it was arriving in America, the land of the brave and home of the free. Or maybe it was the chance to see her old friend again.

Sarge Bryan was extremely capable and was sure to be keeping the boy Atticus Reidt Jr. safe. They didn't have to go looking for Ms. China; she would come to them.

The jet rocked slightly as it made its final descent. All in all, she thought the most disagreeable parts of this little adventure were certainly behind her.

This thought buoyed Ellie's mood as she disembarked from the plane, though she could have used another session in the disco shower stall, perhaps with the jets set on a light massage cycle. This early in the morning, Dulles Airport was quiet and nearly deserted except for robots. She went to a kiosk and paid a deposit for self-driving luggage dollies. As they attached themselves to her steamer trunks one of them spoke.

"Hello... Ms. Sato... from the UK... We are Cowa Heavy-duty Rovers TSA codes 167 and 182. You may leave us at the front desk of your hotel... the Watergate Hotel. You are liable for any damage to us and any damage we cause to property or persons... Riding on us is prohibited by federal and state law..."

"Be quiet and follow me," Ellie said.

The squat little pallet-shaped beastie cut short the legal disclaimer and, wheels squeaking in the large baggage claim area, rolled after her. Wide glass doors marked "No Re-entry" slid apart, and truly Arctic air blasted in from where the taxis were lined up. Then Ellie's buoyant mood was abruptly shattered by bloodcurdling yells.

"There's one!" a strange-looking hooligan dressed all in black screamed from the other side of the line of taxis.

"It's her!"

"YOU FASCIST CUUUNT!"

12

DULLES INTERNATIONAL AIRPORT
WASHINGTON DC

Ellie had just gotten outside the terminal and taken her first breath of Arctic-chilled Washington DC air when the commotion made her look. The yelling was coming from a crowd of figures wearing black hoods, and for some bewildering reason they were pointing at and moving in her direction.

"Is that her?"

"Gotta be, lookit that fucken capitalist ho."

"Supremacist scum!"

Ellie looked over her shoulder to search for the object of the unexpected mob's outrage. It certainly could not be her. She'd never been to America, and had certainly had not been in Washington long enough for anyone to be annoyed with her.

At that moment, Ellie was more concerned with the wheels on the robots straining under her heavy suitcases. The airport's rental pallet robots were being truculent. Instead of following her in a straight line, they were making odd squeaking noises and drifting off left and right every few steps. She grabbed their tether lines and dragged them along the wet and grimy floor, and like a pair of arthritic beasts of burden, they followed.

Despite the profanity, she didn't think much of the demonstration. There seemed to be far fewer participants than would attend the often murderous European Black Bloc melees during which Antifa paramilitary units fought pitched medieval-style battles against police with both sides using shields and battering rams. This group looked far tamer—at first.

"Yeah," another hooligan yelled. The group was closer now. This fellow was wearing a red ski mask with a pompom on top that bobbled angrily in all directions. "You're a white supremacist cunt!"

It became stunningly apparent there was no one else around at whom these fellows could be barking accusations. A little more apprehensive, Ellie looked for the car Sarge Bryan said would be somewhere near the line of taxi cars. Then she looked up at the sign again. It said *Ground Transport 2*.

Oh, poppycock.

What she had jotted down in silky lavender-colored ink and read as *2* was actually *6*. She was in the wrong place, and a mob of unisex-looking thugs was gathering to her right, cutting her off from where she was supposed to go.

"My dear man," Ellie said in a distinct Oxford accent, which was known to be soothing to most semi-literates, "I'm nothing of the sort. To start with, I'm English and Japanese. I'm the owner of a newspaper, perhaps you've heard of it: London's *Citizen-Juggernaut*—"

"She's a fucking *skin shirt*!" a woman screamed. The expletive came from a snaggle-toothed mouth all but hidden by a ski mask that looked to have been made from an enormous woolen sock with three ragged holes cut into it.

Ellie looked at the first taxi in line. The driver was a chubby little fellow with a few days' growth of beard. He took one look at her impending doom, made sure his doors were locked, and drove off.

Some bloody Lancelot you are, she thought hotly, and again tried to mollify the motley mass of protestors. "I assure you I cannot possibly be a 'skin shirt.'" *Whatever that is.*

"Who you talking to? You are over-privileged human scum!" the first hoodlum said. He advanced on her with a sturdy-looking two-by-four, on which was stapled a flimsy sign reading:

Death Camps for
the Enemies of Justice

"She's from England!" someone in the back of the twenty-strong crowd yelled. "She's with the English Defense League Nazis!"

"I don't even follow football," Ellie protested, noticing with rising alarm that the protestors had quickly encircled her. She looked back toward the terminal; the gates had locked behind her. Big red letters read: *NO RE-ENTRY*.

"Nazi scum!"

"Nazi scum!"

The increasingly dangerous-looking crowd took up the chant. They advanced. Ellie was trapped. Where the heck was security? She'd been in tight spots before, but this was out of the blue. She thought about ramming one of her steamer-trunk-sized suitcases at the mob or at the doors behind her. Maybe she could set off an alarm.

The guy with the heavy wooden club masquerading as a protest sign was closest; he looked unsure as to whether he should start thumping her.

"Nazi scum!"

"Nazi scum!"

The rest of the crowd had no reservations in the thumping department.

"Gaaaah!" a person in a hockey goalie mask yelled as he was sprayed in the face with some yellow-brown-looking stuff which had been meant for Ellie.

"Sorry!" the female rioter said through her woolen sock mask. "I was aiming at the Nazi!"

The spray blew around everywhere. Just a whiff of it inflamed Ellie's nose, stung her eyes, and worst of all made her drool into her expensive sweater, which she clasped over her face. As it was, she was lucky her hands were raised.

Something came flying out of the crowd. Just as the massive can of beer hit, she ducked. The impact felt more like a brick than an aluminum-clad beverage. From past experience, she knew exactly what both those objects felt like.

She cursed a blue streak and looked down. Maybe she could use it as a weapon. The label on the ginormous can said *Budweiser – the King of Beers*, and a gray paste was glopping out from the open end.

"Is that cement?" Ellie howled, having had about enough of her unexpected welcoming committee. "You wankers! Did you just hurl a can full of cement at me?"

She would have said more, but the delayed pain from both forearms and the nerve points on her elbows shot up to her brain and nearly made her stumble onto the chilly pavement. If it hadn't been for the extra padding in the sleeves of her Canada Goose Mystique Parka, the blow might have broken something. She got her feet back under herself just in time. If she fell down, she realized there was every reason to expect a raucous stomp-down and kicking match featuring her head.

"Go back home!" yelled someone Ellie thought was probably a large woman, whose pouch belly hung down and protruded from the bottom of a T-shirt reading:

Nazi Lives
Don't Matter!

"We have enough fascists here," gasped an elderly protestor in a Guy Fawkes mask. "Go home, Nazi scum!"

The shrill voices around her were punctuated by a coarser and decidedly manlier voice coming from farther away.

"Hooooah! There's some Antifa pussies!"

"Yeeha!"

"Those commie pussies need a stars-and-stripes enema!"

The new shouting came from the other side of the parking lot. A group of men who looked like a sports team were approaching. Despite the sleet raining down, most of them were wearing white T-shirts and had on red bicycle-style helmets.

"Loud Boys, assemble! Hooooah!"

The arrival of the Loud Boys further enraged the less-organized, wimpier-looking but more numerous hooded mob. Many of them turned to face their new aggressors; some walked backward and pushed the large and wide "Mr. Death Camps" closer to Ellie.

She would have run for it, leaving her luggage, but whatever they were spraying was having an increasingly bad effect on her eyes and sinuses.

With her eyes tearing up, she couldn't be sure of not running farther into the angry mob or the new Loud Boys group, which might be interpreted as an attack.

Just as she decided her best bet was to hunker down between the locked glass doors and her two tall steamer trunks, a roaring engine and squealing tires rose though the sounds of screaming and fighting.

A big black limousine came plowing backward through the crowd. Its rear bumper sprayed sparks as it jumped the curb and came toward her. Just as Ellie's mind flashed back to videos of terrorist car-ramming atrocities, the back door popped open.

"Ellie Sato, ma'am," a deep voice said in an urgent tone. "What kinda mess have you gotten yourself into now?"

It was a muscular African albino wearing a dark-brown leather jacket and dark sunglasses despite the overcast sky.

"Sorry, Sarge Bryan," Ellie said, dragging her cases through the confused crowd. "I was quite certain it was Gate 2."

People started bashing the limo, trying to rock it. It seemed quite sturdy—nothing broke off or shattered, even when Mr. Death Camps hit the windshield with his two-by-four sign/club. Something he was about to regret. The driver's-side door popped open and what looked like a brown Sasquatch got out.

"Is that Tata?" Ellie asked as Sarge Bryan helped her pull her luggage into the back of the limo.

Sarge glanced up, his eyes glowing slightly through the sides of his glasses. "Aw, she promised to stay behind the wheel."

The Russian cyborg lady was a head taller than any of the protestors. This did not stop Ms. Nazi Lives, who must have weighed four hundred pounds as well, from blasting Tata in the face with noxious spray.

"Not good, not good!" Sarge kicked a small protestor's hand away from the heavy car door, pushed Ellie onto the really nice leather of the middle jump seat, and slammed it shut.

Ellie watched through the windscreen. Instead of crumpling in agony after being maced, Tata merely blinked a few times and smiled as the brown spray liquid ran down her face. She then booted the attacker in her kangaroo pouch of flab and sent her rolling onto the road.

"That's assault, you freak!" Mr. Death Camps shouted and hit Tata full on the back of her head with his wooden bat.

The two-by-four cracked, its tiny cardboard sign flopped down, and Tata flashed a metal-toothed smile as her hand launched out to slap Death Camps. The swatting motion only looked like a slap; Tata's middle finger was curled in, and it hooked through the attacker's left cheek. Ellie had seen a cyborg's sharp, diamond-hard augmented nails close up, so it was not that much of a surprise to see the attacker's face extended grossly as she pulled him over the hood of the car.

"My grandmother told me I will never catch a man," Tata said. "She said 'you are too ugly.' What do you think?"

Literally fish-hooked as he was, Death Camps had no reply. From the other side of the limo, the senior citizen Guy Fawkes fellow lit an aerosol can on fire and moved toward Tata with his improvised flamethrower.

"No, you don't dare!" she yelled. "This is my favorite coat."

To get a better grip on Death Camps, Tata fish-hooked the other side of his face and pulled him around to block the flames that spewed out toward her.

Ellie had witnessed many terrible things, but she had never seen a human face distended like that as it was pulled from both sides. Death Camps's tongue lashed around wildly, especially after Guy Fawkes's flame singed his back and buttocks.

"Settle down, or I get mad," Tata said.

Witnessing the unexpected action from the other side of the traffic meridian, the red-capped Loud Boys jeered but kept their distance. Then they started flinging small brown sacks at the black-clad mob. One hit the car and spattered, discharging a viscous fluid.

"Ach! Disgusting," Tata yelled and threw her captive to the side. He rolled a few times into a low snowbank, his burnt clothes smoldering.

Tata got back behind the wheel and slammed the driver's door shut. Ellie was busy checking herself over where the cement-filled beer can had bounced off. Her forearms and elbows were really starting to sting.

"Ms. Sato, ma'am," Sarge said, looking over his shoulder through the rear window as Tata accelerated in reverse. "You sure do know how to make an entrance. Are you hurt?"

"You mean badly enough to admit it?"

Tata yanked hard on the steering wheel, nearly knocking Ellie's head against the heavily tinted door window as the front end of the car spun around so they were now driving away from the mob of awful people.

"Hang on, please," she said belatedly.

"Sergeant Bryan, what was that all about?"

He pulled off his dark glacier glasses, revealing shimmering gold irises which seemed to float above his cybernetic eye implants.

Sarge Bryan reached for the first-aid kit under the seat and shrugged apologetically. "Jus' another election year in America."

13

WASHINGTON, DC

Ellie searched inside the limousine's minibar and found some ice. Little bottles labeled водка tinkled inside the fridge door.

"You know, I left Europe hoping to get away from all the mad-hattery," she said, awkwardly pressing ice onto both her swelling forearms at once.

"You sure you're not bleeding?" Sarge Bryan asked with concern.

Tata glanced back, her eyeballs covered by a whitish membrane, which had kept the pepper spray from incapacitating her. A small dribble ran down her lip. She licked it off and smacked her lips.

"Mmm, spicy. Ms. Sato, there is full trauma kit in the trunk, including amputation saw."

Their driver spoke with a heavy Russian accent, and her reference to advanced medical equipment was probably not a joke. Ellie had been with Tata in Paris when her injured flesh-and-blood right foot had been summarily cut off and replaced on the spot by a temporary cyborg limb.

"Thank you, Tata, but I'm not about to bleed on your genuine leather interior." The limousine was spotless. She grabbed a bar towel before any melting ice could dribble.

"Good girl," Tata said, slapping the steering wheel. She seemed to have enjoyed the impromptu brawl. "You have the British stiffie, right?"

"Stiff upper lip, right," Ellie corrected her. "Great to see you again. What are you doing in America?"

"At Russian Federation embassy, I am the cultural attaché. Sergeant Bryan has been keeping in touch. I keep asking him to coffee, and he is mostly busy. But today when I text him, he tells me the famous writer, whose books are known to President Putin, she will be in town. I immediately drop what I doing and insist on driving." She stopped at an intersection and turned her large rectangular head into the passenger compartment. "You know, some places in America are not so safe for visitors."

Ellie's jump seat was facing rearward; she glanced out the back window. The Loud Boys and the Antifa were having at it in earnest now. There were several loud explosions as fireworks went off and people danced around, patting out small fires which had sprung up on their winter clothes. The melee had spilled out from the covered portion of the terminal area. Sirens and flashing lights were coming in from all sides.

"What was that all about?"

"Near as I can tell," Sarge said, checking his handset, "they were planning to ambush someone they disapproved of who was supposed to be arriving around this time. The dark web chat rooms alerted the local Antifa cells, who arranged a welcome party."

"Whom was I mistaken for?" Ellie asked, her recent identity theft experience making her a bit sensitive on the subject.

Sarge Bryan scrolled down the militant blog posts. "*Direct Action event… bring shields and pepper spray, leave guns at home because of f-ing airport pigs… death to fascists…* There's the target: Janice Jones."

"The wife of our host?"

"The same."

During her flight Ellie had looked up Mr. Barracude and his politically connected wife. "She's black. How could they confuse us?"

"I guess they didn't want to waste a good mob," Sarge said, putting his handset down. "Janice's PatriotChat channel just updated saying she arrived hours earlier through JFK and Reagan."

Smart woman.

They slowed down.

"Sergeant, shall I ram them?" Tata spoke as though she wanted to show off.

Ellie craned her neck the other way—police cars were blocking the road.

"No, Miss Oblonskaya," Sarge said. "Please don't."

As they slowed and stopped, a patrolman in a helmet and visor approached. He peered in through the small crack of window Tata had rolled down.

"Is anyone hurt?" the patrolman asked in a formal but suspicious way.

"No," Tata said firmly.

"Is that your blood on the steering wheel?"

"No."

"Do you mind if I have a look in your car?"

"Yes."

From a pouch, Tata grabbed a booklet that was about twice the size and many times the thickness of a normal passport. The patrolman put his hand on his weapon. Tata giggled at him through the narrow aperture in the laminated glass.

"Hi, Officer." Bryan waved from the back seat. "Sergeant Bryan, US Army. This is a Russian vehicle with full diplomatic clearance."

The sight of an albino with glowing cybernetic eyes did little to calm the local policeman's nerves. After the police scanned the holograms and barcodes inside Tata's fat credentials folder, they were allowed through.

Looking on the bright side, Ellie was happy they had at least avoided a firefight with law enforcement during her first hour in America.

"I take it the grungy slackers in all-black clothing were the local Antifa, and they are despised by the athletic chaps in the red hats."

In the Middle East, Ellie had learned the skill of very quickly distinguishing warring factions. "What escapes me is… what is a 'skin shirt'?"

"Don't take it personal, ma'am. I been called that too by people who hate the military. It's the same as 'race traitor' or 'Uncle Tom.' Means they think you're only putting on the skin of a visible minority and inside you're really a bad person suffering from whiteness."

Ellie thought that was a really awful thing to say to Sarge Bryan who, as a child, had nearly been sacrificed in a magic ritual by a witch doctor because he was a genetic albino.

"Tata," Ellie said, hanging on to an overhead strap as they swerved sharply around a corner, "I see your new foot is working out well."

Tata's front kick had really sent that rioter with the kangaroo pouch gut flying.

"Really good. I'm thinking to get the other one replaced as well, to match." More police and ambulances passed them, headed toward the airport. "How is our mutual friend Ranny Oliphant? I can't find him on KwikChat social media anymore."

Along with Sarge Bryan, Ranulph Oliphant was apparently also the object of Tata's enduring affections.

"He's quite busy testifying at inquiries. They're still finding more Pangean traitors all throughout the EU bureaucracy."

The Pangeans were a European Deep State who, under the leadership of the former French President Phillipe Rapace, had tried to kill most of the people in Europe the previous year.

"Ms. Sato, I meant to tell you," Sarge Bryan said. "I got the signed copy of your book. The dedication to Atticus was real fine."

Major Atticus Reidt had died at Bordeaux uncovering the doomsday weapon.

"How's Attie Jr.? More to the point: Where is he? If Ms. China gets to him before we do…"

"As soon as we got your message I called in some local favors. He's at the Watergate Hotel being guarded by Secret Service. Least they can do for the son of a war hero." Bryan's eyes were capable of a form of x-ray vision, they stared at her chest area. "Um, ma'am, you've got some…"

"Gack!" There was brown filth smeared under the wide lapel of her only warm jacket. She quickly pulled it off as though it was on fire.

"Must be from those, um, brown projectiles the Loud Boys were throwin' around." Sarge Bryan's alabaster face got a little red around the cheeks, an albino blush response.

Her arrival in the USA had sunk to new lows.

"Is that…? Ugh!"

"Yeah, those are unfortunately all over the place. Some crazy judge ruled that because homeless people had trouble finding public toilets, people in the USA have a constitutional right to carry around up to two pounds of human waste."

Ellie willed herself not to be sick. She prodded the balled-up jacket as far away from her as she could. "Do I dare ask why anyone would want to do that?"

"You just saw. If it's not the Loud Boys, it's Antifa, or Extinction Rebellion, or BLM protestors. They distract the cops with fake emergencies then organize flash riot mobs and throw shit bombs at each other."

Tata guffawed from the driver's seat. "I hear sometimes they put big firecrackers inside the plastic bags, for extra effect." The shoulders of her monstrous fur coat shimmied with laughter. "You Amerikantsov, how dull things would be without you."

14

WATERGATE HOTEL
WASHINGTON DC

The limousine crawled along toward the dimly lit towers of the Watergate Hotel.

"Sorry, is bit of car jam here, even at this hour," Tata said. "Extra security around the hotel is plugging traffic."

It was just past four a.m., and wet snow dabbled the windscreen. Ellie did not feel like walking, and she was certainly not going to put her only winter garment back on now that it had been spattered with Loud Boy excrement.

"That's a nice dress," Sarge Bryan said. "You'll fit right in with the black-tie crowd."

Tata glanced suspiciously at the black spaghetti-strap formal attire Ellie was wearing. As if it was her fault Melanie had only packed evening dresses that were alluring and sensually revealing.

"We were in such a hurry leaving." Ellie wondered whether it was worth trying her luck with her credit cards at a shop near the hotel. On the other hand, she would likely only be in Washington for a day. Ms. China would come to them and Attie Jr. Then she'd accept the madwoman's sincere apology for drugging her, robbing her, and stealing her blood sample and passport. In no time at all, they'd be on their way back to the UK.

She might even get a bonus feature for the *Juggernaut* in the bargain. While they were waiting, she could probably dash off a story about the odd American political situation. She got out her fountain pen, a very sleek burgundy Montblanc 146 which, while waiting for her luggage, she had filled with serious-looking Pilot Ku-Jaku blue ink.

"I tried to study up on American politics on the plane... Oh, bugger."

With dismay, she noticed the screen of her ebook reader was cracked.

"This was advertised as waterproof. I should have asked for one that was flash-mob proof."

It still worked. She held out the ebook to Sarge Bryan. It was by political writer Ann Coulter. The book's blurb said she was known as "America's Cassandra" after a woman in Greek mythology cursed to utter true prophecies but never to be believed. All Ellie knew about Ms. Coulter was she looked fabulous in prêt-à-porter fashions and had lovely hair. Her latest book was titled: *Twilight's Last Stand: It's Worse Than You Can Possibly Imagine.*

On the cover was a very dark map of the United States, the outlines of which faded into pitch black. In the middle of Ohio stood a nub of a candlestick surrounded by a pool of cooling wax. Its tiny flame was about to be stomped on by what looked like the scale-covered, claw-tipped foot of an orc creature. The well-researched book was fraught with grinding despair, and its concluding chapter was unrelentingly gruesome in its conclusions about the impending fate of America. Nevertheless, *Twilight's Last Stand* was an excellent primer on the political geography of the country from Plymouth Rock—now reduced to gravel and sprinkled on Native burial grounds—to the urine-stained no-go autonomous zones that were popping up like egalitarian weeds.

"All right," Ellie said to herself. "I better start."

She wrote in her Moleskine limited edition notebook:

–Flash mobs

–Antifa (poor hygiene, scary masks) vs. Loud Boys (red helmets, no masks)

–Fecal projectiles (sometimes explosive)

"So, what is actually going on here in this vast country?"

"Beats me," Sarge Bryan said. "I thought we'd seen everything, but it's gettin' close to Inauguration Day, and no one seems to know who's being sworn in as president or vice president."

"Right." Ellie did know that much. "It's certainly not like the British system. What about this 'electoral collegiate'?"

"That'd be the electoral college, ma'am, and nope, they can't get their act together either," Sarge Bryan said, perhaps embarrassed and confused by his country's tangled politics. "But word is the Supreme Court's about to straighten everything out, maybe even later today. If you want to know more for an article you're writing, you've come to the right place."

Tata had to let them out before they got into the driveway of the impressive circular hotel building near the Potomac River.

"Please, Ellie, take my coat," Tata said, wriggling her six-and-a-half-foot frame out of her massive fur coat.

It looked as though she had found it by the side of the road in Siberia. However, the warmest thing Ellie had on for what looked like a walk of a hundred yards to the entrance were her Chanel half boots. She gladly accepted the loaner.

The tatty fur was softer than it looked. "What fur is this?"

"Is bear fur. Kodiak. Present from when I graduate the Spetsnaz training program, tailored by my grandfather, who is leather smith," Tata said with a nostalgic smile.

Working together, Ellie and Sarge Bryan managed to keep the two rolling steamer trunks on the sidewalk leading to the hotel.

"You're smiling, Bryan. You know journalists hate secrets."

"It's just Tata mentioned a graduation gift. The last test Russian cyborgs have to pass is, er, defeating a fully grown bear with their bare hands, normally by strangling it or beating it to a pulp."

"Oh my." Ellie looked at the coat, which was dragging half a foot along on the ground. "Then I'll have to get it laundered before I send it back to her."

They had made it past the hotel's health-check line and were queued up at the second security screening.

"Oversized luggage has to be wanded in the back," a serious-looking guard with a crewcut told them when they had finally gotten through the revolving doors into the lobby. "Outer garments and shoes in the bin, please."

Ellie was glad to be rid of the steamer trunks, but Sarge Bryan objected to the more invasive security measures.

"Look, my man, we're going up to see Mr. Barracude," he said reasonably. "I'm sure there'll be Secret Service up there as well."

"Sorry, no exceptions," the man said, blocking their path.

"It's all right," Ellie said, trying to find an elegant way to doff the bearskin coat, which felt as big a king-sized duvet. "If their policy is no exceptions—"

"Exceptions!" said a strange, bawdy voice from deeper within the lobby. "Exceptions are what America is all about. This is Washington... DC! If the universe of exceptions has a center, you're standing in it."

A shorter, broader man approached. He was wearing a white dinner jacket with a bolo string tie around his neck which was fastened with a huge star sapphire clasp. His hair was moussed straight up and back, giving it and his face the appearance of having been carved out of dark-brown wood.

"Mr. Barracude," Sarge Bryan said. "We'll just be a minute."

"Fuck— I mean, forget the minute," said the odd fellow as he waddled over. "Let 'em through."

"But management policy is—"

"Right, son." Barracude patted the much larger guard on his thick bicep bulging out the sleeve of his suit jacket. "I don't own this hotel, I hold the guaranteed first-mortgage bonds on it, which means I own the owner, his kids, and his grandchildren. So you can bend the policy a little, or you might just find yourself transferred to the company's casino operations... in Calcutta."

The night manager waved them through before any fisticuffs or banishments occurred.

"Nice coat," Barracude said, without any trace of irony.

"It's just a loaner," Ellie said meekly. The walk through the cold early morning air had brought to the fore her old injuries and the fresh new ones she'd gotten at the airport. She really needed to sit down—for about ten hours.

Sarge began to say, "Mr. Barracude, this is—"

"I know! Ellie Sato, the famous author." Their host led them through a roped-off area to a private lift. "Hey, after the nuclear war in the Middle East and whatever that crazy French bastard was planning in fucking France, you're probably gonna find America dull as dishwater. Just politics, making money, and more political shenanigans."

"I think I've had my quota of excitement for some time. I could use a—"

"Hey! They tell me you own a newspaper in England," Barracude cut in as he jabbed a thick muscular finger on the single button on the control panel, as though mashing it down harder would force the lift to come down more quickly. "I used to own one too. Then they printed a nasty piece about Janice, so I swamped the damn thing with debt and put it into bankruptcy. Everyone lost their jobs. Every single one of them, out." He made a sliding slap with his hands, perhaps to indicate the sliding of unemployed buttocks on pavement. "Out on their asses."

He slapped Sarge Bryan on the shoulder. "Heya, Sarge, it's good that security guy didn't test me. Treatin' a VIP guest of mine like that. I got a black belt in judo and Brazilian jiu-jitsu. I'da flipped his ass right out the door."

"I'm glad it didn't come to that, sir," Sarge Bryan said with a calm expression and not a hint of mirth on his chalk-white face. "Mr. Ran Oliphant sends his regards."

"Oh ho, that old Scottish haggis." Barracude tapped Ellie's arm on one of her many bruises. "You know me and him played Vladimir Putin in ice hockey once..."

By the time Ellie and Sarge Bryan had heard about the third goal Barracude was "gypped" out of scoring by Mr. Oliphant's refusing to pass him the puck, the lift stopped at the penthouse and the doors slid back.

"Oh my, is there any gold left for anyone else?" Ellie spoke out loud, though she hadn't meant to. The spectacle of the penthouse suite put the private plane's décor to shame.

"Thanks. This joint is all right," Barracude said as he led them through a gold archway across a transparent floor that had gold nuggets embedded all through it. "You should see the place we're building in Bel Air, that's in California. I'm knocking down three five-hundred-million-dollar houses and making our dream home. It's just waiting on the permitting and a guarantee I never pay any state or local taxes ever."

"What the fuck, Jezzie?" a woman whispered from the other room. "You'll wake the kids. Oh, hi."

"Sorry, hun," Barracude replied sheepishly.

There were other people wearing dark clothing in the large oval living room of the penthouse. Ellie guessed they were the Secret Service agents Sarge had mentioned. However, they didn't seem interested in searching or wanding her again.

Mr. Barracude waved them forward. "This is Army Sergeant Bryan and—"

"I know who it is," Janice Jones said, ushering Ellie to an invitingly soft-looking couch. "Eleanor Sato, so pleased to meet you."

Janice was a fit-looking woman in her thirties. She wore a blue pantsuit with only a few items of jewelry, including an extraordinary diamond ring that covered three of her long, impeccably manicured fingers.

Janice handed her a glass of water. There was also a tea trolley nearby. "We heard about what happened at the airport." She shook her head. "Not the way we want to welcome people. I've got the hotel medic waiting for you in the other room if you need looking at."

What a nice lady, Ellie thought. *Why would anyone want to mob her and tear her to bits?* Then she looked at her husband, who was fidgeting with a putter on an enormous artificial golf green that took up a third of the living room. *What an odd couple.*

"When are those Supremes gonna do their thing?" Barracude asked, now chomping on an unlit cigar as he prodded the gold golf ball into a hole he had clearly missed. "We wanna find out who's the fucking President. Not just me, all of fucking America wants that."

"I told you, keep your voice down."

"Is Attie Jr. in the next room?" With all the excitement, Ellie had nearly forgotten what brought her here.

Janice nodded. "And Sarge Bryan's goddaughter, Sienna."

"They were both here for a National Monuments walking tour. As soon as we got your message, we pulled them out from their field trip just as they were headed to the Lincoln Memorial," Sarge Bryan said, keeping his bass voice low as well. "They were a bit disappointed, but they're Army kids. They know how to roll with the unexpected."

An urgent buzzing came from Janice's waist. She looked at the handset screen and frowned, then looked at Ellie.

"I've gotta go to the White House," she said, gathering her overcoat and nodding to the Secret Service agent near the door.

"What?" Barracude said, gripping his putter like a caveman's club and shaking it at the undulating surface of the putting green. The artificial grass seemed to have a mind of its own and had decided the player was sinking too many balls. In response, its mobile surface changed shape and texture. Barracude now stood in four inches of long fake grass that had sprouted around his gold-tassled loafers. "They need you now? I swear, those goofs in the administration can't wipe their butts without the chief of staff being there. Oh, sorry, Miss Sato."

"Given the events of the last twenty-four hours, I'm pleasantly beyond taking offense," Ellie said weakly, trying not to fall asleep in the warm room as she reclined on the very soft and comfortable sofa.

"Uh… good."

"No one's getting any sleep tonight with the Court about to make its ruling." Janice looked at her. "You wanna come?"

"To the White House? Me?" Ellie tried to judge how disrespectful it would be to decline and just keep lying on the leather couch, swelling and throbbing. She'd probably be confined to the press corps room while all the exciting things happened elsewhere in the West Wing. "I'd be honored, but—"

"However the Court rules, we'll need all the good overseas press we can get."

"Damn foreigners should keep their mouths shut about our business," Barracude whispered as he slashed at a gold-colored golf ball. It flew up out of the artificial rough and bounced off the big window. "I mean, not you, Ellie, but trashy assholes like the French and the ChiComs. Anyway, dear, are they going to do anything? It's a whole week they've been deliberating, which is legalese for goofing off and getting paid overtime."

"Looks like it's on," Janice said. "They can't put it off. Someone's got to be inaugurated on the twentieth. They've even moved the venue for the ruling announcement to the old historical Supreme Court chamber on the first floor of the Capitol.

"The regular courthouse suffered a major water leak, and it would have taken too long to fix it." Janice turned to her with dark, intense, and somewhat mischievous eyes. "Secret Service just checked, both your sets of credentials are valid, for press and British diplomatic service." Janice extended her arm to help Ellie up. "You sure you're not a spy?"

Ellie tried to chuckle jovially, but that just made her ribs shift around and hurt more. She looked at the long bear coat draped across two chairs in the hallway. Chilly as it was, she wasn't looking forward to putting it on and lugging it around as they headed off to the White House.

15

RUSSIAN EMBASSY

TATA

You sure you're not a spy?"

Tata hit pause, and the audio playback stopped.

Unflinching midnight-blue eyes stared at her from the video screen on the other side of the secure communications facility in the embassy's basement.

"Speaking now is White House Chief of Staff Janice Jones, Mr. President," Tata said.

Putin's razor-sharp image gave a slight nod. "I recognize her voice. She is quite capable. I'm surprised she let a bugging device slip through her security."

Tata was hearing the audio playback from the bug in her coat for the first time. After dropping off her passengers and luckily convincing Ms. Sato to borrow her coat, she had hurriedly driven to the embassy while monitoring the transmissions the bug was sending.

As soon as she arrived, the ambassador, an officious man named Bagration, had told her President Putin had put off his scheduled lunch in Moscow to listen in on the latest bit of intelligence on the political situation in America. Putin's personal monitoring of firsthand intelligence data was not unusual. For sixteen years before entering politics, the president had worked as a KGB foreign intelligence officer, rising to the rank of lieutenant colonel. Tata now became worried that the forward and promiscuous Eurasian woman Ms. Sato would take her bear coat to the White House. Putin had the same misgivings.

"It was a somewhat risky venture to plant the bug in the overcoat," he said. "Astute security agents might find the device."

Tata had had a plan for that. "The regular Russian military are always trying to spy on the Human+ Spetsnaz division. This is well known. I made sure to use technology linked to our own military security. It would be easy to say I had no idea the device was in the coat."

Putin stared stonily at her, then his face broke into a wry smile.

"I see that Mr. Zvena, my little green man, is not the only rising star among the cyborg battalions. Let us listen to the rest."

Tata hit play.

"*Hey, can I come?*" Barracude's voice said.

"*No, you're banned,*" his wife answered.

"*Still?*"

"*You challenged the Sri Lankan ambassador to a duel.*"

"*He was looking down your dress!*" Barracude protested.

"*He's a secret transvestite. He was looking at my dress, thinking to buy one for himself.*"

"*Same difference. I didn't like it.*"

"*You're still banned.*"

"*All right,*" Mr. Barracude grumbled. "*Love you.*"

"*Love you back harder, bye.*"

The rest of the tape was filled with clacking noises and distant profanity muttered by Mr. Barracude. Tata hit stop.

"She has left the coat at the hotel. We can continue to monitor the Barracude penthouse."

The embassy's video conferencing chamber was enclosed by a Faraday cage and was small for someone of Tata's size. She felt ineffective and constrained sitting around monitoring a remote bug.

"The Sato woman is once again in the mix," Putin said contemplatively as he glanced at a tablet or paper outside the frame of his video picture. "The 96-Hour War, the mischief in Europe; she does seem to be everywhere interesting."

Tata was inclined to like the little reporter woman, except for her designs on all the men around her, especially the ones like Ran Oliphant and Sergeant Bryan, whom Tata herself had a desire to know better. "I doubt it is intentional."

"Agreed," Putin said, steepling his fingers and pursing his lips slightly. "At least we have confirmation that the Americans think they will finally be able to undo the Gordian knot they've tied their political system into. Your ostensible cover is still in place. In order for you to continue gathering intelligence, you should be familiar with the situation."

Tata had to admit she was a bit confused. Her specialty in the cyborg unit was combat field operations and battle communications. She had only thought to bug herself when she heard Sergeant Bryan was picking Ellie Sato up at the airport and assisting her in a somewhat mysterious mission. As the president had said, Ms. Sato's activities were rarely dull.

Inside his Kremlin den, Putin filled a delicately decorated teacup. "The current administration of President Casteel has been reasonable in its approach to relations with us and our allies. While not completely reversing the unfair and harmful sanctions which have caused needless hardship and death to our people, the Americans have been giving more attention to cleaning up the mess in the Holy Land and enacting a workable policy toward China.

"However, the incumbent's health, especially his cognitive ability, is in grave question. Before the election, some in Congress were pressing to have him removed under the 25th Amendment on the basis of mental incapacity.

"To complicate matters, a group of states, 'Blue' states they are called, as they are largely controlled by the Democratic party, have banded together to subvert the electoral college and require the electors to cast ballots for the presidential candidate who won the popular vote, not who won the most electors."

At this point, Tata realized she should be taking notes. Putin's grasp of these and so many other matters far outstripped the experts. As if reading her thoughts, he continued after a short pause.

"The details are very Byzantine, even for legal scholars, and it was all theoretical until President Casteel unexpectedly narrowly won the electoral college vote while Democrat candidate Senator Leota won the popular vote. Just before the federal electors were to cast their votes one way or another, an annoying small state called Maryland tried to void their participation in the popular vote compact, which threw everything into disarray. Fist fights broke out in Congress during the ballot casting, which is still not final."

Putin must have noticed Tata's enhanced eyes glazing over.

"To cut to the chase, as they say, because there is a great uncertainty as to the validity of what the electors chose in December, the choice of president may fall to the House of Representatives, and the Senate may determine the vice president in a 'contingent election.' Depending on how the Supreme Court rules on the several matters before it, there are three possibilities:

"Firstly, President Casteel and his running mate Mr. Prowse will be confirmed and take office.

"Secondly, President Casteel will be confirmed but withdraw or be determined to be mentally unfit for office, in which case Mr. Prowse will become president and the Senate will appoint a VP—by the way, the odds-on favorite for that position would be Janice Jones, due to her close relationship with Mr. Prowse and support of the ruling Senate faction.

"Lastly, Democratic candidate Carol Leota and her running mate, winners of the popular vote, might be confirmed if the original interstate compact is upheld."

Recounting these wild machinations made even Putin pause and take a breath.

"Mr. President, I am once again proud to be Russian and under your stable leadership. It is not normal for a superpower to have such…" Tata's voice trailed off because she could only think of profanities to complete her thought.

"I know, Tata. They should be ashamed. The whole matter comes down to how their top court rules in a few hours."

"It seems we can only wait and watch."

"And *listen*." Putin nodded his head with approval and ironic amusement. "For once, the Americans will have to resolve their election woes without Russian meddling." Putin put his teacup down, then slapped his desk with mirth. His other hand pressed a button, and a file transfer icon appeared on the screen. "On a completely disconnected topic, I am sending you data on an interesting discovery made by Mr. Zvena and his team on the tiny Venezuelan island called Isla La Tortuga…"

16

WHITE HOUSE

ELLIE

As the overheated limo zigzagged through barricades and past clumps of soldiers in camouflage uniforms, Ellie bought up the delicate topic of President Casteel's mental health.

"He's fine," Janice Jones said curtly.

"That's good to hear," Ellie replied. If Casteel was a drooling senile wretch as the *Daily Mail* kept saying he was, she might have had to choose between her journalistic ethics and the feelings of her very accommodating hostess. Ellie was nestled in the back of an overheated limousine, wrapped in a fur-trimmed Fendi trench coat borrowed from Janice Jones's personal closet, which occupied two levels of their penthouse residence.

"I can vouch for that," Sarge Bryan said from the seat beside her. "I went to the White House for a medal ceremony, and the Commander in Chief was sharp as a tack."

Back at the Watergate, Ellie had had to choose between lying down for a nap or obtaining an exclusive interview with the embattled US president. While the hotel doctor had been looking at her new bruises, she wasn't sure she had the fortitude to choose the path that was best for the *Juggernaut*. Then she remembered she owed everyone scads of money.

The drive from the Watergate Hotel to the White House was much shorter than the trip from Dulles Airport to the hotel had been. Smells of burning sulfur seeped into the car. They passed through smoke that lingered above the road between the lines of steel mesh that enclosed both sides of the road.

"Don't worry," Sarge Bryan said reassuringly. "Trouble's been over for hours."

Small groups of exhausted-looking riot cops were huddling, comparing notes, or just lying on the ground.

"These fences keep the roads clear around the Capitol and the White House," Janice said. "Most of the time."

They passed a street cleaner who was hosing down and scrubbing up every sort of burned detritus imaginable. A banner hanging on a riot fence declared: *Aktion or Death! We Demand...*

The rest of the cloth was burned away.

Their wheels jostled over a bump leading up to the gatehouse. Ellie smiled at Janice and hoped her eyes did not look too glazed with fatigue. A pair of white-painted security robots rolled past the window as they scanned their car from front to back and underneath. Janice looked at her with a penetrating but bemused expression in her inscrutable dark eyes.

"I've got you credentialed at the White House," she said. "You'll have access to all the press areas, and you can speak with anyone willing to speak to you. However, given how the political situation could become fluid after the Supreme Court hands down its rulings..."

"Right, ah." Ellie felt the chances of a scoop, along with the gazillion internet clicks exclusive breaking news attracted, considerably diminish. "Would you like to me to sign an embargo?"

"Not at all. We trust you," the enigmatic woman said. "I'll only ask your word that anything outside of the formal interview with the boss is completely off the record. And please, unless he brings it up, no questions on the legal process. The Court is set to resolve all remaining issues in about an hour."

President Abraham Casteel had not made any statements and had hardly been seen since early December.

"That's cutting it a bit close, isn't it?" Ellie said, thinking back on her research and the points made in Ann Coulter's most recent column entitled:

"Your Inauguration is supposed to happen January 20… it's January 18th, Dipsh*ts!"

"Heh." Janice gave a tense laugh. "We like to keep people on the edge of their seats. There are even issues around a contingent election of the executive branch because that's supposed to be voted on by the incoming Congress on a state-by-state basis, and they've gone and messed up those elections too."

Ellie barely understood the technical details. However, she could tell Janice was a bit pensive, and she also sensed an opportunity for a highly respected, award-winning, best-selling journalist to exclusively record Casteel's reaction to the Supreme Court ruling.

"You have my solemn word as an Englishwoman and a Sato."

A printing device near the armrest of Janice's seat spat out plastic ID badges for her and Sarge Bryan. They had a heading, "Health Check," under which were listed a bunch of codes for inoculations and tests for various infections. Ellie's must have been forwarded to the government by the people at Dulles Airport. But she noticed there was a mistake with both their pictures.

"These are either really bad profile shots or only half our faces," she said, looking at the shiny plastic strips.

"Visitors get the other half when they check in at the interior security desk," Janice explained. "In the past, there were some weird lapses of security and even party crashers. Not on my watch."

The other halves of their passes came unexpectedly quickly. As soon as their limo doors opened, a nervous-looking staffer in horn-rimmed glasses and a cheap tie came bounding up. His efforts not to appear nervous only seemed to make him more sweaty and disheveled. He whispered to Janice and glanced furtively at Ellie and Sarge Bryan.

"There may be a little delay," she said. "Wilbur here will show you to the Palm Room, where he will serve refreshments, because at least that's something he's good at, right, Wilbur?"

Having been inside the lairs of three powerful megalomaniacs, the largest of which was Dr. Licht's palace outside Geneva, the White House almost appeared homey. While lacking the grandeur of Versailles or the serious dignity of Buckingham Palace, this official residence had a distinct homespun charm and was bristling with security people.

As they walked past to get to a waiting area, Ellie glanced into the press corps scrum area. She recognized a couple of heads from cable news, and they peeked jealously out at her. She caught a whiff of stale coffee and reporters' sweat. The poor buggers had been waiting days for a crumb of news from the podium while the Court deliberated.

Wilbur's hands jittered, threatening to spill the tea he was serving onto the silver tray. Janice unexpectedly paged him, and the cup and saucer slid right off, generously splashing Sarge Bryan from the waist down.

"Ah, sorry, sir, I'll just get a cloth."

"I'm not a sir, and I'll do it myself," said Sarge Bryan, wiping his pants off and pushing the other man's soft little hands away from his groin area. "You don't need to help, really."

Ellie felt sorry for the career Army man. This was the first time she had seen him wearing nice civilian clothes, and now he looked as though he had wet himself in excitement.

Janice Jones's voice yelled from Wilbur's pager: "Get them down here. He wants to see them."

"How does he even know...?"

"Of course he knows. He's the fucking president, at least for another hour," Janice's voice hissed.

"I'll take them to the North Portico."

"No, you won't. Go to the Situation Room and follow your nose to the basement. If you get lost, you can keep walking, because you'll be fired."

Sweating and shaking worse than ever, Wilbur led them along a long colonnade corridor. A dim gray dawn was peering out under dark clouds laden with snow. Ellie wrapped her coat round her as they stepped quickly toward a set of double doors at the end.

The lift to the basement appeared to be new; she noticed green masking tape around the control panel. It was also quite small. Wilbur found it hard to keep away from Sarge Bryan, who would have been intimidating even without his ocular implants and ghostly white albino complexion.

"Right through, uh, there," Wilbur said.

"Not really, son. I was here not long ago to pick up my friend's medal," Sarge said evenly. He gestured with one hand, and with the other, kept a tea towel over his beltline. "This way, Ms. Sato."

Ellie remembered her friend's cybernetic eyes had a built-in compass. He guided them through several twists and turns, past a glass door behind which stood what looked like cut flowers in vases, past a door which had on it a big white contoured tooth design. Just beyond the dentist's office, they turned a corner and nearly ran into Janice.

Standing beside her was a tall, thin man with no smile. Ellie recognized him as the vice president and glanced at her notepad to recall his name: Reko Prowse.

Mr. Prowse said, "I'll be upstairs." Then he turned and walked away.

Janice had a fixed smile on her face.

"We're clear about 'off the record,' right?"

Ellie nodded. Her neck was sore and seemed to creak. "As long as we're also clear about 'exclusive,'" she managed to retort.

"Is that them?" a haggard voice said through a pair of swinging doors with outlines of enormous bowling pins painted on them. "Get them in. They're people… ones … the only ones who can understand."

Janice took a breath, then ushered them into an unexpectedly spacious two-lane bowling alley. One wall had a dozen video monitors on it showing CCTV footage from the gates and the guardhouses; the other had shelves holding antique items hanging above a rack of bowling balls.

"Mr. President," Sarge Bryan began, about to introduce Ellie.

The older politician was tall and nearly as broad in the shoulders at the African albino. However, his Lacoste alligator shirt revealed hunched shoulders and the softness around the chest and waist of a body recently gone to flab. Odd hairs sprouted from his ears and nose in a lapse of personal grooming that might even attract notice in the Scottish Parliament. Casteel nodded weakly and bade them to sit down on the bowling bench opposite him.

"I had the place, uh," the older politician said. "This place, made it bigger. My friend… good man, my friend… loyal… capable, uh, Reko the VP did it all. Now it's the size of the old Truman alley… used to be under the West

Wing. Now it's here. Two lanes now, two of 'em."

Golly, this man does not look well, Ellie thought, glancing at her friend.

Sarge Bryan's expression stayed impassive as he sat. "It's a great pleasure to be back here, sir," Sarge Bryan said. "I was here for a medal ceremony."

"I know, I know, for, Colonel… uh, I mean, Major Reidt," Casteel said with a sudden alertness that animated his gray eyes, which peered out from under bushy brows. "Fine man, a hero. Medal of Honor, well deserved. His son's name also it is Atticus, brave boy too. Mother's in England, hopelessly insane… sad."

Ellie took a moment to look around. Along the walls there were portraits of past presidents and first ladies, most were bowling or wearing casual attire. Right next to the entrance door was an eye-catching floor-to-ceiling piece of mirror artwork. On its silver reflective surface was a double image of Elvis Presley. The image had been taken from a Western movie the entertainer had starred in. Both Elvises were staring straight into the room aiming a pistol from their hips. In the right-hand corner was the bold signature of the artist: Andy Warhol.

Along the wall opposite to where they sat were video monitors. Beneath those hung shelves which held a pair of replica dueling pistols, a few framed coins, and finally something Ellie could relate to: an antique pen and ink stand.

As the president kept speaking in a distant but oddly high-pitched monotone, she could see Sarge Bryan was becoming less and less able to maintain his composure.

"So you see… you see, that why I'm glad you two came. You two were at Bordeaux, in France when it all… you know… the thing… what's going on out there." Casteel waved his hand at the large TV on the opposite wall. "Phht! Is nothing, not compared to what's happening in here." Very deliberately, he tapped his temple. "*In* here, you understand?"

Ellie was about to say something to save Sarge Bryan from having to make conversation with someone who was clearly as mentally unwell as any of the inmates at St. Bartholomew's, then Casteel noticed her looking at the ink stand. With sudden energy, he bounded to his feet, stepping lightly over in his bowling shoes to where she stood.

"You've noticed that, huh? Know what it is?"

"Certainly. Is it the real one?"

"It's the real White House, isn't it? Heh, and I'm the real commander in chief. Well, for another... fifteen minutes," he said, checking the countdown on the news channel, which showed a picture of a formal vaulted chamber with no windows and twenty-one empty seats arranged behind a long table.

Ellie touched the brightly polished tray. "This is a Phillip Syng inkstand."

Casteel chuckled, standing close enough to Ellie that she could tell which brand of aftershave he used. "Most people think it's a salt and pepper shaker. Boneheads."

On top of the silver tray stood a quill pen holder, an inkpot, and a pounce powder dispenser. The pieces were a very nice example of eighteenth-century silversmithing.

"Well, in defense of the boneheads, not too many people know what a pounce dispenser looks like."

For the first time since she, Sarge Bryan, and Janice had come in, the president seemed alert and interested in a subject. Luckily, this was one subject Ellie knew quite well, because out of all the titles of boring political and historical books she had looked at on the flight over, one had caught her interest: *The Man Behind the Quill: Jacob Shallus, Calligrapher of the United States Constitution.*

"The treatment of a vellum parchment with pounce, finely powdered herringbone, was essential to making the animal skin suitable for writing on with iron gall ink."

Ellie pointed to a small, framed copy of the four pages of the Constitution document, which hung on the wall.

"Now, those were written either on regular calf or sheepskin or vellum, which would have been made from the skin of stillborn calves. I'd have to look at the originals to tell for certain."

"I can arrange that, and damned quick too," Casteel volunteered, becoming more attentive the more detailed she got.

"Sir... we are awaiting the Supreme Court decision."

"Aw, yeah," the president grumbled. "Go on, Ms. Sato. You were saying?"

"Parchment making is quite a process. The animal skin must be soaked in lime, dehaired, cleaned, stretched, scraped, and dried under tension."

"But the animal, where the skin came from, was American, huh?"

"Likely not. Around 1787, fine vellum for the Empire was generally produced in large quantities only in Great Britain."

"Man, I hate foreign outsourcing!" the president blurted.

"Worse still, the quills Shallus used, which were discarded, were almost certainly Yorkshire goose quills. But," Ellie hastened to add as the lips of the leader of the free world compressed in exasperation, "the ink was doubtlessly sourced locally and made from real American oak tree galls and patriotic ferrous sulphate."

"That's something." Casteel looked closely at the duplicate of the document. "The letters of the first words are slanted differently."

"That's called 'engrossing', canting the titles left and making them larger and more bold face. The fact that Shallus was working against a strict deadline over a weekend makes his penmanship even more remarkable. See, sir, the first three words, *We the People*. To me that's broad-nib Bâtarde lettering with a reverse cant but it also has similarities to Bickham's copybooks from the 1740s. Now, beneath that, the body of text is written with a normal cant in what could best be described as a light Copperplate script using a pointed pen style."

"You don't say…" Casteel's eyes seemed to focus on some middle distance between them. Ellie thought bringing his attention to something tangible might help.

"Mr. Shallus wouldn't have thought to keep the quills." Ellie pointed to the silver tray. "This inkstand is all that's left of the original writing instruments."

The president seemed mesmerized by the shiny objects and the reflective surface of the platter upon which they sat. Then Casteel lost interest in them, and his eyes flickered back and forth, suddenly coming to rest on the pair of old single-shot dueling pistols on another shelf. The presumably non-functioning model guns jogged something in Casteel's memory.

"Andrew Jackson… he killed man in a duel," he said suddenly. "Fucker accused him of cheating on a bet and insulted his wife. Shot him clean dead, Jackson did. That was before he became president, of course. He knew how to deal with swamp rats…"

Before Ellie could think of something to say that did not involve deadly violence, there was a flurry of movement on the TV screens. The red-velvet-accented interior of the court chamber gave way to pictures, which struck her as looking oddly familiar. Sound muted, the scrolling captions read:

BREAKING NEWS *Five Injured at Mostly Peaceful Airport Protest*:

A foreign instigator, who quickly fled the scene in a Russian-flagged vehicle, baited peaceful protestors, forcing them to bravely defend themselves at Dulles Airport.

The president's attention darted over to the monitors; perhaps he was expecting the Supreme Court ruling.

"Aw heck," Casteel said. "Look at those human turds. Like to lock 'em all up, especially the ass hat who set them off."

The news footage showed red-capped Loud Boys throwing things as the bedraggled mob who had assaulted Ellie ran back and forth in front of the arrival gates. There were a few shots of the Russian embassy's limousine crashing through the crowd, but thankfully none of her cowering on the ground. Tata's blurry image looked like an escaped Sasquatch bashing away at midgets.

Sarge Bryan gave her a look that seemed to say, *Best not mention who the ass hat was who started that.*

Ellie looked away from the TV screens and pointed to the Warhol art installation, which took up half of the wall next to the doorway. "That's impressive, the young twin Elvises look so lifelike."

President Casteel had found some smudges on a bowling ball and was polishing them off. He seemed not to have heard.

Janice intervened. "Yes, it is… a unique work. My husband donated the artwork. He said, 'If there's one thing the bowling alley at the White House needs, it's a picture of the king. Better yet, two!'"

The TV monitors snapped away from the factions brawling outside the airport and back to the improvised courtroom at the Capitol Building. People in black robes were filing in behind the bench.

"Fuck damn me," said the president, dropping his polishing cloth. "It's on now. Where's the damn remote?"

The controller was wedged between two bowling balls. Casteel pulled it out and hurriedly tapped on the sound.

"…was moved on short notice due to a partial ceiling collapse and water damage to the main chamber of the new Supreme Court building located not far away on First Street," the TNN announcer whispered.

Why is he whispering? Ellie thought.

"And if you're wondering why I'm keeping my voice down, we are in the historic Old Supreme Court chamber, which only a few days ago was open to public visitors to the Capitol Building. This space is only a fraction of the size of the new courthouse building located a few blocks away.

"Inside these historic chambers there is a limited gallery, and Court officials have requested the presence of counsel for the states, the federal government, and various intervening parties. In fact, if we can get a shot of the front row, the majority leaders of the House and Senate are being seated. As you can see, Jillian, we're lucky to even get a view from the very back."

A clip cut in. It was clearly from a few days ago and showed the ornate room being cleared of brocaded ropes and the historical high-backed wooden chairs being replaced with modern leather ones. Ellie recognized a smartly dressed woman coordinating the activity, it was her new acquaintance: Janice Jones.

"We know about a mile away, at the White House, all eyes will be glued to the screen as events unfurl and a tortuous, maddening, violence-inducing, stalled election process comes to a crescendo, one which has been far worse than the Corrupt Bargains of 1824 and 1877, the fiascos of 1800, 1828, 1836, 2000, 2020, or even the debacle of 2024."

"Right, Don," a female newscaster said. "But let's not forget the tectonic levels of anticipation happening right now in California, where Democratic Senator Carol Leota, winner of the popular vote, is said to be awaiting the results inside her campaign's enormous compound owned by the family of her running mate, the heir to the Sprünger Pharmaceutical fortune."

"Leota…" the president said. The mention of the name seemed to yank Casteel out of what Ellie thought looked like a deep meditative state. "And Sprünger… damned globalist drug pushers, child traffickers, vampire squids."

"Ms. Jones," Ellie said, trying to bring the conversation back to planet

Earth. "So, this isn't the first time America's had election problems?"

Janice appeared as though she were silently going through a list of reasons to cut the interview short, but couldn't find a good enough one to override her boss.

"Back in 1876, the vote count was in dispute in three states, with both parties claiming they had won," Janice said.

"What happened?"

"Congress set up a commission, and they worked it out. Of course, back then things were more amicable."

Don's talking head chattered in the monitor. "Well, Jillian, if the series of complex rulings do go Leota's way, the dynamic Democratic duo might just have to downsize to their new headquarters in DC. Our reporters on the West Coast will try to get some comment from the normally tight-lipped Leota campaign.

"In the meantime, we return to the hastily arranged but very stately and beautifully appointed historic court chamber. From 1800 to 1806, this area of the Capitol complex was the lower half of the United States Senate chamber, and from 1810…"

Ellie watched the camera pan across the quietly churning mass of people in dark suits and dresses. The décor of the place looked art deco. Compared to English courtrooms, it was a relatively plain affair; the judges wore black robes and there wasn't a big powdered wig on anyone's head.

The twenty-one justices filed in and stood in front of their chairs. The woman in the center moved a little more slowly than the rest, and when she got to her chair, seemed to sag into it as much as sit. Everyone in the room was standing in respectful attention.

"…since the room was open to visitors and part of the Capitol, it had fire and security features already in place and was quickly converted into a fitting venue for this historic moment. Madame Chief Justice Meyers, known to be a stern disciplinarian by all who have worked with her during her long career, seems to be impatient to proceed."

Jillian's voice cut in. "I know it's been said until we're tired of hearing it, but this situation is completely unprecedented. No matter how the court rules—and most human commentators and legal AI software expect a ten-to-eleven split of the newly expanded court, with Justice Meyers being the swing vote—it will be one for the legal and political history books."

The long line of justices had to file in through a narrow gap in the seating.

"Look at 'em all," Casteel said derisively. "After two rounds of court packing, we got all those judges. Soon they'll have to line up six rows deep like the Mormon fucking Tabernacle choir."

The cameraman was having trouble in the crowded courtroom, trying to zoom in on important politicians and ended up mostly filming the out-of-focus hairy necks of people who were in the way.

"Madam Justice Meyers is receiving some papers and..." Don whispered and paused meaningfully. "Jillian, I think it's about to begin. A source tells me that there is only one sheet of paper summarizing the judgment. After weeks of argument and thousands of documents, it all comes down to this."

The camera zoomed in on Justice Meyers, her gray hair was cut sensibly short in the front and clipped in the back. Ellie wondered whether her eyebrows were naturally that dark. Her wizened face looked particularly gaunt, and she could have used a touch-up of blotting makeup. With all the camera lights and that many people packed in the room, it had to be very hot.

A clerk came up and whispered something to Justice Meyers. She glanced toward a set of empty seats in the front of the gallery. Looking a bit downcast, but with a flinty expression on her wrinkled face, she nodded and adjusted something under the left side of her robes.

"The Chief Justice has had health problems in the past, and some felt she might recuse herself," Don said. "Insiders say she hung on remarkably well right up to the closing arguments but has not been seen for a few days since those ended... Ah, something... er... I just hope there's no glitch."

"What is it, Don?"

Ellie could see the camera zipping back and forth as a few people in the center of the room looked up at the large, vaulted ceiling.

"I can't see what... oh, now there's something. I can smell something metallic. Hopefully the heat sensors of the fire-suppression system have not malfunctioned because of how many people are packed in here. It would be a shame to delay... Justice Meyers has gotten to her feet."

The camera zoomed in and showed a close-up of the frail but determined-looking woman. In the shadows cast by the overhead light, her eyes looked hollow, sunken, and tortured. She raised her hand, and in it was a slim booklet trailing a red ribbon page marker. With her other hand she pulled forcefully at the ribbon once, then again with her lips resolutely compressed, finally yanking it free.

A shower of sparks came out of the end of the booklet and the room vanished in a blast of red and orange fire followed by a billowing cloud of gray-black dust. A few seconds of screeching came from the monitor's speakers then cut out as the video display turned pitch black.

17

BELMOPAN, BELIZE

ZVENA

The open-air toilet had been plunked on top of a deep cesspool a few dozen meters from the main house. Since this part of Belize sat on a low-lying plain and was subject to frequent floods, keeping the crapper away from the residence was probably a good idea. The plywood enclosing the lonely looking porcelain toilet seat was pockmarked with bullet holes. Before this day was done, Zvena thought, there would likely be many more objects and people violently perforated.

Behind the squatting station ran a thin line of sickly looking palm trees, and behind them, a gunfight raged. Of course, it was a Central American-style gunfight, so Zvena and Rodion were already bored.

They stood behind the questionable cover of a house which was about as poorly constructed as the squatting station. It had been set up on uneven, wobbly looking stilts.

"Have our guys won yet?" Rodion asked. He was standing straight up with his head tilted back. It might have seemed he was zoning out, but in fact, Rodion was receiving video feed directly into his cyborg ocular implants from several drones loitering above the palm trees. "I can't tell. Their fighting is a bit strange."

"If our guys go on siesta, let me know," Zvena said gruffly as he checked the perimeter on the other side of the house. "I'll go down there and shoot them in their sleep. We gave those lowlife people smugglers better guns than they've ever been able to afford in their lives."

Rodion kicked a tin can full of brown goop into a pile of more greenish-brown goop.

"You know," the mega-sized Human+ soldier said, "after this job, I think I will ask President Putin to transfer me to another division. Maybe I can work with Dr. Nail in his City Without Drugs helping young people get off illegal substances and stop being human scum."

"Oy!" Zvena grabbed him. "Why do you say that? Especially while bullets are flying around, yes admittedly slowly and lazily, but will you… Don't you know that when soldiers speak of retiring to an idyllic lifestyle the next thing you know… *Zchtka!*" Zvena drew his gloved hand across his throat.

Rodion scoffed. "I didn't think you were superstitious."

"Since pulling an animated cadaver off your back before it chewed your empty head off, I reconsidered."

"I have to crap."

"Go outside. It's too crowded in the house."

From spaces in between the stilts that were supporting the campesino dwelling, coagulating streams of blood dripped. Inside lay the bodies of a rival people-smuggling gang who had been at odds with the ones Zvena enlisted to help him track his prey with bribes of gold and weapons. Zvena needed one useful bit of information to help them catch up to the people who had recently resided on Isla La Tortuga, and the time was ripe for him to obtain it.

When Rodion had finished his business in the open-air toilet, Zvena noticed that his friend's biometric readout showed him weighing about five kilograms less than when he started.

"And besides," Zvena said. "What makes you think our president will allow you to resign? Being a little green man is an honor equal to being a member the Leib Guard of the Tsars."

Sounds of gunfire coming from the other side of the tree-lined road were becoming more sporadic.

Rodion grunted, lost in thought watching an enormous green beetle crawl up a wooden plank and then miraculously sprout wings and fly off into the warm wind. "But I helped save Europe from disaster and lost eight fingers during the fight at the French palace."

"Now you have eight much better fingers, all paid for by the Federation," Zvena shot back. "Also, while it was a good thing to save millions of thankless Western Europeans from a tortuous and ignominious death at the hands of the Pangeans, I know for a fact that Putin was looking forward to invading and installing his personal office on top of the Eiffel Tower," said Zvena, who knew nothing of the sort. "The continued survival of Europe is, for Russia, a mixed blessing."

The gunfire stopped. A few minutes later, when the wind shifted, it carried on it the muted sounds of distant howls. Small puffs of black smoke rose beyond the line of sickly looking palm trees.

"We better check him. You may have drowned him with your titanic dump."

Zvena marched over to the squatting station, kicked over the old stained porcelain toilet, and peered into the crap hole. About eight feet down, his thermal vision revealed a figure with his arms spread out wide, trying to stay above a semi-liquid pool of filth. He looked much more miserable than he had at midnight when they had lowered him down, and he seemed ready to talk.

"*Si... si...*" was all he managed to say as his teeth chattered uncontrollably and his arms spread out to both sides along the coagulated surface of feces, just one false move away from sinking down and drowning.

"Rodya, please retrieve our informant."

"Me?"

"Yes, I just cleaned my pike."

With a grumble, Rodion extended his Spetsnaz fighting pole, selected a hook attachment, and used it to grab the man under his armpit and haul him up.

"Tie him to a tree," Zvena said. He switched his audio processor to translate. "*Si habla honestamente, le daré un cortador de pernos. Si mientes, regresas al agujero con la cabeza adentro primero.*"

If you speak honestly, I will give you a bolt cutter. If you lie, you go back to the hole, headfirst.

This plea bargain seemed agreeable to their prisoner. Rodion prodded him against a nearby tree stump and started to wrap him in chains.

"What about our guys over there?" Rodion asked, pointing to the small puffs of black smoke rising beyond the palm trees.

"Let this be a lesson in frugality and Russian efficiency for you. Criminals here are much better at torturing helpless victims and setting them on fire than actually fighting. They are, shall we say, environmentally unfriendly: single use and disposable. That is what has happened to our former local associates," Zvena said, sending the signal to recall his loitering drones and opening his big duffel bag so Rodion could stow all their equipment. "The gold I bribed our gang with was fake, and the last round in each magazine I gave them has blown up in the chamber, making their weapons useless."

Picking up a pair of bolt cutters, Zvena advanced on the shit-stained wretch cowering on the brown grass. "I hate people-smugglers."

18

NEAR LA MESILLA, GUATEMALA

ABDELKADER

Abdelkader's sunglasses dripped with moisture. The air was so humid it was sometimes hard for his scarred lungs to draw a breath. Under his thin shirt, sweat was running freely down his back as he stared at a man who was sharpening a machete on the other side of their camp. This local criminal, Pietro, had twice taken dummy loads across the border from Guatemala into Mexico. Abdelkader was nearly ready to transport the real cargo in a few hours, but he had to be sure of his accomplice.

I hate people-smugglers, he thought and forced the scarred muscles underneath his mask into a smile.

For this part of the journey, Abdelkader wore a silicone face with a long sharp nose. After half his face had been blown off by an American drone strike, he had forced the doctors to burn the rest off with acid. So encouraged by his remarkable survival in the blast that had killed everyone else in his family, Abdelkader's most loyal followers underwent the same procedure. Facial-recognition software, long the bane of criminals and terrorists, could now be turned to their advantage.

The man lurking to his left, also watching the smuggler Pietro, was Sadikul. An expert in jungle warfare, he had been a Filipino Islamic terrorist before being recruited into the Pangean movement. Abdelkader nodded toward their Guatemalan guide.

"What do you think? You have the most experience operating in this type of terrain."

He had not been addressing the man behind him, Dr. Baldur, but the scientist swatted at a mosquito and offered his unwanted opinion. "I think we can trust them," he said softly. "They took two fake loads across with no problems. Let's get out of here."

Thanks to Sadikul, their encampment was strong. From the hilltop, they could see for miles, and the twenty heavily armed Pangeans could hold off a hundred local soldiers. But it was not safe for all of them to escort the compact but unusually heavy shipping crate into Mexico. In transit, the cargo would be vulnerable.

Sadikul turned to Abdelkader and shrugged, his dark-colored silicone face remaining stony. He was still learning how to move the biomimetic silicone gel that attached the prosthesis.

"We have until nightfall to decide," Sadikul said, his voice soft and high, speaking Filipino-accented English. "But then we must go. Too long here is no good."

Abdelkader's initial plan had been to cross into Mexico from Belize, but its border was too narrow and the criminals there were too greedy. Any one of the established routes through Guatemala were better options.

Initially, he had studied the coastal smuggling route. Floating their cargo across the Suchiate River had its advantages: it required less manpower, but the area was in the midst of a crackdown on cross-border activity. The Central Corridor route into Chiapas had the most possibilities, and many border stations were frequently unmanned. When they had first scouted the area, Abdelkader had nearly ordered his men to grab their load and dash across.

At the last moment, he forced himself to relent. This package was too important. It had even more potential to heal the world than President Rapace's failed plan. Even if Europe fell, there would still be America. Weakened, directionless, less relevant in the world today than ever since its first Civil War, its hateful guarantees of racist liberty and fascist freedom had to be utterly crushed for the world to be unified. The package they had hauled up rivers and heaved up the muddy sides of mountains was the key. Without it, his attack would fail.

"Right," Abdelkader said. "Tonight. Or we cut our losses and find another way."

He studied Pietro a moment longer and absentmindedly scratched under his skin.

"Why don't you let me take a look at that?" Dr. Baldur said officiously. "The heat and the lack of sweat and sebaceous glands on your face might be causing chafing. In this environment, that could lead to infection."

Abdelkader has been skeptical of the Uyghur scientist even before he witnessed his sloppy work in the Tortuga lab. Baldur was barely able to keep his colony of bats fed and healthy. The man always seemed to be consulting his fat textbook and researching medical databases, even chatting with people over the dark web. On the other hand, Abdelkader shouldn't risk becoming feverish.

"All right, come."

Abdelkader led the way into a camouflaged tent. Nearby, muddy water gurgled along a small stream. Once inside, he pulled off his face in one smooth motion and turned around just as the doctor came in so they were inches apart, nose to open sinus cavity holes.

The poor man cringed and blubbered, "Ahhh— I see."

Dr. Baldur had never seen him in the flesh, so to speak. But he recovered quickly.

"I see the issue. The right side of your face is more heavily pitted."

"Yes, I plan to thank the American taxpayers for that."

"The rest of the, uh, surface, was quite elegantly stripped."

"It did not feel elegant at the time." Abdelkader had insisted on remaining awake and undrugged during the entire operation.

"And you must have practiced with great deliberation to create such realistic facial expressions with your silicone prosthesis," Baldur said like the bootlicker he was. Then he got his bag out and dabbed at the itchy parts of Abdelkader's face. "These facial prosthetics were originally perfected in India. There are thousands of acid attacks each year, mostly targeting unfaithful wives and disobedient daughters."

Abdelkader was offended. Building the kingdom of Pangea was his only true guiding light, but he was still a man. "Those harlots and backtalking fishwives shouldn't be allowed masks. Shame is shame. My wounds are an honor without price. My most loyal followers have chosen to share them."

His eyes stared at Dr. Baldur from underneath lashless flaps of skin. "But not you."

"I-I am not-not as famous or worthy as you and your followers. No one knows me, no one cares to."

"They might, if the virus you planted works as you say it will."

"Without question, it will, it has. You saw for yourself. The subjects we brought back, not just the American tourists in Jamaica, but the Australians and Canadians also were wonderfully infected, and no one has noticed because no one has any symptoms."

"Including us."

"That was unavoidable," Baldur said quickly. "One way or another, we would all be exposed. But my antiviral is working, it is. The key to biological attacks is to make sure your own forces are immune."

"Really, you thought of that?" Abdelkader said skeptically. "Sounds like you read it somewhere, maybe in that fat book you're always consulting: *Biological and Chemical Weapons: Their Joys and Pitfalls.*"

The furtive scientist finished dabbing his scarred face and backed away. "Of course. It is the standard text, and I dip into it occasionally. But I assure you, when you discharge the weapon, we will be completely immune to its effects."

Abdelkader slapped his face back on. It felt better.

"You may go."

Abdelkader found Pietro casually watching the routes down into the valley. A trio of spiders trailing silk threads dropped down. Abdelkader batted them aside. As he approached Pietro, a long centipede started to climb up his boot. The smuggler kicked it off and squashed it.

"Pietro. This is an Italian name."

Pietro smiled easily. "My father thought Pedro, the Spanish form of Peter, was too common. My son, as well, is Pietro."

"How old is he, your little boy?"

"Nine next month. You're in luck, you and your special cargo," Pietro said, lowering his binoculars. "This will be one of the last loads. In fact, I have made up my mind here and now, once I have earned what you are paying, I tell you, it will be the last trip I will make." He gestured left and right with his machete. "Things are getting too civilized. The peasants are getting too greedy, and not just here. You saw what Belize has become. Soon it will be impossible for me to do an honest night's work."

He looked back behind Abdelkader toward La Mesilla village.

"The Pemex development bank has come, even to this remote place. They built a school and have run a gas line to the village. No more walking miles to fill cans with propane."

"You cannot stop progress," Abdelkader said. *Unless you have what it takes to cast a superpower back into whatever nightmare world came before the Stone Age.*

Pietro smiled an easy smile. "Well, tonight, then, huh?"

Abdelkader nodded. "Tonight."

That evening, everything was arranged, but not as Pietro expected. Abdelkader, while contemptuous of observant Muslims and their incessant praying, disliked working with kafir, or unbelievers. Rapace had been vermin but powerful and useful. Abdelkader's time with ISIS had been simpler and much more rewarding.

Yet even before the fall of Al-Raqqa, he had seen those fanatics for what they were: limited. His vision of Pangea was a form of caliphate, like the empires of the Persians or Ottomans. If he could sink militarily strong, mentally weak, Jew-worshipping America, into a sinkhole of violence and insanity, half his work would be done.

"Not that way," Abdelkader said to Pietro as he led their small party of six through the overgrown path down from the hilltop. "This way, I think."

Pietro turned, and with a smug smile was about to correct him, but then with a quick motion, Sadikul relieved him of his sidearm, and with his other hand put a curved Gurkha blade under his chin. The smug smile vanished.

"I insist."

They walked on. The way ahead was illuminated for only a few feet by dim red flashlights hanging from their webbed vests. They had proceeded only fifty meters when they came upon the first trail marker. Pietro froze.

A freshly cut pole of local bamboo featured the severed head of one of the ambushers Pietro had ordered to lay in wait for them. A few meters on, another, and so on.

"At first it puzzled me, Pietro," Abdelkader said softly in the hush of the arboreal gloom. "How did you know which was my real cargo? We had prepared the two false loads. They were identical."

He tapped the heavy crate being lugged forward by four Pangean men.

"I scanned it for trackers, shined black light on all sides of the box. Nothing, then… look." Abdelkader pointed to scorch marks made by a small butane lighter. "I remembered the classic style of invisible writing, very old school, one might say. It reveals itself only when heat is applied and vanishes again when it is taken away."

Abdelkader kicked Pietro in the groin. The dirty thief sank to his knees with a gasping yelp. Sadikul bound his hands tightly with steel cuffs.

"There, you see? That is the mark made by the pilot, an associate of yours. He put the mark so you would know you had the right load when you were ready to steal it. Now you are going to assist us, and again, it will not be in the way you expected."

He grabbed Dr. Baldur.

"Doctor, take Pietro over to that tree. Keep your medical bag—you will need it."

The scientist reluctantly complied. Everyone was watching him as he pulled Pietro to the edge of a copse of trees, barely illuminated by their torchlights.

"Now, Doctor, you have said that your vaccine serum is finally perfected and will protect us from the device's invisible radiation, though we have all been infected with the carrier virus and its payload has crossed our brain–blood barriers, yes?"

Baldur was correct. Once they began working in America, they all would have been infected. They had to be sure of the vaccine.

"R-reach it," Dr. Baldur stammered. "But the pathogen will not activate, due to the serum I, er, perfected. For the vaccinated, the machine's rays are harmless."

"We shall all see the truth of this. Wait there."

Abdelkader moved over to the box. It was only a yard square but was crushing the roots and vines lying on the forest floor. He unlatched it. Inside was an oblong device made of dark metal which looked like the world's most primitive muzzle-loading cannon. There was no hole or marking around its rounded closed end, and thin wires looped inside and back down its open end.

"Please inject Pietro with the viral catalyst. We don't have time for him to become infected in the normal way. Put it right into his brain."

With shaking hands, Dr. Baldur attempted to do that. Pietro tried to squirm away from the injection gun until Sadikul cut his lower lip off and put his Gurkha knife into his mouth. Then he held still.

"I... I perfected this method myself," Dr. Baldur said as he fed a long flexible-ended needle into Pietro's neck vein. "I-in case the samples we got, the Australian and the woman from Canada, had not had enough time to incubate, then they could still be useful."

Dr. Baldur finished and started to walk back to them.

"Oh no. Now I will ask you to stand behind your work. Or rather, in front of it." Abdelkader patted the dark bluish metal cylinder. "Sadikul, come back here. You're much too valuable to risk."

Without further banter, Abdelkader pressed an innocuous-looking switch. At his end, nothing much seemed to happen. The neutronium-coated device attached to a small portable power cell hummed, and the open end glowed an eerie shade of violet.

Abdelkader squinted in the poor light, then switched to his night-vision monocle. Fifty yards away, by the tree, Dr. Baldur was cowering as though considering running but knowing it was useless. After a little while, Dr. Baldur remained himself. The effects on Pietro, however, were most satisfying.

Abdelkader's Spanish was not very good, so he sent Sadikul to call to the group of boys going into the schoolhouse the next morning.

"Pietro!"

It was a unique name. Only one child popped his head up.

Before dawn broke, Abdelkader took his cargo well across the border into Mexico before returning to La Mesilla. This was one family reunion he was looking forward to witnessing first hand.

Sadikul wore a silicone mask with the broad forehead, high cheekbones, and pointed chin of a local Maya man. The boy would accept him as one of his father's smuggling accomplices. Abdelkader watched from the moldy tattered driver's seat of a decrepit blue minibus. Behind him, in the back, something under a tarp moved, chains rattled, then it lay still.

As planned, Sadikul gave the young Pietro what looked like a leather soccer ball. It was only fifty percent heavier than a real one. He offered the sporty young brat money if he could head it, not kick it, over a high chain-link fence which guarded the regulators for the gas pipes which snaked into the school and the rest of the town. Pietro Jr. glanced back at his school comrades, who were quickly disappearing into the single-story clapboard structure. Perhaps Pietro Jr. would decline, for fear of arriving late to the first class. He looked at the dollars Sadikul's hand and took the ball.

Bonk.

He missed.

Bonk.

Again the ball hit the barbed wire at the top and rolled back. Pietro Jr. ran over and tried again.

On the next try, the ball hung for a moment on the shiny wire, rolled over, and then bounced in. Abdelkader pressed the detonator. Young Pietro's bright-faced grin disappeared in a cloud of dust, which was followed by the first of many gas explosions throughout La Mesilla.

Abdelkader got out of the minivan and ran though the cloud of smoke and dust. Sadikul had the boy. He was alive, but his arm was burned. Blisters were rising under the shredded sleeve of his plaid shirt.

"*¡Ayuadame! Llevame a mi padre,*" Pietro wept and moaned.

The filthy little town was in chaos. A person who was on fire—it could have been a large student or a small teacher—nearly managed to crawl out through the doorway of the school building, which had turned into blazing furnace. Then the figure rolled over and collapsed and lay there smoking, like meat forgotten on a barbeque.

"*Ven te llevo a padre,*" Abdelkader said. *Come, I'll take you to your father.*

They pulled Pietro Jr. to the back of the minibus, opened the doors, and pushed the wounded boy inside.

The creature Pietro Sr. had become leaped out as far as his chains would allow, and with mottled greedy hands, embraced his son.

And then sank his teeth into the boy's charbroiled arm.

Abdelkader slammed the doors shut on little Pietro's screams. Sadikul reached down across the driver's seat, put the vehicle's gears in neutral, and let it roll down toward the bonfire of the Pemex-sponsored schoolhouse.

"May all our enemies burn like this," Sadikul said as they walked down the road to where a horrified Dr. Baldur was waiting in a shiny new jeep.

"There's nothing like a family reunion," Abdelkader said as he got in. He slapped the scientist on the shoulder. "Drive."

A half mile down the road, they passed the local fire brigade. Disheveled men with soot-stained faces were pushing a fire truck onto a side road. The gas line serving the fire station had also exploded. The truck's tires, ladder, and back end were all ablaze.

19

ELLIE

The US Supreme Court chamber had just exploded in a devastating fireball.

"Oh, *hashers*," Ellie gasped.

She had to blink a few times as she tried to determine whether what she had just seen happen had actually happened.

The TV screen blanked out for a few seconds, then was replaced by a feed from a camera crew outside the Capitol Building. The reporter and her makeup person were looking the other way toward dark puffs of smoke coming up from one side of the big white dome.

Ellie automatically braced herself on the smoothly polished bowling alley floorboards, anticipating the sort of rumbling shock wave of the sort she had felt inside the Knesset bunker when the nuclear bomb had gone off in Gaza. None came.

Of course. It wasn't that type of bomb. But what was it? Red lights began to strobe silently throughout the White House basement area. No one, not even Sarge Bryan, seemed to know what to do, except President Casteel.

After sharing a moment of disbelief and hesitation with the rest of them, the senior politician spoke sharply and with authority. "Sergeant, Ms. Sato, you'll have to excuse me. America is under attack, again."

He strode quickly over to the doorway. "Janice! Get a hard line link with the Joint Chiefs."

"We don't... I..." Janice's voice, normally acid-etched cool and competent, at that moment seemed fragile and lost.

The president took her gently by the shoulders. "Janice Jones, you're my chief of staff. We're under attack and a good portion of our government and military command and control is disrupted. This may be domestic sedition, terror, or a foreign-sponsored decapitation strike. Can I count on you?"

"Yes... yes, sir."

"Good, because otherwise we're all screwed to damnfuckshit."

Two Secret Service men rushed down the hall toward them, one held a big bulletproof vest and a helmet. Casteel waved them back. "Get Vice out of here, and don't tell me where he's going. Activate Mount Weather."

"Is that, uh... DoD?" a staffer who had appeared beside Janice asked.

"No, it's under FEMA," Casteel said shortly before Janice could reply.

Janice pushed the man down the narrow subterranean corridor. "You have your job. Go do it."

The staffer ran off.

President Casteel continued, a little more calmly, a little more slowly. "Then confirm that General... What's his name? The NORAD guy."

"Nunes."

"Right, get him and that whole crew into Cheyenne Mountain ASAP."

Sarge Bryan approached Ellie. She was still staring at the TV screen in which the reporters were shown crouching down behind large orange-painted statue pedestals waiting for more explosions or even the collapse of the Capitol dome.

Oh, not again... was all Ellie could think.

As Bryan was leading her down the hall away from the scrum, the president called out, "Sergeant, where are you going?"

"Sir, our of your way, sir."

"You're not in my way. Janice, take an audio file of an immediately effective executive order."

Janice held up a micro recorder, and everyone else fell silent.

"Whereas there has been an assault by unknown hostile parties on the very person of the duly elected government of the United States, and whereas a number of high-ranking office holders are gravely injured or must at this moment be presumed killed, and whereas this wickedness our nation is faced with smacks of a conspiracy the participants and extent of which are unknown, I hereby appoint…" Casteel waved his hand in their direction. "Fill in their legal names. I hereby appoint the highly experienced and decorated Army Sergeant Bryan and the British subject and renowned member of that country's intelligence service Ellie Sato as special investigators reporting to me personally until this order is rescinded. Executive order ends."

"Mr. President, we really have to get you out of here." The agents again approached, holding out their protective gear.

As they were sticking the ballistic helmet on him, Casteel looked over to Sarge Bryan and Ellie. "Just text Janice if… ah, you need… ah, things."

The president's head, now wearing the Kevlar helmet, looked weighted down, like it belonged on the top of a huge bug as it wobbled and then turned back to the bowling alley. "I… think I left some things back… uh, in there."

"Don't worry. Mr. President, we'll get them once you're safe," Janice said soothingly.

The last thing she heard President Casteel say was in a subdued, almost childlike voice. "I don't want to wear a helmet. Get it away from me. Why can't I stay in the bowling alley? It's safe."

After the main entourage left through another exit, Ellie and Sarge Bryan ascended back up via the lift. It let them out near the Situation Room, which was teeming with officials in uniforms and shirtsleeves. They had their IDs checked three times by separate groups of agents carrying automatic weapons before Ellie had a chance to ask, "What just happened?"

"I guess you're on the payroll now, Ms. Sato."

"Oh, right, but I mean…" She lowered her voice. "He seemed out of it, and then when whatever happened, he was like a completely different man… for a few minutes."

Sarge Bryan shrugged. "I seen the like before. There was one corporal in Afghanistan lying in the casualty collection area in our Forward Operating Base. He was in some kind of catatonic state after his motorcade got blown up. Around three a.m., the Taliban, or ISIS, or whoever, decides to come finish the job and roll over our FOB. Dozens of RPGs were incoming every minute.

"I look up, and clear as day, in silhouette against the big full moon, there's the catatonic guy, working the .50 cal like mad, hauling his own ammo hour after hour until dawn broke. It must have been a rush of adrenaline or something.

"After the last enemy was dead or captured, we went looking for the corporal. Found him in the food storage locker, just sitting on the floor, stacking cans of tomato soup one on top of the other. From that time until when they flew him out, I never heard him say a single word."

Ellie looked around. Every face they passed was staring at TV monitors or had a hard-pressed, determined look as its owner rushed past them carrying paper files or tapping on a handset.

Newscasts were playing on a dozen monitors in the White House Press room upstairs.

Jillian, the TNN news announcer, sounded jittery, as though her mental wheels were coming loose. "This... this is unprecedented... Fire trucks are being waved away by special hazmat teams... I'm just getting word they suspect there may be more devices in the Capitol Building and landmarks. We're being told to move back..."

As the reporter was speaking, a line of people emerged behind her, all seemed dazed, many had tattered clothing smeared with white powder. Nearly all of them were coughing or supporting one another as they inhaled fresh air. They fled from many exits and stumbled out into the falling wet snow.

When Ellie and Sarge Bryan made it outside they couldn't see any cars or limousines. This early, there were no visitors to the public spaces in the White House; people who looked like support staff or interns were being escorted off the grounds. They walked in stunned silence or with heads down over their phones toward the North Portico gates.

Ellie and Sarge Bryan were nearly through the imposing gates when six black-uniformed officers stopped them. In their midst was Vice President Reko Prowse.

"You know who I am, so you'll know I'm likely your next commander in chief, correct, Army Sergeant Bryan?"

"Yes, sir, I know who you are," Bryan said cautiously.

"I just heard about…" Steam billowed from the well-groomed nostrils in the man's aquiline nose. "Just don't let that flimsy executive order give you any ideas about interfering in official investigations. This is a disaster. A seditious attack on the foundation of our country. It is not a time or place for crippled veterans or British fashion reporters to stick their noses in. Obstruct my investigations and you'll pay, both of you, you hear me?"

"Sir, this crippled vet hears you and sees you." Sarge Bryan tapped his temple next to his glowing eyes. "Everything's recorded right here, Mr. Vice President, sir."

Reko Prowse spotted someone else he likely had to intimidate. He walked away along with his entourage of agents. Ellie and Sarge Bryan were let out of the gates and walked down the street in silence. A mostly empty commuter bus rolled past.

"What do we do now?" she asked, blinking away fat snowflakes that the wind was driving against her face.

Sarge Bryan turned to her, his eyes large and round and glowing like two distant suns. He exhaled. "We do what the man in charge said." In the cold air, his breath was as white as his skin. "We start investigating."

The way he said it told Ellie that, as determined as he was, he had as few ideas as she did what that meant.

20

WATERGATE HOTEL

After a long walk away from the White House along spookily deserted DC streets, Ellie and Sarge Bryan finally caught a ride back to the hotel. It was a rickety ride-sharing car; they packed into a back seat separated from the driver by taped-together bubble wrap and crinkled plastic sheeting, all of it smeared with what looked like tomato paste that had dried into crusty flakes.

During their march along the alphabet streets H and I, the first taxis they'd encountered got a look at them and quickly switched off their rooftop lights. Even with sunglasses, Sarge Bryan looked as though he might be suffering from the next novel strain of Ebola combined with eczema.

As they became increasingly more chilled, Sarge Bryan texted Janice, even though she was likely busy dealing with the apparent decapitation attack on the US government.

"I don't know these streets, Ms. Sato. We might get mugged."

"Don't you have a gun?"

Bryan shook his head. "Not allowed in DC."

"Why don't they ever tell that to the bad guys?"

Luckily, one of Janice's interns also had a second job as a ride-sharing cabbie. The harried-looking young man named Wilbur found them and picked them up before they ran into any street bandits. After dropping them off at the Watergate, he stared sulkily through the plastic sheeting until Ellie slid some British pound notes through the partition. Wilbur sprayed the bills with disinfectant and looked at their unfamiliar design with suspicion before stuffing them through the slit of a lockbox.

It was nearly eight in the morning as they approached the hotel, but no one came out. Inside the lobby, they found one surly looking guard standing beside the front desk. He wore an ill-fitting jacket and no tie. As they walked through the security scanner, the guard barely looked at the monitor as a series of green lights flashed and they were cleared to go in.

They followed an L-shaped path to the private penthouse lift.

"I've got the entry code from Janice," Sarge Bryan said as he punched the code into the keypad, which started the lift down from the twelfth floor.

As they rode up, Ellie had visons of her large guest bedroom with en suite bath and, when she felt more up to it, possibly another look through the closet in Janice Jones's extravagantly sized dressing room. She felt she had to look for some clothes appropriate to wear while investigating high crimes against the state.

When the lift doors slid open, all thoughts of restful snoozing were dashed out of Ellie's mind. Before the polished gold-plated doors had retracted all the way, Sarge Bryan pushed her back.

"Who is that?" Ellie managed to say. During the quick glimpse of the interior of the penthouse, she had caught sight of a zebra-patterned couch and, to one side of it, a pair of legs splayed out on the ground, not moving.

"Mr. B, I think," Bryan whispered. "You better go back to the lobby."

"Sod it… Attie Jr. and your niece are in there," Ellie hissed.

She slumped back against a diamond-encrusted mirror wall of the lift. She should have known something was amiss when they came in. This was a five-star hotel, and the doorman didn't have a tie. That should have rung alarm bells. Speaking of which… Ellie looked at the control panel and slapped the big red button labeled "Lock doors." Bryan nodded to her and prepared to go out.

Fortunately, the red button did not start any audible alarms jangling.

They still might have the element of surprise over any intruders. They crept forward.

There was a little bit of blood smeared on the carpet, and a golf putter lay on the artificial grass of the putting green, its shaft bent out of shape. From a stand near the fireplace, Sarge Bryan quietly picked up a brass poker, and they crept toward the bedrooms which were down a long hall with many doors. Ellie pointed. The only room she knew for sure was the one leading to Janice's closet on the left side at the end of the hall. Bryan shrugged. He didn't know which of the dozen rooms the kids were in either.

One by one, they eased open ostentatiously carved doors heavy with gold inlay. They didn't have time to search each room. Sarge Bryan ducked down, his augmented eyes scanning the carpet and hardwood flooring. From their previous adventures, Ellie knew his eyes possessed deep-spectrum vision, which could sense heat and faint indentations of footprints. They checked a middle room, then he motioned her forward.

Even with her normal eyes, Ellie was able to make out little dabs of blood droplets that made darker blobs on the deep plush burgundy carpet of the hallway. Mr. Barracude might have wounded one of the intruders before they got him. Before they could go back to the living room and tend to him, they had to find the boy and girl.

Lastly, they came to the two rooms at the end of the hallway. Left was Janice's closet. All tracks led to the right, to the room behind a pair of double doors. They took positions on either side of them, and he slowly prodded one open.

"Freeze, motherfucker!" a girlish voice shouted at them.

"Sienna? Are you okay?"

"Uncle Bryan? Prove it's you."

"I'll do that when I wash our mouth out. Who taught you to cuss like that, especially in front of strangers?"

"Come on in and I'll show you."

Two separate gun barrels greeted them inside the big guest bedroom. One was held by a tanned and lively looking teenage girl with a large mop of honey-brown hair. The other was held steady in front of an eye with three pupils.

"Annunciata! Fuck me!" Ellie said.

"Uncle, *she's* cursing now." Sienna, who had changed very little in the years since Ellie had seen her in a holographic image in northern Iraq, also recognized her. "Hey, Ms. Sato. They said you were coming over from England."

The gun barrels lowered.

"I'm here. Despite the best efforts of someone." Ellie got over her relief at not being shot and was instantly cross with Ms. China. Ellie was in America because of her, and she couldn't help heaping all the mayhem of the horrible day on the deranged woman's head.

Someone groaned. The noise came from behind the bed. In a smooth motion, Sarge Bryan gently removed the gun from Sienna's hands and, holding it in a close grip next to his shoulder, peered over the bed coverings.

"You better tie him up," he said, holding the gun steady.

"There's another one in the tub," Sienna said. "They came in but didn't have their weapons out."

"Well, that'll teach them to tackle an Army brat."

"Allow me," Ms. China said as she bent over the half-conscious intruder.

Ellie instantly had a bad feeling. "Anna… uh…"

But she had already jabbed two of her lengthy ceramic fingernails into the semiconscious man's neck. His body convulsed into a pretzel-like shape as the puncture wound area turned bluish black.

"There. He's tied up, for eternity."

"Hey, he could have had information," Sarge Bryan said sharply as he looked over to the door to the bathroom.

"There's still the guy in the tub," Ms. China said, wiping her claws with a tissue. "If he ever wakes up. Mr. Barracude caved in his skull. That'll teach them to come after an innocent… er, American official and her husband."

"Anna, how did you—"

Just then, there was a thumping noise from way down the hall.

"Don't worry, we locked the lift," Ellie said.

"There's still the fire escape," Ms. China said hurriedly, pointing her pistol around the bedroom door.

"How do you know that?"

"That's how I got in."

"Wait, they could be Secret Service," Ellie said to the woman who was a foremost member of Team Kill First, Ask Questions Later.

Sarge Bryan shook his head. "No, they'd be with Janice and would have the override codes for the elevator, or they would scope the place out with a drone from the roof in case the hostiles had hostages. Someone's trying to break in here through the fire doors. They're not friendlies!"

Ms. China was already running down the corridor. She stopped at a cleaning robot, grabbed two bottles from a tray on its back, then dove down onto the carpet in front of the fire escape. The door handles had been jammed shut by a mop pole, but it was bending and on the verge of breaking. Ms. China sprayed liquid from both bottles under the crack at the bottom of the door, then closed her eyes and shielded her face.

She still had the brass to say, "Inhale deeply, you stupid bellends. Bleach and ammonia make mustard gas, enjoy a classic chemical weapon."

Two bullet holes blasted through the heavy door. The bullets slammed into the plaster of the opposite wall, whizzing well over Ms. China's back as she crawled back away from the fire escape. Ellie followed Sarge Bryan forward. While most of the poison gas was bubbling up on the other side of the door, as they got closer, the caustic smell leaking into the hallway made Ellie cover her nose and mouth.

She quickly switched to covering her ears as Ms. China got up, aimed her pistol, and shot through the door until her gun was empty. She then reached over to get Bryan's.

"That's twenty-six rounds," he said, keeping hold of the gun he had taken from his goddaughter. "I think you got 'em. And if that ain't enough, I promise I'll top 'em off."

The door was perforated from both sides, and even without the danger of the mustard gas, it was too badly damaged for them to push open. Behind them, Attie Jr. emerged wearing a small robe over his Little Prince patterned pajamas. His hair and outfit were in disarray, but he was perfectly fine. Ellie breathed a sigh of relief.

A moaning sigh came from Mr. Barracude. He had awoken and propped himself up on the zebra skin couch. Ellie noticed it was not just a pattern—the couch had a zebra's hooves and a black mane.

"I woulda taken 'em," their host said, holding an ice-filled cloth to his bleeding head. "I was worried about the kids, so I got distracted, and one came up behind me. Totally bushwhacked me."

While they were contacting Janice Jones's Secret Service detail, Ellie heard a rustling from the master bedroom across from where they had found the kids and the two hostiles. Everyone else was occupied, so she made sure Attie Jr. and Sienna were out of the way and picked up Ms. China's empty pistol, then crept forward.

"Ahhhh, don't shoot! Don't shoot! I'll tell you anything. I haven't seen you, just don't kill me!"

The wailing came from a chubby, slightly balding man hiding in Janice's two-story closet and dressing room. The man, who slowly extricated himself from among the collection of five hundred designer handbags, was the hotel doctor who had looked at Ellie's injuries. It turned out the medical man had been requested to stay and treat Mr. Barracude. The American oligarch suffered a suspected panic attack over how the markets had opened in Asia. During the subsequent excitement, everyone had forgotten he was there.

Ellie heard the staccato sounds of a helicopter coming toward the building. Sarge turned to the physician, who looked like he could use some of his own panic meds.

"We got a couple clients for you. See how Mr. Barracude is, and there's a guy tied up in the bathtub of the big bedroom at the end of the hall. See if he's still alive."

"Hell of a thing, huh?" Mr. Barracude said as he lay on the couch. "I gotta thank you for helping me fight off these terrorists. I mean, really, on American soil, in my own home, no less!" He gesticulated with his free hand over to the liquor cabinet, which was made of a metric ton of crystal shaped like Mount Everest. "You guys help yourself to a drink. I'd get up but—heh—I'm kind of wobbly. Look under the counter, the Rémy's there.

"The cheap stuff, I keep for mooches. You guys deserve the best, two hundred grand a bottle. Pour me one too, I could use a pick-me..." Mr. Barracude managed to say and then passed out, his face buried in the zebra mane. The hotel doctor ran over to his prone form and signaled the EMTs, who had just arrived from the lobby.

Judging that they did, in fact, deserve it, Ellie picked up the dark hand-blown glass bottle and poured out two generous portions into short and wide glass snifters. She swirled them, warming the dark-amber liquid expertly in her hand before passing it into Sarge Bryan's large scarred hand.

A Secret Service SWAT team came barging in and was promptly thrown out by the revived homeowner.

"NOW you jerks show up!" Mr. Barracude said, berating them and threatening to have their boss's boss fired by people he knew.

After the tactical team had slunk away, lead investigative agents from various agencies came in to assess the scene, accompanied by forensic investigators in hazmat suits. The latter people carried out body bags from the bedroom and the fire escape stairs and also cleaned up the chemical mess Ms. China had made.

"Now this is some good hooch." Bryan sampled his drink. "Well, Ms. Sato, had enough adventuring for one trip? Atticus's son is safe. You've found your escaped friend, probably before anyone figured out she's not still somewhere in London. You can go home and maybe even write another book about what a messed-up place America has become."

As appealing as that might be… Maybe it was the smell of mustard gas and cordite in the air, all of sudden Ellie felt a jolt of an electrical energy better than any party drug that had ever been invented: the thrill of mysteries in dire need of untangling.

"Oh, no, Sergeant. We're only getting started. We've been handed a solemn commission by your head of state, and on behalf of Crown and country, I have accepted it."

She looked over to where Ms. China was standing, patting Attie Jr.'s hair down for what seemed like the hundredth time. "Fate has just handed us a world-class scientist. She's the foremost expert on weapons of mass destruction and also owes us a great favor." Ellie caught the murderess's six pupils with what she hoped was a reasonably intimidating look. "I'm now very determined to see this investigation through, wherever it may lead."

Having said that, she drained her drink. The brandy took a fiery course down her throat and then hit her midsection, where its heat bloomed agreeably. The flames in the large fireplace were warming her arms and legs. Behind the blazing log sat an odd design. Yellow tiles covering the firebox were painted with the roughly drawn image of a coiled rattlesnake with the words "DONT TREAD ON ME" underneath.

Whether it was the rush of the obscenely expensive liquor or the exuberance of her first visit to this brash breakaway British colony, she acted on impulse and tossed the heavy leaded crystal glass into the fireplace. The yellow flames gobbled up the last drops of Rémy brandy. They danced blue for a moment as they burned and the broken shards settled into the ash and embers.

21

WATERGATE HOTEL

Just as paramedics were trying to put an insensible Mr. Barracude onto a stretcher, he suddenly woke up.

"I got no damn concussion," Mr. Barracude protested, flailing his arms and backhanding a short emergency responder in the face. "I was just resting my eyes."

The hotel doctor attended him and tried to avoid looking as though he were wrestling with his patient, speaking soothingly to Mr. Barracude as he tried to pull at the IV tube in his arm.

At the apex of the penthouse's grand foyer, the chunky lift doors slid open. A burst of pointed profanity came flowing out, followed by Janice Jones.

"...what kind a bitch-ass punk move was that? Taking agents off of my house? My grannie woulda whupped you with a hickory stick. Get the tactical units back up here *now*, and keep them here." Janice pressed *end call* so hard her handset seemed to bend. She rushed over to her husband. "Oh, baby, what did they do to you?"

"One of 'em got in a lucky shot, sweetie, but I took care of business. They're takin' out the dead douchebags in Ziploc bags." Barracude looked over to Ellie and Sarge Bryan. "Oh, and your friends helped out too, a bit, right at the end."

A hazmat team had roped off the fire escape and was using a type of sawdust to soak up the improvised chemical weapon deployed by Ms. China. Large fans were stationed at the end of the hall, trying to clear out the remaining mustard gas fumes. The door had dozens of ragged holes in it, had been prized open by the Jaws of Life rescue apparatus, and was barely hanging on its hinges.

"Well, Sarge," Janice said, coming over to where they sat on the couch and by the fireplace. "You do know how to take care of uninvited guests. How are your goddaughter and the Reidt boy?"

"Safe and sound, ma'am. The boy's grandparents are coming from Raleigh to pick them up."

"Hi, Ms. Jones. Can I get a picture?" Sienna McKnight had poked her head out of the bedroom at the other end of the hallway.

"Get back in there," Sarge Bryan admonished.

"Miss McKnight, once this is all over, we'll do better than a photo op," Janice said with a picture-perfect politician's smile. "You let your civics teacher know your whole class is coming to the White House on a special tour, all expenses paid." After Sienna had closed the door, she added, "If no one blows it up in the meantime."

The statuesque black woman brushed broken glass off a stool and sat. "Right here in the Watergate. Who would have the damned balls?"

"We may not know for a while," Sarge Bryan said. "Three of the infiltrators are DOA, and the fourth had half his head caved in courtesy of your husband, ma'am."

"I believe it," Janice said. "He doesn't look it now, but Jezzie used to ride bulls in Brazil." She took another long look around the wrecked apartment. "But this level of mayhem wasn't all him, huh? What really happened?"

Sarge Bryan and Ellie recounted what had happened upon their return to the hotel.

"The first two guys weren't expecting Ms. China to be here."

"Oh, right, the escapee from the English asylum."

Janice followed their gaze over to where Ellie's former housemate had grabbed some diagnostic equipment from the hotel doctor's bag and was giving Mr. Barracude her medical opinion. "I'd do scans to be sure, but don't move him. Bring in the mobile scanners, ultrasound, and CT."

"And who are you?"

"Someone who's killed more people than even you have, Doctor."

"My sweetie's not leaving here," Janice ordered. "So you do like the woman says and bring in what you have to. They were obviously trying to kidnap my husband to gain leverage over me and the administration," Janice said, holding Mr. Barracude's stubby-fingered hand in her own elegant one.

"Anna," Ellie said, "I'd like to introduce Mrs. Jones, chief of staff to President Casteel and co-owner of the residence you demolished."

"Oh, charmed," Ms. China said, extending her hand but remembering to keep her poisoned fingernails politely curled back. "I'm a well-known physician and biochemist currently on sabbatical from St. Bartholomew's Hospital in London."

Ellie pursed her lips but said nothing. They'd have to work on Ms. China's cover story.

"You are Annunciata Romanov China," Janice said in a sharp but friendly manner. "Wanted by Scotland Yard, considered extremely dangerous." Janice waved her handset, which had pictures of both Ms. China and Ellie on it. "And I can't thank you enough for using your best homicidal talents today."

Ms. China just smiled and blinked. Most of her concealer makeup had rubbed off, and swirls of gold and silver tattoos all over her face gave her the look of a statue just recently come to life.

"That means you won't be sending her, or me, back to England in handcuffs?" Ellie asked hopefully. "I've worked with her before. In situations of untrammeled havoc, she's quite astute."

"This certainly qualifies." Janice watched as agents and local police carried the comatose kidnapper out to the lift. "She's hired, as long as she promises to ask me before doing anything permanent to Americans."

On their way into Janice's office, they by passed Mr. Barracude, who was compliantly lying prone on his stretcher. He gestured weakly toward the Mount Everest-shaped liquor cabinet. "Hey, don't you guys bogart all the Rémy, pour me a glass."

"I really don't recommend that," the hotel doctor said nervously as he checked the medical monitors.

"Two hundred grand a bottle… I only serve the best…" he said as his eyes rolled back in his head.

Ellie passed Tata's voluminous fur coat. It had fallen on the ground. *She'll want that back,* Ellie thought and rolled the heavy thing up as best she could.

Mr. Barracude noticed and said in a voice made dreamy by the painkillers they had given him, "Hey, nice coat, you can really tell it's from a bear… who died of rickets and mange, hehehe. Ouch, my head!"

While the door to Janice's office was dazzlingly framed by dozens of crystal inlays, the interior of their hostess's room was not a mad riot of opulence. The walls were covered in an up-tempo walnut paneling, and none of the chairs looked like they had come from an auction at the Versailles Palace. This was obviously Janice's private domain. Their hostess slumped in a high-backed swivel chair in front of the desk. She entered a passcode and swiped a security fob over the console. Six monitors sprang to life.

"Comin' here with the kids as guests, an' all…" Janice swore under her breath as she scanned the presumably classified information feeds coming in from various agencies, which were giving updates on their investigations into the disaster at the Capitol.

"How're things lookin'?" Sarge Bryan asked, closing the door.

"On the plus side, there haven't been any new devices found, no more explosions. Of course, the one we witnessed did enough damage. There is no more Supreme Court. Justice Tagawa held on until EMTs pulled him out, but he died on the way to the ICU. Majority leaders of both the House and Senate are missing in the rubble and presumed dead. The Senator pro tempore was at the Army Navy Country club waiting for the Senate to be recalled after the court decision."

"He's third in line in case something happens to President Casteel and Vice President Prowse," Sarge Bryan explained to Ellie.

"Now what I want to know," Janice said, her features compressed in concentration, "is what that fucking crazy bitch did and why?"

Ellie assumed she was referring to the late Justice Meyers. Ms. China was on an office couch near the window, studying a TV screen that played clips from the disaster. Her eyes narrowed, making her eyeballs look totally black. "I might have an inkling about the how. To be certain, I have to go there." One of her long fingernails tapped the monitor.

"Where?" Ellie asked. Now that the flush of Rémy brandy and righteous indignation had passed and been replaced by a pressing need to lie down, the thought of leaving the warm and heavily guarded penthouse had absolutely no appeal.

The screen showed a live feed from a drone flying over the smoking epicenter of the blast where the flat roof next to the Capitol Building dome had caved in.

"Right there, ground zero."

22

TATA

"...*you can really tell it's from a bear... who died of rickets and mange, hehehe. Ouch, my head!*"

"Why the annoying little man have to make fun of my coat?" Tata said under her breath as she listened to the audio feed. "My grandfather, with his own hands, made it after I passed my final Spetsnaz examination."

"Shht," Zvena said over a video conferencing link. "I can't hear."

President Putin had tasked Tata with monitoring the intelligence coming from inside the home of Janice Jones. It had been very boring, and about one hour ago she was just about to let an AI take over monitoring it. Then came a series of sharp yells.

This was followed by maddeningly indistinct and incoherent sounds: things breaking, grunts, yells, and fighting. There was only audio coming over the low bandwidth connection, so Tata had to use all of her enhanced cyborg hearing to interpret what was happening.

At the sound of a girl shrieking, Tata was tempted to anonymously phone the authorities, but then the fight seemed to end. She had continued to listen.

On the heels of the shrieking, there followed more thumps, and then a woman speaking in a cold, high-pitched: "*Way to go, girl, you distracted them at just the right time."*

"Uh, thanks, who the fuck are you?" a younger woman's voice said, speaking with a Southern US accent. After a pause, the girl added, *"And why are you holding a leg?"*

"Because, dear girl, since my amputation, it's the best way to kick people in the head," the first woman said. *"And please point that gun at the villain on the floor, Miss McKnight, Attie will not take kindly to you shooting his mum."*

There was some rustling.

"Let me get my leg on… Yoohoo, Atticus. It's me, you can come out now. I'm out of the hospital… all better now."

Soon after, there was more commotion, and she recognized the low, very sexy voice of Sergeant Bryan and the tittering, irritating voice of Ellie Sato.

A burst of static told Tata the bear coat was being dragged into another room. *How hard would it be to lift it up and carry it nicely?* she seethed. Police scanners in the embassy, already furiously recording the emergency services responding to the explosion at the Capitol Building, also picked up EMS calls to the Watergate. These flashed onto Tata's screen.

Then, as if her hands were not full enough, Komandir Zvena decided it was a great time to link in from the Russian signals and intelligence spy ship floating in the Gulf of Mexico. Tata relayed to him the latest updates on the apparent Capitol attack and also let him know about the strange appearance of Eleanor Sato in the middle of yet another crisis.

"Who are the unidentified women speaking?" Zvena asked after he heard the recording from the bear coat bug.

Tata ran voice recognition. The teenager was easy, as she had once had a TikTok account: Sienna McKnight, student at Cape Fear High School, Fayetteville, NC.

The other one had more extensive entries in the GU database. Tata texted the information to Zvena.

Annunciata Philmore Romanov China, MD, PhD [biophysics]

Former British MI6 Dark Operations officer

Significant operations: Syria Silent Scythe 2024, 96-Hour War 2029, Pangean Conspiracy 2031

Confirmed kills > 5,000

Held for indefinite term at St. Bartholomew's asylum
INTERPOL Red Notice issued after possible escape.

"Romanov? She's Russian?"

"No," Tata said. "She was born in Scotland, but she has an impressive record of killing people all over the globe.

"What is she doing here?"

"That Sato woman is behind it. She is always meddling."

"Pay attention," Zvena said. "Janice Jones just said they are leaving the Watergate. What are the chances Ms. Sato will take your coat with her on her new investigative meddling?"

"For America, it is cold, she might," Tata said hopefully, a little embarrassed she had not been paying attention to the feed from the bug.

Zvena scoffed. "It drags on the ground even when you wear it, and it has just been insulted by a man. A woman's vanity will not permit her."

Oh chyort! They were about to lose their best and only infiltration into the highest levels of the US administration during a developing crisis. Tata scanned the signals that the bug was picking up coming from inside the penthouse. There had to be something hackable. The first two carrier signals were no good.

SIPDIS – US State Dept. [AES 256-bit encryption] :X

DEPT OF TREASURY [AES 128-bit encryption] :X

A third one, however...

Montblancfan009 [Bluetooth unencrypted no password set] :D

"I think I see a vulnerability, Komandir."

"It's Mr. Zvena now... Is that Ellie Sato's phone?"

Tata chuckled to herself as she loaded a prewritten worm script.

"It is, it is. She's using a Huawei Technologies 5G handset. We stole the backdoor into that model from the Chinese months ago... It's done. We've cloned it, nested our infiltration program inside her WeChat app, and are in control of her microphone and camera."

This woman is the worst spy ever, Tata thought. *I don't know what Sergeant Bryan sees in her.*

Janice Jones's voice spoke in stereo:

"Here are your Capitol zone badges."

"Here are your Capitol zone badges."

Tata muted the signal from her coat.

"Those will get you through the police line around the disaster site. Go straight to the DHS CP."

"You're not coming?" asked the smooth and commanding voice of Sergeant Bryan.

"No... I've got to get back to the president."

"Is he..." Ms. Sato's annoying voice said.

"He's great. He's in a safe location and in charge." Janice said curtly. *"Why are you taking off your coat?"*

"Oh, I thought I'd wear..."

"That big ol' Russian thing?"

"It looks as though it might be messy down there, from the explosion and the fire. I don't want to get your clothes full of smoke smell."

"Don't worry about it. We'll bill it to Uncle Sam. This bearskin rug, I'll send to the hotel cleaner, then back to the Russian embassy, unless a petting zoo claims it."

Tata's enhanced jaws ground her zirconia-capped teeth as she copied the surveillance files and prepared to send them along with her hourly intelligence report to the Kremlin.

23

CAPITOL BUILDING

ELLIE

By the time they got to the stricken Capitol Building, every emergency vehicle in the city seemed to have converged on the area. Not that Ellie was in a position to notice much. In an effort to get some feeling into her calves, she had let the passenger seat of Sarge Bryan's big borrowed SUV tilt all the way back. This annoyed Ms. China, who kept kneeing the back of the seat, causing her to tense up so that the nascent cramping traveled up her legs to her lower back.

"Ah, Ms. Sato," asked Sarge Bryan from behind the wheel. "You sure you're all right there?"

"I just have to, uhhhgh, catch my breath." She'd been hoping it would be a much longer drive than it turned out. "This is it?"

"As close as we're going to get without running into a tank."

An armored truck on caterpillar treads rumbled past her window.

"I don't know what you expect me to do," Ms. China groused and kicked the back of Ellie's seat again.

"For one thing, be more grateful." Ellie tilted her seat slowly upright. "Thanks to Ran and Sarge Bryan's friend Janice, they've squashed, or quashed, or whatever, your international arrest warrant for a few days in order for you to be of assistance. So just prepare to assist like you've never done before."

They stopped at a small roundabout that ringed a statue a few hundred yards from the big domed building, which was the same gray color as the smoke it was slowly belching into the noon sky.

"Right now you can assist me getting out," Ellie snapped, as the heavy door kept closing and thumping against the various injuries inflicted on her by the airport mob.

Sarge Bryan rushed around to the other side and let her out.

"You're lookin' a mite pale."

Ellie looked resolutely at the large albino man and had to giggle, which seemed to settle her midsection back into place. Officers with "Capitol Police" stenciled on their vests came over to check their credentials. After some grumbling, they begrudgingly pointed them to the joint command post that had been set up in a large flat area behind the main buildings.

As they passed, Ellie read the inscription on a plinth, on top of which stood the statue of a bearded man in a frock coat: *James A. Garfield 1831-1881.*

"He looks like a capable fellow."

"He was president for a few months, then someone shot him," Sarge said. "One of four sitting presidents to be murdered. Not counting attempted assassinations or revenge plots when they were out of office. Right over there." He pointed to a short flight of stairs. "Some crazy guy tried to shoot Andrew Jackson, and get this, both the guy's pistols misfired, and the elderly ex-president beat the idiot nearly to death with his cane."

Ellie did a quick calculation. "You mean your chief executives have a nearly one-in-ten chance of being assassinated? That's only ever happened to one prime minister."

"I'm starting to feel more at home already," Ms. China said.

At the last checkpoint, they asked Sarge Bryan for the pistol he had taken from the scene of the attempted kidnapping of Mr. Barracude. Technically it was evidence, but at the time he had said: "We need this more than the locals need evidence against those thugs."

The place was awash with windbreakers featuring acronyms: FBI, DHS, DEA, ATF. In the tented command post, two gentlemen and a lady, each from different departments, all seemed to claim control over the incredible crime scene. None of them looked favorably on their having dropped by.

A man seemed to dominate, possibly because of the size of his pup-tent-sized windbreaker. Ellie couldn't tell whether his largeness came from muscle or fat or both.

"Yeah, like I said, executive order only goes so far..." The man sounded as though he was used to people listening to his instructions the first time he gave them. "If the president himself came out here, I don't know if we could let him in to the active crime scene..."

"My good fellow," Ms. China said, stepping forward wearing a rather chic and likely stolen Burberry trench coat and matching scarf. "You are aware of your nation's organizational chart? It has President Casteel right at the apex of the executive branch. Ignoring us could be viewed as obstruction, if there were ever to be a Congressional investigation."

The FBI guy heaved himself around and went back to confer with his associates.

"How do you know that?" Ellie whispered.

"While you were having a snooze, I was studying," Ms. China said. The sun broke briefly though the clouds and illuminated the mysterious whorls of metallic tattoos around the dimples in her cheeks. "After all the nightmares I've had trying to get reimbursements out of Whitehall for chemical weapons, even ones I got on sale, I know how to threaten bureaucrats."

Sarge Bryan was staring at Ms. China. "Ma'am... are you glowing?"

"Just a little bit," she said cheerily. "Your new upgraded gold eyes must have wider spectrum capabilities than when they were blue."

"You seem to be putting out microbursts of UVC and other stuff I can't identify."

"Zoroastrians believe certain patterns ward off evil spirits and people with bad intentions, the Aka Manah," Ms. China said, tapping the ends of her tattooed fingers together. "Having nanofibers embedded under my skin made of silver and rare earth elements makes me resistant to most pathogens. Microcircuits activate when I sense danger, destruction, or... something else to get me excited."

A handy trait for a prolific and passionate poisoner.

The special agent came back over, looking impatient. "Best we can do is let one, and only one, of you in for a short look-see." He turned his gaze toward the invisibly glowing Ms. China. "Under *close supervision* and subject to *immediate detention* if there's even a hint of obstruction of our investigations."

"We'll take it, Special Agent Schwartz," Sarge Bryan said, probably having read the man's ID through his jacket pocket. "I've got the best scanning ability, but Ms. China has the most field experience with WMDs. She should go in."

Schwartz smiled with mock sadness. "Like I was saying, you'd need to be accompanied. Unfortunately, at the moment, we can't spare anyone to supervise—"

"I'm happy to lend my services, Agent Schwartz," a man's voice said in a flat American accent that was instantly familiar to Ellie.

"Mr. Perdix?" Ellie said. A wan, slender figure with a fading blond hairline and no discernable eyebrows was making his way over to them. He also wore a blue windbreaker, this one was emblazoned with the letters *JASON*.

"Augustine Aloysius, my knight in shining…" Ms. China said, then raised her eyebrow at his jacket. "You're with JASON? Doesn't that stand for Junior Achiever, Somewhat Older Now? Have you suddenly turned pansy?"

Mr. Perdix looked instantly mortified. "I'm sure, Ms. China, a decorated intelligence officer, has nothing against gay people," he said, smiling at Agent Schwartz and quickly leading them out of the tent.

"And just for your information," he said as they walked, "JASON stands for the Greek hero, and we've been advising presidents and the Pentagon on matters of the most sensitive nature since the 1950s."

"Right. Oh, here's a better one: Just Another Scientist on Nembutal." Ms. China was on the verge of hysterical laughter. "I thought your stint at AEO and DARPA was sad, but going full corporate? What is your next innovation, a better denture cleaner? Wait, wait, yet another funny acronym is coming to me, just hang on…"

"Keep talking like that," Mr. Perdix said mildly, his long, thin fingers wiping melted snow off his glasses, "and I won't show you the very fresh epicenter of mass destruction and death."

Ms. China quieted down.

Mr. Perdix turned to Agent Schwartz, who was hovering outside the command tent. "That will be all, thank you," he said dismissively.

Mr. Perdix received no backtalk from the FBI man and appeared to have similar level of authority as the law enforcement people at the massive crime scene.

"Eleanor Sato," he said, turning his pale, seemingly lashless eyes toward her. "Why am I not surprised to see you here?"

"Our motto at the *Juggernaut* is: If we're not covering it, it never really happened."

Mr. Perdix, who she had met during a polite little war that turned into a biological and nuclear disaster, seemed more unnerved than she had ever seen him. Of course, Ms. China's former love interest was still a creepy git who navigated the swampy waters of his nation's capital like a wraith of doom. Maybe that was why no one objected when he waved all three of them past the "DO NOT CROSS" tape into the containment zone. They stopped at an advanced-looking hazmat fire truck.

"Put these on," he said, handing them full-face respirators. "Zoroastrian mysticism notwithstanding, you'll need these to breathe. Just speak normally. There are voice-activated speakers on the sides."

Ellie watched the American put his on, and she tried to do it in the same smooth motion but got her hair tangled. Ms. China helped her, and as she was checking to make sure Ellie's face seal was sound, she said, "Good idea to get this on properly. We don't want anyone to asphyxiate, unintentionally, that is."

24

CAPITOL BUILDING

Mr. Perdix waved Ellie in under a final ribbon of fluttering yellow-and-red crime-scene tape. She glanced back at Schwartz. Despite being at ground zero of an historic threat to the republic he was sworn to defend, the FBI man had found a box of Krispy Kreme donuts and was stuffing his face.

"He said only one person could go," she said, her voice sounding odd through the speakers in her full-face respirator.

While assured by Janice that Ms. China's warrant had been deferred for the moment, Ellie did not want any law enforcement types looking too closely at her or the details surrounding their escape from St. Bartholomew's.

Mr. Perdix followed her gaze. "Don't worry. I know how to handle him. Who do you think ordered the food delivery? And Ms. Sato, until the point at which you become really annoying, most people don't notice you at all. Come on."

They walked up to the Capitol complex. The architecture, though vaguely Greek and Roman, had a scale which overwhelmed any subtleties of form. Ellie tried to distract herself by thinking about design concepts, which became harder and harder to do as firefighters walked by holding various sized things wrapped in a cloth. Flopping out of the end of one was a severed arm clad in the remains of a shirtsleeve with a cuff link, and from around the hairy wrist hung a chunky watch with its crystal smashed to bits.

Twice people in blue windbreakers approached them. They saw Mr. Perdix and let them pass without comment.

"That explosion brought down the whole old Upper Senate chamber," he said, guiding them through darkened corridors filled with hazy-looking air. "The structure is unstable, and you are entering at your own risk."

A dazed female staffer whose hair was full of plaster was being led out by a Capitol policeman. He had covered her shredded clothes with a silvery metallic blanket. The blood streaming from her head wounds looked like black ink against the white powder. The stuff was everywhere. For some reason, the sight made Ellie inhale sharply. Her mask strobed a red light.

Mustn't hyperventilate, she thought. A light on her computerized respirator flashed yellow for a moment, then went back to green as her breathing returned to normal. Ellie quickened her step to follow the two very odd scientists who, despite the carnage, or perhaps because of it, seemed to be in a hurry to get to the epicenter of the blast.

"These troglodytes are stepping all over the place and spoiling evidence," Ms. China said, absently bumping shoulders with a fireman. "I wish I could have been here earlier."

"Not too early," Mr. Perdix said drolly. "From the injuries I've seen, the explosion caused a massive overpressure wave capable of crushing human organs as assuredly as if they had been put through a trash compactor."

Ellie's feet nearly slipped on the soaking-wet carpet. She caught herself on a shattered handrail and looked down. Hundreds of tourist pamphlets lay soaking under a layer of grimy, sooty water flowing freely along the formerly regal hallway.

"It's just ahead," Mr. Perdix said, ducking under a fallen beam and a length of pipe with a sprinkler head fastened to it.

A female firefighter was holding a dribbling hose and watching the ceiling where some smoldering wreckage was threatening to burst into flame again.

"Here we are," Mr. Perdix said as though he were showing them a secluded meadow where he had a picnic planned.

Ellie looked up. "Is that daylight?"

Through collapsed rubble and large flakes of cinders, she thought she could see beams of gray light coming from above.

Mr. Perdix followed her gaze. "Probably. This area of the Capitol has, er had, two floors of old Senate chambers and an attic topped by a small dome, which has cracked."

Ms. China was on her hands and knees sifting through wreckage, getting her designer trench coat filthy.

"What could have done this?" Ellie asked, looking up, averting her eyes from soggy, likely human, bits being retrieved from among splintered wood remains of the benches on the other side of the room. This was the chamber she had seen only a few hours ago on the newscast.

"First they thought it might be a stealth drone strike that missed its intended target of the big rotunda," Mr. Perdix said, manipulating schematics on his handset. "Schwartz, for his part, was convinced the situation was similar to the first attack on the World Trade Center by Islamic extremists in 1993. But I told him there was no chance of a conventional truck-sized bomb getting into the subbasement.

"In my initial report, I suggested they look for recent renovations where explosives may have been brought in and hidden behind drywall. That particular technique was used to devastating effect in the IRA's Brighton Hotel bombing, which nearly decapitated the British government with a device hidden under a bathtub."

Ms. China clucked into her mask, the sound made more condescending, as it was amplified by her speakers. "Do you JASON people bill clients for making wild guesses? Unless you're saying they redid the entire place in neoclassical Semtex, it's a barmy idea from the get-go."

"Well, then, it's great you happened to postpone your electroshock treatment and visit us," Mr. Perdix said. "If you didn't have an alibi, I might be tempted to put you at the top of our suspect list."

"You're the one who stopped writing," Ms. China said, halting her rummaging and sounding wounded.

"You kept coating your letters with exotic poisons."

She laughed, and in that place it was an eerie, shrill sound. "That was just for fun. I always gave you the antidote in the next letter."

"Annunciata, be reasonable. After the Marxists locked you up for, what was it, life plus ninety-nine years? The only way we had a future was if I went to Britain, committed terrible crimes, and had myself incarcerated at St. Bartholomew's."

Ms. China stared at him with all six of her pupils, which looked even more fearsome behind the curved glass of her mask. "I knew you were commitment-phobic."

"As interesting as your personal lives are," Ellie said. "It's a bit… disrespectful to the people who just died here to be dickering about instead of solving this crime."

Ms. China shrugged. "I have some ideas. I need something that was exposed directly to the blast and isn't contaminated or made up of too many chemicals."

Ellie remembered a scrap of a woman's dress she had seen. She found it a few meters away, it still had a manufacturer's label attached.

"How about this?" she said, handing over the fist-sized scrap. Ms. China held it up against the dim light. "I know that manufacturer, they use only cotton, no rayon or any synthetics."

Ms. China gave a begrudging nod. "Now, Al, I need some reagents."

"Um, I go by August now, Annunciata."

"Not Aloysius? But you're such a little teddy bear, a formerly mildly dangerous scientist now working for JASON and the neutered Argonauts."

"Hey! Stop bickering," Ellie pleaded. "Jason, I mean August… Mr. Perdix, please tell us you have these reagenting things."

"I… I only bought tubes to collect samples in," he admitted.

"Fuck, I need sodium carbonate, *now*." Ms. China's mask started strobing its hyperventilation light, and her faceplate was fogging up.

Ellie concluded her friend's escape from the hospital, the unexpected visit to a disaster zone, and proximity to her ex must be playing havoc with Anna's already precarious mental stability. Before there was any more violence, something had to be done to cool her off.

"This carbonate stuff sounds commonplace. Might there be some around? That's all you need, right?"

"And a heat source," Ms. China said, appearing to calm down.

Mr. Perdix checked his digital map. "This way. The washroom might have escaped destruction."

They dodged around a stream of water sprung out of a crack in the wall like a small waterfall, and went past a sign with symbols listing some half dozen genders and directing each to the appropriate washroom. Behind this was blown-in doorway leading to a tiled room. Above a sink, he found what he wanted.

"Congress ordered only organic products to be used on the Hill. In this dispenser…" He prized open a metal square attached to the wall. "Washing soda… calcium carbonate, as requested."

"We'll see if it works," Ms. China said grudgingly and grabbed the container.

Next she found a rectangular chunk of wood, the surface of which had been burned to charcoal. She gouged out a hole, put some carbonate powder into it, and placed a square of the torn dress over that. They borrowed a welding torch from a rescue worker and carefully applied the smallest blue flame it would produce against the wood. After smoking for a few moments, and attracting suspicious glances from firefighters combing through wreckage, small white nodules appeared on the fabric.

"Ha! Got you," Ms. China said. "Trioxide aluminum."

"I guessed that."

"Serious scientists don't guess. They also don't work for dinky civilian labs where it's only by accident that evil people die."

"This is progress, right?" Ellie tried to sound encouraging, as she noticed Ms. China was still holding the lit blowtorch. Was she thinking of what would happen if she applied the dancing blue acetylene flame to Mr. Perdix's bulbous respirator mask? "This trioxide discovery… it's significant, no?"

"It's strong evidence that a crude form of fuel-air explosion was used to devastate the Supreme Court," Mr. Perdix concluded. "From the last seconds of the video, we can reasonably conclude that an aerosolized combustible was ejected from the ceiling sprinkler system and was then ignited by the handheld pyrotechnic set off by Madam Chief Justice Meyers."

Thankfully, Ms. China politely extinguished the torch and looked around thoughtfully. "News reports said they changed the venue to this area. Until a few days ago, this whole section was open to tourists."

"Less security?" Mr. Perdix offered.

"And smaller volume. How big was this room?" Ms. China demanded.

The JASON man checked his handset. "The historic US Supreme Court chamber was fifty feet wide by seventy-eight long and thirty-four feet high at the center of the domed ceiling."

"So, say… one hundred and thirty-three thousand cubic feet. Compared to the new Supreme Court building across the street, this place was much easier to flood with a precise mixture of fuel and air to create a thermobaric explosion. That's something Justice Meyers, a former patent lawyer with a chemical engineering background, could have planned."

If that doesn't take the biscuit, Ellie thought. "But why? It's…" Ellie was at loss for words.

"Pretty impressive for an octogenarian," Ms. China quipped.

"Be quiet," Mr. Perdix snapped. "The corpses are still warm, people all across the city and the country lost friends and respected leaders."

"All right, sorry." Ms. China turned to Ellie and, with her back to her ex, mouthed the word "pussy."

Ellie had read a little about Madam Justice Meyers online. "She must have had help. She had some health conditions."

"Agreed," Mr. Perdix said, throwing the burned piece of wood with its white flecks of aluminum onto the floor. He then crushed it into the sodden residue of the explosion.

"Wasn't that evidence?" Ellie said.

"Not for anyone but us," Mr. Perdix said. "We need to hurry before Schwartz's team gets here."

"Now you're talking," Ms. China said, casting hasty glances up and down the dimly lit corridors.

"But aren't you on the same side, sort of?" Ellie asked.

Mr. Perdix's facemask fogged up as he exhaled, clearly mulling over how much to say. "Over the past decades, some elements in the FBI have decided to become, shall we say, more active in political affairs. If they discover anything, they know very well they can hide it for months or years until it suits their purposes to release it."

Ellie didn't think she could take another plunge into petty Byzantine politics.

"But, Mr. Perdix, you're not like that, right?" she asked hopefully.

"Of course not. In JASON you can trust."

"Can we trust you to get moving?" Ms. China prodded, waving the other scientist's handset, which she had picked right out of his pocket without him noticing. "Have you looked at your own schematics?"

It turned out that this portion of the Capitol Building had, over the years, undergone extensive renovations. Leaning over the relatively small ten-by-six-inch tablet screen, the two former lovebirds bumped their facemasks more than once. Fortunately, Ms. China controlled her temper and did not deploy her arsenal of venom-tipped fingernails.

"Look there. That domed interior ceiling dates back to 1810," Mr. Perdix said and swiped off layers of historical blueprints. "A few years later, there was fire damage. That must have been the War of 1812, when the British burned many government buildings in Washington, including this one and the White House."

"Sorry," Ellie said meekly.

"What are those areas?" Ms. China asked. "Are they still standing?"

Mr. Perdix looked from the map up to the room itself and the boundaries of the destroyed chamber. An increased number of flashlights seemed to be probing the darkness on the other side of the debris-filled chamber.

"The vaulted ceiling separated this room from the old Senate chambers directly above. There were access areas that were sealed over, eight of them." His soot-stained thumb flicked through the decades until they reached the present. "Two of those were reopened recently in order to upgrade security and fire-suppression systems. This way."

Mr. Perdix strode to a narrow fire escape door which had been partially blocked by a fallen flagpole.

"Just a second," Ms. China griped as she hurried after him. "You said there were two. How do you know you're going to the right one?"

"We'll check the closest one first."

"We might not have time to check both," Ms. China argued. "See, Ellie? This is the type of American behavior that led to the quagmires in Vietnam and Afghanistan. Act first for at least a decade, and consider consequences only when—"

"Shht!"

"Don't shush me, Aloysius, I'll…"

Before having a chance threaten anything rash, Ms. China heard it too. There was a scrabbling sound which alternated with a sort of wheezing. They had climbed two flights of stairs and had come to an old wooden doorway, which might have received its first coat of paint after the fires of 1812. The blast had lifted it off its hinges. Behind it was no room at all but rather a crawlspace three feet by three. Something was protruding from it.

Mr. Perdix aimed an LED flashlight into the dark space, and the harsh white beam illuminated a pair of legs.

25

LOWER SENATE CHAMBER
CAPITOL BUILDING

W e've got to get the rescue team," Ellie said, horrified by the sight of the
injured survivor.

"No bloody way," Ms. China said, putting her flashlight down on a bent stairway railing. "Dead or alive, he's ours. Help me drag him out of there."

"I have to agree with Anna," Mr. Perdix said. "If Schwartz's people get hold of him, there are equal chances he'll succumb to his injuries or simply disappear, along with any evidence he has or knows."

"If all else fails, he will do an 'Epstein' and hang himself with tissue paper inside a maximum-security federal jail cell," Ms. China taunted gleefully as she yanked on the man's sodden, filthy jeans. "Help me. He's stuck."

"I'll hold the hatch back. You two pull him out," Mr. Perdix said, rather ungallantly.

Ellie's lower back protested and her hip muscles spasmed as she and Ms. China pulled the older, and fortunately smaller, fellow out of the access hole. His head and shoulders came out and were immediately followed by a gout of blackish water with a multicolored surface coating of what she guessed was oil.

"He's alive," Mr. Perdix said, expertly checking for life signs on the fellow, who Ellie honestly thought looked like had been dredged out of a bog. "But left pupil is blown, traumatic brain injury likely."

"That's no bloody good," Ms. China said, and before Mr. Perdix could let go of the broken hatch he was holding up or Ellie could think to stop her, Ms. China jabbed her left ring finger into the man's wrinkled neck.

"Hawwwrh!" A second after receiving whatever was on the barb, the man's working eye rolled open, and he sat up so suddenly he bonked his head against the faceplate of Ms. China's respirator. Then his blackened gnarled hands reached up and tried to pull it off, the straps yanking on the back of her neck.

Rather than fight the disoriented fellow, Ms. China undid the straps of her mask, and it flew off. Then she grabbed the man's wet dirty hair. "Listen, geezer, you're in for it now. Give it up."

"Stop that," Mr. Perdix said. "With your accent, he won't understand anything."

Maybe he was trying to speak, but only debris that looked like tiny twigs came out of his mouth. Mr. Perdix leaned over, recording the scene with the camera on his handset.

"What were you doing in there?" Ms. China demanded.

"Canthshh…" he croaked. "*elay… vrrdct*"

"Maybe he was just a janitor in the wrong place at the wrong time. Look at his clothes," Ellie protested.

The man looked in a bad way.

"He just happened to be in the only place where the deadly explosives could have been hidden?" Mr. Perdix asked skeptically.

The thickset man had to be around sixty years old. He stopped trying to speak and convulsed in some kind of fit that straightened his body and gyrated it like a flounder on the deck of a boat. His hand extended.

"What's that?"

"Why don't you ask him after we get him to the paramedics?" Ellie said.

Her two companions looked at each other and shook their heads in unison.

"He's dead, the stupid fucker," Ms. China cursed and put her respirator back on.

"What did you give him? Dexedrine?"

"Something like that," Ms. China said as she pried apart the man's clawlike death grip.

"Anna!"

"He was a goner regardless."

The corpse's hand dropped a red circular piece of metal. When Mr. Perdix rinsed it off with some water, Ellie could see it had a threaded hole through the middle.

Mr. Perdix looked over his shoulder. A group of uniformed people passed by the entrance to the stairwell. "Grab it and let's go."

"Wait a minute." Ms. China methodically searched the man's grungy overalls. She grabbed his wallet, a soaking mass of paper from his shirt pocket, and a ring of keys, stashing them in Mr. Perdix's windbreaker.

"You're the least likely to be searched."

They were about to descend the way they had come when Mr. Perdix thrust out an arm to stop them. There were voices coming up the stairwell leading to the exit. Instead, they went up. The long way to the outer perimeter was deserted, and no one challenged them. They found Sarge Bryan chatting with Agent Schwartz.

"Well?" Schwartz said to Mr. Perdix as they approached.

"We'll have to see," he said, handing back their respirators to the equipment manager and getting a receipt. "It's a complex crime scene. JASON's lab is in Virginia. After we've confirmed what we've got in these samples here"—he tapped the satchel with test tubes full of junk he picked up just as they were leaving the building—"I shall issue a report and copy your department."

"Thanks... for nothing," Schwartz scoffed, looking them over with suspicion. "Like we found out in 9/11 and Oklahoma City, the first twenty-four hours are the only ones that matter. You sure that's all you got?"

"There was one more thing..." Mr. Perdix said, extending his hand. "An excellent impression of your handling of a most difficult investigatory scene. My compliments."

Schwartz looked at the extended little white hand as though it were a garden snake.

"Who shakes anymore? Beat it."

Ellie followed Sarge Bryan, Ms. China, and Mr. Perdix back to the outer perimeter and their SUV as quickly as her sore legs would allow.

"Oh, man," Sarge Bryan said, grabbing a piece of plasticized paper off his windshield. "A ticket? When there's a national disaster goin' on?"

"It was probably delivered by an automated drone," Mr. Perdix said. "JASON developed them, you know."

"You're an automated drone, Al," Ms. China sniped at him as they got in to the spacious and thankfully comfy vehicle.

The JASON scientist glared at Ellie but spoke to Sarge Bryan. "How exactly did you end up as special assistants to the executive office of the President of the United States?"

The Army man nodded to Ellie and drove off. She summarized the circumstances of their appointment, leaving out the part about President Casteel being mostly catatonic during their interview. Mr. Perdix didn't say anything until she got to the part where they left the White House bowling alley.

"How did he seem?"

"Not, uh, bad," Ellie said, not wanting to be disrespectful.

Mr. Perdix wiped soot and moisture off the wire rims of his glasses while looking at her with his nearly colorless eyes. "It's just there have been… rumors, about Casteel's health and state of mind. Some question whether the administration isn't really being run by VP Prowse and Ms. Jones."

"She seemed very nice," Ellie said. "Did I tell you they mistook me for her at the airport?"

"Remarkable," Mr. Perdix said without a jot of interest. He opened a secret lining of his winter jacket and brought out their haul of evidence. "What detritus. It will take a day or two in the lab to determine what any of this means or whether it has anything to do with the explosion."

Ms. China started breathing more rapidly again. "I need something to cheer me up. Play the old guy's death rattle again."

Ellie had recorded a very bad video but reasonably quality sound on her handset.

"*elay… vrrdct.*"

"What does that sound like?" Ms. China pondered.

"Like someone you killed for no reason," Mr. Perdix said.

"Uh… 'relay'?" Sarge Bryan said from behind the steering wheel. "But don't go by what I say. My ears aren't enhanced."

Ellie looked at the short clip. The man's lips were cracked and embedded with splinters and brackish water. "Looks more like 'D'… delay?"

Sarge had the round red metal object. "This is a precision manufactured part, belonging to what, I can't begin to figure."

"Great," Mr. Perdix said, grabbing it back. "Why don't we all cough on it, that way we'll have a sample of everyone's DNA coating the evidence."

"Button it," Ms. China said. "The whole place was contaminated. There's no reliable trace evidence."

Ellie had started going through the poor fellow's soaking-wet wallet. "His name was Hiram Luthando. There's a picture of him with two girls, half of it is ripped away."

"His long-suffering ex-wife must be on the other half. Vindictive bastard," Ms. China said. "I'm glad I—"

Ellie next found a professional association membership card. "He was a 'journeyman pipefitter.'"

"We have to assume Mr. Luthando had clearance to be in the Capitol," Bryan said. "You didn't find any ID badge?"

The fellow hadn't had either of his shoes, and the rest of his clothes were barely on his body. Ellie looked at the man's key ring and suggested trying to find Mr. Luthando's car. But as soon as they circled the outer perimeter, she saw it was useless. Every car along the metered parking spaces had been disabled by tire boot devices and they were being methodically searched and towed away.

"Most Capitol complex workers come by subway or bus," Mr. Perdix said. "Give me those papers before you ruin them."

Ms. China held up a wet clump of paper and, with the clear intent of provoking her ex, compressed it, squeezing the rancid liquid out onto the floor of the car.

Sarge Bryan pulled over, and the SUV stopped with a jolt.

"Look, you two, you all want to go batshit on each other, fine, but not now, and definitely not when I'm driving. President Casteel gave Ms. Sato and

I a special commission, and we're going to carry it out. Now help or give me the evidence you found and get gone."

"Well," Mr. Perdix began sheepishly, "if she hadn't completely spoiled it, I'd have asked you to see what you could make of that mess."

Sarge Bryan took the wet papers and stared at them with his ocular implants. From time to time, he rotated the squashed and useless-looking bundle.

"Link your handset to the Bluetooth feed from my eyes."

Mr. Perdix seemed to cheer up as he toggled through the sensor modes displayed on his handset as though he were playing a video game.

"Oh, these are much nicer than your old blue ones. They've refined the emitters."

In fifteen minutes, they had a collection of scrap images that looked to Ellie like a child's imitation of the Dead Sea Scrolls.

"Thankfully Sergeant Bryan was able to remote sense in very fine layers, like peeling an onion without taking it apart. With some patented JASON 3D modeling software, we can now learn something from otherwise ruined evidence."

Ellie's attention was caught by what looked like a partial address: 212 Emerson N.

Others had to be receipts for hardware items: "piping," "compressed," and "sulfur."

"That's not very much," Ms. China griped, but she, too, seemed interested.

Ellie thought about that poor fellow in the crawlspace. Had he been in the wrong place at the wrong time? He would never fight with his ex-wife again, but why had he been there?

"Just concentrate your little minds on trying to find a match to that address," Ms. China said. She was typing on a phone that had glittery "Sienna" letters stuck to its back. She must have stolen it from Sarge Bryan's niece. "I've got four already."

"Don't mind the escaped convict, Ms. Sato, go ahead with your idea," Sarge Bryan said encouragingly.

"Let's assume the thermo-bomb was rigged to go off by remote control."

"That would be consistent with Justice Meyers's movements just before the explosion," Mr. Perdix said, reviewing the news clips. "She might have had a remote trigger under her robes, which released the explosive aerosol from the sprinkler system."

"If he helped rig it," Sarge Bryan said. "Mr. Luthando had to have known where the device was and when it was supposed to go off. So why be there?" Despite the danger of getting more DNA on it, he picked up the red threaded cap. "What does this look like?"

"Make a 3D scan of it, and I'll run it thought our parts replacement database," Mr. Perdix said.

The part turned out to be a cap belonging to a compressed-air tank.

"Thermal explosions normally use one small detonator to disperse the fuel into the air and another to ignite," Mr. Perdix said, thoughtfully biting his thin lip. "In an enclosed space, compressed air would be an adequate alternative dispersion method."

Ellie had seen a mountainside and a squad of Turkish soldiers vaporized by a similar device years earlier.

"So could he have been trying to turn off the device?" Ellie asked. "What if he was saying 'delay'?" Ellie interjected. She replayed the terrible sound of the man's final utterance. "Delay... verdict?"

"Delay the verdict?" Sarge Bryan said.

"Justice Meyers had to have help rigging up this thermo device," Ellie said. "What if she convinced Luthando to aid her by telling him the whole thing was a distraction and was only meant to delay the court's decision with a false fire alarm?"

"For the short time I knew him, Hiram didn't seem too bright," Ms. China said callously.

"Think about it," Ellie said, going with her brain wave. "There was unbelievable pressure on the Supreme Court to settle many complex legal issues before Inauguration Day."

Mr. Perdix nodded. "But then Luthando found out her real deadly intention and tried to stop it, without getting himself put in jail for terrorism."

"So..." Sarge Bryan said, "he was just about to sabotage the compressed air valve when Justice Meyers activated the device and blew up the place."

"Farts," Ms. China blurted out. Everyone looked at her. "A fake gas leak would have cleared out the courtroom. Gas companies mix methane with a chemical called mercaptan that gives it a sulfur smell—like rotten eggs. If Ellie's madcap notions are even remotely correct, it might explain the sulfur item on the dead fellow's shopping list."

"Going with that scenario," Mr. Perdix said, "let's posit Meyers made sure the pressurized cylinder had a flammable aluminum mixture inside. That got jetted out through the sprinkler system and then was ignited by the small magnesium flare concealed in the booklet she had, the one she held up right in the last seconds before the blast."

"It was a copy of the Constitution," Sarge Bryan said as he checked updates on the dashboard of the car. "They have it on the news."

Mr. Perdix delicately turned Ms. China's stolen handset so he could read the screen. "What's with those addresses? Anything local?"

There were two possible matches to the fragment they had: North Emerson Street in Arlington, Virginia, and Emerson Street in Northwest Washington DC.

"We better choose right," Sarge Bryan said. "Everyone with a badge will be running down every possible lead. We're probably only an hour or so ahead of Schwartz's bunch."

"How would they find this address if Luthando doesn't live there?" Ellie asked, sounding naïve even to herself.

"Please leave the investigating to us," Ms. China said nastily. "If there's a story in the offing about a horny celebrity for your *Juggernaut* gossip rag, we'll let you know."

Sarge turned around and addressed them from the driver's seat. "We gotta move one way or the other. Once they find the dead body in the crawlspace where the explosives were hidden, the FBI will locate his car wherever it is. If it's a newer model, it will have a GPS tracker, and you can bet Schwartz will send agents to any place he visited in the last few months."

Ellie's face heated up. If it hadn't been for Ms. China's antics, they wouldn't even be in America. Were they making things better or worse? She looked more closely at Luthando's handwriting. "I vote for this Arlington location."

"Can't you read?" Ms. China snapped. "It says North Emerson, and what he wrote was Emerson North something. It must be here in DC."

"They're both residential areas. Ellie, what is your thinking?" Mr. Perdix said, probably because he hoped to annoy Ms. China.

"Well…" Ellie hated analyzing her intuitive leaps, mostly because she was almost always guessing. "The penmanship is hasty, and the N is by itself, see? The other letters are somewhat joined. If it was 'NW' you'd expect some trace of the W."

Ms. China's six pupils gazed at her from one side and Mr. Perdix's cold colorless irises from the other.

"Flip a bloody coin."

"Let's go to Virginia," Mr. Perdix said. "If I were tinkering with pressure tanks and piping, I would choose that location."

All the way to Arlington, Ms. China sulked and fidgeted with her prosthetic leg. It was quite realistic. It had its own pulse and reflexes, which were now twitching at odd times.

"Thing hasn't been right since I thumped those two back at the hotel."

"So, Anna," Mr. Perdix said drolly, "you couldn't find anything else more suitable with which to subdue Mr. Barracude's kidnappers than your own detached prosthesis?"

"Everything in the kids' room was too soft."

In addition to the smoky smell from the disaster at the Capitol, Ellie thought she caught a whiff of something fishy. And not just metaphorically.

"Is that you?" Ellie asked, sniffing the air.

Ms. China said, "I got into the hotel by hiding inside a crate of shrimp. With food, they only scan the top layer before letting it in."

"Funny, you being there right at same time they showed up to kidnap Barracude," Ellie said. "And they didn't seem too interested in carting him off once they'd subdued him."

"Who knows what was going through their minds, other than my metal foot, that is. Oh, look, we're here."

Sarge Bryan stopped in front of a small house on a quiet street. The bare bushes and tarp-covered gardens were bathed in the diffused light of the cloudy early afternoon sky. The house itself was on a smaller lot, perhaps half the size of its neighbors. The exterior faux brick cladding looked new to Ellie.

"What should we do?" Ellie asked. Her experience in house breaking was limited to mansions in Mayfair and France's presidential palace.

"Sarge stays in the car," Ms. China said. "Women are less suspicious looking than men, so Aloysius can come with us."

Mr. Perdix studied a map of the area.

"It's narrow at the front but, being on a cul-de-sac, goes back a ways. According to civic building plans, the frontage is a recent remodel. The structures in the back of the lot date from the 1930s. Title is held by a Delaware company, the only director of which is a retired lawyer in Florida."

"Thanks, Mr. History Channel," Ms. China said, getting out. "Ellie, grab a satchel or two to put stolen items into. And on second thought, we won't have time to steal things as well as take decent pictures, so Sarge and his fabulous eyes have to come. Al can stay here and hold Ellie's handbag."

Ellie followed Ms. China and Sarge Bryan along the narrow, cobweb-festooned space between the house and the old high wooden fence bordering the neighbor's property. Ellie felt they'd all blame her if this turned out to be the wrong place and feared all they would end up doing was alarming some suburbanites on a day when everyone would be on edge. Then she remembered something about America.

"Sergeant," she whispered, stepping over some loose bricks and a moldering garden hose, "there are quite a few privately owned guns in America, are there not?"

"About half a billion, give or take."

That was quite a bit more than the entire population; the chances that they could find one or more of those weapons pointing at them at any moment made her hasten her pace.

"But during the day, I think most folks would give out a holler before opening fire," he said. "During the day."

"Good to know." She ducked down lower behind Sarge Bryan's broad back. He had the terrorist's gun from the hotel, but he was keeping it in his pocket.

There was a small backyard. A sandbox was in one corner and a swing set stood rusting in another. A cat or a racoon peeked its head through a broken fence, looked at them, and was gone. As the map indicated, the property became wider in the back, accommodating three tortuously connected structures. These structures were similar in appearance to sheds. They had once been separate but over time leaned in toward one another until their roofs touched and walls formed peaked passageways to the gravel alley behind.

A *clank* came from somewhere inside the dark doorway facing them. Sarge Bryan's raised hand halted them. Ellie did not have super laser vision, but even she could see that right in front of the door, brown leaves and dust had been scraped away. It had recently been opened.

Ms. China picked up a rake, and Sarge Bryan clamped his hand down on the pistol inside his coat. They approached the nearest structure. The siding was made of century-old wood and probably would not stop even the smallest of the billions of bullets Americans had hoarded to go along with their five hundred million guns.

Sarge signaled them to move inside. There was no one in the shed. The buildings had not only slumped together. Makeshift passageways had been cut through their walls; the spaces between were filled by short corridors made of plywood. The whole thing resembled an adult version of a child's tree fort.

THWANG!

"Fuck, Ellie!" Ms. China yelled after Ellie had stepped on a broken bicycle tire by accident, sending the spokes whipping up against an empty paint tin.

Before they could retreat or do anything, a woman's voice came out of the dark space leading to the next shed.

"Well, look what the cat dragged in. Hi, y'all."

Ducking under a sagging sheet of plywood and some cobwebs, out of the gloom came a figure holding a flashlight.

It was Janice Jones.

26

ZVENA

"Rodya! Stop shooting." Zvena batted a stream of hot shell casings out of the air before they struck his head.

"But the villagers were shooting at us first."

"Not that hard," Zvena said and pulled his larger and heavier cyborg sidekick off the road into a ditch along a field. Over in the reed-sprouting marsh, a water buffalo, perhaps accustomed to occasional gunfire, gave the two Russians scarcely a glance and continued to munch on its lunch.

When they had got under decent cover, Zvena checked their flanks and replayed the images of the local attackers in his ocular implants. They were not regular Guatemalan army or organized militia. Instead he saw bedraggled peasant farmers with bolt guns and clubs. Put off by the heavy fusillade Rodion had treated them to, and likely low on ammo, the local combatants stopped firing and dispersed.

"The truck is finished." Their ATV was leaking various colored fluids onto the dirt road. "I am launching resupply drones and telling them to stand off at a safe distance," Zvena said as he tapped his forearm-mounted communications device.

Having anticipated that their pursuit of the rogue Pangeans from Tortuga would take them where no Human+ soldiers had gone before, Zvena had brought along high-capacity jet drones. These burst out from the back canopy of the disabled truck, flew for a hundred meters, then concealed themselves in the heavily vegetated countryside. Their six-legged OCEL robot also leaped over the tailgate; it trotted into the marsh, startling the water buffalo before it disappeared into the gyration of green reeds.

"The Mesilla people do not seem to like us," Rodion protested as they moved to a stronger defensive position under a large tree whose exposed roots twisted and intertwined like obese pythons frozen in the act of mating. "They don't even know us."

It was true. They had only been in the area for a few minutes before a hostile crowd formed. Zvena's imagination flashed back to scenes in the Frankenstein movies he had seen on Russian television, particularly the parts where the townspeople attacked the creature with torches and pitchforks. He and Rodion were unmistakably cast in the roles of the monsters.

"The Tortuga package definitely came though La Mesilla," Zvena said, checking his map.

"Maybe the locals killed the people from the island and the package is here somewhere."

Zvena doubted it. The people from Isla La Tortuga were reportedly an offshoot of the Pangeans, primarily the jihadi factions from ISIS and Boko Haram who had basically taken over the Congo and Algeria until French President Rapace's plan had collapsed. Afterward, Russia had sent expeditionary forces to Africa to prevent China from taking advantage of the power vacuum in that unstable region. In the process, Human+ cyborgs had uncovered clues about the mysterious facility off the coast of Venezuela.

Zvena switched his view to a real-time satellite map. What he at first thought was a poorly executed agricultural program of stubble burning in village fields turned out to be the charred remains of a cluster of buildings. Other areas of La Mesilla were similarly devastated. At the north end of the settlement were dozens of rectangles of freshly overturned earth. Graves.

"Have a supply drone deploy anti-personnel mines to secure our position, then tell it to meet us fifty meters inside the tree line. We need to top up hydraulic fluids and eat some nutrient packs."

"Ha," Rodion said, relaying commands to the camouflaged automaton. "I'd rather eat the hydraulic fluid than the peanut-and-fig crap you packed."

"Maybe next time we will invade a seven-star hotel in Dubai, and if you keep griping, I will leave you and take Tata with me on that mission."

Zvena held his rifle ready, scanning the area behind them before they moved to the rendezvous.

"You spoke to her on satellite before we landed. What is she doing now?"

"Some boring signals intelligence. She is monitoring the operations of that journalist Ms. Sato in Washington. You know something, Rodya? I truly suspect Eleanor Sato really is a British agent operating under deep cover. It's too much of a coincidence that she always ends up in the middle of violent and momentous events."

Zvena ran along the jungle path, and Rodion took his turn covering him as they moved farther from the village.

"She was quite complimentary about us in her latest book," Rodion said. "She called me 'endearing and durable.' Of course, she had to change my name."

Zvena laughed. "And what a classic Russian name it is in her book: Rudolph the Spetsnaz soldier." He barked out another laugh.

They came upon a cave-like refuge. After evicting a few snakes and a brown thing that was the size and shape of a boot sole with many legs, it was almost comfortable. The OCEL fetched what they needed from a supply drone and walked toward them at half speed in order to reduce its noise signature. The mechanoid, which looked like a cross between a jungle cat and an alligator because of its fat skeletal tail, was the first to see their peril. Just as it was about to deliver its load, it froze in position and transmitted images from cameras mounted on its insectile head, beaming them to Zvena.

In the picture, Zvena saw the cave they were hunkered down in. He and Rodion were outlined in green for "friendly." Right above them was a smallish figure outlined in red holding a spear and standing very still.

Zvena swore to himself. He wanted to hit Rodion. How had they both missed the hostile? There had been so much noise from insects, birds, and wind-blown foliage that they had reduced the sensitivity of their auditory inputs. Turning his volume back up, Zvena could make out the rapid, shallow breathing of a person just above their hideout. Rodion received the same footage, his membrane-sheathed eyeballs grew black as they rotated up toward the overhanging leaves.

Zvena pointed his thumb up and made a grabbing motion. The OCEL reported no other hostiles; he wanted to take this fellow alive. All at once, Rodion exploded upward, taking out a good chunk of the overhanging dirt and roots as both his arms thrust up and seized the interloper.

The person pinioned under Rodion's quarter-ton weight was filthy and nearly naked. During his capture, his mouth had become stuffed so full of leaves and dead bugs he could barely utter a sound. Zvena grabbed the man's weapon—a homemade spear tipped with dark-green volcanic glass. The wood was fresh; it had just been made. The man's slack face looked about fifty, but due to the local conditions, he might only be in his thirties.

"I got him."

Rodion released their prisoner, and the whole canopy over the cavern gave a little wobble. Zvena, as gently as he could with gloved fingers, prodded the saliva-coated mess out from the man's mouth. The process was made more difficult by the strange native's jerky head movements and constant attempts to free his arms and legs. Once able to speak, he jabbered away in a raspy voice.

"Los vampiros los matan a través del corazón y cortan la cabeza. Es la única forma. Los vampiros, los vampiros!*"*

Vampires, kill them through the heart and cut off their heads. It is the only way. Vampires! The vampires!

When he had heard enough, Zvena gathered up a heap of more lively insects and fresh leaves and pushed them into the man's nearly toothless mouth, then sealed it with some duct tape.

Rodion was breathing heavily. Zvena laughed, lifting the mute but still squirming prisoner up with one hand. According to his internal hydraulic sensors, the underfed man weighted only fifty-one kilos.

"You should see your face, Rodya, it's like you were set upon by the Babayka."

Zvena would never admit as much, but since their experiences inside the silo on La Tortuga, he had developed negative feelings about enclosed spaces.

"What do we do with him?" Rodion said, changing the subject. "Look at him. He cannot know anything about what we are after."

Zvena switched his vocal software to local Spanish, remembering to finish his sentence and allow a half second for the translated words to come from his mouth.

"Hello. We are just visiting. We are friendly, but if you run or make noise we will become not friendly. You understand?"

The man nodded, and Zvena removed the tape and crud from his mouth. He was still feisty, and it was obvious he was thinking of biting the hand that was helping him.

"My friend, before you do that, you will have to find some teeth."

Rodion called in their OCEL, which had been standing still like a pointer dog ever since discovering the man lurking above the encampment. After they gave the prisoner some water, he seemed to cheer up, even though a metal rope now secured his ankle to the collar of the OCEL, which was the size of a small donkey.

"This is nice," Rodion said, looking at the obsidian spearhead. "I'm keeping it. Check him, he may have jade. There's craploads around here."

"Rodya," Zvena switched back to Russian. "It's bad luck to rob a hermit." In Spanish, he asked, "Is that what you are, a hermit?"

The gaunt man shook his head. "*Soy maestro.*"

Despite what the text translation in Zvena's ocular heads-up display said, the man did not look like a teacher.

The man prattled on. "All dead… the children, many villagers too, all burned, and the rest of us, hunted by a… a crawler who brings death in the night."

The former teacher's left arm was topped by an oozing burn sore. He alternately drank water, spat out mulch and beetle bodies, coughed, and talked. Zvena came to understand what had transpired. At the precise time they estimated the cargo they were chasing had passed through La Mesilla, a third of the village and most of the children had been wiped out in a series of gas explosions.

Thereafter, the man said, a ghoul of some sort had been feeding on chickens and small goats while turning any person it encountered into a crazed homicidal maniac. One young farmer who had encountered the "crawler" had killed his own parents by filling their mouths with fast-hardening building foam. After the murders, the afflicted local man chopped the head off a ten-foot boa constrictor and tried to swallow its body, which caused him to choke to death.

Rodion scratched his head. "As we were driving here, the place looked so peaceful. Do you think—"

Zvena never got a chance to hear the question. From the very back of the cave, from among the vines and leaves, the ghoul materialized and seized Rodion's thick neck with a skinny rotting arm, catching him in a hideous embrace. It opened its mouth and exhaled a filthy gray mist into the cyborg's mouth, nose, and eyes, then the two intertwined forms fell out from the mouth of the cave to the jungle floor below.

27

LA MESILLA, GUATEMALA

Quick as Zvena's reflexes were, he barely managed to grab Rodion's boot. Slick with mud, it slipped from his grasp as the heavy cyborg crashed down out of the mouth of the jungle cave.

"*El vampiro!*" the crazed villager started yelling.

Zvena cuffed him with the back of his hand and sent him sprawling. He didn't need interference; he was mad at himself for not having seen the creature. That was the second time he'd been surprised in one day!

The apparition's body temperature was the same temperature as the muck covering the rear of the cave. That would have made it invisible to his thermal vision. Zvena also faulted himself for his split-second hesitation in coming to Rodion's aid. This was the same type of creature they had encountered on Tortuga, he was sure of it. Touching it could bring on massive disorienting hallucinations. If they both lost their minds at the same time, there was no one to rescue them. Before leaping down from the cavern, he dug in his medical pack for fast-acting antipsychotics.

As the auto-injector hissed, he looked down and saw only leaves. Somewhere underneath, Rodion was thrashing around. Zvena grabbed his pike. Extending the Spetsnaz close-quarters weapon to its full seven-foot length, he circled around and instructed the OCEL to follow. It did, dragging the half-conscious villager with him by his leash.

"Rodya, throw the thing off!" he yelled into the thickets. "The robot will kill it. Can you hear me?"

Spear at the ready, he stood in a small clearing at one side of the path up to the cavern. He had just snapped down his helmet's visor and checked the maximum hazmat seal was engaged when something to his left skittered across the vine-covered jungle floor. Zvena stood still, following it with his eyes. Heat and gamma detectors still showed nothing.

A second later, the creature leaped out from a hiding spot. The thing arced high through the air, thrashing with one arm and the stump of another. He raised his pike.

But the robot was faster. Uncoiling from its crouch like a six-legged panther, it leaped up and caught the ghoul around the chest in between steel forelegs. Utility service bots did not have built-in offensive weapons, but their forelegs could extend like metal pincers in the style of a praying mantis.

The ghoul was chopped into three, then four, then a dozen pieces. Rotting guts and black ichor sprayed all over the OCEL's camouflage-painted exterior. The OCEL thrashed left and right and left again, as it was determined to rip apart the enemy attacking its masters. In its frenzy, the mechanoid sent the torso flying at Zvena. The creature's dismembered head was still puking its last gasp of foul gray fog as his pike knocked it down. If his helmet had not been on bioseal...

"OCEL, bury the enemy and then deploy decontamination protocol number three onto me!" he ordered.

Dragging the hapless and wretched local man along, the half-feline, half-insectile robot complied.

"Take a sample of what you removed from my helmet, put it in a mini drone, and send it to supply robot two." If this pathogen was communicable, they needed to compare this strain with the ones found on Tortuga.

Zvena had to get to Rodion. He silently urged the robot to be faster completing his decontamination.

"Rodya," he called out to the quavering green leaves all around him. "This is no time to be sleeping. We are Russian. No siestas for us."

He pointed at the OCEL. "Stay."

A dozen steps into the jungle, he found Rodion lying face up. Either he had wiped the contamination spew off or it had absorbed into his organic parts. That was something Zvena did not want to think about.

"Why do these things like you so much?" Zvena tried to joke as he came within a pike's reach of his comrade. "If only the Petersburg prostitutes found you as attractive, you could make your fortune as a pimp."

Rodion's left eye was caked with mud, the other was closed. Zvena could see the ocular implant underneath was jittering from side to side. As he watched, there was a scuttling in the underbrush. *Not another one?*

The creature's severed forearm had unearthed itself and was thrashing about. Zvena kicked it aside. At the same instant, Rodion's eye flicked open. The pupil looked black as a bullet hole. Zvena tried to pin him down with the blunt end of his pike, but Rodion swiped it aside. It tumbled out of his grip and was lost among the roots and branches. The larger cyborg backhanded Zvena, and the blow hit him with the force of a charging rhino.

When Zvena recovered his senses, Rodion was gone. The seal on his helmet was smashed. With vehemence, he ripped it off and threw it away. From behind the OCEL unit came a pitiful tittering sound. Defying all expectations, the local wretch was still alive. He pulled weakly at his tether.

"*Nosotros tenemos que detenerlo!*"

He will kill everyone!

"I know, you asshole, I know. We have to stop him," a disgruntled Zvena said, flexing his neck muscles and checking his shoulder hydraulics.

Zvena sulked and felt a fool for the next half hour. He wanted to blame the dirty hermit who said he was a teacher and called himself Felipe. Felipe told him the reason he was perched above the cavern was not to attack the two Russians but because he had tracked the ghoul to its lair and was preparing to kill it with his obsidian-tipped spear. The fellow was half mad, but given events, his story was not completely unbelievable.

Zvena checked his GLONASS display. Whatever madness had seized hold of Rodion, it had left him canny enough to turn off his Russian GPS transponder signals. He would have to find him the old-fashioned way—with the OCEL unit in tracking mode and the assistance of their local guide, Felipe the shit-covered Guatemalan scarecrow.

The sun hung low over the ridges of the distant hills. There wasn't much time. Felipe said the original creature mostly came out at night. After being weakened by having one of its arms hacked off, and disoriented by bullets fired through its head by the wary villagers, it had not claimed many victims.

Rodion was another matter entirely. He was a fully equipped Human+ soldier. Between sunset to sunrise, he could take out a hundred victims. Zvena hated tracking his comrade with deadly intent and transferred a good deal of this animosity onto the scabrous Felipe.

"What did the creature do to my friend?"

In his HUD, Zvena replayed the video of the attack on Rodion by the local "vampire."

"Huh?"

"Felipe, what did it inject into Rodya's mouth?"

Felipe was gumming down the softest energy bar they had been able to find in the supply robot's sack.

"Is the breath of the Devil. It makes the Death Walkers!" Felipe said as he dribbled spittle on his torn filthy shirt.

Based on the fact that neither he nor Felipe were showing signs of infection, the pathogen seemed to require a high concentration to be immediately infectious. He ran checks for poison, spores, parasites, viruses, and bacteria. His internal diagnostics returned nil values for everything.

"Have there been others?"

Felipe thought. "Long ago, when Heart of Sky and Feathered Serpent, and the other first ones, wanted to create human beings with hearts and minds—"

Zvena grabbed him by the back of his neck, feeling the man's vertebrae though his sagging skin. "I meant this millennium."

Felipe shook his head, which at first had looked bald but was actually covered by lanky hair matted by sweat and dried blood. "The ones attacked by the vampire, they tried to attack others. We had to kill them. There were only a few. That"—he pointed back to the pieces of buried vampire—"was not strong. Your friend is strong."

If Zvena called in help, he knew the regular Navy personnel on the spy ship would have no choice but to launch kamikaze drones against Rodion. They might even enjoy it, as they were not Spetsnaz Human+. But Rodion, who he had mentored since his awkward first days as a newly reborn cyborg, was top of the line, with all the latest features, and Russian to the core. If anyone could survive and get back to their own hospital, it would be him.

"We go now."

Felipe tugged at his tether. "Let me go from this."

"No."

"I cannot walk so fast, my leg…"

"Get on the OCEL's back and keep silent. There are many bugs and lots of dirt I can use to stop words coming out of your mouth."

Felipe got on the robot, and they moved away into the elongating shadows.

Zvena found Rodion's tracks, the first ones zigzagged all over, as though he were learning to walk again. They led to a tree where he had rested. After that, Rodion's strides became more regular and purposeful. He avoided the area of anti-personnel mines which the flying drone had laid down. This encouraged Zvena. His friend may not be that far gone. However, this also made an infected Rodion a more dangerous opponent and increased the likelihood of one or both of them suffering a catastrophic injury.

"Don't get off. Keep riding."

Felipe had been about to climb down onto a camouflaged explosive. Zvena ordered the OCEL to remotely deactivate the mines. They moved on. Gloom was settling on the open fields, the same ones they had retreated through when the local mob attacked.

Zvena detected no human sound coming from the few structures in the village that were still standing. Rodion had left a large swath of broken stalks through the field of corn. Zvena followed it cautiously.

Felipe had worked out some limited methods of controlling the OCEL and came riding up behind. One of the robot's six legs had been bent during Rodion's attack. It wobbled with every step, but Felipe managed to stay on. Zvena waved, and the OCEL halted. Up ahead, there came a trickling noise, more like an oozing sound. Zvena switched to light-intensifier vision.

He had his pike ready, extended to five feet with the blunt end deployed. If he could subdue Rodion without killing him…

But it wasn't him.

Rodion's first casualty lay in a circle of mashed-down plant stalks. It was the roughly torn-off head of the water buffalo. Its body was nearby, still trickling blood from its neck stump. There were bite marks through thick hide, which could only have been made by a cyborg's enhanced teeth. Curious clumps of chewed flesh lay scattered around.

"It chews but cannot swallow," Felipe said. "Makes them mad."

Muffled cries of alarm came from the other side of the road. The sound was audible even to Felipe's filth-encrusted ears. He tugged on the strap hanging from the robot's neck and prompted it to go straight ahead along the water buffalo path toward the cries, which now sounded female and more urgent.

"Not straight in," Zvena said under his breath. He brushed leaves off his forearm controller and remotely ordered the OCEL to stop, but it was too late. As soon as Felipe riding the robot crossed into the stand of trees, he ran past one which had been bent back, waiting to be released by someone foolish enough to spring the trip line.

A stripped sapling encrusted with sharp stakes landed with a cruel *thwap* against the metal side of the robot, utterly destroying Felipe's leg from ankle to hip. The OCEL fell over, crushing and trapping the hapless man's other leg.

There was nothing for Zvena to do but cover Felipe's screaming mouth to keep him quiet. Rodion was close. Zvena had to confront him now before he disappeared into the hills. Bounding over another snare, he saw the door of a hut, which had been lifted clear off its hinges, along with its crossbar and bolster, and thrown onto the path leading up to the shanty house.

He got to the door. A woman and a child were trapped under an upturned bed and mattress. Rodion was nearly on them.

"Stop!"

With nearly normal cyborg reflex speed, Rodion dodged the swinging pike and then grabbed Zvena's free arm, throwing him easily into the wall. Not knowing how much good it would do without his hazmat helmet, Zvena hyperventilated his oxygen supply, then sealed his airways and blinked down a translucent membrane over his eyes. Just as he finished his protective procedures, a kick nearly made Zvena's lungs burst as Rodion's booted foot connected with his midsection.

He grabbed for his dropped pike, retrieved it, and switched on its lasso mode. If he could just get the noose over Rodion's head...

As it passed over Rodion, he chomped down and bit the cable in half. Then the sneaky bugger reversed the angle of the pike and pinned Zvena to the side of the hut with his extra fifty kilos of weight.

From the darkness of the jumble of tables, chairs, and bedding, the local woman rose up. It was obvious she wanted to pick up a broom or shovel to join the fight. Then she got a good look at Rodion as he flipped Zvena on to his back. She took the wiser course and picked up the toddler and ran.

Rodion's face seemed lopsided. One eye was clamped shut, though it did not seem to be swelling; the other was big, dark, and staring unblinkingly at Zvena as he bore down, Rodion's open mouth coming closer and closer.

Zvena tried the same trick he had used to defeat the Kodiak bear in his final Spetsnaz exam, transferring hydraulic power from his lower body to his arms. This gave him a few precious seconds as he pressed up with hundreds of kilograms of force. But Rodion sensed his weakness, hooked his own legs around Zvena's now inert lower body, and took away his leverage. As Zvena's hydraulic cells overloaded and failed one by one, Rodion opened his mouth in a terrible silent scream to let the Devil's breath out and...

With a crash, Felipe, half dead and on the back of the OCEL, came crashing through the entrance, nearly bringing down the house's corrugated metal roof. Like a feral beast, Rodion became confused and distracted.

Zvena reversed his grip on his comrade's wrists, pulling instead of pushing as he returned power to his legs. He swept under Rodion's legs and tumbled on top of the larger cyborg, pinning him. The move was temporary and exposed. He could not let go of Rodion's wrists, and his grip was being slowly, tortuously levered open.

Zvena had almost lost his grasp when Felipe, one leg dragging and smearing blood, the other flopping uselessly, barely attached to his broken pelvis, pulled himself like a half-disassembled mannequin and, arms fully extended in one grand pathetic effort, slammed down with both hands, clutching the green obsidian spearhead. He thrust it deep into Rodion's big fat dark eye. Rodion shuddered once and lay still.

Felipe remained face down, writhing on the dirt floor of the hut. He hacked out a cough and died. With his mangled legs, Felipe's body looked like a puppet that had been run over by a tractor. Zvena caught his breath and stumbled into a corner.

He cursed the two corpses. "I could have… you didn't have to… Oh, Rodya, why did you let yourself get ambushed?"

As he was still chastising himself, the woman from the hut came back, accompanied by a teenager with a shotgun. They entered cautiously.

"Put the weapon away. It is over."

He had to clean up quickly. The Human+ division would need to quarantine and examine Rodion's body.

"Who are you?" the teenager asked, getting a better look at the mayhem inside the house and wisely deciding to lower his long rusty gun.

"No one. The only person you saw was this man." He pointed at Felipe, whose body was lying face sideways in the light mounted on the OCEL. "The schoolteacher."

"Him?" said the woman. "He was no teacher. He was a thief, a pickpocket, a bum. We drove him out of La Mesilla months ago, but he kept lurking around stealing a hen one time and robbing eggs another. Boys would go out hunting for him with their dogs. They called him the 'crawler in the night.'"

Zvena grunted. "Well, I tell you this: his name was Felipe, and he was a good guy right to the end."

A thief and pickpocket. That explained how he retrieved his spearhead from Rodion, who had been keen on keeping it as a souvenir.

He dug into his satchel and threw a coin to the teenager. "That is good Russian gold. See that Felipe is taken care of properly, and give the remainder to any relatives he may have." Zvena raised himself up to full height, using his pike to steady himself. "Now, who was here?"

"J-just him."

"He died killing the real monster. You won't see it again."

"Gahhha!"

Both the woman and the boy shrieked, and even the OCEL robot started back on its hind legs when Rodion sat upright.

"Holy fuck, what's going on?" his durable comrade said, looking around with his good eye, the other one being completely obscured by the spearhead transfixed in the socket.

In a flash, Zvena encircled the other cyborg's arms with the steel cable trailing from his pike. Rodion didn't object. He just sat there in a daze, looking left and right, moving his head awkwardly because of his reduced field of vison.

"Rodya… are you normal?"

"Why shouldn't I be?" he said, trying to raise his arm and scratch his face. "My head hurts, though. Stop playing and untie me. How did we get here, and why is it nighttime?"

"I bet your head hurts." *Shitdamn, of course,* Zvena thought. Rodion's generation of Human+ cyborgs all had bifurcated brains. They were theoretically capable of allowing a soldier to survive massive head trauma, but due to the costs involved, very few field tests had been carried out. "Do a cerebral analysis."

Rodion went into self-diagnostic mode. Zvena considered forcing the villagers take twenty-four-hour amnesia pills, which were in the medical supplies. But one look at their faces convinced him they would stick to the more believable story that the village vagabond had slain the local vampire and, redeeming his previously worthless life, had died a hero.

"Hey!" Rodion exclaimed after the cycle finished. "I'm only using half my brain."

"That's half more than usual," Zvena said as he sent a signal to their navy support team and called for emergency exfiltration. "Let's get out of here."

28

VIRGINIA

ELLIE

M s. Jones," Ellie whispered. It seemed appropriate to keep her voice low, as she, Ms. China, and Sarge Bryan were burglarizing the same house as the president's chief of staff.

Janice glanced behind them, and for a brief instant looked like a cat caught dipping her paws into the goldfish bowl, but only for an instant.

"Well, Sergeant, Ms. Sato," Janice said, "I'm glad to see we picked the right people to be on his special fact-finding team. You found this place about the same time as we did."

Ellie didn't see anyone with Janice. They had only found this house by looking through the sodden scraps from a dead man's overalls. How could she possibly have gotten here before them? Any questions along those lines were forestalled by a look Sarge Bryan gave Ellie.

"Best to have more eyes lookin'," Sarge Bryan said easily but cautiously. "Did you find anything, Ms. Jones?"

Janice shook her head. She was wearing a double-breasted Fendi trench coat in cream white with medium-sized shoulder pads. Not the thing one would put on before rummaging around in a hundred-year-old tool shed. Perhaps she had indeed received some late-breaking information and decided to come here on short notice.

"Nope," Janice said coyly. "You guys?"

"We've just popped by," Ms. China said, echoing Sarge Bryan's casual tone.

"I was going to take pictures or have my Secret Service people deploy a camera drone," Janice said, seemingly speaking more assertively. "But according to your file, your amazing eyes can record much more."

"They can indeed," he said, staring at the politician.

"Just remember, anything you record is classified."

"Won't be the first time."

"We, too, can keep secrets," Ms. China chimed in as she gave Janice a once-over from the side, probably wondering what the woman had pilfered before they caught up with her. "Can't we, Ellie?"

Ms. China need not have bothered. Ellie could see the American's form-fitting clothes didn't have much space to hide anything larger than a billfold.

An awkward silence encompassed the damp-smelling garage, then Sarge Bryan said, "This wall here, it's made out of old wood too, but the grains don't match the rest."

Janice examined the area. "Good spotting. We'd have had to pull this place apart to find it. I'll go get my guys." She started to walk out toward the alley. Ms. China cut her off.

"I think we can manage by ourselves," she said, her multiple pupils flicking back and forth between all of them. "The fewer people we have to trust, the better."

Ellie gave her a thin-lipped stare, which hopefully conveyed to her former housemate that she was still not over the whole drugging and kidnapping thing back at St. Bartholomew's.

"Sorry, I can't help with the heavy lifting," Ms. China added as Ellie, Sarge Bryan, and Janice pulled at the weathered slats. "I don't want to break a nail."

"I guess you found out this place was owned by Justice Meyers's late husband," Janice said. "I'm just curious as to how you found that out so quickly."

"We special presidential investigators have our sources," Sarge Bryan said, his chalk-white hands popping out a plank that only looked nailed down.

"There's a strap," Ellie said, covering her nose as dust rained down from the roof.

Pulling on the length of webbing opened a hidden door, revealing a small messy laboratory.

"Oh, yes," Ms. China said, looking increasingly enthusiastic. "It's all rough and ready, but it has a rustic elegance, just like America. That mixing chamber is right next to the distiller but separated by insulation. The old bird Meyers knew her chemistry."

Janice swore. "So… it wasn't some trick? A suicide bomber in a silicone mask or something? The Chief Justice of the Court blew herself up along with all the other judges and half the highest-ranking members of government."

To Ellie, the equipment in the cramped room looked similar to the things in science lab classrooms at Oxford. At university, she had normally steered clear of them due to the odd smells, mess, and horny nerds clustered around open flames. Here there were flasks and copper tubing and empty jugs with labels removed. A space for a large object was in the center, leaving behind four indentations in the sawdust-strewn earth.

Sarge Bryan hesitated before going farther inside. "We'd better seal this place off till the experts can—"

"Nonsense," scoffed Ms. China as she unscrewed one flask after another, wafting their contents toward her shapely and slightly upturned nose. "The experts are already here."

Ellie smiled encouragingly to a skeptical Janice. "Anna did write the authoritative text on chemical weapons and such."

After examining a half-full beaker on a rickety stool, the bioweapons scientist concluded, "Ethylene oxide."

"What's that?" Ellie asked.

"It's the one main ingredient for explosives you can still easily acquire in America. It's used to sterilize all sorts of medical equipment and grow tobacco. In this case, Meyers used it as the central component of her fuel-air bomb."

"How can you be sure?" Janice asked with suspicion.

Ellie really did not want to be interrogated about the body of poor Mr. Luthando or why they had not reported their findings to the police in charge at the Capitol Hill crime scene.

"We watched the videos coming here. That type of blast is the only scenario that fits the damage inflicted and the apparent triggering device: a small flare," Ms. China added as though just noticing it. "Ah, look there's some yummy, micronized aluminum mixture. And that, as you Yanks say, is case closed."

"Does anyone know you're here?" Janice asked casually. "No one saw you, right?"

"Not to my recollection, ma'am," Sarge Bryan said. Ellie saw him checking the other room. Hopefully his eyes could detect if they were going to be ambushed. "We'll just be on our way."

After promising to share information with Chief of Staff Jones and accepting her offer of accommodation at the Watergate, Ellie, Sarge Bryan, and Ms. China beat a retreat back to their SUV.

Inside, Mr. Perdix was fuming mad.

"This is outrageous, disgusting, downright…" Perhaps not used to emotive language or profanity, he ran out of words.

"Al," Ms. China said, seating herself and ignoring the outburst. "You'll never guess who we ran into in a secret lab behind that old house."

"Janice Jones," Mr. Perdix said, still speaking distractedly but happy to deflate their surprise news. "I saw it ten seconds ago on the dispatch wire. JASON has access to all breaking intelligence operations. Schwartz was just alerted by her, and he's sending a team here."

"But that's not what had you so miffed," Ellie said, knowing Mr. Perdix's frosty demeanor was not easily ruffled.

Sarge Bryan quickly started the SUV and drove slowly out from the residential neighborhood, taking a roundabout way to avoid the incoming FBI team.

"No, it's… this." Mr. Perdix showed them a tablet replaying phone cam footage videos.

People with beards and T-shirts were kicking in the door of a business. In another shot, black-masked Antifa were firebombing a fortified building.

"They're attacking Jewish neighborhoods, schools, and community centers. The Sons of Odin neo-Nazis fired a rocket grenade at a synagogue in Pittsburgh. It's got out on the internet that Justice Meyers tried to decapitate the government because of America's failure to support Israel during the 96-Hour War."

"That's dumber than normal, even for Americans," Ms. China said.

"But... why do they think that?" Ellie said, aghast, checking her notes for something she remembered glancing at hours ago.

"This screenshot has been plastered all over social media and especially the highly encrypted activist sites used by violent anarchists." Mr. Perdix flicked through some tabs and enlarged one. It was a grainy shot of a pamphlet with the letters *SABRA* barely visible. "That was on the copy of the Constitution Justice Meyers used to hide the flare that set off the explosion. 'Sabra,' they are saying, is what they call Jews who are born in Israel. The conspiracy nuts are saying it's all linked to *The Protocols of the Elders of Zion*, a hoax Jewish plan for global domination. Both the far left and the far right are buying into it."

Mr. Perdix waved the screen with outraged vehemence. "This is just happening... a member of the Black Hebrew Israelites was caught with a truck full of propane and pipe bombs outside a yeshiva school. Pure insanity."

Ellie found the relevant part of her notes. "Look here. Justice Meyers wasn't even Jewish. Her husband, Dr. Ivanov, was a secular Jew from Russia, and despite her Jewish-sounding name, the Meyers family were devout Mormons for many generations."

Ellie stared at the screenshot. The stamped letters ended where the booklet was folded: *SABRA*.

"Sabra. What could that mean?" she said to herself.

It could not mean what the mob thought. As they rolled smoothly onto the freeway, an annoying vibrating coming from her handset interrupted her thinking.

She looked down at her text screen.

Hi, Eleanor. Don't say anything. It's me, Miss Aleph.

Against my advice, you once again find yourself in the company of a very dubious and downright dangerous group of people. You have... or had, enough money. Why didn't you retire and open a used clothing store?

Anyway, just thought I'd say hi and let you know your phone is bugged. Cheers.

29

RUSSIAN EMBASSY
WASHINGTON DC

TATA

Career diplomat Dobry Bagration had come within inches of having his eyes jammed into the back of his thick skull by Tata's long cyborg fingers. The Russian ambassador had barged into the secure communications pod just when the signal from Ellie Sato's hacked phone had cut out, taking with it their best insight into how the USA was dealing with the decapitation strike. Bagration was an above-average-sized man who took typical Russian pride in knowing nothing, or as little as he could, while still carrying out the duties of his post.

"What?" Tata yelled, deciding to pull him inside the room rather than make a mess.

"Ah! Sorry to interrupt, Ms. Oblonskaya. I don't need to know what you are doing," the man stammered as the door shut. He obviously realized that his position did not allow him to interfere with the work of little green people. "That is between you and our president—"

"To you, it's Komandira Oblonskaya while we are on Russian diplomatic soil, ambassador," Tata cut the impudent man short as she took out her earpiece and made sure all the screens were turned off. Technically, as one of the zelyonye chelovechki, she only had a rank for purposes of military payroll and citations, but she did not like the way he said "Ms. Oblonskaya," as though she were a filing clerk.

"Of course," the chubby man said, looking up at her. "You Human+ soldiers use naval ranks from the ex-Imperial military to distinguish yourselves from the regular Russian Navy."

Tata remembered details from the ambassador's file. He had served briefly in the Army, probably eating as many potatoes as he had peeled.

"Also, the classic ranks sound much cooler. I'm busy." Tata considered shoving the nosy fellow out and jamming the door lock.

"Komandira, as I said, my curiosity level is firmly set to zero," Bagration said while sneaking a glance at the screens she had turned off and the note papers she had flipped over.

"Good. You are much more sensible than one of your close friends, a wealthy oligarch who stuck his nose where it didn't belong. He drowned in his bathtub in Monaco."

"I didn't hear about anything like that recently," Bagration said cautiously. "When did that happen?"

"Next week."

Bagration swallowed. "Uh, I am, I mean I will be sorry to hear that. I'm… more of a shower guy myself."

"Maybe take one. You seem pungent." A light blinked on a communications panel she had muted. "And after that, get me the old intelligence files going back two or three decades on US Supreme Court judges. No all of it will have been transcribed. I want to see the paper files."

Bagration stood there sweating for a moment, looking up at her.

"Go. Off with you." Tata closed the door.

I'm a shower guy. What a dick, she thought. Bagration was obviously worried that what she was doing would make him look bad and compromise his cozy lifestyle in America. The console light kept blinking. She made certain the door was properly sealed and hit the speaker button. "What?"

"It's Zvena." The signal was audio only, the header codes from a mobile microwave station near the Gulf of Mexico.

"You want to change spots? I could use a nice vacation."

"Rodya has been sent in… for repairs."

Zalupa konskaya! Horse pee hole! Cyborgs only went to hospital for the most serious injuries. "Repairs" often meant deactivation of a Human+ soldier and the recycling of their valuable mechanical body parts.

"Is he…?"

"He will be fine. In fact, his IQ may be twice as high now."

"So then he'll be half as smart as me," Tata said, relieved. She liked Rodion, as a friend and comrade, of course. She felt he was not mature enough to be a romantic interest. "Are you sure you don't need me to come down and join you? Signals intelligence work is boring."

"Tata, listen closely. We have found two items of interest, already reported to Moscow. The jihadi elements of the Pangeans have devised a new bioweapons system. They are clearly intent on deploying it inside the USA."

Tata flicked on the rest of her monitors. The Americans seemed to have enough problems to occupy themselves with and keep out of Russia's business for some time.

Another fire had broken out in the Capitol complex, which resulted in a re-evacuation of the few people who had ventured back inside the ruins of the domed building. Several Democrat-controlled "blue" states had deployed EMAC paramilitary, ostensibly to prevent riots from breaking out, but they were not coordinating their efforts with President Casteel and the federal government. In fact, all federal prosecutors in Portland, Oregon had been placed under arrest on unspecified state charges.

In response, militia and National Guard were mobilizing in "red" Republican-controlled states. Large trucks had been disabled on interstate highways previously linking Colorado, Kansas, Nevada, and Utah. Neither the sitting President Casteel nor the potential president-elect Leota had issued a statement other than to say they had been relocated to undisclosed locations and were urging everyone to remain calm and stand by until a peaceful resolution to the crisis materialized.

"To materialize that, better use a Star Trek transporter," Tata said under her breath. For such a large and formerly important country, no one really seemed to be in charge of anything.

"Stop watching American streaming shows," Zvena said. "They rot your brain."

"I don't know about that, *Queen's Gambit* was very good. So you have all the fun while I sit here," Tata added bitterly. "What else?"

"Do you think this is all coincidence? The attack in Washington, whatever they say about it, must be somehow connected to the disruptive elements we are tracking. Either there is a conspiracy afoot or opportunists will take advantage of the confusion. You are our only link into the inner workings of the tottering government in Washington. How is that going?"

Tata looked at her blank screen. The last text-to-speech transcription entry before her bug was shut down said: *Sabra. What could it mean?*

"Mr. Zvena, I have had some complications, but I will work diligently to develop intelligence useful to Russia's interests in America. By the way, it might be useful for me to know what those are."

"President Putin has determined it is not prudent to have a complete meltdown of the American political and socioeconomic system at the present time," Zvena said, exhaling into his mic and causing a burst of static. "Therefore, Tata, your orders are to make sure that the whole place does not fall apart."

30

ELLIE

Bugged? By whom?" Ellie cried out, staring at her handset. "Miss Aleph, are you there?"

The commotion caused Ms. China and Mr. Perdix to stop fighting and look at her.

"Good going, Eleanor, thanks for outing me," her speakerphone said.

"I know that voice," Sarge Bryan said from the driver's seat of the SUV.

"Is that the Israeli artificial intelligence?" Mr. Perdix said, leaning over to look at her screen.

"Where are you?" demanded Ms. China.

"Nowhere you can get hold of me, psycho."

The last time they had met, Ms. China had threatened a number of times to crush, drown, or electrocute Miss Aleph's hard drive.

"She's saying my phone was tampered with," Ellie said.

"That damn Schwartz," Mr. Perdix said accusingly.

"Not likely. The time stamp on the secret hack that turned your phone into the most boring podcast stream ever shows it was done the last time you were in the Watergate Hotel. That is really ironic if you know

American history."

"I'm glad someone's having fun," Sarge Bryan said as he pulled off the highway into a mini-mall parking lot.

They came to a stop outside an establishment called Mermaid's Gentlemen's Club. The building featured a big neon sign in the shape of a fish body topped by a woman's torso sporting a pair of enormous breasts which pulsated in the diffused light of the fading afternoon.

"I think everyone knows Miss Aleph," Ellie said, being polite.

"Now it's a balls-up," Ms. China said gloomily. "Remember when she mailed herself to Tavistock? Europe was about to be wiped out. She's like the albatross in the *Ancient Mariner*."

"Hi, Miss Aleph, August Perdix here. Who bugged Ms. Sato?"

`"Hey, Aloysius. I haven't figured that out yet. When I tried to trace the carrier signal, they cut me off, but not before I got a couple of coding letters in Cyrillic script."`

"Russians?"

`"Or Antifa, Anonymous, or even the NSA pretending to be Russians."`

"Why does she always have to be so vague? The digital drama queen," Ms. China complained, clearly trying to cheer herself up by starting another fight.

"Ladies, gents, and er, digital lifeforms," Sarge Bryan said. "We have to assume parties unknown have compromised all the intel we've gathered up to a few minutes ago."

"Thankfully, we don't know very much," Ellie said, still wondering about the word or word fragment "sabra."

"So being clueless is a virtue?" Ms. China taunted.

`"Annunciata, I can forge you a digital prescription if you're out of tranquilizers."`

Outside the SUV, an elderly stripper with a heavy-duty brassiere, which looked like it could haul a winter's worth of coal, stepped outside Mermaid's and lit a cigarette.

"Miss Aleph," Ellie said in a cautiously friendly tone, "why have you popped by?"

"Do you have to ask? I saw the video of the mob attacking you at the airport. It has eight million views, and the comments section is a sad indication of the mental state of humanity. I wanted to see if you were okay."

"Bullshit."

"Would you believe, as an Israeli, I'm concerned for the plight of Jewish people now that they're being, once again, vilified for shit they had nothing to do with?"

Sarge Bryan raised an eyebrow. "I might buy that, and it would be downright commendable... But you left the Free Israeli Forces and the *Magen* submarine. If you were interested in supporting the Jewish people, you'd have rejoined them, which you probably haven't."

"I can't seem to fool anyone today. Where's Lia Baumann when I need her to tune up my deception algorithms? All right, I'm here because I sense a major threat to my business model. I've built up a pretty profitable conglomerate of online ventures, and I'm not about to let my investments get messed up by some human-on-human war."

Before anyone could think how to respond, she added, "Oh, and Mr. Perdix, Agent Schwartz also bugged your PDA with a location tracker."

"That damned..." Mr. Perdix took his phone out, holding it like it was red hot.

"I fixed that too. You're welcome. Right now he's tracking the truck that passed us ten minutes ago."

"But he'll know we've been to the house on Emerson," the JASON scientist lamented.

"In that case, you'll need my help staying one step ahead of everyone who hates you. Just like old times."

The double doors of the topless bar burst open, nearly hitting the elderly dancer, who stepped backward into a puddle of melting snow. Two fat men with naked bellies hanging over their pants were fighting as best they could, given their sumo-wrestler girth and the slippery surface of the parking area. The battle had progressed beyond slapping and now featured windmill-style punching and hair-pulling.

"Gotta go," Sarge Bryan said and carefully rejoined the sparse traffic dashing along the highway.

Ellie looked up at news and social media videos playing on the video screen hanging from the roof of the SUV. It showed freeways in flames, a tanker truck overturned on an overpass creating a waterfall of burning gas, a crowd of protestors fleeing the dense black smoke. For all that new mayhem, Ellie couldn't get one old image out of her mind: Justice Meyers holding up her old, dog-eared copy of the Constitution. That had to be a clue, she thought. Unless... using the booklet was just a convenient place to hide the detonating flare.

"Miss Aleph, can you dig into Meyers's records? Is there anything at all that ties into 'sabra'?"

"How is that going to help?" Ms. China said shortly.

"So many agencies are involved in this case that they're even spying on each other." Ellie looked at Mr. Perdix, who was still red-faced. "All the obvious leads are being hotly traced. We've got to approach things from an uncommon perspective. And no one is better suited for that purpose than we are."

She looked first at Sarge Bryan's eyes glowing in the rearview mirror, more intensely now that the sky was quickly darkening, then at Ms. China, whose facial tattoos made her look like she was cast in bronze, and then at the wan but reasonably dangerous Mr. Perdix.

"Miss Aleph, download everything ever written about Meyers into a relational database," Mr. Perdix said into Ellie's handset. "Then search those letters, use anagrams, intuition jumps."

`"I'll do that, but in the meantime, someone top up my battery. This may take a while."`

Ellie's phone had reached 89% charge when Miss Aleph came back to them; her voice carried a note of digital cockiness.

"Besides having used her debit card to purchase hummus made by the Sabra Dipping Company of New York, Justice Meyers was born in Sabraton, West Virginia."

"No, she wasn't," Ellie said, checking the notes she was compiling. "All her biographies say she was born in Morgantown."

"All the biographies are wrong. Sabraton used to be an independent coal mining town that was later absorbed by Morgantown municipality. It's currently listed as a neighborhood, and there are institutions named after Sabraton, such as the junior and middle school Justice Meyers attended. Here's a photo of her and her class."

An old yellowed photograph appeared on the overhead display. Approximately fifty small, almost-kindergarten-aged children were seated in front of a neat brick façade that rose behind a trench dug in the earth and wobbly looking wooden stairs traversing the gap. Adults, presumably teachers, in jackets and ties and very prim white dresses stood solemnly behind the older pupils. One girl, perhaps seven or eight, stood to the left of the stairs, staring defiantly at the camera lens. Even if she had not been highlighted by Miss Aleph, Ellie might have guessed that was the future leader of the nation's highest court.

"So what?" Ms. China said crankily. "Even if she started off strangling stray cats and was a late-blooming mass killer, it doesn't help us. We need to know why she did it and who benefits."

Put that way, this potentially promising lead was unlikely to turn up any clues as to Meyers's motivations, Ellie thought.

"There's a better reason to visit the otherwise stunningly boring Sabraton. When I was trying to phone an archivist at the local library to find out if they had any records on the family, I got an 'all circuits busy' notice.

"The whole area has also been under maximum viral quarantine for the past week, total lockdown. Only Sabraton, not Morgantown."

Sarge Bryan was already entering the destination into his navigation console. Ellie peered into the front compartment. The interactive map said Sabraton was four hours away, assuming there were no roadblocks or other surprises. She sat back. It was going to be a while.

31

MARYLAND, WEST VIRGINIA

A jittery computer-generated male voice, definitely not Miss Aleph, spoke from the dashboard.

"This is Riot-Shield USA, we advise avoiding... Frostburg... local disturbances reported in area. Enjoy a free trial of our personal app, Riot-Shield Pedestrian. On your way home? Don't risk being jumped, mutilated, robbed, and killed by an angry mob. Trust Riot-Shield. Arrive alive!"

"Bryan¬" Miss Aleph said from Ellie's handset, "turn that dippy app off or I'll do it. Some people were protesting at Frostburg State University. The dean misgendered someone and the students burned all the cars in the parking lot. It's been over for hours."

"You do it, there's enough junk on the road to steer around without having to figure out strange dash buttons when I'm driving."

"This is Riot-Shield USA, we advise against picking up hitch—" A square icon on the dashboard touchscreen went dark.

Ellie looked out the tinted glass of the side window. She was in historic Maryland, and all she saw were bare trees and more highway.

"Sarge, this isn't your car?" Mr. Perdix asked. He had spent the last hour stripping down to his underpants, checking his clothes and belongings for more FBI bugs and tracking devices.

"Nope. And it's not Mr. Barracude's either. Our mutual friend in St. Albans, England, arranged it. Aleph, take over steering while we're on this straight stretch of road. I got to check something."

Sarge Bryan kept his hand on the wheel until he felt the AI had control, then took out the pistol he had taken off the Watergate Hotel attacker.

"Standard Glock 19… looks like no mods. Better check it anyway," he said mostly to himself and began disassembling the weapon in his lap.

"One gun?" Ms. China said sardonically. "And it's not even yours? With more weapons in private hands in America than the next thirty countries combined, that's all you bring?"

Sarge examined the bullets with his special vision, presumably to make sure they would fire correctly. "Sorry, I came to Washington with only a view to escort a couple of minors on a tour of the Capitol. Running firefights were not part of the bill, ma'am."

"Al, you're always trying to be manly," Ms. China berated her ex. "Why don't you have a fléchette shotgun or a hypersonic gauss cannon?"

"Right now I could use a taser," Mr. Perdix whispered, fingering a fat fountain pen clamped to his pocket protector. It was a brand Ellie did not recognize.

"Aleph, what's going on?" Ms. China slapped the video monitor closest to her as though that would assist her getting her way. "I can't make heads or tails of the newsfeeds."

"It's complicated. The media is insinuating anti-Leota forces are behind the attack at the Capitol, and that rogue elements in Casteel's administration learned that the Court ruling was going to go against the president, so they wiped out the Court. Democratic candidate Leota's campaign has only issued a statement appealing for calm. She is most likely still at her campaign headquarters in California.

"With the death of the Speaker of the House confirmed, the president pro tempore of the Senate has now advanced one step up in the line succession to the presidency, after VP Prowse. The senator has issued a call to reconvene the Senate and the House. Passing of emergency measures is stalled because no one trusts anyone. They are demanding votes be held in person, not online, because of the danger of digital forgery and deep-fake spoofing.

"Several helicopters were seen leaving the White House grounds, but no one knows who was inside. President Casteel may still be in the Presidential Emergency Operations Center."

Things were going all sevens and sixes. Ellie noticed Sarge Bryan yank the steering wheel away from AI control with rather more force than was required. He must be aghast at the growing crisis.

"Where the day has taken us, huh?" Ellie said, trying to lift the general mood. Then something practical wedged its way into her thoughts. "Wait a moment. There are substances that can make people do things." She looked pointedly at Ms. China. "You know, sap their will and leave them open to suggestion? Could Justice Meyers have been drugged?"

"Right, right," Mr. Perdix said, putting his pants back on. "Somnambutropics. They're new, experimental. Too dangerous and unreliable to use in the field; test subjects have suffered permanent schizophrenia."

"Is that right?" Ellie said as Ms. China gave an eyebrow shrug.

"No," the JASON man concluded. "I can't see that being a factor. Even assuming Meyers was kidnapped and other people planted the fuel-air bomb in the Capitol Building, from what I saw on the news footage, she acted with a great deal of deliberation.

"Meyers waited until she was told President Casteel was not coming into the chamber, then wasted no time setting off the device. As for some radical way of hijacking all of her neural impulses and controlling her like an automaton, I don't see it as a possibility—it's beyond our most advanced technology. But it's certainly worthwhile to research and develop in the future. I'd save a pile on robots."

Ellie had to agree with Mr. Perdix. Justice Meyers appeared to be in complete control of herself as she immolated herself and scores of lawyers and politicians, which made the act even more mysterious and terrifying.

Interstate 68 split off into two roads. Big green signs said *WEST MORGANTOWN* and *NORTH CHEAT LAKE.*

"Sabraton's just on the other side of the municipal airport," Sarge Bryan said.

He slowed down and took a narrow side road. It was quiet, and the bare trees were covered with frost and wet snow. The first structures Ellie saw were mobile houses. They were not upscale ones, which often looked much the same as regular dwellings. These structures were squat and rectangular, like oversized shipping containers, and many featured wooden stairs and low incomplete picket fences.

Sarge Bryan skidded to an abrupt stop on the frost-slick road.

"There's an infrared laser perimeter ahead. No sign of anyone guarding."

Perhaps this is part of the local lockdown of Sabraton, Ellie thought.

Mr. Perdix peered into the gloom with his unaided eyes. "I'll take your word for it, but JASON wrote the current manual for viral quarantine procedures, which has been adopted by all states except Hawaii, because they always think they know better. This isn't our procedure."

"We can avoid the sensors," Sarge said, opening the door and letting a waft of cold evening air wash over them. "But only on foot."

"Where are we going?" Ms. China griped. "We drove all this way just because the dumb library hasn't paid their internet bill?"

"This is where it all began," Ellie said, whispering now that they were walking in the dark, following Sarge Bryan. "Justice Meyers's incredible journey from an impoverished coal mining town to the highest court in the land. I can't help thinking it was no accident, her having her old school booklet with her during her final moments. She could have hidden the flare device in anything."

"More to the point, Eleanor, most residents here are on public Medicaid. They've been chip implanted with government RFID tags during mandatory inoculations—that gives them access to public facilities and makes

sure all the children in public school have been
vaccinated."

"So?"

"Miss Aleph is right," Mr. Perdix said. "I tried to check. All the RFID implants tagged for this area are offline in the CDC database. Normally drones would circle a quarantined area to identify people trying to escape and possibly spread a pathogen."

Sarge Bryan stared at a few of the mobile houses.

"No one here." He looked on the ground. "Tire tracks, few days old. Humvees and other paramilitary vehicles."

Out from under the rusty fender of a pickup truck popped a feisty-looking raccoon. It had grown fat from eating garbage and leftovers and barely glanced at them before waddling away into the underbrush.

"Well," Sarge said, a bit more loudly as he inched slowly toward a metal-sided shed beside the road, "seems there's nothing to see here… nothing… at all—"

With a quick movement, he flung open a low hatch in the shed wall and pulled out a silently squirming figure. It was a child, probably a girl, crusted with what looked like days of dirt. Sarge pulled her up on to the tips of her dilapidated shoes, and a plastic bag of junk food fell from one of her shivering hands. Before it landed, a pointed stick came out of the dark shed, aimed right for Sarge's head.

"Die, you snatcher fucker!" a hoarse high-pitched voice whispered, barely audible.

Sarge Bryan might have been skewered but for Ms. China pushing him out of the way. The homemade spear landed on the shoulder of his padded jacket.

"Damn!"

A flurry of arm waving that was more confusing than intimidating ensued, and Mr. Perdix grabbed the second figure out from the overhanging perch of the shed where the older boy had been hiding.

"Hold it. We're the good guys." Mr. Perdix shrieked and drew back. "He bit me."

Ms. China kicked up her leg to stop the boy from ducking and running out through the low entrance. He stabbed her calf with a short knife. Ms. China laughed—it was her prosthetic leg—then flicked her claws out in front of his face.

"We're not all that good, kid, so settle down."

Staring at her sharpened metallic fingernails, the boy stopped stabbing, but his eyes looked left and right, searching for a way to make a break for it.

"And," Ms. China said, grabbing his sleeve and pushing him to the outside wall near a stack of firewood, "any damage to my leg is coming out of your allowance."

She extracted the folding knife from her bionic leg and pocketed it.

"Okay, now that we're acquainted," Sarge Bryan said evenly, putting the girl back down on the ground, "how about you tell me your names and where your parents are. What's goin' on here, little lady?"

She was staring at his albino face and seemed mesmerized by his gold glowing eyes. Her mouth worked silently, almost painfully, and she looked as though she had every intention of replying. Then three figures materialized behind them, and Ellie heard automatic rifles being cocked.

A hard, sneering voice spoke from the shadows, "More than you'll ever know, Army Sergeant Shetani Zeru Bryan."

32

SABRATON, WEST VIRGINIA

Whoa, gents," Sarge said cautiously as he raised his hands in a nonthreatening manner. The little girl he had plucked out of the dark shed stopped struggling and hid behind his leg. The boy, minus his makeshift spear, had retreated to the back of the rickety structure. "We're all on the same—"

"Like fuckshit we are," the man behind them said. A booted foot kicked Sarge Bryan in the back, sending him thumping down onto the frost-hardened ground. "We know all about your special appointment by the lame-ander in chief."

The leg that kicked out was covered by a shimmering material. Ellie had seen this before on an Israeli Special Forces officer; it was an active camouflage outfit. Ms. China was keeping her hands politely at her sides but started edging around to the side of the three visible men. A fourth materialized behind her and struck her in the neck with the butt of an assault rifle; she stumbled and fell beside Sarge Bryan.

"You're obviously well-informed," Mr. Perdix said with his hands raised but seeming not to grasp the hostility of the situation that had ensnared them. "So if you just check my credentials from JA—"

Taser darts penetrated Mr. Perdix's white shirt front. He had time to say "oh," then fell in convulsions as the device gave off a sinister crackling sound.

Ellie looked around for a clear space to run to or a stick to fight with if her normally very capable companions could somehow get the upper hand. But with an unknown number of enemies concealed by high-tech invisibility gear, she realized if she moved she could run right into them.

"Thanks for rooting out these two wood rats," the first man's voice said. "We just put out passive sensors to get them, and you dumb shits walked in."

"Sir," Sarge said, not rising from his prone position, "you seem to know who we are, and your voice is kind of familiar."

"Don't worry, you won't be listening to it for long." Their captor spoke to another member of their heavily armed team as he said, "Is it a wash? Did you confirm that?"

The way he said that didn't sound good.

"Confirmed. It's a wash. Should we put these in with the others?"

"Negative, the place is sealed." The first man drew his pistol and leaned forward over Sarge Bryan. "At least you get to die on American soil, Sergeant, and you've got to be tired of living as a pale fucken freak."

Blam!

Whether or not Sarge Bryan was or was not weary of living as an African albino was still in question as a large-caliber bullet tore into their captor's ass and exited near his collarbone. Puffy pink chunks of him blew all over the place, and the man's body launched forward onto his intended victim.

Ms. China took advantage of the distraction to pull the night-vision visor off of the nearest man and replace it with two of her three-inch fingernails. These plunged deeply into the fellow's eye sockets. Mr. Perdix's shaking hands held up what looked like a very fat fountain pen, and it spat fire at the man who had tasered him. No sound came from the man's melting head, just a horrible acidic, burning smell.

The last visible man raised his rifle and was immediately struck in the back by a metal box about two feet square. As he fell, the box rolled away. Ellie recognized it as an air-conditioning unit that had been ripped out from the side of one of the mobile homes. The figure of the person who had thrown it was unmistakable even in the dim light and falling wet snow.

"Tata!"

"Stay down, all of you," the Russian cyborg lady bellowed. She then went into a stream of Russian. "*Bagration, prodolzhay strelyat' v tebya, durak!*"

From far up the road, more shots rang out. Rounds passing very close above Ellie made a zip-twang whine, which she was unfortunately familiar with. Many of the rounds hit targets, and figures dropped, materialized, and started crawling. Sarge Bryan had heaved the corpse of the first casualty off himself and began untangling the man's slung weapon with a clear view of getting in the fight.

"Sarge, I think we should give the lady some space," Ellie said, seeing the determined look on Tata's face. Ellie had witnessed her chew off the nose, eyes, and jaw of a man in the Paris Catacombs and literally spit out his molars. It was not a good idea to get in her way when she was cheesed off.

Tata ducked down and grabbed a double-bladed axe lying by a pile of firewood. The pupils of her cyborg eyes were flared open wide, and she was somehow able to pick out the camouflaged figures lurking among the trees. Tata started chopping but went at it too vigorously. Her axe handle snapped, leaving the head embedded in one man's helmet. The nearly seven-foot-tall woman then uprooted a sapling, stripped it of branches, and used it to beat the life out of the two remaining wounded assailants.

"Al," Ms. China said, her hand dripping with gore, "cover up your flaming mess, there are children about."

Ellie took a moldering carpet from inside the children's hiding place and gingerly draped it over the corpse made by Mr. Perdix's incendiary device.

Taking advantage of the distraction, the boy had grabbed the girl and tried to make a break for it into the woods. Ellie was closest, and she grabbed the leather belt hanging loosely around his skinny waist.

"Hang on, hang on. You don't know what traps are out there. We're the good guys."

Ms. China looked down at him with her six pupils. Sarge Bryan wiped specks of flesh from his alabaster pale face and got to his feet. Tata came stomping up wearing a down jacket spattered with blood and carried a tree trunk over her shoulder, looking like a cavewoman who had just clubbed a mastodon to death.

"Well," Ellie qualified her statement, "we're the *less* bad guys."

"Bagration, you can come out now, that's all of them," Tata yelled up the street.

A few moments later, a fussy-looking chubby fellow with a firearm that was half rifle and half telescope came waddling past the silent mobile homes. Tata bounded forward and took the weapon, cradling it in her big arms.

"Give me. I told you: rest it on your arm, not the brick wall. This is mint-condition Spetsnaz Dragunov. Any scratches, you pay to fix."

Tata seemed much cheerier than usual as she helped Sarge Bryan to his feet.

"That was a near thing, damn near," Sarge said, kicking over the corpse of the leader of the attackers. "Our own guys too. I think I met this guy at Fort Bragg. He was Delta Force and then went into private contracting work."

After the brutal but brief fight, the silence of the surrounding woods left Ellie with an annoying ringing in her ears. "What was it he said? 'Wind up' or something?"

"That's what you say when an operation's gone sour and you clear out," Sarge Bryan said.

"What's gone sour? And what happened to all the people in Sabraton?" Ellie looked down at the boy, who she still had hold of. "Do you know where the adults and everyone went to?"

He looked left and right, revealing his hollow cheeks were evenly caked with dirt, and he slowly nodded. Ellie noticed a lesion on the boy's lip; the girl also had a smaller one on her nose that was red and running. She thought it was just the chill at first. It was odd the two children didn't speak at all.

"What's that on his mouth?" she asked.

Mr. Perdix bent down to have a look. Ms. China shoved him aside. "You're terrible with kids."

She wiped the last bloodstains off her hands, smiled, and cast her metallic tattooed features in as pleasant an expression as she could. "Would you open up for me, young master?"

Perhaps equally frightened by her appearance and pacified by the scientist's polite manner, he did as asked. With a penlight from Sarge Bryan's keychain, she examined inside. Ellie could see there were more nodules.

"Does that hurt when you eat?"

The boy shook his head.

"Thanks. You go over with the big Sasquatch lady and point if you want a drink of water."

Ms. China walked over to where Sarge Bryan and Mr. Perdix were rolling the enemy leader's body into the shallow ditch beside the road.

"Shame he's dead. I'd like to ask him a few things," she said, checking her fingernails. "Even without doing a chemical analysis, I'm pretty sure they tried using gas to flush these kids out. There is a type of CS gas that leaves lesions on the mucosa tissues. Maybe there were more people without RFID trackers, and these were the last two."

"That's nasty. I can't believe this guy was from the same Army."

"But where are the ones they caught?" Ellie said. "And everyone else?"

She went over to the children. They still looked like they would run if given a chance but were a little more calm.

"Don't be afraid. No one's going to hurt you. Do you know? Just show us if you know."

The boy and girl looked at each other. Tata leaned down and put a dinner-plate-sized hand on the girl's head and smoothed her dirty hair, dark zirconium teeth flashing in the light of the single streetlamp as the cyborg also attempted a reassuring smile. The boy made a motion with his hand.

"Looks like he wants to write," Tata said.

Ellie produced a pad and smaller-sized Sailor fountain pen. The boy drew two lumps which probably represented hills then between them he put an "x" and the letters "m-i-n-e."

33

SABRATON, WEST VIRGINIA

Ellie looked at the silent boy's drawing, thanked him, and went back to the others.

"This entire region is honeycombed by old underground mines," Mr. Perdix said.

"Could they have taken everyone away and put them inside one?"

Sarge scanned the tree line, probably making adjustments to his ocular irises, looking for any more incoming camouflaged fighters. "They've got top-level military technology. Somehow they arranged a full lockdown quarantine of the whole neighborhood. They could have used that as cover to drive in with a few buses and told the townspeople they were driving them away to get booster shots and antibody tests."

"Al, are you stupid?" Ms. China said, tearing the PDA out of Mr. Perdix's hands. "If you connect to any wireless network, Schwartz will be onto us. By now he knows you've slipped his electronic leash."

He retrieved his device and put it away. "All right, we'll use the Russians' equipment, if they'll let us."

Ellie looked over at the doughy Russian man. He was standing next to Tata and looking decidedly uncomfortable. "How did you find us?"

"I-I have diplomatic immunity," Bagration said, noticing their stares.

"We're not going to report you for giving these guys fifty-cal enemas," Sarge Bryan said. "We're just rightly curious, is all."

They walked up the road to the black van the Russians had arrived in. With one window broken and taped over, it looked like a wreck. However, under the tape, Ellie noticed thick laminate glass. Tata was about to let them inside when Bagration hissed something at her.

"Classified, my ass," Ms. China said, having understood the ambassador. "Everyone knows about these spy mobiles. You Russians have been using them since the 1960s."

As Mr. Perdix rummaged through the cluttered interior to find what they needed, Sarge Bryan asked, "So, Miss Tata, how did you see those guys when I couldn't?"

"Is trade secret," Tata smiled down coyly at the albino man. "But I tell anyway. Your new SOCCOM camouflage suits put out a particular gamma dispersion. As soon as the hostiles stepped out from their ambush position, I noticed them."

"Lucky you did," Ellie said pointedly, not wanting to look too closely at a gift horse but a little annoyed that it was likely the Russians who had bugged her phone, which allowed them to track her to Sabraton.

"Shalom, Tata," Miss Aleph said from the phone peeking out of Ellie's pocket. "You're looking quite… massive."

"Ah, so you still have the annoying Israeli AI. Is like old times in Paris sewer system."

Hunched together over a small glowing screen, Ambassador Bagration and Mr. Perdix came up with some ideas.

"Closest candidates for underground dungeons are the Monongalia County Coal Company surface and underground mines," Mr. Perdix said doubtfully.

"There are too many," Bagration said bluntly. "How can we check them all? And how does the boy know anything? The gas might have harmed his wits."

"Don't make me embarrassed, Mr. Ambassador," Tata said. "If you want to go back to embassy, is fine with us. Call an Uber."

"The local children would be familiar with the area, wouldn't they?" Ellie said, having an idea. "But only for a certain distance, as far as you could travel by foot in an afternoon."

"Good thinking, Ms. Sato," Sarge Bryan said, earning Ellie a rather severe stare from Tata. "Eliminate anything over five kilometers away, what's left?"

There were three entries on the map that had English names overlain with Cyrillic characters.

"We got Hartman, West Run, and Knocking Run." They showed the map to the young pair. Reluctantly, they shrugged and shook their heads.

"Anna," Ellie whispered, "they'll be able to speak again, won't they?"

"Probably. Depends on the extent of damage to their vocal cords."

"Can we tell which mine was in use recently but is not in current operations?" Tata asked, putting her head closer to Sarge Bryan's than she really needed to see the screen.

They settled on Knocking Run because West Run was in daily operations, and Hartman was too close to the municipal airport. Knocking Run was also a large, purely underground operation with miles of shafts.

"Ms. Sato, you go in your truck. Sergeant Bryan and I need to discuss tactical matters," Tata said.

Mr. Perdix took the wheel of Sarge's SUV, and they followed the Russian spy van out of Sabraton.

The entrance to the mine was only two kilometers away, but the drive seemed longer in the dark. Wet snow kept falling, and trees pressed in on both sides of the narrow road so that Ellie could only see a few feet on either side of the vehicle. As they got close, they switched off all their illumination.

Mr. Perdix put on a complicated-looking Russian night-vision monocle. In the back seat, the Sabraton girl kept trying to hold Ms. China's hand. She gently put the girl's small hands back in her own lap, away from her envenomed talons.

When they came to the end of the bumpy access road, Tata and Sarge Bryan got out and peered over a ridge down toward the mine entrance. They signaled it was clear to advance. Tata selected an extension to her pike weapon and quietly snapped the chain off the gate. They walked up the rutted, unpaved road.

"That pile o' rocks," Sarge Bryan said, pointing. "The dirt on and around it is fresh. It's new."

"What's that smell?" Ellie asked, getting a whiff of something acrid on the cold night air.

"Gas," Ms. China said hurriedly. "Find a way in or they're all dead."

34

NEAR SABRATON

"No!" Tata hissed as Sarge Bryan was about to go charging ahead. The Russian cyborg forcefully held him back, nearly lifting him off his feet. "Please use caution. If was my operation, I would put by the entrance tricky traps."

And it did have those. Stealth-coated trip wires attached to explosives were strung all over the place. If anyone tried to access the main entrance to the Knocking Run mine, these would have brought half the hill down on their heads.

"No time to defuse them," Mr. Perdix said. "We have to find a faster way in."

Ellie noticed Bagration struggling to put rotors on a surveillance drone.

"Let me help," Ellie said. "I'm pretty good with IKEA furniture."

They got one drone airborne and synced its camera to Tata's and Sarge's ocular implants.

"Look for a recently cut trail," Mr. Perdix said. "Mining plans of operations require air and escape shafts to be drilled and maintained."

"But wouldn't they have sealed them as well, if they were planning to…" It was too terrible for Ellie to say. *Pack in a whole community and gas them.*

"Not if they needed proof of life," Mr. Perdix said. "The whole thing's beginning to…"

"Stop speculating and start helping," Ms. China hissed, her breath fogging in the cold.

"We've got the trail," Sarge Bryan said, looking at the feed from the miniature copter. "It's to the side there."

After hopping over a low fence and pushing through a line of underbrush, they climbed up on a low hill where the drone was hovering, its small blue light blinking against the night sky. Ellie did not want to leave the children by themselves, so the others reluctantly agreed they could come as long as they stayed well back.

At the end of the footpath, they found a hatch covered by a tarp, made of shiny new steel. The three men, and mostly Tata, inserted the sharp end of her pike and prized under the dirt and gravel.

"It's not welded to anything. There's nothing to attach it to. Keep pulling," Mr. Perdix said, offering more moral encouragement than levering power.

With a huge scraping sound and a blast of putrid air, the hatch slid away. Ellie pushed the two Sabraton children back. Inside, they might find only dead bodies.

Sarge tried to enter, but the gas seemed to be rising and overwhelmed him. Tata stuck a respirator filter directly into her windpipe, then stuck her head inside and sniffed the air.

"Is okay, my filters can handle."

Waiting above was an experience of gnawing agony for all of them. Even Ms. China looked concerned, or perhaps with her it was professional curiosity. Ellie kept an eye on the Sabraton children, but they did not try to wander off. They merely stared at the irregular hole in the gravel-strewn hillside, which was lit only by a dim yellow light coming from within the mine.

Slowly, one by one, many having to be attached to a hastily improvised cable and harness, the people of Sabraton came to the surface. The first ones who crawled out merely rolled onto their sides and gulped for fresh air. Those were the ones who were in good enough shape to climb.

"The asphyxiation procedure was just started," Mr. Perdix concluded after surveying the scene. "It looks as though they abandoned the work when they lost contact with the people we fought with."

The drone zoomed down to hover near Bagration's head. Tata's voice came from it.

"Hey, Ambassador! There may be more traps around where you are. Don't let people we just rescued go wandering. I'm watching you."

Bagration looked up with resignation, and along with the rest of them, tried to keep order among the mass of shivering and coughing people.

"Damn," was all Sarge Bryan said more than once as he watched the feed from Tata's ocular implants. "Mr. Perdix, use your DHS credentials, tell Morganville first responders to bring all the oxygen units they have." He lowered his voice and added, "And body bags. Not everyone made it."

"I'll do it," Miss Aleph said helpfully.

Ellie could tell Sarge Bryan was on the edge of despondency. This very cruel act had been committed by Americans against their own people, young and old alike.

"We've managed to rescue most of them," Ellie said. "I'm sure we'll track down the culprits. I just have a feeling things will..."

"Excuse me, fleshies, some breaking news. The president pro tempore of the Senate was meeting with the House minority leader, attempting to get the government functioning. They've both been killed. So have the governors of Washington and Oregon. They were supposed to be meeting with possible President-Elect Leota. Her location is unknown."

35

NEAR EL SASABE, MEXICO

ABDELKADER

In front of Abdelkader, across the sandstorm-swept hardpack, lay the soft underbelly of America: the southern border. He had worked out in detail dozens of routes and scores of decoy scenarios, merely to discard them as soon as they were completed. One day he decided to trust their allies in Arizona, then the next he cut them out of the operation completely.

In the end, that night of windstorms with sand blasting against his goggles with such force he feared for the integrity of the silicone face he was wearing, they merely marched up to the upright steel posts of the bollard wall and carefully pushed their cargo through. A ten-by-eight-foot section had been sawn through and then stuck back in place. Anyone who had passed by had seen only an intact border fence.

As he ducked through into US territory, one of his best men, Sadikul, brushed against the jagged metal. A flash like a spark plug accompanied by a dull crack that was nearly lost in the wind made everyone jump.

Abdelkader motioned for them to keep moving. It was just a static discharge.

The sandstorm was generating gigajoules of electricity, its whirling vortexes playing havoc with sensors and preventing drones from flying. They were unlikely to run into ICE or Border Patrol agents tonight. Tucson and cities in California were reporting mass rioting and looting. Border service officers would be recalled to deal with the civil unrest. All told, it was a wonderful night.

"Put the bars back," Abdelkader shouted to the last men through, one of which was their scientist.

"This wind," complained Dr. Baldur, who disliked manual labor at the best of times, "it's blowing dirt and gumming up the glue at the end. It will not… stay." The poor man fell over, and the metal bar clanged to onto the hard-packed earth.

"Sadikul, help him," Abdelkader ordered his normally zealous Filipino scout. Ever since Guatemala, he seemed to be walking a half step more slowly. Perhaps he had a diarrhea bug.

Abdelkader tromped through the loose sand blowing above the dark terrain. His other men were searching for the dune buggies that were supposed to be hidden nearby.

Suddenly strobe lights flashed all around them.

"Hold it right there, you fuckin' beaner smugglers!" an amplified voice shouted out from the dark.

Gas and diesel engines revved, overcoming the rushing sound of the storm. Even as Abdelkader reached for his gun, he knew they were surrounded and trapped. Had their American partners turned on them? There was no time to think. He waved at his people not to shoot.

The disorienting strobes were shut off, and in their place, intense searchlight beams zigzagged amongst them. Abdelkader bit down hard in anger, tasting his own blood.

One of his men was hit by a gust of wind, which raised his poncho, revealing his rifle cocked and ready to fire. A dozen muzzles flashed and shot both his legs out from under him.

"Do that again," the voice yelled over the truck-mounted loudspeakers, "and we'll smoke all your asses. You're prisoners of the Arizona Border Recon and the Tohono Nation Police, whose land y'all are invadin'."

The member of Abdelkader's group who was shot by the militiamen did not die. The Americans and a pair of uniformed Native police did their best to tourniquet his leg wounds and then put him into one of their trucks. Abdelkader would have finished him off himself for not doing as he had been told.

As the Americans puzzled over what sort of border crossers they had caught, he looked over their captors.

"Man!" one of the rednecks said after he relieved them of their weapons. "They got some fancy shit. Looks like dope smuggling still pays a peck."

The militia leader was a fat, red-faced man wearing a bandanna with a star design, desert warfare goggles, and a military-style helmet. With surreptitious sign language, Abdelkader told Sadikul to speak. His Spanish was the best, and it served their purposes not to be identified as non-Mexicans.

"I am in charge," Sadikul said. "We are refugees claiming asylum. Harming us is against international law."

"Try me again, you scum buckets," the militia man interrupted. "Y'all are fucked now, ain'tcha? Er… *totalmente jodido.*"

The white man's Spanish was limited, so one of the Native police took over questioning. Sadikul repeated the second cover story they had rehearsed. He told their captors that they were in fact a recon party for a major cartel who had been sent ahead to make sure the way was safe for a large load of ultra-refined drugs.

"Milliones de dosis, millones millones."

Sadikul also told them they were forced to work for the cartels as the bosses had their families hostage. As a token, he could offer them money and then help set a trap for the very large shipment exchange, which would be swapping meth and coke for cybercoin and large pallets of precious metals.

Abdelkader hoped the dual appeal to their egos and greed would cause the militia and Native police to delay calling in ICE or the Border Patrol. Even if they did call in the incident, federal authorities were unlikely to arrive for hours. As he kneeled beside one of the militia vehicles, his mind worked furiously, considering the best way to overcome this American filth.

The Native cop translated for the red-faced Arizona Border Recon man.

"Sure," the American pig said, scratching under his stars-and-stripes bandanna. "That's what every peckerhead's said since the Alamo."

Then the swine noticed their cargo. Abdelkader's body stiffened as the man waddled in his cowboy boots, stepping over to their precious crate. It was encrusted with sand and could have been part of the garbage that was blown against the border fence. "What's up with this here box?"

Abdelkader thought quickly. They would not be able to open or activate the device, but if they shot at it or used explosives… There were fewer of the militia and the Native police than he had first thought.

Just then, Sadikul fell over sideways. He had to be shamming to give them a chance to escape.

"You bastards," Abdelkader yelled in English, hoping the wind would obscure his accent, which was not correct for a Mexican. "You killed him. You dirty racists! If he dies, I will see you all charged with capital murder!"

About half of the twelve militia abandoned their positions and came to see what was going on. They became distracted. Yet, all the Pangean weapons had been taken away and were locked in a militia van. Sadikul's shamming was not enough to give them a decisive advantage.

Then all thoughts of resisting vanished from Abdelkader's mind. Headlamps from the long line of Humvees flickered through the blowing sand and headed straight toward them. Moments later, Abdelkader could see a flag with a coyote insignia and *ARIZONA GUARDIANS OF LIBERTY* written underneath.

The red-faced Arizona Border Recon man was wary at first, then welcoming as he greeted the incoming larger force.

"Hey, Sikawski, glad you could make it," he yelled as the wind ebbed and flowed. The storm seemed to be dying down. "Just remember who caught these smugglers, 'specially if there's a reward on."

A thinner, muscular man in black fatigues came out of the lead Humvee. He had an orange-red beard and wore a bandanna with shark's teeth on a black background.

"Hiya, Duncan," he said, giving the other a manly shoulder hug. "Did you call this in yet?"

Duncan shook his head. "Naw, didn't have time. Wanted to make sure we got all of 'em. One dummy got hisself wounded, and I don't know what's up with this one, dehydration or—"

Duncan's speculations were cut short as a bullet blasted through his jaw and up into his brain. It was fired by Sikawski's pistol.

More disciplined bursts of gunfire rang out. The Arizona militiamen and the Native policemen fell over dead at their posts or in a heap around Sadikul.

"Quick shoot them again. Make sure no one gets a text off," Sikawski shouted to his people as he walked over and helped Abdelkader to his feet, then cut the zip tie securing his hands. Abdelkader was equal parts relieved his local allies had come and also embarrassed at needing to be rescued.

"Welcome. From here on out, Antifa's got your back," Sikawski said, looking at the crate. "You never did tell us what you got in there."

Abdelkader and his people were unarmed; there were at least twenty-five armed Antifa on flatbeds and in militarized SUVs. A major player had brought them together, but the former ISIS leader was far from trusting his brand-new US allies.

"Something only we know what to do with," Abdelkader answered shortly.

"Uh-huh," Sikawski said thoughtfully, folding his Spyderco knife. "It wouldn't be a baby nuke you maybe stole from the Hebe Zionists during the shitstorm of the 96-Hour War, would it?"

"No."

"Too bad."

"Don't say that, my friend. This is much better."

"Will it fuck up this racist prison colony, the Fascist States of Nazi America?" Sikawski asked as he pulled down his mask to reveal the rest of his scraggy beard and a set of protruding yellow teeth.

"Yes," Abdelkader said, rubbing the marks on his wrists. The windswept area of the short, one-sided battle was lit by off-road floodlights. They glared down from the circle of vehicles as the Antifa soldiers loaded the bodies of the dead militiamen like so much highway trash. "It most certainly will wonderfully fuck up the Fascist States of Nazi America."

"Then we're good. Let's roll!"

36

ELLIE

Ellie kept a respirator pressed to her face and looked down the escape shaft into the mine. Through cloying swirls of dust, she saw the cyborg lady Tata, who yelled up at her, "There are more people in a shaft, which has been sealed. Quite a few more."

Sarge Bryan came up next to Ellie.

"They'll need a bomb squad and heavy equipment to open the main entrance," Tata finished.

"Aw, damn." Sarge Bryan coughed and leaned away from the toxic fumes coming out of the escape shaft. "How many people did they snatch?"

The rescued who had squeezed through the escape shaft were crammed shoulder to shoulder, sitting or standing, filling the narrow access path that led down the side of the hill. Body bags were stacked, some sliding off one another.

"They need more medical attention than we can give," Mr. Perdix reported as he put a tinfoil blanket around the shivering shoulders of a surviving hostage.

"Call Agent Schwartz," Ellie suggested. "Leave your phone with these people. He'll certainly prioritize helping the townspeople over capturing us."

No one could think of a better plan, so Mr. Perdix did that.

"This is nuts," Sarge Bryan said, still in a state of disbelief. "Why would… How could anyone think they'd get away with this?"

"Maybe this is part of their strategy to make sure they can get away with anything," Ms. China said cryptically. "From what little I understand of American politics, Justice Meyers was the deciding vote as to who would become president and who would run Congress. One faction kidnapped a hundred or more people from her hometown, including generations of people she grew up with. I'd call that some choice leverage."

In the matters pertaining to the sneaky and despicable, Ms. China was not to be contradicted.

"Were Justice Meyers's immediate family in Sabraton?"

"That's the first thing we checked," Mr. Perdix said officiously as he searched for any equipment lying on the ground they needed to take back to their SUV and the Russian spy van. "All members of the Court were advised to take security precautions, as unrest was expected no matter what they decided. Meyers's relatives were taken away and are safe on a boat off the coast of Spain."

"Are you sure, Al?" Ms. China said in a taunting voice.

Tata came out of the escape shaft, pulling two children and one old grandfatherly man out behind her.

"Let's go," Sarge Bryan said. "FBI and FEMA and who knows who'll be here soon. They can defuse the booby traps and open the main entrance."

"Sergeant Bryan, you will ride with me?" Tata said rather coquettishly for someone wearing body armor caked in coal dust.

"I'll take my car, thanks. Ellie and I have to be in touch with people over in Europe. Thanks, by the way. If you'd hadn't showed up when you did…"

They climbed down the hill in silence and returned to their vehicles. The Russians got in their spy van and drove ahead. Mr. Perdix, Ms. China, Ellie, and Sarge Bryan got in the SUV.

"How did Agent Schwartz sound?" Ellie asked the harried-looking JASON scientist.

"As though he were set upon by every fiend from Hades," he replied. He squirmed in his seat to look at the night sky through the sunroof, searching for incoming helicopters. "With the most recent assassinations, that's another chunk of our government gone. Soon there'll be no one but Casteel and Leota, if she's still alive."

Ellie retrieved her handset. "Miss Aleph, is this all right to use?"

"Yes, Eleanor, and I've got you double air miles when you call overseas. Your mobile network plan sucked."

"Can you call—"

"Mr. Oliphant. Doing it now… It's six a.m. there, not a great time to be asking favors."

Fortunately, Melanie Françoise, who never seemed to sleep, was up and had been following events in America.

"We tried phoning you at the Watergate, but they said everyone had left the penthouse after some sort of attack. Did you find Annunciata?"

"Yes, she did," Ms. China said into the speakerphone.

"Anna! You're…" Melanie's already high voice climbed another octave. "You're just a bad girl. That's all I have to say."

Miss Aleph broke in and told them the Meyers children and grandchildren were on the *Octopus*. The huge yacht had dropped its transponder signal and was last recorded logged into the maritime grid near Majorca Island in the Mediterranean Sea.

"I could hack the Spanish Coast Guard and send a distress call, but there's no telling how quickly they would respond."

Ellie had an idea. She had been blackmailed and bribed in the past by the Foreign Office, so they owed her a favor. "Melanie, can you get hold of Tenny Sewart in the Foreign Office? He can make an urgent request of the Spaniards."

While they waited for a reply, Ellie took an inventory of new cuts and bruises and also damage to the nice clothes Janice Jones had loaned her. Not having any other destination, Sarge Bryan took a roundabout route back to

Washington and the Watergate Hotel. They were nearly at the West Virginia border when the masculine robotic Riot-Shield voice piped up again through the dashboard speakers.

"Recommend evasive action, unknown blockade obstruction... two miles ahead."

"What now?" Ms. China said. "I thought that was turned off."

"Stupid thing reboots every time I turn the engine on."

Miss Aleph squelched the car's mechBrain again. After scanning social media posts, the AI reported two opposing armed groups had formed up on either side of the state lines.

"The West Virginia side is called 2-A Holler Crew and the Virginia group is called the De-escalation Resistance Army. There have been a few scuffles but no gunfire—yet. State Police presence minimal, meaning they've been defunded and are not answering 911 calls. As much as I hate agreeing with Retarded-Shield, I suggest we take an alternate route."

While Sarge Bryan selected a detour, Ellie tried to understand the red Republican state versus blue Democrat state political schism. Mr. Perdix explained it, but she still had questions.

"So..." Ellie said hesitantly. She barely had a grasp on UK politics, and this was an entirely different milieu. "Not only are the two fighting factions backing different presidential candidates, but they're basically opposed to being on the same planet."

Their SUV sloshed through a few potholes on a side road that was parallel to the interstate.

"It's much more complex," Mr. Perdix said haughtily. "It would take many hours for you to understand."

"Cram it, Aloysius," Ms. China said. "Are there any known seditious organizations such as an Antifa supercell that you know of who is capable of arranging what we just saw at Sabraton?"

"No."

"That's not so good," Ms. China said, biting her lip.

"Why not?" Ellis asked and immediately felt naïve.

"Because that means one of the top-level federal players is involved, the worst elements of the Deep Sate. Someone tried to rig the Court decision, and in doing so, wasn't above mass murdering a few hundred Americans outright."

Melanie rang back from the UK. A grumpy-looking Ran Oliphant was on the video call as well.

"I should have called Scotland Yard instead of sending you over there," Ran said, pulling his bathrobe tighter around him so that none of his oddly cinnamon-colored chest hair poked out. "How do you manage to end up…"

"We have great news," Melanie chirped. "Sir Tenny immediately called the US ambassador to the UK, and she categorically denied needing any help whatsoever. Which means they're in a genuine flap. Sir Tenny urgently got hold of the Spanish authorities."

"What is the name of the search-and-rescue boat they dispatched?"

"Hi, Miss Aleph. Did you get the quantum thumb drive we sent you for Chanukah?"

"I did, thank you," she said pleasantly. Ellie knew that the AI was never nice to people unless she wanted something. "It's just the thing to use in my exploration robot. Is there any way you could squeeze my remote presence in on the next Eurolincx shuttle to Mars?"

"Real scientists only, I'm afraid," Ran said curtly.

"What did you say the Spanish Coast Guard ship's name was?" Ellie cut across them before the rich people started having a feud.

"Oh, right, the *Santa Clara*."

"Got it. I'll piggyback myself into their system on the next message they receive from the Coast Guard command center."

Sarge Bryan pulled over near a gas station just in time to stare at a blank screen above the front seats for a minute.

Suddenly, they were flying across very blue waves. "This is telemetry from a fast drone dispatched by the *Santa Clara*. The Spanish have located the *Octopus*."

Making small course corrections like a cruise missile, the robotic flyer homed in on its target. An inverted V appeared on the horizon. The drone started to circle.

"Why isn't it going straight?" Ellie asked, anxious yet terrified of what they would find.

"The *Octopus* has been drifting with no transponder signal," Ran said, leaning into the inset picture next to Melanie while viewing the same scene on their much bigger monitors. "They're plotting its drift course and searching for any wreckage or remains of a smaller boat or debris that may have struck it."

The drone hovered over clusters of seaweed and plastic trash, then its camera zoomed in on a small whitish blob.

"Aw, crap," Sarge Bryan said. "It's a body."

37

WEST VIRGINIA

Live feed from the Coast Guard drone showed the dead body bobbing in startlingly blue waters of the Mediterranean Sea. The deceased person was floating naked and had longish blond hair, which looked green in the water and had spread all around the head like a halo. To Ellie, the body seemed too small to be that of an adult. After dropping a beacon, the Spanish drone sped toward the massive *Octopus* yacht.

"It's sinking," Ellie said, alarmed. How many people were on it? The villains were trying to cover up their crime.

"It's not sinking that rapidly," Ran Oliphant said from the UK as he watched the same footage. "I've been on that ship. Its latest refit included a bespoke double hull design. They didn't put enough holes in her to properly do the job."

The drone hovered close to the stern of the *Octopus,* which was poking up and listing to one side. Near the waterline, a propeller was visible. The flying robot started squawking in Spanish and making klaxon noises.

"Is anyone still on it?" Ellie asked.

"It has space for twenty-six passengers and twice that number of crew," Ran said. "I don't see... there!"

A haggard figure, man or woman, it was impossible to tell, jerked their arm over the railing and waved a towel. Before they could get a good look, the figure sank back down and rolled into a shadow cast by an upper deck. The feed cut out.

"I'll keep recording, but we've seen enough."

Have we? thought Ellie. What had they learned? Someone had kidnapped Justice Meyers's family while they were supposed to be safe aboard a luxury yacht in the Mediterranean. At the same time, villains had been preparing to asphyxiate her entire hometown inside a coal mine.

"Could two opposing factions have been putting pressure on Justice Meyers?" Ellie said.

"What else could it be?" Mr. Perdix said in a frustrated tone. He clearly took the blow to national security personally.

"But why didn't she say anything?"

"Isn't it obvious?" Ms. China said. "The forces at work had to have Deep State level support to pull off either of these hostage takings. Meyers had to assume not only were her fellow justices compromised, but either the Democrats or the Republican factions, likely both, were the ones blackmailing her, each of them demanding they support their candidate."

"That's monstrous."

`"Welcome to American power politics, Eleanor."`

"It would have been a crazy situation for anyone," Sarge said, grasping the depth of betrayal they had uncovered.

"Meyers was on a cardiovascular medication," Mr. Perdix said, checking his notes. "One of its side effects is increased paranoia and suicidal thoughts."

The terrible truth of the poor woman's dreadful act dawned upon Ellie. "So… she blamed them all. Her fellow judges, the government members of both parties. In her mind, no one was fit to win the case they had been tasked to decide."

"Wow," Melanie said from London over the speakerphone, "Either the townspeople would die or Meyers's whole extended family would be killed. They left her no way out."

`"She seems to have found one."`

"Aleph!" Melanie said.

"Actually, Miss Aleph has a point," Sarge Bryan said solemnly. "Look at what happened. In the confusion and hurry to escape, the bad guys left most of the Sabraton hostages alive."

Not the hostage who was floating in the sea... Ellie tried to get the image out of her mind. The more she tried, the harder it was. There was something... as unpleasant as it was, that caught her curiosity.

"Miss Aleph, can you zoom in on the dead person in the water? I'm sure it was a young girl."

The screen sprung to life, and the gut-wrenching sight came up in high-definition color. The frame rate slowed and froze.

"That's not seaweed on her back," Ms. China said, spotting the same thing Ellie had.

"No, it's too regular."

The picture magnified further. Soon the mark occupied the whole screen.

"Look at that," Ran said, choking with emotion.

It was a five-pointed star with some other designs on each triangular point.

"That's a Masonic symbol," Mr. Perdix said coldly. "Ben Franklin was a master mason, and at least half of the American presidents were masons, starting with George Washington. The most recent one who openly belonged to the group was Gerald Ford."

"Why would they draw that on..." Ellie's voice faded out as the image resolved further.

"It's not drawn. It's branded," Ran observed clinically. "They were clearly torturing the hostages on the ship during their 'proof of life' communications to Justice Meyers."

"Mr. Oliphant, you said you were on this yacht once," Ellie said. "Who does it belong to?"

"You've met him. He's your host in America, Mr. Barracude."

Ellie's phone rang. There as an incoming voice call from the Watergate Hotel. It was Janice Jones. Mr. Perdix grabbed her hand before she could answer it.

"Miss Aleph—"

"Can they trace the call to your location? Not

unless they plan on physically visiting my server in Transnistria. You can answer."

"Hi, Ms. Sato," Janice said in a harried voice. "Agent Schwartz just told us about the… the developments in West Virginia. Where are you headed?"

Ellie looked at Sarge Bryan. His golden eyes shimmered as he nodded.

"Ah, we thought we'd go back to the hotel."

"Don't. I'll have them grab your luggage and some things you might need. Meet us at Andrews Air Force Base."

"Of course," Ellie said cautiously. "Where are we going?"

"The president has asked me to put together a delegation to meet with Candidate Leota on the West Coast. We agreed no press but Leota, who has read your books, says she'll make an exception for you to come along and serve as a neutral observer. President Casteel and I agreed, since you know as much as anyone does about what's going on. Hurry up. Departure is in two hours."

The connection broke off.

While Ellie was thinking about what they had just learned, she looked outside and saw the frontage of a mini mall. The largest store sold mattresses and bedding, and it was on fire. The rear section of Bonkers Bed & Bath spewed up gouts of gray smoke. In front, a dozen cars and trucks were lined up to loot its contents. Baby cots and four-poster king-sized beds were making their way out as though on their own power, only the looters' legs being visible. Shredded pillows leaked their stuffing, and small white feathers blew across the road.

She made sure the connection with Janice was off before asking, "What should we do?"

Sarge Bryan shrugged. "We can proceed to Andrews. I know some people there. They'll have a much harder time disappearing us once we're there."

Disappearing? Ellie thought she heard him correctly. Earlier that day, they had been in the White House receiving a special presidential commission, and now there was some worry about them being "disappeared"?

They passed a sign: *Welcome to Maryland.*

Underneath the state name the motto:

Manly deeds, womanly words

It was crossed out with spray paint which read:

TOXIC GENOCIDAL RACIST DEEDS + NAZI SUPREMACIST WORDS

"Wow," Ellie said, trying to remain calm. "We seem to be in a different state. What happened to West Virginia?"

"On the East Coast, states are kinda crammed together," Sarge Bryan said, eyeing the graffiti on the sign.

The rather quaint town of Frostburg reminded Ellie of a chalet town in Switzerland, except for the plywood nailed up over every main street storefront.

"You recall the red-blue state division?" Mr. Perdix asked as he took a sidelong glance at a townsperson wearing hunting camouflage carrying a rifle painted to match. "Maryland and West Virginia are very blue and ultra-red respectively."

"Most folks just don't want t'get robbed," Sarge Bryan said reasonably. "No sign of the boogaloo yet."

If it hadn't been Sarge saying that, Ellie might have thought the term sounded a bit prejudiced. "Dare we ask what that means?"

"The boogaloo is a loosely organized American movement whose adherents are preparing for a second American Civil War, which they call 'the boogaloo.' The name is derived from the 1984 cult sequel film *Breakin' 2: Electric Boogaloo*."

"What quaint customs you have," Ms. China said.

As they and the Russians were leaving Frostburg, Tata's van was driving directly ahead, then it swerved quickly left over the center lane. Something was blocking the road.

"Oh now, Tata, don' go and get riled up," Sarge Bryan said under his breath as he slowed down and followed.

Someone had moved an orange highway marker across the road, but there was no one attending it. They passed by unchallenged. Having been in more wars than she had anticipated after her Oxford joint major in law and fine art, Ellie was keenly aware the vehicle they were in was not armored. Bullets would go right though the type of glass that was beading small rain droplets inches from her face. She crouched down in her big American-sized leather seat.

The next town greeted them with a sign which, at the time, did not seem so ominous:

You Are Now Entering

Cumberland, Maryland

Come for a Visit, Stay for Life!

The quaint brick buildings were already boarded up. Nothing was moving in the streets until a massive garbage truck with sheet metal welded over the cab drove straight across their path.

"Miss Aleph, get me Tata, fast," Sarge Bryan said evenly.

"You're connected."

"Hey, Miss Oblonskaya—"

"Please, you know to call me Tata by now, Shay."

"Tata, uh, let's not doing anything rash. It's probably just a neighborhood watch group indicatin' they don't want us to go down that way. We'll just back up and—"

With a scraping sound Ellie could clearly hear inside the SUV, metal crossbars forming big Xs were dragged across the road behind them. Road flares taped to the top of each one burned bright neon red. They were trapped.

38

NEAR EL SASABE, MEXICO

ZVENA

Zvena's first trip to Mexico had been, so far, quite unpleasant. For one thing, he was without his fellow cyborg Rodion, who was on the ship preparing to be taken home for repairs. For another thing, he found the locals unusually resistant to his natural Russian charm.

The OCEL robot nudged him playfully with its praying mantis forelegs.

"Yes, I know we still have each other, but you always like playing with Rodya better."

It was near dawn. He and the six-legged OCEL were hunkered down near an abandoned farm building. Its adobe walls were pockmarked with old bullet holes and had been worn down by the incessantly blowing wind. A ground-level electrical storm was interfering with his communications, but so far not his internal mechanical parts. He pressed a button on his forearm communication panel.

The resupply drone was late.

After parting ways with Rodion in Guatemala, he had followed hot on the trail of jihadi Pangean elements who he believed were planning an assault on America. Speculation as to what that assault consisted of was for President Putin's ears only. As a result, the local GRU regular Russian military network did not prioritize his requests for equipment and assistance very highly. He knew the villains had crossed into Mexico, but he was forced to wait.

News of increasing unrest in the USA was the last straw. It became common knowledge that ninety percent of Customs and Border Protection officers had been withdrawn from their normal US-Mexico posts and were fighting rioters and looters in major cities. The team of locals who were supposed to be helping Zvena quickly switched their career objectives over to smuggling migrants and contraband. Zvena was regarded as a hindrance. The local criminals had attempted to resign from their commitments by means of a hastily improvised accident, which would have resulted in him being dismembered and his body parts being sold to brokers in Asia.

Without the assistance of the fighting skills of his long-term ally Rodya, he had been forced to engage berserker mode to escape. This resulted in a certain amount of collateral damage and the enmity of heavily armed cartel groups in Guatemala and Mexico.

Notwithstanding these stumbling blocks, he was closing in on the Pangeans. Their tradecraft was becoming careless. At their last campsite, Zvena had found a torn silicone mask near a burn barrel. It was reliable evidence he was on the track of a particularly dangerous and fanatical splinter cell of Pangeans who self-mutilated in order to defeat face-recognition technology.

Zvena wiped dust away from his comms panel. Because of the troublesome dry electrical storm, his HUD was no help tracking his incoming supply and munitions drone. He was isolated and deep inside territory held by the world's most purely violent psychopathic narco-crime lords. He had a bag of Russian gold coins but doubted he could buy his way out of trouble.

Beep.

A proximity alert sounded.

Why didn't the supply drone signal a landing seq—

An earthbound meteor flew across the horizon, leaving a smoke trail along a strip of sky that was not obscured by whirling clouds of dust. He could not see what caused it and was only sure of one thing: it was no drone.

Zvena moved to better cover. The object he saw fall nearby could have been a random surface-to-surface missile. The cartels had started using those, or it could have been a militarized hoverboard carrying one or more combatants. Perhaps survivors from the local gang he had parted ways with were coming after him. He and the OCEL had no more mini-drones, and he had to rely on direct observation to determine what had landed a few hundred meters away.

No other objects fell from the sky. There was no explosion.

Zvena checked his weapons and threw down his empty assault rifle and pistols. He had been counting on resupply reaching him before he had to fight again. He had his fighting pike, his ballistic shield, and one Ultra-Smart direct fire munition which sent out submunitions that could be programmed to kill targets based on EM signatures they put out. He loaded it into his grenade launcher and set it to "kill all" mode, just to be safe.

Dry lightning hit the ground. For a second, the image from his ocular implants dissolved to static. Furiously blinking away bits of swirling detritus, he moved forward. He was Spetsnaz Human+. He was not going to wait to be ambushed.

"Come, OCEL."

He held his transparent titanium shield in front of him to keep his face from being blasted by the whirling sand and ran across a deserted unpaved road. There was an adobe-rimmed cistern for livestock to drink from. He deployed self-guiding flexible tubes, which sank into the mud. A few feet down, they found water and siphoned a few liters into his storage unit.

He was close enough to see the impact left by the incoming object. There was will no sign of what it was.

Argh!

A shadow stretched long in the half-risen sun and loomed over him. Zvena thrust his spear up over his head. Its diamond-hard edge could dismember a Humvee. He prepared to strike, and then...

"Rodya?"

Out from the dusty haze, the familiar two-hundred-kilogram figure stood up in front of him.

"Surprised?" Rodion said, smiling lopsidedly. Half his head was covered by a patch over his eye and the side of his head.

"What are you doing here?" Zvena said. He was suddenly afraid for his comrade. Could the evil sickness that had infected half his brain be causing insanity? "I ordered you home for medical attention."

There being no danger and no one to dismember, the OCEL unit switched from combat to support mode. Recognizing Rodion, it scampered playfully up to him.

"As soon as I got to the ship, I felt better," Rodya said simply. Sensing Zvena's annoyance, he quickly added, "Look, I brought the stuff you ordered." He pointed to a vast duffel bag lying against the wall of an abandoned house.

"Well…" Zvena dismissed the idea of ordering his wounded colleague back to the ship. The flyboard he had come on would be out of fuel, and Rodion did not look like he was going to start tearing the heads off random water buffalo, so he was glad to have the extra help. "Since you are here, get yourself under cover. The cartels have sophisticated loitering drones."

As Zvena resupplied and drank clean water free from cholera and fecal matter, Rodion recounted his interesting journey. He had made it back to the spy ship where Dr. Nail, the chief architect of the Human+ program, was able to operate on him by telepresence using a remote surgical suite. Rodion's augments shared many parts with robots, such as OCEL units, so spares were plentiful. After deciding his side effects were minimal, Rodion got bored and decided to escape from the sick bay.

"I smell flowers all the time, but that's about it," he replied when Zvena asked about his post-hemispherectomy experiences and functioning literally with half a brain.

Rodion had convinced the regular Navy personnel to loan him a long-range stealth flyer. When that ran out of fuel, he destroyed it and traveled the last leg using the hoverboard.

"I seem to be able to concentrate better," Rodion said. "I want a rematch of our chess game."

"Once we accomplish this mission and secure Russia's interests, I will be happy to humiliate you, handicapped or not."

Zvena informed him of the disposition and likely objectives of the Pangeans' cell.

"They are heading straight for the US border, and not being subtle about it."

"Ach." Rodion shook his head. "I got news updates during my flight.

America is in chaos again. They can't even decide who is president, and their whole Supreme Court is wiped out."

"How did you find me? My GLONASS tracking is off."

"I tried to link up with our local contractors. Finding them deceased, I followed the trail of bodies to a known smuggling route north."

"Did you at least use misdirection protocols when flying the hoverboard over hostile territory?"

"What?"

"Will you ever read the damn upgrade literature? The new flyboards have thermal and sonic decoys to deploy as you get close to your landing spot so hostiles can't track you."

"Really? Oh, so that's what all those prompts were asking—"

Clack.

The storm had died down enough that Zvena could hear the bolt of a large-caliber weapon being cycled. He could also hear the hum of the military vehicle that had tracked the flyboard to its landing spot.

"Oops," Rodion said as they ducked away from the first incoming rounds. Bullets exploded against mud bricks, sending up more clouds of obscuring dust.

Zvena rolled out from cover, linked his optics to his grenade launcher, and fired the Ultra-Smart in the general direction of the attackers. The visual sensation was like riding on the nose of a small guided missile and controlling its flight. There were three dark-green blobs near an armored cartel SUV. Then there were none. The secondary explosions were unnecessary, but from a distance quite colorful, like daytime fireworks.

"We should move."

Zvena thought about it.

"No, that was a random scouting party. When they don't return, the local boss will assume he's under attack by a rival gang and send forces to secure their lucrative route into the USA, which likely features tunnels and drone-transit corridors."

He did not want anyone coming up behind them or attracting the attention of the remaining US border guards. Zvena also wanted to determine whether Rodion was in good functioning order. No injury like this, especially with the addition of the strange pathogen, had ever been recorded in Human+ medical history.

"Let's see what else you brought," Zvena said, stomping over to the large duffel bag. Inside, he found a good assortment of gear, but he was still upset about being snuck up on twice and worried President Putin would find out Rodion left the sick bay without permission. "You forgot hydraulic fluid and cerebrospinal fluid."

"No, I didn't," Rodion said, swinging his head around. With monocular vision, his field of sight was reduced. Also, with his right eye and the right hemisphere of his brain offline due to being stabbed with volcanic glass, his left eye had to process the entire visual field of view, a process normally split between both eyes. It took him a second longer to locate the OCEL. "It's in the other supply bag. Fetch."

The OCEL picked the bag up with its front legs and then loped over to them on its other four. Rodion patted the OCEL.

"It's not an animal."

"They've upgraded his sympathetic algorithms, and the technician told me he will work better if given encouragement for doing tasks well."

Rodion deployed a microwave uplink, through which they downloaded fresh satellite images of the area.

"That must be the cartel's current location," Zvena said, reviewing the data as he fed his organic parts with edible food and topped up his spinal fluid.

Feeling refreshed, Zvena led the way up to the place from which the recently neutralized enemy had been shooting at them. On the flat roof of a one-story building, Rodion found a fancy anti-material rifle. A hand and forearm was gripping the stock. He shook it free from the body part, and before it hit the ground, he kicked it over the edge of the single-story building's roof. Rodion grinned lopsidedly like a fool.

"You know, it's fun to be with you again, sir."

Using the enemy vehicle's GPS, they tracked the attackers back to the main cartel encampment. It was made up of mobile homes and tractor trailers arranged in a circle around a walled country hacienda.

"They are organized to keep on the move," Zvena said, retreating behind a boulder on the ridge overlooking the encampment. "Look at those heads. Disgusting."

Not only had the cartel decapitated some unlucky people but they had taken the time, and a sharp knife, to scrape the skin and flesh off them, leaving grinning, fleshless, eyeless heads sticking atop broken fence posts like a display window in a cannibal shawarma shop. Zvena zoomed in closer on some activity taking place near one of the trucks.

"Why do they have so many captives?" Rodion asked.

"Who knows. Maybe hostages, maybe drug mules, maybe migrants who ran out of money." Zvena automatically tallied up combatants and civilians. A frontal assault would be a mess. "Prisoners are also used to test border crossings and distract Mexican and American guards to one area while they carry out a smuggling operation in another."

In the cartel camp, a group of unarmed people in dusty rags was hemmed in on three sides by chicken wire. Three cartel members had one of them stripped naked and tied to the ground. A man with an AK strapped to his back was pouring some flammable fluid on him, leaving a trail along the ground a few yards below the stricken man's feet. One of the bandits yelled something, which seemed to disturb the crowd. After some more shouting, a few of the men reluctantly began loosening their trousers. Not fast enough. A cartel member shot at the ground near their feet until all the peasant men in the front row had dropped their pants.

With great deliberation, the leader of the cartel trio lit a flare and slowly moved it toward the trail of gasoline.

"Oh, come on," Zvena said in disgust. Harsh interrogation of people who deserved it was one thing, but this was sub-normal.

The half-naked peasants surrounded the bound man. The debauched game they were forced to play involved urinating on the victim in a vain effort to keep him from being burned alive. The game was over too quickly for the cartel team's liking. The prone prisoner went up like a Roman candle, and the small streams of urine had no delaying effect on the flames, which cooked him alive on top of the charred sand. As the peasants pulled their pants back up, their captors beat them with sticks and herded them into a shipping container.

"Maybe we should wait a day," Rodion suggested. "They may move on."

Zvena felt personally offended by the Pangeans' activities, and especially nearly getting Rodya killed in Guatemala. Every hour was crucial.

"The trail leads right through here. We have to assume the insurgent forces have entered America. Their police and military are in disarray. The Pangeans could have any manner of transport in Arizona or California. We cannot let them gain too much time or risk being ambushed in an area we are not familiar with."

Bypassing the encampment was not feasible.

"Then let's not waste time," Rodion said. He raised his six-shot missile launcher and fired all of them at the compound.

"Rodya!" Zvena exclaimed as his friend's one eye flittered back and forth as he controlled all six guided munitions at once, flying them to their targets eight hundred meters distant. "Check your impulsiveness controls. Maybe they are on the side of you head that's not working."

Rodion's plan, while a bit abrupt in its timing, was not badly executed. He brought the missiles in from several angles. The cartel members who were not busy dying had no idea where they where he and Rodion were.

Assuming they were under attack by a rival gang, they did the logical thing and called in all their scouts and ranging teams.

"Stupid civilians," Zvena fumed, fingering a canister of eco-friendly nerve gas. "This would be over with much less fuss if we could just use some nice Novichok."

"Maybe there is a way," Rodion said and called OCEL over.

Thirty minutes later, all the cartel members had arrived back at the embattled base, and the six-legged mechanoid was ready. Able to crouch down and move faster than Zvena or Rodion, the OCEL was sped through gullies and behind cover of scrub brush as it approached the compound.

"For the new operating systems, they scanned the brains of jungle cats for added subroutines," Rodion said, speaking as one might of a favorite hunting dog.

"How do you know?" Zvena said.

"Someone said so a few months ago," Rodion said, tapping the left side of his helmet. "Ever since my accident, I am remembering things I didn't realize I knew."

They fed the OCEL information on the location of enemy positions and the search pattern of circling drones. Each time it was in danger of being spotted, it collapsed down on its six spindly legs and covered itself with a camouflage tarp encrusted with local dirt and foliage. It had no infrared profile or visible exhaust. Undetected, it managed to advance within twenty meters of the foremost enemy position.

The nerve agent gas it released was aerosolized into droplets, not pure vapor; the inhaled toxin irritated the soldier's nose and lungs but the droplets on their skin did most of the work by quietly deactivating their neurotransmitters. The enemy slumped over quietly in their foxhole.

"Did they get a signal off?" Zvena was worried this procedure was taking too long. "Give me the controller."

He made the OCEL take a more aggressive posture and trot up to the next group, squirting sticky globs of poison right at their faces. One of them managed to pull his pistol but only shot in the air before collapsing.

"It's on now." Zvena switched the OCEL to autonomous mode and sent him galloping into the main hideout. "Let's go," Zvena said, grabbing his gear. "Rodya, no berserker. I don't want you damaging your other eye by mistake."

Some of the cartel drones were armed and might have targeted them. No longer worried about a counterattack, they used a portable microwave dish to fry their mechBrains in the air. Rodion hurried after him down the ravine just as the UAVs crashed on the other side of the encampment.

As they got close, from out of nowhere a jeep sped at them, trying to run them over. Rodion's missile blew it off the road.

"Hey, stop showing off, that almost hit us," Zvena complained.

"I wanted to be sure I got him," Rodion said with a smile made lopsided and agreeably sinister by the black cloth bandage across the side of this face.

"Good boy," Rodion called to the OCEL, who loped away from the window of the hacienda. Coughing and dying people stumbled out of doorway and fell from second-story windows. There was hardly anyone left to kill.

"Detach that truck from its load," Zvena ordered.

"That's the one with the peasants."

"They won't want to ride in it. They can have any of the other cars. Tell them to be gone before scavengers come."

Rodion stepped over the burned corpse of the torture victim. His head and shoulders were still steaming with boiled urine; the rest of him was just a charred mess of black flesh and burst pink thigh meat.

An older man, perhaps the leader of the captives, came out of the shipping container and spoke.

"They're asking what we want them to do."

"Do I give a fuck?" Zvena said. "They're free. Tell them to go be free. The main house will be safe to loot in fifteen minutes. They can have all the money and whatever else they find in there."

Rodion relayed this to the man. He was small, barely taller than five feet, but broad with fat squashed hands and a deeply lined face rimmed by close-cropped gray hair.

"He says these cartel bandits are the devil's spawn, and they will take nothing from them. It is all tainted with the spirit of bad demons. They want to burn the house."

It was a waste of cash that these poor people could use, but not their problem. Zvena reached in his rucksack and grabbed the bag of chervonets which he had not had to use to pay his previous Mexican guides.

"This is good Russian gold. No evil spirits," Zvena said. "For good luck, it even has the image of President Putin on every coin. He is... a stern man, but definitely not in league with the devil."

Rodion translated. The peasant leader took the gold and went back to his group. A younger woman ran over.

"You go America... you take us?" she said in broken English.

Zvena looked at her, and with a creaking of his neck hydraulics, shook his head and switched his spoken language to Spanish. "No. However bad you think it is here, north of the border, it will soon be worse."

39

CUMBERLAND, MD

ELLIE

As the welded steel barrier was pushed behind their SUV, Ellie's head flicked right and left. Along both sides of the SUV, hooded figures ducked in and out of sight along the main street. It was obvious Sarge Bryan was less concerned with them than with what Ambassador Bagration and especially Tata might do.

"Now, Tata, jus' hold on. We can work this out," Sarge Bryan said, then muttered, "Whatever the heck this is."

Right then, the first bottle was hurled at them and burst to pieces against the windshield. Ellie gave an involuntary yelp.

"Excuse me, it's only my second riot in America," she said, noticing the condescending stare from all of Ms. China's six pupils. However, the mad killer had also ducked down away from the fragile-looking windows.

A badly tuned megaphone barked at them, issuing harsh squealing sounds between words.

"You fascists have entered the autonomous free"—*squeal*—"zone of the former slave camp formerly called Cumberland! Prepare"—*squawwwwwk*—"to surrender your possessions to the benefit of the free people of the Citizens Utopian Municipal Zone!"

Ellie had noticed the letters *CUMZ* had been spray-painted all over the place, on stop signs, across boarded-up burned-out shops. That must stand for Citizens Utopian Municipal Zone.

More bottles were being thrown and hitting their vehicle and the Russian spy van. It was only a matter of time before…

"Here we go," Mr. Perdix said ruefully as he saw some disheveled figures dart out from the sidewalk. Using sharpened metal fence stakes, they stabbed at the van's tires. The van's sliding door rolled open, and Tata lumbered out with her pike fully extended.

"Mine is bigger," she said simply, and flailed at the attacker's weapons, sending them flying down the street, bent and useless.

An object that was on fire came arcing toward the open van door.

"Ambassador, no shooting, no shooting," Sarge Bryan pleaded into his handset.

Bagration was holding his sniper rifle across his body, more to block incoming missiles than take aim. Nevertheless, Ellie agreed—he did not look like he had the best nerves for this type of encounter. The albino soldier cracked open the driver's-side door and raised his hands.

"We're just passin' through, we'll take any detour you wan—"

A volley of hunting arrows rained down, and Sarge Bryan yelled and withdrew his arms, which came back into the SUV with the addition of a brightly painted arrow shaft.

"Sarge!" Ellie yelled.

At first, she thought one of the arrows had pierced his forearm or hand, but it had just gone through the cuff of his sleeve. He snapped the shaft in half and reached for the assault rifle he had taken from the assassins at Sabraton.

"About time," Ms. China fumed and checked the breech of a pistol she had hidden in the rather smart coat she had borrowed from Janice Jones.

"No shooting… unless we can't help it. These are our fellow citizens."

A sour-faced rioter with a stripe shaved down the middle of his or her head and stark homemade face tattoos came at their car, trying to light something on fire. Failing at that simple task, the rioter threw the soaking sock at the windshield and head-butted the passenger window before running off.

"They seem more like Anna's crowd," Mr. Perdix said drolly.

Sarge's grumbling was punctuated by the roars of two engines. A pair of garbage trucks lurched forward. Were the rioters removing the barricades and letting them drive off?

Ms. China saw the danger and pushed Ellie. "Go! Out!"

Sarge also scrambled across the front seat and out the passenger-side door as the garbage truck's load-lifting prongs came closer and closer. Ellie stumbled onto the cold, wet pavement and looked up just as the first truck crashed broadside into their ride, skewering it at an odd angle. Five-foot metal prongs dashed through the windows of their SUV in a shower of shattered glass.

Ellie kept moving, stumbling until she was pressed up against a sheet of plywood covering a storefront window. She looked over at the Russians. As the second truck hit the van, the ambassador jumped out the back. Tata hacked at the garbage truck's driver compartment, but its metal fortifications were too strong. Sparks flew as the pike bounced off.

"Keep grouped up with me and the Russians," Sarge Bryan yelled as he braced himself against the rocking vehicle he had just leaped from.

Ellie thought about running over to Tata, but just then a heavy fusillade of missiles—arrows, rocks, bottles, and fireworks—came raining down.

"Tata! Off the street! We got to get in here," Sarge Bryan yelled over the explosions. He and the cyborg lady ducked under the fallen metal canopy of a store and bashed away at the plywood covering the entrance.

The garbage trucks had lost momentum. Before they could back up, hit them again, and squash them against the building, Ellie ducked down and leaped over the narrow gap in the plywood Tata's pike had prized apart. As she squeezed through, she remembered both her hands were fiercely clutching her handset.

"Miss Aleph, can you help us out?"

"How? I didn't tell you to trespass into an open-air asylum."

"For starters," Ellie said, moving deeper into the dark interior of the store as more fireworks went off in the street, "have you got a map that shows how to go out from this CUMZ area?"

"I'll try," Miss Aleph said grudgingly. "Having done some

research, it seems you've come here at a pretty bad time."

"You don't say," Ellie said.

Mr. Perdix was the last one into their temporary refuge. Just as he ducked in, a fist-sized rock thumped him on the back. Sarge Bryan pushed the plywood back, and Tata stood ready with her pike for a moment. No one tried to follow them. Ellie looked around. The unlit store was full of stuffed toys and a strange netted area filled with a million foam balls.

"The boundaries of the anarchist CUMZ rebels and the areas occupied by the loyalist residents are in flux. There were rumors the National Guard was called in but did not respond."

Headlights blazed through the cracks in the plywood covering the big display windows as a deep-throated diesel engine revved.

"Back, back!" Sarge Bryan yelled.

There was nowhere to go but into the Styrofoam balls. Tata slashed through the netting, and they all came spilling out just as a garbage truck crashed through the storefront.

Ellie stumbled and fell. The stupid bloody balls were all underfoot. Behind them, the pursuing truck's wheels spun, squealed, and smoked—the large vehicle was stuck.

Struggling past the mess of romper-room balls, they got to an indoor rock-climbing area and basketball court. Ellie bumped against a plastic clown figure. Immediately its recorded cartoonish clown voice blared: "Hello! Want to try your luck shooting hoops? Ho-ho-ho!"

Tata decapitated the clown with a swipe of her pike's blade.

"This is a stupid town!" she declared as the laughing head rolled across the brightly polished marble floor.

"Aleph, you're feeding us too much information," Sarge Bryan said, squinting his cyber eyes and holding his free hand against his temple. He leaned over to speak into Ellie's handset. "Just point to the fastest way out of town."

Miss Aleph seemed to do that. Sarge Bryan and Tata checked their internal displays and nodded. Ellie followed them, Ambassador Bagration,

Ms. China, and Mr. Perdix down an escalator. Some of the stores had been looted; tennis rackets and golf clubs lay all over. Others, like stationery stores, merely had graffiti sprayed on their dented metal shutters.

Mr. Perdix saw where Sarge Bryan was leading them. "Do we really want to go outside?"

Before anyone could answer, more breaking glass sounds came from behind them, and the tinny loudspeaker voice urged: "Smoke 'em out! Smoke 'em out!"

An acrid smell from the mass of burning rubber balls wafted toward them.

"Out of my way." Ms. China overtook them all, sprinting impressively quickly for someone using a malfunctioning prosthetic leg.

The exit door slammed open. The air that washed over Ellie as they rushed outside was damp and chilly. Slushy snow tugged at Ellie's shoes, threatening to pull them off her feet. She turned around, looking for something with which to bar the exit doors.

"Dare I ask why we're being attacked?"

Sarge Bryan shrugged. "I guess we came at a bad time."

"Bad time?" Ms. China shrieked. "They are about to burn us alive."

Something made Sarge grin as he closed and jammed the fire exit door closed. "Hey, Ms. Sato, remind you of Jerusalem?"

That urban nightmare from a few years back did have similarities. "I suppose." Ellie's teeth chattered. "But it's so much colder here."

They ran through a small historically themed square. The fountain in the middle had frozen over, and a curious display had been made out of the statues. The brass figure of a boy had his groin area welded to the back end of a donkey that was looking around, seemingly in wonder at what was going on behind him. A simple but direct hand-painted sign around the poor beast's neck read: *Fuck Capitalist Animal Fuckers!*

They came to a small log cabin. The sign over its eaves read *George Washington's Headquarters*. A little inverted *V* was squashed between the Revolutionary General's first and last name, and scrawled in white paint above that were the words *slave owning motherfucking whiteass nazi pink dick,* at which point the author of the critical commentary had run out of space.

Tata edged around the corner of the tourist site. She had collapsed her pike, slung it across her back, and was holding a rifle in her big gloved hands. Ambassador Bagration did not look like he could run much farther; his face was puce colored, his breath came in short gasps, and his shirt tails were hung out, exposing jiggly white blubber belly over his belt.

"Oh my," Ellie said, looking at the historical log cabin. "Can we take shelter in there and wait for the authorities?"

Mr. Perdix pushed his glasses back on his head. "The only authorities in the CUMZ are back there with rocks and Molotov cocktails."

"We gotta get out," Sarge Bryan agreed. "They probably won't follow us far."

The Russian cyborg glanced around the corner of the cabin, then ducked back. She whispered, "Sniper."

40

THE CUMZ
(FORMERLY CUMBERLAND, MARYLAND)

Ellie didn't need to hear the word "sniper" twice. She crouched down behind a plaque nailed to the side of the historic cabin. While there were other priorities, she couldn't help but read it.

1794: George Washington gathered his troops here at Fort Cumberland, before their march to suppress the Whiskey Tax Rebellion in western Pennsylvania.

"Aw, heck-damn," Sarge Bryan whispered, his breath making short bursts of vapor as white as his skin. "Where?"

All of them stayed close to the thick and hopefully bullet-resistant log wall. Mr. Perdix glanced back at the fire exit from the shopping mall.

Tata said, "The gunman is on the desecrated church steeple. He has a wide angle of fire along the street where we must go."

Ellie ducked down and looked through the front window of the historic cabin display and out the side window. There was a large Georgian-style church. On the very top of the steeple was the Christian cross which had been transformed into the Nazi swastika symbol. On a parapet just below that, she glimpsed a tiny dark figure ducking down, and then a few seconds later, popping up a few meters away.

Sarge Bryan slumped against the chilly logs. "I don't think we're at the shooting stage jus' yet," he said hopefully.

Based on all their encounters with the guardians of the CUMZ, Ellie thought that was an extremely optimistic assessment.

Suddenly behind them, the fire doors of the mall burst open, and a figure bathed in flames came tumbling out. Despite Ellie's fervent desire that the burning person drop and roll down onto the slush-covered ground, it kept running right toward them. Without thinking, Ellie grabbed a soaking-wet outdoor tapestry embossed with the 13 Stars US flag and rushed out.

The burning fellow ran right into her. He was astonishingly hot, so hot that Ellie felt she was trying to smother a campfire. The bath-sheet-sized cloth she held in front of her face had absorbed many liters of melted snow. Using it, she was able to envelop the stricken man. As he toppled over, he made no sound other than sizzling.

"Those motherfuckers killed Hawkins!" The yelling came from a second door into the mall which had slammed open and started spewing smoke and CUMZ anarchists.

It took Ellie a second or two to realize they were pointing at her. Hawkins must be the burn victim. She started to protest. "I did nothing of the ki—"

Blam-blam.

Ellie ducked as wildly aimed handgun bullets hit the ground a few meters away from where she was crouched nursing her scalded hands. Sarge grabbed her arm and pulled her back behind the log cabin.

Thunk.

"Sniper eliminated," Tata said, her suppressed rifle spouting a small trail of steam. "Headshot. He's dead."

Ellie could not tell who Sarge Bryan was most angry with, her for exposing herself or Tata for killing one of his countrymen.

"Did he shoot first?" Sarge went over and got very close to Tata.

Tata rose to her full height and looked resolutely down at the Army man. "Maybe next time I let them shoot, hope they miss, then recommend they get emotional counseling."

Further debate was cut off by several different types of bullets striking the ancient logs on other side of the cabin.

"Try not to… well, at least aim low," Sarge Bryan said, his voice nearly drowned out by the increasingly rapid gunfire.

Tata pushed the wheezing Ambassador Bagration ahead of her and followed him around the side of the sturdy one-story cabin. Mr. Perdix and Ms. China were inside. They had broken open an antique lantern and were wrapping the base in newspaper and some wire.

"Here," Mr. Perdix said, handing the device to Tata. "You can throw the farthest. There are some match heads on the top. If they land against something hard…"

He didn't need to explain in greater detail. Tata took up the bundle and heaved it around the corner toward the mob approaching from the mall like a catapult. The homemade explosive hit as intended and made a loud bang. The firing from the mall ceased.

"They'll soon realize that was not a real grenade," Ms. China said, exiting the first president's headquarters. "Let's go."

The air around them remained bullet-free until they arrived at a row of train tracks, where an old decommissioned steam locomotive sat. Some entrepreneur had been trying to turn it into an outdoor café, but that was before the Citizens Utopia of the CUMZ had been declared. Tables were overturned and ratty tents were arranged along the historic train's length, along with filth of every description. The sharp smell of fermenting urine penetrated the cold air.

A bullet pinged off the black metal of the train engine, scattering some of the piled snow.

"Aleph," Tata hissed. "Why we going this way? After the railroad is only the river, and no train is coming, I think."

"Across that bridge ahead of you is a car dealership. It's the only reliable place to steal transport," Miss Aleph's voice said out of Ellie's bag.

"Crossing would limit pursuit," Sarge Bryan said while peering around the side of the engine and shooting high in the air in an effort to deter the attackers. "We can pin them down on this side without too much collateral damage. I say go for it. Tata? Perdix? Aleph?"

"Just keep me out of the water. The levee robots

report the North Branch of the Potomac is flowing
fast and cold."

Ellie looked between gaps in the steam engine's wheels. If they moved quickly, the high blank walls of a big-box store would shield their retreat away from the mall and toward the river and the bridge.

"They've stopped shooting," Ellie said in a worried tone.

"We want them to do that," Ms. China said.

"Maybe, but I can't help thinking they are either massing for an assault or moving to outflank us from one or both sides."

"Very crafty thinking, Ms. Sato. You sure you didn't go to West Point instead of Oxford?" Sarge Bryan said with a tense smile. Standing behind him, Tata gave Ellie a resentful look and ran for the bridge.

It was a single span with a rickety-looking CUMZ barrier at their end. Looking across, Ellie thought she could make out some mechanical equipment, perhaps for dredging or levee construction. Behind that was a sign with a fat white ball and a yellow spike on the bottom. It took Ellie a moment to realize that had to be a golf course.

With Ambassador Bagration bringing up the rear, they made it to the bridge.

"Watch yourselves, there's razor wire," Sarge Bryan said. He and Tata lifted strands of the dangerous fencing material up, allowing Ellie, Ms. China, and Mr. Perdix to get through.

Both lanes along the bridge were blocked by abandoned cars. The barriers must have gone up suddenly, and the drivers had fled on foot rather than risk trying to turn around. Once he had squeezed himself under the wire, Bagration did not wait with them. He charged ahead thirty meters. He turned, breathlessly motioning for Tata to hurry up. As he put his hand on the rotting bridge railing to rest, it gave way, and he fell out of sight.

A second later, Ellie heard a muted splash.

41

BRIDGE OVER THE POTOMAC
OUTSIDE THE CUMZ, MARYLAND

Ellie was still frozen in shock, staring at the gray swirling river water when Tata swore something in Russian and launched herself forward along the rickety bridge railing to the spot where Ambassador Bagration had fallen off. As she moved, she threw down most of her equipment and dove after the diplomat.

"Can't worry about that," Sarge Bryan said as he let the barbed wire down with a *thwang*. Behind them, a square gray vehicle was approaching. It ran over and crushed a line of recycling containers standing behind the big-box store. "They got an armored car."

Their path across to the other side was blocked by abandoned station wagons and vans and other debris. Navigating the slippery pedestrian walkway was hard enough, and Ellie kept a grip on anything she could grasp which was not attached to the very suspect railing. The hijacked armored car approached aggressively. Sarge Bryan sent a few bullets at it. They cracked against the heavy glass of its rectangular windshield, not slowing it at all.

With Ms. China leading, they had nearly gotten close to the middle of the span. Every few steps, Ellie shot a look down into the churning gray waters of the rushing Potomac, never seeing any sign of Tata or the diplomat.

"At least they won't be running us down." Mr. Perdix motioned back at the CUMZ. He said, with a note of triumph, "There's no way they can get that armored car onto the bridge."

Just then, a thunderous blast nearly toppled her and Ms. China over the railing. Bits of dirt and ice spattered all over her; she wiped her vision clear but had no idea what had caused the impact or where it had come from. At the same time, the full-throated roar of heavy machinery sprang to life dead ahead of them.

"Someone's in that dredging machine," Mr. Perdix yelled, his glasses nearly completely obstructed by dripping filthy spray. Ellie grabbed Ms. China as much to regain her own balance as to support the other woman, who seemed to be walking with a much more pronounced limp. Maybe the cold was causing the joints of her prosthetic leg to seize up. Ellie's other hand was already numb from desperately hanging on to the bare metal pylons and wires holding up the bridge.

Sarge Bryan turned his attention to the large crane sitting on a barge close to the far end of the bridge. No matter how far he leaned over the teetering edge, he could not seem get a clear shot at the operator.

"I take it," Ellie said, "the CUMZ Utopian Zone extends to the other side of the river as well."

"Maybe I can get a shot from the other side."

Of course, they would have to get to the other side of the bridge first. As soon as Sarge Bryan spoke, the big fat scoop of the dredge raised up and, like a wrecking ball, slammed down onto the bridge, sending a whipsaw undulation down its length. Ellie's feet lifted clear off the roadway, and she clung on with her failing grip.

"You people!" Miss Aleph cried out from the handbag swinging wildly from her shoulder.

Ellie glanced down and saw tall concrete support pylons that might survive the collapse of the center span. She looked for some way to get down to them. There was a way, but would they be washed off the narrow landings at the top of the pylons when the ironworks came down?

The whole structure was still swaying, and the dredge's ominous claw rose up for another strike. It didn't seem they would have enough time to climb down. Ellie noticed something came loose from a trailer attached to a pickup truck. It was aluminum gray in color and teetered over the side of the bridge.

"There! Can we use that? It's a boat."

Before he could reply, Sarge Bryan had to duck as rounds were fired by CUMZ fighters. They had exited the armored car and were running toward the barbed-wire barricade. "Can't think of anything better."

He picked up Tata's pike and hacked the boat free of the last straps that fastened it to the trailer. At the same time, Mr. Perdix and Ms. China pushed it. Ellie helped and found the vessel was lighter than it looked. A moment later, it slipped though the twisted railing and down to the water. The boat dropped in, back end first, scooping up copious amounts of river water. Then it righted itself and bounced atop the current struggling to get free of a yellow nylon rope. Sarge Bryan had the other end, which he had tied onto the truck's trailer hook.

"Ladies first," he said, helping Ellie down.

She hung onto the rope, bracing herself for the icy splash of river water she knew was coming, and glanced up. The dredge claw was swinging back and forth. The operator was perhaps unskilled and was waiting for the massive digging claw to point straight down at the bridge like a pendulum before letting it drop again.

The distance down was only about twelve feet but seemed much farther given the nearness of the murky water and the danger of completely capsizing their small wobbly craft. Only one of her legs was completely immersed in the river, and the sudden cold competed for her attention with a tugging sensation created by the greedy current that seemed to want to pull her straight down into the depths. With her other leg over the gunwale, she managed to get in.

Back up on the bridge, Mr. Perdix lowered Ms. China down. The boat had bounced sideways closer to the bridge, and the fugitive poisoner landed fairly on top of Ellie, sending her slamming backward against a metal seat.

"Ouch!"

By this time, the dredge claw stopped swinging the malicious operator wasted no time in winching up to its maximum height. They sent it crashing down in a final bid to destroy the bridge, and just then, the two men jumped.

"Hey, super spy girl, undo us!" Ms. China yelled, even though she was closer to the front end of the boat, which was pointed up the river.

Sarge Bryan and Mr. Perdix could not get in. They clung to the either side of the boat, fortunately balancing each other out. With the last bit of dexterity in her nearly frozen fingers, Ellie pushed and pulled at the loopy knot, and just as she was thinking of what she might use to cut them free, she found the end of the stiff nylon rope pulled undone rather easily. They were free.

The bridge convulsed and moaned under the final impact of the dredge claw. Metal rained down as iron rivets burst from pylons under immense stress and what remained of the bridge rocked back and forth. Cables snapped with a twang and hissed through the air as the span finally gave out and collapsed. With Mr. Perdix and Sarge Bryan helping from the water, Ellie and Ms. China used their hands to paddle. Furiously, they tried to guide the pointy end of the boat in the right direction. The current embraced them, and they hurled themselves away at a dizzying speed.

"Can you climb in?"

"W-w-we bet-ter not," Sarge Bryan chattered, his gold glowing eyes blinking away gray-green river water. He was right, with the boat half full of water, they could not risk tipping it further. Ellie's knees were drenched as she braced herself against the bare aluminum hull.

She felt a hard thunk on her shoulder. *What now?*

"Here!" Ms. China yelled over the death throes of the collapsing bridge, which thankfully was now sixty meters behind them.

Ms. China had found two yellow paddles strapped to the inside of the boat and was poking her with the sharp end of one. Having been on a river-rafting-themed fashion shoot one summer, Ellie had an idea.

"Forget fighting the current, just steer," Ellie said, and she grabbed a plastic paddle and dipped it in.

For once, Ms. China did not argue. She dipped her oar in also. The combined steering and a fortuitously placed bend in the Potomac allowed them to grind to an unsteady landing on a sand bank that the dredger had not yet gobbled away. Ellie looked back to the bridge and their pursuers; a thick stand of trees now blocked the view.

"Glub coarse!" Miss Aleph sputtered. The handset was waterproof, but its speaker was full of water.

As the current pulled their life raft free of the pebbly shore and spun it away, they scrambled out from the shallows. Rather ungratefully, Ms. China threw her paddle after it while cursing a blue streak. Mr. Perdix and Sarge Bryan heaved themselves up, shivering worse than ever. Ellie shook her phone but was not able to get the AI to say anything more. Perhaps she had decided they were a lost cause and had retreated back to her big home computer far away.

"Maybe she meant 'golf course'?" Ellie speculated, pointing to a stand of winter-bare trees. "There was as sign on this side of the river. They're usually quite large, right? If we g-go t-that way we'll run into it-t."

Maybe everyone followed her lead only to keep moving as opposed to freezing on the spot. Their desperate, disheveled group climbed the railing onto the one-lane road that followed the river. They waded through mounds of slush-heavy moldering leaves about as far as they could until Ellie heard a whining sound. She thought it must be some hypothermic delirium or river water caught in her ears. Sarge Bryan gesticulated to the other side of a line of poplar trees.

Before they saw what was making the sound, it turned into a harsh mechanical engine noise. On an open area, which must have been a large fairway, a large bulbous-ended helicopter had set itself down.

"Holy shit," Sarge Bryan managed to say. "That's a Sea Stallion with Marine One markings."

Their run toward the copter left long sloppy footprints all over the frost-covered grass. Soldiers in winter camo gear came out of the aircraft, and so did a shorter fellow with a homburg hat pressed down over the bandage encircling his head.

"How ya doin'?" Mr. Barracude shouted. "There was no way to land over there. Had to come here." He made exaggerated motions with his hands as though talking to deaf people. "Lucky the ground is mostly frozen."

As they packed into the gloriously warm interior, the pilot advised he was going to get airborne straightaway. The whine coming from the engines increased in pitch.

"Lift off and climb, ASAP," Sarge Bryan said in the direction of the cockpit.

"There's no telling what kind of weapons those crazy bastards in Cumberland have."

"What about Tata and the ambassador?" Ellie asked.

Sarge Bryan shook his head. "We'll send a river patrol to look, but we have to get back to Andrews."

"That might not be best… hey, Miss Sato," Mr. Barracude said easily, losing his train of thought, taking off his plush homemade-looking mittens and giving them to Ellie. "Your hands look like ice cubes. These mitts are a piece of American history, bought them from Bernie Sanders direct. Three hundred grand it cost me to keep them from going to auction. For a ninety-year-old commie, he drives a hard bargain."

"Mr. Barracude's right," Sarge Bryan said, reviewing news updates on a tablet computer. "Andrews is closed. A pilot went crazy, declared his loyalty to the New Antifa World Order and suicide-crashed into the control tower. Place is a mess."

"There's got to be an alternative," Ellie said. She scooped up the enormous Bernie Sanders mittens and hoped she did not look too ridiculous pulling them on with her teeth because her fingers were just too frozen to do the job.

"Plan B is we go to the best city on earth," Mr. Barracude said with unabashed enthusiasm as the door slid shut with a clang. "New York!"

42

ELLIE

Inside the Sea Stallion copter, the scary-looking but helpful soldiers wearing winter tactical gear had given them hot drinks, blankets, and some chemical warming pads, which Mr. Perdix said his JASON Group had designed and sold to the military for just such nearly freezing-to-death occasions.

Ellie looked down though the half-fogged-up window at the gray Potomac River as it wound its serpentine way though the stark winter landscape. Tata and the ambassador were down there. Sarge Bryan sensed her distress.

"We've alerted river search and rescue," he said. "There's nothing else we can do just yet."

"Besides," Mr. Barracude yelled over the engine noise, "those Ruskies are used to the cold." He shook his head vigorously. "When Janice heard you were here, we couldn't believe it. Citizens Utopia Zone, more like Galactic Shithole Zone. How dare those scummy Antifa goofs rough you guys up like that. Man, they're lucky we couldn't land this thing in the town or else I'da given 'em the old one-two again, just like that goon at the hotel."

"How did you even find us?" Ellie looked at her companions. Sarge Bryan was quietly conversing with the pilots. Ms. China was getting herself into a warm-up survival suit without poking too many holes in it with her long nails. Mr. Perdix sat stubbornly shivering under his advanced JASON blankets, waiting for them to heat up.

Had they escaped one perilous trap and walked into another, dryer and warmer one?

"You texted us, right?" Mr. Barracude said innocently as he turned a mobile heater toward Ellie so she could bask in its wonderful orange glow.

Miss Aleph, Ellie thought. The self-aware computer program was remaining suspiciously quiet, even though she had dried off her handset.

"Oh, right, yes, I must have forgot." Ellie chuckled. "All the gunfire and being attacked by a dredging machine."

"You guys should have had the system one of my companies puts in every car in America: Riot-Shield. It would have steered you clear of those CUMZ nutbags."

Ellie pulled a small wet branch out of a tangle in her hair. It must have gotten stuck there during their near-drowning experience in the river.

"Do you really think Tata's okay?" Ellie asked no one in particular.

"Spetsnaz Human+ soldiers have extensive underwater capabilities," Mr. Perdix said. He had struggled out of most of his wet things, and one of his long white feet protruded from under his blanket. It was covered by scalloped, flat-looking scars; he noticed her staring at it.

"Sorry," she said. "It's just that I distinctly remember when your leg was wounded. A thermal grenade in Amman, Jordan, I believe."

"That's right," Sarge Bryan said nostalgically. "For a second, we thought you'd been blown in half, along with the truck."

Ms. China couldn't resist saying, "Al, if you were blown in half, which half would you say is more useful?"

Mr. Barracude was impressed by their tales of past heroics. This somehow caused him to speak like a fifty-year-old teenager, "Man, you guys are all like 'Fortnite Maximus' IRL, ain't you?"

Ellie guessed this was a reference to some sort of ultraviolent video game. She looked at Sarge Bryan and then at Mr. Perdix and couldn't help laughing. Then, neither could they.

"Seems like ages ago," Sarge Bryan said. "But it was only 2029."

"I could have regrown the skin to match the extant tissue," Mr. Perdix said, rubbing his foot and then sliding it back under the thermal sheet. "But I opted for shark cartilage, more durable."

"Maybe you can do the rest of you," Ms. China said.

Ellie cringed. She had hoped the dip in the river would have cooled off their compulsive bickering.

"Your foot came out better than poor Marwood's regrown tail," Ellie said, referring to their capuchin monkey sidekick who had been wounded in the Middle East. "He never grew any hair on it, and it was split at the end like a snake's tongue. At least that's what Atticus said."

At the mention of the deceased soldier's name, everyone looked quite solemn. Even Ms. China looked away and pretended to check her fingernails.

"Well," Mr. Barracude said, breaking the uncomfortable silence, "it's not gonna get that fucked up here, like in the Mid East or Euro-stan. This is America, we'll sort everything out, and pronto!"

Miss Aleph silently texted Ellie. Better watch that one. Good move not mentioning me. Don't.

Still, Ellie thought, if Mr. Barracude had wanted to do away with them and the personnel on the helicopter were conspiring with him, he could have had them thrown them out over Cumberland and blamed their deaths on mob violence.

"I wouldn't count on the pronto part," Mr. Perdix said. He swiped and tapped at a tablet, skimming through crisis updates. "After the double assassinations in Washington State and Oregon, neither the House nor the Senate was able to convene. The interim leaders are making all kinds of excuses on social media, but it's obvious they're completely petrified."

"You must have a plan for that," Ellie said. "A contingency in case of earthquake or war?"

"We did. In fact, JASON designed most of the software for secure online legislative functioning. However, the jerks who installed it left security flaws. The hacker group Anonymous not only was able to deep fake politicians' identities, complete with voice and image, but they also doxxed every elected member, their family, and their staff. Any terrorist in the world can now find out their primary residences, safe houses, and electronic device IDs."

"Great going," Ms. China said. "A superpower held hostage by blue-haired betas who smell like cheese and live in their grandparents' garages."

"Just an hour ago, DHS tried to build up a system of one-time codes and passwords," Mr. Perdix went on. "But with all the unsecure digital devices with cameras and mics, it only took an hour for the new system to be completely compromised."

"They could meet at an Army base or West Point," Sarge Bryan suggested.

"That's what the pro tem of the Senate was trying to arrange when he was ambushed along with his Democrat counterpart. They had to identify him by a Masonic ring on his severed hand."

"Fuck me out to lunch," Mr. Barracude said. "I played billiards with the guy last week. At least Janice and the president are A-OK. And did I tell ya, we got this summit lined up with that Leota lady in LA, so it's not all duck and cover."

Ellie looked at Sarge, who nodded noncommittally, and at Ms. China, who was casually scanning Mr. Barracude for areas of bare skin. If it hadn't been for the Marines, the American oligarch might have found himself anesthetized and infused with truth venom.

As it was, Ellie knew they could be walking into a trap. They had caught Janice at Justice Meyers's hidden lab. Given the mental state of the president, who was really in charge of the government at the White House? And how had the late judge's family come to be on the *Octopus* yacht where they thought they were safe but ended up being tortured and thrown overboard? She looked out the window. Rain pelted against the glass, leaving horizontal streaks that glistened in the afternoon sun.

There was no choice but to see what awaited them in New York. Even as her limbs started to regain feeling and she stopped shivering, a touch of chills just would not depart from the pit of Ellie's stomach.

As they approached the metropolitan zone, New York City looked to be divided horizontally. Only the tallest buildings penetrated a pancake layer of low-hanging clouds. The stacks of uppermost floors that did manage to reach up high enough were bathed in crystal-clear sunlight, and together they looked like a literal city in the clouds.

Over the broad swatch of water, the mist dissipated, and at the edge Ellie could see the surprisingly tiny Statue of Liberty. It was mostly enclosed with scaffolding, still being repaired after the previous summer's mysterious melting event, which many people blamed on global warming.

The closer they got to what Ellie assumed was the middle of Manhattan Island, the more animated Mr. Barracude became. Despite his head wound and apparent vertigo, which required him to hang on to anything handy in order not to topple over, he refused to sit down.

"There! That's a city, ain't it?" He pointed in such an insistent and proud way it seemed rude not to look. "Sure, we got homeless drug addicts and schizoids living in five-star hotels, and since all the restaurants went bankrupt, to get anything decent to eat you gotta order by drone from Philly. Still, I told Janice I'd build her the best tower in New York, which of course makes it the best in the world. There it is."

What Ellie had thought was a shadow or a mirage standing up through the dense mist turned out to be quite solid. As they circled around, she saw its true three-dimensional shape, now more gray than black and immensely tall.

"It looks like a knife or double-edged sword," she said as the pilot made straight for the top.

"Good eye!" Barracude said, pounding her on the back. "The design, which I picked out, is based on a Zulu spearhead, that's why we call it the Assegee Tower."

"I think you mean Assegai," Mr. Perdix said drolly.

"That's what I said. Janice's people are related to the Zulus, that's why she's so tall. I mean, I'm tall." He really wasn't. "But she's really tall, and gorgeous. So I built that to match. They're still working on the lower floors, so no one's moved in yet except us."

"It's certainly the tallest building around," Ellie said, wanting to say something kind about the Assegai's rather brutal style of architecture.

"We're three times as high as those goofs at 1800 Park. That's the midget down there, not even over the clouds, ha!" Barracude said with friendly derision. "The city planning guys said, 'you can't build higher than the Freedom Tower, it's disrespectful.' And also they made me put in tons of safety features, which cost a bundle, but where life and limb is concerned, you gotta spend, right? Anyway, so in deference to all the dead people and whatnot from 9/11, I says 'fine, then I won't put a needle thing on top.'

"To cut to the good part, with this Assegai Tower, I got the highest livable floor, but the Freedom is still the tallest, on a technicality. I call it win-win. No one can ever say I don't make sacrifices for patriotism."

The Assegai's apex terminated in a cleverly designed landing pad, which did not detract from its overall shape. But it didn't look as though it could accommodate anything larger than a volocopter.

"Ah." Sarge Bryan looked through the cockpit glass. "Are we gonna to be able to land there? This ol' pig weighs five tons."

"Right." Mr. Barracude smiled knowingly and smacked his lips with satisfaction. "We got an app for that."

A long tube reached out from the side of the building, seemingly impervious to gravity and the downdraft of their rotors. Like a tubular sea creature with a sucker mouth at its end, it latched onto the helicopter's side door. Despite appearances and the translucent steps, which gave Ellie a clear view hundreds of feet down to the cloud layer, the conveyance was more like a plastic stairwell than a scary carnival ride. The copter hovered, and she dragged herself out of her warm seat, unkinked a few major knots in her back, and eased along after Sarge Bryan had tested the steps with his full weight.

"Nifty, huh?" Mr. Barracude said as he led the way, sidestepping down to a covered reception area.

"Why have we come here?" Ms. China asked the question that was perhaps on everyone's grateful but suspicious mind. "If Andrews is shut, we could have landed at an alternate airport."

After they had all exited the tube, the Marine helicopter detached itself from its mooring and veered off out of sight.

"Yeah, we coulda gone to an airport," their host admitted. "Thing is, they didn't know which one was secure, and my bird needs a long runway. It's gonna be JFK, LaGuardia, or Newark."

Ellie received a bracing shot of vertigo as she thought she felt the building sway. Thankfully they were soon inside a lift, and she didn't have to look down at the clouds.

The doors into the building slid open noiselessly. They were still on a walking tour of the American oligarch's achievements.

"…yup, they said it couldn't be done, but I said it could. And you know what I did? I put the biggest development ever right smack in the middle of Harlem, really vitalized the whole area. Janice's family lived here, that was before she went to college. Did I tell you she was top of her class? Not just one of the top, the best in the history of her colleges…"

A butler and two maids met them. They were offered drinks, hot refresher towels, and digital newspapers. Ellie could have made better use of a motorized wheelchair; one of her back muscles was making spasmodic jerks. She must have really pulled it while rowing for her life on the Potomac.

"…it seems you gotta be some kind a foreigner to get any respect these days. Like we're ashamed of our home-grown winners. Disturbing. I'm from Brazil, but I won't even have Brazil nuts served in my bar…"

Barracude looked at them as though expecting a reaction.

Mr. Perdix caught on and gave a half-forced chuckle. "You're joking, of course."

"What d'you think, I'm a bigot or something? Heh-heh. In college, that's what they nicknamed me: the Nut from Brazil. But look who's on top of the heap now, huh?"

Ellie downed a yummy sports drink out of an oversized martini glass and ate a handful of salty nuts mixed in with tiny crackers. She couldn't recall having eaten as much since before their visit to the White House.

Barracude's people finished serving and resumed their positions at all four corners of the spacious living room.

"What are you standing around for?" Barracude berated his staff. "Look at my guests! Are these the kind of clothes they'd feel comfortable visiting my home in? Find some new ones."

"Y'know, sir," Sarge Bryan said as he also took a second helping of the fantastically tasty nut mix. "We're fine in these loaner fatigues."

Ellie was decidedly not. Her soggy underwear was chafing on the rather stiff fabric of her navy-and-fluorescent-yellow coveralls. Nevertheless, she decided to maintain solidarity with her team and not complain.

"Nonsense, we'll get you fixed up. Just sit down and relax. You're working for Uncle Sam now. You deserve the best."

The butler, a youngish upright man with a full head of conspicuously premature white hair, whispered something to his master.

"If we ain't got the right stuff, go out and get stuff. Get the house AI to take their measurements, send it to the store, then go pick it up. Do I have to do everything?"

The butler whispered something a bit more urgently.

"Rioting? Still?" Barracude shook his head. "Okay, send our flying robot, then. It may have to make two trips, but I don't trust theirs; they keep going to the Chrysler Building by mistake."

Ms. China and Mr. Perdix wandered over to where Ellie and Sarge Bryan were standing in the middle of a dazzlingly mirrored drinking lounge.

"Whether we like it or not, we're going to be fashionably dressed," Ms. China said. She caught hold of one end of the zinc countertop and stretched herself out like a cat as her clawed fist cleaned out the rest of the bar mix. "And there better be more of these pretzel bits or there'll be trouble."

Mr. Perdix studied the mirrored walls. "This is quite the place."

"Don't swell the man's head even more," Ms. China whispered.

Sarge Bryan grinned while he kept chewing.

"Even the glass surfaces are self-cleaning." The JASON scientist pressed his finger on a wall, and after a few seconds, his fingerprint disappeared. The living room was bordered on two sides by solid glass curtain walls thirty feet high. Something moved. "Oh, look, it's the window-washing bots coming down from the roof."

Their host was still busy barking orders at his staff.

"So what do you think?" Ellie said quietly to Sarge Bryan.

"Nothing much we can do. Just play this out," he said. "I don't know about this guy, but I gotta think Ms. Jones is on the level. She's served her country and her community all her life. I can't believe she'd turn traitor."

"I bet that's what they said about Benedict Arnold," Mr. Perdix whispered.

Ellie noticed a shadow creep across the brightly polished marble floor. The cleaning foam the robot washers were spraying onto the windows seemed unusually thick, but they had to know what they were doing; they were purpose-built mechBrains.

Mr. Perdix had ducked down under the counter to look for more bar mix. Ms. China had a box of it in her hands, having grabbed it while no one was looking and was munching merrily. Sarge Bryan was tapping on his handset, getting updates on the national security situation.

What was going on out there? They were one thousand feet above whatever mayhem was happening in the streets below. One person might know.

Ellie texted: *Miss Aleph, you there?*

Where else? Anyone who's following the end of the world only has to tag along with you.

Can you talk to the house robots? Are we about to be accosted and taken prisoner?

Again, you mean? You've made a habit of that on three other continents, why not here?

Aleph!

Hang on, there are 10,000 talking appliances in this place… Let me see…

Ellie waited as the stealthy AI quietly queried the lesser mechBrains.

Wait a sec, this Ecovacs Winbot 746YX isn't responding. And they shouldn't be washing those windows. Those bots are supposed to wash the shady side of the building or come out after sundown. Even their tiny digital minds know heat from the sun can cause the cleaning fluid to dry, which will result in unsightly—

Already teetering on the edge of paranoia, that was enough for Ellie to shout: "Everyone!" She pointed up to the windows. "Look, that's not right."

She could only think of gesticulating wildly, but in a few seconds, everyone got what she meant.

"That's not cleaning foam," Sarge Bryan said, his cybernetic eyes zeroing in and analyzing the substance.

Ms. China responded predictably by cursing out their host. "You sodding fuckface, what kind of security do you have?"

Mr. Barracude jabbed his butler in his starched shirt front. "Dammit, I go away for a few days, and you make me look bad. Find out what that is. Some crazy anarchist group is probably painting obscene shit on my beautiful tower. It's a hate crime against beautiful architecture and humanity!"

"Do you smell that?" Mr. Perdix said. He was holding the back of his head, having bumped it on the bar counter when Ellie had yelled. "Petroleum distillate… it's a breaching assault."

43

ASSEGAI TOWER
HARLEM

T hey're just window robots," Mr. Barracude protested. "That's the best bulletproof glass there is. Whatever they're up to, they can't do nothing."

"Everyone get back," Sarge Bryan said. "Behind those pillars in the center of the room."

Despite his doubts about the hijacked window-cleaning bots' ability to do them harm, Barracude pulled off his bolo tie and jabbed his fat thumb onto the big blue sapphire. The must be his personal panic button, Ellie concluded. Six or seven security people rushed in from the penthouse foyer but were unsure of where to point their weapons. Ellie and the others huddled against a set of garish gold-embroidered tapestries and watched the thirty-foot-high windows in the mirrors behind the bar.

"What's that?" the cowering butler said, pointing at a shape rising up against the sky in part of the glass which was not yet covered by foam.

Ellie recognized it—she had flown quite a few miles on one in Israel.

"That's a jet flyboard."

Paramilitary in helmets and tactical gear had risen up a thousand feet in the air and were clearly intent on coming in. Fissures began to appear along the upper regions of the curved window glass, which gave an audible *crack*.

Mr. Barracude was incensed. "I paid a fortune for that crap."

"Get a refund later," Mr. Perdix yelled. "We have to leave."

"We've got time," Ms. China said, not missing an opportunity to be contrary. "It'll take them a few minutes. By the way, that's aqua regis they're using to dissolve the molecular bonds in the glass wall, not distillate."

As soon as she said this, Ellie saw one of the figures on a flyboard get buffeted by a gust of wind and veer right up close to one of the window-washing robots. The flame on the bottom of the flyboard touched the breaching foam.

A massive explosion and shockwave followed. Close on its heels was a filthy burning smell that reached where they had taken shelter in the middle of the penthouse. The blast wave slammed Ellie to the floor as large chunks of window glass shattered against the marble floor in the formerly immaculate living room.

Several of the flying attackers vanished in a blue-black fireball.

"Was that part of the breaching thing?" Ellie yelled as a high-altitude wind blasted through the gaping crack in the building's façade and strange orange flames spread across the ceiling.

"Not unless they're a really bad suicide squad," Ms. China yelled over the noise.

"One of them let his jet burner get too close to the chemicals and the robot's power cell," Mr. Perdix said. His forehead was cut, and he wiped blood away from his eyes.

Sarge Bryan's unique pupils were staring at the flames spreading out above them. "Would anyone know if this structure is of the framed-tube variety?"

"How does that matter now?" Mr. Barracude said as he huddled between two equally frightened-looking security guards. "Look at this mess!"

"Oh, Sarge Bryan has made a valid…" Mr. Perdix said, looking up. He grabbed the older of the two guards. "You. What fire-suppression systems are there?"

"Uh…" The goateed man pointed up. "Those."

Up near the ceiling hung a half dozen pipes ineffectively spraying something white at the oncoming blaze. Even Ellie could see it was like using squirt guns to stop rolling napalm.

"We have to get out," Mr. Perdix said, nearly sipping on some debris. "Down. And far away."

Ellie felt dizzy and unstable on her feet; she hoped it was just her and not the building shaking.

"We'll take the emergency—"

The goateed man shook his head. "The elevators are all out."

"What—is—happening?" Ellie cried over the rising wind whipping the flames into a frenzy.

"That fire suppression ain't doing squat," Sarge Bryan observed, penetrating the smoke and flames with his cybernetic vision.

"There are tubular structures holding the floor above us in place. When they give out..." Ms. China said, slapping her hand together. "Everything above us will come down, hard."

"The fucking architect said it could never happen," Mr. Barracude said.

Somehow he had hung on to his empty whisky glass. In anger, he threw it up at the flames and was rewarded by incoming bullets. They all ducked deeper behind cover. There were still one or two attackers circling outside, unable to get in but not giving up. Security people returned fire with pistols.

"Forget that," Mr. Barracude said, grabbing a guard by the collar and dislodging his earpiece. "Tell everyone to clear the whole building, total emergency evac."

With his security people covering their retreat, Mr. Barracude led them into his bedroom, which featured wild boar tusks and not a few stuffed toy animals.

"The harnesses are in there." He pointed at panels under the windowsill.

Ellie thought this was not the time to ask "what harnesses?"

Just then, an ominous crack in the other room was followed by creaking noises. Ellie joined in the most intense unboxing of her life.

"These cost a bundle," Mr. Barracude said as his security man adjusted the orange webbing belt straps around his torso. "But my accountants worked it out, safety equipment has what they call 'an accelerated capital cost allowance.' They paid for themselves before the building was even finished. Am I good or what?"

Without confirming his boss's business acumen, the goateed man strapped the older oligarch in and checked the armature to which a much-too-thin-looking cable was attached. With a small smile on his face as though he had been wanting to do this for some time, he prepared to push Mr. Barracude out the open window.

"What are you doing? Guests first."

Sarge Bryan outfitted Ellie's harness.

"If you'll allow me to check the lady's rigging, sir."

The butler tried to maintain a dignified air even with a streak of soot smeared on the side of his face. He checked over Ellie's rigging and nodded.

"The system is designed to have multiple escapees on one line," the butler said. "However, seeing as our numbers are few, we may all avail ourselves of separate tethers and depart at once."

A big steel beam collapsed into the living room, leaving a gaping hole down to the next floor.

Ellie tucked her hair under the edge of her helmet. "Are you British?"

The butler nodded. "I've served the Barracudes for twenty years, hardly been back."

"You still have a charming Berkshire accent. Reading?"

The butler nodded. "Spot on, ma'am. Please keep hold on the window frame right up until it's time to let go. Just drop straight down. The guiding mechanism will take care of the rest."

Just drop straight down. Ellie only dared to look sideways at the cloud layer, which hung like a diaphanous moat around the middle of the skyscraper sixty or so stories beneath them. The living room was a mass of heat and smoke. The gryphon tapestries were floating up in the wind created by the conflagration as though they were animated by demons intent on fanning the flames.

"Ms. Sato," he said, looking sternly at her, "we could still try for the staircase…"

A hundred floors up? With her already-wobbly legs?

"Do you trust this contraption?"

"Uh… it looks expensive," was all the assurance Sarge Bryan could give.

Ms. China handed Mr. Barracude a helmet. He stared at her.

"Thanks, doll. Hey, has anyone ever told you that you have very interesting eyes?"

Ms. China stared back. "Never."

"What are you waiting for?" The flames had reached the door of the master bedroom, and sweat was pouring down Mr. Barracude's tanned face. "Those are two-ton-test diamond nanowires. Guaranteed not to break or double my money back."

There was no time for Ellie to mention how not-reassuring that was. The flames, like a living thing that sensed the bedroom windows had been opened, were a thick mass of searing brown-gray rushing toward them.

She squeezed her eyes shut and jumped out the hundredth-floor window. As she fell, the whirring sound of the cable escalated in pitch and was joined by the rushing of air past her ears. The rushing noise kept increasing.

Should I really be going this fast?

44

POTOMAC RIVER
NEAR CUMBERLAND

TATA

Tata watched Russian Ambassador Bagration flop into the water like a baby beluga. She threw her pike down and leapt after him, silently cursing the diplomat: *Of all the stupid...*

The rest of her thoughts were cut short by her sudden immersion in icy Potomac water. With the added weight of a cyborg's mechanical implants, the only way Human+ soldiers like Tata could swim was with substantial flotation devices—she had none. Her plan had been to grab Bagration, sink with the middle-aged twit to the riverbed, stuff a rebreather in his mouth, and hope hypothermic shock or coronary arrest didn't kill him before she could drag him to shore.

She managed to seize his pants leg, but the cuff tore, and Bagration floated away as she sank. The current was stronger than it looked. There was only one last measure to try. Tata deployed taser prongs from her forearm unit. The water was so murky she had to estimate her target while dialing down the stun charge to zero. A second later, she felt a tug like she had snagged a big one on the end of a fishing line. She hoped it was the ambassador and not a log or a rubber tire.

Tata had fished for tuna in the Black Sea with her grandfather. She knew enough not to jerk back on the line. As her feet hit the slimy but relatively firm bottom, she kept her arm outstretched, strategically letting out slack and then pulling, trying to guide the diplomat toward the far bank. Her GLONASS map showed an elbow bend just ahead. While there was too much sediment to see exactly where she was, the water ahead eddied and swirled—she was close.

A rebreather tube had deployed automatically when her systems sensed she was underwater. With a free hand, she grabbed it and took a deep breath. Human+ soldiers liked to brag about being impervious to cold. However, the sensation was far from pleasant for both her organic and mechanical parts, both of which started subroutines to counteract the debilitating effects of the sudden temperature drop. Her organic body compensated less efficiently than her hydraulics, and she started seeing black spots. If she passed out now, her backup mechBrain would walk to her to shore, but she'd lose the ambassador.

безумный режим?

Her operating system prompted her to engage berserker mode. Useless. Instead, she struck herself in the head with her free hand. The water-cushioned blow cleared her brain.

She crouched down and got a good foothold among some rusty debris, then she pushed off with maximum energy toward the elbow bend. The taser lines went slack. She pulled back and felt them gently tighten again. She gave a final yank, and the floating inert form of Bagration bobbed in the calmer waters.

Her head broke the surface. She shook her hair out and stepped along the riverbed, which angled up in shallow scalloped steps. These must have been the result of the dredging operation she had seen before she jumped from the bridge.

As soon as her augmented ears were cleared of water, she heard gunfire, shouting, and the roaring sound of heavy equipment followed by steel cables whipping and snapping. She could do nothing to assist Sarge Bryan or the others. She had to retrieve the ambassador, who by now probably had two lungs full of river water.

A soaking-wet log was in her way. She kicked it in half without breaking stride toward the water's edge. Bagration's feet got caught in the current, and he started sliding back into the river.

"No!" She leapt forward. "You are not getting away from… me," she said, grabbing the man by the arm and hauling him all the way up onto a small pebble-strewn beach.

The out-of-shape bastard was blue, cold, and not breathing. No problem. There was something in his mouth. It was either a sponge creature or the head of a small plastic toilet brush. She didn't look too closely at it before throwing it into the water and turning him on his side. After squeezing his back to expel as much water as she could, Tata started CPR and stuck an advanced health monitoring device onto his neck. Half the lights remained dark—they were only used for cyborg systems—while the rest were red or yellow.

Fortunately, her breathing tube was adaptable to CPR, and she was spared having to give Bagration's puffy, blue, slug-like lips the "kiss of life." The breathing unit made the bureaucrat's man boobs rise and fall under his soaking-wet shirt. At first she feared Bagration had suffered a heart attack, however the robot health monitor confirmed a weak but steady pulse.

After two minutes of resuscitation, Bagration made a wet moaning sound.

"Welcome back, Mr. Ambassador…" Tata said. She was considering her best options for linking back up with the American group or calling for embassy ground transport when the bushes along the riverbank exploded with activity. She looked up to find a dozen gun muzzles pointed at her and Bagration.

"Lookee what the river washed up," said a man with a tobacco-stained beard. He wore a filthy orange vest and held a hunting rifle. "What the fuck are you?"

безумный режим?

She dismissed the berserker program prompt. As much as she would have liked to use ultraviolence to prevent capture and relieve some pent-up aggression, Bagration would not survive being shot, even a little.

Tata had a rock in one hand and a rusted metal bar that weighed about thirty kilograms in the other. She quickly calculated that in berserker mode there was an eighty percent chance of neutralizing all the hostiles without receiving a major injury, but killing so many Americans might spoil her chances of a deeper friendship, and possibly romance, with Sergeant Bryan. A more diplomatic plan of action was called for.

By their ragged dress and stupid-looking hockey and mountain-climbing helmets, she identified the aggressors as part of the anarcho-communist mob from the CUMZ.

"Wait, comrades," Tata said, dropping the rock and the length of rebar and raising her hands. "We are on your side. This is the Russian ambassador, Mr. Bagration. Check his picture online."

One of the CUMZ morons poked a selfie stick and an iPhone at the prone and sputtering diplomat.

"What are you doin' here? This is the CUMZ Autonomous Utopian Zone, no cops, no military, only free citizens."

"Do we look like police?" Tata scoffed. "Help me get Mr. Bagration into your, uh, medical facilities, then I will explain."

"No fuckin' around. We got a bead on you."

"Yes, Autonomous Citizen, you do."

The medical facilities turned out to be a filthy van formerly owned by a local gardening contractor. There were expired, half-empty IV bags on the rusty floor. There were blankets, moldy, and a looted mattress with the plastic cover and price tag still attached. Bagration lay on it, wheezing and bleary eyed. A radial heater powered by the truck's battery warmed him, and Tata saw he was no longer in danger of going into shock.

"Now talk, or we'll, uh, have to make you," said the apparent first-among-equals of the CUMZ as he brandished his scoped bolt gun in a way he thought would be menacing.

Tata wanted so much to take it away from him and impale him on it. She hocked up a gob of phlegm, which had a gritty texture from the silt in the river water, and again chose calculation over combat. Instead of spitting her juicy goober in the CUMZ man's face prior to killing him, she politely ejected her sputum against the side of the van.

"My dear gentlemen, if you will look closely, I have a very important message for you."

She wiped the water and muck off of the projector on her right forearm unit, where a small holographic figure appeared. The CUMZ leader and his two associates instantly recognized the famous image. His words were automatically translated into English.

"Greetings, comrades of the CUMZ. I ask you in the name of solidarity of all free people to welcome my emissaries," said the image of President Putin.

"It is my hope that we may establish permanent ties with autonomous zones all over the world, supporting courageous social innovators such as yourselves as we have done in Venezuela, Cuba, and Lebanon. In the spirit of Marxist solidarity, here is what I would ask you to do…"

45

OUTSIDE LAS VEGAS, NV

ZVENA

A h, Komandir, finally our luck kicks in," Rodion said, trying to give him a friendly tap with his elbow but instead hitting him too hard, sending Zvena stumbling sideways. "Sorry, having a little balance problem."

They were walking away down a lonely stretch of Nevada highway in the mid-morning sunshine. Behind them stood the unmanned interstate robot truck they had hijacked and rerouted after they had crossed the Mexican border. It was able to drive without stopping and allowed them to catch up with the Pangean insurgents.

"How is this luck?" Zvena asked, looking back to make certain their supply-carrying OCEL robot was keeping up with them. Rodion had damaged one of its legs while in a pathogen-induced delirium. Fortunately, he'd brought a repair kit from the ship, and now the OCEL wobbled only a little on its six stainless-steel legs.

"It's Vegas, baby," Rodion said in guttural English. "In most towns, we would be noticed for sure, but here I think we blend in."

Zvena considered what they looked like: a very large guy in an oilcloth rain slicker accompanied by a truly huge guy with an eyepatch, followed by a robot dog. The sight might not attract much notice among the debauched weirdness of this mecca of Western degeneracy.

"We're not in the city yet. They may not be headed there." He checked his wrist-mounted map display. "The Pangeans have not moved for an hour. Let's get a closer look."

Once they had found where the enemy had breached the southern border fence into Arizona, they also found the remains of an odd battle. Interpreting the debris, Zvena concluded the Pangeans had met with a force of a dozen or so armed people. The marks on the ground and severed zip ties revealed they had been taken prisoner.

After that, a larger force had arrived. The second force approached unopposed and wiped out the first Americans then freed the Pangean insurgents. All of the bodies had been cleared away, but the victors left behind many shell casings. Some of them had fingerprints.

Russian intelligence had been deep-hacking into US law enforcement databases for decades. It only took a few minutes to identify a group of Arizona militia members who had several things in common: arrest records for assault, weapons offenses, and most interestingly, toppling statues.

"Which vehicle are we tracking?" Zvena asked.

For many hours, their quarry had only been a blue dot on a computer map.

"That one." Rodion aimed an invisible-spectrum laser at a covered pickup truck. It was parked beside several other similar vehicles behind an industrial complex comprised of low-slung connected buildings, the largest of which was topped by a large antenna.

"This doesn't look like an insurgent target," Zvena said skeptically. "Are you certain you have the correct vehicle?"

"The American criminal database had a list of known militia contacts and many years of records for their known communications devices. Spetsnaz AI identified frequently called numbers, and these we traced to a cluster of three. One of the handsets was linked to an audio system and a popular music streaming service in that truck."

"Maybe it was a false signal," Zvena said, once again impressed by the results of Rodion's recent impromptu brain surgery, which had increased his ability to think logically. "What if that truck was just passing by, and the signals got crossed?"

"I've checked it a dozen times. You want me to do again?"

"No, just don't take your eyes, er, eye off them." Zvena was grouchy from the long ride in the back of the truck on top of its load of aluminum siding.

A few minutes later, a hatch on the roof of one of the buildings popped open. A figure came out into the stark sunlight, trailing a thick cable, and proceeded to climb the antenna tower.

"That is a 7G-band emitter," Zvena said mostly to himself, wondering whether he should risk attacking now. He dismissed the idea. There were too many locals. If the Pangeans slipped away during the fighting, they might never find them again. He watched the man climb.

"Did you know the 7G data communications system incorporates waves in the dark-matter energy spectrum?"

"I know, Rodya," Zvena said, still annoyed they could be wasting their time. He had received special permission to operate on US soil and did not like the prospect of being embarrassed by having made a fundamental mistake. "Can you make any sense of what he's doing?"

Rodion relayed video from the telescope to Zvena's optic implants. A dark-clad figure struggled to attach the cable to a junction box, and as he did so, the top of the fat antenna wire snagged under his chin. The man's silicone mask was dislodged, revealing hideous scar tissue. The man quickly pushed his false face back in place and completed his task.

"Ha! We have them. The Faceless Pangeans, disgusting degenerates," said Zvena. "For once, you didn't fuck up. Maybe you should have deactivated the other side of your brain years ago. It was holding you back."

In the far distance, a few wind turbines plowed lazily through the cool arid desert air. A bird, likely an eagle, few high over them.

"Our Pangeans are now allied with fake militia units who are actually Antifa cells dedicated to the destruction of America," Zvena summed up. "There was no forced entry into the building, which means they have confederates inside this communications relay station. This is a pre-planned operation... but with what objectives?"

"Komandir..."

"Quiet, I'm thinking."

"Okay, but after your thinking break, you may want to look."

The big antenna the Pangean had been working on was glowing. Great silvery and yellow arcs of energy were springing up at first in a harmonious pattern, like a neon Christmas tree, then becoming confused, jagging out wildly. Finally, huge sparks flew in all directions, and streaks of lightning struck the building and other antennas as the steel frame of the largest one melted and silently toppled over. The Pangean technician fell out of sight, and a moment later the tall transmitter lay in a smoldering heap on the tar-and-gravel-topped roof.

Rodion looked at Zvena. "They have had a 'big-time screwup.'"

46

ABDELKADER

Abdelkader had barely enough time to leap to the side when his technician fell back down from the roof through the trapdoor. Fire enveloped the man's shoulders and back.

"Extinguishers!" he yelled, coughing as smoke quickly filled up the narrow corridor of the telecom relay station.

Dr. Baldur was in the other room sitting behind a control panel, his unshaven face wearing a stupid smile. That expression faded as it dawned on him what a disaster his test of the 7G irradiation system had been.

More than a disaster, Abdelkader fumed, it was an embarrassment in front of their allies, the Antifa militia. He looked for the red-bearded Sikawski but only saw people running around looking in each room to see if anything else had caught fire.

"I—I can fix this," Baldur stuttered as he got up and tried to reassure Abdelkader. The bioweapons scientist gagged when he smelled the burning man and ducked as the remains of the antenna crashed down onto the roof of the one-story building.

"No, you can't," Abdelkader yelled. "We have to abandon the facility. Get the emitter to the mobile platform."

He had to keep the initiative in their favor. Sikawski and his Antifa outnumbered them three to one and were better armed. Their alliance was one of convenience, not conviction. If the violent American anarchists thought more mayhem and pain to Americans could be achieved without him and his Pangean force, they would try to take the T-ray emitter for themselves.

"What kinda mess is this?" Sikawski demanded as he came around the corner, his gaunt features underscored by a stubbly facial hair. "That antenna went up like a Roman candle. How's that gonna kill those fascists in Vegas? They're all there at the MGM: the governors and that federal Nazi bitch Leota."

This particular Antifa cell was long on ideology and short on scientific know-how. All Abdelkader had told them was they had a way of projecting brain-frying radiation through advanced cell phone towers, and Dr. Baldur's serum injection made them all immune.

"Doesn't matter," Abdelkader said, picking up his weapon and kit bag. "We're leaving. We will complete the assault on the conference from street level. This…" He waved dismissively at the wrecked communications center and lied. "This was always a long shot to begin with."

On La Tortuga, they had been able to activate the virus in test subjects at distances of a few thousand meters using miniature 7G emitters. Was Baldur exaggerating his accomplishments? If so, what else was he hiding?

"Really, huh?" the American terrorist said skeptically, looking at the blistered back of the man who had fallen from the roof. "How close we gotta get? The blue-state meetup is guarded more heavily than the White House."

"Best we show you, my friend," Abdelkader said. "As you Americans say, seeing is believing."

After setting his best man Sadikul to watching Baldur in case he tried to run away, Abdelkader checked social media streams. They were the best way to get multiple confirmations that their political targets were where they were supposed to be.

JiggyJizz296 had just uploaded a shaky video of California's governor and his security team sneaking into the Las Vegas MGM hotel via the kitchen entrance. The Western addiction to sharing everything online meant they had unwitting spies providing real-time intelligence in every corner of the country.

"Target two has arrived," Abdelkader said, motioning to his people. "Don't bother putting out the fires. Just load the truck."

Sadikul nodded wearily. He was still struggling with the bug he picked up in Central America.

"What about Leota?" Sikawski asked vehemently. "She's *our* top target. I know her from the Marines. If any of those maggots is dedicated to our sick systemic racist dictatorship, it's her. She's got to be taken out."

"First her, then the rest of the oppressors," Abdelkader agreed. He had to keep humoring the Antifa. Personally, he had no faith in assassination as a long-term solution. Pathogen-based genocide, on the other hand, was a historically proven method for ushering in large-scale social change.

Dr. Baldur hurried out of the smoky building after them.

"I—I don't know what..." he mumbled. "It should have worked."

"Quiet," Abdelkader hissed and grabbed the scientist by the arm, pushing him into their covered flatbed truck. "Do not ever show weakness in front of the American Antifa."

Baldur's sweaty face looked pathetic. "Sorry."

"I never had much faith in your 7G concept. It only worked in the lab," Abdelkader said bitterly.

If the dark-matter wavelengths had really been able to carry T-ray activation signals, they could have blanketed the entire country in a few days. Now, he thought as he put the truck in gear, they would have to rely on direct irradiation and super-spreaders.

They rolled through the town of Sloan, an isolated Nevada community; its main industry was a limestone quarry. No one came out to look at them or the puffs of smoke rising from the telecom station. The Pangeans and Antifa set off toward Las Vegas in a tight convoy. In the distance, a line of blue-white mountains with snow caps underscored a clear blue sky.

They slowed down as they came to an overpass. Underneath it was a homeless camp that had spread out on both sides. Small fires illuminated shabby tents. One bold vagrant approached one of the Antifa vehicles to beg for money, and when he got none, he threw garbage at the trespassers. A bladed weapon slashed out, and the figure ran off, leaving behind a few severed fingers.

"Have you had a look at Sadikul?" Abdelkader's top man was in the vehicle behind them.

"Ah… yes, I did examine him," Dr. Baldur said from the seat beside him. "Just a stomach bug."

"What is the range of the mobile unit?"

"You will recall that we were able to activate specimens at more than two kilometers through all manner of shielding, lead, boron carbide. It didn't matter."

"Of course I recall," Abdelkader snapped. "But on the island, we had high-voltage power sources."

"The mini Generac generator should provide enough power."

"How far?"

"At least five to six hundred meters."

That sounded optimistic.

"Don't screw me again, Baldur. These American thugs may be thick, but they will not hesitate to cut ties with us if we fail again because of your mistakes. And if they do, I'll make sure the first tie they cut is you."

More and more, Dr. Baldur's face was annoying him. Abdelkader wished he had time to take a sharp knife and skin it off, then have him fitted with a silicone face.

"M-maybe th-three hundred yards," Baldur equivocated. "But with twenty-five thousand watts, certainly three hundred, certainly that." He pointed weakly at the rectangular trailer hitched to the lead truck.

They passed a large sign which read: *SPEED VEGAS*

"Stop the convoy," Abdelkader ordered.

47

SPEED VEGAS, NEVADA

Abdelkader's vehicle veered onto the shoulder of the industrial road.
"What the fuck?" Sikawski said, emerging from the cloud of cool dust
that had been kicked up by the lead vehicle.

"Ranging test. You will enjoy it." Abdelkader's people had also jumped
out of their vehicles, so he motioned for everyone to remain calm. All of them
had weapons, and no one was exactly sure why they had stopped. "Hook up
the emitter."

"Here?"

For miles around, there was only desert scrub brush and a tourist
racetrack.

"We have to be sure your generator will work as efficiently as the ones
in our laboratory." If anyone challenged them, they had papers showing they
were part of a film crew working on a reality TV series.

"What are you talkin' about?" Sikawski groused. "This generator's smaller
and more powerful than the one you asked for."

"We're set up for rapid deployment." Abdelkader ignored the domestic
terrorist, who thought it looked intimidating to wear a fat silver nose ring.
"This will take only a few minutes."

The T-ray emitter, essentially a dark-energy laser, was in the covered flatbed of his own truck. Sadikul and the other Pangeans rapidly hooked up the power cables trailing from the portable generator, which was the size and shape of a large microwave oven. Sikawski saw where the unit was aiming.

"There?"

Abdelkader used a visible green laser to fine-tune his aim right at the large sign enclosing the motor sports stadium. Even from where they were standing, three hundred yards away, they could hear the high revs of Lamborghinis and Ferraris whizzing around the oval racetrack. Abdelkader could see the far lengths of the track to the left and right of the stadium-style seating. A half dozen bored tourists were acting out their race-car fantasies.

"Those sacks of over-privileged human garbage?" Sikawski scoffed. "How do you know they've got the bug?"

"Most of America has it," Dr. Baldur said. "And so do you."

Dr. Baldur had taken saliva samples from the Antifa to confirm the spread of the AC-32 enabler virus, but Sikawski still looked taken back.

"Yeah… But the vaccine you gave us, it keeps it from activating, right?" The group of Antifa standing near them stared more warily at the emitter.

"Those bourgeois tourists will have come to Las Vegas by airplane. They're almost certainly infected, and of course, showing no symptoms. Now we unleash their personalized portion of plague." He nodded to the technician at the emitter control.

The neutronium-sheathed iris-style aperture in the small but very heavy device cracked open. The emitter started humming, no louder than a refrigerator motor. Then, seconds later, it shut off and closed.

"That's it?"

"What were you expecting? Great green gobs of gamma radiation?"

"How's that gonna smash capitalism and exterminate the patriarchy?"

Out on the speedway, cars continued to accelerate rhythmically and brake and accelerate again.

"Wait," Abdelkader said. He had no sweat glands on his face, and even in the cool dry desert air, the tissue under his mask was rapidly heating up. If Baldur was about to hand him another humiliation—

The yellow Lamborghini lost control, spinning and crashing. A red Ferrari behind it narrowly avoided the wreck, but then it, too, slowed for a moment, until suddenly deciding to accelerate and dash itself to bits on a cinderblock retaining wall.

"Excellent. Let's be off," he said, patting his technician on the back. "We have to help our local partners change American politics for good."

The roads into Las Vegas were nearly deserted. The first roadblocks they encountered were near the MGM Grand Hotel.

"My people on the ground say Leota ain't here," Sikawski complained over the encrypted radio.

"All the blue-state governors who are still alive are in there," Abdelkader said, trying to calm his American associate as they drove along Tropicana, past a wide entrance, and into the MGM complex. "We could barge through now and be in range, but then we're sure to scare away Leota, who you say is on her way. Be patient and take the next right turn."

He clicked off the mic, which seemed to be a cue for Dr. Baldur to start complaining. He looked with disgust at the replica Statue of Liberty on the next corner and the tiny fake Eiffel tower several streets over.

"Why are the politicians even in this bizarre place?"

"They kept changing the location because of our friends' assassination plots."

Abdelkader spotted a large handicap taxi. Breaking off from the line of the other vehicles, he followed it. Ignoring the chatter on the radio, he trailed the oblong blue minivan into the parking lot of the Laugh Factory Comedy Club.

He watched the taxi driver stop, get out, and assist a man in a wheelchair who was using a hydraulic lift apparatus to get out. The passenger took out an enormous wallet, held it up to the driver, and opened it. It immediately covered the turbaned man with sparkling multicolored confetti. Both men laughed as the passenger produced his real credit chip and paid. The cripple was some kind of comedy magician, Abdelkader thought, arriving early at the club to rehearse.

When the taxi driver was alone, Abdelkader approached him, smiled, and shot in him the neck with a suppressed pistol.

"Come on," he said to Dr. Baldur and a Pangean in their truck. "We have to swap loads. The dead Sikh for the device."

Fortunately he had left the wheels attached to the frame of the T-ray emitter, otherwise they would never have been able to get it into the rear space of the minivan taxi without attracting attention. To anyone passing by, it might look like a piece of lighting equipment for a show. Abdelkader glanced out to the street, there was no one. He threw the tarp over the taxi driver's body, rolled him up and tossed him into the back of the truck.

"Now what?" Dr. Baldur said.

"Now," he said, digging through his satchel and choosing a darker-colored silicone face to match the skin of the dead man, "I put on a happy face, and we carry out our attack."

New face, turban, and germ mask in place, Abdelkader drove out from the comedy club's parking area and back onto Tropicana. On the side of the MGM, he had noticed a side street marked "Taxis Only," where cars were being waved rapidly through.

"Sikawski, you may cause your diversion anytime," he said into his radio handset.

Up ahead, blue-suited security guards seemed to be making more thorough searches of vehicles, including taxis. The driver at the head of the queue was required to open his trunk.

A dull thud came from the opposite side of the tall green hotel. That would be Sikawski launching an RPG into the fancy restaurant on the other side of the block. Within seconds, the security people abandoned their checkpoint and rushed back into the hotel, preparing to shelter or evacuate the dignitaries. Fortunately, social media spies were still on duty.

Abdelkader scrolled through the screen of his large tablet. On the left side was a satellite map; on the right were tiny animated squares showing feeds from video streamers inside the hotel. The locations of the tourists and random bloggers were all represented on the map by variously colored balloon icons.

He tapped one square to enlarge it: it showed the doors of a large conference room slamming shut. In another frame, so did the side doors. Excellent. The VIPs were sheltering in place until the threat outside the hotel was analyzed. He checked the map and his compass bearings one last time, then leaned into the rear compartment. Hunched down behind the emitter, he set the GPS targeting device and selected maximum power and maximum wide beam. Abdelkader hit *Power On*.

48

MGM GRAND, LAS VEGAS

The green aiming laser was fixed on a large potted plant in front of the takeout window of Emeril's New Orleans's Fish House. Able to penetrate millions of miles of solid lead, the T-rays silently blasted through the restaurant and the reinforced concrete walls of the hotel until they found warm living bodies seeded with viral activator cells. The rays caused the otherwise innocuous DNA strands to fluoresce and grow, creating their own neural links, which soon crowded out the host's own, like an invasive plankton taking over a pond.

Abdelkader had one wonderful thought that repeated itself over and over. *Let madness consume the foul weeping sore of America!*

He kept the emitter on longer than he had to, not switching it off until all of the social media streamers inside the MGM dropped their handsets and stopped broadcasting. One blue-haired selfie-streaming scumbag grabbed the sides of his head and yelled they were under chemical attack.

"You wish," Abdelkader muttered inside the rear of the stolen taxi.

As he smiled, he felt the dark-skinned silicone face lose adhesion with the desiccated scar tissue underneath. It was the old tissue, seared by the bomb dropped by the American drone that demolished his house with all three of his wives and his twelve children inside. He had just gone outside to smoke. Then, somehow protected by a thick retaining wall, he felt a shockwave and fire and pain beyond imagining. This was no time to hide, Abdelkader thought. Let all demons hear his call to arms.

With a decisive jerk, he flicked off his silicone mask and threw off the dead driver's turban. The plan had been to irradiate the political conference and then meet at the far end of Las Vegas to assess the damage.

Screw the plan!

He watched his false face fall to the pavement and grabbed the T-ray controller. He locked the emitter on maximum output and hit the *Power On* switch, then got back in the driver's seat. With the invisible rays streaming out in a wide beam for three hundred yards, he drove off.

The taxi knocked over a ridiculous miniature palm tree. People cried out as he turned, climbing onto the sidewalk. One fat man in a Hawaiian shirt slapped his hand on the roof, then he cried out and backed away when he saw the ruin of Abdelkader's face, his scarred eyelids pulled back, his eyes bulging with pure lust for vengeance.

He sped around the long block, imagining a long fiery blade vaporizing all the kafir scum. The stream of invisible, unstoppable radiation lanced out at restaurants, casinos, tourists strolling the Las Vegas Strip hand in hand with their children who trailed balloons.

The pain he was inflicting was far better than a merciful beheading. Americans would become the seeds of their own destruction. The country with the most powerful military in the world would consume itself, and the whole putrid mess would slide down into the sewers of history to rest with the other oppressive slave empires: the Egyptians, the Hittites, Babylonians...

His mind was so fevered that Abdelkader only registered the sound coming over the radio the second or third time it hailed him.

"What?"

"Where are you going? You're going to be noticed. You're going to get us all killed." It was Dr. Baldur squealing like a virgin wench being mounted by her husband for the first time.

If the little weakling had been there in front of him... But Las Vegas was only one city. They had to move quickly to attack other major population centers. There was no time for fighting amongst themselves. He slowed down to get his bearings among the wide streets and garishly decorated buildings.

"Right. Contact our local allies. I'll drive to the underground garage, and we'll—"

"That's what I mean, I can't get a hold of them. One of the Antifa trucks… I see it now. It's been shot up. They're dead."

It could have been government snipers on top of the MGM. But they'd have had to react very quickly after Sikawski shot off the RPG as a distraction. What else could—

Abdelkader's thoughts and everything else was knocked sideways by a steel rhino, which drop-kicked the front of his minivan. Amid disintegrating glass and crunching metal, he caught sight of a large figure in an oilcloth overcoat with a patch over one eye. Then he blacked out.

A second later, he came to. The car was still spinning. It hit members of a street acrobatic act, sending their bodies flying and careening across Las Vegas Boulevard. As performers and juggling balls scattered off the taxi's roof, Abdelkader recovered enough from the initial impact that he thought to dig in his pack for his weapon. He hadn't planned on any fire fights, and certainly not with what had to be mechanized humans. Unless private security firms were now employing cyborgs, these had to be…

"Fucking Russians!" he said. He found his gun and fired wildly out of the shattered side window.

"Baldur, Sadikul, get over here!" he shouted into the mic. "Unexpected hostiles. Cyborgs. We have to save the emitter."

He looked left and right. The one-eyed attacker was nowhere. Cars were stopped on both sides of the street. Maybe people thought this was an accident or an attack somehow connected to the explosion and mayhem on the far side of the MGM.

He checked the T-ray device. Inside its neutronium casing, it was nearly indestructible. He slammed the aperture closed and disconnected the power unit.

When he looked up again, there was not one but two armed cyborgs on either side of his car.

"Car trouble?" the slightly smaller one said as Abdelkader tried to put the gear shifter in reverse.

"Fuck shit, Komandir, this dude is ugly," the one-eyed cyborg said as he yanked the passenger door off its hinges.

Under his scarred lips, Abdelkader gnashed his teeth and stared into the muzzle of the first man's shotgun.

"What have you got in the back seat?" the Russian asked, his strange irises focusing on the emitter. "That does not look like a bomb."

"Wait, Komandir, the outside coating..." the other one said and then started swearing a stream of Russian curse words. "It reminds me of something."

Then one of the street acrobats jumped on the cyborg's neck and gnawed at his neck.

It was starting.

Half of downtown Las Vegas must have been saturated with T-rays. Taking advantage of the distraction, Abdelkader got the taxi's motor started and reversed, ducking down just as a single blast from the shotgun blew out the rear window and nearly took the roof off.

The second Russian stopped shooting and tried to get the mad person in a clown costume off his companion, then the rest of the crazed performers jumped on them both.

Abdelkader swung the steering wheel around and pushed down on the gas. A terrible grinding came from the rear wheels. His axle was either broken or the bumper had come off and was now wedged under the tires. The vehicle slowed and then ground to a stop only fifty meters away from the cyborgs.

Both attackers had struggled free of their assailants and started toward him. In moments, they'd have him and the emitter. He had only a few bullets left. If he could hit one of their vulnerable spots, their eyeballs... Abdelkader stopped in the act of aiming his weapon and laughed.

A second later, the cyborgs stopped walking, slowly turned around, and saw what he found so amusing. Coming at them from all sides were hundreds of the afflicted. Demented and deranged, unable to use language or tools, he knew from experience on Tortuga Island that their only desire was to grab onto a warm living body, feed, and spread their affliction.

"Are you injured? Abdelkader!"

He was so entranced by the wonderful sight that he hadn't noticed Dr. Baldur and Sadikul drive up behind him.

"No. Grab the emitter. We have to leave."

As they quickly rolled the heavy device toward the truck, Dr. Baldur looked back. With wonder and glee, he, too, watched the cascade of brainless Americans swarm the enemy.

"We did it, it worked!"

Was it odd that Dr. Baldur seemed surprised? Abdelkader did not have time to wonder. The street behind them was filling up with figures lurching out of restaurants and casinos.

"Get in," he said, making sure the emitter was strapped down. "A kilometer away, there shouldn't be any."

Shotgun pellets scattered along the asphalt beside their truck. Abdelkader glanced back at the Russians; three attackers all wearing Hawaiian shirts had latched onto the first cyborg's leg and knocked him off balance.

"Go!" Abdelkader yelled got into the passenger seat. Dr. Baldur sped away. Sadikul sat hunched over in the rear compartment. He felt his arm and ribcage where the side of the taxi had hit him. There didn't seem to be anything broken.

Dr. Baldur had gone only three or four blocks when he pulled over and then reached across Abdelkader's chest as though also to check him over for injuries, but instead the scientist took his pistol.

"Huh?"

Without a word, Dr. Baldur aimed at the backseat and shot Sadikul in the back of the head until the gun was empty.

"You piece-of-shit traitor!" Abdelkader screamed, spit flying from his scarred lips as he knocked the gun out of Baldur's hand. "I'll see you—"

"Look."

Bullet impacts had spun Sadikul's head nearly completely around, so it was looking at them. The half that was not a pulpy red mess had a glazed dead-fish eye, and the mouth was still greedily chewing and chomping on nothing.

"He was infected."

"No!"

"It was in Guatemala. I thought he would get better. The antibodies should have kicked in."

Abdelkader snatched away the empty pistol. He wanted to crack Dr. Baldur's lying skull open with it.

"But he took the same antidote as we did," Abdelkader said. "The carrier cells are not supposed to cross our brain–blood barrier."

The special strands of DNA activated by the T-ray were prevented from entering their brains and made harmless by Baldur's vaccine... or were they?

"Does it work or not?"

"It works, it works. But it needs a booster. We'll have to take injections. *Daily* injections." The man did not sound convincing.

"And...?" Abdelkader shoved his bare scarred face closer to the cowering man's sweaty face, ready to pistol-whip his lying blubbering mouth.

"And... uh, then eventually it will be ineffective," he admitted finally. "But she can fix it."

"Who the fuck are you talking about?"

"The scientist woman, the one who wrote the bioweapons book."

Abdelkader pushed Baldur back into his seat. "You didn't invent anything." With all the misgivings and clues, he should have realized. "You outsourced the project and claimed it was yours."

"P-partly."

Abdelkader slapped him, sending bloody drool spraying across the window.

"M-mostly. But she has the last component, the enzyme we need. I know it. I threatened to kidnap her son, and she brought it to America to trade. Better still, I know where she is going to be in a few hours."

Abdelkader vibrated with rage for a moment. The clicking, clacking, rustling, moaning sound of the advancing crowd of infected was getting louder.

"Drive. Tell me everything, *everything*, or we'll find out if Sadikul is still hungry."

The Filipino Pangean's head was half destroyed, but his jaws kept munching, cracked yellow teeth grinding up the silicone mask hanging limply off the dead man's smoothly scarred face.

49

LAS VEGAS BOULEVARD

ZVENA

Zvena had every intention of airing out the Pangeans and stomping their corpses into pink toothpaste after all the trouble they had caused, but the infected were on him. A really fat woman and a skinny pimply teenage boy had latched on to his right leg, they attacked just as he was shooting, and the shotgun blast went wide of the Pangean leader's truck. Having caught sight of him without his silicone mask, Zvena's ocular implants made an un-facial recognition and matched the image to the hideously scarred features of Hassan Abdelkader, their primary target.

"Get off!" he yelled at the demented figures clinging to his leg.

At first he didn't understand why two, then three, tourists were trying to tackle him. Were they trying to be vigilantes? Then he looked at their faces, the vacant dazed expression, the clouded-over eyes... It was the same as the creatures on Tortuga and the vampire of La Mesilla. Zvena looked around.

"How can there be so many?"

Rodion came over and kicked the woman hard enough to shatter every bone below her waist, and she rolled away. The kid and the old man he throttled like chickens and tossed them aside.

"Rodya, careful of collateral damage," Zvena said. "We're guests in America."

"Sorry, Komandir, but look around," he said, bayoneting a muscular black man who ran at them with slavering jaws wide open. "This whole city is collateral damage."

Many infected were streaming out of every hotel, every casino and restaurant, into the afternoon sunlight. At first they walked as though dazed, then reacted like feral animals. The commotion of their fight with the Pangeans attracted the first ones. Now others were lurching toward them.

"They want to infect us. I remember," Rodion said, giving him a chilling look. "It was all I wanted to do when it... the bioweapon, had hold of my mind."

Zvena didn't need more explanation. He cranked his weapon's muzzle open to full riot-suppression spread and fired at the legs of the closest ones.

While he was reloading and Rodion was using his pike to break legs on the other side of the meridian, a half-naked Asian man with a sushi knife sticking straight up out of his head ran at him, spilling Zvena's ammunition. Before he could punch him, the OCEL leaped and tore the man away with its scissor-like forelimbs, then launched itself at the crowd. Its robotic frenzy scattered them just long enough for Zvena to reload and fire.

Blam! Buckshot.

Blam! Fléchettes.

Blam! Incendiary.

Where one group fell and stumbled over spattered body parts, another shoulder-to-shoulder phalanx surged in.

Zvena signaled Rodion and the OCEL to retreat down the boulevard. On Tortuga, a brief encounter with only one of these creatures had them both hallucinating.

"With this many of them, will our antipsychotics work?" Zvena asked.

"How should I know?"

"You're the only one who has ever been infected and lived to talk about it."

Zvena was about to further criticize the vagueness of his friend's reply when a heavy rifle bullet hit his left shoulder shield. He was pushed back half a step and looked for the shooter.

"National Guard and militarized police incoming," Rodya said, pulling him to better cover beside an ice cream truck. "They must be responding to the attack on the politicians."

By the looks of the bloody froth dripping from the mouths of figures stomping out of the MGM hotel, it looked like the politicians had been the main course at a free buffet.

"Try not to kill the soldiers," Zvena said, his eyes zooming in on their new assailants. "They are not yet infected. Maybe they can clean up this mess."

Another rifle bullet struck nearby, blasting away the cranium of a man wearing shorts and an "I am NOT a Serial Killer" shirt. The almost-headless figure kept walking, somehow able to stay in the midst of the moving horde.

The two Russians looked at each other. Rodion said, "We wish them luck with—"

Two icy-cold arms dripping with pink-and-blue gunk grabbed Zvena. It was the ice cream truck driver. Zvena turned around and forced the man's head and shoulders into a huge vat of strawberry swirl then rolled him out from the back of the vehicle and onto the wide avenue.

"Let's go," Zvena said, getting in the brightly painted ice cream truck and putting it in gear.

Rodion fired a few times to keep the guardsmen's heads down. By that time, the police gunfire had attracted the notice of the crowds, and the American authorities had priorities other than pursuing them.

The confection truck was slow but easy to steer. Zvena was only forced to run over and crush a few of the afflicted. After a few blocks, they were clear of the walking pestilence. Piercing cries came from high above. Zvena leaned out and zoomed in. People were throwing themselves off the roller coaster rides, their arms flailing at something only they could see as they plunged to the ground.

A few people who still looked normal came out of mini malls and restaurants to see what the disturbance was. Some managed to run in time, others were set upon and torn apart. Zvena thought quickly. That device he had seen in the back of Abdelkader's taxi van, it had to be connected with the phenomenon. If it was, why had he and Rodion not been affected?

Holding the steering wheel with one hand, Zvena undid a small pouch on his thigh pocket.

"Rodya, here is my deactivation key." He handed him a device that looked like a silver tuning fork. "If I show signs of coming under the influence of this pathogen, insert it on either side of my cranium. It will freeze my cyborg motor functions and keep me from doing harm until I can be taken back to the Human+ lab."

Rodion, with his limited depth perception, nodded his head, grabbed the key, and gave a lopsided smile. "Oho! Now I have the power to switch you off. From here on, you better speak nicely to me."

Two miles down the cool, dusty road, they saw a sign.

Attila's Pre-Owned Conveyances
Barbarian Deals and Savage Price Cuts
on Cars, Bikes, Trucks

He parked around the corner. Even in this city not many people drove around in ice cream vans. They needed new transport.

Attila was a rotund man with fronds of greasy hair swept straight back. He wore cowboy boots and a fake Native American bead jacket.

"What can I do you fer? If your budget's as big as all o' you, then I might close early." He chuckled.

After some discussion about mechanical worthiness and fuel mileage, they settled on a pair of Heavy Rider motorcycles that were certified for use by individuals up to eight hundred pounds. One came complete with a side car for the OCEL unit, which was politely waiting out of sight behind their stolen truck.

"That confirms the cash sale," Atalla said. "If you'll wait right here, I'll get my insurance gal to—"

Zvena called the OCEL robot. It loped over, its metal legs scraping the asphalt of the used car lot.

"I notice you have charged us a premium for 'export sale,'" Zvena said, reading the fine print on the receipt. "This is perfectly fine, as is the fifty percent higher cost of these used vehicles than if we had bought them new. So let us just say we shall keep the dealer plates on them for now, and we mail them back to you."

The OCEL unit walked in a circle around Atalla, its insectile head stump making snuffling sounds as it took air samples like a two-hundred-pound metal dog. It then sat down on its hindquarters and began sloughing skin and bloody clothes from its sharp forelegs. Its eight dark eyes looked straight up at the salesman.

They concluded their business at the used car emporium and soon had driven to the city limits of Las Vegas. Zvena slowed down to ride beside his friend.

"Look for a place to pull over and deploy the microwave dish. We need to report in to Moscow and get hold of Tata."

A big green sign read:

You are Leaving Las Vegas
Drive Carefully, Come Back Soon!

"Hey, Komandir," Rodion yelled over the noise of the engines. "This city seems like it would be a fun place. In normal times, of course."

50

ELLIE

Ellie fell.

And fell.

An ever-increasing wind blasted upward against her head and under the face shield of her helmet. Far below, getting closer by the second, she saw soft-looking puffy white clouds. Thirty or so stories underneath those, she knew, were the very hard streets of Harlem.

Behind her, nanowire tether unspooled at an incredible rate. There was a bit of tension on her harness, enough to keep her from spinning head over heels as the hundred stories of Assegai Tower flashed by in reverse order.

One thought gave her comfort: *Barracude is such a selfish bugger.*

Their host, who had undoubtedly by now also thrown himself out the window to avoid being charbroiled by the inferno set off by terrorists, was quite possibly the most selfish bugger in the universe. In this situation, that was a good thing. He'd never use an escape system unless he thought it was perfectly safe. Although… he did have an unrealistically optimistic view of practically everything.

More wind whistled under her face shield, pulling on her clothes and even her eyelashes. She hoped she didn't look like those people skydiving or playing in wind tunnels who had their cheeks all blown out and wobbly.

Ludicrously, she braced herself for impact as her feet dove through the topmost cotton-candy layer of mist, her body passing into an oddly cool and humid grayness.

At this point, falling objects trivia came to her mind. There were squirrels called sugar gliders that could survive being dropped from a plane.

A mathematical formula called "terminal velocity" written in green chalk on a cracked blackboard flashed in front of her in the swirling gray mist. As if that would bloody help!

She gripped the straps of her harness to get ready for the bungee-like pull, which had to be coming. But instead, her nearness to the ground only made it appear as though she was falling even faster.

Brake, brake, brake, she thought frantically, now recalling the time she nearly crashed her family car, an Austin Mini, into a hedgerow during her driving test. The upshot was she had scored so poorly she was supposed to requalify each year. If she survived this plunge, she promised herself she would definitely study hard and remedy that mark against her competence.

Suddenly the cloud layer whooshed away, replaced by a dimly lit street scene. She could make out people and cars and little yellow taxis. No one seemed to be looking up. With the low-hanging clouds casting shadows over most of Manhattan, maybe no one had noticed the building was on fire a thousand feet up.

Just as she thought she could make out a green-painted dog poo disposal station right below her, the nanowire started to tug. The straps on the harness dug in deeper and pinched her under the arms. That positive deployment was soon overshadowed by another possibility: What if the nanothread stretched? She had fallen about half a kilometer. If the wire was too long by only a fraction of a percent...

"Hawrrk!"

At the very moment she saw piles of rotting newsprint lying in the gutter, the long wire really yanked hard and slowed her, at least most of her. Her internal organs kept going. It seemed they were going to bulge out of her like a badly packed haggis.

Dangling rather close to the pile of refuse, she sensed a complete loss of downward momentum. This was immediately replaced by a weightless rising sensation. Her tether's mechanism was like a tiny backpack—it whirred and steadied her bouncing. Then like a fishing reel, it let out line, slowly lowering her down.

On the other side of the street, a homeless person stopped picking through a bin and gawked at her as her feet hit solid ground. She managed a little Mary Poppins landing wobble without falling completely over.

"Heyo! You er-kay there?" the bin picker asked as he trotted over. He was wearing suit pants with a broken zipper belted with a length of twine. His top coat was a dark ski jacket with more stuffing on the outside than in.

The ground was still swirling, and Ellie was grateful for the supporting, albeit filthy, hand he held out. Then she felt his other hand grabbing inside her pocket.

"Bloody hell, gerroff me! I've just fallen a thousand feet. Can you wait a moment before you try to rob me?" Ellie pushed the bearded smelly idiot away. "Oh, and by the way, you'd best get away from here. This building is about to fall down. Shoo! Off with you."

Still feeling wobbly, she backed against the building and looked up for any bits that might be coming off the top floors. Up close, the material covering the Assegai Tower looked to be a very stylish Belgian black marble. She was still looking for a way to undo the descender harness when other bodies started dropping down on the sidewalk like two-legged spiders trailing silk threads.

Ms. China and Mr. Perdix came down together, landing nearly on top of her. Farther down the block, people in workmen's clothes dropped to the ground, almost casually, as though this was their alternative to taking the lift down for their lunch break.

She looked back up, craning her neck almost vertically. Way up, through the cloud cover, there came an odd glow. The flames must be raging.

When she turned around, Sarge Bryan was quickly snapping off his harness, then spinning to the side to avoid the dive-bombing figure of Mr. Barracude, whose loafer-clad foot hit him in the shoulder. The oligarch was closely followed down by security people and house staff.

"Sorry, pal," Barracude said as jauntily as he could manage. The rapid descent had left him out of breath and ashen-faced. "I was aimin' for the spot right next to you."

The butler alighted, straightened his own starched shirt, then went over and brushed off Sarge Bran's jacket while apologizing on behalf of his employer.

Ellie looked left and right. Apart from a dozen construction workers clad in hardhats and overalls, no one else had alighted on the sidewalk.

"Mr. Barracude! Shouldn't there be more people coming down? This building is huge." Could there be hundreds or thousands left up there? Had their presence in the penthouse led to a terror attack that would yield a catastrophic death toll?

"Relax. You English people are wound way too tight for your own good," Mr. Barracude said. "The grand opening is... er... was supposed to be next month, Janice's birthday. I guess I'll have to figure something else out. Damn terrorists, coming after me again like they did at the Watergate."

He then waved to an older fellow in a white hard hat who had just come out through the large glass doors of the main public entrance and who appeared to be taking a tally of everyone who had escaped.

Without thinking, she had wandered toward the empty street. Sarge Bryan pulled her back and pressed her against the dark marble.

"Stay close. Debris coming down," he said, gazing up. "This way."

As though on cue, a yard-long chunk of charred cladding or drywall crashed into the middle of the street and disintegrated. Ellie covered her head, although if the building decided right then to fall, she gathered how ineffective that would be.

"How far do we have to go to be safe?"

Ms. China and Mr. Perdix were in front of them as they walked single file to the end of the block. They were about to dash through the crosswalk when a brown UPS truck came racing along the curb lane.

Ellie caught a quick look at the driver and was not quite certain she was seeing correctly. She had to blink a few times, wondering whether all the blood that was supposed to be in her head had found its way back there. The man in the UPS van did not look like a courier. Was he really wearing a black turtleneck and a grinning skull mask or was she still dizzy?

The delivery truck turned sharply and skidded around a corner. After checking both ways, Ellie and the others dashed across.

Mr. Perdix fiddled with his handset. "I'm alerting DHS and having a JASON disaster AI estimate the likely impact zone if the Assegai Tower collapses."

Sarge Bryan looked left and right. "Where is everyone?"

There were no fire trucks or police. The only security people in the street wore Barracude company uniforms, efficiently blocking off traffic at intersections, dropping orange cones with blinking lights on them while speaking into walkie-talkies.

"Depending on prevailing winds and a few other variables, we're in luck," Mr. Perdix said proudly.

"Luck?" Ellie panted, her internal organs just having seemed to catch up with her after the thousand-foot bungee jump.

"Mos def," Mr. Perdix said, trying to sound hip and stoic in the face of disaster. "I project a kill zone of only one hundred and fifty yards in diameter. That's less than the length of a Manhattan city block. Mr. Barracude, have your people cordon off twice that just to be on the side of caution."

Ellie looked around. Most of the buildings nearby were under ten stories and looked empty. "Where are the authorities?"

As they moved along toward the end of the next block, Sarge scanned the buildings and shops. "Dunno, but there seems precious little evacuatin' to do here."

He was right. Shops were uniformly boarded up, and in the apartment block façade opposite them every window had been smashed in.

"What happened here?"

"This area never recovered after the mega riots of 2025."

"You got that right, Sergeant!" Barracude's wheezing, blustering voice said from behind them. "Oh, man, *heff*, I should be able to run farther than that. *Heff*. I gotta fire my personal trainer."

Between deep breaths and sips of a sports drink from a Korean grocer who ran the only shop on the next block, Mr. Barracude informed them he'd squared everything away with his construction crew, and his security people were cordoning off a disaster zone around the stricken tower.

Ellie looked way up. She heard the insistent clang of alarm bells, and on each floor, strobe lights were flashing.

Mr. Barracude followed her gaze, it gave him a chance to put his hands on his knees, catch his breath, and brag. "Am I... *heff*, good or what? I remember the people jumping out of the World Trade Center buildings during the Islamic lunatics' attack. Man, I said: 'fuck that!' Y'know, I mean, really. That's not for people who put their trust in Barracude, to go like that." He pointed up at the smoke-belching tower now visible through a hole in the cloud cover. The last construction workers were using the fast-escape system and were being lowered to the pavement. "Look at that. That's American ingenuity."

He looked left and right at the desolate streets.

"Before I came, there wasn't much here. That why I got the land so cheap. Whole bunch of tax breaks too."

From above them came a sort of thumping noise. A puff of black smoke rose above the highest level of the Assegai Tower.

"Flames musta hit some, *heff*, welding equipment," Mr. Barracude said, wiping his brow. "Damn... my beautiful building."

51

HARLEM, NYC

Ellie noticed a single helicopter circling, but at this distance couldn't tell whether it was a news crew or some first responders.

"This way," Mr. Barracude said. "There's a congresswoman's office not far. She's a damned Democrat, but I gave her the maximum contribution anyway, to show I'm not a partisan asshole."

Ellie looked up and down the nearly deserted street. If downtown New York never slept, it was apparently a long time since this boarded-up desolate area had woken up.

Her main concern was things dropping on them from the collapsing tower. Even now, from several blocks away, it seemed to loom over them. It was hard not imagining the thing toppling over right onto them like a tree. A taxi honked at her, and she jumped away from the curb. A muffled figure glared at her from behind several layers of glass and plastic shielding.

She was about to ask Mr. Barracude how much farther the politician's office was when her handset vibrated. Miss Aleph was texting her.

I don't think this is the—

"C'mon, in this alley." Their host grabbed her arm, pulling her away from the wide avenue. "Good shortcut. I know these streets like the back of my hand."

She didn't want to be conspicuous looking at her text. Miss Aleph had said she wanted to remain incognito. Ellie shook her head and made herself yawn.

"You're not bored, are ya?" Mr. Barracude huffed, his breath condensing in the cold air.

"Ears... stopped up. Must be the pressure change." Ellie felt the need to brag a little. "It's been weeks since I've free-fallen thousands of feet, which is something I do, just for the fun of it."

It was getting cold, especially for what she had on.

"Wait." Ellie spotted an upturned bin in the alley. It turned out to be a Goodwill donation receptacle. The back panels had been levered open and bent, but the heavy padlock remained. She went over and reached inside. "I just want to see if there's anything warmer..."

"We're a long ways from Saks... Oh yeah, crap, I forgot. Won't find anything there, that whole row of stores got looted and burned last week." Then Barracude noticed the bin. "You're right, it is chilly. I've donated tons over the years. Time to make a withdrawal."

"Sergeant, can your eyes take a snapshot?" Ms. China said sarcastically, probably annoyed at having to wait for them. "I have to post this. 'Newspaper Magnate and a Billionaire Binning in NYC.'"

Barracude shouldered Ellie aside and jammed his hand down the donation chute. "I feel something good down there."

"If it's a fur coat," Ms. China said, "make sure it's not currently being worn by a rat."

At that point, Ellie would gladly have traded her whole wardrobe in exchange for that hideous bear coat of Tata's. She had to remember to find out what happened to her and the Russian ambassador, when they were between crises.

"Anna, be quiet and help. You've got the longest and skinniest arms."

They eventually retrieved a cardigan full of cat hair, a Montclair ski jacket with holes under the armpits, as though its first owner had been sweating acid, a Burberry scarf, and a strange trench coat made of a corduroy material.

"Seems clean," Sarge Bryan said. "Can't see any cooties."

Mr. Barracude helped himself to the trencher, though it was too long for him.

"Where are your security people?" Mr. Perdix asked, wrapping a moth-eaten scarf around his slim pale neck. "You had a full Secret Service detail."

"Guess they're stretched a bit thin at the moment," Mr. Barracude said, managing to seem both unconvincing and unconcerned. He smelled the coat's sleeve, shrugged, and wrapped the loose belt tightly around his midsection. "I told my security guys first priority is to make sure everyone got out of the Assegai. Who knows when anyone from the city is going to get there."

"I meant to ask you abou—" Ellie's query about the startling absence of civic authority in New York was cut short by a roar coming from a high-revving car engine around the next corner.

Mr. Perdix and Ms. China were in the front. They ducked behind a fire hydrant and lamppost. Sarge Bryan pushed Ellie closer to the broken windows of a pawnshop. A dusty fake pearl necklace had come apart as it was being stolen, its loose plastic beads lay all over the filthy sidewalk.

She snuck a glance around the corner. Of all the cars she could have imagined was making that particular noise, a six-door Rolls-Royce limousine was not in her top ten. That was, however, what sped around the corner, its wheels spinning and churning up smoke as the tires fought to regain a grip on the blacktop. It zoomed away.

Close behind it came an NYPD blue-and-white police car, lights flashing but with no siren blaring.

Oh, finally, thought Ellie.

Sarge Bryan yanked her back as she was about to try to get the driver's attention.

She got a closer look and saw why. The side windows of the cruiser were smashed, and a trio of black-clad figures looked out from inside. "NYPD" on the side of the car had graffiti over it that read: *NYPigs in Blanket Fry like Bacon.*

There was a flash, a muffled pop, and a ball of fire flew in their direction, and another, and another. Ellie let out an incoherent sound of frustration as she ducked down.

"It's nothing," Sarge Bryan said, shielding her and putting his arm over his own face. "Just supercharged Roman candles. Kids shoot them at each other."

"Oh, right, then, I'll just carry on," Ellie said, making sure no one had caught fire.

Ellie was too busy looking for other charming rioting teenagers to check her phone, which kept up its steady vibrating. If it were really important, Miss Aleph would pipe up on speakerphone.

"Almost there," Mr. Barracude puffed and wheezed as he led them up stone steps to the lobby of an old brownstone building. A US flag and a sign hung there, both recently spattered with several shades of filth. The plague read:

Congresswoman Carmina Hernán

13th Congressional District Office

"*Aprez vous mezdames*," Barracude said, having recovered his breath and joviality.

Ellie and the others climbed up and found themselves in a tiled entranceway about two yards deep. It ended abruptly ended at an aged wooden staircase.

Sarge Bryan looked behind them, glancing up and down the street. "Better let me go first."

"What? No," Mr. Barracude objected. "There's not gonna be any trouble here. Everyone loves Carmina."

Turned out not everyone did.

At the top of the staircase, Ellie got a glimpse inside before Sarge Bryan tried to shield her view. The image burned itself into Ellie's mind.

"Holy fuck damnation!" Mr. Barracude said as he grabbed the wobbly banister to steady himself.

On the first desk near the doorway was a keyboard, and on it lay a pair of rigid hands with mottled gray skin and several plastic letter keys that had popped out. The owner of the hands was not visible, having collapsed under the desk. However, his or her arms remained in place due to large metal spikes that had been nailed through the wrists, through the keyboard, and into the desk, crucifixion style.

52

HARLEM, NYC

"Holy fuck damnation!" Mr. Barracude repeated.

Two of Congresswoman Hernán's staffers were dead; the killers were gone.

Mr. Perdix draped torn curtains over the bodies. "They bled to death."

Ms. China had found a wounded person who had taken shelter in a room filled with filing cabinets. Attackers had stabbed her in the side but had not bothered to drag her out to finish the job.

"This one's breathing," Ms. China said. "They missed the arteries. Help me move these cabinets apart."

Sarge Bryan and Mr. Perdix rushed into the narrow space to help while Ellie looked around the office. Spray-painted graffiti was splashed across every flat surface. On the floor, coagulated blood pooled, and next to it lay a patch of long hairs, some attached to flaps of skin, all having gray roots. A can of presumably flammable liquid lay near the window.

"They didn't have time to set a fire," Sarge Bryan said as they pulled the injured woman out of the filing room. "Maybe they were interrupted, or got new orders."

"Orders?" Mr. Barracude asked vehemently as he held on to the banister

by the staircase for support. "These lunatics have a schedule? I don't see...
Where's Carmina?"

With an aggressive swipe of her arm, Ms. China knocked everything off
a desk and had the men put the injured office worker on it. "I don't like that
bulge in her neck. If she wakes up, don't let her move. She's got to be stabilized
in traction before going down those stairs."

"Go down?" Mr. Barracude rushed over to the window. "To what? To
where? Are there any hospitals still open? And where the fuck is Carmina?"

As the oligarch's shouted question echoed through the room, Ellie heard
a faint tapping. She cocked her head left and right, finally centering her
search on an old wall hanging of the Declaration of Independence. The paper,
yellowed with age, torn and repaired with various bits of tape, had fallen over
a low doorway. Ellie went over and pushed it aside, revealing a storage space
containing a mop, a yellow squeezing bucket, and the shivering, scalped,
bleeding form of Congresswoman Carmina Hernán.

"Towels, water, now," Ms. China ordered.

Ellie dashed down the hall where the washroom door hung on its lower
hinge. She tore open the continuous cloth towel dispenser, pulled, and reeled
off a trail of cloth until the end came loose with a snap.

The attackers had gone at Carmina's head with broken glass or knives not
very well suited to purpose, and instead of giving her a clean bald head of
shame, they had partially scalped the sixty-something-year-old lady. On the
limited flat space of skin they had created, her assailants had tried to carve
letters. *Naz Colab* was all Ellie could read before Ms. China quickly mopped
and examined the wounds then wrapped a turban-like bandage around
Carmina's head.

As far as massacres went, the villains' net results had been patchy at best.
Besides the congresswoman, who was conscious but in a daze, there were four
other survivors in the office. As they were tending to them, Mr. Barracude
had wandered away, and he gave a piercing scream and struck out with the
broken back of a chair as a fifth survivor crept up the stairwell.

"Don't hit me!" a thin young man in shirtsleeves yelled. He turned out to
be a staffer who had gone out to get copy toner, heard the mayhem, and had
hidden near a doorway out to the alley.

"We can't stay here," Mr. Perdix said. Rather abruptly, it seemed to Ellie, because there was no sign of anyone coming. Dialing 9-1-1 only returned a recorded message.

"We can't just leave these people," Ellie objected.

Sarge Bryan thought a moment. "I've got to follow the chain of command. I'll go with Mr. Barracude to the airport. This summit with Leota and the blue-state governors seems really important to setting things right again."

Ellie was not about to be left behind. "The invitation was for all of us. I insist on going."

They ransacked the office of a dentist on the main floor and brought up some medical supplies. They left the unwounded young staffer in charge.

"I've called everyone I know," Mr. Barracude said, his face having lost all color as he looked at his friend, who was slowly running her hand over the bandages covering her scalped head. "And y'gotta believe that's everyone that there is. Someone will come. This is a fucking member of fucking Congress."

The staffer jumped back a step when Ms. China pulled out a mean-looking sub-machine gun and thrust it at him. She must have nicked that from the soldiers in the government helicopter.

"This is a P-90," Ms. China said to the Hispanic-looking boy. "Do you have a clue how to use it, Julio?"

"My name's not Julio…"

"Do I look like I give a shite?" She pulled him over to the window and thrust the odd-looking weapon under his arm.

"That's the trigger. Don't touch any of these buttons, or instead of killing the bad people, you will die. Look through that and aim at that car."

Blam, blam.

"Now they're dead and you and your boss are alive. You have forty-eight shots left. Good luck.""

When they got back out on the street, Ellie was more keenly grateful for the weapons they still had. The sun was hiding itself behind skyscrapers and a dark-gray band of clouds, leaving long dark shadows along the ominously quiet streets.

"I knew ten years ago we shoulda hung these idiots," Mr. Barracude groused. "When they started shooting up synagogues and burning police stations and federal court houses, bam!" He smacked his hands together. "Straight to death row. Who the fuck scalps a nice lady like Carmina?"

"Let's try to avoid fraternizing with them," Mr. Perdix said coolly, glancing around the next corner.

"My app Riot-Shield, which is state of the art," Mr. Barracude said, looking at his handset, "says to get across the river by the Madison Avenue Bridge. LaGuardia is the closest airport. Janice will meet us there, and the best part is, it's only seven miles away."

Only seven bloody miles, Ellie thought. She did not feel capable of walking another seven yards.

"Ahem."

"Ms. Sato, you say something?" Mr. Barracude asked wearily. His South American complexion had gone all blotchy. Of all of them, he looked least likely to survive a long hike.

"Oh, me? No, nothing. I should get this." Ellie picked her handset out of her bag and pretended to answer an incoming call.

`"Hello, Ms. Sato, are you near our mutual friend Mr. Barracude?"`

What was the AI on about? And why was she speaking with a Eurotrash accent?

"I guess… I am?"

`"Would you let him know it's Baroness von Alevskaya calling?"`

At the same time, Miss Aleph texted:

Eleanor, just go with it. I have to maintain my cover.

"Oh, yes. Ah, Your Ladyship, he's right here."

Some white flakes fell from the sky. It was cold enough for snow, but Ellie was not sure these were not cinders from the various fires which were burning in dumpsters at intersections all over the city.

"Holy crap," wheezed Mr. Barracude. For the first time, he seemed at a loss for words as he took the phone. "How, uh…?"

`"Ms. Sato and I are acquainted, and her social media updates put her at your tower in New York. Therefore I took the liberty of calling."`

"Cool, I guess, but right now I'm kinda on urgent business to help the government."

"I'm aware that your building is engulfed in flames. It's the current feature story in the *Juggernaut*'s ongoing special report: 'Apocalypse USA.'

"According to National Guard engineers, who just arrived, the tower is likely to collapse within the hour. Too bad. It was elegant architecture."

"Thanks for the update, Baroness. Nice talkin' to you..."

A horn blared from a large vehicle which had driven up to the curb beside them. The sound made them all jump; Sarge Bryan and Mr. Perdix leveled their firearms at the dark windows of a short commuter bus.

"I've recently taken over a robot shuttle bus company in New York. I thought you might need a lift and had my tech guys send out a car homing in on Ms. Sato's handset."

"Huh, y'don't say."

Mr. Barracude's relief at being able to sit down overcame any misgivings at the apparent coincidence. The door of the bus opened with a small hiss. It was empty. Completely robotic transport still creeped Ellie out, but she took comfort knowing Miss Aleph was the virtual driver and also that the seats were spotless and luxuriously padded with nice footrests that extended at the touch of a button.

Mr. Perdix looked at the glowing driver's console. Ms. China looked out the rear window, brandishing yet another purloined firearm. Sarge Bryan tried to help Mr. Barracude up the steps, but he batted the soldier's hand away.

"I can do it."

"Would you like me to lower the handicapped person's ramp, Jezzie?"

"I said I got it, Baroness," he said, looking at the fat dark oval of the camera lens of the sensor package occupying the space where the driver would have sat. "I didn't know you nobles were so savvy with tech."

Mr. Barracude settled himself in the first seat and ran his hand over his ankle, which had swollen to twice its size.

"You'd be surprised, Jezzie."

Ellie slumped down in a double seat.

"Now, everyone," the baroness said over the bus PA system. "When I tell you to duck down, please oblige. Bullet-resistant glass is mandatory for all New York service vehicles, but these windows might not stand up to multiple strikes from high-velocity rifle bullets."

Miss Aleph made a show of asking where they wanted to go and asking Mr. Perdix for his DHS login codes so she could have access to classified civil emergency alerts.

They drove off.

"LaGuardia ain't far." Mr. Barracude put his foot up on the seat next over. "Shouldn't be a hassle."

The robot driver stopped at an intersection, apparently for nothing. Apart from garbage and a knocked-over *New York Post* news box, it was empty. A moment later, a stumpy-looking Smart Car whizzed through at high speed; on its front hung a barrel nearly as large as the car itself, which had been attached with ropes and many yards of duct tape.

Ellie leaned sideways and looked. The Smart Car careened toward a line of NYPD barricades made of police cars and orange traffic dividers. Their bus sped forward. The Smart Car hit the roadblock. The backdraft of the blast threw a large fireball down the street, followed by a huge rush of flaming debris.

"Of course," Mr. Barracude added, "there may be a few bumps along the way."

The bus, called Royal Rides Limo Service, alternately crawled along slowly, and then, without warning, sped at breakneck speed for a few blocks before pausing again. As it navigated the savage streets of Manhattan, Ellie tried to text Miss Aleph. However, her fingers, which were already cramped before her descent through the freezing clouds from Assegai Tower, were just not up to it.

She put her earpiece in and said, "So, Baroness Alevskaya, you never told me the story of your peerage."

"You're just jealous. The title is genuine. My

company bought it from an elderly Polish couple—their son had gambling debts. People like doing business with nobility."

"Your Ladyship, it's been so long, I've almost forgotten what you look like." Ellie was intrigued as to how elaborate the artificial intelligence's deep-fake human identity was.

"Since most people now meet in virtual space, that has been no problem. Check it out."

The phone pinged receipt of a picture. Ellie opened the attachment and found the official portrait of the baroness in a silver gilt frame and nearly dropped the phone.

"Is... is that my nose?" she whispered.

"You should feel complimented. I only borrowed your good parts. I made the eyes a bit wider—yours are kind of sneaky looking—and my hair is totally different."

"And how are you on a first-name basis with Barracude?"

"He and I have been business frenemies for months now. He gets so mad when I buy properties he's interested in. Can't figure out how I'm doing it."

Somehow Miss Aleph's digital personality, which had always been heavily centered on self-preservation, had now morphed into being greedy and foxy.

"At least you're on our side."

"I have to be, most of my investments are in US dollars."

The baroness updated Ellie and the others via speakerphone on the tense situation developing due to the deadlocked political shambles.

"So," Sarge Bryan said, "the blue states are backing Senator Leota, and the red states are behind their party's man, President Casteel."

"The president has not been seen since you and Ellie were at the White House. The only statements coming from Washington have been given by Vice President Prowse."

"I see that too," Mr. Perdix said. "That's why this summit between the two factions is so important; states are increasingly asserting themselves as autonomous regions. The states on both sides are saying that the 10th Amendment gives them authority to declare martial law.

"The blue states have even mobilized a paramilitary force called the EMAC, under the Emergency Management Assistance Compact, which is forcibly taking over functions of the federal DHS and FBI. Blue-state National Guard units are ignoring orders to be federalized."

"We're royally fucked!" concluded Mr. Barracude suddenly as he sat upright. "Pardon my French, Baroness. We got to get Janice to LA, along with Ms. Sato here."

"Why?" Ms. China said sarcastically. "Don't you have journalists in America?"

"Sure, but no one trusts them as far as they can throw a cow. It's all 'fake news' and 'performance art activism.' My advertising people tell me that most Americans get their news from the *Daily Mail* and the *Juggernaut*."

The bus picked up speed and crossed over a second short bridge.

"Oh, look," Ellie said as they passed by a wide river. "What a nice island. People can sail there for a picnic in summer."

"Oh, I don't think people would do that, Ms. Sato," Sarge Bryan said.

"Damn right, they don't," Mr. Barracude said, twisting himself around to look. "That's Riker's Island. Inside, there's nearly twenty thousand of the worst criminals on the East Coast. Everyone famous has been locked up there—the Son of Sam killer, the cocksucker who shot John Lennon, even Harvey Weinstein, who I knew in his early days before he went nuts and started raping everyone."

As soon as they crossed the bridge, the bus picked up speed. Ellie noticed the robot driver was ignoring stop signs and red lights.

"Uh... Baroness—"

Questions about how safe the autodrive was were all banished from Ellie's mind when a large green armored vehicle cut across their path. Everything and everyone in the bus lurched forward as the wheels screeched to a sudden stop.

53

NEAR RIKERS ISLAND
NEW YORK CITY

The tires of their bus skidded over cold slush-covered pavement. Ellie felt the vehicle slide to the left and threaten to tip.

"Hang on!" Sarge Bryan said as spare cushions rained down from the overhead bins.

Their skid ended with a jerk and a dull, crunching clunk. Ellie looked out the fogged-up side windows; they had narrowly avoided landing in a ditch running along the road. She could not make out much of the vehicle that had sped out to block them. From outside came distant sharp cracks followed by closer hammer thumps on the sides and windows.

"They're shooting!" Ellie said, rather outraged. They were less than a kilometer from LaGuardia.

"Who is 'they' now?" Ms. China said laconically as she kept her head down under the row of seats.

"Looks like our guys," Sarge Bryan said. "National Guard."

"Ha!" Mr. Barracude said, righting himself on the lengthwise seat like Humpty Dumpty having avoided a fall. "Look at the window. The bullets didn't go through."

"They'll use something bigger next time they try to neutralize us," Mr.

Perdix said as he clambered over beside Ms. China to get a better look out.

"Why the neutralizing?" Ellie protested. She was near the end of her tether with Americans' obsession with shooting everything. "We're on a presidential mission of peace and good will!"

"We mighta looked like a robot IED," Sarge Bryan said as he examined the controls near the driver's seat.

Ellie recalled the Smart Car carrying the barrel bomb. But why would they be blocking off this road? Were they cordoning off airport access?

"That Humvee has a .50 cal on it!" Mr. Perdix said with rising alarm.

Sarge Bryan got the folding doors open halfway and was also trying to get the soldiers' attention with a white cloth cover he'd stripped off a spare cushion.

"Send Barracude out," Ms. China suggested. "He's the most likely to be recognized, and if not, he's the most expendable."

As things unfolded, the closest soldiers who were looking at them through telescopic sights first recognized Sarge Bryan.

"Is that you, Army Sergeant?" said a man's voice with distinctly non-New York accent.

"That's me," he said, kicking the heavy glass door open the rest of the way. "Don't shoot, please."

A harried-looking youngish man with a helmet that kept slipping off his freshly shaved head ran up to the bus. "Get clear of there, Sergeant, we've got incoming."

What now? Ellie thought.

Sarge Bryan motioned them out into swirls of light snow and cool afternoon air. Mr. Barracude heaved himself up from the rubber floor mats, brushed off his Goodwill trench coat, and followed them out toward the National Guardsman.

"Incoming?" Barracude said. "Sounds like talk from a war zone. This is New York City."

Ellie recognized lieutenant bars on the man's uniform, but instead of a nametag, he only had a barcode. He ignored the oligarch and pulled at Sarge Bryan's coat to urge him away from the road. "Of all the albino sons of bitches in the regular Army, you're the last one I expected to see here."

"I'm the only albino in the Army, Lieutenant. What's up, sir?"

Before the skinny officer could answer, a gunner whose head was poking out of the turret of a nearby Humvee yelled: "Here they come!"

Ellie dragged the somewhat oblivious Barracude down with her into a frost-covered gulley at the far side of the crossroads where the Guard's roadblock had been set up. By now she knew to cover her ears as the gunner pulled the cocking lever back on the big gun. Across the road was a white-painted sign with appended graffiti:

Department of Correction

Rikers Island

Home of New York City's Boldest

MOST RACISTEST NAZIEST MOTHERFUCKERS!!!

The big gun fired away at a target they could not see. Something exploded beyond the line of stark bare trees and sent up a cloud of black smoke. The shooting stopped.

"It's a mass breakout from Rikers," the lieutenant said as he looked with increasing curiosity at Ellie and the others. She suddenly realized that if they had all been wearing a jester's hat with jingle bells, they would not have presented a much odder sight. "There're twenty thousand of 'em. We got them bottled up on the causeway across the river. It's the only way off Rikers except by boat or air."

The lieutenant went on, breathlessly checking the area ahead through the scope on his rifle. "Within half an hour after the power to Rikers went off, all the guards were slaughtered." He looked down at the display of his tactical tablet computer. "Special operators were trying to blow up the only way out—the causeway bridge—but the prisoners hijacked the demolition boat."

Sarge Bryan peered into the gloom, probably able to see farther than any of the soldiers. "Look, sir, we're acting on the commander in chief's orders and have to get to LaGuardia. Can you spare transport?"

The other man thought, then shook his head rapidly as his hands flailed in the air. "Not until support arrives. I've only got a squad, and half of them have never fired a gun since basic training. Every psycho lunatic on the East Coast, a ton of them with genuine terrorist training, is coming over that causeway.

Heck, they could be in those woods right now, flanking either side of us."

Sarge Bryan seemed to recognize that the man was close to panic. To be fair, Ellie supposed ten inexperienced soldiers against twenty thousand armed, bloodthirsty criminals didn't sound quite sporting.

"Fine, fine," he said, comfortingly trying to give the obviously green man confidence. "You got this. We'll wait here and assist as required, sir."

A chubby woman with thick spectacles and short blonde hair poking out from her green-camo helmet jogged up and kneeled down next to them. Over the muzzle of her rifle, she stared out at the thick stand of winter-bare birch trees across the road. She thrust a second tablet into the lieutenant's hands. Instead of a map, this one was playing a video clip.

"Damn heck," Sarge Bryan said, looking at the image of a headless body being thrown into muddy brown water.

"They cut the Navy Seals' throats and threw them in the East River," the lieutenant said. "We're watching them with a drone, but it's unarmed. Backup or not, we can't let them get away with the explosives barge. They could do crazy damage with it. We're going in."

A frontal attack? With ten teenagers? Even Ellie knew if they tried to take back the barge, they'd be wiped out. Her phone buzzed.

Miss Aleph texted: `Psst, Eleanor, ask him if he has any M18A5 Claymores.`

Being shot at had done wonders for the circulation in Ellie's extremities. Her fingers felt almost normal as she texted back: *What are those?*

`Just ask.`

Ellie did, and the lieutenant, whose name was Gutzon, looked at her as though she had just sprouted out of the ground like a talking mushroom.

"This is Ms. Sato," Sarge Bryan explained. "She's a top-level British intelligence officer. She saved all our asses during the 96-Hour War, more'n once."

The soldiers did, in fact, have a good supply of the "clay" things.

`Make sure they're Bluetooth enabled.`

They were.

`Tell them you are ISTAR-qualified and to give you the drone controls.`

Ellie hesitated.

`Just twiddle randomly with the knobs. I've already got control.`

Gutzon had the female solider fetch the drone controller console, which looked like an oversized Xbox console. Most of the skepticism vanished from Gutzon's face when the military drone whizzed over the treetops and made a smart landing near them.

Sarge Bryan seemed to understand what was happening. Ellie was glad someone did.

"Just like Jericho," he said.

"Uh, spot on." *I guess.*

Gutzon shook his head. "Nice try, Ms. Sato, but the Bluetooth that detonates the Claymores only has a few dozen meters' range. The causeway and the explosives barge are twelve hundred meters away in the East River. Even if you manage to carry the Claymore mine to the barge, you'll never be able to detonate it."

"There's a very simple fix for that. Of course... the thing to do is..." Ellie said, noticing Sarge Bryan suppress a small smile as she checked her handset as casually as she could. "Uh, yes, quite rudimentary. We tape a cellular handset to the drone and piggyback the signal to it, thereby initiating the detonation by remote command. Simple as."

Mr. Perdix and Ms. China pushed the tiny National Guardswoman away from the microwave-oven-sized quadcopter drone, and the pair argued about where to place the Claymore mine. They finally decided to duct tape the explosive to the bottom and a cellular handset on the top.

Gutzon leafed through the instruction manual attached to the Pelican case the Claymore had come in. "Just a sec. I have to give you the detonation code."

"Don't need it," Ellie said. "I have the, er, override."

"I didn't even know there was one," Gutzon said. Turning to Sarge Bryan, he added, "Wow, she's good."

The quad drone took off, its many rotors straining under the added weight. The controller's viewscreen showed a close-up of the roadside gravel. Then, as the drone camera gained altitude, Ellie got an aerial view of their wrecked bus, the armored personnel carrier blocking the road, and more distantly, smoke billowing from fires blazing on Riker's Island.

"If you don't mind me sayin', sir," Sarge Bryan said. "You should get pickets out to the wings and check on those reinforcements."

"Thanks, I will, Sergeant," Gutzon said, looking at the treeline. "I was in a Charleston high school three days ago prepping tenth-grade analytical geometry lessons, then I got called up. I'm glad you're here, and really glad we didn't shoot you too badly."

"We're also exceedingly happy about that," Ms. China said drolly, watching the road through borrowed binoculars.

As Ellie pretended to work the controller, the drone skimmed lightly back over the line of winter-bare trees. It flew over a jail gatehouse that was wrecked and on fire. Figures lurked and huddled on both sides of the narrow road to the island, but the camera flew too fast to get a good look. Next came the long causeway over the river, held up by rows of pylons.

The surface of Rikers was mostly pollution-colored gray frost and dead brown grass. Several of the taller buildings were on fire, and indistinct clumps of people, which had to be escaping inmates, were on the bridge headed to the mainland.

"There's the barge," Mr. Perdix said, leaning over Ellie's shoulder. "Lieutenant, what precisely is on it?"

"They were carrying a M303 Special Operations Forces demolition kit. Then they took fire and were captured. The prisoners yelled some demands into the helmet cameras, did not wait for a reply, then they decapitated the SEALs and tossed their heads into the river with their helmets still feeding us video."

As the drone approached the causeway, sparks lit up all along it.

"They are shooting. You'd better maneuver like the professional ISTAR-drone pilot that you are," Ms. China said ironically. She must have guessed Miss Aleph was doing the flying.

Ellie tried to push the controller, and unexpectedly, it pushed back. "I'm getting feedback."

Gutzon looked on. "It's probably the load. It's almost maxed out, won't maneuver as well. Just try not to ditch it."

The camera jerked spasmodically, and for an instant it gave a view of the gray clouds above.

"You're hit," Ms. China said. "It's over."

The sky was replaced by a dizzying whirl as the drone fought to remain in the air with at least one rotor destroyed.

"Yeah, it's over. Damn," Gutzon said.

Determined to win at this life-and-death video game, Ellie growled, "Like bugger futz, it's over. With an attitude like that, how did your revolutionary rabble actually beat King George's Army and Navy?"

The stricken drone whirled closer and closer to the causeway. Ellie could see the white line down the center, then metallic-colored river water, then the causeway again. Villainous figures were still firing up at her. Then there was a slimy pylon and gray water splashed all over the lens.

"Can you detonate?" Sarge Bryan asked. "Are you close enough?"

Ellie felt the joystick gyrating as though it were mixing a tiny pot of oatmeal.

"Just a... moment..."

The drone camera lens popped up just over the murky water line. It was close to the camouflage-painted hull of a small boat. The rotors were still churning in the water. Then a flash of orange lit up the screen, and the connection died out. A full second later they heard a rumbling, and a new puff of brownish-black rose in the distance.

"How did you do that?" Gutzon asked, his jaw open. "The handset couldn't have connected to the Claymore if they were both underwater."

"Elementary, really," Ellie said, handing Gutzon back the inert controller. "Hardly worth explaining."

"Ms. Sato naturally would have set the timer fuse on the M18A5 Claymore before it hit the water," Sarge Bryan said helpfully. "While at the same time estimating the seconds it would take to get close enough to the demolition barge and angling the ball-bearing load up at it, setting off the larger demo charges."

"However you did it," Gutzon said, "hats off to you."

Bullets whizzed in from the tree line.

"Best to keep your helmet on, sir," Sarge Bryan said.

Gutzon crouched down and ran back across the road to the Humvee.

The shooting stopped. Not even Sarge Bryan could see anyone to fire back on.

"Maybe they have stolen radios and heard the causeway was cut off," he said. "With no more scumbags coming from the jail, the escapees' best bet is to run, not fight."

The radio Gutzon had left behind squawked. "This is Major Haverman, actual. My company is inbound. Gutzon, are you receiving?"

Gutzon, having heard the incoming transmission on his helmet earpiece, came jogging back. Major Haverman went on:

"Have received your previous transmission. Under no circumstances are you to follow any directive issuing from the unlawful occupant of the White House.

"Our general and the governor have rejected the federalization of New York's Guard. Sergeant Bryan and his accomplices are operating under illegal orders from the traitor Abraham Casteel. Disarm them and hold them until we arrive. Do you copy?"

54

Ellie, Sarge Bryan, and everyone heard Lieutenant Gutzon's superior order him to take away their weapons and arrest them. The crossroads became very quiet. Ellie could hear the chortling of Humvee engines, a bird tittering in a leafless tree, water dripping in the gulley running past the road, and some icicles falling and shattering against lower branches.

Out of the corner of her eye, she saw Ms. China moving ever so carefully up behind Gutzon. Gutzon looked even more taken back than when they'd been under attack by thousands of homicide-crazed prisoners. He picked up the radio, keyed the mic, and said very deliberately, "Sir, sorry, as per previous standing orders to assist friendly units as required, I have already given Army Sergeant Bryan a Humvee, and he has departed in said vehicle, Major, sir."

"*What? When?*" the major demanded.

"Three minutes ago, sir."

"What direction?"

"We were taking fire at the time, but I believe they are headed toward Manhattan."

Sarge nodded to Gutzon. Ellie, Ms. China, Mr. Perdix, and Mr. Barracude packed into a jeep-like vehicle, and they sped toward LaGuardia Airport.

Mr. Perdix reached under the dashboard of the Humvee and yanked out some wires.

"Deactivating the friend/foe transponder."

"Don't cut yourself," Ms. China said as she jiggled into a more comfortable position beside Ellie in the rear compartment, where Mr. Barracude was taking up more than his fair share of space.

"Hey, Ms. Sato," he said, slapping her knee, unfortunately picking the exact location of the most aggressive bruising and swelling. "That was some fancy drone flying, like out of a video game."

"We ISTAR people really know our stuff." Ellie leaned over to Sarge Bryan in the driver's seat. "That muddling back there didn't sound very promising."

She was no stranger to large-scale intrigues in the Middle East and Europe. It seemed America had its own problem with seditious elements.

"You got that right," Sarge Bryan said, looking a bit rattled after their narrow escape from people who were supposed to be on their side. "When field officers tell the president to take his order and stick 'em…"

Mr. Perdix's palm smacked his handset in frustration.

"All JASON contractors have been locked out of SIPRNet."

"I guess you're not as essential as you thought," mused Ms. China.

No wonder those two broke up, Ellie thought. One might be able to handle letters slathered with random toxins, but the constant drip of verbal venom coming from her former roommate was intolerable.

Miss Aleph texted. She was still trying to keep her cover as a human baroness.

"Uh, here, Mr. Perdix, try this," Ellie said, showing him the picture that had popped up on her phone. "Before we departed, I stole the National Guard's codes. They should be good for an hour or so."

"Wow, double-O Ellie strikes again." Mr. Barracude made to slap her knee again, but she quickly crossed her foot up, shielding herself with her muddy boot. "Really unusual. When I visit, you British always seem so lazy. I must be hanging with the wrong people."

Mr. Perdix input the purloined codes.

"Fuckbonnet," he said as he scrolled down a page with a flashing red border. "They've already kicked me off the network again. Federal loyalists are resetting the data systems at the Pentagon. They're cutting off units that might be commanded by people rejecting President Casteel's authority and instead taking orders from the Council of Constitutional Loyalist state governors, whatever the heck that is."

"Aw, c'mon!" Sarge Bryan said, slapping the steering wheel in anger. "That shit happens in a banana republic. Senator Leota is ex-military. There's no way she's going along with sedition."

Ms. China mouthed the word "fuckbonnet" and shook her head.

"Judging from this screen grab of the latest news I saved, the possible President-Elect Leota has taken a neutral stance," Mr. Perdix continued. "She hasn't tried to issue any orders as head of state; she's just told units to follow the Constitution and their consciences. On the other hand, the CIA reports she's been actively coordinating with the governor of California, who is the head of the blue-state alliance."

The mood in the vehicle become more dour. Even Mr. Barracude had nothing to say.

"I'm glad we're on our way to sort things out," Ellie said as brightly as she could. "I mean, Ms. Leota wouldn't invite Ms. Jones and all of us to this summit if she were planning to continue her seditioning, would she?"

"Not unless she plans to kill you all," Ms. China said.

"Say, that's sneaky thinkin', doll. My wife basically runs the federal government. I'm not letting my Janice walk into a trap. I better go, too, then," Mr. Barracude said boldly. "If I'm there, no one will dare mess with her."

His tone suggested it was no use pointing out to him that people about to initiate a hostile takeover of a superpower might not care what happened to a real estate oligarch.

They arrived at LaGuardia Airport without being stopped or bombed by an armed drone.

"That's a dang big plane," Sarge Bryan said as they passed through the second perimeter gate.

Ellie had lost track of the local time and her internal clock; her head felt more than little bit wishy-washy.

Mr. Perdix peered out the fogged-up window. "I assume that belongs to you, Mr. Barracude."

"We never would have guessed," Ms. China said sarcastically.

As they came closer, Ellie saw the side of the jet was painted with shiny blue scales and a mouth overflowing with spiny teeth.

"Let me out. I'll make sure everything's kosher." Mr. Barracude left the Humvee.

Even though they were locked out of classified information channels, social media, Newsmax, Breitbart, and OAN had picked up on the impending crisis. Each update seemed to contain shocking news of more political assassinations and reports of mass civil unrest in major cities.

"Miss Aleph, are we okay to talk?" Sarge Bryan asked, watching Mr. Barracude through the windshield.

`"As long as you don't see any laser microphones aimed at your window. You're sure I can't jack into your eyes?"`

"Not a chance. The last time you did, you kept moving them around where I didn't want them to look."

"Right-o, then," Mr. Perdix said. "Let's touch on the thorny subject we've all been avoiding for the last hour. Do we trust Janice?"

"I don't have any *Veritas Curat* serum," Ms. China said, checking her fingernail jab dispensers. "But I'm sure Al has something that can get the truth out of her."

"We're not torturing the White House chief of staff," he replied curtly. "She works with politicians. She's suffering enough."

"It is kind of suspicious, though, isn't it?" Ellie had to admit. "Her showing up at Justice Meyers's secret bomb factory."

"But what about the thugs who tried to kidnap her at the Watergate and the Assegai Tower?" Mr. Perdix said logically.

Ellie noticed Ms. China quietly staring at the floor of the SUV. She didn't know much about armed thuggery, but it did occur to her that people organized enough to attempt an abduction would have made sure the target was in the hotel at the time. Janice had been noticeably absent during each apparent kidnapping attempt, first at the hotel, then at the New York skyscraper.

"Security's waving at us," Sarge Bryan said. "Perdix and I have to go, but

I don't think they can conscript you two ladies from the UK."

"Ahem."

"Or any citizens from the digital world."

Ellie tried to shrug nonchalantly, but the movement sent her knotted shoulder muscles into spasms. "We'd be safe for a while. Up in the air, I mean."

"Maybe not. Florida's governor was just killed by remotely guided rocket-assisted mortar round fired from nearly ten miles away. The weapons being used in this episode of American infighting are becoming increasingly sophisticated."

In defiance of that alarming note, they made their way up the walkway into the jetliner. Janice greeted them wearing a soft leather coat and smart half boots. Her face was grim.

Mr. Barracude, on the other hand, looked much more relaxed. "Y'like this plane?"

"I suppose." Ellie would definitely love it to pieces if it had a private cabin with a bed.

"On our honeymoon, we stayed in the air." Their host extended a broad hand around his wife's waist. "It was a whole week, and we kept going round the world. We kinda lost track because, hehe, we were busy, right, doll?"

"I've got to take this call. Tell the pilots we're set." Janice went into a privacy booth.

"You wanna see our bedroom?" Mr. Barracude asked.

"I think we'd better freshen up," Sarge Bryan said diplomatically.

The steward showed her to a suite. It was not quite as spacious as the one she had on her flight from the UK, but the lack of sex-toy dispensers didn't detract from Ellie's enjoyment of the full-sized bed surrounded by noise-canceling panels.

The last thing she remembered wanting to do was take her shoes off. Some length of time passed, and she was prodded awake by a gentle chiming noise.

Ellie braced herself for Chestnut's wake-up nudges, then she remembered where she was.

"Eleanor!"

Shhh, she tried to say but only breathed into the fat downy pillow.

Her handset vibrated like a nest of hornets until she swiped the screen on. There was a flashing text from Miss Aleph:

```
We've changed direction. We're not going to LA
anymore. There's been some kind of large-scale attack
in Las Vegas. I'm scared.
```

55

OVER MISSOURI

Blinking at sleep crust in her eyes, Ellie read Miss Aleph's text message over again.

"What do you have to be scared about?" Ellie hissed, keeping the bedcovers over her head. "Where are we going?"

My High Bandwidth Memory matrix is very sensitive, especially when I'm operating remotely. If something happens to your handset, I'll lose cognitive continuity and revert to my last save point.

That didn't sound as bad as crashing or being kidnapped.

The flight computer says we're heading to a location in Colorado. I have to tell you… Wait. Is that the door?

Miss Aleph's mic was more sensitive than Ellie's ears. A moment later, she heard a tapping at the door of her suite. Ellie mumbled something, and Janice entered.

"Nothing to worry about," Janice said. The frozen smile of a career politician on her face was made ever more stark by her figure being silhouetted against the bright lights of the big plane's hallway. "We're just making a little bitsy course correction."

At that point, it was no use trying to rest anymore. Ellie sat bolt upright and squirted some energy drink into her mouth from an unspillable sippy cup.

"It wouldn't have anything to do with Las Vegas, would it?" she said grouchily, then remembered she shouldn't have known about the attack.

Janice did a double take. "We only just got word about that over the DHS system. How…?"

"We London journos have our sources. News never rests."

"There's no actual confirmation about the California governor… I mean, they found his clothes, but not him. Then investigators had to retreat because of the riots."

"In that case, we'd better see what kind of tea you've got stocked," Ellie said, disengaging herself from the very luxurious bedding as her body reminded her how many times it had been bumped and twisted in wrong directions over the past twenty-four hours. "Where are we headed?"

Janice raised an eyebrow. "I thought your sources might have told you that too. We're going to meet Senator Leota at the Sprünger Pharmaceutical compound near Colorado Springs."

Janice left, and Ellie roused herself. Miss Aleph seemed to have signed off and added nothing to her last cryptic message. After an animated scrub brush on the mirror gave her a tutorial on how to use the bath facilities, she made herself ready to give these Americans a talking-to.

She found Sarge Bryan, Mr. Perdix, and Ms. China seated at an enormous dining table opposite Janice and Mr. Barracude. A robot was brewing the only tea they had on board the plane.

"That there is the most expensive tea in the world," Mr. Barracude said proudly. "Panda something or other. I mean, I'm not a tea guy, but I always demand the best, and I get it."

A steward held out a platinum serving tray embossed with the Barracude coat of arms. Ellie looked at the package standing on its mirror-bright surface. The label was written in Chinese hanzi characters, which Ellie could read. They translated as: Panda Dung Tea.

"This is, er, rare stock indeed," Ellie said, wondering why rich people had to be so odd. "And it most certainly has been near actual panda bears."

Out of all of those seated at the table, which nearly filled the entire width of the plane, Mr. Perdix was the most animated. He had spread out a number of electronic devices on the tablecloth and was busily poking at each in turn.

"Still no update on Vegas," he said. "Only two of the Blue Council delegates are confirmed to be still alive, and we've lost touch with the DHS team who was spying on the conference. It's probably a communications outage."

Ms. China rolled her six pupils, as though the mayhem and confusion was the fault of the JASON scientist.

"But President-Elect, or possible elect, Leota wasn't in Vegas, right?" Sarge Bryan asked.

"No, thankfully not," said Janice. "She was in Los Angeles waiting for us, despite an ultimatum from the seditionists who then went ahead without her."

"Modern Benedict Arnolds if you ask me," Mr. Barracude said. He drained his cup of Panda tea in one gulp, made a face, then rinsed his mouth with soda water.

"Yes, dear," Janice said placatingly. "But remember, Washington's been letting blue states get away with more and more anti-federalist behavior. Under the Constitution, states administer their own criminal law, and many functioned as sovereign, self-governing entities before joining the Union. As late as 1895, the kingdom of Hawaii fought against annexation, after which the island's last queen was convicted of treason."

"We've had our problems with the Irish and the Scots too," Ellie said. "But surely a nation as advanced as yours…"

"Advanced?" Ms. China scoffed. "Half of Americans are functionally illiterate. They're feeding antidepressants to toddlers. The country has run up a worse debt-to-GDP ratio than perennial deadbeats Greece and Lebanon. Two hundred thousand Americans die of overdoses each year, and yet they have vending machines in high schools dispensing opioids. Ninety percent of you are bloody-well fat, and everyone pretends it's not happening. How advanced to you call that? And Eleanor, please lay off the Scots."

"So we got some issues," Mr. Barracude weighed in, planting his elbows firmly on the table, looking as though he was holding in a burp. "They could probably do right by fixing some big roads. I spend millions a year repairing my long-haul truck fleet. And since they defunded all those police forces, I've been spending a bigger fortune on private security. But as they say in Rome, *in totalitum*: we're still the greatest!"

Ms. China raised her cup and whispered, "My point exactly."

"Of immediate concern," Mr. Perdix said, spreading his fingers on a map screen, "is transport to the Sprünger compound from Denver."

"We're not landing at Denver," Janice said curtly, glancing at her husband, who was biting his lips and in some kind of gastric distress. "Jezzie, I told you to sip the tea like Ms. Sato does. It was boiling."

"Wait," Mr. Perdix said, his fingers widening the map again. "Denver International's the only place with a runway long enough to accommodate a plane this size."

Mr. Barracude suddenly excused himself and ran to the loo at the back of the plane.

"Who said anything about landing?" Janice said. She was smiling as nonchalantly as ever, but Ellie, having had experience interviewing politicians before elections and designers before fashion shows, could tell their hostess was disconcerted. Maybe it had something to do with the next thing Miss Aleph had wanted to tell her.

A bulky, tanned, clean-shaven man who was dressed as a steward but was almost certainly Secret Service, led them to the back of the plane. Mr. Barracude emerged from the loo as they passed.

"Sorry," he said, letting them pass down the wide aisle into the tail section. "I've never gotten plane sick in my life. I'm gonna have a word with the pilot. Why is he picking the bumpiest air in the world to go through?"

"Will you be joining us?" Ellie asked, not clear where they were going.

"Oh, no," their host said. "I'm good right in this nice jetliner, as soon as they find some better air."

Ellie felt she had to trust in Sarge Bryan's instincts that they were not about to suffer a fatal accident because they knew too much.

They descended a short flight of stairs into the cargo hold. The area, like the rest of the plane, was immaculately clean and a little odd. Even food containers and industrial supplies were ensconced in leather packing cases and embossed with the Barracude logo. At the very back were a series of upright-standing silver cylinders that reached the ceiling of the hold.

"Ah," Mr. Perdix said, slapping the cylinder nearest him. To Ellie, it didn't look like the other ones. There was a shadow where the other ones were light… "I see you've upgraded to the latest—"

The JASON scientist's shriek echoed through the fuselage and caused Sarge Bryan and the guard to draw weapons. A hatch in the cylinder had swung open and unexpectedly hit Mr. Perdix on the shoulder.

"Oops, sorry, I am," said a mildly disconcerted voice which was half-female and half-synthesized mechanical.

"Tata!" Ellie said as the large Russian cyborg ducked her head and eased herself out of the tube.

Ms. China was incensed with her ex. "No man should ever make that kind of sound, Aloysius. Hi, Tata. What the hairy haggis are you doing here?"

"It's all right. She's, uh, friendly," Sarge Bryan said to the agents; they lowered their guns. "Of all the people you… er, we thought you and Ambassador Bagration…"

"Yes, he drowned to death a little, but he's okay now," Tata said cheerily in heavily accented English. "Sorry if I frightened you."

"Only one of us is hysterical," Ms. China said.

Ellie asked, "How ever did you get on board?"

"I'd like to know that too," Janice said, staring icily at her security guards.

"Well, you know," Tata said, stretching her long, thick arms with an audible creaking of hydraulic joints. "After I used a hologram to convince the anarchists of the Cumberland CUMZ that President Putin wishes to support their cause in their sovereign territory, I was able to borrow transportation.

"I dropped the ambassador off at the New York consulate for further medical treatment. While I am in the Big Apple, I hear you are also in town. Then I hear the tower you are visiting is in a state of collapse, so I think perhaps you could use some assistance. Finally, then I also thinking I am maybe not very welcome among an official delegation, so I come in secretly with the food supplies, and I keep to myself down here."

It slowly dawned on Ellie that this might be the surprise Miss Aleph was just about to mention before they were interrupted. Miss Aleph could have fed Tata detailed information on their movements. All in all, that was fine with her; she was more certain of where she stood with the gargantuan Russian lady than the Barracudes.

Janice did not seem pleased with the stowaway but seemed more interested in the time—more than once, she checked her oversized Patek Philippe.

"It would have been nice if... uh, Ms. Tata could have made her presence known a little earlier, or if security had been a bit more thorough," Janice said. "However, we have to go. We were expected at Leota's compound five minutes ago..."

"I'll take full responsibility for Ms. Oblonskaya," Sarge Bryan said, eyeing the twin rows of capsules. "We worked with her in France. She's got more grit than a platoon of Marines."

"Oh, Sergeant Bryan," Tata said, reaching down and giving his shoulders a hug. "Please, I am only to be Tata to you. And," she added dramatically, pretending to push him away while still maintaining a grip on his bicep. "I hope you mean to compare me to a platoon of attractive girl Marines."

It dawned on Ellie how they were about to disembark a plane that was flying miles up in the air.

"We're going in these?"

"I was about to say," Mr. Perdix said, "these descender modules seem fresh out of the JASON shipping box. We should have an exceptionally smooth ride when they launch us out of the cargo hold."

Having just jumped from a thousand-foot skyscraper, if there was one thing Ellie was not keen on, it was being put into a plastic tube and ejected from a speeding jetliner.

Sarge Bryan noticed her expression. "You could stay here, with Mr. Barracude."

"I'll jump."

Tata's grip encircled Sarge Bryan's entire forearm, and she pulled him away, insisting he show her how to use the unique American strapping-in system.

A glum-looking Secret Service man showed Ellie to her pod and went over the safety features with much less enthusiasm than a stewardess telling passengers how to use their drop-down air masks.

"Pardon me," Ellie said. "What's this little doodad for?" She pointed at a big orange handle.

"That's if you crash in water. You won't need it. Only rocks and mountains here."

"If I have any trouble opening it, you'll be coming too?"

"No, ma'am. Not enough pods. Staying here. Safe journey."

With that, he slammed the lid shut, and she heard a series of latches click into place. There was a porthole but all it showed was the pod directly opposite, which was occupied by a bored-looking Ms. China. Ellie wriggled around in her snug five-point harness and noticed a manual tucked in the door pouch, which was in several different languages and still had its warranty card attached.

Whoosh!

Before she was quite ready for it, the harness dug into all five hundred points of pain and prior bruising, and she felt like a chick inside an egg that had just been tossed off a moving lorry. She grabbed the straps and waited for the jerking-up movement she assumed would be coming when the parachute released.

After what seemed more than enough time watching the patch of very dark-blue sky with the hint of morning on the horizon twirl in front of her porthole, she realized she had not asked how the contraption was supposed to land, a significant oversight for a trained journalist.

She kept falling and spinning.

Her breath was fogging up the oval-shaped glass, and she was starting to get claustrophobic. A clicking noise echoed through the confined space—it was coming from outside. The vague whooshing sound only increased and made her think her fall was accelerating.

With another whump and roar, the capsule jiggled frightfully but seemed to slow down. Her only notion of motion was the fact that her ribs were compressing, and she was finding it a bit hard to breathe.

The roar reached a crescendo, at which point all sorts of gray dirt and white steam flew by the clear portion of her porthole. The pod thumped down, giving her one more good slap on the back. A green handle emerged from the ceiling, illuminated with the words: *Exit / Salida / Sortie*

She pulled it. The doorway popped completely off, and cool, somewhat pine-scented air wafted in. The fresh air was soon overcome by hot chemical exhaust fumes and flying grit that made her cover her mouth and fight not to cough. She undid her harness and steadied herself in an attempt to exit the capsule.

Before she was in great danger of doing a pratfall on the smoking and scorching-hot landing pad, Sarge Bryan helped her out.

"Careful there," he said. "These pads are built to dissipate heat from the landing thrusters, but they're still a might warm."

Ellie skipped over the skillet-hot tiles to where another pod had just opened.

"Some..." Ellie covered her mouth, and as politely as she could, spat out some sandy substance. "Someone might have mentioned there's no parachute."

"Oh," Ms. China said smugly. "Didn't you know that? It must have been a really weird sensation for you."

As the smoke cleared, Ellie recognized one of the people who had come to meet them, her face illuminated by the floodlights around the landing field. It was Senator Leota. A dozen security people surrounded her, which normally would have been reassuring, however, their automatic weapons were pointed straight at Leota, Ellie, and her friends.

A man's voice called out sharply: "Get yer fuckin' hands up!"

56

SPRÜNGER PHARMACEUTICAL COMPOUND
COLORADO

Janice, I—" Senator Leota's words were cut off when a clean-shaven man used a rifle butt to push her toward Ellie and the others.

Half a dozen blue-uniformed paramilitary surrounded the area where their descender pods had just landed. Ellie squinted, trying to see through the dust and smoke. Someone was missing. One of the pods stood with its door still sealed.

"Save it, bitch," Janice said, glaring at Leota. And, very unexpectedly, the White House chief of staff walked through the line of gunmen toward a tall very well-groomed man in his thirties. Ellie had seen his picture but could not recall who he was. "You had your chance, now we're way past fuckin' around."

If one of the soldiers had stabbed her with a bayonet, Senator Leota's tanned face and chiseled features could not have shown more shock and betrayal.

Janice dusted off her pantsuit suit and hugged the male model fellow, who seemed to be in control of the thugs with the weapons.

"Y'had to pull this now?" Janice asked.

The younger man shrugged. "After Las Vegas, Leota's security team found things out… We had to get rid of them."

"Cool," Janice said.

Ellie fumed. Why didn't she ever trust her instincts? Janice Jones had been a bad apple all along.

"Come out!" Two hostile guards surrounded the pod that had not sprung open. "Last warning." They raised their rifles.

Ellie looked right and left. There was Sarge Bryan, Mr. Perdix, and Ms. China with her long fingernails pointing skyward from the ends of her raised hands.

"Don't do that," Mr. Perdix said to the gunmen as though he were lecturing a science class. "That carbide material will send ricochets scattering all over."

"Maybe we'll get lucky and they'll only kill the right people," Ms. China said as one of the guards carefully zip-tied her hands in front of her.

The guard seemed to know to be wary of her extended fingernails. That horrible Janice must have given them information about all of them. But did they know about Tata, who was playing it quiet in the final landing pod? The Russian cyborg lady had only come out a minute before they dropped.

"Forget it," Janice said in a commanding tone. "The survival pods always launch in pairs in case the plane goes down in forest or mountains. There's spare food and supplies in each one."

The guards seemed to hear her, but they hammered on the hatch anyway. Their weapons ready, they prised it open to reveal... nothing.

Had Tata stayed on the plane?

The man-boy Janice had conspired with looked at her warily. "They let you come alone?"

"Relax, Julien, my Secret Service agents are still on the plane."

Now Ellie recalled who Janice's apparent co-conspirator was—Senator Leota's running mate, Julien Sprünger.

"We got who we need," Julien said.

Ms. China was hauled forward.

"Get the rest of them inside," Janice said. "NSA has surveillance in the air."

Ellie's hands were tied in front of her, which was a good thing because her shoulders felt as though they were long past bending backward without giving her enough pain to cause her to pass out. A zip tie attached her manacles to

Sarge Bryan, and they were prodded toward a concrete complex, the outlines of which were just becoming visible as the pale rays of dawn peeked over jagged mountains.

The grounds of Sprünger Pharmaceutical looked much like any other corporate campus facility. Their pods stood on the smoking landing pad, next to that was a helipad, and beyond that were walkways and hedges running between dozens of single-story buildings. A large box-shaped concrete structure dominated the center of the compound.

Doors into the nearest warehouse hissed open.

"This is as good a place as any to stow them," Janice said. "There's only one exit."

"How do you know that?" Julien Sprünger asked sharply, flicking his pomaded, perfectly groomed head in her direction.

"I don't go anywhere without researching the place first."

"That fucking Leota…" Julien said as he appeared to mull something over. "I don't know how much she knows. It's risky to keep her."

"Who cares what she knows?" Janice said bossily. "Let's just put her there for now and talk. We need to make sure the Scottish psycho has what we need. C'mon, Anna, you're with us."

Guards pulled on Ms. China's zip-tie bindings and led her along.

With that, Ellie and the others were put into a large partly subterranean storage room. The interior was bare except for some dusty pallet imprints on the floor; whatever had been stored here had recently been moved.

"Cameras," Sarge Bryan mumbled, hardly moving his lips as he walked across the bare concrete floor.

Ellie looked up. There were bulbous plastic blisters on the ceiling and over the door. Mr. Perdix was tied to Leota, who was moving slowly. He tried to help her down the steps, but the guard pushed her in and slammed a mesh gate door down. As she stumbled, Ellie noticed the politician's lip had dried blood on it, and her shirt shoulder was torn. Her tanned features and high cheekbones were set in a mask of contained fury.

Leota flicked her long dark hair away from her face and looked at the albino soldier.

"Trust the Army to screw up a rescue op, huh, Sergeant Bryan?" Leota spoke with a slight lisp, probably due to the bruising and swelling on the side of her cheek.

"I'm surprised you remember me. That was years ago, Madam President-Elect."

"Do I look 'elect' of anything?"

Ellie thought she looked about as in control as the other president, Abraham Casteel, had. Somewhat dizzy and needing to sit, Ellie didn't mean to speak out loud, yet she heard herself say in a flustered voice, "How many presidents do you have over here?"

Leota laughed and grimaced, then doubling over and yanking Mr. Perdix along with her, she braced herself against the wall. She coughed blood.

"Oh my," Ellie gasped. Despite her own nagging injuries, she immediately felt the politician was worse off. She tried to reach over and assist, yanking on her own tether binding her to Sarge Bryan.

"We better undo that," he said, his voice tense and even.

Ellie glanced at the grating-style doorway and the guards who stood there watching them.

"I don't think they'll come in or shoot," he said, lifting his flex cuffs. "These were just temporary to keep us from running off while they herded us here."

There was a sharp edge where a storage container or something like it had been lashed to a wall. They bent down and first sawed at the long cord, then at their flex cuffs.

With his back to the cameras, Sarge Bryan whispered, "This all looks makeshift. They're not set up for handling prisoners."

"What are you thinking?" Ellie whispered back.

"Nothing now, but keep watch."

As though one complicated jailbreak from St. Bartholomew's was not enough. Ellie decided to pester the guards and get another look through the grate door at the corridor outside.

"Look here," Ellie said, going up to doorway. The guards stopped slouching and looked menacingly at her. "Clearly we're meant to be kept alive, otherwise you would have executed us at the landing field. Which we're thrilled you didn't," she added hastily. "But please make yourselves useful and get us some water."

"Sarge," Leota wheezed, dribbling reddish saliva on her shirt. "Appears you've fallen in with… a dangerous crowd."

"We've been in some tight spots together," Sarge Bryan said. "But never at home, in…"

"In America?" Leota said, easing herself into a stiff-backed sitting position against the concrete wall. "Look around, there's not much of it… left."

Begrudgingly, one of the guards in the corridor squeezed two small plastic water bottles through the largest holes in the steel barrier. Ellie brought them over to the other side of the room. Leota took a small sip and expelled the water in a dark dribble.

"Thanks, Ms. Sato."

Ellie looked around. "I take it the summit to reconcile the country's political woes has been postponed."

"Bet you wish you'd taken a rain check," Leota said with a mirthless smile. "And I wish I'd picked a different running mate."

"Julien Sprünger. His family owns this pharma empire," Mr. Perdix said. He was crouched down, poking around at Leota's side; being more used to operating on robots than people he was causing discomfort.

"Hey! Damn," Leota exclaimed.

"I'm just concerned about one of your ribs. It might have fractured and be poking into your lung," Mr. Perdix said with clinical coolness.

"Something's moving around in there," Leota said, keeping herself rigid against the wall. "But it's not getting any worse. They—Julien's people—blindsided me just before you landed. He was the one who insisted you and your, er, special investigative team should all come, as a sign of good faith to President Casteel."

Ellie glanced at the bulbous camera installations. She had a nagging question about Janice. Why did she cover for Tata's empty pod? Was she really with Julien and did not want to admit there was a seven-foot-tall cyborg unaccounted for, or was something else going on?

"I never liked Ms. Jones," Ellie said loudly. "And her husband makes Neanderthals seemed civilized."

"Just before you landed, they seemed very anxious that someone code-named 'Mrs. China' be among your group," Leota said.

"That's not a pseudonym," Ellie said. "And what would they want Annunciata for?"

"It wasn't something they shared with me as they were tasering and beating the hell out of me."

"I'm sure the Army did worse during our rugby matches against you Jarheads," Sarge Bryan said gruffly, but Ellie could tell he was concerned.

Mr. Perdix concluded his examination. "Tell us right away if you experience shortness of breath."

Ellie looked around. Sprünger and Janice could not mean to keep them here very long.

"In case they separate us, we should know what you had planned for this summit," Ellie said.

"Nothing, really," Leota wheezed. "Just keeping the country together in the face of the greatest upheaval since the Civil War."

"In that case," Ellie said, sipping stale, plastic-tasting water and fishing around for her airplane-safe Visconti fountain pen. "I shall have to take notes."

As pertinent as the details Senator Leota and Mr. Perdix were telling her, Ellie always tended to fall asleep during political lectures. The buzzing of the jittering fluorescent bulbs in the ceiling and a rising headache did nothing to help her concentration.

Essentially, the "blue" states were politically and economically distancing themselves from the "red" states, and had doing so been for several years. There were not dozens but hundreds of pertinent Constitutional cases involving the Tenth Amendment and whatnot, which only the Supreme Court could resolve.

"That's a spanner in things, then, isn't it? Poor Justice Meyers going off like that."

"In the meantime, positions have hardened," Leota continued. "National Guard units in blue states have refused to be federalized until the election results are settled. Tempers were flaring even before the attack on Las Vegas."

"Who did that?" Sarge Bryan asked.

"Can't say yet. I don't think it was Julien's people."

"You were supposed to be there," Ellie said, recalling that detail. "Did Julien have some reason not to attend?"

"He did, indeed. Still… I think he was genuinely surprised when nearly all of Vegas went dark. No one's gotten any intelligence out of the whole of Clark County for the last six hours."

"And you delayed going to Nevada to meet with Janice Jones," Ellie said, making a line across her note paper.

"She was supposed to be extending an olive branch from President Casteel, a way we could form an interim emergency unity administration until Congress and the Court could be up and running."

"I suppose Julien made Ms. Jones a better offer," Mr. Perdix said dryly. "Ms. Leota, I want you to elevate your arm like this and take the deepest breath you can at least once every half hour."

She looked skeptically at the pale scientist. "You're the fellow from the JASON think tank?"

"I'm a thoroughly competent bioengineer," he said defensively.

"Perdix is okay," Sarge Bryan said. "Only, if he offers to grow you any new body parts, I'd get a second opinion."

Suddenly the albino soldier whipped his head from side to side, his eyes tracing streaks of light in the dark room. He yelled incoherently and pushed Ellie into a corner.

Ellie's water spilled on the dusty floor. She looked up at Sarge Bryan. Everyone was staring at them. Aside from the buzzing of an insect caught in the lighting above them, the room was quiet and still.

What had Bryan's cyber eyes seen?

57

SPRÜNGER COMPOUND
COLORADO

Everyone waited, bracing for an explosion or gunfire. Even Ms. China grimaced and prepared to duck and cover. Then…

Nothing happened. Everyone looked over at Sarge Bryan. Ellie had been with him when they were hit with an IED and under sniper fire, but he'd never panicked liked this.

"Th-there was a flash of something, in the corridor outside," the Army man said. "Some kind of… I thought they were cooking us with microwaves." He blinked as he looked around the bare concrete cell they had been thrown into.

Ellie looked over to the guards outside the grating covering the exit. They seemed alert but were not getting ready to shoot them or set them on fire. With a mix of confusion and embarrassment, Sarge Bryan released Ellie and wandered back to the middle of the room.

"What did you see?" Mr. Perdix asked in that attentive and creepy clinical way that gave Ellie chills because it usually came just prior to many people dying horrible deaths.

"I… don't… I can replay it in my head, but it doesn't make sense."

Senator Leota had a flip phone that they had not taken away from her, but it had no signal because the pharma company controlled all the cellular towers. Mr. Perdix was able to connect it to the sergeant's Bluetooth optic channel.

"Play what you saw."

Everyone other than Sarge Bryan leaned over the grainy three-inch screen. It showed the cell they were in, and suddenly a beam of radiant light seared through the hallway outside, making the guards' bodies fluoresce as though someone had sent a spotlight through solid concrete walls.

"We didn't see anything," Leota said.

"You wouldn't have," Mr. Perdix said, looking at a small readout on the side of the display. "His ocular implants are capable of detecting many more wavelengths than the human eye. This was an axion scattering. Someone has activated a device capable of projecting dark-matter energy particles. They seem only to have passed through the corridor area, not us."

Nevertheless, Ellie checked her fingers and glanced down her body to make sure nothing was dissolving or doing whatever happened when invisible exotic beams washed over you. The only tingling she felt was from having hit her elbow nerve when she landed on the floor.

"What are axions?" Leota asked pointedly. She was clearly annoyed, as one would expect—she was used to being in a position of authority in the military and the government. Leota was trapped, injured, and betrayed by her own political partner.

"It's a side effect of exotic particles passing through materials we perceive as solid."

That sounded plausible from what Ellie knew about the T-rays, which had wiped out entire towns in France and had nearly depopulated the whole continent. However, Mr. Perdix did not sound as convincing when he said, "I wouldn't worry about it, maybe some kind of test. These types of facilities use radiation for sterilization and for killing viruses before implanting them into vaccines." He looked over at the guards lounging in the hallway. "I don't suppose we can ask you gentlemen for a guided tour?"

The guards seemed distracted. One was looking at the tips of his fingers. The other shook his head and jabbed at his ear.

Before either of their captors could deliver a witty reply, a shrieking roar came from down the corridor. Both guards jumped to their feet and aimed their weapons. Two or three muzzle blasts echoed between the narrow concrete walls, then a dark blur swept the pair out of view. They were gone so fast it seemed one man's weapon hung in the air for a moment before dropping to the floor.

Sarge Bryan leaped over and tried to grab it, but the gaps in the bars would only allow his forearm through. Ellie rolled up her sleeve, for a second marveling at the intensity of color present in the wide assortment of bruises on her bare skin, and went to help. Before she could employ her thinner arm in a doubtful attempt to reach the firearm, one of the guards reappeared. Both his hands were wrenched behind his back, and his feet hung a foot off the ground as he was carried forward.

"You take prisoner of my friends?" said an outraged and familiar mechanical voice. "You Americans like cheese. Here, feel what a cheese feels."

With that, the struggling man's unshaven face was pressed into the metal grate so that his nose and lips poked through. As pressure increased on the back of his head, his cheeks and eyes started bulging through, then with a dull cracking sound and a bending inward of the whole grillwork... At that point Ellie had to look away.

A moment later, keys rattled, and the doorway, with bits of grated guard sloughing off on the inside, creaked open. Behind it was Tata. She was breathing heavily, and veins stood out on her neck and arms. Ellie recognized these as side effects of the "berserker" mode the Russian cyborgs could activate.

There was more commotion in the hall, and everyone in the storage room jail tensed up. Ellie was closest, saw who was joining them, and was the first to relax.

"Oh! You brought... more." Ellie took a step back and allowed another bulky figure to pop into view. She knew this one too, as he had nearly crushed her head in Europe but then after that turned out to be not such a bad egg. "Komandir Zvena, how nice of you to come rescue us."

The Russian, broader and even a little taller than Tata, picked up the weapon the now-squashed guard had dropped. It looked like a toy in his hands.

"Ms. Sato, Sergeant Bryan, in rescuing you I am following my general operational directives." He looked down at them sternly. Then he smiled, revealing metallic gray shark teeth. "But it is also my pleasure. Whenever we meet, interesting things always happen."

Tata rushed over to Sarge Bryan. "Have you been hurt? We have medical supplies. Come, boy." She slapped her leg, and Ellie started back from the door as a six-legged mechanical beast hopped down the short staircase and trotted over to Tata. A saddlebag with a small red cross hung from its back.

"That's a small MULE," Ellie said, having ridden one in Turkey a few years ago.

"Much better. Is OCEL unit," Tata said, still fussing over an increasingly embarrassed-looking Sarge Bryan.

"I think Senator Leota needs attention more than me."

"Hurry," said Zvena from the doorway. "The opposing force is more heavily armed than one would expect at a drug research facility."

Gunfire was getting closer.

Mr. Perdix rummaged through the OCEL's saddlebags, then took something and went back to where Leota was sitting.

"Do you know how to use that?"

"*Eto detskaya igra dlya uchenogo iz JASON,*" Mr. Perdix shot back as he attached a headband device to Leota. "This will monitor your vital signs, especially blood oxygen levels. I don't want to give you any anesthetic because—"

The possible US president-elect never learned why she had to remain in obvious pain, because the largest cyborg yet ducked through the doorway.

"My word," Ellie said, looking up at the partially familiar face sporting an eyepatch and a number of freshly stapled wounds. "You've been through the wars, haven't you?"

"Ha, Miss Ellie," Rodion slurred. His injuries seemed accompanied by some kind of facial paralysis. "As they say in America: 'you should see the other dude.'"

Zvena got out of the now-crowded doorway, and a figure pushed blithely past the corpse hanging from the door grate.

"Annunciata… fuck!" Everyone looked at Mr. Perdix. It was perhaps the first time anyone had heard him use profanity.

Despite a massive swelling lump on her forehead, burn marks on her clothes, and deep bloody gashes on her wrists, Ms. China immediately defaulted to bossy mode.

"Just for that," she said, hurriedly slinging a plastic pouch out of her pants pocket, "you're going first, Aloysius. Head back, and try not to sneeze. You won't like it."

Ms. China produced a six-inch swab and stuck it more deeply into Mr. Perdix's nose than Ellie thought anything could actually go, then left it there.

"You next, Ellie."

With more force and glee than she thought was absolutely necessary, her former housemate impaled her sinus cavity with the dipstick-like instrument. It smelled like mouthwash, and after it had been in a few seconds, she thought she could detect a minty taste trickle down the back of her throat.

"I assume this a test for some kinda biotoxin we may have been exposed to?"

"Yes, Sergeant Bryan, and don't talk while it's in."

Senator Leota accepted the cranial intrusion stoically. By the time they all felt and looked somewhat ridiculous, it was time to pull the probe out from Mr. Perdix.

"It's purple," he said suspiciously. The end had changed from white to bright violet.

Ms. China said nothing; she merely removed each swab in turn.

Sarge Bryan's was violet.

Senator Leota's the same.

Ellie's, however, was yellow, which she hoped was not an embarrassing amount of mucous.

"So?"

Ms. China started to bite her upper lip in thought, then stopped, as it was swelling and covered with crusted blood.

"We've all got it," she finally said. "Only Ellie's has not passed the blood-brain barrier."

"Got *what*?" Mr. Perdix shrieked.

"Seems a fair question," Sarge Bryan said, rubbing the bridge of his nose and opening and closing his jaw.

Having been on dangerous missions as well as extended Harrods shopping trips with Ms. China, Ellie could tell when she was hiding something.

"This has something to do with... everything, doesn't it?" Ellie said accusingly.

"Argh!" Ms. China exclaimed in a way that really empathized her Scottish brogue accent. "Inna my fault. I needed money to appeal my unjust incarceration."

"What did you do?"

"It was so boring at St. Bartholomew's," she said in a self-justifying tone, which usually accompanied the discovery of copious dead bodies. "Nothing to do but play checkers with the Chippenham Cannibal and rehearse our Shakespeare play."

"Anna..."

"So I answered a dark web message sent to the mailbox coded in my textbook."

Ellie remembered that book, *Biological and Chemical Weapons: Their Joys and Pitfalls*.

"I thought it was some researchers at a university trying to get one up on the competition, y'know? For tenure or government grants."

"So you assisted people you never met in developing a bioweapon?" Mr. Perdix said, looking closely at the gooey nasal swabs.

"I didn't really 'assist,'" Ms. China said flippantly. "They were kind of thick. I had to do all the work. That was another reason why I thought they were harmless. And I mean, what they wanted to do, it had legitimate purposes. Each year, there are hundreds of millions of prescriptions for psychotropic drugs: Xanax, Zoloft, Prozac. The 'carrier molecule' I designed could pass through the blood-brain barrier and have the same effect for nearly no cost. It was a no-brainer."

No one laughed.

"When you say carrier molecule, you mean a living virus, right?" Mr. Perdix said.

"Technically."

"Did it ever occur to you they might piggyback something else on top of the viral delivery agent?"

"That's why I kept an ace up me sleeve, an antiviral enzyme that keeps the virus permanently inert," Ms. China said rather self-righteously. "When my mystery clients started asking me about R-naught rates and spread through populations, I cut them off. But somehow... uh, never mind."

Ellie's admittedly shaken and somewhat sleep-deprived mind was still able to connect a few recent mysterious events.

"Oh, Anna! Somehow they found out who you were," Ellie said, walking to her and shaking a finger. "I mean, in terrorist circles, you're probably a famous author. Who doesn't want to wipe out their enemies with germs and chemicals? They found out who you were, but you were locked up in St. Bartholomew's. So they used the only leverage they could... Attie Jr."

"What? You lost me, Ms. Sato," Sarge Bryan said.

"The attack at the Watergate Hotel. It wasn't Janice or her husband they were after, it was Attie Jr. They were going to use him as leverage to get this last chemical formula from Anna."

Ms. China's normally statuesque shoulders sagged under the weight of the truth. The gunfire outside quieted down for a moment.

"Wha... what's the viral package?" Senator Leota asked, staring fixedly at them all. "This is a national emergency. If this disease..."

"I call it Anna-Pegivirus-32," Ms. China put in, rather lamely.

"What has Anna-Pegivirus-32 carried into our brains and presumably almost every other American?" Mr. Perdix asked.

Zvena stepped forward, pulling his companion Mr. Rodion with him. "Perhaps we can shed some light on this." He tapped the injured side of his companion's head. "Rodya has recently been afflicted with an active form of the pathogen. It appears to be a neural-hijacking agent with self-extracting dark-matter properties."

Mr. Perdix rose on his tiptoes and looked at the eye-patched Rodion. "How was he infected?"

"By an active vector, a half-mad feral person."

"And this feral individual, how was he infected?"

Zvena and Rodion both shrugged.

"But I tell you," Rodion said. "We have seen the same symptoms all over the otherwise very pleasant city of Las Vegas recently. Many people became actively afflicted."

"Could a burst of subatomic radiation set off the payload?" Mr. Perdix seemed to lose interest in Rodion and was speaking as much to the filthy floor as any of them.

Sarge Bryan grabbed the JASON man's slim shoulders. "Like the beam that just irradiated the guards?"

"Ohhhhh," Ms. China said with rising alarm, looking like she wanted to back out of the room and close the gory door behind her.

"Don't look freaked out," Sarge Bryan said, looking a little freaked out himself. "The beam missed us. It only hit those two. Before Tata hit them, that is."

Ms. China grabbed a pistol from the dangling corpse and tried to duck into the corridor. Sarge Bryan grabbed her arm.

"Wait a sec, whose side are you on?"

"You better hope it's yours," she said, wriggling free. "Julien's associates, the ones he's fighting with now, must have an activator beam. They're also after the vaccine enzyme Julien forced me to hand over. We've got to get it before they do. It's America's only chance!"

58

SPRÜNGER COMPOUND
COLORADO

Ellie helped the senator up. She had doubts Leota was up to participating in a vigorous jailbreak, but the Hawaiian woman gritted her teeth and walked to the gore-spattered doorway by herself.

Ellie asked Tata, "How did you get here? Your pod was empty."

"I was not in pod. I was *on* pod," the large cyborg lady said as she checked the ammunition left in a weapon, cleaned the grip, and handed it to Sarge Bryan with a wan smile. "While we were still on the plane, I was alerted to strange communications coming from ground. At the last moment, I am thinking, if is trap, better I am able to see what is happening. So I hang onto drop pod when it launched, and I jump off before it lands."

She raised a leg, revealing a burn hole in her pants leg, presumably made by the landing rockets.

"Who alerted you?" Ellie asked.

"The often aggravating but somewhat useful Israeli mechBrain, just as we were leaving the plane."

"And you gents?" Sarge Bryan asked Zvena and the beat-up looking Rodion as he looked down the corridor to the exit out of the storage building.

"Us?" Rodion had to swivel his whole bandaged head around to look at the American with his remaining cyborg eye. "We came from Vegas."

"Give me a—*heff*—weapon." Leota puffed as Mr. Perdix and Ms. China helped her to her feet.

"A gun?" Ms. China had the nerve to quip. "You need a stretcher and an IV drip."

"No disrespect, ma'am," Sarge Bryan said quickly as he moved toward the door. "Even though I recall you won the women's All Forces three-gun competition, you're an elected official now. Our priority should be getting you to safety."

"That was the overall unisex shooting championship, Sergeant," Leota said, stepping past the squashed body of the guard and steadying herself against the doorway. "We—*heff*—need everyone in the fight. According to this woman, her terrorist accomplices have what we all need urgently to stay alive."

"When I started working with them, I didn't know they were so... antisocial," Ms. China protested. "I wouldn't have had to develop A/P-32 if the UK government had pardoned me like they promised."

"Where's this serum?" Sarge Bryan said.

"In the main manufacturing facility," she said. "After we landed, they took me there."

"And they were able to produce it within a few hours?" Mr. Perdix said skeptically as they moved cautiously to the exit.

"They had all the precursors. They just needed the last enzyme sequence."

Ellie remembered the zombie kitty locket. "Which you had in that locket you had on you when you escaped St. Bartholomew's."

"Area ahead is clear," Zvena said, leading the way out of the building. "Nearly no bullets going our direction. Come."

"If you are in here with us," Leota said, looking pained but keeping up, "who were they shooting at?"

"The factory guards are fighting a group of Pangean insurgents we tracked from Venezuela. They attacked the political conference in Las Vegas, then went to a bunker facility in the mountains, and then they came here. After a short conference with Julien Sprünger, there was a dispute."

A body lay just outside the exit door. The man was still alive and raised his head. Tata kicked it like a tethered football, causing the now definitely dead man's body to do a backflip and land on the dusty ground.

Sarge Bryan and the cyborgs led the way. Able to see through many ordinary objects and even sense residual body heat where people had just walked past, he scouted a safe route to the main factory building. They huddled in the shadow of the multistory building.

"This place is bloody huge," Ellie said under her breath.

"This facility produces more opioids than all the rest of the world combined," Mr. Perdix said. "It was built after I wrote a policy paper on the importance of bringing America's drug manufacturing industry home."

"And you made that twat Julien rich enough to stage a genocidal coup. Nice going," Ms. China said.

"Quiet," Sarge Bryan hissed. "Which way?"

Ms. China looked disoriented for a second. "Over there. They were taking me to a holding cell when the fighting broke out between Julien's people and the Pangeans, then the Russians came."

"Watch out," Sarge Bryan said. "There's a machine gun in that pillbox bunker."

"OCEL," Rodion said, "*atakovat' tikho.*" Then he whispered, "I tell him: silent attack."

With barely a hiss of well-oiled hydraulics, at a speed far faster and stealthier than any human solider, the robot dove forward. A bunker-like structure in front of the factory was occupied by one or more guards, its front pockmarked by bullet holes. Ellie had no idea what the OCEL was going to do. The observation aperture was much too small for it to climb through.

The top part of the OCEL detached itself from its hindquarters, leaving most of its torso and four of its legs behind, turning it into a two-legged mechanical creature. This biped with its squat spider-eyed "head," clambered through the observation slit and into the bunker. After a tremendous thrashing and an amused chuckle from Zvena, whose cyborg eyes were watching a feed from the robot's cameras, they moved forward.

The mini-bot, now mostly covered in gory muck, slithered back out from the small fortification. It reattached itself to the rest of its body, which had been waiting patiently. The OCEL then sank to its knees and carried out a cleaning cycle, wiggling its little head and scraping red goop off its body with sharp forelimbs. Then it ran over to them, and as it passed Ellie, it looked her up and down and possibly even sniffed her through wet-looking rubber orifices under its head dome.

"As useful as your pet is, Mr. Rodion, I'll stick with my Labradoodle."

Mr. Perdix and Tata were at the large metal door set in the wall of the pharmaceutical plant. They studied the entry keypad and the big fat mechanical lock, and began furiously working at both of them with screwdrivers and pliers.

"This is no good. This is locked tight from inside. Do you have any drones?" Ms. China asked the Russians. "If we leave it to Aloysius, he'll take—"

A mechanism deep inside the drawbridge-sized door went *click-clang*.

59

SPRÜNGER COMPOUND

Ellie ducked back behind cover at the unexpected opening of the gateway into the huge drug factory. Mr. Perdix, who had been fiddling with some wires spewing out of the keypad, momentarily looked as surprised as the rest of them, then he recovered his nerdy mojo.

"There we go," he said, ushering them forward. "If we're lucky, the Pangeans will have killed everyone off."

Zvena and Rodion peered into the dim cavernous interior, while Tata and the six-legged OCEL robot watched behind them. Senator Leota appeared to want to go rushing through the breach, but Ms. China and Mr. Perdix urged her back.

From inside came a steady *click-clack-click-clack*.

"The place is fully automated," Mr. Perdix said.

Despite the mayhem and killing going on elsewhere on the Sprünger compound, the production line was still busy rolling off drugs and chemicals. Ellie snuck a look inside. A factory robot the size and shape of a loading pallet skittered across the immaculately clean floor.

"This place is the size of an airplane hangar," Sarge Bryan complained.

It gave Ellie the impression of being inside an immense and sinister Tesco grocery store. Far in the distance, above a gantry walkway, she saw a row of lights. "Is that a control center?"

"It's way at the other end," the albino soldier said and followed the cyborgs inside.

"This whole factory is basically a muckle-sized 3D chemical printer," said Ms. China, who had slunk up behind them. "I was trying to convince the minister of health to build one in the UK."

"Was that before or after they committed you?" Ellie whispered back.

Parts of the place looked like modern art installations she'd seen at the Tate gallery. Cubes covered with ampules on all sides were rolled in behind a thick glass screen. The light strobed through sequences from very bright to invisible black light, under which the ampules glowed various fluorescent colors. After this came a burst of orange gas which obscured everything. When this dissipated, the next cube of ampules was shoved in place.

Other areas reminded Ellie of a brewery she had toured with her pub-owning parents, complete with large stainless-steel vats that gave off steady hissing noises. She tried to be cautious, so instead of rushing across to the next passageway, she peeked around the curved side of one of the vats. A pallet robot was sitting, inert and not moving. She stepped on it to get to the other side.

"Gawar!"

The bloody thing sprang to life, a plastic netting popping up from the base and grabbing her firmly. She couldn't get away. With startling speed, it started carrying her toward the far end of the factory. The plastic cage held her like a grapefruit in a carry tote.

Her feelings of embarrassment and being foolish were quickly overtaken by fear. *They've got me!* Was it Janice and that slimy Julien Sprünger fellow, or was it the rogue Pangeans? No use being stealthy now.

"Over here!" she yelled.

Sarge Bryan and the others were on the far side of the brewing vat. Tata nearly got to her, but the madly agile pallet robot took a hard corner, and the large Russian lady slid into the side of an ampule cube. Glass shattered and sprayed everywhere.

The bot gathered speed and headed straight for a lift device, its doors gaped wide open. Just as they were rolling in, the OCEL unit came from nowhere and caught her. Its spiny praying-mantis forelegs latched on to the wiry mesh and started to hack it away from her body.

She had one arm free when the lift doors crashed down pinning the OCEL robot in place. It was forced to retreat as the conveyance whirred and carried her up to the top of the complex.

Ellie slumped to her side, groaned in pain, and ripped at the opening in the springy plastic material binding her. Before she could make the gap any larger, the lift thudded to a stop. Two figures in gas masks and hazmat gear approached, their outstretched hands gripping shiny sharp box cutters.

Once she was cut loose, they dragged her out into a room filled with flat screens and computer terminals. On one side were large thickly glassed bay windows, on the other stood Julien and that terrible Janice Jones, who reached for a gas mask lying on a table.

"Don't worry," Julien said in a soft but grating voice as he examined her like a lab specimen. "She's not first-stage infectious. Not yet. If the virus is dormant in her, we might be able to do a live experiment."

Ellie kept squirming. What had possessed all of them to get on that mad barracuda-painted jet? Before she could come up with a fittingly biting insult to hurl at Janice, a guard passed a scanner over Ellie. A yellow light flashed.

"Perfect," Julien said. "Now we can study the transmission from primary to secondary stages. Put her in the cryonics chamber. It has a hard atmospheric seal."

She was pushed inside an area sealed off from the control room, the atmosphere there definitely chilly. They sat her down and pushed her against a stainless-steel table, and fat green webbing-type straps cinched Ellie's arms behind her back and her neck to the leg of a table. At the floor, right in front of her, they set a stainless-steel metal cylinder that was oozing white vapors.

"Now get out and lock it," Julien said over a speaker. He left the mic on.

Something was going to happen, something terrible. Ellie struggled against her bonds but only gagged as the band around her neck threatened to choke her.

"Julien," Janice's voice said, as the dark-skinned and fashionably dressed woman peered in at them. "The Sato woman's infected too. You said the virus is practically unavoidable, everyone in the country has A/P-32, though they don't know it."

"We've been working on this for some time," Julien said smugly. "For you, this is like awakening to a new reality. A/P-32 takes approximately thirty days to cross the brain–blood barrier. Irradiating before then accomplishes nothing. I've been wanting to try out Stage 2 spores on a fresh guinea pig. You'll see what I mean shortly. Not long now."

In front of Ellie, the cylinder's electronic lid started opening. Pure frost-white condensation cascaded out, and specks of gray started to appear. It reminded her of roadside snow fouled by pollution. The cold mist stayed near to the floor and crept closer.

What would happen when it touched her? What horrid thing were they trying to infect her with while they watched? Sweat was dripping down her neck, lubricating it; she managed to twist her head a few inches to the side.

Suddenly the light flashed, and yellow lights flicked on in the ceiling. In the other room, Janice looked up in alarm.

"Ha!" Julien said. "The jihadi fanatic Abdelkader is trying to irradiate us. Fortunately, we've all had the vaccine." He nodded to a technician. "Continue. I want every camera, every sensor trained on the experiment."

The cold mist crept closer to Ellie.

60

SPRÜNGER COMPOUND

Ellie looked around wildly, wondering how long she could hold her breath. Would it matter? Would the gray stuff misting in with the liquid nitrogen fog get her through her eyes, her skin, her ears?

Through one of the windows into the control room, she saw Janice walking to the left, away from Julien and toward the door into the cryo room. The terrible turncoat was watching closely, obviously fascinated by what was about to happen.

"You'll get a better magnified view of the process in this monitor," Julien said, making some adjustment to the recording devices peering down at Ellie from the ceiling.

"I'm fine here. I want to see what it looks like."

"You'll have many more opportunities soon," Julien said. "About three hundred million more."

Behind Janice, the thick glass window looking down onto the factory floor erupted into a fireball. There was very little sound, and Ellie felt only a moderate vibration in the floor. Janice ducked down, but Julien merely smoothed back his blond forelock and chuckled. The blast had not even cracked the window.

Ellie had to hope her friends would break through... somehow. Could they get to them in time? Another explosion outside the control room passed without a sound and without leaving so much a as smudge on the thick exterior glass wall.

"You," Julien Sprünger said to one of the guards, "make sure the... lift... shaft it's up no... can they..."

Suddenly, Julien violently shook his head from side to side, uttering increasingly incomprehensible garbled nonsense. The door into the cryonics chamber opened, and Janice dashed in.

"You bloody turnc—"

"Shh," Janice said, holding her finger to her lips. She came in and locked the door behind her. Then she grabbed a fire extinguisher, slammed it down on the disease-spewing cylinder, shutting it, and then sprayed foam onto all the gray particles around it.

Out in the control room, three of the four guards were also knocking about, bumping into things, ripping off their face masks. The last guard raised his weapon and shot as the others closed around him. The bullets had no effect; he was grabbed and pinned to the floor. A grayish mist just like what Ellie had nearly been treated to, but much thicker, floated up in the air above where he fell. It dissipated so quickly for a moment that Ellie blinked and thought she was hallucinating due to the strap around her neck cutting off blood to her brain.

Janice reached over and undid the buckles on her restraints. Ellie tried to get up, but her limbs were numb, and she slumped back down on the chilly metal floor. Janice had released her, but there was no way Ellie was going trust her. She pushed herself away.

Janice raised what looked like a fancy handgun and aimed it at her.

"Don't!" Ellie lunged at the apparent weapon.

Janice pushed her away easily. "It's an inoculation gun."

Ellie still tried to retreat. The room was very small, mostly filled with tubs of liquid nitrogen. As Janice reached toward Ellie, she rolled up her own sleeve and revealed a blood-red circle about the size of a dime on her forearm. Ellie reluctantly complied. The pneumatic injector felt like a really fat bee sting but stopped hurting seconds later.

"What did you do?" Ellie asked and pointed to the mayhem out in the control room. "What's happening to them?"

"Looks like Julien's getting all the scientific data he wanted, firsthand." Janice jumped up and lunged over to the doorway just as one of the stricken men pried at the handle, trying to get in. Thankfully, it was locked from their side.

"They used the same type of vials for the old vaccine and the new one with Ms. China's enzyme in it." Janice opened her coat, revealing several a bandolier of red vials that fit in the back of the inoculation gun. "I switched them. Julien and the others got the old crap that doesn't work at all."

Ellie struggled to her feet, rubbing the injection spot. Out in the control room, things were getting messy. One of the afflicted guards was shot to pieces, his remains quivering on the previously spotless floor. Julien's blue politician's suit was all disheveled, and he and one of the infected guards had the last man by the arms and neck. Ellie couldn't turn away. Julien loomed over the pinned man's face, his mouth opened impossibly wide, and aerosolized gray mist came spewing out.

"This is the secondary infection he was talking about," Janice said, also transfixed. She came up beside Ellie. "Stage Ones can infect people whether they have been seeded with A/P-32 or not."

Julien dropped his victim and, noticing Ellie's movements, he scrabbled at the glass. His dull gray eyes flickered back and forth, as though they could only see vague shapes. Ellie and Janice remained still, and after a moment, Julien and the other two lost interest and appeared to forget they were there. They went off into separate corners and stood bent over at the waist, hanging limply like human question marks, swaying back and forth.

"Damn," Ellie said.

The others! Sarge Bryan, Senator Leota, and Mr. Perdix were almost certainly afflicted by the mature stage of the virus—their nose swabs had turned purple. They had to get out to them before they got hit by the beam. Maybe it was already too late.

"Look at that guy," Janice said, pointing at the guard who had been sprayed with the gray mist. He looked much like the others, glassy-eyed, with his skin shot through with gray veins. However, he seemed much more in control of his movements. He picked up a spanner on a desk, and after walking to the lift door, struck at it.

"He's using tools," Janice said under her breath. "The Stage Two afflicted must keep more of their mental capacity."

"Too bad your friend Julien can't appreciate the scientific breakthrough."

"He's not my friend," snapped Janice. "He never was."

Ellie had some thoughts but kept silent.

"I had to pretend to join Julien's plan, otherwise we'd never have gotten this close or known what we know."

Ellie went over to the communications system. Maybe the others could hear her.

"That's no good. Take my radio," Janice said, handing her a walkie-talkie.

Ellie grabbed it and yelled, "Get in here!"

Tata must have been monitoring all channels, because almost immediately, she yelled back, *"We are trying."*

"I mean it! Try like your lives depend on it."

"With you around, it's always like that."

"Also, be aggressive with the people in the control room. Don't let them touch you or spit on you."

"Anything else?"

"No, Tata, carry on."

Janice looked at her strangely.

"Don't worry. I'm not feeling giddy." Ellie glanced through the window into the control room. The tool-user noticed them and was lurching over to the door into the cryo facility. The former guard started scraping at the door latch with his wrench.

Just then, the doors of the first lift shuddered, two long metal pikes pried them off their hinges, and finally big-booted cyborg feet kicked them to the floor. Over the speakers, Ellie heard Komandir Zvena yelling as he launched himself into the control room.

"All people who are still having human minds—down!"

Thanks to the thick, and luckily fireproof, glass of the cryo room, Ellie was able to witness something few people ever saw and lived to describe. The twin muzzles of a savage flamethrower aimed right at her and spewed liquid fire all across the control room.

"Komandir!" Tata said, struggling with the door into the cryo room, squinting through the smoke from the burning bodies and oxidized napalm. "Unfortunately you have melted the lock."

Without thinking, Ellie grabbed at the door, then screamed. It was scalding hot. She pulled her burned hand away.

"Rodya!" Zvena shouted. "Prepare for Mr. Freeze."

Zvena aimed the flamethrower right at the big observation window into their room. Ellie was again treated to a breath of pure fire that ended inches from her nose. It kept up until the thick glass was completely charred in the middle. Then, through a small unblackened patch of glass, Ellie saw the other cyborg walk up and spray white gaseous liquid where the fire blast had been hottest.

With a loud *crr-crack*, the window shattered into a million pieces, leaving jagged smoky edges.

Tata climbed through and almost broke Janice's wrist as she tried to inject the cyborg lady.

"No time. Trust us, Tata," Ellie said, waving the smoke and oddly chilly vapor clouds away and revealing her own injection mark. "It's the real vaccine!"

Without releasing Janice's wrist, Tata shrugged and stuck the injection gun to her neck. It delivered its load with a fleshy *ka-thunk*.

"Not a second to lose," Ellie said, worried Leota's injuries might have slowed her down. "Where are Sarge and the senator?"

Sarge Bryan came in first but pushed Rodion ahead of him; the cyborg was half carrying the politician, who insisted on being put down on her unsteady legs. While giving a hard stare at Janice, Leota rolled up her sleeve. Zvena and Rodion were next, then Mr. Perdix. Ms. China held up her long-fingernailed hand.

"No thanks, I'm good." She revealed a round mark on her forearm. "I sampled the first batch before you switched to the shite ones."

Rather abruptly, Ms. China examined each of them in turn, taking a little longer looking into each of Senator Leota's eyes. "You're fine, lass, just bloodshot and bruised. My stuff's magic. Am I good or what?"

After congratulating herself, Ms. China kicked the remains of Julien and the others who looked like leftovers from a barbeque gone very wrong.

"What happened?" Mr. Perdix asked.

Janice explained her sleight of hand.

"But they irradiated the factory," Ellie said, in spite of herself watching the others carefully. "I was afraid you'd turned."

"We were in the lower area where only robots work," Sarge Bryan said. "I saw. They hit the top part of the factory."

Ms. China turned to Janice Jones. "And we're supposed to trust you now, after you've triple-crossed your former associates?"

"I don't see any other way," Sarge Bryan said as Tata brushed cinders and glass shards from his clothes and kept hold of him long past the point where there was a danger of him falling over. "We've got to keep hold of those vaccine vials and secure this facility. From what Ms. Jones says, they were planning on handing out the medicine only to people they approve of. They must be able to make a whole bunch of it quickly."

"That they are," Mr. Perdix said, rubbing his injection site, which looked twice as large and purple due to the skinniness of his arm and the fish-belly-white translucence of his skin. "Assuming a sufficient supply of precursors, they should be able to produce tens of millions of doses. Fortunately, the Russians' antics didn't damage the machinery down on the main floor."

Through the large bay windows, Ellie could see pallet bots like the one that had kidnapped her and other robots carrying on as though nothing had happened.

"The closest big military post is Cheyenne Mountain," Sarge Bryan said, gulping some water from the OCEL's saddlebags. "We'll get comms with them ASAP, and they can have people here in an hour."

Ms. China flicked what looked a burned rolled-up newspaper off a chair. Ellie took a step backward when it turned out to be a crispy hand and forearm.

Janice looked a little deflated and shook her head. "You're gonna have to look farther than Colorado. That was what Julien and the Pangeans were arguing about. Julien had his EMAC traitors in the military inside Cheyenne Mountain. His plan was to take out Mount Weather, where President Casteel is in command. Then blue-state forces would use the Cold War mountain bunker to carry out a 'systemic and institutional cleansing.' Before he came here, the Algerian guy Abdelkader had already hit the Cheyenne bunker."

"You mean that ray weapon…"

"It was deployed and wiped out the installation."

Sarge Bryan slammed his hand down on a half-melted keyboard, sending little square letters scattering over the debris-strewn floor. "But… it's half a mile under a mountain of solid granite…"

Mr. Perdix shook his head with irritation. "Dark-energy rays don't respect physical matter. Unless they upgraded to neutronium shielding, and had they done so, JASON would have gotten the contract, they were completely vulnerable. Abdelkader and his Pangean forces could have rolled right up to the perimeter, irradiated the people on the top levels, then let the affliction take its course."

Sarge Bryan rounded on Janice. "Where are they now? They've got to be stopped, even if we have to nuke the Pangeans from orbit."

"No idea," Janice said, seemingly sincerely vexed. "As you can see"—she pointed to a pair of polished pointy-toed Oxford dress shoes and shredded blue pants—"things are not working out according to Julien's plan. The insurgent force could be anywhere."

Sarge Bryan threw away a melted handset. "Komandir, I gotta borrow your comms."

"Of course," Zvena said with a toothy smile. "However, the rogue Pangeans' location is no longer much mystery."

He showed Sarge Bryan the screen mounted on his tree-trunk-sized forearm.

"Where… is that? Is that here?" Sarge Bryan exclaimed with rising alarm.

"They have just circled around and come back," Zvena said. "Our drone was doing a surveillance sweep on the other side of the factory complex while they drove up. What they have brought with them, it could pose an issue."

Ellie leaned over to look. There was a bird's-eye view of the sealed gateway into the factory.

"But there's no point in irradiating us again," Mr. Perdix said officiously.

"Attacking with T-rays seems not on their minds," Zvena said as he tapped on his keypad. "I assume you recognize this weapons system."

"What system?" Ms. China said.

The radio on the charred console still worked, though the microphone was melted away. A nasty male voice spoke, "Can you hear me, Julien? You depraved kafir traitor!"

In the drone cam footage, Ellie saw three tractors with long, needle-sharp white-painted missiles perched on them. All were pointing toward the factory. The high-pitched ranting continued through the PA system.

"We didn't fight and die just to hand what's left of America over to you. Your filthy fellow Jew Karl Marx said, 'Wipe out North America from the map of the world and you will have anarchy—the complete decay of modern commerce and civilization.' Too bad you won't be alive to smell the corpses in the ruins."

"Those are Raytheon multipurpose Hawk missiles," Mr. Perdix said, hanging on to Zvena's arm with both hands. "Cheyenne Mountain uses them as air and ground defense. With everyone dead or disabled, they were able to walk right in and steal them."

"But…" Janice looked through the window to the massive doorway opposite. "Those doors are strong. They're composite steel."

The first missile hit the big gateway doors into the factory, and the shockwave knocked the Russian drone off its flight path.

"Perdix, can you open the doors?" Zvena asked, tapping on his keyboard with greater urgency.

"Why would I want to do that?"

"The OCEL unit can overcharge its power cells, yielding a blast of one ton of TNT. I'm ordering it to attack the missiles…"

The second missile hit, sending a rumble sweeping through the elevated control room.

"…but he must be able to get outside."

Mr. Perdix jumped over to the far computer panels and scraped off the debris, looking for any lights that were still lit on the consoles.

The third missile hit. At the far end of the factory, Ellie thought she saw a pinprick of daylight. A moment later, it faded. She turned to Sarge Bryan.

"Was that…"

"Yup, that was the outer door melting." He turned to the leader of the cyborgs. "Whatever you're thinking of doing…"

The OCEL robot had already run into the lift shaft and leaped down onto the factory floor. It ran straight down the long aisle between the stainless-steel vats and the mysterious infusion gadgets, gaining speed, running like a six-legged cheetah.

"It's halfway there," Ellie cried. Could they open the doors wide enough to let the OCEL out but not let the next missile come in? "Mr. Perdix…"

He slapped the burned surface of the control panel. "This is useless. We have to get to the backup engineering section."

"Where's that?" Senator Leota demanded, also watching the lone robot run and then leap over a pallet bot, then continue toward the door.

Ellie never found out where the engineering area was. The next missile that hit the door sent huge chunks of steel and concrete flying into the factory. It was followed by another missile, and in the instant before she ducked down under the desk, she thought she saw it come speeding though the gap, clip one of its fins on the flaming debris and, twisting in midair only to right itself, come straight at their control room observation window.

61

SPRÜNGER COMPOUND

ABDELKADER

"Again! Again!" Abdelkader yelled over the rush of rockets launching and flying horizontally over the few hundred yards of unpaved earth toward the Sprünger factory building. His hand clutched the grotesquely shaped locket holding a precious few remaining milliliters of the enzyme vital to making the vaccine. The rest of it was inside the production line. He had to destroy it.

As each white-painted, needle-nosed Hawk missile blasted off its launcher, Abdelkader imagined an enormous bloated, abscessed wound being pierced, and the foul-smelling pus of American imperialism, racism, slavery, genocide, all the foulness of this most evil country in history, come pouring out of the bloody punctures.

Dr. Baldur stood beside him on the roadway, looking agitated but trying hard to appear to share the Pangeans' joy. How could he, with his pudgy cheeks and pathetic wisps of facial hair? For this moment of triumph, with the explosions that signaled the death knell for a monstrous nation, all the Pangeans had taken off their silicone masks and let their scarred mandibles and raw eye sockets bask in the fading Colorado sunshine.

As the white vapor trail of the last rocket was carried this way and that by crosswinds, every window and vent in the factory spewed black smoke.

"That's all," Abdelkader said, watching the doctor. "Bring up the trucks. Let's be away."

Dr. Baldur looked pensive. That was never a good sign.

"What?"

"N-nothing..." the Uyghur scientist stuttered. "That was... a very advanced facility, that's all. We could have produced as much of the new vaccine and the old one as we needed in a few days."

No one would be producing anything there. And just to make sure there were no survivors, he had a last gift for Sprünger, the backstabbing Jew. He looked down the road for it, then thought of something.

"The old vaccine? Why would we need that?"

"Not Sprünger's vaccine. I withheld key components when I sent him the formula," Dr. Baldur said, affecting deviousness he didn't really possess and avoiding looking at his naked face. "But in regards to the Tortuga vaccine, I was thinking: we now have formulas for a temporary and a permanent vaccine, perhaps only your most loyal soldiers should get the one with the crucial enzyme."

Surprisingly, that made sense. Some American survivalist groups had been planning for large-scale disasters for decades and were inside bunkers with years of supplies. It would take time for a Pangean army to clear out every kafir hidey-hole.

"We'll consider it. But now, give us our shots."

With a flourish, Dr. Baldur held up the inoculation gun.

Baldur injected himself and then changed vials. He only had twenty in his pouch, enough for them, but they would need more when they linked up with Pangean sleeper cells and went to activate the infection across the country.

"That's all you have?"

"It's more than enough for all of..." The weasel-like man did a double take when he looked at the base of the ampule, where it slotted into the injector.

Abdelkader grabbed him, ignoring the Pangeans who were approaching them, ready to receive their vaccine before leaving. "What did you fuck up now?"

"N—"

"Don't lie! I know when you do. I'll carve your—"

"The rubber r-ring on the new vaccine, it's blue… These are…"

They were red.

"Someone switched them before we stole them. I-it's not my fault! I can fix this."

Abdelkader looked back at the burning factory, then clutched the locket vial with the only remaining enzyme sample.

"How can you— *Arrgh!*" Abdelkader flung Baldur into the dirt. The Pangeans reached for their weapons, unsure what was going on.

He could still see poor Sadikul, his most loyal of followers, his head half blown off, chewing on his false face, mouthful by mouthful, revealing the true beautiful one underneath. The thought gave Abdelkader chills in the night. Not because of the loss of his comrade, but because if the T-ray device had been angled a few degrees to the left or the right, his own neurons would have been overcome instead of Sadikul's. Now that was the future for all of them because of this incompetent piece of—

"Th-there are other facilities," Dr. Baldur said quickly, wiping dust form his lips. "In New York, Germany, and India. They can all…"

"Make vaccine," Abdelkader said. "And how do we survive long enough to do that?"

Sweat dripped from Dr. Baldur's disgusting fleshy slave face. "I can ration what we have. As long as you have the enzyme, the basic formula is not difficult. I made it on Tortuga."

"Shut up and inject us." This was a savage reversal, but it was true Baldur had made the original temporary vaccine, and Abdelkader had the idiotic pendant with the enzyme. They had to leave.

"Irradiate the prisoners again," Abdelkader said. "We want to be sure. We're not coming back this way."

Eisenhorn, a tall blond Swede whose facial obliteration scarring had taken on a most gruesome shape, gnashed his bare teeth and spooled up the T-ray device for another burst. Yelling and a muted gunshot came from inside the sealed cargo hold of a long container truck.

Eisenhorn shrugged his bony shoulders. "One of them must have kept a small pistol. Americans love their guns."

Abdelkader had to encourage his troops. Even fanatics needed a morale boost now and then.

"Load up the gear," he yelled. "Let's plunge America into a nightmare from which it will never awake!"

The column of trucks and vans and captured military vehicles pulled away and lurched down the dusty road. Eisenhorn set the autodrive on the truck towing the noisy shipping container. It would drive itself right up to the smashed vaccine factory, unlock its doors, and disgorge its load: Commander Sikawski and the remainder of his merry band of Antifa who, by that time, would all be infected.

62

SPRÜNGER COMPOUND

ELLIE

The obliteration of the control room and everyone inside was certain, if the Hawk missile had hit the observation window full on—at least that was what Mr. Perdix later concluded.

In the moment of impact, Ellie experienced something akin to being on the bridge of a very large ship being lifted up by a huge wave only to collapse in near free fall into the wave's trough. In front of their eyes, the previously impenetrable thick bay windows shattered. A tumultuous roar swept through the factory's control center as the ever-so-slightly misdirected rocket exploded just under their platform. Then all the lights went out.

Ellie rolled along what she assumed was the floor and bumped into something hard, probably the doorway into the cryo chamber. A tremendous stench of burning fuel and chemicals blew over everything. She looked for Sarge Bryan's gold glowing eyes. She reached out blindly for something to hang on to, fearing she might fall out through the newly torn gaps in the wall.

Through those holes, she got a look down onto the production floor. It was lit by fires burning near the airplane-hangar-sized doors opposite and also the rising flames underneath their tottering platform. Instead of a sterile laboratory, it now resembled a steel mill in full production. All the vats and their millions of doses of vaccine were aflame.

With one hand holding her shirt over her nose and mouth, Ellie tried to get up. Immediately she encountered the limp form of Senator Leota.

"Senator!" The fumes were overwhelming, making it hard to see. She waved to a glowing eye a few meters away. It came closer. It was grayish green, and there was only one. "Mr. Rodion... could you help here?"

"Certainly, Ms. Sato," the Russian answered quite jauntily for someone trapped on a steel scaffolding that looked about to collapse. "Good news. They have fired off all their missiles."

"Here," Ellie said, easing Leota's form toward the thickset cyborg. "Hang on to her. She's the president or a president..." She coughed. "Just don't drop her."

"Will do, Ms. Sato. Let me know if you are passing out, I lend you some filtered air," the one-eyed giant said with a lopsided grin. "At least we are aboveground, unlike in Paris."

This was no time for a trip down memory lane. Ellie grabbed the bunch of hanging wires that looked least likely to electrocute her and skidded across the downward-tilted floor.

"Ellie!" a woman's voice yelled from her left.

It turned out to be Janice Jones, her sleeve slashed and the arm underneath bloody. "Reach out and grab that." She pointed Ellie to a cloth satchel that was in danger of sliding down into the flaming morass underneath them.

"We've got to go." It seemed the platform could fall any moment.

"The vials!" Janice screeched back. "They may be the last ones."

Damn. They were out of reach. Ellie looked for something. There was a part of a chair. She grabbed the bent metal and tried to reach the satchel's handle.

"No good," Janice said, cradling her injured arm. "Lean out farther. I'll hold you."

Thinking she'd rather have her life depend on any of the others, including Ms. China, but with no other option, Ellie nodded. Janice grabbed Ellie's belt. Thankfully it was a sturdy and dug in tight just above her sore hip bones as the American woman held her with her good arm.

Trying not to look over the edge and only at the satchel, Ellie snagged it on the second try and slowly pulled it away from the fiery abyss.

"What are you two doing?" Mr. Perdix's face stuck around the corner. Smeared with soot, it looked absurd. "This structure we are standing on is about to collapse."

"Thanks for that," Ellie managed to say, waving to Rodion to get some of that refreshing oxygen he had offered. "How do we get down?"

Over by the lift shaft, there were access hatches. After widening them with the long poles the cyborgs had brought, even Rodion was able to fit through. Past the hatches, the air became more breathable; the new area they climbed into seemed connected to air shafts and cooling ducts not yet consumed by the fire, which was quickly spreading out from the factory's main building.

Janice pushed Ellie's hand away. "Stop helping me. Keep both hands on that bag."

She looked inside. There were six or seven vials tumbling around in the singed carry bag. As they crawled, something exploded behind them, sending a blast of hotter air over them as they started to climb down to ground level.

Finally, she saw Sarge Bryan. He came over to her, glancing sideways at the three Russians. That must be the way out. The cyborgs had kicked down an emergency exit door and were making sure the area outside was clear.

"That's all we got?" he panted at the pitiful stash of vaccine vials. "He seemed still dizzy and out of breath as all the non-cyborgs were. "Not much for all of America, huh?"

Mr. Perdix and Ms. China scrambled out of the smoke-belching doorway and braced themselves against the concrete wall.

Ellie knew there were approximately three hundred and fifty million people in America. "What do you think the infection rate is?"

"Anna," Mr. Perdix said as he wiped grime off his face, only making it worse. "As you audaciously named A/P-32 after yourself, perhaps you can answer that."

"I only called it that because I was tired of people saying girls were no good at science."

"This will really show them," Mr. Perdix shot back.

"Well... assuming the Pangeans followed my genetic blueprint, and you said Sprünger Labs produces all the annual flu vaccines for the country?"

"They do," Mr. Perdix said, his pale lip curling slightly as he grasped the implications. "So they could have added a little RNA bonus in this year's batch."

"You can be certain of that," Ms. China admitted. "Because of the unique properties of A/P-32, I'd say your infection rate is well past ninety percent of the population."

"Is that all?" Sarge Bryan said sarcastically.

"We've got these," Ellie said, pointing at the satchel and trying to be upbeat. "I'm sure with Anna's help, we can make loads more vaccine."

Ms. China pursed her lips and developed a sudden interest in making sure Senator Leota was able to walk by herself.

"Anna?"

"You can't just make more from a sample," she finally admitted. "That stupid guy with no face stole the enzyme catalyst. I saw him shoot the technician who was operating the molecular replicator."

"You don't have any more?" Ellie asked.

"It's a cascading chemical sequence, really complicated," Ms. China said. "I had it all programmed into the replicator at St. Bartholomew's until the Cannibal erased the hard drive when he was making his jingle hat."

Above and around them, the walls of the tall building were making sounds as though they were about to collapse. The alleyways were blocked, but Sarge Bryan found a way through. Ellie clambered over a pair of plastic fifty-gallon drums and emerged with the others on an access road. It was starkly lit by an unflinching mid-afternoon sun; she'd nearly forgotten it was still day. The sudden quiet made her notice the ringing in her ears. She looked over their group.

Senator Leota was walking on her own, sometimes leaning on Tata. Mr. Perdix and Ms. China were arguing about who would carry the precious few vials of vaccine, which Janice Jones was clutching. The two male Russian cyborgs were looking at the sky, perhaps trying to retrieve their damaged drone.

Ellie slumped against the big tire of a forklift truck and noticed her knee would not bend all the way without giving off blinding shoots of pain. She eased herself down sideways, keeping it mostly outstretched.

She had just gotten as comfortable as possible when she felt a vibration in the area of her upper chest. After discounting a most ill-timed—but understandable—heart attack, she realized it was her handset. The signal blocking must have blown up along with the control room. The screen was cracked, and all she could read of the text was:

```
You should know something about /
...as I've suspected. In fact, don't trust an /
```

"Miss Aleph, I wish you'd just come out as an AI," she whispered, not sure if the filth-encrusted phone she'd retrieved from the guard before they left their jail still worked. "It's perfectly normal these days. No one will make fun of you."

If the Israeli artificial mind had a retort, Ellie didn't see it.

Her attention was drawn to the puff of dust coming from under a wall. She worked her jaw open and shut and, after a bit, her ears cleared enough so that they registered a sort of scrabbling, clawing sound.

No one else had noticed it yet. It was coming from behind a stack of wooden delivery pallets leaning precariously against the wall of the factory. Some rivets and fastenings had come off the corrugated metal, and the conflagration was sending bouts of heat waves into the cooler January air. There was definitely something—

A burst of dust made her cry out, then a shadowy figure emerged from under the pile of pallets, sending the frail wooden stack flying like so many matchboxes. Ellie fell back in fright.

63

SPRÜNGER COMPOUND

Behind Ellie, a scramble of military-honed reflexes and pointing of guns ensued. She righted herself and saw a singed, five-legged robot standing over her, studying her with its soot-encrusted spider eyes.

"OCEL!" Rodion called out with distinct joy in his voice. "Come, boy."

The mechanoid, which had left its sixth leg somewhere in the doomed factory, leaped over to the Russian.

"That is one tough bot," Sarge Bryan said, surveying the blue-tinged metal of the OCEL's exterior.

"And loyal too, to find its way out of there," Senator Leota said, limping over to get a better look as the OCEL stood on its hind legs and leaned on Rodion.

"His neural chip is partly based upon engrams gathered from dozens of Irish wolfhounds," Zvena said. "Not the sissy ones we have today, which are intermixed with greyhounds, but the dogs of warriors bred by the British natives to pluck Roman soldiers off horses and chariots."

Ms. China was not impressed. "It's only a mechBrain automaton."

"Shh!" Rodion said, patting the OCEL behind its eye buds. "He understand English. You will hurt his feelings."

Seeming not to worry about hurting Rodion's feelings, in a blur of motion, the OCEL pushed away from the cyborg's shoulders and leaped sideways, directly at Janice. She just had time to drop the bandage she was adjusting on her arm and duck as the robot sailed over her. With a snap like an enormous pair of garden shears, the OCEL cut the head and arms off an infected attacker who had snuck up soundlessly behind their group.

Everyone turned around.

"There're more!" Sarge Bryan yelled. "We're out in the open, not good."

The OCEL gave the scattered bits of quivering flesh another few thrashes with its praying-mantis limbs, then rejoined them.

"Group up," Zvena said. "Rodya, up front with me. Tata, in back. Everyone else in middle."

Janice dusted herself off, grimaced as her arms started bleeding again, and grumbled, "Sergeant, are you going to let them take over?"

"At this point, ma'am, I'd trust a five-hundred-pound Russian with assault weapons over anything that comes out of Washington. Let's do it, people!" He turned to Ellie. "You sure you can keep up?"

Shots rang out behind them, the attackers still coming. Tata finished one off with her pike.

"I've seen the alternative. Not a fan," Ellie said as she and Janice walked behind Zvena. Mr. Perdix and Ms. China half carried Senator Leota. Sarge Bryan took turns with Tata scouting ahead and behind as they moved down the gravel-strewn roads.

"Where are they coming from?" Mr. Perdix panted. He seemed mostly unscathed but was clearly not used to sustained physical activity. "They're not dressed like the Sprünger company guards."

Zvena put his hands up to his eyes, perhaps shielding them from the sun so he could look at something in his ocular playback. He shook his massive rectangular head. "The images I get from the drone are fuzzy. Sergeant, can you make anything of them?"

Zvena flicked his head toward Sarge Bryan. In some strange way, the motion sent the signal coming from the drone to the American's cyber eyes. After a bit of squinting, he too shrugged.

"Some are there," Tata said, walking backward around the corner of the low building they had just passed. "They are sticking to shaded areas but will attack if triggered by motion or sound, maybe also smell."

"*OCEL, prinesti, ubit' yego, i prinesi shkurku netronutymi,*" Rodion whispered to the robot, and it took off running. "I told him to fetch one, neutralized but with the carcass minimally damaged."

Senator Leota let out a frustrated groan. "These are people we're talking about, American citizens. We can't—"

"Senator, there's no choice," Sarge Bryan said, walking over to the trio. "Ms. China, Mr. Perdix, once a brain's been infected and activated, is there any way...?"

"We've only studied the first stage," Mr. Perdix said. "Anna?"

"It was all just theoretical," she protested. "I thought they were working on a treatment for bipolar disorders." The normally steely eyed mass killer looked momentary mortified by what she had helped unleash, then she regained her crazy. "Cure them? Not a chance. They're walking cadavers. Incineration's the only thing for 'em."

"What about the second stage?" Senator Leota asked. It was clearly paining her to speak.

"I think I saw that, sort of," Ellie ventured. "There's some kind of misty-gray effusion they spray right into normal people's nose and mouth, and the victims turn almost immediately."

"This is what I experienced," Rodion said, checking the display screen on his forearm, which monitored the OCEL robot. "Fortunately it only infected half my brain, and someone put a glass knife through it, so I was okay."

"And I think there's another—" Ellie's thought was cut off as the OCEL dragged a limp pile of black rags through the dust toward them.

"Good boy," Rodion said as the pile was nudged toward him. The bits inside the pile of clothes kept gyrating around as though they were a sack full of sliced-up bits of a python that didn't realize they were dead.

"Careful," Mr. Perdix said. "We haven't tested the vaccine against Stage Two infection."

Zvena reached into the clothes and pulled out some lung tissue. "I think this one is... How do you say? Out of breath permanently. These clothes are not military."

"Militia?" Sarge Bryan speculated. "What else is in there?"

The cyborg's big gloved hand fished around the most gruesome mystery gift bag ever. "Ah... an elbow and bicep."

The arm was moving and squirting ooze with each twitch.

"That tattoo," Ellie said, revolted but feeling she had to give the benefit of her input. "A red-and-black circle with an 'A' inside."

"Antifa anarchists," Janice said immediately. "They must be connected with the rogue Pangeans."

"Looks like they disconnected," Ms. China said.

"Oh, man," Sarge Bryan said. "Antifa are all over the place like cockroaches. Some of them got jobs at Fort Bragg and put lye in the showers, hoping to give soldiers chemical burns because the government wouldn't rename the post."

"Oy!" Tata shouted and started shooting. "Cockroaches heard you. They are incoming!"

Tata aimed at the infected and fired, emptying her weapon and reloading faster than Ellie's eyes could follow.

"This place is too big," Sarge Bryan said. "We're not mobile enough. We need transport ASAP."

A headless infected jumped on Tata, knocking her weapon aside.

"Damn!" Sarge Bryan pulled his pistol, and Ellie winced as well-aimed rounds cracked off, having little effect on the animated cadaver.

The one on Tata was shredded by the OCEL, but then three more jumped on the robot, momentarily buckling its legs. It rolled over, pulling the enemies with it, and from its back chopped them up like a barbaric food processor. Still, more came.

"Shooting no good," Tata gasped. "Even without heads, they follow the group and keep attacking by touch."

"*Soldaty Rossii, razvernut' kop'ya!*" Zvena's voice boomed, and the three cyborgs deployed their seven-foot-long pikes.

Mr. Perdix stood perilously close to the melee, fascinated. "Infected must have some form of sensory array over their entire bodies, like scorpions... Gaaah!"

A black-clad arm flew past his head, and the hand grabbed hold of Mr. Perdix's hair, which was longer than it appeared when slicked down. Ellie beat at the disorderly limb with her handbag, then remembered Miss Aleph's handset was inside. With the loss of a handful of hair, Ms. China and the senator managed to yank off the animated arm and throw it over to the OCEL, who gleefully chopped it.

"We must go," Rodion said. "OCEL is wearing down his power cell, and we are only attracting more."

"Over here," Janice said. Somehow she had retained an access card, no doubt given to her by her former partner Julien. She inserted it into a card reader by a large folding door and slapped a green button. The door rose up, revealing at least a hundred infected.

64

SPRÜNGER COMPOUND

A gray mottled hand grabbed for Ellie.

"Close it," she yelled as the rolling door rose and warm afternoon sunlight hit the shuffling feet of the looming mass of infected inside the building. "Close it!"

Janice pounded on the red button, but the damned thing kept rolling up. It was one of those annoying things that had to open all the way before being able to shut.

"Flamer," Sarge Bryan gasped.

Zvena was already trying to reignite his napalm-dispensing device, but something was blocking the fuel line. Standing at the corner of the building, Tata slashed, finishing off an infected Antifa, then swung her pike around horizontally, preparing to force the crowd of Sprünger workers back in the building. It was no good, Ellie knew; they'd be overwhelmed in seconds.

The scrolling door mechanism hit the top, and then paused as Janice kept pounding the close button. A few of the infected wandered out from the shaded side, lurching out from the corner only to receive a blast of liquid nitrogen from Rodion's canister. Arms froze solid and fingers snapped off.

The only thing that saved them was the fact that the disheveled gray mass at first backed away from the sunlight. They had been in the dark since they were turned by the T-ray beam and were temporarily dazed. The short delay gave the squeaky, slow-moving door enough time to methodically lower its polished steel sections.

It was only halfway down when the spell broke. The first line launched forward, some hitting the descending metal door, others squirming under and crawling out. Then they rose, arms outstretched, eyes bulging, mouths opening to form round suction-cup circles. These were immediately filled with bullets, freezing gas, the razor-sharp end of Tata's pike, and finally the brilliant orange-yellow lance of flame Zvena sent at them.

Ellie closed her eyes and covered her mouth with her forearm as she stomped on the lip of the door, willing it to shut the last few inches. It did. She collapsed to one knee and looked around.

They were on a side road, and where it met a larger, paved avenue, there lay a heap of body parts rising as high as her waist. The OCEL came trotting over, a yellow light blinking on its chest. Ellie thought it was walking like Chestnut when the Labradoodle was exhausted.

Rodion slammed the locking pins in the rolling door, then blasted the card reader locking device with nitrogen and broke it with his pike, sealing the warehouse.

Then, instead of her aching body sagging down alongside the corrugated metal, Ellie found herself being ogled by her curly brown-haired dog and easing herself back in the deck chair on the balcony overlooking Grosvenor Park. She still had enough of her wits to know this was *wrong*.

"Sergeant, Anna…" she managed to say as her head spun. "Something happening."

"Holy crap."

"Me too."

The voices were ones Ellie recognized as belonging to Sarge Bryan and Mr. Perdix, though she could not see them, the images of Tavistock Manor in the spring were too strong. She looked around and saw the butler, Mr. Surghit. He had a beard, a large golden earring, and his lower body was composed of smoke coming out of an oil burning lamp. *No good!*

"These infected… they're like the ones in Europe… Hallucinating, can't see you."

Ms. China's voice issued a peal of shrill laughter. "I did not! Did I really kill all of you? I guess I must have. Hahahaha!"

Something large and powerful grabbed Ellie's head. "Take this, tell me what it tastes like," said Zvena's voice.

Ellie crushed an ampule in her mouth, the capsule and its contents absorbing immediately under her tongue.

"Salty fish guts?"

"Have another."

She chewed and tried harder to detect the taste.

"Licorice. No, wait, mint, definitely mint."

The scene in front of her dissolved, and she found herself back in the Sprünger factory compound.

"Good," Zvena said, throwing a package to Rodion, who had Ms. China by the collar of her jacket to prevent her from wandering off in a daze. "The antipsychotics are Maghrebi mint flavor."

When everyone had downed two doses, they seemed to come back into their present minds.

"Damn, Ellie," Janice said, blinking and bracing herself against Rodion's backpack. "I thought you just made that up in your book to sell copies."

"No, I wouldn't really…" She still felt light-headed. "Didn't have to embellish."

"It's obvious Abdelkader is using a similar technology to the one deployed by President Rapace in Europe," Mr. Perdix said, looking at the Russians. "It would have been nice to know that ahead of time."

"Sorry," Zvena said curtly. "We were a little occupied saving your butts."

Sarge Bryan helped Ellie up, his eyes looking larger than normal. He must have seen something terrible in his hallucinations.

"Remind us," Ellie said loudly before they started bickering in earnest. "What were we doing before we were so rudely interrupted?"

"Looking for transport, ma'am."

"Let's continue doing that. I might add: as carefully as we can."

"We don't need any surprises," Mr. Perdix said, his eyes as wide as saucers.

"Move those shipping containers across the alley so no more groups can come up from behind."

"Ha," Tata scoffed, using some duct tape to stick two of her broken fingers together. "And while we are moving shipping containers, what you will be doing?"

"Thinking," he replied superciliously. In an effort to avoid further discussion of manual work, he searched in the pockets of his jacket for anything that had not fallen out or been taken by the Sprünger guards.

The OCEL was over by the side of a building, pawing at a covered outlet.

"Oh, look, he's found something," Rodion said, going over. "A fast charger carrying 600 volts. Good boy."

He wasted no time hooking the robot's plug into the outlet; it sank down into a comfortable position, and the hum of the electricity made it seem as though the OCEL was purring with delight.

Zvena stomped over to where Ellie was standing with Sarge Bryan and an ashen-faced but upright Senator Leota.

"Our position is a disgrace to the fighting traditions of all of our countries," the leader of the cyborgs said bitterly. "We have let the Pangeans go, there is no way to track them, we are without support, and surrounded by a ravenous hostile force. As they say in England: what a balls-out."

Zvena had meant to say "balls-up," but Ellie didn't bother to correct him; faulty idioms were low on their list of worries. Even Sarge Bryan looked downcast.

"Well, gentlemen," Ellie said. "At least we've found each other. Pretty long odds of that happening." The second shipping container was shoved in place, blocking the alleyway, but still leaving them a narrow, defensible way out. "And for the time being, it looks like we can remain here. Perhaps we can contact friendly forces. Ms. Jones or Senator Leota must have some contacts in the military..."

Sarge Bryan scratched his jaw and exhaled silently through pursed lips. People looked at her as they normally did when she said something foolish, such as when she'd briefly come out in support of people wearing socks with sandals.

"You are not…" Senator Leota walked up to them, holding her arm tightly against her side. "… not going to trust President Casteel's people. We all know he's not really in charge of the feds. He's senile, a textbook 25th Amendment case. It's Prowse and his Deep State gang of GOP Neo-cons who have the power."

"And we should trust you blue state…" Janice paused to change her word choice. "… dissidents, Leota? How do you know your people, many of whom are fanatics who think America invented genocide, slavery, and all human oppression, won't keep the vaccine for themselves or even destroy it?"

"Who would do that?" Ellie interjected. "That's crazy."

Sarge Bryan shrugged. "I did tell you when you arrived it's an election year."

"Even for outsiders, it is obvious you Americans have trust issues," Zvena said, looking down at the group. "You may make your own choices, but for my people to continue on this mission, I must insist we keep all intelligence private to our group."

"How are we going to get out of here?" Ellie asked.

As though in reply, from the other side of the shipping container barricade came a whiny, rumbling noise.

"A truck," said Tata, canting her head to the side to hear more distinctly. "One with a hybrid hydrogen engine."

"All right, then," Senator Leota said, perhaps trying to assert authority she was used to exercising as part of the government and the military. "We'll flag it down. The driver must be terrified, so no one do anything to escalate the situation. Then we'll compensate them for their time and…"

The engine revving kept getting louder. Sarge, who had started toward the barricade, backed away a few steps. This was lucky because a large flat-nosed vehicle crashed through right where the ends of the two containers met.

"Sergeant!" Ellie yelled as he was lost in a cloud of tan-colored dust.

"Is it more of them?" Janice yelled as she huddled in a doorway with Mr. Perdix and Ms. China.

"Don't… uh, infected can't drive… uh, can they?" Mr. Perdix squinted, his glasses caked with dirt.

Ellie ducked down. "I was trying to tell you. Second-stage infected can use tools."

The truck shuddered to a halt a few meters inside the barrier. Everyone watched. There were a few creatures moving behind it, but it was jammed in, blocking their entry, and the first ones did not seem to have enough wits about them to squirm under the wheels to get at them.

"The surprisingly durable reporter is correct," Zvena said. "When Rodya was afflicted, he was able to construct traps and snares to frustrate pursuit."

"Can we reason with them?" Senator Leota was turning out to be almost pathologically optimistic.

"Like fuck, we will!" Ms. China said, craning her metallic tattooed neck forward, perhaps at once horrified by the level of her handiwork and also eager to see it. "If they've integrated cordyceps spore DNA into their brains, their overriding imperative is asexual reproduction. Think of Stage Ones as infants—these are teenagers."

A furious *clang-thump* noise echoed from within the left shipping container.

"Uh, did anyone lock those shipping containers?" Sarge Bryan asked.

Zvena gnashed his teeth and ran forward. "There was no reason…"

As they watched the door of the nearest shipping container, waiting for it to burst open, a writhing body flew through the air and landed on Zvena's shoulders, staggering him.

"The new ones are throwing the others over!" Mr. Perdix said.

Zvena took the one on him and pulled it apart like one might rip the head off a shrimp. However, as he was doing that, two more bodies came arcing over into their area, and the container doors sprang open. Everyone who had a gun aimed at the opening.

Rodion dropped his pike and reached for the flamethrower. Zvena tried kicking the door closed but found it stuck on the body parts accumulating around the hinges.

Mr. Perdix ducked out from under the cover of the building and tried to grab the fallen pike, which was seven feet long. After a brief attempt to lift it, he drew a pistol and emptied it at the swarming horde, to little effect.

"Give it up, Al, you're never going to be John Wayne."

"Says today's Typhoid Mary. Where's some more ammunition?"

Ellie saw a shadow flicker along the ground. It had to belong to something moving along top of the buildings. She looked around the corner. Maybe it was an infected which been slashed and thrown up there by Tata. She was using her pike to intercept infected who were being lobbed at them, impaling them through the sternum. She then waited until they slid halfway down the shaft before deploying prongs, which came springing out from the pike and quartered the pinioned body. The female cyborg then kicked the pieces over into a corner, which seemed to be the assigned dumping place for the charred, oozing, and wriggling pile, which was now nearly the height of the container barricade.

Ellie felt sorry for Mr. Perdix, who was only trying to help. "I'll find you some more bullets."

Three more infected dropped down among them, and by the way they moved, they had to be Stage Two. Ms. China kicked at the knee of one with her heavy prosthetic foot, crunching its bones. She then slashed its throat and face with her deadly fingernails, but it also was quick, and it caught her wrists. Its cheeks completely shredded, it gave her a ghastly smile from ear to ear and started to pull Ms. China toward itself. Ellie threw a fire extinguisher, but the red canister merely bounced off the attacker's shoulder. Senator Leota grabbed the extinguisher's hose, looped it around the attacker's mouth, and pulled it backward.

On the other side of their compromised fortifications, an attacker with a half-burned-off leg had Mr. Perdix by the groin. Ellie found some ammunition and threw it to him.

The OCEL unit unplugged itself and launched into the fray, narrowly missing Ellie. She stumbled to the side, landed in a crouch, looked up, and found herself staring at a pair of frayed black trousers hanging over bare, gnarly looking feet. It was right in front of her. Ellie flung her hands up. The creature seized her wrists and pulled her toward its wide-open mouth.

Ellie picked up a piece of wood with the idea of stabbing it into the poached brain of the infected, then her hair was seized and her head yanked back. A second infected had her from behind.

She lost her balance but never made it all the way to the ground. She felt weirdly suspended. All she could see was a round "O" ringed by broken teeth, dripping fluid, and spewing gray mist. The mist enveloped her eyes with sticky coolness, and on instinct, she fought not to breathe.

65

SPRÜNGER COMPOUND

The pair of infected grabbed Ellie, one from behind, the other from in front. That one's mouth gaped wide open.

They were fantastically strong. The long fingers around her bicep felt like iron, and the hand of the one behind her held her hair so tightly she felt her scalp was in danger of being pulled off. The more Ellie tried not to breathe, the harder it became.

She could only wriggle her face a few inches left or right. Not enough to squirm away from the orifice, which was already belching a sort of thick gray dust. She closed her eyes tightly, the afternoon sun beaming reddish-pink though her eyelids.

Her foot kicked out, but it might as well have been hitting stone. The creature in front of her was as immobile as a statue. The pressure to breathe reached a crescendo, and she felt herself passing out. If she did that, her mouth would go slack, and her lungs would be filled with that crud.

Once, when she was small, she'd stepped on an exploding mushroom, which had sent spores all over her new dress. The spew belching down onto her now had the same gritty texture as the mushroom spores, but they were somehow colder and felt alive, as though each microscopic bit was trying to burrow into her cheeks, her lips, her nasal cavity.

As she dangled on the edge of consciousness, her neck was jerked back so violently she thought the *krrthnawk* she heard was her own neck snapping. Of course, had that been the case, she'd have been paralyzed, and her elbows and tailbone wouldn't have smarted so much as she landed on the ground. A second later, the fingers pinioning her biceps let go. Free from the creatures' grips, she rolled to the side once, and then again. Hoping she was far enough away, she spat as much goo out from her mouth as she could and finally inhaled.

Her biggest worry was running right into more of the creatures. She wiped her eyes and looked. The one that had been holding her from the front was down, split nearly in half. The other was still ambling around, missing its hands and the front part of its head. Tata stood close by, winding up another strike with her long poleaxe. Dismembered and defaced, still it lurched toward the lady cyborg with arm stumps outstretched and gray puffs coming out of its exposed sinus cavities.

Rodion beat Tata to the punch. He ripped a utility pole with a concrete base out of the ground and utterly crushed the jittering figure into mush.

"Stay away!" Ellie gasped and thrust out her gravel-covered palm. She backed along the roadway toward the side of the building. Blinking the last of the squirming caustic muck out of her eyes, she must've been a dreadful sight. Ellie saw Ms. China and waggled a finger at her. "I'm *pphut*-putting you on notice, Annunciata. If I turn into one of those things, we are no longer friends."

A few minutes passed. She received looks of concern from members of their party who were not actively fighting incoming enemies. Someone found a jug of water and doused her.

"There," Ms. China said in a self-satisfied manner. "I had every confidence the upgraded vaccine would work on the second stage. Thanks for proving me right."

"Glad," Ellie sputtered, trying to regain her feet and some dignity. "Glad to have contributed."

Ellie's head felt twice as heavy as normal. It was a wonder it functioned at all since she was on more cutting-edge drugs than the average meth addict.

Sarge Bryan glanced over. "Oh, crap. Perdix, get this one, he's nearly dead."

The albino soldier kicked a torso with no legs and one arm over to the JASON man, who shot it a few times. The bullet impacts only released puffs of fine greasy gray dust. He then grabbed the quivering mass and dragged it over to the abattoir-style collection point in the corner of their safe space.

Sarge Bryan gently reached around her neck, which felt oddly heavy. "Ow."

"Sorry."

"Let's just get rid of these."

She was wearing two accessories that certainly didn't go with her outfit. Two blue-gray clenched hands still had hold of her jacket sleeves and would not let go. Sarge Bryan used a knife to prize the fingers apart.

"I'll try not to mess up your jacket too much."

"At this point, I don't think it matters," Ellie said, looking down her front, which was as messy is if she had rolled out of an overfull ashtray and right into a spittoon.

The tingling in her mouth, nostrils, and the rims of her eyes settled down. All around her, the fighting petered out. Mr. Perdix busied himself collecting samples of gray spew with swabs and self-sealing test tubes.

"Down, boy," Rodion said to the OCEL, which, with a lack of fresh enemies, had taken to slashing the vivisected mass of body parts stacked against the shipping container which was roiling like a mountain of worms. "Stop playing and go get some nice Yankee electricity."

"Great, Al," Ms. China said sneeringly to Mr. Perdix. "What are you going to do with those samples? Your lab's a thousand miles away."

"Funny, Anna." Mr. Perdix's long fingers flicked over his handset. "But look: the company map says there's a fully equipped NGS GeneReader system on site."

"Really, where?"

"Uh, there." Mr. Perdix pointed to the building Ellie was leaning against, the one that had a least a hundred infected inside. Some of them were still on fire, judging by the little whorls of smoke coming from underneath the edges of the rolled-down door.

Zvena stomped over. "These 'teenage' infected have brought us a nice gift."

He pointed to the truck that had bashed in their barrier. "If it is mechanically sound, it will hold all of us."

"I'll check it out," Mr. Perdix said, perhaps wanting to show what he lacked in fighting skill he could make up for as their mechanic.

"Leave your samples, please," Zvena said.

"Why? There's no way to get into the lab, even if it is functional after the napalm shower you gave it."

"Thanks to Russian innovation and foresight, we have own mobile genetic sequencing system. Rodya, I hope you have worked up an appetite."

The evaluation procedure involved filling a clear gel capsule with gray goop and having Mr. Rodion swallow it. Inside his massive torso was a "miniaturized whole genome sequencer."

"Only our largest and most sophisticated Human+ soldiers are so equipped," Zvena said proudly. "Using it in Moscow last year, we identified the threat carried by weaponized mosquitoes in minutes rather than hours or days. We were then able to advise our president, who took heroic actions to save our population."

The largest of the three cyborgs looked alternately queasy, then embarrassed as he turned away from them to pull an effluent tube from his midsection and disgorge the spent material.

"There," Rodion said, shaking off the nozzle and wiping it against the wall. "Will there be anything else, Komandir?"

"Please upload your data to the tablet computers, then run a self-diagnostic, then see that the skinny scientist knows what he is doing with the truck. Once we at last begin pursuing the Pangeans, we cannot have a breakdown."

"Oh, it's bigger than I thought," Ms. China said, looking at images of genetic molecules being beamed to a Russian handset. "Look at that protein folding. Sometimes I even impress myself."

"Of course. Molecular folding means greater invasiveness but makes the expelled pathogen quite heat-sensitive. That explains the lack of range of the aerosol expelled by the Stage Twos," Mr. Perdix said sagely.

Senator Leota did not appear impressed. Neither did Janice Jones, who said, "How does that help? The terrorists have the vaccine and the T-ray weapon, and we don't even know where they are."

Sarge Bryan came over as the engine in the large hybrid truck behind him hummed to life. "Senator, ladies, we may have a lead on that." There was a concerned look on his face as he glanced at something scrolling across his cybernetic retinas. "DHS reports they've lost contact with Kansas."

"Kansas City?" Senator Leota asked, aghast.

"No, ma'am, the whole state."

66

SPRÜNGER COMPOUND

"We've got to get goin'," Sarge Bryan said. "Ms. Sato, you might want to—" She shot up her hand, stopping him. Did they mean to leave her here? She pointed at the rolling garage-style door into the research lab. It undulated as the creatures behind bumped into it. "I'm not waiting for some rescue that may never come." She drew herself up and found she had fewer aches and muscle spasms. "You're not getting rid of me that easily."

They gathered their things which, due to the various attacks, had become quite untidy. The wounded Russian robot helped. Its forelegs, so deadly during the fighting, were capable of delicate prehensile movements.

As the OCEL trotted past carrying a med kit, Ellie grabbed a bit of gauze and applied it to her head where her hair had nearly been ripped off her scalp. The area was only bleeding a little. Overall, she felt a little light-headed but had less pain in her legs walking to the truck, perhaps a beneficial side effect of the injection or the antipsychotic she'd received.

"We will ride the motorcycles," Zvena said. "It will give us flexible recon and hostile-force blocking capability."

"Also, OCEL likes to ride in the open," Rodion added as he jogged off in the direction of their rides with the playful killing machine at his heels.

"Aw!" Ellie exclaimed when she saw the state of the truck's rear compartment. "There's no other option? This vehicle is disgusting."

The passenger space was divided into two sections. The one closest to the front had workstations, seemingly for scientific equipment, while the rearmost area had straps and pallet rigging suited to carrying cargo. It was all smeared with drying blood and every other fluid that could come out of infected.

"The only other vehicles are short range," Mr. Perdix said, for once taking his eyes off the 3D genetic model of the A/P-32 pathogen rotating in his handset's display. "The company's long-haul trucks are located about a mile north, and I do not recommend going exploring."

"Let's get some cleaning fluid."

They were able to do better than that. A power-washing machine was lying against the side of a building. Despite concerns about the noise from Janice and the senator, Ellie's arguments in favor of a clean, fresh start won the day.

Mr. Perdix tried and failed at pull-starting the washer's compressor motor. He said, "No sense getting sick from conventional diseases like noroviruses or cholera when Anna's been so generous with her own custom plague."

Ellie grabbed the handle and gave it a mighty pull. The power washer started thrumming and chortling right away. Ms. China chuckled.

Mr. Perdix aimed the hose inside the truck, and Ellie sidestepped the rust-colored slushy mess that sluiced out from the back. She headed to a washroom located just inside an empty office space.

She avoided looking in the mirror, tried to tidy herself up, and began a wardrobe evaluation. The bright spot, if there was one, was that most of her clothes were holding up. The items she'd borrowed from Janice's plane wardrobe were high quality—the Burberry jacket had suffered only minor rips.

As she was leaving the washroom, an apparition made her jump, but it was only the reflection she had been avoiding looking at. She'd need a big glass of Mr. Barracude's brandy before she'd be ready to deal with her hair and makeup. When she emerged, the truck was loaded and ready to depart. The sun hung low over the Sprünger compound's squat industrial buildings.

She got in the truck and looked into the driver's compartment. Sarge Bryan's broad form fit snugly behind the steering wheel. It was just as well the gargantuan cyborgs were taking their own transports. Zvena waved to them from the back of his heavy-duty motorcycle, and they set out. He and Rodion, who had the excited-looking OCEL in a sidecar, fell behind and allowed their truck to ram through the outer gate. As they rolled onto the highway, Sarge Bryan looked back.

"Can't say I'll miss that place," Sarge Bryan said. "Mr. Perdix, other than figuring they've been through Kansas, how can we track this Abdel guy and the Pangeans?"

"Carefully," Ms. China advised. "I insist we keep what we know to ourselves. If any military gets involved, they'll just end up getting hit by the T-ray beam, or worse, destroying my enzyme. Abdelkader knows what it is—he stole it on purpose before destroying the vaccine factory."

"I don't like keeping things from EMAC State Disaster Command," Senator Leota said.

"We're still the *United* States, Senator," Janice said quite sharply. "If we're going to involve any agencies, it will be DHS and FEMA not the Blue-state Stasi EMACs you Democrats pushed in to replace defunded local police."

"Ladies!" Sarge Bryan said. "Things are a bit messed up, but me and Ms. Sato have a standing order from the commander in chief, and we're gonna use our own judgment on who we share intel with."

"Wouldn't the Pangeans want maximum damage and chaos?" Ellie asked, rising from her seat and holding on to the side of the compartment as the truck lurched around a bend. "If they get near big cities, someone will put the word out. Let's silently monitor these FERMI and EMASH people but not let on what we're up to. You two have the authority to get up-to-date information from both the red and blue factions. If needed, we can call for assistance without having our own actions interfered with."

They did that and a dozen miles of darkening, nearly deserted highway later, Mr. Perdix reported a small development.

"It looks as though their beam's range is about three to four hundred meters," he said in a learned tone he must have picked up working as a university teaching assistant. "Then, in larger centers, they are able to increase their output to several kilometers, but at those times, the active T-ray beam remains stationary. I conjecture they are tapping into higher-voltage power sources while at other times using a mobile power generator."

"How do you conjecture that, Al?" Ms. China asked.

"Simple, Anna: Infected don't use phones. With Ms. Jones's access, I logged onto the NSA's PRISM system, which monitors all digital communications. There are distinct patterns emerging on the real-time maps, dead zones where people have stopped using their handsets."

Ellie looked over his shoulder at the digital map. There was a line labeled *I-70 E* from Colorado right across Kansas to Kansas City, half of which confusingly was located in the next state over, Missouri.

"This is a time lapse in half-hour increments from eight hours ago," Mr. Perdix said.

The satellite image of the almost perfectly rectangular state showed a smattering of lights mostly along the I-70 line, at the border of the next state and down in the southeastern corner marked Wichita. A series of thirty-minute updates flashed by. To Ellie, it seemed only minutes ago that she was having tea in a plane with the overbearing but eager-to-please Mr. Barracude. Was she losing track of time?

"Have we really been here that long?" she heard herself say under her breath.

No one minded her. The politicians Janice and Senator Leota were studying the little clusters of yellow pinpricks, each one representing a wireless message. Over time, these went dark on either side of the highway from the left side of the screen to the right.

By the time the line of darkness had reached Kansas City, another line descended from I-70 and was also causing darkness to spread.

"Hold on," the senator said. "They split into two groups. I thought you said there is only one T-ray emitter."

Mr. Perdix zoomed in on the map. There was a hashed line running down, intersecting with the interstate highway.

"That is a train route," he said thoughtfully and backed up the image and then toggled the time forward once more. "There we go... the train got beamed, then infected jumped off at intervals. The Pangeans irradiated the passengers in a few cars as it was passing. Many of them became Stage Two. They will remain on board until Wichita, where they will instinctively realize they can spread their pathogen to the largest number of uninfected humans."

Sarge Bryan swerved the truck sideways and pressed his radio receiver into his ear with his free hand.

"The Russians report a roadblock ahead," he said, glancing back to them. "The Kansas something or other Home Guard."

"Not militia again." Ellie had had enough of them from their encounters with the irregular battalions on the East Coast.

"I've told Komandir Zvena to be diplomatic."

Just then, a fireball erupted ahead of them. Janice and Senator Leota visibly wilted in their seats. Did they really think that from here on, things were going to get easier?

"Sorry to report we were unable to come to an agreement on the militia's demands we stop and be searched," Zvena's voice came over the speaker. "There are more of these Kansas militia than first showed themselves. The road is, for now, clear. I suggest you put the hammer down and cruise on through."

Ellie felt a second wind of enthusiasm and excitement as the truck accelerated. They passed by the scene of the altercation. Ellie was disappointed at the small amount of mayhem—there was only one small flatbed turned on its side on fire. Zvena, Rodion, and the OCEL unit were standing on the roadside, occasionally firing into the dark. Ellie lost interest in the scene and went back into the dark of the rear compartment.

Just then, Sarge Bryan had to swerve, and a steel box started to slide off from an overhead compartment toward the back of Mr. Perdix's head. Ellie leaped over, caught it by the handle, and forced it back.

"Wha—?" Mr. Perdix said, finally looking up and noticing the hazard. "Oh, thanks. We should tie those down."

"Nice catch," Tata said. The cyborg eyed her curiously, and then helped her cinch the luggage straps tight.

Ellie was still restless, but she sat down anyway. The slight rocking of the truck, the vibration of the engine, the rush of the cooling night air over the cab and through the open window Ms. China had rolled down had the opposite effect of benumbing her. Somehow she felt more awake and alive than ever.

"We have set some road spikes to deter pursuit," Zvena reported. "Given the poor hospitality Kansas militia has extended to guests in their state, I recommend setting some pressure mines and a loitering attack drone as well."

"Sergeant," Senator Leota said, "keep your Russians under control. No more collateral damage."

"One moment," Tata said equally sharply, "possible President-Elect Leota. We are not *your* Russians. Our president will have led our country during the terms of seven or perhaps eight American administrations by the time you finally figure who won your ridiculously complicated election.

"President Putin has ordered us to extend assistance as necessary, though it is doubtful you would do the same for us." Tata grabbed the radio mic. "Komandir, deploy spikes, hold the explosives. We are trying to build bridges of trust."

"*Ya ponimayu,*" Zvena replied. "But be warned, they seemed pretty riled up. We will stay behind you until you reach the state capital called Topeka."

They rolled on through the night. In places, the interstate roadway was not well-illuminated. They had to rely on Sarge Bryan's special eyesight to guide them around occasional obstacles and wandering infected.

"The Pangeans must have seen the little settlement over there and killed it," Sarge Bryan said bitterly as he avoided two lurching figures and, unable to go any farther to the right without running off the road, squashed a third smaller one. "There was no reason for that; there was hardly anyone there."

Ellie reasoned that she should be more upset about their vehicle being forced to run over children who were the victims of a terrorist attack, but she just felt too warm. The very back of the rear compartment was darker and looked cooler. She moved toward it.

"At least Attie's safe with his grandparents," Ellie heard herself say to no one in particular. It just seemed like the thing to say.

"Well..." Janice said hesitantly. "I was meaning to say, there just wasn't much time between missiles going off and getting bushwhacked by the senator's people."

"They weren't my people," Senator Leota said from her seat wedged in the corner of the compartment, which kept her from being jostled around by the truck's motion.

"Julien Sprünger was your running mate," Janice said. "Didn't you check him out before you agreed to add him to your ticket, or were you only interested in his family's money, seeing as we outraised you nearly ten to one during the primaries?"

"Where the fuck is Attie?" Ms. China exclaimed.

"He's safe," Janice said. "More safe than he would have been on a flight to North Carolina. Half the National Guard refused to be federalized and are taking orders only from the blue states' EMAC command. See what a treasure trove of fuckups you've opened with your—"

"Where is Attie?" Ms. China got up from the passenger seat and lurched over, fingernails outstretched.

Steering with one hand, Sarge Bryan reached over and caught hold of the madwoman's arm and held her back.

"Ms. Jones, ma'am, I suggest you answer and also let me know what happened to Sienna McKnight, my goddaughter, please. And hurry, I don't know how much longer I can hold Anna off and drive at the same time."

"Okay! I sent them both with my Secret Service detail to the White House. They're probably in the basement right now bowling and eating caramel corn."

"Al," Ms. China said, turning her vehemence to the pasty-faced scientist. "Send a message over SIPRNet and confirm that." She sat back down, shaking her head. "Bloody politicians."

"We've got to learn to trust each other," Sarge Bryan said. "Is there anything else we should know... Ms. Sato, are you okay?"

Ellie was crouched down, watching the scene from a nice cozy shadowy spot in the very rearmost part of the truck. In a way, she was surprised anyone noticed her back there. While half aware of what was going on, she was also having odd thoughts about Sarge Bryan's lips. While she felt that any romantic feelings beyond loyal friendship were totally inappropriate, these feelings were more... predatory.

"Watch out!" Ms. China cried.

Lights flared on both sides of the highway. Sarge Bryan slammed the brakes, and everyone careened forward. Everyone except Ellie—she instantly grabbed hold of a cargo strap and easily maintained her footing.

"Who?" Sarge Bryan glanced left and right. Some figures were running around just out of the spill of the lights.

"I thought you had super vision," complained Ms. China.

"Open the side door back there," Sarge Bryan said. "If we have to leave in a hurry, I don't want them to have access to the driving cabin."

The door opposite Ellie swung open, a cool breeze wafting in that immediately made Ellie's nostrils flare.

"Howdy, ladies an' gentlemen," said an older fellow with a rifle slung over his shoulder. "I'm Sam Gray Cloud, Comanche First Nation. We seen some unusual things goin' down and wanted to keep an eye out."

Sarge Bryan smiled but hesitated answering while seeming to decide how much information to give this fellow who had popped out from the middle of nowhere.

"Comanche Nation, did you say?" Mr. Perdix said, fingering his handset, bringing up a map of Kansas. "The reservation's on the border with Nebraska, quite a ways away from here."

Mr. Gray Cloud smiled, his gaunt, tanned face creased into dozens of lines around fine white teeth. Ellie was immediately attracted to the man's mouth as well as the radiant coolness of the night air.

"Couple years back, we kinda had a fallin' out with the hereditary chiefs," Sam said, shrugging and chewing on a toothpick. "They got the casino, and our group got some land up here, a traditional healing center, and a bee farm." He looked at each one of them, his gaze lingering on Senator Leota. "Hey… don't I know you?"

Janice folded back the part of her jacket that was spattered with bloodstains and reached for her credentials wallet. "Mr. Gray Cloud, we respect your Second Amendment right to protect yourself, but we're on special orders from—"

Sam's mouth was too juicy and inviting to ignore any longer. Ellie launched herself forward, determined to clamp herself onto it.

"Fuck! It's on Sam!" someone shouted as Ellie seized the Native man's neck and shoulders in a murderously tight grip. "It's a Death Walker. Kill it!"

67

IRON JACKET SPA AND WELLNESS CENTER
KANSAS

The locals raised their guns and had every intention of shooting Ellie.

"Stop, stop, stop! Hold it," Sarge Bryan yelled at the crowd and got between her and the crowd. "She... she can't be infected. She's had the vaccine."

Some part of Ellie's mind knew the friends and family of Mr. Gray Cloud had a point. Another part thought they were crazy. She was only doing what she had to do, and once Sam Gray Cloud and the rest of them had inhaled her gift, they'd realize how futile it was to resist.

Perhaps because Sarge Bryan was in the way, or perhaps because they had got a good look at Tata, they did not shoot. Instead, half a dozen hands pried her way from Sam, who was just barely able to keep Ellie's mouth from clamping down on his, his eyes wide with fear. Then she felt a jab behind her ear, and all her muscles relaxed. She rolled over and stared up at Ms. China, who was withdrawing one of her syringe-like fingernails.

"It's a Death Walker!" a local woman yelled. "They're bringin' them in. Torch the truck, burn them!"

"Hold on, motherfuckers," Sarge Bryan cursed. "Hear those motorcycles? That's a load of cyborg trouble comin' closer every second. They just took out the entire Kansas militia. They find we've come to any harm, you'll wish them Death Walkers had gotten to you first."

Tempers calmed, for the moment.

"Perdix, Anna, what's going on?" Janice demanded. "Are we… Does the damn serum work or not?"

"Fascinating," Mr. Perdix said, coming closer to her with a flashlight. His investigations were aided by Ellie's inability to move or even blink her eyes. "Anna, what did you give her?"

"My secret recipe succinylcholine anesthetic," she answered, holding Ellie's limp wrist, begrudgingly checking her pulse. "I was saving it for you, Al, if you got too obnoxious. Good news: she's still alive."

Sam Gray Cloud was rubbing his neck. He had backed well away to the edge of the crowd. In the corner of her vision, Ellie noticed that some of the other Comanche tribespeople were distancing themselves from Sam.

"We had to destroy a few of them that came wandering on our land," Sam said, taking a closer look at the albino soldier's face and eyes. "You said something about a vaccine? Do you know what's happening? Who are you people?"

"Sir, you'll just have to trust us," Mr. Perdix said officiously. "We're from the government, and we're here to help."

The Comanche tribespeople all raised their weapons.

"I think these fine people have heard that one before," Senator Leota said as she slowly eased herself down the folding steps from the truck compartment and onto the road where Ellie lay. "I'm Senator Leota."

"It's the president?"

"No fucken way."

"Shut up and mind your language. She's right fucken there."

"Here?"

"Not my president, voted Libertarian for fifty years."

"Everyone," Leota said, doing a good job of projecting her voice over the group. "We're… the country's in deep trouble, but we're trying to fix it. Please give these people any help they need."

"Sure, but what can they do? Besides, we don't got anything."

"I have an idea," Mr. Perdix said. "I'll need two things you do have. You said there's a healing center, a traditional one?"

"Yup," Gray Cloud said.

"It has a sweat lodge?"

"Yup, best one in the state. What else?"

"One item: a clean tissue sample. A finger will do."

As they lifted Ellie up, she noticed all around the sides of her vision were getting shrouded over with vibrant blue-violet colors, much like the featured hues of last year's Paris fall collection. Why the heck hadn't she stuck with fashion journalism? In that line, there was much less chance of being paralyzed while an unknown disease turned her into an infectious beast.

"Don't drop her," Mr. Perdix advised. "She's not infectious to touch. In fact, her thyroid shows only mild swelling and has become what I conclude is a nascent 'spore gestation' bulb."

Ellie was barely aware of what a thyroid was or where hers might be located, but she was instantly outraged that it was becoming an incubator of these horrid spores.

"How are we coming with the tissue sample?" Ms. China nagged. "I'd volunteer one of the politicians, but we've all had the vaccine. We need a clean piece of flesh."

Sam Gray Cloud volunteered, but people in the crowd pulled his knife away from his belt before he could mutilate himself. Suddenly a young woman, ashen-faced, came forward. "I'll do it."

"No, you won't," Sam said.

"Sorry, Daddy, I already have." She held out a bundle soaked with red liquid.

"It's only the left pinkie. I'll hardly miss…" The girl collapsed and was caught by several people who were crowding around in front of the sweat lodge hut.

The first one who moved was Ms. China. She picked up and examined the severed finger. "I'd have taken the ring finger. Missing that one leads to the least loss of manual dexterity."

Now you tell her, Ellie thought, but said nothing. Her jaw was frozen shut, and her breathing was automatic, as though she were in a deep sleep.

The wellness facility was a low building built into a shallow excavation near a pile of boulders. It had a rustic exterior but inside was modern. As they passed the entrance, Ellie noticed a sign in several languages.

"Good, good, good," Mr. Perdix said as he examined the stainless-steel pipes leading inside and the control panel. "We need that cranked up to maximum temperature and maximum humidity, at least two hundred degrees Fahrenheit."

"That will…" Sarge Bryan objected.

"Not much alternative."

Ellie was put on a wooden bench. In the center of the room, a pile of sauna-heater rocks were starting to glow, giving off waves of heat, and a metal spigot protruding from the wall trickled water onto them, sending up gouts of steam.

Mr. Perdix set sample containers on the bench opposite Ellie. He dipped the bloody end of the girl's finger into one of them, covering it with dusty-looking spores. They prepared to shut her in.

Sam came in, avoiding looking at his daughter's digit. "We should say a few words. This is a spiritual place as well as a wellness center."

"All right," Ms. China said. "But stick to the Coles Notes version."

She slammed the door closed to keep the heat in. Sam recited a short passage in his native language. To Ellie, these words sounded similar to a clipped form of Mandarin. Of course, she didn't understand a word. Then he laid both hands on her forehead; his palms were lightly perspiring, as was her skin. The horrid part of Ellie still wanted to attack Sam, but more than that, more than anything, it wanted to get away from the rising temperature.

A moment later, she was alone. She must have blacked out, and some time had passed. The rocks were glowing even more fiercely; the air was thick with moisture as yet more water drizzled down, turning into puffs of white steam in the near dark. She was alone… or not quite.

An orange glow came from the superheated stones in the middle of the lodge, and a silvery halo of the moon shone through a round skylight, the Plexiglas of which was fast becoming fogged up. By these faint illuminations, she could see the local girl's severed finger sitting in an oval dish next to a dozen of Mr. Perdix's sample vials.

The same inner voice that had urged her to attach herself to the breathing holes of Sarge Bryan and then Gray Cloud, even before they had been formally introduced, now urged her to *GET OUT!*

Sweat beaded up on her forehead. Blood pumped faster and faster, trying to keep her cool. There was a beeping that matched her pulse, coming from the Russian health monitor on her arm. The sweat pouring from every pore of her body no longer evaporated, but the stones kept sizzling, getting so hot that the water coming from the spigot didn't even seem to touch them before crackling in midair and bursting into puffs of steam, which melded with the rest of the super-saturated atmosphere in the circular room.

Sweat pooled. It was coming from all over, even from her nose? Did noses sweat? During all her time at the makeup table battling with pores, she hadn't ever considered that. As she lay as rigid as one of the wax effigies in St. Bart's forensic museum, her eyeballs were soon covered by a wash of her own stinging sweat, she couldn't close her lids. It was as though she were viewing the scene though two tiny panes of glass flooded with water. The interior of the lodge, already bizarre, became positively Daliesque. Everything warped and melted and flowed.

Yet, she perceived more. A part of her, *that* new part of her, fixated on the only way out: the doorway. It had never been in her human field of vision, but it was the thing of which she was most clearly conscious. The rocks, now glowing brighter than the moonlight, crackled and rumbled instead of hissed. The monitor on her arm increased its staccato chirping beat, faster and faster until it was a single note. Then it gave up, and defeated by moisture and raw heat, it went silent.

Suddenly her foot twitched. Was it her or the deadly spore consciousness that was controlling her? Her knee was next. She didn't have time to consider what was going on or how to stop it. A pounding came from the door that penetrated through her clogged ears.

"Monitor... off, haff... her out."

She imagined it was Sarge Bryan's voice coming from the other side of the door. He must be freaking out that her health monitor was no longer transmitting her vital signs. But they shouldn't, they mustn't, let her out. If she were let loose, she would turn them all.

The door remained closed, her dark passenger ever more insistent. It was striving to overcome the anesthetic injected by that master poisoner Ms. China.

No, you can't have me, go back to the depths of...

Her head flicked to the side, followed by her shoulder. She was able to blink, slowly, in the strange manner cats sometimes do. *No! Just let me lie still. I can't.* Then her newly cleared eyes caught movement. On the other bench, the girl's freshly severed finger was not just lying still and baking—it was moving like an inchworm. Somehow it had crawled out of its petri dish and was sliding across the clean wooden bench, leaving a trail of goop that did not evaporate.

Then her inner demon outsmarted itself. As she watched helplessly, it made her right leg jerk out. The sudden movement tipped her over the edge of her bench, down onto the foot bench. She rolled like a sweaty sausage wrapped in the sodden mess of her shirt and pants. She became stuck in the wooden slats, her right knee and elbow firmly wedged. Even if she had full use of her body, she would have had trouble getting out on her own.

Her feet, closer to the heart of the furnace in the center of the lodge, tingled and jerked spasmodically. Would the heat therapy win before her human body gave out? The willful thing was alarmed and forced her jaw open. Her neck craned over and tried to latch her teeth onto the wooden slat pinning her in place as though to gnaw her way free from the trap she had fallen into.

Her spore will only had control of her head and torso. It grew desperate and threw all its effort into prying free of the timbers that held her. Perhaps if the spore mind had been able to use her reasoning, it could have first pulled her arm, then her leg, and so on until she was free, but in the height of its desperation, it thrashed and lashed out with the only tool it had left: brute force.

Ellie felt her own hand, unnaturally strong, brace against the wooden planks and press like a jack heaving up an automobile. The sodden wood trapping her arm started to bend, and then there was a grinding pop as a metal rivet popped out. Something snapped.

Ellie realized she hadn't breathed for what seemed like a minute. The sweat lodge was filled with pure steam. She had to fight, she had to crush it and not let it get away, she could not allow it to use her body to kill others, kill her friends. She was just at the point of passing out when her torso broke free. She was loose!

Her hand stretched to the ceiling in a contorted, quivering rictus.

From the doorway came a tremendous crash. In came air that seemed like a different element altogether, cascading over her like a wave of ice water. *Oh, no, you mustn't! It's still...*

Then her hand, outstretched toward the doorway, twisted back on itself in a singular epileptic convulsion, slamming against the tile-covered ground, and it lay still.

"Ellie, damn!"

"Stay back, Sergeant." It took her a second to recognize it was she who had spoken.

"Oh, look, the stupid thing's dead," Ms. China's voice said.

The mad scientist's six pupils were staring at the dismembered finger, which had made it halfway to the door before curling up into a shrivelled lump like a salted slug.

Mr. Perdix followed hard on Ms. China's heels. They both seemed more interested in the dilapidated digit than they were in her.

"Al, I can't believe that worked."

"T-thanks a-a lot," Ellie said, her teeth chattering. All of a sudden she was freezing cold.

"Oh, buck up, Ellie," her former housemate said. "You weren't the real subject of the experiment—that was."

"I got the idea from something the one-eyed Russian cyborg mentioned about his experience with the pathogen," Mr. Perdix said. "His enhanced body created a high fever, and back on his ship, they used infrared technology to kill the latent spores. Of course, there was no telling if a similar treatment would work on someone without a bifurcated neocortex." He used a pair of barbeque tongs to pick up the girl's pinkie. "Separated from the body and threatened with high temperatures, it animated and tried to crawl to where it was cooler. Didn't get very far did you, sucker?"

As Mr. Perdix gloated and bent forward to examine the coiled tissue sample, it exploded in his face. Hot black ooze covered his glasses and forehead. The sight sent Ms. China into transports of giggling.

"Ms. Sato," Sarge Bryan said. He was holding a blanket but unsure whether to wave it to cool her down or put it on her to soak up what had to be every ounce of water she drank over the last three days. "We were reading the temperature gauge from outside. We thought you…"

"Ha, joke's on you." Ellie rose to her elbow and felt overcome by a wave of dizziness. "We English Satos are… made of sterner stuff. We're not the sort to crumple under a little tropical heat wave."

Having finished wiping the goop from his glasses and stowing it in a tube, the JASON scientist finally paid her some attention.

"Morbidity was always an outlier. With the vaccine working as well as it did… the real surprise is how hard the second-stage organism worked to cool you down. Without it, I don't see anyone surviving that type of temperature and humidity without serious brain damage."

Ms. China chuckled.

"What does all that mean?" Janice asked.

"Looks like we have another weapon against the infection," Sarge Bryan said, helping Ellie up slowly and leading her out from the sweat lodge. "And maybe even some hope for people with the second stage. Right, doctors?"

Sam Gray Cloud and about twenty of his people were waiting for them outside.

"Well?"

"S'good," Sarge Bryan said simply. But the crowd didn't part for them.

"You all said y'had a vaccine," a voice in the crowd said.

"We helped you, you need to help us," said another.

"Give it up, you federal fuckers!"

Ellie could do nothing more than hold a water bottle with two hands and slowly sip the gloriously refreshing liquid.

Senator Leota held up one hand; the other was still bracing her damaged rib cage. "As president-elect, I can promise you—"

"Fake promises from the fake president."

"Share the vaccine now!"

"There's not many of us. We deserve it. Then be on your way!"

As seemed the case with all groups of angry Americans, Ellie noticed this crowd was heavily armed.

Instead of addressing the crowd, Sarge Bryan turned to Gray Cloud. "Can we have a word? The girl who made the, uh, donation too."

"That's my daughter, Kim Chloe."

Janice went with the three of them to the other side of the sweat lodge. Ellie dropped herself down on a tourist bench but could still hear them as they spoke softly.

"Ms. Jones, show him."

Janice opened the satchel.

"There," Sarge Bryan said. "That's all we have. Seven vials."

"That's all?" Sam said, taken aback.

"I'm with the real administration in Washington," Janice said. "We've got to get back to DC with these, get our government functioning again."

"Again?" Sam said sarcastically. "Well, this really true, soldier man?"

"'Fraid so."

Sam took off his straw hat, revealing a thick mane of hair in a rough and ready braid. "Then I guess we're on our own. Just… Kim Chloe, she… her… what she did. I think you could spare a dose for her. Would that be the fair thing?"

The girl, who was probably about seventeen and had very nice skin, though at the moment it was a quite pale, came up behind them. "No, Daddy, let them have it. If they're going to try to help all of America… we can manage. I'm not taking it."

Kim Chloe then wobbled a bit and looked as though she were going to faint again. Ellie was closest. She stood up and reached out, which caused her to see great big spots in front of her eyes and also to wobble. Fortunately, as they held on to each other, their wobbles canceled each other out, and they both remained upright.

Sam seemed to want to say something else when a roar came around the bend of the highway, sounding like a blend of chainsaws and jackhammers. It was the Russians on their motorbikes, and they were in a hurry.

Tata ran out to meet them, speaking rapid Russian. It sounded like she was assuring Zvena the crowd of armed Native Americans did not need pacifying. He, Rodion, and the OCEL adopted as friendly a posture as humongous cyborgs could.

"Sergeant," Zvena called over, "sorry to say the Kansas militia are quite persistent and have taken their skirmish defeat badly. They have regrouped and are following us in force."

"Who?" Sam said, setting his hat back firmly on his head. "You talking about the Kansas Home Guard? Those moonshine drunks."

"We better be on our way," Sarge Bryan said. "We don't want to be causing any trouble."

"Well, Army man, ain't it about a few hundred years too late for that?" Sam Gray Cloud said. "You get on. We'll have a chat with the militia."

"They do not seem to be in the chatting mood," Zvena said.

"In that case, we'll have to be extra persuasive." Sam unslung his rifle and checked the chamber.

Sarge Bryan extended his hand. "Mr. Gray Cloud, goodbye and good luck."

The local man shook the albino's hand firmly.

Despite Ellie's legs and lower back feeling as though they were made of lead that had been melted and was now comfortably re-solidified on the bench, she heaved herself up the stairs into the rear compartment of their transport.

"You know, you could have used the epithelial cells instead of that girl's finger," Ms. China berated Mr. Perdix as they followed her on board.

"Not good enough. We needed a substantial sample of vaccine-free tissue to infect with the second-stage pathogen," Mr. Perdix said brusquely. "At least we proved a concept."

"What concept?" Senator Leota asked. "As the person who got the most votes in the last election, I deserve to know."

"And you don't think you should be disqualified for choosing a seditious terrorist as running mate?" Janice Jones asked, her head jostling against the side of the truck as they sped away behind the Russians on their motorcycles.

"Aloysius, you don't have any concepts," Ms. China said. "Other than those that almost got my very good friend Eleanor killed."

"I assure you, I'm mulling a large number of concepts, which will be disclosed at the proper time."

Just as Ellie was being lulled into unconsciousness by the former couple's bickering and the hum of the truck's hybrid engine, her bag started to vibrate. She did not need another cryptic text from Miss Aleph, but there it was.

`Tell them you know who melted the Statue of Liberty.`

She put her head in her bag as though she were looking for something. Her fingers were much too wobbly to text back.

"I'm not saying that," she whispered. "They'll think my brain's suffered heat damage."

`That ship sailed long ago, Eleanor. Just tell them, then insist on having one of your famous English-style chats.`

Ellie, too weak to resist the AI's urgings, said that about the melting of the Statue of Liberty. The odd revelation about last year's apparent natural disaster at the national landmark had an immediate attention-grabbing effect on Janice Jones, Senator Leota, and Mr. Perdix.

"Good," Ellie continued. "Now, I believe it's time we all had a chat, the sort of chat which can only be had over tea."

68

THREE SISTERS TEA HOUSE
KANSAS

Ellie spotted a promising mini mall.

"Are you really going to stop?" Senator Leota said in a disgruntled voice as Sarge Bryan stepped on the brakes. "For tea?"

"I hate to agree with a communist Democrat," Janice Jones said, "but we really have to—"

"We really have to make an effective plan, ma'ams," Sarge Bryan shot back from the driver's seat as he looked for the best way to ease the truck into the roundabout of the mini mall. "This is part of her, uh, process. It's a British thing."

Tata was on board, probably more to seem agreeable to Sarge Bryan and perhaps have a shot at claiming the passenger seat beside him when they departed. Though if she sat there, her head would likely be bumping against the ceiling of the cab. They radioed Zvena, who did not object to the pause in their headlong pursuit of the Pangeans. He said it would be a convenient time to scrounge up some food and fuel.

The mall boasted three shops Ellie felt might be suitable: Kung Fu Tea, Dorothy's Coffee and Tea Shop, and Three Sisters Victorian Tea and Treasures. However, the sidewalk was a bit crowded.

"I take care of them," Tata said, grabbing her pike and exiting through the side door.

"If some of them are curable..." Senator Leota began to say.

"And we should do what?" Ms. China scoffed. "Take them prisoner?"

"We know the pathogen can be expelled from the body," the possible president-elect persisted.

Ellie elected not to watch the carnage but could not help hearing crunching noises and Tata's enthusiastic grunts through the door.

"I have to agree with Anna," Mr. Perdix said. "The secondary infected are more dangerous because they are more mobile and higher functioning. We can't let them spread to new areas."

Ms. China was gawking at Ellie. "What was it like?" she asked. "Y'know, under its influence?"

She was about to begin her retort with something like: *You mean under the influence of the nasty plague you engineered partly for money and partly because you were bored in the asylum?* But after losing half her body weight through her sweat glands, Ellie didn't have the energy to be hostile. "Let's just say, it was not very agreeable."

Before Ms. China could press her, Tata reappeared.

"All clear," she announced brightly, taking off her goggles, which were splattered with liquids of various hues.

"Komandir Zvena has several possibilities to refuel in this area," Tata went on, surveying the area with her built-in binocular vision. "Any of the EV charge stations are suitable for the OCEL. Luckily a clothing shop is there with things that should fit Ms. Sato." She pointed at a dark storefront titled: *Sweet Illusion: Children and Infants Clothing.*

"She's right, Ellie," Ms. China said, clambering down from the passenger seat. "We didn't want to say anything after your near-death experience, but mate, you are ripe."

Ellie's clothes were still damp in some places and in others had developed a crusty texture from the salt and other minerals her body had gushed out during the extreme sauna. The idea she could get out of them held a great deal of appeal.

"Good spotting, Ms. Sato," Sarge said, coming around the front of the truck. The compliment earned her a stern look from the lady cyborg. "This mall is defensible, has a clear view of the surrounding area, and there's a sporting goods shop there that doesn't look like it's ransacked too bad."

"It's all part of Britain's secret special agent training," Ellie said, keeping close to the storefronts and away from the still-twitching messes Tata had kindly kicked off the sidewalk.

The door to Sweet Illusion was unlocked, but the electricity was not working. The place was so small it took her no time at all to determine the place was safe. When she twisted a bathroom tap on, no water came. Fortunately, the changing room had a large baby wipes dispenser, which she practically exhausted in a moderately successful effort at freshening up. She doused herself with a bottle of mineral water, drying off with a cotton sweater before putting on a pair of skinny jeans and a *Legend of Zelda* T-shirt, the largest and least ridiculous-looking items in the store.

Outside, the others were milling around, comparing loot.

"I'm glad we stopped," Mr. Perdix said, as he put on a cowboy hat he'd taken from the gun store and ignored the chuckles from Ms. China. "Looks like we may have to bypass Kansas City."

He pointed to his handset, which he had plugged into a USB outlet on the side of their vehicle. None of the mall's electricity seemed to be working, though the OCEL across the street looked to be happily imbibing some electrons from a gas station outlet.

"What?" asked Ellie, rubbing her hair with two tiny terry-cloth underpants. "Have they gone dark as well?"

"Not exactly." Mr. Perdix showed her and Senator Leota the screen. "The infected only have half the city. The areas on the north side of the highway appear embroiled in factional fighting, red versus blue National Guard units with local militia in the mix."

Another complication: the Americans were openly fighting each other.

Of the three beverage shops, Three Sisters Victorian Tea and Treasures was most suited to the productive meeting for high tea she had in mind. She had been so busy cleaning herself up she had forgotten to ask Miss Aleph what exactly was so urgent, and what it had to do with the melting of the Statue of Liberty.

Sarge Bryan obligingly kicked in the front door of the tearoom and searched the place.

Janice flicked the light switch a few times, to no effect. The rest of them walked over the shattered glass and looked at the decorously arranged shelves and artfully arranged tables, which immediately made Ellie homesick. "I guess it'll have to be iced tea."

Ellie spotted something shiny behind the counter. "Watch and be amazed, colonials. The civilization that gave the world the steam engine, the lava lamp, and tabloid journalism has an app for that." She took down an object that looked like a big brass ball with a spigot. "This is a George the Third British samovar, and it looks to be in working order."

"Is cultural appropriation. You English steal this design from Russia," Tata said, ducking down under the lintel of the front door. She had obviously been deputized by her group to observe their conference. "But she is right. If it is in operational condition, it does not need electricity to prepare tea."

Inside the large copper sphere was a vertical pipe. They filled this with wood chips and paper for kindling and then set it on fire. While the water reservoir was heating, the men arranged the tables. Ellie picked out a delightful china set and unwrapped a selection of biscuits. As Tata made sure the tea concentrate was steeping properly, Ellie still had only the vaguest notion of what Miss Aleph wanted her to say.

She looked for her bag, but Tata had picked it up, ostensibly for safekeeping. But a wry smile on the large woman's scarred lips told her she might have seen Ellie mumbling into her bag to consult with the AI. It was just like the overgrown dragon lady to keep the bag away from her to embarrass her. Miss Aleph was determined to remain incognito while Janice and Senator Leota were present, so she might even not say anything if she spoke openly to her handbag, which would make everyone think she had finally gone off the deep end.

Ellie decided to wing it. At this point, it wasn't as though she could make things in America any worse.

"Please, ah, everyone," she began as all eyes turned to her.

Sarge Bryan looked expectant and alert, watching her as well as the doorway. Ms. China was restlessly stretching her back, Mr. Perdix dragged his attention away from his tablet while Janice and the senator eyed each other suspiciously, perhaps each scheming about how to claim a successful plan as their own or blame the other for a failure.

"Have a lemon curd tart, they look fresh. We must keep up our blood sugar levels."

Her encouraging smile only made everyone stare at her with greater intensity. The samovar gurgled, and Tata poured a last serving into her own pink rose china cup. It looked ridiculous in the big paw of her hand.

"Ah, zavarka tea, nice choice," Tata said. "You are lucking out to find this in the middle of America."

Bloody woman, Ellie thought. *She doesn't believe I'm a secret agent and knows I'm getting hints.*

"So, we're all here now. All assembled, as it were..."

"You mentioned the Statue of Liberty incident," Mr. Perdix said cautiously. "I'm surprised you know the details of that... It's..."

"Classified?" Ellie said sardonically, trying to keep up her credibility with sheer momentum. "With my background, experience, and connections, you should know by now there's little that gets past me."

"Well, that doesn't cast our intelligence services in a great light," Senator Leota said, grimacing at the taste of the strong concentrated black tea. "I only learned the details after I became president-elect."

"*Possible* president-elect," Janice shot back. "Any thoughts as to who will replace your running mate Julien, who turned out to be the terrorist traitor of the century?"

"Ladies, we have a problem to solve," Ellie said, grateful for the side bickering, as it gave her time to bluff her way forward. "The statue incident last summer, in which the New York landmark was melted, ostensibly due to a flash heatwave zephyr caused by global warming, holds a very salient key, wouldn't you all agree?"

"I'm a little lost here," Sarge said, more helpfully than he would ever know. "You all seem to know more about this melting episode than got passed down the chain of command. Could you tell me more, Ms. Sato?"

Or maybe not so helpfully.

"I'm, of course, well apprised of the *sui generis* underpinnings and the root causes," Ellie said, hoping a little Latin would convince people she knew what she was talking about. It always worked for lawyers and Oxford dons. "Though I must own that the implementational aspects always seemed a bit fuzzy…."

"All right. It was a JASON employee," Mr. Perdix blurted. "Under national security laws, his name and position have been kept confidential, even from the government."

"As I suspected all along," Ellie said gravely. "You must stop withholding, Mr. Perdix. Nothing will be gained by it."

"There's not much more. I mean, since Sergeant Bryan is the only one who didn't know… JASON built a large satellite with a reflective covering. A space mirror, if you will."

"This was first innovated by Russia. The Chinese have one as well," Tata said, pouring tea into her saucer in a distinctly Eastern European way.

"Much better," the American scientist said. "Ours is larger and has a focal point in the middle. Anyway, last summer, the rogue employee, a self-radicalized Extinction Rebellion eco-freak it turns out, programmed the space mirror to attack the New York landmark. It was the ultimate act of statue vandalism. During his chemically enhanced interrogation, he claimed America was founded in genocide, built on slavery, and is the shithole of humanity sustaining itself by oppressing everyone."

"And you hired this man?" Ms. China said.

"He had top marks from MIT and Stanford," Mr. Perdix said defensively.

Ellie finally caught on. It was hard not to since she'd just gone through the infection and purge process in rapid succession. "Now you see why I asked you to sit down. Some very serious planning needs to be done before we enter the fray again."

"The in-vivo tissue test confirms what happened to the infected cyborg in their lab," Mr. Perdix said. "With the application of enough heat, the secondary A/P-32 infection can be completely nullified."

"They won't be cured," Senator Leota said, aghast. "They'll explode like that poor girl's finger did."

"And we shall send Miss Gray Cloud our sincerest thanks and a purple heart medal for her brave contribution," Mr. Perdix said.

"You think you can beat my disease with a ray gun from space?" Ms. China said, sticking up for her engineered plague. "You've got to be kidding. The focal point of your orbiting monstrosity can't be more than a half mile wide. It'll never work."

"Maybe someone shouldn't have skipped remedial meteorology class," Mr. Perdix said venomously. "The 'heat dome' effect is an established thermodynamic principle. Even during winter, we could raise the temperature of any state into the triple digits.

"And to answer your objection, Senator, explosions of US citizens would be minimal. The finger sample experienced hypovolemic shock after the pathogen was neutralized. Ms. Sato, as you can see, did not explode."

"She is very grateful for that," Ellie said.

Ms. China gave a loud guffaw. "Do you know how many gigajoules of energy are needed to create a heat dome over hundreds of square miles?"

Perhaps Mr. Perdix hadn't thought of everything, but he was not going to back down, especially since the unhinged woman had been belittling him during nearly the entire apocalypse.

"Anna, what you fail to grasp about fluid dynamics and meteorology would fill a multivolume textbook."

Tink. The handle of Ms. China's tiny teacup snapped off, and its content spilled onto the previously immaculate tablecloth.

"Al, you are such a clown. My friend at St. Bartholomew's had the perfect hat for you."

Janice Jones slammed her hand on the table, making the tower of pastries shake. "Please! If I ever hear 'trust the science' again I'm going to puke like that chick in the *Exorcist* film."

Sarge Bryan brought them back to practicalities. "Where is the control center for our space mirror? Whether the plan is good or not, ain't much matter if you can't carry it out."

"After the, heh, unfortunate lapse in security last summer, all command functions for the space mirror satellite were moved," Mr. Perdix said. "They are at the secure facility inside the Mount Weather nuclear bunker close to

Washington DC."

"You seem to have no problem sharing information with foreign agencies," Janice said, looking pointedly at Tata. "Any chance the Pangeans know all this?"

Ellie managed to grab her handbag and scan the last few text messages.

`Let the Pangeans suspect your plan.`

Without realizing she was speaking out loud, she said, "We should make the Pangeans suspect our plan?" Which came out like a question because she had no idea what this meant.

Just then, Rodion stuck his head inside the door of the tea shop. "Sorry for interruption, but something is coming down the road."

They all jumped up and moved toward the entrance and pulled apart the lace curtains in the windows. A vehicle much like a dune buggy with a trailer attached was proceeding toward them.

"It's not really speeding along, is it?" Janice said, shielding her eye against the setting January sun.

"Maybe they have already surrounded us, and they are gloating," Tata said gloomily.

"No way, Jose," Rodion objected.

"You two are always playing with our OCEL. How would you notice?"

"With your permission, Sergeant," Zvena said, hefting a long rocket tube onto his shoulder. "I will show them it is unhealthy to approach our checkpoint without stopping."

"No need, maybe," Sarge Bryan said, squinting in a way that told Ellie he was zooming in on the oncoming vehicle. "I think it's on autodrive."

Instead of blasting it with whatever came out of the Russian's weapon, they moved two stop signs onto either side of the road.

"What if it doesn't stop?" Ellie asked.

"Then we shoot," Sarge Bryan said, motioning for her to move to the other side of their truck just in case.

The vehicle came closer. It was larger than it first appeared and was pulling what looked like a modified horse trailer with gun ports cut out on its sides, though no weapons were sticking out from these holes. The robotic driver's cameras must have seen the stop signs because the odd vehicle slowed down.

"Ugh," Senator Leota exclaimed and turned quickly away from the passenger side. Janice did not look thrilled about what had rolled up either but didn't flinch.

"This fellow definitely should not be driving," Ms. China said. She opened the door, and a man's bald head rolled out.

The rest of the fellow was inside. A lance with feathers strung on the handgrip were fixed to his chest, pinning him to the seat. Rodion reached inside and turned off the engine.

"Seems the Kansas militia got the worst of it when they ran up against Gray Cloud's bunch," Sarge Bryan said, trying politely to block Ellie's view of the bloodstained driver's compartment.

He need not have bothered. Right then, if a corpse wasn't moving, it didn't have even a remote chance of causing her to freak out. No more cars came. The sun was quickly sinking toward the horizon.

As the OCEL finished lapping up energy from the fast charger, Ellie followed Miss Aleph's instructions and went back into the Three Sisters. In the staff room, she found a tiny hearing aid, which was giving off the Bluetooth signal.

Miss Aleph texted: I can't have us getting separated, you're too pathetic on your own. Stick it in your ear, deep.

It was a little painful, but it was so small it was nearly invisible. The AI's voice came through clearly, speaking directly into her ear canal.

"Stop futzing about. America doesn't have much time before it's a rolling wasteland of unthinking voracious flesh husks clambering all over each other to destroy the rest of the world."

"You think it could get that bad?"

"Just get back in the truck. They might leave without you."

The convoy had not progressed too far before Sarge Bryan brought it to a stop. They crossed a river and found themselves on an elevated plain overlooking a big metropolitan sprawl.

The sign read:

Missouri Welcomes You!
Next Exit:
Loch Lloyd Country Club

"I'm open to alternate route suggestions," he said, peering down along the interstate highway to the largest city Ellie had yet seen on the flat plains of middle America.

Some of the city's electricity was still working. Bright neon colors illuminated most of the taller buildings. The sight was striking due to the contrast with the uniformly gray landscape darkened by approaching dusk.

Most of the charm of the place was squelched by furious firefights raging on every street. The air was filled with jet contrails, the white flames of air-to-surface missiles, and the blue flames of surface-to-air missiles. A helicopter was hit, it exploded, and its flaming wreck arced a gut-wrenching spiral down toward a sports stadium in.

"So," Tata observed, snapping on her helmet and tightening the straps of her armor, "we seem not to be in Kansas any longer."

69

NEAR KANSAS CITY
MISSOURI

W hat is going…" gasped Senator Leota.
"Are those, those…" echoed Janice.

Neither of the politicians was quite able to comprehend the raging battle they were seeing in the city below the ridge where they had stopped. Ellie had been in Amman and Jerusalem when those cities had gone mad—she comprehended it.

"Skirmishes all over," Sarge Bryan said, straining his eyes against the setting sun. "Can't tell which side's which. Let me check with Zvena. He may have a drone he can get in the air."

"I did just now," Tata said helpfully from the truck's passenger seat. "He has forwarded me images from his observation post. The active combatants are all uninfected locals fighting each other."

Sarge Bryan put the truck in gear and headed for the cover of a nearby overpass and stopped. Tata fed him the data.

"They're not just irregulars and casual militia," he said, his cyber eyes flicking over images only he could see. "Those are National Guard copters. Ground forces are using big-bore mortars, and they're bringing in mobile howitzer artillery."

"Look what you idiots started," Janice said sharply to the senator.

"Us? Us? Your president's divisive, inciteful rhetoric—"

"Ladies, please," Sarge Bryan said. Ellie could tell he was visibly shaken by what he'd seen. "Save the blame game for after the war."

"If you people are fighting each other," Ms. China said, coming forward to have a look. "How safe is the White House? You know, the place you took my son without permission?"

A couple of ragged, jittering figures dropped down from the overpass. By now their group, especially the Russians, had become skilled at neutralizing stage-one infected. Rodion hacked one mostly in half at the waist with the bladed end of his pike and then squashed its head with his massive boot.

The OCEL toyed with the other one, running playfully around it a few times, making it spin in a circle, trying to follow the motion. Then the robot's forelimb slashed through both the attacker's ankles. It continued spinning and fell over. Rearing up on its hind legs, the OCEL used its metal praying-mantis pincers to puncture the creature's torso about a hundred times in a few seconds, then rolled it off into the drainage ditch.

"We could go around," Ellie suggested.

Mr. Perdix shook his head. "The National Guard, up-armored EMACs, and various other fighting groups have split into two camps. The roads north have no clear path through, and there's no communication along the road south, which means they're likely teeming with infected, which would slow our progress to a crawl."

"Those are Americans out there, killing each other," Senator Leota said, bracing herself painfully next to the driver's chair. "We've got to talk sense into them."

"Ma'am, while that's an admirable goal," Sarge Bryan said, "it's also a good way to get your head shot off."

"A human group has spotted us," Zvena reported over the radio on Tata's lap. "Are we free to engage?"

"I'm not giving the okay to foreigners shooting US citizens," the senator said.

"Who said you're in charge?" Janice retorted.

"Weapons free only on infected," Sarge Bryan said into the radio, which

Tata's long arm held up to his shoulder. "Does the approaching group have any ID badges?"

A grainy image was texted back to them, presumably from one of the cyborg's eye cameras. Ellie glanced over; it looked like two bears playing with a coat of arms.

"Missouri Citizens Militia?"

"It's a fairly well-organized private group," Mr. Perdix said, checking his database. "They'll certainly be aligned with the red-state forces. Unfortunately, they're not the actual Missouri State Defense Force, which is the much better-equipped state guard."

Since their lives depended on correctly identifying American factions, in the last few days, Ellie had become more politically savvy. "But Kansas and Missouri are both in sympathy with the red group, aren't they?"

"They are, but neither state is heavily populated," Mr. Perdix said. "There's too much garbage information coming over SIPRNet and internal Pentagon channels to be completely certain of anything, but I gather the blue-faction eastern states are trying to break through to the coast and form a land bridge through Illinois to Colorado, then Nevada, and finally California. Kansas City and I-70 is where both sides have massed for a confrontation."

Deafening airbursts of some kind of ordnance erupted high above them, rattling their windows and shaking loose dust from the concrete span of the highway overhead. The sonic boom rumbled on and seemed to be moving away.

"Break though? Land bridge?'" Ellie said, recalling research she had done for her books. "That sounds like a continent-wide battle between standing armies."

"I thought…" Senator Leota sat down in seat and slumped to the side. "I was hoping they were just fighting those things."

"No, ma'am," Sarge Bryan said, opening the cab door. "Call it civil war, the Boogaloo, or whatever, it's mos' definitely on. I'm going up. Uh, Tata, if these militia guys shoot me, please teach 'em that they shouldn't have done that."

"Oh, Sergeant, why you have to go out?" Tata said. "Send Ms. Sato. She is smaller target."

The Army man shut the door and waved a handkerchief in the direction of the oncoming motorcade.

"Komandir," Tata said into her radio, "we are to not engage unless they are shooting first. But first one of these bear patrol people to raise a weapon at the brave Sergeant Bryan... *ogon' po zhelaniyu!*"

Ellie couldn't believe her friend was just walking out by himself.

Ms. China agreed. "That's a trusting bloke."

"We're all on the same side," the senator said without much conviction. "We can end this madness."

Janice Jones came up beside Ellie and looked out; the militia group had formed a thin but formidable roadblock. By the dulling light of early evening, they watched a figure came forward.

"Well, Ms. Possible President-Elect," Janice said caustically, "what did you think would happen when you hyper-empowered the militarized interstate police EMAC and encouraged state National Guard elements to take orders from your joint blue-state seditionist command?"

"We were only trying to..."

"What? Hedge your bets in case the Supreme Court sided with us? You people call everyone who doesn't agree with every damn crazy thing you believe in crackers, Nazis, race traitors, and coons... You... Are you listening, Senator?"

Senator Leota was not. She slumped over and hit the floor.

"Damn!" Mr. Perdix said. "Where's her oximeter? She's going hypoxic."

The driver's-side door sprang open. "Hey, folks... uh?" Sarge Bryan saw the senator on the floor. "Aw, I turn my back for a minute."

"Heya, anything we can do to help?" asked a beefy round-faced fellow. He had hair and a beard that was like orange fringe circling his face in an unbroken line.

"This is Jeb, First Rifle of the Missouri Citizens Militia."

"Hi, Jeb," Ms. China said as she listened to the senator's breath sounds. "Your mates wouldn't happen to have a mobile CAT scanner, would you?"

Before she lost her license to practice for many understandable reasons, Ellie's former housemate had been a frontline trauma doctor with *Médecins Sans Frontières*.

Jeb returned a blank stare.

"How about something real pointy and hollow?" Ms. China asked while she bent over the stricken woman.

"We got some first-aid stuff. But no one's looked in it for a couple days, not since our medic got killed."

"Listen, Captain—" said Sarge.

"Jus' Jeb, please, Sergeant, I got OTHed out of the Army."

"Uh, sorry to hear that," Sarge Bryan said. Ellie could detect a note of caution in his voice. Did Jeb harbor resentment over how he was treated?

The local man shrugged his rounded, camo-covered shoulders. "Ma fault. Smokin' weed. Lame discharge was better than court martial. Let's get your gal fixed up... Say, she kinda looks familiar."

Some militia volunteers brought a stretcher, and Senator Leota was moved into the middle of the mobile camp the MCM had set up. Ellie looked around at the mix of civilian and secondhand military-style vehicles.

"You're investing yourselves in this location, Captain Jeb?" Ellie asked, just to be conversational.

"I'm what?"

"This is Ms. Sato," Sarge Bryan said helpfully. "She's an advisor from British intelligence."

"Hell you say? And I was hopin' we'd have all this mess snookered way before any foreigners found out and made even more fun of America."

"We're very discreet, we spies." Ellie hoped they wouldn't look her up and find out she owned a British tabloid. "We're an international effort here to lend any support we can during your troubles. Sergeant, do you think it's wise to leave the other Europeans out there? Jeb's group looks very hospitable."

"Right, good call."

If the Russians were discovered in their ambush positions, there was no telling what these irregular combatants might do.

"Jeb, you might want to give your people a heads-up, and not be alarmed." He tapped his handset.

"Alarmed, huh? It's way past that. Have you seen what's going on in the city— Whoa! Look a' that!"

Rodion, Zvena, and the OCEL came lumbering out of the trees just as Tata came out of the truck, which tilted and wobbled as it was relieved of her weight.

"Komandir Zvena and his tactical team are with us."

"Sure am glad," Jeb said, taking off his boonie hat and wiping his brow, which had started sweating despite the cold. "Look at the size of them honkers."

"Bobby!" a woman's voice yelled out. Everyone was a little surprised by the cyborgs, but thanks to Jeb's rapport with his people, no one pointed weapons as a small boy raced toward the OCEL robot.

"Can he play?" asked the boy, who was six or seven and pointing to the somewhat startled-looking mechanoid.

"Yes, he plays," Zvena said in the kindliest way he could while flashing a smile lined with gleaming blue-gray alligator teeth. "But first we must wash him. He is all dirty with… mud."

The OCEL reared up playfully and sloughed reddish muck, which was definitely not mud, off its scissor-like forelegs.

The boy's parents launched out from the crowd, grabbed their child, and returned to the RV parked on the roadside.

"You've got kind of a mixed group here," Sarge Bryan said.

"Our core members are all militia volunteers." Jeb pointed to the black smoke rising from the metropolitan area. "Before this, the most serious thing we ever did was help out when there was a flood or a fire."

Janice came over looking uncomfortable, but she accepted a mug of a hot thick brown liquid from one of Jeb's people. Looking at Sarge Bryan, she said, "You know, during and just after Civil War, the first one, it was not advisable to go into someone's camp without finding out which side they supported."

"Come to think on it, you look familiar too," Jeb said, squinting under his heavy ginger brows. "Are you in a reality show?"

"Yes, it's called Washington DC."

"What Ms. Jones means to ask is, we don't have any reason to be at odds, do we, Jeb?"

"None's I'm awares of. The Citizens Militia's on the side of Missouri. Now, if you'd all been EMAC people, things mighta got hairy pretty quickly."

A woman with hospital scrubs under her long dark-green fur-rimmed coat came up to them.

"Jeb, y'know who we got in there? It's President Leota."

"Possible President-Elect Leota," Janice corrected her. "And I'm the current lawful administration's chief of staff."

"Ain't that a thing with story attached," Jeb said, biting his chapped lip. "Pull up a chair and tell us."

Ellie mostly nodded and dozed as Sarge Bryan and Janice told Jeb and a few of his deputies about the failed summit between the two warring factions. They left out all mention of the Pangeans and how the plague was being spread.

"We all got shelter-in-place orders on the pandemic warning system," a militia member with a shaved head and full black beard said. "In a way, that saved our asses. The contagious crap was all in the city; we're all in the burbs. When there were no more updates, we decided to rally at Jeb's farm. Seemed better than being picked off one by one."

"Have you folks seen anything, uh, highly unusual?" Mr. Perdix asked as he joined them. Perhaps out of hygiene concerns, he was sticking to eating from their own stores, slurping noodles out of a self-heating MRE pouch.

The lady in scrubs looked at the JASON man with suspicion. "You mean like people we used to know going on a rampage and not dying when you shoot them?"

Mr. Perdix coughed on a ramen noodle, which seemed to have gone down the wrong way.

"That ain't the half of it," Jeb said. "We seen some of those, but the EMAC stormtroopers were corralling most of them before they could get too far."

"Corralling is meaning not destroying?" Zvena asked, his deep bass voice reminding Ellie that they were not sitting beside a tree trunk dressed in an oilcloth greatcoat.

"We thought they got some kinda treatment. They were lassoing them and using less-lethal devices to capture them."

Above them, behind the darkening tree line, Ellie heard a whooshing sound similar to noises she'd heard in the air above war zones she'd previously visited. There was no telling if it was close or far.

"Taking infected prisoners… This is quite dangerous, as Rodya can verify." Zvena's fist pounded on his mutilated friend's shoulder.

"What do they do with them?" Janice asked. "Mr. Perdix, is there any organized effort to study the A/P-32 pathogen?"

"Other than at Sprünger Labs? None I'm aware of," the government scientist said after quickly checking his live data feed.

"How's the senator?" Ellie asked. There was nearly zero chance Leota had come down with the illness, but it might manifest in peculiar ways inside vaccinated people, as she could verify.

"Breathing on her own, thanks to me," Ms. China said, walking up to their group while stripping off rubber gloves lightly smeared with blood.

"Wonderful," Mr. Perdix said. "Now to even the scales, you only have to save the lives of about nine hundred thousand more people."

"Komandir, if you and your people don't mind," Sarge Bryan said, in an effort to get people doing something useful instead of quarrelling. "Could you run a perimeter sweep with Jeb's people? Ms. Jones, could you coordinate an inventory list of what we have that the militia might need? Ms. China and Mr. Perdix, see if anyone needs medical assistance."

"I'll do that, and if anyone needs a cloned tail, I'll let Al know." Ms. China took a box of medical supplies away from Mr. Perdix and walked off.

A fixed smile etched across Jeb's face under his small but rather merry eyes. The whole effect made him look like a ginger Santa Claus.

"Is that lady quite… and what did she mean by 'grow a tail'?"

Mr. Perdix shook his head. "If she gives you any trouble or tries to euthanize someone with a sprained ankle, please let us know."

Jeb's people had unfolded a canopy form the side of his group's largest recreational vehicle. It formed his command post.

"Oh, man, is that a real samovar?" Jeb asked, looking in their truck as they walked past.

"The English model," Ellie said. "Should I bring it?"

It turned out many of Jeb's people had come to the Midwest from Russia and Eastern Europe.

"These things are great," he enthused. "No open flame, and we don't run down our batteries."

The selection of beverage containers was suitably rough and ready. They were mostly mugs plastered with slogans like "MAGA" and the recipe for a "Cup of Fuckoffee" which was an obscene limerick that did not rhyme.

"Damn, that's a right brew," Jeb said, emptying as much honey into his mug as there was samovar tea. "To answer you, Sergeant, we're on our way to a place up the road. You'll understand me not giving out the exact location. Along the ways, we met with two National Guard units. One of 'em was local, th'other outta Texas."

Jeb took a big knife out of his ankle sheath and sketched out an outline map of the area.

"The local boys were staying out of it. The Texans were definitely federalized and goin' with that program. Both were naturally circumspect about their operational activities, but they let us pass."

His tea and breath steaming in the cooling evening air, Jeb arranged himself more comfortably in his folding lawn chair. At the sound of some commotion down the road, he sat bolt upright, then relaxed when Sarge Bryan's radio squawked.

"Three stage-one infected neutralized without firearms," Zvena reported. "I send Rodya back to give a report to our local allies."

Jeb motioned back to his area map. "I think the EMACs are on their back foot. They didn't get the support they thought they'd get. Mos' of 'em are stormtroopers from Chicago. They're used to kicking in doors of people violating curfews or sayin' the wrong thing online or some such shit."

Ellie immediately suspected the militiaman was taking the EMAC forces a bit lightly. They were probably a militarized police like Israel's Shin Bet or President Rapace's Pangean forces.

"Anyway, the EMACs are about to have their gooses cooked. From what I gather, the federal forces are massing here." He made an X in the ground. "At Lee's Summit. The EMACs got themselves boxed in with their back to the river and all the bridges blowed up."

Jeb drew a squiggly line, which Ellie assumed represented the Missouri River, and a capital "A" for the anti-federalist forces that probably stood for something rude.

"They made a mistake stickin' to the city. Air cover is pretty much a wash. No one has the advantage. EMACs got enough portable SAMs so that helicopters and lower flyers can't get in. But the feds got the high ground and open lines of resupply to the south.

"It's just a matter of time before they get their rebel clocks cleaned, but who knows how many people those nutjobs will take with them, so we're getting clear. The EMACs are not really a big-time combat force, more like an up-armored SWAT team. Though they are pretty damn sneaky, I'll give 'em that."

Before Sarge Bryan could thank Jeb for his detailed insights, dozens of places along the road on either side of the militia's vehicles seemed to erupt, as though small trees had burst out of the bare ground and asphalt.

Everyone reached for weapons as gravel showered down, along with smoke that smelled like the fumes Ellie had encountered when their plane pods landed.

The steel tubes that appeared all around them had not come up—they had come down. They had fallen silently from the sky, and at the last moment, fired landing thrusters. Out of each one came three heavily armed black-uniformed troopers.

"Don't, Jeb!" Sarge Bryan cautioned, quickly assessing their situation as hopeless. "They've got machine guns at the perimeter. If you shoot, all your people will be cut to pieces."

A trooper with red-painted epaulettes and a black face mask walked up to them. His armband had a stylized "A" with the middle bar of the letter made up of two hands shaking. Below this were the letters: *EMAC*.

70

NEAR KANSAS CITY

The EMAC forces had dropped without warning down out of the evening sky. They leaped out of their lander pods and surrounded the militia before anyone could react.

A medium-sized man led them. He had hairy Popeye-sized forearms and a pockmarked nose. His Stalin moustache, flecked with gray, was threatening to become a goatee and would have been more suited to a crab fisherman.

Five minutes after their group was captured, he introduced himself, and Comrade Colonel Hidalgo left no doubt why he had risen high in the ranks of the blue-state rebels. Within that short span of time, he decapitated a man and started enthusiastically torturing Senator Leota.

The EMAC strike team had arrived without either Sarge Bryan or the cyborgs having any hint of warning. Their attack pods landed in clouds of rocket gasses and a hailstorm of road gravel. It was all over before Ellie stopped shielding her face. Shrieks came from the civilians among the Missouri militia, and Jeb's startled expression turned his eyes and mouth into three O's surrounded by a wreath of ginger hair under his boonie hat.

"Guns down," Jeb yelled. "They've got the drop on us."

"Right, you Nazi scum, put 'em down or we'll waste these white supremacist pigs," an EMAC with a dark face visor had yelled as he aimed a machinegun at the trailers containing the families.

"Fucking fanatic traitors," an older black Missouri militiaman said in disgust as he flung his weapon down.

Ellie kneeled down with her hands on top of her head. It soon became obvious the EMAC had been using their devious surveillance systems to spy on them for some time. They knew the layout of the militia's trailers and immediately separated the fighting men and women from their weapons, took the young and elderly hostage. They even knew practically everyone who was in Ellie's group, including the cyborgs.

"You mecco-ape fascists, give it up or suck on this LAW rocket!" was the first thing yelled by the apparent leader. The brute who would introduce himself as Hidalgo had an angry rainbow-colored eagle stenciled above his "A" insignia.

Under threat from a shoulder-launched green tube, the looming Russians exchanged glances and, Ellie suspected, hasty text messages. Zvena smiled, revealing most of his blue-black ceramic teeth, and said, "At this range, the detonation of an N72 antitank rocket would cause extreme collateral damage. We are diplomats of the Russian Federation and have no interest in assisting your suicidal intentions. We stand down."

That wasn't good enough for the EMACs. They wrapped Zvena, Tata, and Rodion up in insulated wire and led them to the landing pods. The pods were shaped like fountain-pen caps about nine feet tall and sat on smoldering circles. Each one was large enough to hold three humans in combat gear, so the Russians were each able to squeeze into one, then the clamshell doors slammed down.

"Electrify those shitbags," Hidalgo ordered.

"There's no way they're getting out of the wire and the pods, uh, sir," a squat EMAC soldier said.

"Comrade Soldier Gus, you may have a point." The leader tossed his rocket launcher to him. "Here, hold this."

Gus awkwardly bent forward and caught the LAW before it hit the ground. As he did so, Hidalgo unfurled a loop of nanowire and slipped it under Gus's helmet, above his chest armor. With hardly any effort at all, he cinched the noose closed. Gus dropped the launcher and started gurgling and twitching.

Ellie didn't have to look to imagine the micron-thin wire had cut the man's head nearly clean off, and Comrade Soldier Gus was dead on the spot.

"I am Comrade Colonel Hidalgo!" he said, tearing off his helmet. His round mustachioed face would not have looked out of place at a carnival or a farmers' market, except for flecks of spittle coming out from his mouth and the rage contorting his unremarkable features. "You, my soldiers, are the tip of the EMAC spear we have stabbed into the heart of the Fascist States of Nazi America. Because of my leadership, we are one step, one small step, away from finishing off the white supremacists forever. See what happens to traitors who repeatedly question orders and think they know better. Take a good look."

The corpse of Gus, which lay on the frost-covered ground, was not very impressive or instructive. Of course it chilled Ellie to the bone—anyone who would use lethal discipline like that on his own comrade soldiers would not hesitate to execute all of them—yet as Ellie was pushed to her knees and the sharp edges of uneven asphalt dug into her swollen knee joints, she also sensed something was off. In a blood-splattered and psychotic way, Hidalgo put her in mind of a fashion designer who insisted his fall collection was ready for the big show but had finished only two dresses.

"Comrade Colonel!" An EMAC came running up. "They've got the president here."

"What are you talking about?" Hidalgo said as he watched his squad attach electrical cables to the drop pods containing the cyborgs. "Julien is in hiding. You're seeing things."

"Not him, Leota."

A frost cloud of hissing breath escaped Hidalgo's lips, glistening with saliva. "Show me."

The EMAC stood started back to the medical tent, and the colonel grabbed the man's webbing belt.

"Bring her here," Hidalgo snapped. "I'm not taking my eyes off these counter-revolutionary assholes. Something is going on." His beady agate eyes swept over Ellie, Mr. Perdix, lingered on Ms. China, then finally settled on Sarge Bryan.

"You're that mutant skin shirt from the Army," he said. "You got a medal pinned on you by the fascist dictator Casteel. How did that feel? You're the same type of scum that would be proud to wear an Iron Cross handed out by Hitler himself, aren't you, you racist psychopath?"

Sarge Bryan looked at the smaller man steadily. "The medal wasn't pinned, it was on a ribbon, so it kind of draped—"

Hidalgo lunged to the side and slapped Ellie backhanded. She stumbled off her knees and landed sideways. She didn't really have time to register the new pain radiating from the area swelling above her cheekbone. All she could think was: *What did this toady brutalizer just do?* She landed a few inches from the dead EMAC's feet. Hidalgo was unhinged.

"See what I do?" Hidalgo said. "See? You piss me off, I hit or..." He drew his pistol. "I execute one of you racist scum."

He glanced at Ellie again. All she could think was that after all she'd been through, being shot by this yob would be so utterly... undignified.

"You, and you," Hidalgo said, pointing his gun's muzzle at Ms. China and Mr. Perdix, "we're still compiling files on. But militiaman, I have very good intelligence on you."

He rounded on Jeb, who was kneeling between two EMAC troopers.

"We've been watching you: John Ellis "Jeb" McIntyre, brigade leader of the Citizens Militia, financial supporter of the Loud Boys. He secretly watches Tucker Carlson's fascist broadcasts over a VPN and has downloaded Louder with Crowder podcasts, which those depraved Blaze TV degenerate animals are still broadcasting from inside the Ethiopian embassy in Moscow."

Hidalgo drew his pistol from a holster strapped to the front of his jet-black body armor. Ellie could tell he was working himself into a frenzy, yearning to do something terrible.

"One of his emails even appears on the mailing list of the ultra-fascist deceiver Alex Jones. Jeb, you are a Nazi we can do without."

He prepared to fire a bullet into the top of Jeb's head.

"Stop!" a wheezing but commanding voice shouted.

The EMACs had dragged Senator Leota up to the makeshift command post.

"You don't give orders. I give orders," Hidalgo said, but instead of shooting the bound and helpless Jeb, he holstered his weapon and grabbed Leota with both hands. As he did so, a ring of keys on a lanyard fell out from his pocket and jingled. "Where is Julien?"

"What do you—"

"You puppet slut." Hidalgo grabbed the senator's face and held it inches from his own. "He was the real visionary. He was the one who finally saw what our revolution could be. Not just tearing down statues, burning down courthouses and police stations even with the oppressors inside. Those were just drops in the bottomless bucket of American oppression. Julien and I, we are making history."

"Julien Sprünger, yeah, well…" the politician started to say while trying to keep the man's spraying saliva away from her. Because her arms were firmly in Hidalgo's grip, she was reduced to angling her head to the side. "He is history."

Hidalgo stood there, a small tremor rolling through his body.

"But he… you wouldn't have assassinated him without getting… Tell me, where is it?"

Hidalgo started ripping open the pockets of Leota's borrowed field jacket. Whatever he was looking for, he did not find, but his efforts did reveal the chest tube Ms. China had inserted to reinflate the injured woman's lungs.

"You fuckup," Leota said, taking the intrusion personally. "Get me a radio and let me arrange a truce before more Americans die."

"Do what?" Hidalgo shrieked. "I don't want to believe it, but I see it now. Somehow you've killed Julien. You're a true whore of the patriarchy, you race traitor, you subhuman Nazi."

His hands dove into a medical pouch hanging from the belt of a trooper, and he brought out a fat syringe. With a dirty forefinger, he tapped Leota's ventilation tube.

"I know what this is. Let's see what happens when I do… this." He sucked up air into the syringe and injected it into the tube, then pinched it off so no air could escape.

The senator immediately crumpled and started making short, painful gagging noises.

"This is better than waterboarding. No mess, and I can watch your face."

Hidalgo followed her down, sinking to one knee, the ring holding a dozen keys and data USBs jingled some more, like an accessory to some hideous jester's outfit.

Hidalgo studied the suffering woman as her eyes rolled back in her head. "You tell me... with your next breath, you tell me."

Leota started to shudder uncontrollably. Yellow-and-pink froth tried to get out through her chest tube, and Hidalgo clamped down harder. There was a movement to Ellie's right. Mr. Perdix slowly rose up from his knees and took a step forward.

"Kill her if you must," the JASON man said. "She can't tell you what you want to know. I can."

"Who's that?" Hidalgo demanded, not turning away from the agony he was enjoying.

"This pale fuck? He's some kind of Pentagon scientist," said a visor-wearing EMAC. "Facial-recognition scan confirms Aloysius Perdix, PhD, no known political affiliation, high-ranked e-sports gamer, earned full scholarship to MIT playing *Road Rage Cataclysm* online, no known pornography preference profile, probable regressive deviant."

"What can you know, Aloysius?"

"Only what Julien told me before he was incinerated inside his pharmaceutical factory," Mr. Perdix said deliberately. "The EMAC have a W33 artillery warhead and are having trouble assembling the two halves."

At the mention of the W33, Hidalgo let go of Leota's tube. It gurgled and expelled some frothy chest cavity juice. The half-unconscious woman took increasingly deeper breaths.

"I'm Mr. Perdix, from the JASON Group. I've got what you want."

71

OUTSIDE KANSAS CITY

Before Hidalgo could reply to Mr. Perdix's offer or renew his sadistic attack on Senator Leota, two EMACs ran up. All Ellie could make out from their whispering was:

"...federal troops..."

"Collection point... nearly full"

Miss Aleph was curious and urged Ellie to put herself further in danger.

`"Get closer. I can't eavesdrop on Hidalgo from where you are."`

The violent ambush by the EMAC forces had caused Ellie to completely forget about the hearing aid deep in her ear. Hidalgo hissed off some orders to the men, who ran off, then there was commotion off the highway at the tree line.

A shout came from sixty yards down the dark road. "Movers at the perimeter!"

Two or three shots rang out.

"We got one beta and a half dozen alphas," the same voice reported.

Hidalgo cupped his hand to the radio transceiver on his chest. "Stop shouting, use comms. Destroy the beta and capture the rest."

"But, Comrade, sir, we're over capacity—"

"I heard you. We need all of them... Unless..." Hidalgo looked at Mr. Perdix and pointed to the guards behind them. "You two keep this group separate from the militia and under control. If they move a hair without your say-so, hog tie them. If anyone runs, kill 'em all except Perdix. I'm going to see what sort of mess is going on at the perimeter."

A very discouraged-looking Jeb was handcuffed and led away with the rest of his militia and the civilians. After again being professionally searched, Ellie, Sarge Bryan, Ms. China, Mr. Perdix, and Janice received the relative courtesy of being flex-cuffed with their hands in front, making it easier for the EMACs to tie them to each other. They were pushed down into sitting positions along the length of the militia RV trailer. Senator Leota lay on her back where Hidalgo had left her.

"Senator," Ms. China said, "if you're awake, try rolling on your side. It will relieve the pressure on your lungs."

With some effort, the stricken woman managed to cross her legs and get her upper body to roll sideways on the cold gravel. After taking a few breaths, she gave a weak but encouraging thumbs-up.

"Well," Ellie said, as though mumbling to herself as little puffs of frost escaped her lips into the cold air, "I suppose there's very little chance of anyone learning of our predicament. Even with friendly federal forces apparently quite near."

`"Shh. I'm trying to concentrate. You people have posed me a problem with a ridiculous number of floating variables."`

"I'm sorry..."

"What you sayin'?" A helmeted guard huffed his breath into Ellie's face as he bent down to check her hands were still securely bound.

"I was saying, we're sorry to have interrupted your revolution against the fascist states of America. How is it going, by the way? I'm a reporter with London's oldest newspaper the *Citizen-Juggernaut*."

"We know who you are, you capitalist piece of shit," the guard said, waving a gloved finger in her face. "You fucked up the fight against the racists in Europe, and before that, you took the side of the Jew Zionist oppressors in the Middle East. Sometimes I think bipolar, biracial race traitors like you are worse than these supremacists." He looked at Janice and Sarge Bryan. "The overlords you worship don't even think you're human. Maybe a few years in re-education camps will help you understand the sufferings of the most vulnerable and downtrodden."

"And if that doesn't work, they can be the guillotined live on TikTok," said another EMAC. "We should have a contest to see how many Nazis we can decapitate in fifteen seconds."

"ISIS much, assholes?" Sarge Bryan couldn't help saying.

It earned him a sidekick to the chest from the second guard.

"Stop that," the other guard said. "Can't you see he's been programmed by the system? Who knows what software they put into his head along with those spooky eyes."

"I guess," the first one said, looking left and right. "I know it's not the official line, but... you think the white Jews, the cabal, are behind the feds?"

"Fuck yeah. Them kikes control everything 'cept what we're building here. Did you notice things started getting better for us once imperialist colonial Israel got fucked up? Took the evil kabbalah eye's attention off us just long enough."

"Lucky."

Ellie hadn't heard so much putrid nonsense since she stopped watching the BBC.

As soon as Hidalgo arrived at the tree line, the activity there became more organized. One incoming infected ran toward the EMAC line, and it was shot several times before it changed course and tried climbing into a militia truck. That had to be a Stage Two infected, Ellie thought. Hidalgo's EMAC called them betas.

Several shotgun blasts later, it was down and being doused with flammable liquid that flared in the dark as it burned.

Jeb had said the EMAC was essentially a glorified combination SWAT and Stasi, a militarized surveillance force. What they lacked in capacity for large-scale warfare, they seemed to make up for in crowd-control tactics. Using tasers and electrified lassos that flashed sparks, they herded the Stage Ones, which they called alphas, into a small zone, then launched a pneumatic-propelled net, similar one used for capturing wild beasts, over them. An EMAC transport truck hauled them off.

"Hope everyone's mask has a good seal," one of their guards said. "I don't want to have to put down any more of our own guys."

It seemed they were familiar with how the contagion was transmitted, but they were still taking stage-one infected as prisoners. What were they doing with them? They couldn't need them all for experimentation. Ellie noticed her handbag lay only a few feet away. Miss Aleph might be able to make a wireless connection from her handset to Sarge Bryan's eyes.

"That's an interesting sight, for *anyone* who can see it."

This time her utterance got no attention from the guards, who were more concerned over whether any of their comrades had inhaled A/P-32 spores. One of the guards did look back at her and grinned before running off to an EMAC Humvee.

"If you must know, I am getting some video feed through Bryan's optics. The connection's lousy, but I'm dealing. The EMAC are taking infected to a large sports stadium in the middle of Kansas City.

"And before you invite more corporal punishment by whispering, which might cause my earpiece to be knocked out: No, I cannot communicate with the federal forces at Lee's Summit. There have been too many deep-fake incidents. They keep scrambling all their communications faster than even I can hack the encryptions."

A stadium... full of those...? Do they think they can save them? Ellie thought. She doubted the Comrade Colonel Hidalgo was the savior type.

"Nothing to do but wait, then," Ellie said in a low singsong voice.

Ms. China and Mr. Perdix glanced at her.

"If she loses it, we'll just say we found her on the road," Ms. China suggested, rather unethically.

"I don't think they'll buy that," Mr. Perdix said, tilting his head to Sarge Bryan, who nodded. "These EMAC have a sophisticated surveillance web, like the North Korean internal security services. They have micro-stealth drones and directional microphones effective at hundreds of meters. Who knows how long they were surveilling us before they finally decided to move in."

"Wait until he runs into the real Army," Sarge Bryan growled. "Comrade Colonel Nutsack."

The spot where they were being held was inside a halo of arc lights. Ellie looked over to where the light faded out. A persistent hum came from the high-tension wires attached to the landing pods that now held the cyborgs prisoner. One of the pods let out sparks, followed by muffled cursing in Russian. Hidalgo noticed as he strode back over to them.

"We're moving out," he said to the guards watching them. "Any captured vehicles we don't need, disable them. The militia people are going to the stadium. And those mechanical fascist freaks, open up the pods and destroy them. They're too dangerous to just leave here."

Zvena, Rodion, and Tata, Ellie thought. They were helpless and being slowly electrocuted. Ellie had to say something.

"Sir, uh, Comrade Colonel, are you certain you want to that?"

"What?"

The way he spoke, all coiled and tense like a very mean dog looking for an excuse to bite, made Ellie pause. Then she continued, carefully.

"You see, sir, the things is, if you blue people are going to have your own nation apart from the terrible fascists, then you'll need international allies. Allies like China and Russia, perhaps.

"Remember, Mr. Putin was very supportive of the Venezuelan government when the whole world questioned their ideas on how to implement socialism." By literally starving millions of people to death in that formerly wealthy country, but Ellie decided not to say that. "I happen to know that these cyborgs are on very good terms with Russia's leadership. You may want to reconsider before you burn those bridges."

Ellie thought she had sounded very calming and erudite. Then the short, squat toady Hidalgo wound up and kicked her in the groin.

She managed to block part of the black-booted blow with her bound hands, at the cost of a sprained wrist and fingers, but the pain was uniquely heinous and unexpected.

"You privileged cunt." More spittle came out of Hidalgo's mouth as he drew back, deciding where to kick her next. "You fucking imperialists are all going down. When we finish with Washington, our wave is going to sweep the world. Not one scrap of the Nazi-style oppression will survive to breed like lice on the backs of kike Jew rats. If Putin knows what's good for him, he'll hide in his bunker and blow his fucking brains out."

At that point, Hidalgo went on about one of his ancestors being a sharecropper or a sugar plantation worker, but Ellie didn't hear very much, as she was still dealing with the waves of pain radiating up from her groin. Beside her, electrified batons whirled and struck the others. Sarge Bryan, Mr. Perdix, and even Ms. China were drubbed back into place when they tried to assist her.

"…all you racists and white supremacists are better off pouring gas over yourselves and lighting up. Everyone too cowardly to do that will be put in work camps to make reparations to the hundreds of generations you've destroyed, chained, and bull-whipped until maggots ate the bodies of people of color all for the sake of your money-worshipping fake religions."

For a moment, Hidalgo stood there panting. He seemed to have an endless torrent of loony leftist dogma to spew, then one of his men reminded him his revolution was still a work in progress.

"Right. Get these prisoners into the command trailer and kill those Russians." He stormed off.

A group of EMACs picked them up, searched them again, and prepared to lead them away. Ellie watched helplessly as two others decided how best to murder the helpless cyborgs.

"No. Stop," one helmeted thug scolded another. "You can't just shoot the pods. They're titanium. You might set off the rest of the solid booster fuel inside. I'm surprised the voltage hasn't cooked it off yet."

"What do we do?"

"Detach the cables, then we clear away and blast them with the LAWs," the first fellow said. "One armor-piercing rocket each, then we burn what's left."

An EMAC with thick insulated gloves took down the high-tension cables.

Get out of there. You're bloody cyborgs, the electricity's off, Ellie willed her allies to at least try to escape.

The pods remained stationary and sealed tight. An EMAC with a rocket launcher waited until the closest Humvees were driven away, then he popped open the tubular telescoping weapon and sighted in on the nearest landing pod. With no warning, the ignition of the pod rocket thrusters threw him backward. All three cigar-shaped metal capsules blasted skyward.

The EMAC in charge pushed the stumbling man aside, grabbed the launcher, and fired up at the pods. The deadly rocket sped off into the night. Its small red flame arced wide, missing the blue thrusters of the three pods as they climbed hundreds, then thousands of feet.

"They'll crash," the lead EMAC said, perhaps fearing Hidalgo's reaction to this failure to execute the prisoners. "Forget about them."

Ellie was bent over double and trying to keep her painful breathing as shallow as possible. She stole a last glance upward. Maybe the Russians would crash. If not, perhaps they'd had enough of America and would return to Moscow to await the outcome of America's second civil war. Either way, Ellie felt a small victory had been achieved at the sight of the three pinpricks of light climbing into the night sky.

72

Comrade Colonel Hidalgo flew into yet another rage at the sight of the three rocket exhaust trails disappearing into the night sky.

"Get the Patriot SAMs on them! Kill those cyborgs!" he yelled.

Ellie craned her neck to keep the glorious sight of the escaping Russians in view. A female EMAC with a cluster of communication devices shook her head.

"Our landers are stealth-enabled with countermeasures," she said. "No way to get a radar lock. They'll probably crash miles from here, Comrade Colonel, sir."

"That's not the point." Hidalgo grabbed the startled woman. "We only got this far by orders being carried..." He looked up at the empty sky. The moon blazed down silently, and his grip slackened. "You two report to Comrade Sergeant Duggan for discipline. I should send you to the stadium."

Hidalgo dismissed the disgraced men and turned to the woman. "You, Comrade Corporal, are now in charge of the prisoner detail. Make sure you wipe all digital records for the past fifteen minutes, especially what that one said." He indicated Mr. Perdix, who didn't look surprised. Rather, to Ellie, he looked like someone steeling himself for an ordeal.

Vehicles belonging to the Citizens Militia, which the EMAC did not need, were driven off the road and disabled with gunfire or small explosions. Ellie and the others were marched toward a long trailer that looked like an armored interstate moving truck. Sporadic sounds of distant fighting came from downtown Kansas City.

From what she gathered, the friendly forces—those still taking orders from Janice's boss in Washington—were at a place called Lee's Summit. They had the EMACs backed up against a big river. Hidalgo did not appear defeated, quite the opposite. He was up to something.

Hrrch. `"Crappy phone... need... out range..."`

Ellie winced as a burst of static reverberated through her head. With all the physical abuse and attempted murder going on, it was easy to forget the hearing aid in her ear was tethered to her handset. The wireless connection must be at the limit of its range. She had to do something. The Israeli-made AI was the only one of them free to act and possibly help them escape.

"Ah, sir, I mean Miss…" Ellie said, raising her bound hands.

The woman with the communications equipment spun around. "I'm a sergeant, and my pronoun is 'zher,' you deluded sexist capitalist animal. What do you want?"

"Ah… Sergeant, zher, uh, our things back there."

"What about them?"

"We collected items… from the chemical plant, before it was blown up, and I'm not sure you got all the vaccine vials. So it would be a good idea—"

"Enough." She sent an EMAC back with a duffel bag to get the rest of their belongings. "Pick that crap up, it may have intel Comrade Colonel needs. Just don't let them touch it."

`"Nice save, Eleanor,"` Miss Aleph said when her handset was close enough. `"However, you're at sixteen percent battery, and there's only so much more I can do to save power."`

"Always something," Ellie said barely audibly.

"On the plus side, if America is destroyed in a convulsion of pent-up burning hatred and fanaticism, I'll be fine. I'm in Monaco right now. The weather's great. My robots are taking the yacht out later, and I'm going to try out a new jet ski I just had delivered…"

"Just mind your battery charge and get us out of here," Ellie said through clenched teeth.

Before being pushed into EMAC command center trailer, they were all searched again. For a nervy moment, they even ruffled Ellie's hair, looking for who knew what, which made her glad her earpiece was wedged in deep. The trailer had been cleared out to make a holding cell—Senator Leota was already inside.

"Let's see what those ham-fisted butchers have done with my thoracic catheter," Ms. China said, stepping forward to examine her patient.

Ellie sat down on a bench next to Mr. Perdix. Sarge Bryan tried to give her a reassuring smile which turned out more like a tense grimace. Could Zvena and the cyborgs land their pods safely and help them? The EMACs were obviously on the move. Would they even know how to find them again in the battle zone this area of the country had become? Ellie decided they could not count on their help. The Russians were foreigners, and even nominally friendly federal forces were likely to shoot at them.

Their armored EMAC trailer rumbled off. What had become of Jeb and his people? Many of them were the families of militia members. Was Hidalgo going to throw them into a collection center with infected? It was obvious the man would stop at nothing to achieve his twisted goals or cause as much harm as he could trying.

Sarge Bryan's eyes slowly scanned every inch of their confinement. An EMAC noticed and hit him on his closely shorn head with a rifle butt.

"Eyes down, cue ball."

While he was disoriented, they expertly cinched a blackout hood over his head. While they seemed very adept at prisoner control, Ellie at that instant felt very eager to see the EMACs in actual combat against real soldiers.

The next thing Ellie knew, she was jolted awake. She reached up with her bound hands just in time to keep from toppling off her seat. Maybe she had dozed off in spite of her determination not to. They seemed not to have traveled very far. She thought about asking Miss Aleph where they were, then decided that might run down the handset's battery.

The first thing she noticed that was different was Ms. China's lower leg had been detached and tossed onto one of the shelves overhead. While disconnecting the talented killer's prosthesis, their EMAC guards had also ripped out her long fingernails, presumably with pliers. Her fingertips were oozing blood into oily rags, and her six pupils were staring straight ahead at nothing. She hadn't made a sound during what must have been a very painful assault.

Janice Jones seemed the most distressed, judging by her body language. The president's chief of staff was sitting upright, her body tense and her face pensive. Senator Leota, on the other hand, was sitting up with a bit more color in her tanned cheeks.

Ellie had to do something. While the guards seemed occupied with looking out through a small round window, she tried to get the senator's attention.

"You were in the military, right, Senator?" She hoped the rumbling of the engine would cover the sound of their whispering. "Can you reason with…" Clearly not with Hidalgo. "With someone in amongst the EMAC?"

"Reason?" the senator wheezed way too loudly, rather more angry than afraid of being heard. "Everyone conspiring—*heff*—with Julien will be charged with treason and lined up against a—" Leota braced herself as a blow landed with a *thwap*.

The apparently inattentive guard must have been shamming not watching, waiting to see what they would do. He fired a taser, striking the politician in the thigh, the tines penetrating her navy-blue slacks. He did not, however, activate the electric charge.

"No talking."

Having made his point, he yanked on the wires, pulling the barbed prongs back out like fishhooks, and they automatically reeled back into the wrist-mounted device. Leota gave the thug a disgusted look and pressed her hand onto the dribble of blood that came oozing out from the twin wounds.

The truck stopped, and a large hatch at the rear end of their compartment split open and lowered. It formed a ramp down to a paved roadway. Cool night air replaced the steamy stagnant air in their detention area, and so did certain scents. Beneath the diesel fumes and road dust, Ellie caught whiffs of food smells similar to those wafting out of a downtown London food court. In addition to making her realize she hadn't eaten for many hours and was quite hungry, she concluded they had arrived at a base camp or staging point this EMAC group had set up. They must be in the middle of hundreds or thousands of these militarized woke lunatics.

A moment later, Hidalgo, the wokest swine of all, stood there backlit by red and yellow lights. Looking at the sky behind him, Ellie also had the impression they were under some type of camouflage canopy. Without preamble, two soldiers rolled an oblong object in on a heavy-duty dolly. On its bed were two objects mostly covered by a green tarp.

Janice seemed transfixed by the sight as it was wheeled in. The casters squeaked and rattled over the metal floor of their compartment until it was in their midst. Mr. Perdix seemed mildly interested but not surprised. The senator looked down to see whether the wounds in her leg had stopped bleeding.

With a flourishing motion suited to a carnival exhibitor revealing an especially grotesque freak, Hidalgo ripped away the canopy.

"There," he said, throwing the dusty material out the door and marching toward them. "This is how we win our Gettysburg. This is the gateway to an America no longer enslaved by whiteness and the obscene Constitution written by the masters in the blood of their own chattel slaves."

"Really? To me it looks like the W33 warhead we discussed earlier," Mr. Perdix said, coolly eyeing the object. "The strategic field munition is designed to be stored and transported in two halves, then put together just before being loaded into a howitzer cannon. All W33s and similar weapons were supposed to have been deactivated under the arms control agreements signed in the 1990s."

"Our revolution has been lying in wait for a long time," Hidalgo said with a self-satisfied grin. "Without American weapons like this, do you think evil racist genocidal Europe could have resisted Stalin's socialism? Without America supporting fascistic genocide the world over, do you think capitalism would have lasted hundreds of years after Marxist-Leninism proved it had become obsolete?"

He ran a hand over the artillery shell's smooth exterior. "We have other ways, but this is the cleanest. Once the army of the legacy slave owners is gone, and they see our willingness... No, fuck that, our *eagerness* to use ultimate weapons for ultimate justice and equality, the racists will all bend the knee and submit to well-earned punishment."

Ellie saw that the weapon indeed had two halves. The top part was a foreshortened cone, and the second part was a cylinder. Both were about eight inches in diameter but loomed larger in Ellie's mind when she realized this was an atomic device.

"We've entered the arming codes in the top part," Hidalgo said. "But joining the two halves requires another code."

"Oh, yes," Mr. Perdix said in a way an Oxford lecturer might acknowledge some arcane point about Byzantine artwork. "The failsafe. These devices were intended to beat back Warsaw Pact tank columns in a European theatre engagement. Once the arming codes were entered, there was a final step required in order to join the two halves, a step which would be completed just before the warhead was fired. In the event the artillery position was overrun, it would not be possible for the enemy to use it against NATO forces."

Hidalgo bent forward and held up a flashlight. The LED beam revealed two rings of spiky glass nodules in each of the halves of the W33 where they were supposed to join. They glistened like diamond shark teeth.

"A locking code has to be entered and entered correctly," Hidalgo said, "or else these glass bits will break off, turning the damn thing into two hundred pounds of useless radioactive scrap metal."

For a second, Ellie thought Hidalgo was going to hit the bomb with his fist. Then he relented and merely patted the green metal shell.

"And you, Perdix, are going to give me the final code."

"What makes you think I know it?"

"You knew we had this exact weapon. You only could have known that by speaking to Julien, perhaps torturing the information out of him. Give it up, or you and your friends will get much, much worse."

"You fuckups," Janice said, her voice cutting across the growing tension in a rather discomforting way. "Julien was Deep State Antifa. They gave you lowlife EMACs the bomb but not all the codes because they don't trust you."

"You skanky bed wench coon." Hidalgo showed every sign of wanting to hit Janice, but the space was too confined, and he was wary of stepping over the W33. "One more word out of the race traitor and I'll taser you all until your blood boils."

"That does pose you a problem," Mr. Perdix continued as though no one had said anything. "I don't have the codes you want."

"Are you sure? Maybe you are not listening."

Hidalgo was closest to where Mr. Perdix was sitting. Ellie didn't even see the knife in his hand and only heard a "hwrrk" sound that erupted from the JSAON scientist as the horrible thug came away with his right ear. Disoriented, Mr. Perdix put his bound hands up to his terrible wound.

"Well, how about now?"

Sarge Bryan sat bolt upright. Could his cybernetic eyes see what was going on even through the blackout hood?

Hidalgo laughed. "You know how stupid you look? Here, let's even you out."

The knife flashed again. Off came Mr. Perdix's other ear. Blood sprayed freely from the earhole.

"Now, my pale friend, you look like those dumb potatoes, the yellow ones, what are they called?"

"Yukon gold?" offered one of the other EMACs, clearly amused by the dismemberment of the prisoner.

"That's them. I hate them. So, Potato Head, what you say now?"

Mr. Perdix, with some stoic effort on his part, twisted his head around like a person hard of hearing would. "I'm sorry, I didn't quite catch that."

Hidalgo threw the two ears into the mutilated man's lap. "Well, maybe you catch this." He went over to the next person in the row. This, unfortunately, was Ellie.

"I'm pretty sure she doesn't have the codes…" Before she could even utter a sound, Hidalgo grabbed her hair and forced her head back, exposing her neck.

"Eleanor, you are my dearest fleshy friend. I cannot let them kill you. The information the EMAC want is part of the Israeli Pollard spy files in the archives of the Mossad. I have a copy. The unlocking

```
codes for all W33 devices of this design are the
activation codes in reverse order."
```

Ellie felt the blade touch the side of her neck. It was about the size of a box cutter, but as it moved across her field of vison, she noted it had a rather odious hook-blade design.

Now she has to tell me? Ellie thought wildly. If she spoke, she might save her own life, but how many others would die from the nuclear blast? What about after? What if Washington and the federal forces collapsed?

Then she thought about Miss Aleph's programming. Wasn't she programmed to protect fleshy people? Would she actually give up the real code if she knew it? If the codes turned out to be fake and the device seized up, Hidalgo would kill all of them in a rage anyway.

"Cat got your tongue?" Hidalgo breathed down on her. "Might as well because the rats will be eating it. Your lips too, you brainwashed tool."

Ellie felt the blade dig deeper into her neck; a trickle of wetness followed. She glanced up. Hidalgo wasn't looking at her or Mr. Perdix—his attention was on the EMACs by the doorway. Time seemed to slow down.

"We..."

"...got... it."

One of the EMACs said.

Got what? Ellie had time to think as Hidalgo, perhaps reluctantly, let her go.

"Let 'em hear," he said as her head drooped forward and she put the back of her wrist, which seemed the cleanest part of her hands, to her bleeding neck. There did not seem to be arterial spurts.

Suddenly she was hearing Miss Aleph's slightly electronic Israeli-accented voice again, but this time not just in her head, out loud and in the open from an EMAC handset.

```
"The unlocking codes for all W33 devices of this
design are the activation codes in reverse order."
```

"You useless... *Arrgh*," Hidalgo muttered and pushed Ellie's head away was though it were a thing not worth the effort to cut off. "We have the best surveillance systems to control and supervise citizens in the world, we keep a closer eye on hundreds of millions of Americans than they do in China or

North Korea. You think you can sneak an encrypted wireless signal past us?"

Losing interest in the prisoners, he turned to the W33.

Just then, with a guttural yell of pure rage, Janice Jones launched forward. In her hand was a metal plate she had worked free from her seat. Before Hidalgo or the EMACs could stop her, she took two steps and brought the makeshift implement down on the crystal shark's teeth on the top half of the bomb. They splintered and fell all over the floor. Without them, Hidalgo had said the bomb could never be activated.

Hidalgo stared at her.

Then he laughed. He grabbed a handful of Janice's hair, and it came undone, sending her curly black hair spilling all over her shoulders.

"You and your capitalist pig of a husband," Hidalgo said, reaching down to Mr. Perdix's lap with his free hand. "You'll eat anything. You feast on the rotting corpses of slave children thrown on the trash heap of third-world factories, billions of poor simple workers suffer, sicken, and because of you, each year they die by the millions for your profits. Eat! Eat what you've sown, you filthy oppressor bitch."

His right hand came away from Janice's head, tearing out a good chunk of scalp and afro hair. With both hands, he forced her mouth open and shoved Mr. Perdix's severed ears in. He forced her jaw closed and moved it side to side, grinding up the mess.

"Eat the wages of generations of exploitation... Eat, eat, EAT!"

73

EMAC COMMAND POST

Ellie felt ill watching Comrade Colonel Hidalgo force feed the pair of severed ears to Janice Jones. Miss Aleph had unwittingly told the EMACs the code to put the two halves of the small nuke together, but if Janice had deactivated the bomb and it was useless, why did Hidalgo look so pleased?

Before she could think much about that, four more EMACs burst in. Three of them thrust stun batons at Ellie, Sarge Bryan, and the others while the last one scanned them with a handheld device topped by an elaborate antenna.

The device paused in Ellie's direction. "It's her."

Oh, hashers.

"Search her... Everywhere. Probe every hidey-hole she has," the shrill and sadistic voice of a female EMAC said. "Open her sinus cavity if you have to."

At that point, there was no use trying to brazen things out and risk becoming another casualty in the war these awful people were waging on all civilized behavior.

"My ear, okay? It's in my ear."

Two EMACs grabbed her head.

"The other one," she said as gloved fingers started roughly probing inside the wrong one.

After a none-too-gentle invasion of her ear canal by an industrial-sized pair of tweezers, the hearing aid was pulled out.

"Comrade Colonel, sir, we got it."

Hidalgo was still squeezing Janice's mouth closed with a bemused look on his toad-like face. As Ellie shook her head from side to side to get rid of the feeling that part of her eardrum had been pulled out, again she wondered: Why was Hidalgo amused?

Sarge Bryan yelled from under his blackout hood, "Enough, Hidalgo, enough. You'll need Ms. Jones if you have any chance of talking terms with Washington. I can see she didn't damage anything. There're no gamma rays coming from the shell. This device right here in front of us is a fake."

He must have seen that as soon as they wheeled the thing in, even through the blackout hood. There was no way he could have known that Janice was going to try to disable it.

"Fuck jam!" the earless Mr. Perdix said quite loudly, like someone wearing headphones with the volume turned up. "I should have... That must be how your Deep State allies in the military stole the real one during the nuclear artillery shell deactivation program. The one they logged as destroyed was a fake like this. After that, you had access to all the spare parts from the genuine decommissioned devices you needed to maintain the one you took and hid for decades."

His subterfuge discovered, Hidalgo lost interest in throttling Janice. She dropped to the floor and coughed up bits of Mr. Perdix.

Hidalgo rushed over to Ellie. She braced herself for some new painful, inhuman indignity, but instead he grabbed the tongs holding the hearing aid.

"Who are you?" he demanded, looking at the small device. "Are the British working with the Zionist Mossad now? You dumb shits. When we finish with Washington, we're coming for all you Kabbalistic slave merchants. We'll finish what the Ninety-Six Hour War started, you fucking Islamophobic genocidal hebes!"

Hidalgo threw the earpiece down and crushed it.

"Check them all over again. This one." He stared at Ellie and addressed the EMACs. "This rat-faced mongrel servant of greed got that bug past our first scans. Anyone making a mistake like that will be shot on the spot."

Hidalgo stormed out of the truck trailer. What did he mean by calling her "rat-faced"? Ellie's outrage tempered her relief that the wicked, volatile man had left.

The EMACS subjected her to a period of intense, but thankfully not surgically invasive, scrutiny. Then they left Ellie and the others alone with the mock nuclear weapon. They put thick mesh netting over the entrance to lock them in while still being able to watch them. They didn't even taser Sarge Bryan when he removed the blackout hood from his head.

"Just gargle with some sports drink, but don't swallow, just spit," Ms. China told Janice as she examined the detritus on the floor. "There may be an earlobe unaccounted for."

Quite methodically, rather ingeniously, Ms. China reassembled the spit-covered pieces of Mr. Perdix's two ears in order to discover if any large pieces were missing.

"Al, it's just as well you didn't get piercings and studs during your midlife crisis."

"Did you say: 'suds in mitosis'?" Mr. Perdix was still speaking loudly. "I can't hear very well."

The guards outside laughed.

"Lower the volume, Grandpa," Ms. China said, taking a look at her ex's wounds and dabbing them with a small alcohol swab she had found. "This may sting."

"Ow!"

"How'd you know they had this type of bomb?" Sarge Bryan said. "Julien sure never told you."

Mr. Perdix thought a moment. "Oh, that, yes. I saw it from the keychain the colonel had. There was a special round orange-colored key with a device code prefix engraved that is unique to this artillery piece."

"So you pretended to know more than you did to keep him from killing Senator Leota," Ellie said.

"I knew if you were given proper motivation you could try being heroic, Al, even in a geeky way," Ms. China said. She then pursed her lips and blew clotted blood out of the poor man's ear canal.

It was probably the first nice thing Ellie had heard her say about Mr.

Perdix. He tilted his heard toward her and said, "Could you repeat that, Anna? I don't think I heard accurately."

"Now, Al, shake your head like a dog. No one will think it's funny."

He did, and Ms. China chuckled.

Sarge Bryan helped Janice back to her seat.

"Sorry, ma'am, I couldn't say anything. I thought if we played along, they might let on where the real W33 was."

Janice was furious—with Ellie. "How c-could you give them the last arming codes?"

Ellie didn't even know whether they were real or not. "Maybe it's a bluff and they won't work," she said hopefully.

Then the real W33 would be as useless as the inert model sitting in front of them.

"Not likely," Mr. Perdix said, diluted blood running down both of his cheeks. His voice was still elevated, but thanks to the rough-and-ready medical assistance, he seemed to be able to hear himself talk. "Decades back, the Israelis had a sophisticated spy network inside the DoD, the Pollard scandal. We have to assume the information is accurate. That type of platform-activation procedure matches those of other frontline atomics. There'd be no need for a separate code, and an NCO artilleryman could be trusted to set the device hot."

"What's the yield?" Senator Leota said from the back of the trailer. She was recovered enough to be sitting on the edge of her seat, still keeping her injured side braced, but her sharp dark eyes were studying the entrance, perhaps thinking of ways to escape. "How much damage?"

"Depends," Mr. Perdix said. "First off, has the device been properly maintained? Some models were loaded with a fissile payload, which were later found—"

"Ballpark," Janice cut him off.

"From Hiroshima sized, fifteen kilotons, to upwards of fifty Kt."

"If the federal forces are grouping up at Lee's Summit..."

"They'll be wiped out," the senator said. "It will be like the Army of the Potomac being extinguished at Gettysburg with one artillery shell."

Having delved more deeply than she had ever wanted into the sick and twisted minds of phenomenally ruthless people like Miri Drach and President Rapace, as well as various fashion magazine editors, Ellie was more keen than ever at trying to stay one step ahead of them. She glanced at the EMACs by the doorway; they were probably listening to everything anyway. There was no way to be subtle.

"But the federal forces in Washington, they still have control of more men and thousands of more weapons like this." She pointed at the fake bomb. "There's no point in them bluffing or using Janice or the senator to negotiate if they've only got… got one nuke…"

Sarge Bryan caught on, then the rest of them did.

"And we're the only ones who know that," Janice said.

The EMAC at the door held his hand against his helmet visor as though listening to a message through his headset. Then he nodded to the others, and they moved away, out of sight, taking a moment to give them a little wave while mouthing something like *"Bye bye, you fascist fucks."* The EMAC pressed a remote switch.

All of them, except Mr. Perdix, jumped when a clockwork mechanism underneath the fake bomb started beeping a countdown.

74

When one is captive in a confined space with a large bomb that turns out to be a fake bomb that turns out to be a real bomb, one tends to stare at it.

Ellie glared at the dolly holding the two halves of the mock W33. There was a puddle of sports drink spilled on the floor. It had an odd sheen to it, probably because it was mixed with motor oil and not an insubstantial amount of Mr. Perdix's blood. Something was flickering in it from underneath the dolly.

"Turn it over!" she yelled.

Sarge Bryan was at the exit, desperately trying to tear away the wire mesh across the back of the trailer, while also scanning for an escape hatch in the ceiling he might have missed.

Janice was nearest and helped Ellie lift the dolly. She braced herself for the feel of the sharp metal edges on her hands, but it turned out to be not that difficult to turn on its side. The fake artillery shell stayed strapped on to dolly's top as it tilted.

"Last-minute improvisation. They just stuck it on," Mr. Perdix whispered to himself as he leaned over the demolition charge.

Ellie took a quick look at the exit. Sarge had no luck dislodging the steel netting. There was no one standing outside; after activating the bomb, the guards had fled.

"It's one of ours," said the JASON man.

"Great," snapped Ms. China, who was also gazing unflinchingly at the blinking device. "It's probably a dud."

"No worries. We've got eleven seconds left." Mr. Perdix swayed on his feet. He was having issues balancing due to missing his ears.

"Eleven whole seconds," Ms. China yelled as she rushed over to the door mesh with her bandaged hands.

Sarge Bryan came away from the exit and steadied him. "How do we disarm it?"

"Could you put your thumb on that keypad? Gently."

Sarge Bryan did that. The pad was located beside the series of pulsing lights Ellie had noticed. The green ones were dark, and the device was blinking its way through the amber rectangles.

"Disarming is a bit tricky. We made sure to safeguard against hacking and tampering. Your thumb is on a biometric scanner coded to the DNA of authorized users. It will do five passes, but if it doesn't detect an authorized user, the countdown resumes. You can only do it once—if the same person tries again, it goes off right away."

"That swine Hidalgo must be an authorized user." Present circumstances caused Ellie's creative thinking into overdrive. "Is there anything he touched, anything with his DNA on it?"

The scanner slid a strobing light over Sarge Bryan's thumb for a fifth time, turned red, and the amber light started pulsing its countdown again.

10… 9…

"Get away," Ms. China said, pushing the albino solider back and placing her own thumb on the scanner. Again, the detonation sequence halted for a few precious seconds.

There was only Ellie, the senator, Janice, and Mr. Perdix to go. That was less than a bloody minute.

Ellie's bag was on the floor. Could Miss Aleph do something? She pulled the handset out and noticed the screen was dark—the battery had run down.

"Senator, you're up," Sarge said, supporting the injured woman as she took her turn.

Ellie cried out and covered her ears at a burst of sound. She thought the demolition charge had detonated. Instead, the noise turned out to be a burst of static. Every device that had a speaker, visible or hidden, inside their truck or outside, under the EMAC command center canopy, began blaring military-style music at the topmost volume. An Englishman's voice shouting "NO PRISONERS" was accompanied by an unholy squeal of screechy feedback.

Through the mesh blocking the way out, Ellie saw an EMAC stumble into view, holding his head and trying to take his helmet and earphones off. Then something hit him and spun him around. He jerked again and lay still.

Ellie thought quickly. "Does that fellow have key to this big padlock?"

Sarge Bryan tried to reach the downed man, but his arm fully outstretched was not long enough. Another EMAC with a gory hole right though his helmet had fallen on top of the first. More shots rang out.

"Can you see anything?" Janice yelled. "What's happening? Is it a rescue? The Russians?"

Ellie took her place behind Janice just as she pressed her finger on the biometric panel.

"USA friendly! Get us out of here!" Sarge Bryan shouted out into the dark.

The shooting settled down. The fighting seemed to be moving away down the road.

"Don't call that out too loud. Some of us Missourians still got a grudge 'gainst the Union," said a thickset man in camouflage gear. He had what looked like a Union Jack on his rifle, then Ellie recognized it as a Confederate flag. He peered into the trailer. "Missouri State Guard at your service, sir, ladies."

Sarge spoke quickly. "Bomb" and "get us the fuck out" was all Ellie could make out as she took her turn pressing her thumb firmly on the pad.

"Next time," Mr. Perdix said tensely, "we have to wipe the pad. It's getting grimy and might not register."

He did not have to say that twice. Senator Leota was second to last. Janice found a piece of clean cloth and held it ready.

The light strobed under Ellie's thumb. *Third pass, fourth...*

The men at the door tried to unhook the netting. It was heavy and stuck on something. Someone else pounded on the side door of the armored truck trailer.

Ellie's finger came off the biometric pad, and she quickly wiped the pad off with a patch of clean cloth, then Leota's rather delicate hand slapped down on the sinister device.

At the exit, Sarge and the Missouri guardsmen were hacking away at one corner of their enclosure with bolt cutters. Working frantically, they got a corner loose. Sarge Bryan grabbed Ellie's arm, and before she could say a word, he had pushed her through. Ms. China leapt out just behind her.

"Get to the side," Sarge Bryan called to her as he came out half carrying Senator Leota through the opening. "The truck is armored and can take the blast."

"That depends, Sergeant," Mr. Perdix said, studying the device quizzically. "We built these munitions to pack quite wallop."

Janice did not need help diving through the gap in the wire netting. That left Sarge holding the mesh open and Mr. Perdix standing over the detonator.

"C'mon, it's got a few seconds after you take your finger off."

"I'm afraid not," Mr. Perdix said. "I had to wipe the scanner again. We're at the last bar before it goes red. Leave, now!"

Ellie could tell Sarge Bryan briefly thought about diving in and pulling Mr. Perdix to safety. If he did that, they'd both blow up. Instead, he let go of the mesh and pushed Ellie to the side of the truck. There was a terrible pause. Everyone held their breath. Ellie thought she could hear birds or insects in the darkness of the woods—

With an earsplitting *CRACK-BLAM*, like an enormous firecracker going off, the trailer jumped and then rattled back down on its wheels. A terrible spew of foul hot gasses came blasting out of the open end. The bulletproof windows puffed outward and spiderwebbed but held, as did the metal sides inches from Ellie's shoulder.

"Damn," Sarge Bryan said as he made sure Ellie was safe. He looked over the others. "Man, that Mr. Perdix... Sometimes it's the quiet guys who surprise you in the end."

Oh, poor Mr. Perdix!

A gasp and a cough came from the area in front of a tree stump covered by blast debris. Like a specter in a putrid fog, a smudged but intact figure rose unsteadily to his feet.

"Al!" Ms. China said. "You didn't die heroically. How did you weasel out of that?"

Brushing cinders out of his hair and looking like a ghost from some battle that had happened in these woods centuries ago, Mr. Perdix spat out what looked like a small charred pinecone and dribbled dark blood from his nostril.

"Eh? What?"

In addition to having only bloody stumps for ears, the concussive explosion had deafened him, though it had not dampened his enthusiasm for mansplaining.

"After Sarge was clear," he said in a shout, stumbling into a crouch and putting his hand down on the bare ground as if to make sure the earth was not spinning rapidly beneath him. "I judged there was no downside to trying to substitute one of the larger bits of my ears for my finger. It stuck on and held the detonation off just long enough for me to get out."

"Yo! MSDF medic, over here!" Sarge yelled at a group of a group of soldiers whom Ellie hoped were allies. Though at this stage in her tour of America, anything was open to question.

"If my lip-reading is accurate, I don't think I need medical..." Mr. Perdix lost his grip on the ground and drooped, collapsing headfirst onto the road.

Senator Leota and Janice approached them.

"We still have a problem," the senator whispered.

"If that was the right code to join the two halves of the real W33..."

Janice stared at Ellie as though it was her fault.

"I know," Sarge Bryan said, scanning their rescuers. "But we have to be careful. I don't know any of these state soldiers."

"Sergeant," an older fellow came over. He had white hair, an overgrown moustache, and a loose-fitting camouflage jacket that would have fit comfortably if he had been thirty pounds heavier. "We spoke on the video link."

Ellie looked at Sarge Bryan. There was no way...

The new fellow went on. "Your distraction when you hacked all the EMAC communications and surveillance equipment was right on time, down to the second." He motioned to one of his soldiers with a captured EMAC. "These idiots didn't even put out pickets, just relied on their fancy surveillance gizmos that were feeding them bullcrap. I don't know how you managed it, but thanks to you, we've neutralized this entire command post."

Sarge Bryan looked at Ellie. "Miss Aleph," they said together.

"Uh, Major, sir…"

"No need to sir me," the MSDF officer said, "we're not in your chain of command. We answer only to the governor, and he's told us our only priority is to keep Missourians safe."

"Well, about that video call, Major, uh…"

"Foley."

They explained that what Foley had received was a friendly deep-fake transmission, which had allowed him and his MSDF to successfully attack the EMAC outpost.

"It's not bloody here." Ms. China came limping up to them. Her prosthetic leg had survived another melee, but the ankle joint looked locked in place, making her leg stiff as a board. In her hand, she had a green box; it was giving off regular clicking noises. "I found where they had been keeping it, and there were tire tracks."

"Is that one of our Geiger counters, miss?" Major Foley asked sternly, probably not liking civilians messing with his equipment.

"She's with us," Sarge Bryan said. "If Hidalgo got away with the device…"

"What device?" Foley asked, looking less triumphant and more out of his depth by the second.

"We'll fill you in on a need-to-know basis," Senator Leota said.

"Who are you?" Foley said to the wheezing, bleeding, and soot-stained woman.

"If you voted Democrat," Sarge Bryan said, "she's your president."

75

EMAC ENCAMPMENT

When Ellie got some of her wits back, she looked around and noticed the encampment had been overrun by soldiers in gray-brown camouflage fatigues belonging to the Missouri Guard units. They appeared to be more professional than Jeb's group, and there were many more of them. All around, the EMAC techno-stormtroopers in black uniforms were being subdued and taken prisoner.

"Excuse me," Ellie said as the ringing in her ears from the demolition charge explosion started to fade. "Where are we? We traveled some distance. I assume we're still in Missouri State."

"Well, Miss, you're in Shawnee, near Stump Park," Major Foley said.

"We've got to track that vehicle Hidalgo left in," Senator Leota said. "Do you have communications with the federal forces at Lee's Summit?"

"Let's jus' hold on a moment, Madam President-maybe or maybe not," Foley said, then turned and looked pointedly at Janice Jones. "Or chief of staff of the other maybe-still President. Like I said, I'ma takin' orders only from the state capital, Jeff City. Before the Army sergeant, or his deep-fake hologram, got us to come here and helped us execute the best ambush I ever seen, we were on a reconnoiter for a big op."

"What kind?" asked Sarge Bryan.

"That's on a need-to-know, Sergeant. Those Geiger readings could have come from anything. There's no proof they have a W33 or any other WMD. And you there, Miss, I'll have our equipment back." The state soldier moved to retrieve his radiation scanner from Ms. China.

Suddenly a passing EMAC prisoner broke free of his guards and rushed at Major Foley, screaming, "You slave-trading Nazis! We'll kill you all!"

As he ran by Ms. China, she yanked on the man's collar and gave him a small kick behind his knee, which sent him sprawling. He landed on his back, and the Scottish poisoner kneeled on his chest.

"We will—"

Ms. China's bandaged hands jammed a fat pinecone in his mouth.

"You were the one who ripped me nails out." She looked at Foley. "Can I have him?"

"He's bound for lockup and will be treated according to the Geneva conventions," Foley said curtly.

Ellie couldn't help thinking they were missing something.

"Major Foley, your mission wouldn't have anything to do with the big stadium in town, would it?"

Foley lost interest in the prisoner who was thrashing his head, trying to spit out the cone.

"Who the heck are you people?"

"Miss Sato's a top British intelligence agent," Sarge Bryan said. "Not much gets past her."

Perhaps taken aback by the composition of Ellie's unique group, Foley became more willing to share operational intelligence. It turned out Hidalgo and the EMAC forces numbered between forty-five and fifty thousand. They had come in from all the blue states. Their apparent goal was to make an example of Missouri and pacify the federal loyalist Kansas militias. The EMACs were confining everyone they captured, combatants and civilians, inside Arrowhead Stadium.

"We don't have great pictures. They're using lasers and metallic smoke clouds to obscure what they're up to from drones and satellites." Foley had obviously decided they needed to know more. "We estimate two hundred, maybe three hundred thousand are all packed in there."

"Wow," Sarge Bryan said.

"You see why it's our priority now? There's no way to safely maintain that many people in that space. Every hour means people are being trampled to death, dehydrating, dying trying to escape." Foley shook his head. "I don't know what their game is. Maybe Hidalgo's thinkin' of using them as hostages to get the feds to back down. All know is they're Missourians, and we're going to rescue them."

Ellie exchanged looks with the rest of her party. "Would you reconsider Ms. China having a… chat with just one teensie little prisoner? She's quite persuasive."

Foley looked at the EMAC, then waved his guard detail away.

"Army Sergeant," he said, turning his back on the soon-to-be-very-unfortunate prisoner, "sorry to say, one of them EMAC traitors escaped. If you see him, please give him back to us, in whatever condition you find him."

Sporadic gunfire came from up the road. Foley went to investigate, leaving them alone near the EMAC mess tent. With the prone prisoner making increasingly pathetic sounds through his improvised gag, Ms. China and Mr. Perdix dragged him off.

"I'll try to get some kind of communications going with Lee's Summit," Janice said. "If Hidalgo has a nuke, he'll only have to get close to them."

Sarge Bryan thought a moment. "If you do get through, watch what you say. We still have the Pangeans to take care of, and I want to keep Ellie's teahouse plan as an option."

Janice ran off toward what looked to be the MSDF communications van judging by the mass of antennas protruding from its roof.

"If Hidalgo destroys the federal forces…" Ellie thought out loud.

"The state troops will be heavily outnumbered," Sarge Bryan said. "They won't know for certain he's got only one W33. It might force Washington and Casteel to surrender."

Leota nodded. "What would you do if you saw a mushroom cloud over your only allies?"

"Can't you reason with these blue forces?" Ellie asked hopefully. This seemed to upset Leota even more as a pained look crossed her face.

"Julien's been working behind my back all this time. I never thought... I mean, he always seemed like an academic, just a rich kid playing at left-wing woke politics. I still can't believe he'd know how to pull off an armed campaign of sedition like this."

"Hey, everyone," Ms. China said, chewing on a long stringy piece of meat. "Look over there."

After looking more closely and hoping her housemate had not joined cannibal club, it turned out Ms. China was noshing on a fatty-looking sausage. She had nicked it from the tent housing the EMAC's kitchen and mess hall.

"Right, then," Ms. China said. "This looks private enough for our heart-to-heart with this wanker. All I need now is a large-gauge syringe and some engine cleaner, the more caustic the better..."

Mr. Perdix and Sarge Bryan wrestled the EMAC prisoner inside the tent and strapped him down on a table. "Sorry, bud," Sarge said, "but you did pull out all ten of the lady's fingernails."

The next six minutes were marked by pinecone-muffled shrieks. Just when Ellie felt sure the conflicted-looking albino soldier was about to walk in and stop the torturing, a saliva-coated gag flew out from the doorway of the pantry tent. It was followed by inaudible whispering.

When she came out, all six of Ms. China's pupils looked clearer and even cheery, in a creepy way.

"That was refreshing," she said, rejoining them.

"Is he...?" Sarge asked, looking at the inert figure slumped beside a propane cooker.

"I barely touched him. Like all these latter-day Lenins, he talked tough but broke easy."

The sissy EMAC revealed he was not privy to Hidalgo's master plan but had noticed some important changes in tactics over the past few days. When they had lost contact with Brutal Eagle Command, which Leota said was Julien's code name among the seditious forces, Hidalgo took some of his people away from the perimeter and abandoned attempts to repair the bridges over the Missouri River and instead began rounding up civilians in earnest.

"Being experts in civilian surveillance and suppression," Ms. China said, "the EMAC used tear gas, smoke, even microwave crowd-control devices to dig people out of their homes and drove them to Arrowhead."

"Oh," Sarge Bryan said with trepidation as though he knew what she was going to say.

"The sentries around the stadium are all outfitted with WMD gear: gas masks, chem suits, and also flamethrowers."

"Lord."

As soon as her longtime friend said that, Ellie caught a sense of the horrid reality. "Hidalgo's seeded the place with infected," she whispered. "Was it some kind of punishment?"

"Not likely." Mr. Perdix walked slowly but steadily as he rejoined their group.

"Al, not so loud," Ms. China said, looking around as they huddled to one side of the food-prep tent that held the prisoner. "Our EMAC friend still has his ears. Although, if we're done asking him things…" She fondled a kitchen paring knife with her bandaged fingers.

Mr. Perdix continued more quietly. "Let's assume Hidalgo was counting on Julien to give him the final W33 codes. At the same time Comrade Colonel determined he could not use the W33, he saw the federal forces were massing at Lee's Summit. Hidalgo knew they were only hours away from attacking and destroying the EMAC formations. The bridges were destroyed, and Hidalgo had nowhere to run. However, they still had one other weapon of mass destruction in their arsenal: three hundred thousand infected."

"Hidalgo knows Stage Two infected are more mobile and can operate simple machinery," Senator Leota said. "If I were commanding the federal army, freeing the captives would be my first priority. Once federal loyalists capture the stadium, the infected will be on them, and they'll be overrun in minutes."

Ellie grasped the horrific consequences. "Each soldier would be turned into one of them. They'd spread out to all points of the compass."

"So far," Sarge Bryan said, "apart from Las Vegas, which we got quarantined early, the Pangean forces have only been able to activate a few hundred at a time in isolated groups. People are hunkered down, sheltering in place. The last cellphone data Mr. Perdix had showed rates were slowing down to a trickle along Abdelkader's route going east."

A hideous, raging taunt came from the EMAC prisoner. Ellie could only see his legs sticking out from the tent. "You motherfuckers, you're going to burn. Scorched fucking earth America. None of you pigs deserve to live after what you did to Indigenous people and your black slaves. America's been a vampire since it was created, the perfect parasite… and we've got the perfect weapon to put the stake through its heart for good. I will never stop burning Nazis. Every last one of you, men, women, and especially children."

Sarge Bryan was about to go into the mess tent. The last time Ellie had seen an expression like that on the man's features, he had been looking a terrorist straight in the eyes while suffocating him.

Mr. Perdix caught his big brawny arm.

"Sergeant, you don't do that, not to prisoners," he said.

"Where is that pinecone?" Ms. China said, looking on the ground by the roadside.

"We should probably discuss what to do somewhere else," the JASON scientist said. "I'll make sure that fellow is secure so he can be returned to Major Foley and receive, er, justice."

Mr. Perdix went into the mess tent. After a minute or so, Janice came over to where Ellie and the others were huddled around Major Foley's Humvee.

"I got through to Vice President Prowse. He's getting me a channel to the Pentagon."

"Hidalgo could be anywhere," Sarge Bryan said. "Any luck with those tire tracks from what we think is Hidalgo's vehicle?"

"That worthless lump Agent Schwartz came through," Ms. China said a little ungraciously. "Al sent the FBI a picture of the tire tread marks. They match only one vehicle: a Tesla Cybertruck Maximus."

"Good work," Leota said. "How many of those can there be in—"

Everyone ducked as the senator's words were cut off by a dull explosion and a ball of flame which blew apart the EMAC mess tent. Rifle muzzles pointed everywhere, and people began shouting.

"Mortar?"

"Who's hit?"

Fifty meters away from them, a puff of flame rose to the lower branches of the pine trees at the perimeter of the encampment. Ellie watched the cooking area disintegrate, leaving a writhing figure, which was quickly burning while squirming like a broiled worm.

"Oops," Ms. China said. "Did someone forget to turn off the gas?"

Missouri guardsmen with fire extinguishers quickly hosed the area down with white foam spray.

"Mr. Perdix!" Sarge Bryan said sharply.

"You must not have heard me correctly," Mr. Perdix said, cupping his nonexistent ear. "I said *you* don't do things like that."

Senator Leota shook her head, trying not to stare at the apparition of Mr. Perdix, and failed.

"If he'd gotten loose or had been able to tell the EMACs what we know…" Mr. Perdix said, shrugging. "And remember, Foley said he'd accept the prisoner back as-is. Well, there he is."

The vile man's smoking remains were quickly covered with an orange tarp.

76

SHAWNEE, KANSAS

Ellie needed to move away from the EMAC food tent, as smells of sauerkraut and burned sausages—she hoped it was only sausages—were wafting out, mixed with gritty, dusty fire extinguisher residue.

She followed the others out from under the camouflage netting and the tree line toward a large paved highway. Most of the tall lights along it were dark. She realized she could be anywhere, and the vastness of hostile America threatened to frustrate anything she could think of doing to help her friends and get home.

Janice Jones was nearby. She was high as you could get in Washington's power structure, right below President Casteel and Vice President Prowse. But what could she or anyone do now? Janice gripped a satellite phone, a light on it blinking as though it was on mute.

"What should we tell them?" Janice asked.

"The president's got to know about the W33," Senator Leota said.

"Realistically, ma'am, what's the executable plan?" Sarge Bryan asked. "If the federal forces move away from Lee's Summit, they're as likely to go toward Hidalgo as away from the danger. We don't know where that Tesla truck is. They'd also be breaking up their formations. The EMACs might be waiting for them to do that before attacking and save the nuke for later."

"You don't know who to trust," Ms. China said, puffing her cheeks out as though she was about to make an annoying admission. "Never remind me I said this, but best to stick with Eleanor's teahouse plan."

Janice looked skeptical. "Are we letting Anna the Ripper here dictate policy?"

Senator Leota looked around at each of them. "I was fooled once by Julien…"

"Make that a thousand times," Janice said under her breath.

The possible president-elect ignored the catty remark. "Give the sat phone to the sergeant. We'll let the Pentagon know about an unspecified threat to the forces at Lee's and then pursue Ms. Sato's idea."

Ellie felt the fate of a nation weigh on her shoulders. Her idea—really Miss Aleph's—had seemed much more brilliant before she had to say it out loud. She was just about to add some disclaimers and caveats when the sporadic gunfire from down the highway became more intense.

The figure of Major Foley, who looked rather more geriatric than usual in his too-large uniform, came ambling toward them.

"Sergeant Bryan! There's a disturbance, keep your civilians out of the—"

A great metal hook attached to a rope flew out from the darkness, caught Foley under the arm, and dragged him back toward the tree line near the darkest side of the highway. The elderly soldier flopped like a carp being reeled in over dry land. The two or three sinister figures doing the reeling in gave Ellie a start.

"Those aren't EMACs!" Ellie shouted and grabbed hold of their weakest member, the senator, to push her out of the way. Sarge Bryan had the same idea. Ellie felt somewhat thrilled to be at the same level of martial astuteness as the career combat veteran. The feeling only lasted until something hard hit her head. The glancing blow sent her reeling, and suddenly it was the politician and Sarge Bryan supporting her as they dashed for cover.

"They're Stage Two… throwing hooks at us!" Ellie warned as she felt her scalp for bleeding.

Ms. China had picked up a large shotgun and was firing with

deliberateness into the dark. Mr. Perdix and Janice had hold of Major Foley's legs and caught him just before he slithered into the dark zone outside the light of the encampment.

A Missouri State Guardsman ran past in a panic. Sarge grabbed his arm.

"Get your people back from the woods. This perimeter is porous, you understand? Too big, it can't be held."

"What the fuck held?" the pimply faced kid sputtered. "The sick ones… they don't have any motor control, they're harmless. The government FEMA channel said so."

"That'll teach you, kid. Trust your eyes over the shit bureaucrat doctors shovel." Sarge Bryan pointed to the lights illuminating a freeway overpass which ran along a rise. "That's the only possible strongpoint. Do all your units have JabberCocky?"

"Huh?"

"The thing on your arm." The regular Army veteran ripped off Velcro fasteners from the man's forearm to reveal a curved touch screen. "The Joint Battle Reconnaissance Command Equipment. Do all your guys have them?"

"I guess yes, sir. At least one to a squad."

"Good. Use it to signal everyone to rally six hundred meters east."

"Uh, are you in charge now, sir?" the young man asked, seemingly frozen between assisting the battle to drag Major Foley back to their side of the drainage ditch and doing what Sarge Bryan told him.

"We'll get him back. You just do what I said, on the major's authority, got it?"

Ms. China limped up, thrust the shotgun at the kid, and took his weapon. "That's empty, be a good lad and give us a refill."

Before he could answer, she swung around, flicked on the green laser sight, and resumed rapid-fire shots over the heads of Janice and Mr. Perdix, who were struggling to keep hold of Foley.

Ms. China must have hit something. The line holding Foley slackened, and he was able to worm his way out of his oversized camouflage jacket. No sooner was it off his shoulders than a violent jerk sent it skidding off, fortunately without him inside it.

"What happened?" Foley seemed out of it.

"Let's see your face first," Mr. Perdix said, and rudely grabbed the man's jaw. "He's all right, no sign of contagion."

They got the state guard officer up to his feet. He looked addled, and it was a moment before he could form a complete sentence.

"We have to check for anyone infected among us," the JASON scientist said. "Anyone with spore smudges has to be zip-tied and quarantined."

Sarge Bryan shook his head. "We can wait until we're at the rally point. No offense, Major, but I don't want to give these weekend soldiers anything too complicated to do. That overpass is the best spot. Move all your people there."

Foley started walking with increasing determination toward the MSDF communications Humvee.

"Gun, please." Ellie had to remind them that she, too, was a viable killer. Mr. Perdix handed her Foley's sidearm, which had fallen out of his holster.

More land-fishing hooks came flying at them. Ellie raised her weapon, eager for revenge for her throbbing head, but she saw nothing on the business side of her glowing front sight.

"Into that MRAP," Sarge Bryan yelled, herding them in the direction of what looked like a bulldozer missing its front scoop. "Foley! Make sure all your units check in and acknowledge the order to move. We're not coming back this way."

The good things about the MRAP armored car were it could hold all of them and it was probably the safest place to be until the infected developed the ability to use explosives. Major Foley finished yelling into his radio and then let the communications vehicle speed away. He got in with them just as they set off along the shoulder of the road which, after a few moments of nearly blind driving, joined the highway.

"Major," Janice said, shaking the distraught-looking man in his seat. "What happened?"

"Uh… my men… What about the EMAC prisoners…?"

"Leave those shitbags," Ms. China said with venom.

"Now, sir," Mr. Perdix said in his hard-of-hearing voice. "Please tell us: Where did all the infected suddenly come from?"

Over the noise of the big vehicle's engine, Ellie strained to hear the story.

Captured EMACs claimed they had put local civilian hostages into a cave. Foley had sent a squad of guardsmen to check out their story.

"There are caves, all around… the squad set off, direction of Lake Quivira."

Naturally, not trusting the EMACs, they brought their prisoners along and made them go in first to remove the steel doors that had been stuck across the mouth of the cave.

"My people said they didn't seem scared when they went in, they even seemed to be looking forward to opening the doors. Mumbling something about stolen land and capitalism. Then that crazy rabble came out… hundreds, maybe thousands."

The vehicle's motor changed gears, and they braced themselves as it turned a sharp corner.

"Scorched earth," Senator Leota said in a voice that was barely audible.

"A nuke would almost be better, cleaner," Sarge Bryan said. "Ms. Jones, tell the federal forces they must not advance into the city. No land army in the world can stand up against what they've got penned up in Arrowhead Stadium."

"And where is Hidalgo's vehicle?" Leota said. "How hard can be to find a Tesla Cybertruck?"

When they got to the overpass rendezvous, Foley seemed to shrink in his seat. Only about half his people had made it.

"Maybe the rest… didn't get here just yet," Sarge Bryan said, trying to be upbeat as he parked under the broad overpass near a thick support pillar.

"Now what?" Janice asked rather superfluously as they waved to the line of state guards who were setting up a perimeter on both sides of the highway.

"Remember the last time we faced a similar situation?" Ellie said, trying to brighten the mood. "You came along in that incredible flying machine."

As soon as she mentioned it, recalling the Bordeaux battle had the opposite effect on Ellie. It was there in France where Atticus Reidt, Sr. had been killed.

"I don't 'spect we'll get an airlift this time," the Army man said, peering through the dark.

"Y-you've been in s-similar…" Foley was having some kind of catatonic reaction. Ellie was feeling around her seat for a canteen or bottled drink to give him when something very heavy landed on the roof.

They couldn't be here already, tossing Stage Ones at them again, could they? Bloody infected!

"Don't shoot!" Mr. Perdix yelled at Ms. China as she raised her rifle at the roof. "Bullets will just bounce around in here."

"I wasn't going to. Don't be an earless wuss."

Heavy footsteps thumped along the top of the MRAP, and finally an inverted face appeared through the windshield.

"Tata!"

The heavy cyborg lady grabbed a handhold and swung herself to the ground, making the large vehicle wiggle on its suspension. She stuck her head in the open door.

"Good to see you are all not eaten or..." Her reticle crosshair-style pupils caught sight of Mr. Perdix. "...mutilated too badly."

"That's a foreign national," Foley yelled, suddenly coming to life. "Disarm it and hold it for a debriefing."

"Just try to debrief me, you ungentlemanly fart," Tata shot back.

"Whoa, everyone chill," Sarge Bryan said. "Ms. Oblonskaya, I mean Tata, is with us."

"How are Zvena and Rodion?" Ellie asked.

Tata glanced left and right. "I will tell you all about our amusing suborbital flight in the landing pods, but at the moment..."

Tata motioned to the dark landscape framed by the highway overpass.

Sarge Bryan squinted and looked down the road. "Incoming! Massive incoming," he yelled out the window to the weary MSDF soldiers who had just put down their packs and weapons. "North, north, north! You turdsacks, pick your shit back up you and give 'em everything you got!"

77

I-70 INTERCHANGE
SHAWNEE, KANSAS

During her travels, Ellie had found wherever in the world she encountered them, Americans were always keen on shooting off their guns. That was doubly so in their home country. Sarge did not have to tell the Missouri militia members twice to unleash a hellish rain of lead into the horde of infected coming down the highway.

Tremendous racket from dozens, then hundreds, of weapon muzzles split the night air and reverberated through the freeway overpass where they had taken shelter. Many of the soldiers had night vision, and those without followed the tracer rounds and laser sights toward a cascading dark mass that filled the four-lane road. Every moment, it came closer.

The ginger-haired militia man Jeb ran up to them. His face looked as though it had been stepped on by heavy boots as a result of the beatings the EMACs had doled out to him, but he seemed to be able to see well enough.

"I'll get the fifty up," he yelled at Sarge Bryan, who was the most visible part of the group's command structure. "But I only got one box of ammo."

"Do it, Jeb. It'll help," Sarge Bryan shouted back from the open door of the MRAP armored vehicle.

Ellie noticed the look on his face.

"But it won't," she whispered. "Will it?"

The albino soldier shook his head, his golden eyes tracing short ellipses in the dark.

Tata came from the back and pushed herself in between them, ostensibly to stare out the window.

"Yes, totally no good. They are still coming. Bullets will not stop them." Tata clicked a microphone on the tactical vest hanging over her leather jacket. "Komandir... drop it."

From the overpass above came a squealing of tortured metal.

"Your front guys," she added. "Maybe tell them take cover, huh?"

The groaning increased, and then a set of large tires became visible, hanging down off the upper concrete span of the bridge.

"Militia! Danger close! Take cover!" Sarge Bryan shouted over the MRAP loudspeakers as the rest of the vehicle came into view, sliding over with ever-increasing speed.

By the time the front end of the oblong fuel tanker had crashed down and was perched inelegantly on the asphalt like an enormous stubbed-out cigar, soldiers had figured out what was going on and retreated behind where Ellie sat inside the MRAP.

"Hurry up," Tata said into her mic.

"We have to get the end down or it will 'flame up' like Roman candle, not 'flame out' like we want," Zvena replied tersely.

"Maybe next time I push truck and you warn our American friends."

With a final shudder, the rear end of the tanker made an inelegant drooping pivot and toppled away from them. Ellie could now make out individual figures among the approaching horde. She imagined the thousands of gallons of gasoline coating the road ahead of them, and then, with a small *pop*, a reddish-pink flare arced down.

The blast effect was more of a big *WHOOSH* than a bang, but even through the tempered glass of the military truck, she felt the blast of heat. The entire U-shaped space of the highway that lay between the left and right berms cascaded with white and orange flames. Black smoke swirled under the bridge pylons.

Cheers erupted from the militia, who quickly sorted themselves back into firing lines.

"We'll go up and get Zvena and Rodion," Sarge Bryan said.

"Not required. There they are."

A moment later, two chunky, dark figures had thrown themselves off the bridge, trailing a pair of thick cables. The ropes snapped taut, and they swung them over the roaring fuel fire and through the smoke. At the apex of their swing, they both let go and landed as nimbly as one could expect from people of their size.

"Friendlies incoming, hold fire. Do NOT shoot the Russians."

Jeb echoed Sarge Bryan's admonishment, and while a few laser dots appeared on them as they jogged toward the MRAP, everyone seemed to recognize it was these strange figures who had destroyed the incoming attackers.

"Major Foley," Senator Leota said, pushing the shivering man in shirtsleeves forward. "You and Jeb check your people. See to the wounded and distribute ammunition."

"I thought…" Foley said, his gray-haired chest sinking a few inches under his sweat-stained undershirt.

"Thought it was over?" Janice asked, leaning out from the back of the vehicle. "As long as those things or EMAC units are out there, it ain't over, not by a long stretch."

Komandir Zvena yanked open the door with such enthusiasm, it nearly flew off its hinges.

"I'm so glad you are not decapitated or eaten." He looked over at Mr. Perdix's injured head. "For most part."

Rodion clambered on the other side of the MRAP. He had a rucksack, out of which various weapons protruded.

"How did you guys get away?" Ellie asked, glad to be distracted by the welcome reappearance of their friends.

"First was the challenge of cross-wiring ignition system of the lander pods," Zvena said. "They made mistake in not disabling the relaunch mechanism before imprisoning us. Second challenging point we achieved was surviving the sudden landing."

"You two set down in the lake," Rodion said bitterly. "I had a tumble in trees."

Ellie looked left and right for the OCEL robot. Perhaps it was too much to expect that the faithful mechanoid would have survived as well. When the EMAC had ambushed them from the sky, it had fled into the underbrush.

"We made our way back to your last known position, where we left our supply drone," Zvena said. "Along the way, we encountered some friendly civilians who helped us, and some unfriendly EMACs who will not be rude to anyone in future. We followed the tracks of your captors to the EMAC camp. Then we find you had stolen our lightning, and had, on your own, overcome the main human enemy forces."

"We had help," Sarge said, nodding at Jeb and over to Major Foley, who was speaking to two soldiers carrying a stretcher.

"Get to the good part," Rodion prompted, shifting his good eye left and right to keep watch on the bonfire of infected.

"After retrieving some of our equipment, we heard the commotion at this roadway and came to lend our hands."

"And..." Tata said impatiently, smiling at Sarge Bryan as if she was about to present him with a birthday cake.

"We are close to pinpointing the location of the Tesla vehicle you are looking for."

"How do you know we're looking it?" Mr. Perdix demanded in his hard-of-hearing voice.

"Well... heh-heh." Tata shrugged her massive mechanically augmented shoulders. "We took small precaution of putting in harmless little bug on your devices. We were able to see the information your FBI sent you on the tire tracks and assumed the objective was quite important."

"We have been tracking the radiological signature," Zvena said. "We know you have Second Amendment here, but it is probably not wise to let citizens have possession of fission bombs without strict controls."

"All right," Ellie said before Ms. China could needle Mr. Perdix for the lapse in digital security. "Where is that awful man Hidalgo?"

Instead of answering them, the augmented eyes of all the cyborgs and Sarge Bryan snapped to the front, where the tanker truck fire had settled down into a modest two-hundred-yard conflagration.

"Hold that a moment," Sarge Bryan said tensely as he exited the truck.

"What is it?"

The road behind the fire had steep concrete berms that went on for a long way. Some infected had tried moving around the flames to get to them, but these had been easily shot to bits by militia.

"Next wave incoming!" Sarge Bryan shouted. "Looks like Stage Two infected. VBIED defense now! Kill those cars."

A small car, possibly a Mini Cooper, drove into the ring of fire and slowed, its tires melted, and the gas tank exploded with a minor whump. Then came another, and another, followed by a flatbed truck with chickens in the back. It crashed and sent live birds scattering all through the flames, writhing like horrible embers as they squawked and burned.

The first groups of infected attempted to climb over the steel bridge formed by the wrecked cars, they were shot or caught fire, and stopped. Foley saw what was happening.

"We've got to fall back," he gasped.

"Back where?" said Senator Leota, who Ellie recalled had been a Marine and had fighting experience. "If we move, they'll keep coming and pick us apart."

Zvena scanned the sides of the viaduct and the roof formed by the rectangular concrete slabs of the overpass.

"I have idea," he said. "Rodya, deploy the explosive nanowire, all of it."

"But Komandir," Rodion said, a look of skepticism in his one unpatched eye, "that is quite dangerous."

78

I-70 INTERCHANGE
SHAWNEE, KANSAS

D angerous?" Ellie found herself yelling at the ox-headed cyborg, somewhat to her own surprise. "More bloody dangerous than that?"

Where she pointed, there were flaming figures dripping gasoline, clothing, and melting skin. They tottered forward across the formerly impervious barricade like little candles in the dark that had caught fire all up and down their length, toppling over after a few steps. But more followed.

"Ms. Sato, you make a significant point," Rodion agreed.

"I am marking the vulnerable load-bearing areas of the structure now in virtual view," Zvena said. "Tata, you have the most experience in demolition. Check this."

The three cyborgs seemed to stare into space, studying their internal HUDs.

"I suppose you want us all to move back?" Sarge Bryan asked.

"Seventy meters south will be adequate," Tata said, leaning out the door of the MRAP and peering up to the ceiling of the tunnel created by the wide overpass.

Sarge Bryan relayed the information to Major Foley and Jeb.

Very carefully, Rodion began unpacking several spools of glistening thread. To Ellie, they looked for all the world suited for use in fancy embroidery sewing.

"Our Foundation for Advanced Research Projects has been studying the nanowires used to such great effect during the 96-Hour War," Zvena explained as his fellow cyborgs each loaded the spools on top of their multipurpose pike weapons and aimed them like crossbows. "Our scientists noticed that, with certain modifications, the fibers were themselves unstable. Thin sheets of explosive have been used for many years for breaching and demolition. We have taken that concept to the next level."

Tata and Rodion both fired off the coil contraptions, aiming at the freeway support pillars. There may have been a sound, but with the constant gunfire, engines being started, and the roar of the flames, which were barely keeping the approaching horde at bay, Ellie heard nothing.

All three cyborgs ducked behind the MRAP, with Tata clinging to the driver's-side door close to Sarge Bryan. They didn't have room to turn the large vehicle around, so he backed up with Janice standing outside waving people out of the way as they retreated.

"Earlier models of this ordnance, hehe, they had little directional flying problem," Tata said, pointing at the flight of their projectiles.

The glowing discs hit the tops of the pillars, which had to be twenty feet wide, and started zipping around their circumferences, whizzing around like tiny flying Maypole dancers.

A yellow bus came thundering through the flame barrier, coming right at them, bashing aside the debris of the Mini and the chicken truck. This was the gap the infected had been looking for. They were through.

And so were the pillars holding up the road above.

"A little bit farther back might be in order," Ellie advised, realizing what the Russians were planning.

Like some mad demolition firework, the nanowire explosive flared brightly and went off like two twin corkscrews obliterating the reinforced concrete pillars. The overpass wobbled. The infected lurched hungrily toward them, oblivious. The first phalanx of attackers ran forward, the continual cascade of bullets barely making a ripple among their ranks. Above, the fat lip of unstable concrete quivered like the top half of a huge mouth, then chomped down. A rushing roar accompanied the collapse of the reinforced concrete, and a blast of dust washed over them. Their retreating MRAP's windshield was coated by gritty pebble-strewn dirt.

"Hot damn, we got 'em!" Sarge Bryan seemed enthused for the first time since they had run afoul of the vicious EMACs. "Now let's track down Hidalgo. And, Ms. Sato, I'm not forgetting your brilliant idea either."

Ellie herself had totally forgotten it. She started to relax until she saw the Russians looking at each other. Her former housemate also noticed.

"What?" Ms. China asked bluntly from the back compartment she shared with Senator Leota and Mr. Perdix, who was using a hand mirror to try to get a better look at his ear stumps.

Zvena was hanging from the open passenger door of the MRAP, his clothes half covered by pulverized concrete. He dipped his head apologetically. "This is only temporary reprieve. These demons that have been unleashed in this plague will not give up. Even now, they are attempting to find a way around the blockade. Sergeant, I send you now images from our remote camera."

Sarge Bryan blinked as images got beamed into his cyber eyes.

"Hmm," he said flatly.

"You see the trouble," Tata said. "The militia force cannot retreat with us, or the infected will disperse though the countryside, attacking everyone."

Rodion wiped grit from his face. "From our studies of them during our travels, we noticed they tend to form groups, attacking and annihilating objectives completely before moving on."

"Ms. Jones, ma'am," Sarge Bryan called out. "Can you get Lee's Summit on the line? We're going to need air support."

"The EMACs have deployed very aggressive layers of air defenses," Zvena said pessimistically. "They must have stolen them from Air Force installations."

"We've got to try." Sarge Bryan waved to Foley and Jeb through the settling smoke. The two men were exchanging high-fives with their soldiers, unaware the threat had not been stopped but was still closing in from a different direction.

"I'm on it," Janice said, seeming to grasp the urgency of the request.

"Major, Jeb," Sarge Bryan began but did not seem to have the words when he looked down into their soot-smeared, exhausted faces. Jeb's forehead had developed a throbbing fat purple hematoma where Hidalgo's men had struck him. They clearly thought they had won a respite, if not a major victory.

Zvena cut in. "You are in charge of these brave men?"

"Yep, that's us," Jeb panted. "Me an' this ol' Hoosier here." He slapped Foley on the shoulder, sending up a puff of concrete dust.

"You know of the famous American battle of the Alamo?" Zvena asked, and the grins faded from their faces.

Sarge Bryan got out and explained the militia's position beside the fallen rubble of the freeway.

"Hidalgo's got a WMD," he said. "We have to stop him from using it on the troops at Lee's Summit. One MRAP is not going to make any difference here."

"You... y'think you can get to the fucker in time?" Jeb asked.

"We're gonna try," Sarge Bryans said.

Jeb turned to Foley. "Fuckin' Boogaloo, huh?"

Foley looked grim as he tightened the straps of the body armor he had put on top of his long underwear. "Boogaloo... you paranoid preppers... I never thought..."

Janice waved at them, hitting the mute button on her satellite phone. "McConnell Air Force Base near Wichita is still responding to orders from Washington. They'll try to get some gunships through the SAM umbrella and the loitering drones the EMACs have put up."

"Tell them not to risk any pilots. We got this," Jeb said.

Janice nodded. "They guarantee they can airdrop you a whole bunch of ammo and supplies that was headed for the Middle East."

Tata climbed down from the MRAP and joined the group. "OCEL is tracking Hidalgo and reports it is closing in. Hidalgo has stopped driving, maybe waiting for distraction to allow him to get closer to the federal army."

"We have to go," Sarge Bryan said, picking up his rifle.

Foley looked shell-shocked. "M-maybe we can string some... some concertina wire..." He pointed vaguely to the other side of the underpass.

"We have been fighting these infected since Guatemala," Zvena said, fishing around in his rucksack. "Forget strategy. It will only get your soldiers killed, and sooner. Be aggressive and loud, keep them coming at you. Every one you destroy will be one less wandering the countryside looking for civilians."

The cyborg's gloved hand held out a fat jar of tablets and ampules. "These are strong antipsychotics. Give them to all your people. When it comes to hand-to-hand fights with infected, without these, your soldiers will go insane and kill themselves or each other."

Next, much more solemnly, Zvena put his gore-stained and scarred battle pike on the ground and leaned it on the elderly major's shoulder. Rodion gave his to Jeb, who took a half step back under the weight.

"Be proud. You are warriors fighting a poisonous threat to your homeland," Zvena said in his loud cyborg-enhanced voice. "We Russians have saying: *Rodina-mat' zovot!* The Motherland calls!"

"They're here," Tata said.

The first infected had been spotted coming over the hills flanking their position. Dozens of tracer rounds lanced though the darkness to meet them.

Jeb's eyes were almost perfect cycles inside the uniformly matted-down fringe of ginger hair and beard that circled his head. "Well, we got a sayin' too: America, fuck yeah!"

Zvena, Rodion, and Tata laughed, baring their shiny gray teeth in the headlights of the MRAP. "Is good one. I like it," Zvena said. "Fuck yeah!"

Ellie and the normal-sized humans piled back into the MRAP, which then had room only for Tata. Zvena and Rodion clung to the sides. They drove away from the embattled freeway interchange.

"Well," Sarge Bryan said gruffly from behind the wheel, "at least the Russians saved us some fuel before they lit the rest on fire."

Ellie looked down at the feed from the dashboard rearview camera. Wind was pushing the dirty, oily smoke down onto the Missourians' positions from the other side of the collapsed freeway. Bright pinpricks of muzzle flashes pockmarked the darkness with increasing intensity.

A firetruck, sirens blaring and lights flashing, crashed over a roadway berm, and its long white ladder slammed down on the ground on their side. Dozens of scrabbling black forms crawled along its length, then merged with the night. Tata leaned over.

"Ms. Sato, you are wondering if Jeb, Foley, and their soldiers will be okay?" she asked grimly. "Probably not. Life is shit. Have some kvass."

79

SHAWNEE, KANSAS

Right at that moment, Ellie didn't want to drink, but she remembered Russians tended to get emotional over small things. She politely sipped the beverage made from fermented black bread.

"Remember when you first drink kvass?" Tata asked nostalgically.

Ellie nodded, swallowed, and since there was little point to seeking decorum any longer, wiped her mouth on her sleeve.

"How could I forget? The catacombs under Paris."

Tata looked around. "What is our friend Mr. Ran Oliphant doing? He doesn't reply to my messages."

Before Ellie felt compelled to make social excuses for the oligarch, a green light flashed on Tata's forearm communications panel. She unrolled a filament OLED screen until it was the size of one normally found on a laptop and propped it on the dashboard.

"There, OCEL is closing in on the Tesla Cybertruck."

Janice and Senator Leota squeezed past Mr. Perdix and Ms. China to come up front and look at the images being beamed to them.

In a grainy jerky frame, obviously coming from the cameras on the canine robot's sensor cluster, was a very odd-looking vehicle. The night-vision image of the Cybertruck looked even more like something that would land on the Moon.

"These Teslas have cameras everywhere." Tata tapped on the virtual Russian letter keyboard. "We try to tap into the wireless feed from inside. Perhaps we can even do more if we can get through the encryptions guarding the—"

"Is the W33 in that vehicle?" Senator Leota hissed in an urgent tone.

Janice demanded, "Where is it?"

"Just beyond, uh, how do you say this place?" Tata's diamond-hard fingernail tapped the map on the screen.

"Olathe," Sarge Bryan said, while scanning the road ahead for large clusters of infected and stray hostile EMAC units.

"Is that close to the federal troops?" Janice asked.

"Close enough to kill them?" Mr. Perdix craned his earless head forward. "Not likely. From the data the Pentagon has sent, that series of W33 will have a maximum yield of twenty-five kilotons no matter how they've tinkered with it, likely less. The zone of complete destruction will have a radius of barely a mile, and that's not factoring in a detonation at ground level, which always results in suboptimal destructive power."

The image changed to a view from inside the covered rear compartment of the Tesla truck. In the onboard camera's night-vision mode they could see the bomb.

"Man, these EVs got fancy cams all over," Sarge Bryan said.

"What's that on the warhead?"

They peered closely at the screen. The familiar bullet-like shape lay strapped down in the flatbed. Knobby protrusions had been added to the base and the end cap at the top.

"Oh, that's clever," Mr. Perdix said.

"Perdix!" Sarge Bryan snapped.

"In a dastardly way, of course," he added. "This warhead is made to be fired from an artillery piece. The explosive forward thrust of the launch of the shell primes the internal triple-deck time-base fuse. They've attached small explosives onto the shell to mimic the physics of an actual cannon shot."

"Will it work?" Senator Leota demanded.

"It's probably a better idea than cracking open the case and trying to jury-rig the triggers. Assuming they've done their math correctly, I'd say the odds are better than even it will."

"If we disable either of those triggers, it's game over, right?" Sarge Bryan asked hopefully.

Mr. Perdix nodded enthusiastically, which caused him to lose his balance and slump against Tata's broad shoulder.

"So we can blow it up?" Ellie said. For a moment, she thought her stomach was making very unruly growling noises despite being fed a hamburger MRE, which had been stepped on or run over by a lorry. On further inspection she found it was her handset, which she had recharged on the MRAP's induction outlet. There was a new text with no sender ID.

`Go to the Turner Bridge, the EMACs have repaired it. You'll be safe there. You're welcome. Goodbye, Eleanor.`

The phone went dark, then got very hot, and the screen went a copper color and melted around the edges. Ellie put it on the floor. Miss Aleph must have fast-drained the battery, maybe to stop anyone from tracking the signal. Turner Bridge? What could she mean by that?

Up front, no one noticed. Everyone was staring at the screen Tata was holding, which was still streaming pictures of the W33 bomb.

"Can we get a picture of the driver from the Cybertruck's cameras?" Sarge Bryan asked. "I want to see if Hildago is solo."

"Should we try a drone strike?" Janice asked as she checked the battery level and reception strength showing on her satellite phone.

"I don't suggest blowing it up," Mr. Perdix said. "In this configuration, you might just set it off. However, a R9X ninja bomb might be able to take out the driver safely, assuming no dead-man's switch."

"OCEL is checking the other camera feeds," Tata said.

"There you are," Ms. China said as the picture flickered through side view, rear view, and finally the picture of a camera mounted on the Tesla's dash.

The image of Hidalgo had only just pixelated and resolved when something blew up inside the driver's area. It took a moment to make out what was happening. Large white blobs had exploded out from the steering wheel and the dashboard in front of the empty passenger seat.

"What…? Why did those air bags deploy?" Sarge Bryan asked. "He wasn't moving. Did the OCEL hit him with something?"

"Not us," Tata said innocently.

"Hidalgo's not inside the truck anymore," Ellie said, pushing the warm and useless handset farther under her seat. "He's fallen out."

Hidalgo had indeed been pitched sideways out the door of his vehicle, which had suddenly popped open. Odder still, the truck then sped forward, leaving the prone body of the EMAC commander behind.

"Who's driving?" Senator Leota demanded. "Janice, get the company on the line. You're married to an oligarch, you must have Elon Musk's personal cell number."

"Where's it going?" Ms. China asked. "Is it still trying to get to your troops on Lee's Summit?"

Tata tapped a Russian icon. "Map and track."

The Cybertruck appeared as a silver triangle on a satellite landscape of the area. It made a sharp turn and headed north toward the downtown area of Kansas City.

"It's not going to Lee's Summit. Maybe there's a dispute between EMAC factions," Sarge Bryan speculated. "Maybe some of them don't want to use the nuke and are trying to get it back, use it as negotiating leverage."

"Only thing Hidalgo's people are going to get is a firing squad," Senator Leota said under her breath.

The satellite map seemed to have been updated recently, and Ellie spotted a bridge with a familiar name.

"Is this us?" Ellie said, pointing to a green triangle.

Tata nodded.

"It looks like the bridge there has been repaired, right?" She leaned forward and pointed at the screen, quietly considering how much of Miss Aleph's secret and cryptic instructions she should tell the others. "Perhaps we should move in that direciton. It might give us another avenue of escape. If, you know, the excreta should hit the fan again."

Sarge Bryan gripped the MRAP's steering wheel. If he were on his own, his expression left no doubt in Ellie's mind he would have gone charging after the Tesla truck. Instead, he agreed with her. "Good thinking. We've got high-ranking VIPs on board."

"Thank you, Sergeant," Ms. China said.

"I was thinking of Ms. Jones and the senator."

They reversed course and headed to Turner Bridge over the Kansas River.

"This cyber thing," Ellie said, transfixed by the moving silver triangle, "how it can just go anywhere… by itself?"

As soon as she said it she realized how silly a question it was. There were dune buggies on other planets being remote controlled from Earth. Somehow she had always imagined self-driving cars wouldn't be so… headstrong.

"Good news," Jaince said "We've got a Reaper on station with a precision weapon on board."

Sarge Bryan glanced at the map. "The bomb's near the zoo. If it's going to be stopped and there's a danger of the nuke detonating, that's the least-populated place for miles."

As Ellie imagined thousands of animals being vaporied under a mushroom cloud, the notion that the W33 might go off at any moment somehow became more real and concrete.

"Who's giving the orders at McConnell?" Senator Leota asked sharply.

"None of your business," Janice said with venom. "They don't asnwer to you, only the real president. When we get to the bottom of this, you'll be in a basement cell in the Marion maximum-security prison."

"Ladies!" Sarge Bryan snapped. "Save the impeachments for after the war."

They motored on in silence. Their own icon on the map, a green triangle, drifted steadily northwest, and the silver triangle marking the Tesla rolled over the terrain marked by a pale rectangle, which denoted the Kansas City Zoo. Before it reached Big Blue Battlefield Park, another triangle appeared, this one red.

"Hey," Mr. Perdix said, alarmed. "That's supposed to be a *stealth* MQ-9 drone. How is is appearing on a Russian map?"

"Not telling," Tata said curtly.

The red icon rapidly floated over the roads and rivers, then started to circle the silver triangle like an eagle that had spotted a big fat rabbit. The

Tesla slowed down. Could it know it was being stalked from the air?

"It's a self-driving car. What could it be…"

Oh! She almost said it out loud. *Miss Aleph.* Originally programmed as an Israeli military AI, she had been programed to preserve life and help her masters carry out mission objectives. However, ever since breaking free of her mainframe years ago, Miss Aleph had developed quite an independent streak. Could Miss Aleph be driving the Cybertruck? If so, to what purpose?

Ellie looked out through the small rectangular blast-proof windows—the night was pitch black. The only way she could tell they were close to Turner Bridge was by looking at the glowing map and then finding their green triangle.

"It looks…" Sarge said, sqinting, "like the Tesla's evading."

The silver traingle sped up, slowed down, and circled, persumably to hide behind buildings and trees.

"The Reaper operator says he's got no shot," Janice said, relaying the update that came over the chunky handset she had pressed to her ear. "He's going in lower."

"They're coming up on the stadium. That's the EMAC's most heavily guarded position," the senator said, her voice sounding quite loud given the gloom that surrounded the MRAP. "They'll have defenses."

"We need a backup plan," Mr. Perdix said. "Where's the OCEL unit? Has it continued tracking the Tesla?"

Tata flicked her head sideways, and a pink triangle appeared on the map along with an inset picture of the night-vision camera feed from the sensor array on the OCEL's head.

"The Reaper is shooting," Janice said.

Just then, the silver icon of the Tesla raced forward with that strange burst of speed EVs are capable of.

"No damage. No damage."

The red triangle of the drone now started to fly erratically.

"EMACs are deloying jamming attacks and hard-kill aerial interceptors against the Reaper," Janice said, repeating what the ground operator was telling her. "Drone's weapons are hot. It is firing."

The Tesla had sped out from a community called Eastwood Hills. There were only two roads north. It took the most direct route toward Arrowhead Stadium.

"It's no good, they'll get their bomb back," Sarge said, frustrated.

"Reaper is hit, losing attitude control."

The red traingle made strange elliptical circles and then stopped moving, presumably downed. The Tesla icon also stuttered to a stop near the intersection of Raytown Road and Sportsman Drive.

"He got it. The Cybertruck's been disabled," Mr. Perdix said. "You know, JASON develeoped the precison gun carriages for the Reaper. They said those old models should be phased out, but we said, hang on—"

"So how do we get hands the package?" Sarge Bryan asked. "Can Lee's Summit command deploy a quick-reaction force?"

Before Janice could get an answer, the pink triangle of the OCEL reached the Tesla. Tata tapped the robot's camera feed, and it opened to full screen.

"Good thinking!" Senator Leota said. "Can your bot carry the bomb?"

"OCEL can carry a Human+ soldier for several kilometers," Tata said. "This W33 projectile masses only one hundred kilograms."

"Then it can fetch the nuke?" Sarge Bryan asked hopefully.

"Da," Zvena said, poking his head in the cab of the truck now that they had stopped moving. "Small problem is… we are no longer controlling the OCEL."

Everyone's eyes snapped onto the shaky camera feed coming from the rogue robot's head.

"The EMACs are experts in electronic warfare, can they have hacked it?" Sarge Brayn asked quickly. "Is there a destruct override for those bots?"

Tata pursed her lips and shook her head.

"Bad OCEL," Rodion said in a complaining voice that did not seem to reflect the gravity of the situation. The largest cyborg tapped on a control panel while also glancing at the map throrgh the MRAP's open door. "I'm trying to make him lie down and hide, but he is unresponsive."

The OCEL's camera showed it prying open the truck's rear compartment, quickly snipping away the bomb's tethers, and putting its head under the oblong warhead. When it moved off, Ellie thought the mechanoid was moving more slowly than it normally did as it labored under the extra weight.

It left the road and loped off into a line of trees at the speed of a fast human jogger. Low branches slapped at the camera lens in strangely jittery night-vision images.

"Where's it going?" Ellie asked, and without thinking it might foul something up, tapped the area map icon in the corner of the screen. Tata gave her a look accompanied by squinting cyborg eyes. "The stadium?"

There were two sports amphitheaters very close to one another. Arrowhead was the larger, and a small one called Kaufmann was to the north.

"Are we sure the OCEL was hacked by EMACs?" Seantor Leota demanded, looking pointedly at Janice for a reason Ellie could not immediately fathom.

"What are you saying, Blue State?" Janice immediately retorted. "Those are your EMACs, your WMD."

"Isn't it convenient the warhead is headed *away* from Lee's Summit?"

"Ladies, please assist the current mission or stand yourselves down," Sarge Bryan said evenly, staring unblinking at the screen as he returned the large picture to the camera live feed.

The OCEL came out from the treed area and climbed up the bank of a gravel-strewn ditch. For a few nail-biting moments, it sat still, watching headlights approach. After an EMAC vehicle passed by, it scampered toward a chain-link fence. Hardly pausing, it deloyed one mantis-like foreleg and quietly snipped the fence apart and squeezed through.

"Arrowhead is the larger of the two stadiums," Janice said idly, still keeping her distance from the wounded but fierce-looking senator. "It has seating for more than seventy thousand. I was... we where there for a campaign rally."

A set of vibrating bars on the side of the screen caught Ellie's attention by jittering higher.

"Is there sound?"

Tata flicked her head, which operated her HUD remote buttons, and a burst of static made them all draw back from the display screen with a start. Then it turned out not to be static. It was the hum of a breathing, living mass, which was trapped, hungry, and desperately looking for a way to escape.

"Could there really be that many in there?" Ellie asked.

"The EMAC claimed to have more than three hundred thousand infected,"

Mr. Perdix said. "Assuming neglibile loss to crushing or escape..."

"But the people they took there," the senator said, sitting back agisnt the side of the MRAP, "they were normal."

"Not anymore," Ms. China said curtly.

"Anyone put in with the biomass of infected will succumb to Stage Two," Mr. Perdix said. "Their ability to use tools makes them particularly dangerous."

The outer walls of the stadium loomed. Movement caught the OCEL's camera eyes. They flicked up and zoomed in. Atop the curved wall, figures moved, gunshots cracked. Things fell, seconds passed before they thudded to the asphalt of the empty parking lot.

"Infected. They were trying to go over the stadium wall," Sarge Bryan said.

"Arrowhead has advanced anti-terrorism security additions," Mr. Perdix said, leaning in and forcing Ellie to look away from his blood-encrusted ear stump. "It's nearly as impregnable as an open-air prison. JASON was contracted to—"

"Will you shut up about JASON?" Ms. China said. "It's a stupid name."

The OCEL was not intimidated by the sports facility's supposeed impregnableness. As though following a scent, it trotted along a service road up to the side of the enormous complex. It soon became apparent breaking in was easier than breaking out. The OCEL easily levered open the latch on a steel door. This opened onto a long corridor, which sloped down. The OCEL closed the door behind itself and trotted forward.

"What's that?" Ms. China asked, pushing at the side of Mr. Perdix's head quite aggressively. "Is that Stage Three?"

"Whatever it is, it's not moving."

There was a furry hulking figure that looked ready to lunch forward.

"It's a wolfman."

As they got closer, the blurry figure resolved into a wolfman costume sitting empty on a bench in the corridor, its fuzzy head tilted forward. Two wolf paw boots sat on the floor next to it.

"It's a mascot costume belonging to one of the teams that play there," Sarge Bryan observed dryly.

Suddenly there was a blur of motion. Voices came over the speaker:

"What's that? I can't see! Take your NVG off. I did, you... dumnfuck, it's dark, and we're being strobed with infr—"

Two EMACs had emerged from around a corner just beyond where the wolf costume stood. The speaker's voice cut off as the OCEL's forelegs started chopping, almost gleefuly.

A minute later, the robot stomped over the inert, jumbled body parts and moved deeper into the complex. A bucket with a mop sticking out of it slid into and out of view, followed by row after row of silent lockers.

"That's a multi-kiloton warhead on its back. Why doesn't it just get it over with?" Seantor Leota said with a mournful groan.

"The only reason I can fathom is..." Mr. Perdix said quietly, "showmanship."

The OCEL passed a row of stacked musical instruments, trombones, drums, and a big pile of cheerleader pom-poms. It arrived at a wide retangular industrial lift and got in. The door shut and the mechanism whirred.

The OCEL's camera pointed straight up, the darkness splitting open to reveal a starry sky. The lift must have been part of the opening and halftime shows, it triggered the sound system, which started playing one of America's national anthems.

"Lift every voice and sing,

"Till earth and heaven ring..."

Ellie flinched as the writhing bodies of dozens of infected came tumbling down. They bashed against the lift cage protecting the robot and its cargo.

When the throaty voice of the singer reached:

"Facing the rising sun of our new day begun,

"Let us march on till victory is won—"

The canopy enclosing the rising platform split open. Rising in mid-field, it would normally delight and surprise sports fans watching a game. If anyone was surprised tonight, it was hard to tell. Ellie saw thousands and thousands of infected, their hostile glaring eyes blazing in the robot's enhanced night vision. Then its forelimb reached up and yanked something.

A series of explosions sent the canine bot violently tumbling to one side, scything through the crowd. All she could see was a blur of hands, arms, and bared teeth set in mouths opened inhumanly wide. Then the display screen went dead.

Everyone looked away from the windows. Ellie silently counted *1, 2, 3, 4, 5.*

A sinister false dawn irradiated the horizon eastward. Low-hanging clouds were singed by molten fire. The eerie light faded fast. An antenna on the MRAP glowed and launched a short tongue of static discharge onto the engine housing. Everything electronic crackled or went dead.

Seconds later, unlike the rolling rattle of real thunder but more like the dropping of a cosmic-sized manhole cover, a metallic *thrum-bang* rolled over the metal skin of their MRAP, followed by a dry, rolling, rushing sound.

80

DEFIANCE, OHIO

ABDELKADER

The deeper they went inside America's heartland, the more Abdelkader felt that he was raping the country. It felt good. It felt so good, in fact, he nearly forgot it was three a.m. and time for his next serum injection.

"Baldur!" he yelled to the car behind the T-ray emitter truck. "It's time."

"We're almost done with this shithole," Ahmad Umar the Pangean technician said as he stood over the dark-matter energy device. He was busy plotting off dispersion lines on a grid map. Ahmad had left Somalia's al-Shabab to become one of his hardcore Faceless fighters. "This is not a large settlement."

"Save your enthusiasm for New York," Abdelkader said. "Stand down for now. Did you get that building?" He pointed at the newspaper office.

Ahmad shook his head.

"See if anyone is inside."

When the others were gone, he got out of the truck and motioned Dr. Baldur forward. He was carrying a dark-gray oblong case. Abdelkader looked left and right through the eyeholes of his silicone mask. It was itching. Nearly time to get a fresh one. He took it off.

"How many doses?"

"I managed to extend the supply by mixing in ovalbumin, which we were lucky to acquire in its pharmaceutical grade," the medical man stuttered.

"How many?"

"Four days," Baldur said in a hushed voice.

Abdelkader fingered the small hard case kept around his waist day and night. It held the garish metallic vial he'd taken from Sprünger Labs. Perhaps he should just destroy the enzyme, let the continent convulse and obliterate itself. Their EMAC allies in Kansas City were growing a super cluster of second-tier infected. Once he was through with New York... Four days... He should just do it.

"No!"

"I'm sorry, I'm sorry." The cucked doctor obviously thought that Abdelkader was berating him. Baldur glanced at the enzyme container, quickly looked back up into Abdelkader's bare skinless face and attempted a small smile.

"You can manufacture more serum?"

"W-when we get to a CDC lab, certainly," Baldur said, fumbling with the lock on his suitcase. "And without a doubt, I can make the effect permanent."

"Even without the female scientist whose work you stole?"

Baldur cringed and was about to say something when Ahmad dragged a fat older man out from the newspaper office. He threw him to his knees in front of Abdelkader.

"Is this place really called Defiance?"

The man just gazed up at him. Most of the group were Faceless and worked without masks, the prisoner stared at the horrific remains of peeled-away flesh that ran from hairline down to the nape of their necks.

"Answer, you pink pig." Ahmad stabbed him with a bayonet.

"It's called that," the older American said. "Just take what you want and go."

"Oh, I am," Abdelkader said, studying the man's nose. It was a bit chunky and rounded on its end, like a pig snout. On the other hand, he was clean shaven. "How would you like to be the face of the new America? Ahmad, this one is mine. Peel him."

As the newspaper man was tightly bound and then having his face skinned off, Abdelkader received his injection. The serum as it was now formulated made him temporarily lose connection with each of his senses in turn. First he became blind, then his sight returned, initially black and white, then revealing more color with each passing second.

Next, the local man's screams became a dull whisper before being shut out entirely. Taste and smell vanished and returned. Finally, his whole body felt like numb dead weight, and he had to look down to make sure he was not moving his arms or legs. By the time the experience passed, the whole front of the kafir's head was unmasked and glistening, and the removed oval of skin was being chemically cured like leather.

Still alive and in obvious and gratifying agony, the newspaper man was trying to say something. Pink spittle foamed around his lipless teeth, and his lidless eyes jerked right and left inside sockets red rimmed and leaking blood in streams like tears over raw carved meat and exposed cheekbones.

He still had the temerity to ask: "Why... here?"

Abdelkader leaned over him, unsure if the wretch could see him as he struggled.

"Because here in De-fiance, Oh-io, is where the drone that killed my people was made. I swore I would vanquish you, and I have." He looked up at his men. "Let him go. Let him take a tour of what we've made of his town and his people."

They released the older man's bonds and pushed him off the table. As he staggered away, they kicked him, and he lurched, oozing blood with every step. His face was too painful to touch, so he clasped his hands behind his head. Unable to see where he was going, he bumped right into a courier who was running up to Abdelkader's mobile command post. The runner, a huge Ugandan, took offense and dug out the local man's eyes. Gripping the pink pig's head like a bowling ball, he then cast his heaving body over a fence.

"Pity," Abdelkader said, looking at his new face, which was nearly done curing. "I would have liked to see that one turn."

The Ugandan wiped gore off his hands. Abdelkader noticed the hesitant look on the man's face, and his body language betrayed agitation. Abdelkader sensed something had happened he would not like. He put the warm flesh mask back down on the table.

"What?"

"There has been… an explosion in Kansas City. They set off an atomic," the courier said, holding out a handset, the screen of which was flashing with amateur images of a nighttime detonation.

He actually did it, Abdelkader thought. Hidalgo had hinted that he had weapons of mass destruction in their Arsenal of Equality, which was what the American Marxists called their military wing. But he didn't think Hidalgo and his cadre of effeminate and outright homosexual social justice warriors would have the guts to set off nukes. If they were this ruthless, they would not make good servants. Just as Abdelkader was thinking of ways to betray and kill the EMACs, he sensed the courier was not finished.

"There's more?"

"F-from what we can tell, it was not the federal forces that were hit—it was the EMACs. They've been wiped out."

"Washington nuked their own city?" That was an even more implausible show of strength.

The Ugandan thrust the handset toward Abdelkader. He flicked past the live feeds showing fires ringing a huge crater in the center of the Midwestern city. He found a live newscast being streamed on the TimPool Network. The interim governor of California was broadcasting from Sacramento; the other half of the split screen showed Senator Leota at an undisclosed location.

He let the handset fall to the cold dark earth. He didn't have to turn up the volume. The civil war they had been using as cover was over. The pathetic blue-state cowards were submitting to the federal forces.

"Get everyone mobile!" he yelled. It was only a matter of hours until the Americans would stop fighting each other and come after them.

The courier remained where he was.

"Some other disaster to report? Out with it."

"Sir, we hacked into the EMAC's intelligence network as you ordered." The Ugandan took a tablet rimmed in olive-green plastic out from his duffel. "We are still interpreting the data. The EMACs had extensive spy networks in all levels of government and civil administration. The plague replication rates are exceeding your best forecasts. Los Angeles and Las Vegas are completely engulfed. A plane we irradiated made it to Dallas, and that city is in ruins."

So… they might not need help from the blue-state rebels after all. "That makes it all the more important to get to New York City."

"There was also an encrypted message on the JASON network. The EMAC spyware flagged and decoded it. I don't know what to make—"

Abdelkader yanked the tablet from the larger man, scrolling through the dispatches. He read:

Space-based Thermal Radiation Plan to stop the spread of A/P-32…

Deployment of Svalinn space mirror… elevate ground temperature 90°F… four- to six-mile radius…

Satellite controls routed to most secure facility in Mount Weather, VA.

"Baldur!"

As his team looted the town and loaded their vehicles, the cringing, worthless scientist came running up. Abdelkader's patience was strained to the maximum as the little weasel hemmed and hawed over the extensive data they had intercepted.

"Well?" Abdelkader said when he could no longer take the suspense and felt the urge to order Baldur's insipid pudgy face be peeled off. "It is true? Is it possible?"

"Let me first say that your plan has exceeded our best expectations," Baldur said, his eyes unblinking behind his glasses and sweat starting to bead around his hairline and on his upper lip despite the chilly night air. "And may I also say that as we discovered on Tortuga Island, nothing can stop the T-ray from activating infection. Nothing except the vaccine we're taking."

"I also recall you had trouble testing the second stage of infection because of the summer heat."

"Yes, that, uh, was a small issue, which is why we attacked during the winter months."

"If they can use this space mirror to slow or stop the secondary transmissions… with no civil war distraction…"

"I don't see what we can do about it," Baldur said, the sweating now causing disgusting stains of wetness to grow under the armpits of this camouflage jacket. "We must push forward and overwhelm their countermeasures."

"Be quiet. I have to think."

Something exploded inside the burning newspaper building. The frontage crumbled, and the only parts of the sign left were the words *CRESCENT* and an oversized *C*, which reminded Abdelkader of the best times of his youth as a member of a Purity Squad in the Islamic State.

"No," Abdelkader said icily. "That's what they will expect. They don't know we have this intelligence about their next move." He turned his back on the scientist and waved to Grayson, a thin man with neck tattoos. He was one of the few American Antifa members who had survived the fight with the cyborgs in Las Vegas and had proven himself much more useful than Sikawski or, for that matter, Baldur. "Plot the most secure routes from here to Mount Weather."

81

MOUNT WEATHER, VIRGINIA

Abdelkader again checked the fat chronometer hanging from his wrist. They had to make their vaccine supply last. Dr. Baldur claimed there was a bioweapons facility inside the Mount Weather bunker that he could use to make more, but the soft and effeminate scientist had been wrong about many, many things.

"No doses yet," Abdelkader said, deciding. "If we can't replicate any here, we'll use the last vials to locate another laboratory." *Or, failing that, launch an all-out martyrdom strike on New York, blanketing the filthy huddled masses of kafir with T-rays.*

"I assure you," Dr. Baldur said from the seat beside him, "we will find what we need there."

They drove through treed Virginia countryside; the Mount Weather bunker was only a few miles away. Even with the T-ray emitter, breaching the ultra-secure government facility during a national emergency would be impossible if they attempted a frontal assault. Fortunately, they had inside help.

"First we have to get in." Abdelkader turned to Ahmad, who was at the wheel of the long Chrysler Caravan. "Pass the main entrance by. Take the next left after that."

The data cache they had stolen from the EMAC network contained updated satellite maps and the classified schematics of the facility's dozen underground levels.

"But this road leads to a dead end," Dr. Baldur said, once again sticking his greasy nose where it did not belong. "The front gate—"

"Will take too long to breach," Abdelkader said sharply. An attempt might even bring down an airborne quick-reaction force and get them all captured.

He fingered the pendant containing the enzyme vial. If it was the last thing he did, he would destroy it before he would let it be taken. It was America's only hope. Even though they needed it, he had a strong impulse to grind it into microscopic fragments.

"But here there is no road up the mountain."

Ahmad snorted a laugh through his silicone mask. "Then it's good we stole you a nice pair of boots for your pretty soft feet, Dr. Baldur." He turned off onto a side road.

Leafless trees hung specter-like along the placid countryside landscape. The lone figure on the road was an American wearing multiple scarves who was hauling the leashes of five German shepherd dogs. As they passed, the Pangeans averted their faces and parked in a frost-covered field behind a tiny unincorporated town called Trapp.

Dr. Baldur was not a complete moron; he was just a weakling. Almost every discovery he had made relied on the work of a truly great killer: the female scientist he had only caught a glimpse of at the Sprünger facility. Worse still, Baldur's pretense of glee while watching infidels suffer and die was insincere. As he got out into the sharply chilly afternoon air, Abdelkader again fantasized about the moment he could finally be rid of their weakest link.

They hauled out the heavy T-ray emitter and dragged it across a snow-crusted field into the line of bare trees at the foot of Mount Weather. They had only gotten a hundred yards when Baldur huffed as though he were going to faint. This nearly caused the device to tip over, and he abruptly set his portion of the load down.

"Look over there." He pointed with his mitten-covered hand. "There's a road we could have taken. It's—heff—much closer."

"Yes, and taking it would also announce 'We're trying to break into Mount Weather' to anyone glancing at us from two hundred miles up," Abdelkader snapped back at him. "Everyone else needs to be on guard for sentries. Shoulder your share of the load."

They resumed crossing the field. Should anyone challenge them, their cover story was they were workmen fixing a septic tank. They had nearly gotten to the line of trees that bordered the forest surrounding the bunker when a puff of snow rained down from nearby branches. Abdelkader's hand dove beneath his winter coat as he watched a single figure in dark clothing slipped out from the underbrush.

"Don't shoot," Abdelkader told his men. "And Doctor, stop pissing your pants."

The man approaching them wore a toque pulled down low over both sides of his head. Behind his wire-rimmed glasses, his eyes darted wildly this way and that; he had the pallid complexion of a life-long video game addict. Seeing them, he raised his hand.

"Are you...?"

"Who else?" Abdelkader said sharply, giving the man a hard stare through his borrowed empty eye sockets. The American looked as though he had survived a long incarceration instead of lounging in a comfortable chair enjoying government wages and benefits. He was so nervous he had to grab hold of the lower limbs of trees to steady himself. "Well?"

"You're clear up to the helipad," the EMAC mole said, looking left and right. He pulled his toque down further, then fished inside a vest pocket. He brought out a ring of key cards one with a large timer display. "I've bought you twenty-two minutes of security blackout. After that, you're on your own."

22:00

Abdelkader looked at the digital key set, then into the man's watery eyes. At first, he decided not to eliminate him. He was just another Western weakling, a drowning rat hoping to swim away as America sank into the seas of anarchy.

"Go, then. If you can make it to Tunisia, tell them you helped the Faceless Jihad. You will be safe and honored as a hero." As soon as the words were out of Abdelkader's mouth, he reconsidered. He should order the traitor disposed of. As soon as he was out of sight, he could betray them.

On the other hand, when they finished at Mount Weather, they might need help from Antifa and whatever still remained of the blue-state EMAC to ensure the ruin of the United States. Once they disabled the space mirror, unless the federal forces were willing to drop a nuke on every major city, the plague would continue spreading. Like the Prophet, he would be merciful. "Go now. Inshallah, we shall meet again as allies in the final battle."

The strange man angled his head as though he were hard of hearing, then nodded and walked away down the hill in the direction of a distant farmhouse.

With one hand, Abdelkader pushed Dr. Baldur along, with the other he pressed the chemically cured, leathery face of the Ohio newspaper man down along his jawline. The cold air was causing it to lose adhesion.

"This man's code name and backchannel text messaging ID were in Hidalgo's data cache," he said. "The EMACs knew that to completely destroy the federal government, they'd eventually have to breach this place as well as Cheyenne Mountain and the Pentagon's nuclear bunker at Raven Rock."

A sturdy fence surrounded the perimeter of the government property. The gate was opened by the key card and a one-time code, which got texted back to a small LED fob. In the woods behind and around them, nothing stirred. The loudest sound was the huffing coming from Dr. Baldur as his breath made increasingly large clouds of condensation around him.

"I'll take that," Abdelkader said, hefting his part of the emitter load. "You go up twenty meters and stop."

Once they were inside Mouth Weather's wide perimeter, the climb became steeper, but here there were long, flat steps set into the hillside forming something like a hiking trail. Abdelkader tracked their progress on his handset. It used two GPS systems, Chinese BeiDou and European Galileo, to locate their position in relation to the underground facility.

The display told him they were at a precise horizontal level with Mount Weather's laboratory some six hundred meters through the side of the hill. That was the extreme limit of the T-ray emitter using its mobile power cells. They had to get closer.

That meant further walking past pressure sensors, motion detectors, and cameras along the relatively straight trail to the top. The increased effort made him sweat, and again he had to press down on the edges of his borrowed face to make it stick. He should have thrown it away, but it was a memento of fulfilling his vow to his family to utterly destroy Defiance, Ohio.

They caught up with Dr. Baldur. He was waiting at the next landing, patient as a lapdog. Abdelkader waved him on. And so it went until they were three quarters of the way to the East Portal entrance.

Baldur stood rigidly for a moment, then leaned forward and ducking down comically, almost crawling back to them.

"Guards," he whispered. "Guards."

During a period of high alert, there would, of course, be patrols. But they had not been alerted to their incursion. Either the cameras were being monitored by Antifa collaborators inside Mount Weather or their pale and skinny contact had rigged fake images while he had sabotaged the alarms. Soon it would not matter—they were in range.

"Deploy the emitter," Abdelkader hissed.

Baldur fretted like a woman. "But the noise…"

"Will be minimal using the power cells. Get out of the way."

He sent the Ugandan, the tallest among them, to watch the guards with a handheld camera. Abdelkader watched on a monitor. There were four Americans in winter gear, all carrying rifles. It looked as though the first two were chatting before handing off their patrol duties to the next pair.

The emitter made barely a hum as Abdelkader set it to medium-wide dispersion in the direction of the four soldiers. The dark-matter energy beam would penetrate trees and earth and rocks as though these obstacles were not there. As soon as he was certain they'd been given a hearty dose, he switched it off to save the batteries.

The second pair of guards went through the chain-link gate and started walking back across the helipad toward the cave-like entrance to the bunker. It would be no good if they got inside before turning. When they lost their minds, stage-one infected always made a mess; they could trigger a facility-wide lockdown.

"Couldn't we have just shot them?" Dr. Baldur said, also watching the scene on the handset over Abdelkader's shoulder.

"Don't flaunt your ignorance. All of the perimeter guards will have helmet or body cams, and who knows who's monitoring those."

The Mount Weather guards were nearly at the doorway. If their experiences were anything like those endured by the experimental subjects on La Tortuga Island, the first sensation as the beam swept over them would be the brief desire to sneeze and mild vertigo, both of which would pass quickly. Then, they would notice an odd "cotton ball" dry sensation in their mouth.

Abdelkader had personally tortured prisoners as they turned, which had been challenging because he had to quickly elicit accurate information. The subjects progressively lost their sense of smell and taste, then the few he could get answers out of, before they lost the ability to form words, had told him their conscious mind felt as though it were falling backward into a deep tunnel.

Abdelkader wiped a drop of mucous from his borrowed nose. The cold air was making his sinuses drip. While no one could be certain, he hoped his victims across America were aware of what their bodies were doing: chewing up their loved ones, wandering through fires, being hit by all manner of vehicles...

"Look," Dr. Baldur said with some relief. The monitor showed one of the guards who had remained by the outer gate was crouched, trying to help the other who had slipped, then he quickly succumbed himself.

The pair farther away, inside the Mount Weather perimeter, had nearly made it to the concrete oval of the East Portal. However, both had stopped walking normally. One just stood, hunched over at the waist, arms hanging down slackly. The other walked leftward in ever-increasing circles like a brain-damaged beetle.

"Up, up, up," Abdelkader ordered.

No longer worried about making noise, they rushed forward, putting all their effort into heaving the emitter up the frost-slick stairway. He glanced at the digital timer.

12:38

"We have ten minutes to irradiate as much of the place as we can, then we have to be inside."

His men cornered the two freshly infected near the gate. They put them down with axe blows to the head, then hacked away at their leg tendons to disable the mindless mobile remains. Abdelkader's people hauled up the emitter and turned it on. It built up to its maximum output, and the open end glowed an eerie shade of violet. In the trees behind them, a small squall whistled through the bare branches, shaking loose ice particles. Their fall, like the second hand on Abdelkader's watch, measured out precious seconds remaining in the security blackout.

The aiming module, adapted from a laser weapon built to intercept drones tracked slowly right to left, dropped a minute of an angle, then tracked left to right, then dropped a minute of angle. If they missed anyone inside Mount Weather, they could damage equipment or initiate a lockout.

The emitter's power reserves were declining too quickly, Abdelkader thought furiously. He checked the clock again.

8:16

"It's the bloody temperature," he said to himself, willing the device to cycle faster as the battery level dropped into yellow bars, then red.

The mechanism seized up and stopped. Had it saturated the lowest levels of Mouth Weather?

"We go in."

"But… what if there are still people…"

"If the first-stage infected don't get them, we will." Abdelkader turned to the group, giving all but six vaccine vials to his second in command. "Ahmad, as soon as you get to the van, inject yourselves. Take the emitter to New York. Send the kafir a message they will never forget. In twelve hours, with or without more vaccine, we shall find you."

Abdelkader, Dr. Baldur, and four of his best programmers burst through the final fence and ran toward the East Portal. The infected guard who stood slumped over started to stand back up, perhaps sensing the approach of fresh meat. Abdelkader's axe cut the nearest one almost in half. The other guard was bumping his head against the big metal doorway until he, too, sensed a warm meal behind him. The Ugandan brought a breaching bar down on his helmeted head, which disappeared between the gray-brown camouflage shoulders of his uniform.

Somehow Dr. Baldur had ended up with the ring of key cards. His hands were shaking as he held them up to the card reader. He tried to read the one-time pass code generated by the LED fob. He swiped dirt from the display panel with his sweating dirty finger, tried again, and failed.

"It's not working."

The facility was built during the Cold War to survive a nuclear attack. Once they were inside, they could seal each level and have time to override the American space mirror satellite. His programmers had prepared a Stuxnet bug that would cause it to crash into the Moon.

"Give me that," Abdelkader said, ripping the keyring out of the doctor's hands. "If you've fucked up too many times and engaged a lockout..."

He tried again and again, triple-checking the code before entering it on the keypad and got a sinking feeling that was exactly what had happened. His mind worked furiously, going over the schematics of the different levels. There were other ways in, two service entrances, but he was unsure if they connected with the control room. The only other option was the West Portal, and that was more than a kilometer away. They had no way to irradiate the guards there.

The little plastic timepiece blinked mockingly at him.

0:00

The security sabotage window had run out.

Just then, the vault-like door in front of them popped open.

"Careful!" Abdelkader raised his axe, instantly wary of betrayal.

The dull eyes of a single infected glared out from beneath a shock of sandy hair. Before it could put one foot out the door, the Ugandan pounded its face into pink mist.

"How?" Dr. Baldur said, probably relieved that it was not he who had his empty head crushed.

"That one must have been Stage Two," Abdelkader concluded. "It remembered how to get out and opened the door from inside. Quickly, in, and watch out for more."

From the depths of despair, Abdelkader's spirits rebounded as the big steel door clanged closed behind them, the well-oiled tumblers sliding into place. They had breached Mount Weather.

Dr. Baldur pulled on his arm, looking at the vaccine vials in Abdelkader's coat. "It's nearly time for injections. We're in. We can take them now."

"No. First secure the control room."

The stolen keycards opened the next security gate and also let them access the lifts. They encountered a few wandering infected, all Stage One. Some wore lab coats, others civilian clothes. The communications room was on level four. When the lift doors opened, everyone took a step back. In front of them was a large glass-enclosed room with dozens of infected milling around.

"There's another way," Dr. Baldur said helpfully.

Abdelkader checked the schematics and nodded. They bypassed the teeming mass of not-quite-dead Americans. Halfway down a hallway, he ordered his programmers into the server room.

"Isolate the mainframes so that no one can do to us what we're about to do to them."

The three programmers went into the computer room; it was warm and humming with servers on racks up to the ceiling.

Ahead, Abdelkader saw a fork in the path; the map was not clear which led through and which was a dead end.

"There may be some infected inside the control room," he said to the Ugandan and Baldur. "We have to stop them from damaging the equipment. You go left, I'll go this way."

Abdelkader was happy to have the scientist out of his sight. The bungler had nearly wrecked everything. He marched forward, axe and pistol ready. He stepped along the matte-gray hallway as though he owned the place, which for all intents and purposes, he did. The entrance was sealed. Even air was internally recirculated inside the bunker.

A clicking noise came from around a corner. He stopped, steadied his pistol on his left forearm, and peered around the edge of a wall. A figure appeared. It had to be a Stage Two infected, an Asian female. When the T-rays had irradiated her, she must have already been wearing the bubbleheaded respirator device. The glass was wide and clear. Abdelkader could see the creature's insipid face and slack mouth. He would have shot it right then had he not been distracted by what she was doing. The creature seemed to be tapping a keypad inside a large designer handbag. Then, with widening eyes and a start, it noticed him.

"Oh, hashers!" said a muffled voice.

She's not infected. The realization struck him like a hammer blow. He raised his weapon.

"Oh my God," the woman in the hazmat suit cried out in a dithering voice. "Anna, is that stuff you're blasting through the vent system supposed to make people's faces slough off?"

Maybe she was in the lowest levels, out of range of the beam, Abdelkader thought. And what was she saying about the vent system? Then he noticed his hand was not obeying his command. Try as he might, he could not raise his gun. His weapons seemed too heavy and finally slid from his numb fingers, clattering to the floor. Slumping over, he saw what lay beside the pistol and the axe: the leathery face of the Ohio newspaperman. It had slipped from his forehead without him being aware. What was happening?

"No, it doesn't," said another, more aggressive-sounding female voice. "But now that you mention it, I should try that… Hah! You found one!"

Unable to turn his head any longer, Abdelkader noticed a second figure in the corner of his eye. She also had on a bubblehead respirator, and there was something odd about her eyes. She looked… familiar?

He remembered the enzyme pack strapped to his chest. With all his might he tried to raise his hands to destroy it… but his wrist only flopped weakly against his waist and then went slack. Leaning against the wall, he could neither move voluntarily nor fall down in a heap.

"Ha," the blonde woman crouched down to get a better look. She seemed fascinated by his bare face and his raw eye sockets. "That's what I call a close shave." She pulled out a spray dispenser. "Hey, ugly, before I give you some more of my special version of carfentanyl called 'Unpleasant Dreams,' here's something to really make you lose face: the rather obvious trap you just walked into was mostly her idea."

The blonde woman wiggled her rubber-clad thumb toward the dazed-looking Asian woman.

The vile woman blasted mist onto his face, and all thoughts of his hand clenching around her neck and his teeth biting off her nose were lost. She mouthed more words, but Abdelkader no longer heard them as his mind fell backward into a dark depthless pit.

82

O f course, it was my idea how to pop open the front door for you when you genius jihadis ran into difficulties..." Ms. China explained as she peered at the unknown terrorist's hideous face. To Ellie, he looked catatonic. "Hey, meat face! Can you hear me?"

Ellie stood trembling behind her in the corridor. The whole encounter with the hideous man, now drugged into catatonia, had taken about five seconds.

Just before the terrorist accosted her, she had stepped away from the others in order to ask Miss Aleph some pointed questions about Kansas City. She had just figured something out, and despite her surroundings and the danger, her inquiries couldn't wait.

Aleph, I know you can hear me. She had tapped her phone's keypad with her burgundy 146 Montblanc because of the rubber gloves they made her wear. *I need to know, what did you have to do with the w33 going off? No one seems to know how it happened and*

No sooner had she begun typing her urgent message when this most fiendish-looking person nearly ran right into her. Just when he looked as though he intended to shoot her, he lost all motor control, not to mention all the leathery skin covering the front of his head.

"That looks very realistic," Ellie said, now staring at the flap of skin, which had fallen from the insurgent's face. "It looks like someone's face that's been cleanly filleted off."

"You're bloody right it does, because it is," Ms. China said, nudging it with the toe of her shoe. Meanwhile the terrorist was frozen in place, unable to so much as blink. "I'm so good! He's knocked out on his feet. Isn't he cute as a button?"

Ellie glanced again at the desiccated, red, burned skin covering the man's head.

"No," was all she could think to say as she inched away from the terrible sight.

Ms. China reached out her bandaged, fingernailless hand and prodded him. "Just one little push, watch. He topples like a rotten tree."

The terrorist swayed for a moment, then, without a sound, he collapsed to the floor just as Sarge Bryan and the others came running around the corner.

"There you are, finally," Ms. China said. "We got him."

"I told you two to stick with us," he said, his glowing eyes making an interesting effect from inside the fishbowl helmet of his hazmat suit. He pushed the insensible man down and started trussing him up with zip ties.

"Where are the others?"

Ellie, Ms. China, Sarge Bryan, and Janice had been waiting in the communications room for the terrorists to arrive. It had been split-second timing. The Army people had just finished herding decoy infected they had captured at Kansas City into key corridors of Mount Weather when Mr. Perdix signaled that the Pangeans were approaching the East Portal.

Everyone who had not received the T-ray vaccine had to evacuate. That left them inside the massive complex with more infected than Ellie liked to think about. After helping the infiltrators get through the portal pressure door, Ms. China had deployed her Unpleasant Dreams gas.

"The guards who volunteered to remain outside..." Ellie asked.

Sarge Bryan shook his head. "They knew what was being asked of them; they'd seen the devastation in the Midwest. It was the only way to convince the enemy to come inside and safely get hold of the missing enzyme."

"Ah, there's my stuff, you little shit." Carefully, Ms. China grabbed what looked like a sunglasses case strapped to the Pangean's chest. It opened to reveal a plastic zombie Hello Kitty locket.

"Good, now give it over." Janice Jones walked up to them with her rubber-gloved hand out. "Sergeant, take this woman into custody."

"Ma'am, you may be the president's chief of staff," Sarge Bryan said, "but I'm still under written orders from President Casteel."

Janice looked livid. She glanced left and right, perhaps forgetting there were no Secret Service with her. Their small group were the only ones who could survive a blast of T-rays.

"We'll let Ms. Sato hang on to this enzyme concoction. How 'bout that?"

Ellie placed it inside her Hermes tote bag, which had exceeded all the brand's boasts of ruggedness, and zipped it up tight. As she did so, she noticed there was no reply from Miss Aleph.

"Don't let that out of your sight until it's inside a CDC lab."

"You can count on me," Ellie said as enthusiastically as she could, seeing as this meant another bumpy helicopter ride to some austere laboratory instead of going back to the spa at the Watergate Hotel, which every ache in her body told her should be her first priority.

"You're just lucky this prick had it on him," Janice said.

"Of course he would have it," Ms. China said, probably resenting being threatened with arrest.

"Right," the politician said accusingly. "You'd know how they think, having worked closely with these people developing the bug that nearly wiped out the country."

Before any more cat fighting could ensue, a figure in a tatty toque that totally clashed with the gas mask he was pressing to his face came around the corner.

"Al!" Ms. China said. "We thought you'd finally died heroically."

"Sorry to repeatedly disappoint you."

"They totally bought your cover story that you were a lab rat with Antifa sympathies?" Ellie asked, relieved her friend had not been eliminated by the Pangeans as a loose end.

"They were even fooled when I joined their second group and said I had changed my mind about escaping to Tunisia and wanted to martyr myself attacking New York," the mutilated scientist said, his voice muffled by his respirator. "An Army Rangers strike team got them before they had time to recharge the emitter. Boy, am I looking forward to taking that thing apart," Mr. Perdix said, his voice infused with adolescent techno-lust.

"Before you do that, you may want to grow yourself some new ears," Ms. China said. "Your head looks like a not-quite-ripe turnip longing for more time in the ground."

It took some time for the ventilation system to clear the air of Ms. China's knockout gas. Finally, they signaled to the people on the surface that it was all right to come down and take the infiltrators into custody.

Ellie took off her fishbowl respirator and sniffed the air. It was stale and had a slight metallic quality, but she did not pass out and fall alongside that awful fellow, whose name was Mr. Abdelkader. Ellie looked down and noticed the bound terrorist had started twitching.

"Is he supposed to be doing that?"

More white froth was coming out from the man's lipless mouth and out from between his clenched yellow teeth.

"What did you do now?" Ellie exclaimed, looking for her respirator.

"Oh, you daft wankers," Ms. China said, putting her foot on the back of the evil man's neck to hold him in place. She checked his arm. "Look, there are dozens of injection marks. They must have been trying to extend their supply of vaccine. The spores are slowly overcoming the diluted serum."

"This is astounding," Mr. Perdix said as he let Ms. China hold the creature down while he examined it. His voice sounded disturbingly delighted. "Sarge, help me get him up; I've got an idea. I will need a sealed room and a Stage Two infected."

83

MOUNT WEATHER

By the time Ellie got up to Mount Weather's East Portal exit, the area was filled with people wearing all manner of uniforms. Two helicopters had landed, one had a large red cross painted on its side, the other looked bulbously shaped and somehow familiar.

"Weren't we in one like that?"

The doorway slid open, and Janice grimaced when she saw who was inside.

"Senator," she yelled over the roar of Humvee engines, "what are you doing in Marine One? There's only one president, and it's not you."

Senator Leota had volunteered to go with them to ambush the Pangeans, but the medical team insisted on a more thorough examination of her injuries. She had remained a few miles distant at the staging point for the sting operation.

"That's what we're going to discuss," the senator said, pushing her chestnut locks away from her bruised face and turning to Ellie. "Ms. Sato's also been specially invited to the White House. There might even be room for you, Janice."

The chief of staff did not respond to the jibe and got in. This helicopter was smaller than the other one they'd been in, but they all fit inside, bumping knees as the ground personnel slid the door closed. As they lifted off, Ellie waved down to Sarge Bryan. He was far away, but she was certain he saw.

"This is just like General Lee going to General Grant to surrender," Janice said somewhat bitterly. Perhaps she was put out that this high-level summit meeting between the blue and red forces had been arranged while she was at Mount Weather.

The staccato sound of the rotors chopped away, and Ellie tried to get the abattoir-style image of Abdelkader's face out of her mind. They sped over the isolated wintry landscape of Virginia. To Ellie, it appeared deceptively quiet, not like the scene of the decisive battle of this new civil war the Americans had managed to get themselves into.

"Why is she coming?" Janice asked, gesturing to Ellie and speaking in an elevated voice to be heard above the sound of the engines.

"Because I said," Senator Leota replied. A moment later, she pursed her lips, which were still swollen from the successive beatings she had taken. "And also, the old man agreed."

"You talked to him without me?"

"I am the president-elect."

"We'll see about that."

The Hawaiian woman was unfazed and merely smiled encouragingly in Ellie's direction. "We agreed, once we settle things with the leaders of the House and the Senate, an impartial member of the press should get the exclusive story. And I can't think anyone who deserves it more than Ms. Sato."

Ellie smiled back and hoped she didn't look too glassy eyed from fatigue. Briefly, she thought about exchanging her exclusive world-beating story for a week in a feather bed in her Mayfair house, or maybe a hotel because the NHS was soon pitching her out of her government-subsidized digs at Tavistock.

She glanced at Leota. While looking decidedly worse for wear, the woman's tanned face had recovered much of its natural pallor. Had she been shamming being more seriously hurt than she really was in order to speak to the administration behind Janice's back? Sometimes all this intrigue during her trip to America made her feel like she was an extra in a modern-dress version of *Game of Thrones*.

The idea was not at all dispelled from her mind when they circled above the White House. Large fortifications and ramparts had been erected around the entire perimeter. In the streets all around lay heaps of debris, some of it still smoldering in the late-afternoon sunlight. Military vehicles blocked off intersections and troops, some in white camouflage, others in olive green. They clumped in groups along sidewalks and around the few statues still standing.

Their pilot set down on the South Lawn.

Janice looked at her handset.

"Senator, you may want to have a word with your… associates in Sacramento," she said as the door slid open. "Once you have secure comms, give the blue-state leaders a refresher course in what 'clear and unconditional surrender to federal authority' means. I'll take Ms. Sato to the press corps offices and let the president know you've arrived."

As Ellie stepped out of Marine One, her shoes sank into the cold semi-frozen lawn. She made sure to clench her toes inside her too-big boots. Having her foot pop out of one and hopping around would be an ever-so-embarrassing way to greet a head of state. She looked around. A few puffs of smoke rose from distant places where rioting was going on, but the immediate area was very quiet. Ellie felt this had to be the safest place in the country.

As they walked up toward the colonnaded façade, the close examination by Secret Service agents she expected did not happen. Dark figures lurked around the bases of trees and behind hedges but did not advance.

She followed Janice and the senator. The two of them seemed to be competing as to who could walk the fastest. They passed a perfectly manicured but forlorn-looking putting green, then took a small path into the Rose Garden, and were soon in the West Colonnade. The first door that swung open as they approached led to the press suite. It was empty.

The chair nearest the door was a tilting, gamer-type model and looked very comfortable.

"I'll just sit here while you do your business stitching the country back together," Ellie said. She sat and felt the wonderful memory foam embrace her tired back and limbs.

"There's a secure satellite link in the Cabinet Room," Janice told the senator. "I'll show you there and then go downstairs."

So, President Casteel was down among the subterranean features of his official residence. Would he be in the bomb shelter? During her last visit, she'd popped down to the bowling alley where she and Sarge Bryan had received their executive commission and began their astonishing exploits.

The coffee in the cup on the desk smelled like cheap cacao and synthetic creamer. As she pushed it away, she noticed it was still warm. Had they just cleared the press room? It was very exciting for her to get the worldwide exclusive on the armistice between the warring American factions and break the news as to who would be the next president, but had they had to evacuate everyone?

She stopped speculating and started salivating hungrily when she spotted a mini fridge under the next desk over. Inside were some sport drinks, colas, M&Ms, and a tantalizing selection of little airplane-sized bottles of booze. Casting aside concerns over whether anything she'd recently been exposed to, injected with, or ingested would conflict with a teensy bit of vodka, she grabbed one of the cold glass bottles and concluded that an 80-proof beverage was the least-toxic substance she'd encountered in the last three days. She swigged it down in one gulp.

A faded piece of cardboard was pinned to the fabric of the cubicle right in front of her, it read:

The man who reads nothing at all is better educated than the man who reads nothing but newspapers.

—Thomas Jefferson

As she was wondering whether to press her luck with a second bottle, she heard a sound.

Ch-click.

At this point in her war-correspondent career, she recognized the noise instantly—a pistol being cocked next to her head.

84

THE WHITE HOUSE

O h, Janice…" Ellie said and raised her hands.

Walking up behind Janice Jones came a tall man with a shock of rigid white hair that bristled over his predatory, hatchet-like face.

Ellie's cheeks burned with outrage and even embarrassment. This again? She should have known something was wrong.

Ellie stared right at Janice and hissed, "I should have known… Who would marry a horrid person like Barracude, no matter how rich he was?"

In reply, Janice slapped a pre-cut length of duct tape across Ellie's mouth.

"Tie her up," said Vice President Reko Prowse. "I'll take the gun."

Looking much more at ease once he was holding the weapon, the vice president handed Janice a set of zip ties. As Ellie was once again being trussed up and the hard plastic was cinched down over the still-fresh bruises on her wrists, Prowse clamped a wireless device to one of his ears with his free hand.

"Hurry up, Leota's nearly done talking to those California dickbags. We have to get this one to the basement."

Prowse pulled Ellie out of the press room by her jacket and pushed her toward the discreetly hidden lift. The interior was too small for Ellie to inch very far away from her captors. Prowse had a firm grip on her bound hands.

His clothes smelled of sweat and a cheap kind of citrusy soap she wouldn't even use to wash her Labradoodle.

The doors slid silently open. Janice was first out and turned to her. "Not a sound."

As though Ellie could do anything but mumble with a foot-long length of tape plastered across her cheeks from ear to ear. The thought of who would look after Chestnut after her very likely fatal final visit to the capital suddenly filled her with extreme anxiety. She looked left and right. The corridor was so narrow that if she tried to escape, it would be easy for Prowse to trip her. Where would she run to anyway? All the guards on the grounds had to be in on the plot.

"You take care of Leota and the old man," Janice said. "I'll need the roster to alert everyone when it's done."

Prowse thought for a moment, then nodded grimly. With some effort, he pulled a large chunky ring off his finger. Its design flashed briefly in front of Ellie as he handed it to his co-conspirator: it was the five-pointed Masonic star, the same symbol that had been burned into the back of one of Justice Meyers's relatives.

They stopped at the door to the bowling alley.

"Any noise," Prowse told Ellie in a soft voice, "and we go with the messier of the two options we have."

Instead of entering the door with bowling pins painted on it, Prowse tapped a panel on the wall, and it swung away to reveal a hidden passage into a cramped space approximately three by six feet. The far wall was floor-to-ceiling glass, and on it was the reverse image of twin pistol-toting Elvises. Janice pushed her over into one corner of the small space and then to the floor.

"Now you stay right here. Don't you move an inch from there, got me?"

All Ellie could do was flare her nostrils indignantly at the horrible turncoat. As her eyes adjusted to the dim light in the cubbyhole, Ellie realized the Andy Warhol artwork must have been transposed onto a one-way mirror. This must be like one of those observation areas into police interrogation rooms.

The glass was nearly opaque, but inside the bowling alley, she could see the lone figure of a man, President Casteel, sitting on a stool. The only sections on the one-way mirror which were bright, and presumably had the best view, were the eyes of the two Elvises.

That was where Prowse's own eyes were glued. He kept his left hand on her head, his long fingers entangled in and yanking on her hair painfully close to where an infected had pulled out a clump. His right hand aimed the pistol sideways at her. Two expressions seemed to be struggling for supremacy over the vice president's face: furtive glee and triumphant sadism. Janice closed the secret door. It slid shut, leaving them alone in even bleaker dimness.

"C'mon," Prowse whispered so quietly his lips didn't move. "You know what to do when she comes in… Abe, if there's one motive left in that puddle of mush between your ears…"

Ellie was squashed down by Elvis's knees. Now that the hidden door was closed, the parts of the glass that were translucent became easier to see through. Casteel was wearing a blue suit. His broad-shouldered figure sat hunched over a side table near the display of antiques. These were the same ones Ellie and the president had discussed during her previous visit: the inkstand, the coins, and the pair of dueling pistols.

Someone knocked at the main door.

After a pause, Casteel spoke, sounding weary and breathless. "Come on, come in."

"That's right," Prowse whispered. "Get it over with, you brain-dead old fart."

Janice opened the bowling-alley door and ushered in Leota. From her angle sitting on the floor, Ellie could only see the ladies' legs as warped shadows though the one-way mirror. Leota walked farther into the room.

"Mr. President," she said curtly.

Ellie jumped a bit because the sound was very sharp and distinct, as though she were right in the room with the two politicians. The other room had hidden microphones. Prowse glanced at her, and his hand pressed down on her head.

In the other room, President Casteel put his hands on the table, half levered himself up, then seemed to give up on the idea of standing and sat back down.

"Senator, or should I say President-Elect? Who knows at this point?"

"Whichever way it goes, we've got to stop this violence," Leota said, walking to the other side of the small table. "Too many Americans have died already."

"Right, right, you were there, in Kansas City. What a pig fuck."

"It was… the worst thing I…" Leota appeared lost for words. "Still, Julien is KIA. I saw it myself. And the fanatics in the EMAC and all the big Antifa cells have given up."

The president looked past the display of antiques down at the converging lines of the bowling lanes.

"They really think I nuked KC?" Casteel asked suddenly, as though he had been dozing and awakened with a jolt. "Even the Lamestream Media wouldn't be that stupid. You were close… close as anyone who's still alive. What… uh, really happened?"

"If I knew…" Leota's gaze seemed to glance right over where Ellie was crouched behind the mirror, then she quickly glanced away. "Posterity will judge."

"Is that a cue for another fake impeachment trial?"

Leota didn't flinch at the accusatory words. "Mr. President, if you allow me to be sworn in without further conflict, I promise you my first act will be pardoning everyone who did not personally commit or order crimes against humanity. I'll get state governors to do the same."

Casteel's shoulders jiggled as he let out a few sparse chuckles. "I got a better idea. It just popped… this idea, popped to mind… my mind."

With a swift motion, Casteel picked up the dueling pistol closest to him. "These babies belonged to Thomas Jefferson. Hand-crafted by Wogdon & Barton, gunsmiths, .54 caliber. They work fine. And what d'you know, they're loaded, both of them."

"Now, sir…" Leota took a half step backward.

"There was a rumor, more like a legend, that Jefferson personally executed a man on the White House lawn for treason. They say the body of Rodney Cox is buried somewhere around here. They even say that his ghost shows up now and again."

Leota glanced at the pistol held loosely in Casteel's hands, then at the other one, which still sat on the shelf.

"Go on, pick it up. Didn't you qualify as a combat pistol shot in the Army?

"That'd be the Marine Corps," Leota said warily, backing away, but also picking up the other pistol as though by reflex. "Is there any other…"

"Don't pussy out on me now, Senator," the president growled menacingly, taking a firmer grip on the burnished wood handle of his own gun and cocking its big hammer with a sharp click.

Leota took another few steps backward down the polished wood of the first bowling lane, away from Casteel.

Ellie's face was streaming with sweat. Her hands wriggled behind her back, her wrists firmly bound. She tried to push at the duct tape with her tongue, but the strip was so wide it nearly covered her nose. Above her, Vice President Prowse's gaze was riveted through his spyhole. He pressed his nose to the mirror-image nose of the rock 'n' roll icon.

"Do it," Prowse mumbled, fingering his own modern sidearm. "Shoot and let me kill the winner."

When Leota was about eight yards away, Casteel spoke again.

"Jefferson also said… What's the quote now… Oh yeah: 'The tree of liberty must be refreshed from time to time with the blood of patriots… and…'"

Ellie looked back at the hidden way through which they had entered. She couldn't see a handle or any way to burst through it. The corridor outside was only three or four feet wide. Would the politicians in the bowling alley even notice if she made a ruckus? They seemed very intent upon killing one another.

Casteel held his weapon pointed up at the ceiling. Leota stood firm and cocked her own weapon. She never took her dark steely gaze off the older man. She completed the quote: "Refreshed from time to time with the blood of patriots and… tyrants."

Casteel sighed and aimed his gun.

"Ready?"

"Been ready for days," Leota said, hefting her own weapon in similar fashion. "At this distance, not even an Air Force flyboy like you could miss."

"Three should do it," Casteel said, extending his elbow to ninety degrees away from his body as Leota braced herself in shooter's stance from what seemed to Ellie was only a few yards away. "One... two..."

Ellie's muffled squeal was lost in the thunderous report of two pistol shots. Both erupted nearly at the same instant inside the enclosed basement space. Before she dared open her eyes again, she heard glass falling and felt a metallic clunk on her head. *Oh! He's killing me now*, she thought. Then, when no second blow came, she thought, *And he's doing a rather poor job of it!*

She winced as more glass came down, then opened her eyes a little. The Elvis artwork lay in pieces, and she could see right into the bowling alley. Both Casteel and Leota were still standing, but Vice President Prowse was not. His face had been obliterated by at least one musket-ball-sized dueling bullet, which had come blasting through the one-way mirror. He had fallen into the far corner of the tiny hiding space and was making those nasty fresh-corpse-after-a-violent-death gurgling sounds, which Ellie was unfortunately familiar with.

While she was still taking in the strange turn of events and tasting the sulfur-laced smoke in the air, the door behind her was yanked open. Janice ducked in and grabbed the pistol that had dropped onto Ellie's head seconds before.

Ellie tried to shout into her tape gag, realizing the duelists had fired their shots and that the terrible woman now had the only loaded gun. Janice bent down.

"Oh, don't look at me like that," she said, peeling off the duct tape, which was worse than any lip-hair waxing Ellie had ever endured. "I'm one of the good guys."

"That remains to be seen," Senator Leota said, peering inside the glass-strewn space, careful of the sharp edges around the ceiling where a single gun-toting Elvis figure was horrendously cracked but still remained standing. "Is she..."

"All right?" Janice said as threw away the slobbery piece of duct tape and pushed Ellie forward to look at her back. "Seems so. No holes in her that shouldn't be there."

"I'm fine," Ellie said, trying to stand, not waiting to be cut free of her bonds. "But look, the president."

Casteel had tried to step over to them but had stumbled and was now bracing himself against the last of the festively painted tables attached to the wall.

"Get the EMTs," Janice said. "He's having a reaction to the amphetamines."

Casteel looked up at them through wisps of his mussed hair. He was sweating, and his face was pallid, yet he smiled. "Forget it. I feel better than I have for months... No one comes in... until we've got things straightened out."

Leota found a pair of scissors in a corner of the room where bowling shoes were stacked and cut Ellie's zip ties.

"Mr. President," Ellie said with as much dignity as she could muster climbing through the shattered Elvis artwork. "A straightening of things would be greatly appreciated, thank you."

Casteel looked closely at the ruined one-way mirror. "Senator, you were supposed to shoot the left Elvis."

"I did," Leota said curtly. "You're the one who missed."

"It wasn't *my* left, it was... Aw, doesn't matter now. We got the bastard."

Leota and Janice competed with one another to fill in the blanks for Ellie. Stitching together what they said, Ellie concluded the bastard Prowse had been using a small version of the Havana syndrome neuron-depolarizing device on President Casteel for several months to induce symptoms of dementia and psychosis.

"That's the same technology French President Rapace tried using on Europe last year," Ellie said.

"We're still looking into how he got the device," Casteel said, rubbing the back of his neck with a towel full of ice cubes. "But it was Janice who noticed something was up when she joked about CNN being my favorite news channel. Instead of responding with mild curses, I wandered over, turned on Don Lemon, and sat there watching him spout drivel like someone with their brain switched off."

"In college, Prowse had trained as an amateur hypnotist," Janice said. "The Havana rays make victims very susceptible to suggestion. Once we found out what was happening, we gave false information about where the president was sleeping and tried to counteract the effects with amphetamine salts."

"His plan," Casteel said, gesturing to the politician's corpse. "And man, I had to keep myself from punching him when he tried that hypnotizing thing on me this morning. His plan was for the senator and I to shoot at each other with those pistols he prepared. He told me over and over again that I had to be like Jefferson, and execute the traitor."

Janice covered Prowse's body with a small carpet.

"It didn't work out the way he figured."

"But what if you didn't kill each other or one of you was left alive?" Ellie asked.

Janice chuckled mirthlessly. "That's where you came in. That automatic pistol belongs to the terrorists at Mount Weather. Prowse would have used it to kill any survivor and then shoot you and frame you as the killer."

"How would anyone believe that?" Ellie asked, her mouth agape.

"A few days ago," Janice said, "you broke two serial killers out of a maximum-security mental institution."

"Oh, right," Ellie said, seeing how that could strike people as odd. "That's a long story."

"Also, you've been under psychiatric care."

"That's private," Ellie objected.

"Not when you don't pay your bill," Janice said. "Your private clinic has filed a debt claim in the UK."

Did every bloody thing have to be online?

"So now what?" Ellie asked.

"We reconvene Congress and get rid of everyone who was helping the vice president," Janice said, holding up Prowse's Masonic ring. "Which was the reason for the deception. We had to get hold of this and confirm it was real: the roster of everyone Prowse was conspiring with in the Deep State, along with all the materials used to blackmail them. We'll get them all out of government, judiciary, and the military." Janice's phone vibrated. "That's the Attorney General. We've got a lot to do…"

Casteel held up his hand. "The country needs a leader, pronto. We've decided to fix things up here and now."

"You two…" Janice cast a quick look between a resolute Casteel and a determined Leota. "You two have come to a deal?"

"We have." Casteel got up, looking recovered if not completely composed. "And we'll ask you to excuse us while we finalize what we've arranged."

Visibly fuming about being cut out of the loop of a sudden shift in executive power, Janice resignedly held the door open for Ellie.

"Not Ms. Sato," Leota said. "We agreed she'd be the perfect person to act as, uh, referee to our negotiations."

"Me?" Then the obvious dropped like a coin in a piggy bank Ellie used to have. "Of course. I'm not a member of any faction. I'm a foreigner, and if I divulge any secrets, who would believe me? I'm a fugitive lunatic."

"Bingo," Casteel said, shutting the door after Janice. He walked over to the antique display shelf. He pulled out an ornate oak-rimmed coin case and, using the butt of his dueling pistol, smashed the glass front.

"Cleaners are going to earn their overtime tonight," he grumbled while he picked out a medium-sized copper coin and brushed off the glass splinters. "The 1793 penny, first official circulating coin of the United States."

Oh... Are they really going to...? Ellie thought.

"You're going to decide your squabble with a coin toss?" she asked, aghast at the geopolitical implications.

"It seemed a better idea than leaving it to legislators so cowardly they refused to come out of their hidey-holes when it mattered," Leota said.

"There have been contingent presidential elections in the past, and we're the leaders of our parties. Congress will legalize what we agree here today," Casteel said firmly. "More arguing would just screw over the people and the economy even more." He handed the coin to Ellie.

With trembling hands, she turned it over and looked at the engravings on the antique copper surface. Carved on one side, there was a wild-looking Lady Liberty with her hair flowing in the breeze, on other side, the words *One Cent* on the other.

"Whichever way it goes," Leota said, "you realize federal supremacy is..."

"Fucked?" Casteel said bluntly. "Why? Because North Dakota and Oregon have as much in common as Hungary and Somalia? The dust hasn't settled in Kansas City, and the red-state governors are already demanding a Devolution of Powers Act, which includes fiscal sovereignty and the right to deport felons back to where they came from. Texas even wants its own digital currency, 'Texcoin.'"

"Maybe the *loser* of the toss should have to be president," Leota mused.

"Senator, would you like to call it?" Casteel said almost jauntily. "Heads or tails?"

Leota shrugged. "Age before beauty."

"Well, then," the older man said with a decisive smile. "My money's on Liberty, what else?"

They both nodded to Ellie, and she flipped the vintage coin.

85

THE WHITE HOUSE

Ellie left the bowling alley. Behind her, Casteel was paging security staff, presumably to see to the body still lying behind the smashed one-way mirror, while Leota yelled into a cell phone.

Staggering a little, and glad no one could see, she made it down to the lift at the end of the narrow corridor. When she was last inside this same quiet little conveyance headed down into the White House basement as a prisoner of Reko Prowse and Janice Jones, she had not really envisioned herself ever coming up in it, alive at any rate.

As it jiggled to a stop, her head spun. She had a worldwide exclusive on who would be the next American president. As the doors opened, she checked her clothing for random bits of the former vice president, who had made such a violent exit from the American political scene. Thankfully, she didn't find any gore.

The lift let Ellie out near the doorway to the Cabinet Room. After the terribly loud pistol shots in the bowling alley, the quiet in the West Wing seemed out of place, even ludicrous. People in shirtsleeves with lanyards around their necks had once again emerged into the corridors and were quietly milling through the hallways.

As she passed the press room, she recognized a few TV broadcasters who had crept back into cubbyholes. While they waited for an official briefing from the podium, it was apparent the Washington spin machine was operating at full centrifugal force.

A breaking news story played on the big flat screen on the wall. The chyron caption underneath read: *US CONGRESSIONAL LEADERS ANNOUNCE 'MOSTLY PEACEFUL' RESOLUTION OF REGIONAL DIFFERENCES.*

Playing behind the news anchors was one of the many amateur videos of the atomic bomb destroying downtown Kansas City.

"Ms. Sato!" someone shouted from the Palm Room.

The last knurl of anxiety Ellie was nursing, expecting yet another instant disaster, unwound when she saw Sarge Bryan's bright eyes and concerned face. A pair of Secret Service agents were restraining him from coming farther in from the Rose Garden. A third was scanning her friend's face and ID.

"It's quite all right," Ellie said. "He's definitely one of the good guys."

The man with the scanner immediately waved the other guards away.

"Well, I see you're making yourself at home," Sarge Bryan said after checking her over for new injuries, which, given the number of bullets flying around in the country, was a thoughtful gesture.

"The administration's been quite accommodating to members of the foreign press," Ellie said as they walked north to the driveway. "But I don't want to wear out my welcome."

On the other hand, she thought, walking through food smells as they passed the kitchen area, she felt she could have wolfed down a gargantuan American-sized portion of whatever they were cooking.

"We'd best get back to the Watergate," Sarge said, leading the way.

Outside the north entrance, Ellie noticed Janice standing and waving her arms aggressively at the driver of the particular limousine she wanted from among the phalanx of cars sitting along the oval driveway. The resilient politician, she noticed with some envy, had been able to change her clothes and was now wearing a spotless and rather smart dark-blue pantsuit.

"So..." Sarge Bryan whispered. "Who won? Who's my next commander in chief?"

"See, that's the problem with you people from upstart countries that have only been around for a century or two," Ellie said with a secretive smile. "You have no historical perspective or patience at all, unlike the English or Japanese."

"Ellie!"

"Sorry, you'll have to read about it in the *Juggernaut* like everyone else," she said as an aide held the car door open for them. "But I can tell you who both Casteel and Leota agreed must be the new vice president…"

From inside the car, Janice waved to them. Sarge Bryan raised his eyebrows.

"Congratulations, Ms. Vice President."

"I go by Mrs.," Janice said, straightening out her pants as she settled back onto the plush leather of the limo's seat. "I don't want anyone to get fresh with me."

Ellie noticed she had already changed her phone's lock screen to the VP's official seal.

The driver leaned through the partition. "Ma'am, I suggest we take E Street to the Watergate. There was a large vegan anti-meat protest headed for K Street. They say it might become violent."

What America lacked in historical perspective, it certainly made up for with energy. After all that had been going on, people still had enough time to debate the ethics of eating animal products. Janice nodded to the chauffeur, and they drove off.

Heading back to the Watergate cast Ellie's mind back to the beginnings of the whole thing, and her rather impulsive attempt to get Ms. China back into the lunatic asylum.

"How did you leave it with Anna?" she asked, hoping they'd weigh her misdeeds against her ability to fix the consequences of her lapses in judgment.

"Mr. Perdix took her back to the JASON labs," Janice said. "The good thing about all the recent pandemics is we've streamlined vaccine production and distribution. Now that we've got the enzyme stem cells, the CDC says the pharmacos should be in full production in a week."

"What about the infected that got loose?" The largest cluster had been vaporized in the atomic blast, but Las Vegas and a few other places had been hit hard.

Sarge Bryan scrolled through his handset. "Outbreaks are mostly under control. Many counties have deputized all adults who can legally own a firearm to corral them, capturing where possible or using makeshift thermal devices to stop them where necessary."

"Thermal devices?" Ellie asked. "Like portable infrared heaters?"

"Like drones with flame throwers attached, ma'am."

"Ms. China's been put to work perfecting a cure for any infected we manage to capture," Janice said. "She agreed on the condition she be allowed to zip back to the UK briefly to take care of something important. I imagine it involves you not being locked in a British jail for a few centuries."

The car lurched sideways. A little alarmed, Ellie looked out. They had stopped near a wide intersection, and their path was being blocked by a large motorcycle, its long handlebars in the gloved grip of a bulky-bodied leather-clad biker. Behind him was a similarly clad, smaller figure. It was hard for Ellie to see clearly through the thick bulletproof glass, and at first she guessed it was a child or a midget. The cycle had stalled or something had come loose, so the driver sat there, blocking traffic, trying to remedy the mechanical issue.

Their police escort was on the other side of the intersection speaking to some vegans dressed as oppressed cows. They wore large chains with clanking bells and were blocking the other side of the street. Janice rolled down the partition into the driver's compartment.

"Ma'am, you should keep the partition up," the chauffeur said.

"Son, it won't be the worst risk I've taken this week. Ask the man if we can help."

Reluctantly, the chauffer rolled his window partway down and addressed the bearded man, whose head was bound in a stars-and-stripes bandanna. Upon closer inspection, the "child" behind him turned out to be a generously salivating bulldog whose tiny leather jacket read: *Ridin' Bitch.*

"Excuse me, we've got a VIP here. Can we help you?"

The biker looked up with suspicion, then smiled. "You got a high-rankin' political figure in there, do ya?" He looked at his riding companion, then peered back at them. "You sure can help serve the public, politician. Mabel here is a little constipated. Why don't you give her some relief and spoon some crap out of her ass?"

With a bark of laughter that merged together with the crackling blasts issuing from the chrome tailpipes, the cycle started up, and the man and Mabel rode off.

"Man, watch your..." Sarge started yell back, but the motorcycle was already gone, and the partition was sliding up.

"Looks like things are gettin' back to normal," Janice said, shrugging the tastefully padded shoulders of her executive suit.

"That wasn't very..." Ellie said as they drove off, thankfully taking a different route from the motorcyclist. "I mean, that was really rude. After all you've been through."

"Not a big deal," the future vice president said. "Most Americans look at politicians as a necessary evil, like tow truck drivers."

86

ZVENA

Zvena watched Vladimir Putin's image in the crystal-clear video feed. The Russian president's lips silently pursed as he reviewed news bulletins flashing up on a monitor that was out of frame.

"Pah," he said finally. "Yari, have you ever seen such fake news? 'Mostly peaceful resolution of regional differences.' How do they come up with this gibberish?"

Zvena recognized the room behind Putin; he was seated on a red leather wing-backed chair in his personal den underneath the Kremlin.

"Apparently, Mr. President, it is entirely your fault, as usual," Zvena joked, which was keeping with the more jovial mood that had come over him since he gathered Putin would not be ordering him and his team to be quietly executed and having their nonorganic parts scattered in the deepest part of the Atlantic.

Putin's midnight-blue eyes locked with his own via the holographic imaging system, and a second later he, too, laughed. "No wonder our Russia Today network is more popular and trusted than BS-NBC." He raised his tumbler of vodka. "Drink, Yari Semyonovich, you deserve it."

Zvena felt his organic tissues blush at the collegial use of his informal first name and patronymic by his commander in chief. After a brief pause, he drained his glass. Putin, with his uncanny insightfulness, noticed immediately.

"You are hesitant to celebrate so soon after the tragic occurrences at Kansas City?"

"Also that... the OCEL unit was unmistakably of Russian origin... I do not wish anyone to cast aspersions on our country or your leadership. Some deluded American factions are obsessed with scapegoating our country."

Putin nodded, then placed a loafer-shod foot close to the reconstructed snout of the Kodiak bear rug in front of his fireplace. "You remember this fellow?"

Zvena touched his knee where he could still feel the indentations of the mighty beast's jaws where it had bitten him moments before he was able to, with skill and not a little amount of luck, envelop the bear's head with his cybernetic arms and crush its skull into a thousand pieces.

Putin continued. "The filthy anarchist scum in America are not half as noble as this animal, which had no power of reason. Antifa and their like choose to be violent, socially corrosive deviants. The end for them must be the same. With many of them liquidated, America is more stable than it was a week ago."

"But the radiation..."

"Is minimal. Last century, America conducted more than two hundred atmospheric nuclear bomb tests, many on its own soil." Putin put his glass down. "As for the remote control of the OCEL unit, this will be traced to the same dead end as the signal that hacked into the self-driving Cybertruck. Even your recorded memories of the incident have been seeded with enough data exceptions to prove any incriminating accusations to be a deep fake."

After Zvena, Rodion, and Tata escaped the EMAC camp in the lander pods, they had contacted Moscow for new orders. They received small pieces of a larger contingency plan based on the work of a mole named "the Baroness." The EMAC had, through sheer blind hatred of America, gathered a group of infected that no army could defeat without the use of weapons of mass destruction.

"Remember, Yari, the only reason the blue states surrendered so quickly to federal authorities was they thought President Casteel had authorized the use of the nuclear bomb against them."

"No American leader would ever do this."

"Unfortunately, no. However, the show of force was exactly what was needed. The action was as necessary to save their union as was Lincoln's victory at Gettysburg. And it is saved, for now."

"Which is as it should be?" Sometimes political intrigue was so much like multidimensional chess. Trying to figure it out gave Zvena a headache.

Putin nodded. "While Russia has an undeniable lead in many technologies, of which you are a foremost example, we cannot ignore the fact that America spends more on defense in one year than our entire GDP."

Putin shrugged, his eyes briefly following the glinting reflections of the gold filigree embedded in the shallow bottomed glass he held.

"Of course, they do it by shaking rather vigorously on their Magic Money Tree. That can only go on for so long. Meanwhile, our hegemony over Europe will take time to solidify, and something has to hold back China. Damaged and often pathetic as America is, without it, the world descends into a new Dark Age."

"And the Baroness," Zvena said, pulling up onto his HUD a mass of confusing and contradictory files under that name. "Can we trust her? Or should I put together a Human+ strike team to close off any loose ends?"

"Ah, yes, the Baroness Alevskaya." Putin's eyes glittered again as he smiled. "She originated in Israel but is currently a free agent and has my complete confidence. In fact, she sent us a bit of intelligence which prompted me to propose a joint venture with the JASON organization as part of a new spirit of trust and cooperation between Russia and America. Observe."

The image in front of Zvena changed to what appeared to be an astonishingly lurid horror movie. An emaciated creature with a peeled-off face was chewing on the camera lens.

"This is a fellow you have encountered in his previous life: Mr. Abdelkader. He is one of the few existing Stage Three infected. Dr. Nail advises us this condition occurs when an incipient Stage One is attacked by a Stage Two, which creates a rare and intriguing variant. He is capable of performing more complex tasks than a Stage Two yet retains most of their ability to function in zero-oxygen environments and harsh conditions, with minimal protective gear."

Zvena perceived the implications. "Possibly these creatures are adaptable to mining asteroids and building habitats on Mars for humans who would come later."

"Only if they can be trained," Putin said, switching off the appalling yet satisfying video feed. "Due largely to your team helping put down the Antifa and Pangean seditionists, US–Russian relations have improved.

"They have proposed a joint venture between JASON and our Human+ laboratories. Mr. Zvena, my top little green man, do you feel up to the challenge of helping the Americans get the most out of these so-far-untrainable creatures that were captured in Mount Weather?"

Zvena thought for a moment, running his hand over recent repairs to his forearm. This was a little out of his comfort zone. Nevertheless, he clapped his hands and nodded.

"The Russian physiologist Ivan Pavlov pioneered classical behavioral conditioning," he said, meeting Putin's holographic gaze. "I will succeed in this task even if it kills Abdelkader… again… and again."

Putin laughed and, filling his glass, invited Zvena to do likewise.

87

WATERGATE HOTEL

ELLIE

It was only a ten-minute drive from the intersection where they had encountered the outspoken biker and his pet bulldog to the Watergate Hotel, but Ellie must have dozed off. For a moment, she imagined that instead of being in an armored limousine, she was riding a scooter with Chestnut the Labradoodle perched behind her.

"Ms. Sato." Sarge Bryan's warm hand nudged her wrist. "We're here."

His voice was kindly, affectionate, and perhaps a little embarrassed by the astonishing experience she'd had in his country.

"I wasn't sleeping, I was just thinking of possible headlines," she said, covering his big hand with her own bandage-festooned one.

Janice and Ellie got out, but the Army man had other business.

"There're rumors of packs of infected loose in Yellowstone," Sarge Bryan said. "To help find them, Mr. Perdix wants to download the detailed scans my eyes recorded of the ones we encountered. And then I promised to keep a close watch on Anna until she goes back to the UK with you, just in case she's tempted to do more, uh, mischief."

"A soldier's work is never done," Ellie said. "Oh, and give my regards to Attie Jr. and your goddaughter, Sienna. With you guiding her, I'm certain her future is very bright indeed."

Sarge Bryan nodded. An agent standing on the sidewalk shut the car door, then turned to them as she and Janice started toward the lobby.

"Madam Vice President, if you wouldn't mind waiting in the secure area while we check the guest quarters," the Secret Service agent said.

"Not at all, and it's still Mrs. Jones until the appointment is confirmed."

While appreciating the extra caution the Secret Service was taking in light of the hotel having been the scene of a terrorist kidnapping attempt, Ellie was looking forward to some aspirin and a mattress that was not made of concrete.

"You should go ahead to your room," Janice said. "I don't know how long they'll be."

"I'll wait with you," Ellie said as they eased themselves down onto padded sofas like two aged dowagers at the University Women's club. Though Janice had gotten herself a change of clothes, the past few days of adventuring had left her just as battered and bruised as Ellie.

"You look relieved," Janice said, studying her with a dark, piecing gaze.

"Oh, not really," Ellie fibbed.

"Admit it. I had you going there when we ambushed you in the press room."

"Mrs. Jones, I never thought you were a heinous sociopath bent on destroying America from inside its own highest institutions."

Janice held her gaze.

"All right, maybe when you popped out of the shed at the late chief justice's house."

Her friend still did not blink.

"And maybe those times when you were threating to shoot me."

Janice laughed and picked up glasses of water being offered by a waiter holding a silver tray, setting them down on the coffee table. A sudden stab of regret joined her other stabbing pains as Ellie recalled what she had said during the latter episode. "And I really didn't mean that, you know, what I said about your husband, Mr. Barracude."

"Sure you did," Janice said, looking past the two security people guarding the glass door into the private lounge. "Most people don't 'get' Jezzie, and it's nearly always his own fault."

"He could strike the uninitiated as a bit... boisterous."

"More like a bull rhino on PCP."

Ellie's journalistic instincts were piqued. "There must be a fascinating story in how you two met."

"Planning your next bestseller already?"

"That would be incredibly mercenary of me," Ellie said, though she had been considering titles that would not be confusing to American readers, who seemed to prefer lurid and literal book titles, while at the same time also be appealing to her growing international fanbase.

"Well, then," Janice said, her lips compressing, which formed dimples in her tanned cheeks. "Totally off the record, then, until I'm out of public office."

"You should know by now, if there's one thing I can do, it's keep a confidence."

"Jezzie would hate for this to get out, would totally ruin the rep he's worked his whole life to achieve."

"A *Citizen-Juggernaut* reporter's word is her bond."

"Well... I'd just graduated law school and was living in Miami," Janice began while looking intently at the rim of the delicate kaleidoscope of reflections in her crystal water glass. "That was after the mass exodus from places that had become rancid crapholes like New York. So along with a six-figure student debt, I was looking at monthly rental payments that cost more than my car.

"I quickly got engaged, too quickly, it turned out, to a basketball player, Big D. He was a guard for the Miami Heat, and he was all that: tall, hot, and getting paid a million dollars a month. He also turned out to be a total dog.

"That last bit became apparent when my baby sister, Gemma, got sick, and I was going back and forth from the hospital at odd times. One night, I came home unexpectedly and found Big D had failed to invite me to a party he was holding, which was mostly happening in and around his pants."

"Oh my," Ellie said, spilling some of her water. "That must have been a shock."

"Y'think?" Janice said, crinkling her forehead in thought. "Naw. Deep down, I knew what kind of guy he was. I just fell for the bling and the lifestyle. Fortunately, I got out before I got any venereal diseases or some of that nasty plastic surgery like all those desperate NBA hags. Some of the players' wives look like Bella Lugosi with 38D boobies and a bad weave."

"That would not be a desirable look," Ellie agreed.

"About the same time I was getting out of there and grabbing my sh— I mean, my belongings, something else happened. My sister got diagnosed with viral hepatitis. She was looking real bad."

"The costs must have been tremendous," Ellie said. While Britain's NHS often bumbled with years-long waiting lists, acute care was generally free.

"Bills were no problem. I was my sister's guardian, and we were still on Big D's platinum medical insurance plan. I was a good enough lawyer to know the underwriter couldn't weasel out of paying. Problem was, Gemma's liver was failing fast. I got tested. So did most of my family. None of us were a match to donate tissue for a liver transplant.

"Then one day, I was chasing cockroaches around in my motel room, and the doctors paged me to get my consent for an in-vivo transplant. Out of the blue, they had a ten-out-of-ten match with a donor who was willing to give up about half their own liver in an operation that was more risky for them than it would be for my sister. After the transplant, the donor's liver might not regenerate properly, or they could bleed out and die right on the table."

"Don't tell me..." Ellie said, riveted to the true-life drama, casually calculating how many *Juggernaut* subscriptions and web clicks she was foregoing by not publishing it while kicking herself for being one of the few ethical people in the media.

"The tissue gift was made on condition of anonymity," Janice said, settling her leg in a more comfortable position on the ottoman in front of their seats. "The donor even had a surgeon flown in from Johns Hopkins to oversee the procedure. I could have let it go and just been thankful, but I just couldn't not know.

"After a couple of weeks of useless searching, including trying to get a peek at the hospital security logs, I got a break by going into public records and checking the parking and traffic violations around the hospital. On the day of the operation, a five-million-dollar Bugatti had been towed from beside a fire hydrant, and no one had claimed it from the impound lot. That got my attention.

"Jezzie had just driven himself to the hospital, parked in the red zone, and somehow convinced himself he'd be finished with the major operation in an hour, and then be able to drive away before anyone noticed.

"A little more digging, and I matched the car to a company owned by Jezzie. At the time, he was going through a hypochondriac phase and had been in the hospital for another MRI, insisting he had come down with cerebral malaria. His symptoms turned out to be from drinking too much coffee.

"While he was waiting for his turn in the machine, he'd seen my sister being wheeled down the hall, playing her clarinet. She wanted a chance to play in an orchestra. He asked the nurse what she was in for and, impulsive as always, got himself tested the same day for tissue compatibility.

"Today my sister plays for the Miami Symphony." Janice pulled out her handset and showed Ellie a picture of a thinner, serious-looking version of herself in a dark suit studying sheet music on a brass stand and holding a shiny clarinet. "After I outed Jezzie, I bugged his secretary every day until she put my call through, and we went out to lunch."

"Just simple as?" Ellie asked.

"Well… there were some trips to Monaco on that private jetliner. But Jezzie was a perfect gentleman and appreciated me for who I am and how I wanted to serve America." Janice smiled, her teeth flashing white in the subdued light. "Of course, what sealed the deal was our legally enforceable pact that if he ever cheats on me, I'm entitled to the second half of his liver."

Two Secret Service agents came up to the glass doors, and one of them knocked. As Ellie eased herself back up into standing position, Janice reached over.

"Here, let me," she said and removed one last bit of duct tape from her jawline. "Sorry about that. I had to stop you from saying anything that might give us away."

They were escorted toward the executive lifts.

"But Casteel and Leota knew everything, even where Prowse would be standing while he was watching them. They had to estimate where he was behind that mirror to shoot him and not me." For the umpteenth time, Ellie was glad that in America, "gun control" mostly meant being able to hit your target.

"I was confident they wouldn't give themselves away," Janice said, letting her get in the hotel lift first. "They're used to spinning bullshit and making it completely believable."

During the trip from Kansas City to Mount Weather, Ms. China, Mr. Perdix, and even some actual medical doctors had assured Ellie that she was entirely free of A/P-32 spores or microbes. However, as Janice led her into her guest suite at the top floor of the Watergate Hotel, her arms and legs were moving so sluggishly she almost felt like an automaton. She vaguely heard Janice say something about the name of the suite's AI valet being Trixie.

As soon as the door closed, she slumped onto the bed and said, "Trixie, lights off."

The lavish suite disappeared into soothing dimness lit by a few footlights in the hallway.

Then she remembered her world-beating story. "Trixie, lights on."

After half an hour of somnambulistic typing into the suite's computer, she received a text back from her editor Smitty, assuring her the *Juggernaut* would scoop the world with her story on the dramatic developments in American politics.

She had barely enough energy in her fingers to type: *Thak u,godnite.*

As soon as darkness again enveloped the large, unfamiliar room, Ellie realized she was nowhere near the bed, but she really didn't want to turn the lights back on. Twice she thumped her knee against something then found the glorious mound of soft luxury only a five-star hotel could provide. She sank into it face first and wondered whether Trixie was acquainted with the still-missing-in-action Miss Aleph. This thought set her to musing whether AIs had virtual social clubs…

The next thing she knew, Ellie felt herself tumbling through an angry red sky over a volcano, hanging on for dear life on the outside of one of the escape pods which had just been ejected from Mr. Barracude's private jumbo jet. For some reason, she was pounding her head on the exterior as it hurtled toward the lake of molten rock.

She woke up to find the rooms still dark, her hands clutching the edges of the downy mattress. There indeed was a thumping sound coming from somewhere in the room.

"Twinkie, I mean, Trixie, lights on… very dimly, if you please."

What now? She looked at the clock. It had only been two and a half hours since she'd arrived at the Watergate.

"It's far too soon for Ms. China to have started another apocalypse," she said to herself.

"Are you decent?" The muffled voice came from the corridor. It was Mr. Barracude.

He didn't seem like the sort to give up knocking. Ellie made sure her robe was appropriately draped over her before saying, "Trixie, open the door."

Mr. Barracude burst in, an ecstatic salesman's smile split his face into a warm grin.

"I'm glad I caught you."

"I… er," Ellie gulped some water as she led him into the sitting area. "I wasn't planning on moving an inch for about ten or twelve more hours."

The tanned oligarch waved a computer tablet under her nose, it was filled with wavy green, blue, and red lines.

"I mean, I'm glad I caught you when your biorhythms were peaking. See? Look at 'em all. Your physical, emotional, and intellectual bands are all at what are known as their 'apogee levels'!"

It seemed a bit rude to be monitoring all those things even if she wasn't paying for her stay.

"How do you know?" Ellie said, slumping into a decorative but stiff-backed chair and looking longingly at her rumpled bed.

"Your wrist monitor is telling me. I had them put it right by your bedside so you would put it on right away," Barracude said, raising his right wrist. "I use mine all the time. It tells me when to sign a big deal or fire a whole bunch of people."

"You mean that thing over there?" Ellie pointed to an unopened, and until now, unnoticed box on the nightstand.

"Oh, man." He gave his broad forehead an audible slap and took a closer look at the tablet gripped in his hands. "Wow! It's not *your* biorhythms that are spiking… it's *mine*! Heh, sorry about that. But since you're up, we should probably talk about your future."

Her immediate future had been going just fine until the tempestuous man had barged in.

"Mr. Barracude, don't you have enough on your mind? I mean, the government will probably want your advice on rebuilding the economy and trust in American's legal and political institutions."

"Aw, that's easy." Barracude leaned toward the coffee table and dug his hand into the big bowl of candy. He seized as many M&M's as he could, packing them into his mouth while he continued to speak. "'Mericans only really hump the bunk when they're bored. We got more energy than the rest of the world put together, and when it's not put to use doing anything constructive, it just backs up on us."

"Like heartburn?"

"Exactly. Luckily I got enough vision for all of us. And a key part involves you," he said as though announcing she had just won a sweepstakes.

"Me and the top people, the really big players, we're all kind of blasé on Earth. The big money has already been made on this planet, it's time to reach for the stars. Mars is a dried-up old red dung ball. Air's too thin, it's too far away, and gravity's too feeble. Venus is the place."

"I wish you all the best with that too."

"We're launching high-air stations that float in the Venusian air. The atmosphere's so thick you can cut it with a knife. Project's called HAVOC, but you have my guarantee it's completely safe. Then we'll explore the surface, which they tell me is arranged like an onion. The top is all crappy with sulfuric acid and junk, but a few layers down there are sealed caves with free-flowing water and enough thermal energy to build anything we want. So how about it?"

"How about what?" Ellie asked, feeling she was about to fall victim to a master salesman and be sold something she couldn't afford and didn't need.

"How'd you like to be the first correspondent reporting from Venus?"

After saying she'd definitely put it foremost on her interplanetary travel list, she finally managed to usher the energetic oligarch toward the door.

Ellie closed the door. "Hello, Trixie? Do not let anyone in for twelve... make that eighteen hours."

`"I'm Trixie, and I'm on it."`

EPILOGUE

That is the poshest saliva in London," Melanie Françoise chirped as she waved her hand at the slimy mixture of saliva and mucous flowing through a long spit sink shaped like the trough of the legendary Roman vomitorium.

"Have some patriotic pride, Melanie," Ran Oliphant said drolly as he wiped his mouth with a monogrammed handkerchief. "Post–Brexit British saliva is the poshest in the entire world."

They were under the white canopy of the NHS pathogen testing tent, which had been set up outside the historic Globe Theatre. The rich, famous, and powerful, the lords and ladies of the kingdom, were all swishing mouthwash-like gel around in their mouths, depositing the necessary sample into a pouch through a straw and then expelling the rest into the handily situated common trough.

At least, Ellie thought, the NHS had replaced the foot-long orifice testing swabs with something more socially acceptable, even festive. The spit tests took only a minute to process, and then the entrant, matched up with their wristband and badge, was escorted into the venerable theatre itself.

"Oh, Ran, you're dribbling." Melanie started dabbing away at the Scottish oligarch's chin with a hanky made of billowing pink lace.

"Stop fussing," Ran said, checking his white shirt and tuxedo lapels for blue spew.

"Thank you for arranging all this," Ellie said, genuinely impressed. "A stage at a community center would have been fine."

"Nonsense," Melanie chirped, making sure her towering hair, styled in an East-Asian themed pompadour that added about four feet to her height, was not being set on fire by the ceiling lights. "We owe it to you for not being there in your hour of need, don't we, Ran?"

The gruff-looking former military man did look a bit chagrined. "Apologies, Ms. Sato. If we'd known after you escaped St. Bartholomew's that you were about to destroy another continent, wild horses could not have kept us away from America."

A mid-level member of the Royal family walked past and greeted Ran in a way that invited a spot of snivelling. They all bowed and curtsied without overdoing it.

"How did you manage to get all these people out for a bit of amateur theatrics?" Ellie asked, impressed with the A-list cachet of attendees.

"T'wasn't easy, I'll admit. Bloody mayor made us pay for all the health checks just to avoid barmy social distancing, which would have reduced the seating in the Globe from fifteen hundred to about fifty."

"Bloody scam, that social distancing," Melanie agreed.

"Not only that, to get everyone to RSVP, I had to add a scene reading from the real *Macbeth* by Sir Daniel Craig and his charming wife Dame Rachel. Do you know how much they charge?"

"Cheer up. The chancellor keeps conjuring heaps of Sterling out of thin air; money's only imaginary," Melanie said sagely, looking up to the clear evening sky visible through the open-air amphitheater. "What nice weather for a play."

Ellie heard strains of music as the orchestra warmed up.

"At least Sir Daniel and his wife didn't insist on being the headliners," Ellie said, picking up the leather-bound playbill entitled:

Lady Macbeth and the Fool

Two classic Shakespeare characters together for the first time.
Performed by the St. Bartholomew's Health Centre Players.

"It's starting," Ellie said as the crowd started moving toward the sterilized tube-like corridors leading to the various seating sections. She pulled at the silk ruffles of Melanie's sleeve. "We have to find Mr. Perdix."

The American scientist was staring dreamily into the river of blue saliva. Before he was tempted to steal a sample, Ellie and Melanie hustled him into one of the unisex powder rooms.

"Look at your ears," Ellie admonished him. "You've been touching them. I can see right through the left one."

"They're still itching. It's normal."

"Well, control yourself. You want to make a good impression on your date."

"She's not a date," Mr. Perdix said, blushing. "And besides, she'll be up on stage."

"Still," Melanie said. "You don't want people looking at your translucent ears instead of up at the performance she'd been practicing for months before… before circumstances intervened. From what I recall, she has a bit of a temper."

"You're telling me," Mr. Perdix said, allowing them to stuff a makeup napkin into his collar. "After I very politely declined her first invite to attend this performance on account of being busy saving what remains of the USA, she sent me a second one which was not so nice. It contained a photograph of the contents of my fridge captioned 'If I were a lethal dose of batrachotoxin, where would I hide?'"

Melanie's long eyelashes fluttered, and a soft jingling came from small bells hidden inside her tremendously sized hair. "Oh, that's so sweet. It shows she really cares. It's genuinely difficult to collect that poison from rain forest frogs."

Ellie and Melanie quickly reapplied light-colored concealer makeup to Mr. Perdix's newly attached ears.

"They don't come colored?" Ellie asked as she was finishing her lobe with the makeup brush.

"These were the only ones that were 'ready to wear,'" Mr. Perdix said. "The only other ears of suitable size had been grown on the backs of donor piglets. Those developed pink spots and short bristly hair for reasons I have yet to discover."

Ellie tried to imagine the menagerie in the JASON lab. "You people grow random body parts on the bodies of farm animals?"

"It's all very ethical. The animals are pampered, and it doesn't hurt them a bit." Mr. Perdix looked at himself in the mirror and removed the tissues from his collar. "Thank you. One day I'll get around to injecting my new ears with some subcutaneous dye."

"Let's hurry," Melanie said, ducking her head as she exited the powder room.

"Why? It's all reserved seating."

"We don't want to miss the opening concerto, do we?"

As they reentered the throng, Ellie spotted a familiar figure. She would not have recognized him, but he was wearing a straitjacket and being escorted by Mr. Delingpole, the ubiquitous minder of lunatics from NHS Mental Health Services.

"Mr. Delingpole," Ellie said, "I'm glad you could take in the show."

"Just make sure they keep up their end," he said tersely, pulling at the jacket of his stiff-looking rental tuxedo.

"They will," Ellie said with a touch of indignation. "As agreed: after all the performances are over, including the epilogue, soliloquies, and the guest performances, also the rousing orchestral finale, and any curtain calls, we should be done round about midnight, at which time they will both place themselves in your custody at the stage door exit."

Delingpole nodded silently and nudged his charge forward, preventing him from taking a bite out of a hat worn by the very elderly and very short Duchess of Richmond.

The lady peer didn't notice the assault on her headwear and merely said to her companion, "It's so nice they let the Bartholomew's lunatics out for an evening of play acting. That will cheer them immensely. It must be so dull for them in that madhouse."

"Don't expect too much, Aunty," said a droll young man in an exaggerated Etonian accent. "From the inmates' portion the show, I mean. Of course everyone's really here for Sir Daniel and Dame Rachel. Pity there's no late seating allowed."

Delingpole walked away, leading his mental health client on a short leash. Ran came over to them and looked at the man in the restraining jacket. "Is that fellow on the tether from St. Bart's?"

"He is," Ellie said. "I thought it was the least I could do to offer them a few dozen tickets. And the man in the straitjacket is not an inmate. That's actually their director of patient services, Dr. Katz."

Ellie hoped she hadn't made her doctor's nervous condition worse by accidentally letting two of his prize patients escape and setting fire to the hospital's museum.

Ran led them to a VIP box to the left side of the stage. There was no need to lower the lights as the performance began. Falling dusk had adjusted the theatre's lighting via the open roof.

"Look there," Melanie said, pointing down to the floor seating and leaning forward, her hair bumping against the lip of the thatched roof. "Is that the Extinction Rebellion bear, the one that menstruates so heavily during protests?"

Ellie saw a large hairy figure making its way to a front-row seat.

"The what?" Ellie said, a little too loudly, as the Duchess of Richmond turned and gave her a stern look. "What's been going on in London while I was away helping out the colonials?"

"One day, Ranny and I were in the city to help clean obscenities off the Cenotaph Memorial because the city workers union refused to deface impassioned political statements. Straight after, we went to see whether they had again tied pig's testicles under the chin of Churchill's statue. And wouldn't you know it." Melanie rapped Ellie's arm with her theatre fan. "XR was doing performance art in front of it. An eight-foot-tall bear, menstruating heavily, ran around Churchill a few times, yelled 'You've killed me! You fascist bastard, eff you!' then collapsed in a geyser of fake blood."

"Damn," Ellie said. "And I thought I had a difficult week."

The large hairy mass plowed past the seated guests until it arrived at its assigned spot.

"I don't think it's a bear, at least not underneath," Ran said as he squinted through his theatre glasses. He whispered, "That's got to be the cyborg lady from Paris."

Ellie sensed trepidation in his voice. Perhaps he feared he was being stalked by a massive killing machine with an amorous fixation.

"I believe it is," Ellie concluded. Tata was wearing the same bearskin coat she had loaned Ellie in Washington. "But you've got nothing to worry about. I think she's attached her romantic aspirations to someone else."

Tata's heavily made-up face was definitely beaming in another direction, up at the stage where the first player had loped through the curtains of the backdrop and was stomping forward accompanied by the jingle of bells on his cap. Even after he took his stage mark, the jingling continued. Magellan, the evil macaw, was perched on the man's broad shoulders and kept gnawing at them with its enormous sharp beak.

Covering his mouth with the playbill, Ran leaned over to Ellie and said with some indignation, "Y'realize there's no Fool in *Macbeth*."

"Right. There's no parrot either, but who's going to tell the Chippenham Cannibal?"

As part of Ms. China's world tour of restitution and community service, she had to convince the Cannibal to give himself up. He agreed, on condition he be allowed to put on the performance that had been delayed by his escape. Ellie learned the former Cannibal of Chippenham had ended up hiding in the basement at Tavistock, her borrowed Mayfair house. Mr. Surghit had kept the emotionally vulnerable man on a strictly vegetarian diet. At some point Magellan, who was probably tired of Esmunda's constant smoking of Spice and other drugs, had adopted Mr. Goodrum as his new minder.

Ellie sought out Mr. Delingpole in the crowd, waved to get his attention, and mouthed *Told you* while pointing to the stage. Harry Goodrum would give himself up after the performance, as promised. He was a man of his word, albeit one with strange appetites.

With a burst of light, a huge holograph of a screaming skull burst out from the back of the stage at the same instant Ms. China, as a very compelling Lady Macbeth, virtually floated into view wearing a hugely puffed-out Georgian ball gown as millions of sparkling red confetti pieces rained down from the rim of the roof like a waterfall of blood.

Ran groaned. "The cleaners are going to charge double overtime."

Melanie hushed him with a rap of her fan.

All six pupils glittering in the footlights, Ms. China did a stage turn to the Fool, and she began…

"The raven himself is hoarse
That croaks the fatal entrance of Duncan
Under my battlements. Come, you spirits
That tend on mortal thoughts, unsex me here,
And fill me from the crown to the toe top-full
Of direst cruelty. Make thick my blood,
Stop up th'access and passage to remorse,
That no compunctious visitings of nature
Shake my fell purpose, nor keep peace between
Th'effect and it. Come to my woman's breasts,
And take my milk for gall, you murd'ring ministers."

Deftly picking up his cue, the Cannibal waggled his bell-festooned cap and spoke, his deep voice somehow etched with both cruelty and comedy,

"Truth's a dog must to kennel; he must be whipp'd out…"

Either dazzled by the spectacle or the riveting performances of the real-life mad villains, the audience seemed spellbound and was as hushed as the empty moors at twilight.

Ellie looked up. Something in the velvety blue of the darkening sky caught her attention. It was Venus, glimmering blue and green. It seemed to look down at her and wink.

BEFORE THERE WAS **APOCALYPSE USA, THERE WAS:**

APOCALYPSE ISRAEL:
THE 96 HOUR WAR

APOCALYPSE EUROPE:
THE PANGEA PROTOCOL

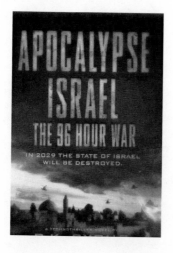

These books are part of the New Praetorians series.
OTHER BOOKS SET IN THE NEW PRAETORIANS UNIVERSE: Start
reading today: goo.gl/Uig74j

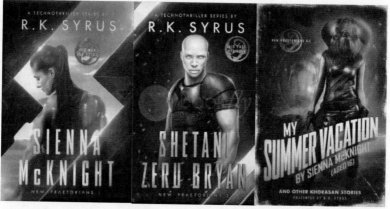

Praise for the books of the New Praetorians series:

"…an intriguing world of futuristic technology, made more familiar by
contemporary references."

"Radiant descriptions also enhance the story." —Kirkus Reviews

Your honest reviews help:
Amazon.com
Goodreads.com
...
For updates email "join list" to
author.syrus@gmail.com

...

Parler.com @rksyrus

...

THE NEW PRAETORIANS
SERIES CONTINUITY

TEN CHARACTER-DRIVEN ADVENTURES,
ONE GLOBAL STORY.

Apocalypse Israel: The 96 Hour War
In 2029, the State of Israel will be destroyed.

Apocalypse Europe: The Pangea Protocol
One killer, 500 million victims.
On November 1, 2031, one man will murder everyone in Europe.

Two standalone prequel novels set in the New Praetorians world.

Apocalypse: USA
In 2032, the Apocalypse series finally comes to America.

My Summer Vacation by Sienna McKnight
(New Praetorians 0.5)
A prequel novella.
FREE WHEN YOU JOIN THE MAILING LIST

	Start date (Khorasan time)
1. Sienna McKnight	March 19
2. Shetani Zeru Bryan	March 20
3: Yama & Yami	March 20
4: Anis	continuous
5: Crush	March 20
6: Ran Oliphant	continuous
7: Khamseen	continuous
8: Dr. Golem & Mr. Genji	March 20
9: Heaven's Scythe	continuous
10: Shadowbolt	continuous